THE OUTCASTS

BOOK THREE OF THE SPARK CITY CYCLE

ROBERT J POWER

DEPAOR PRESS

THE OUTCASTS
First published in Ireland by De Paor Press in 2021.
ISBN 978-1-8382765-5-3

Available in eBook, Audiobook and Paperback.

www.RobertJPower.com

For Rights and Permissions contact:
Hello@DePaorPress.com

CONTENTS

For Jan.
Without you I am nothing.
Everything I write is to make you think I'm cool.
You are my soulmate, my muse.
My one for life.
I'll see you at the rock.

1

THE LITTLE SLEEPING CUB

"Come on, Erroh. Wake up already."

Emir was exhausted. Irritable, too. And drunk. Drunker than usual. It was something to do while missing his friend. Looking at the mangled form of Erroh, he took to watching more appealing things. Like the little glass of clear, burning fluid shimmering tantalisingly in a beam of sunlight breaking through a split in the tent's doorway. There was little in the world for him, but there would always be glistening sine.

"Everyone is waiting for you," he added peevishly. His words shattered the quietness, and he raised a silent toast to both his sleeping guests. They'd earned their rest, he supposed. Hush after a tempest. The bitterness of boredom. Time dragged on without the threat of doom hanging over their heads. Only seven days had passed since the dreadful battle, and it felt like months.

Murderer. His hands shook, thinking of his sins. Not with horror, though. He was a murderer and the title pleased him. The glass almost slipped from his hand. Holding too tightly, hating too much. Shame to drop it, he mused. He had few possessions, but that stolen glass was his. It was pretty and cut in archaic, decorative designs. Mostly it delivered the nicer things in his life. He downed the sine, remembering the slaughter, and savoured the memories. A fine day won for the heroes. They'd suffered few losses in their sudden charge. Who knew a foolish rush of blood was more effective than well-thought-out plans conceived by legendary warmongers? Two battles, equally shared between both sides. There would be more, he imagined, but he was a simple healer and no legend of warfare.

Word would likely have filtered back to the city of the battle, no doubt. Word of a near flawless victory. A good thing in reply to the soul-crushing betrayal by the bastard Wolves. *What comes next?*

The second guest stirred. She hadn't left Erroh's side. She was just like him. A better patient. *A better chest, too.* Grinning at the memories of the dark with his brothers, Emir wiped the sleep from his eyes and placed the glass down beside his tools, then picked it up again.

"Fuk it." He poured another from the steel tankard and enjoyed its watery clink as he hid it back among his healing remedies. As if anybody would really care.

Wretched healer, the absent gods whispered in his mind, and he shrugged. He thought it an appropriate term. He was wretched and broken, but he would heal whom he could. Nobody could take that from him. *Apart from Magnus.*

He felt the exhaustion from the last week. A busy period, without doubt, despite the glory. Only a handful of Wolves had been lost in the battle, but Emir suspected it might have been even less. He felt the stir of guilt and shrugged it away. How many had died because he had sacrificed everything pulling Erroh from the brink? How many hours lost to the cutting and cursing? *While the injured bled out.* It should have bothered him, but his mind was shrewd and he knew he had earned his credit. He opened a little jar of vile-smelling ointment and rubbed the gelatinous, grey contents along Erroh's scorched hands. The Hero of Keri slept through the more painful days, but his body would remember the pain. Would leave the scars to remind him, too. Not too deep, though, if Emir was as skilled as he believed himself to be.

The wind caught the tent's flap, and the murky morning light suddenly stung his eyes. How many days had he remained awake, sitting over a scorched and bloody mess? One might say enough. He drained the second glass of sine and reached for the tankard outright. Everything was easier through a blurry daze. Less tedious. He desired inaction and was granted it. The cots around the sleeping god of Spark City were empty. That could change in fleeting moments were the Hunt to come looking, he imagined.

Save the drink for the thoroughly darker days to come.

"Good idea." He drank from the tankard and, swallowing the bitter ambrosia, poured yet another measure. A healthy one.

Aye, the southerners were still, but he could feel the death in the air. He sensed it like a hound sensed a threat in a brute. It might not be tomorrow, nor even a month from this day, but it was coming, and when it did, it wouldn't stop until the end of times. The absent gods agreed.

Leaning over Erroh's chest, he inhaled deeply. The infections had cleared swiftly. All he could smell was the sharp bite of disinfectant. He listened to Erroh's heart. Strong and constant. Every day filling with fresh blood. Thanking the gods of healing, he hadn't needed to resort to refilling him using careless, ancient practices. Erroh would happily have gambled that both their bloodlines were strong and harmonious, but Emir would not.

3

"Stitches still clean… and strong." He tested his handiwork on the wounds. Providing Erroh didn't move for a few more weeks, he'd recover. *Mostly.* Thinking of his brother of the dark, remaining still, brought a grim smile to Emir's bristled face. As if the Alpha male would not attempt to leap onto the nearest mount to go chase and "kill Oren" the moment he woke. Oh, the words he'd cried out while under the influence of dream syrup. The other words were mutterings from the southern tongue. He could have had a savage prisoner translate. There were certainly enough of those who'd surrendered capable of such a task. Mercy was a beautiful thing, but Emir struggled with it these days. He was not against imprisoning each one in chains; he was also not against slaughtering them for a quieter life, too.

Would I really have them killed?

Lea stirred again. Perhaps she had heard the raging thoughts thundering around his mind. Was this trauma? he wondered, and a fierce anger took hold.

Kill every last one of the fukers!

With a hand controlled by the darker recesses of his mind, he slammed a fist down upon his desk, knocking a clear vial of fluid from its place and shattering it upon the floor. A bitter, sterile aroma filled the room. *Wonderful.*

Instead of pulling himself from his mood, he thought on darker things. And why not? He hated his life and he wanted to die. And he would die. When it was time. Through the sword, through foolishness, or through that bastard age itself. Nothing could sway his thoughts from this eventual path. Being surrounded by comrades wasn't enough. It could never be enough. For a time, he'd forgotten this darkness, but it had returned tenfold, like a nasty infection ill-treated. He missed his home and he missed those he'd loved. Quig was still dead and would always be dead, and so was his beautiful Aireys.

4

"Better than Roja. To the fires with the bitch," he slurred, and caught himself. A bad sign to find a healer muttering profanities to themselves, even if they have good reason.

Have another drink.

"How is he?" asked Lea, stretching in her bedding and immediately feeling the bite in the morning air.

"Same as before… Better colour… Perhaps today he'll come back to us." His voice was slurred. She could see the glazed look in his eyes, and the stench of fresh sine was pungent. She suspected he was drunk again. When he bowed and slipped from his seat to the ground, she was convinced. She heard him mutter Roja's name as he sat in the dirt, picking up little shards of glass carelessly, and she thought him a perfect friend. A better healer, too. Though he was inebriated, his hands remained steady and miraculous. Let him drink all he wanted, she mused, stretching a second time. The aches from the healer's cots were the worst thing about waking up in this horror of a tent. Remembering the world a few moments later was a close second.

The springs creaked loudly as she rolled gracelessly from her bedding. Stretching a third and final time, she checked on her mate asleep in the bed alongside. *Looking stronger.* He had a strong heart—Emir had reassured her as much—and Lea's stomach turned a little. A strong heart, and a little large for her liking. *Wake up, my beo, and meet your whore.* She leaned across and kissed his forehead. He was cooler than the evening before. No deathly cough stealing his breath, no freezing land tearing at his will and no quarter of the world searching for his head.

Most of that is true.

The delicate patter of a light drizzle stirred her from her

memories and worries. She kissed him once more and tied her
boots. The rain would force her from her vigil. She reached
for her cloak and tied it around her neck. Emir craved sine;
she craved something else entirely. At least first thing in the
morning.

"Do you want one?" she asked, reaching for her own
particular tools of healing. Slowly grinding the beans until the
aroma countered other stenches was a fine way to prepare
herself. He shook his head in distaste at the notion and
continued to scramble in the dirt with his shards of glass.
Swiftly, Lea brought the water to a satisfying boil and, as the
ground beans percolated deliciously, she tied her long black
hair into a ponytail and steeled herself for the morning. She
buttoned up her coat and applied a quick coat of paint to her
lips.

I am most beautiful. Pouring two fresh mugs of the
steaming brew before offering a glass of sine for the healer,
Lea, the outcast of Samara, walked out into the rain to face
her captive.

Most of the Wolves still slept off the previous night's
hangover. With alcohol had come welcome cheer and
celebration. Was there anything Wrek couldn't do? Even out
here, in the middle of nowhere, he served the masses. Did his
part keeping morale heightened. Sometimes that was all a
pathetic gathering of soldiers could ask for.

The camp was as desolate as before. Now, though, the
simple act of stepping through rows of erected tents seemed
to bring life to the dismal place. *A fine place to wait until we
figure out what the fuk to do.* As she did every morning, she
followed her path down towards the solitary wooden post on
the other side of the healer's tent.

She heard the jeering before she saw the brutes standing
around the chained beast, and, sighing in frustration, Lea

quickened her pace. As boredom and restlessness stirred among the men, protecting the waif was now becoming part of Lea's routine. They could not leave Nomi with her people at the far end of the camp, but Magnus forbade the girl the right to freedom. After months of supposed torture, she was spending her days as though she was a rabid hound.

Is this wrong?

"Leave her be."

Lea's tone was genial, but they would be wise to recognise the threat beneath her words. She never broke stride, either. She locked away her anguish; her rage; her jealousy. Her face was calm, like a frozen lake of the south. The four Wolves watched her approach, and their grinning, threatening glares fell away to disappointment. All four were taller than she, yet they would not argue. They'd seen her capabilities. Her mate's, too. She was a general in a fractured battalion. And Erroh, well, he might just become the new Master General.

"We were just—"

"What did I say?" she said, and they stepped away from the chained girl, allowing Lea to attend to the captive.

"You said—"

"Leave."

"It's just that we—" The Wolf fell silent under her gaze. "Aye Mydame. As you wish."

Lea offered a bow as they left before setting the cofe into Nomi's shivering hands. "This will keep you warm." *Bitch.* The girl said nothing as she tugged the solitary blanket around her and winced as the chains dug into her neck. *Like a fuken hound.*

"Now you know how he felt," Lea said evenly. The girl wouldn't understand her words, but no matter the language, people instinctively spoke the language of tone, so Lea was always careful not to give anything away.

Blinking through heavily bruised eyelids, Nomi mumbled a thank-you in brutish southern tones before wiping the smear of saliva from her cheek. Her hands shook from cold or pain, and Lea approved of this and thought her thoroughly unimpressive. Emir had done enough to keep her alive, but Magnus allowed him to do little else. She was still the enemy.

Is she a spy? Or a broken waif?

The drizzle had taken what comfort the blanket offered. "Can't have you catching your death out here," Lea muttered, undoing the clasp on her cloak and tossing it carelessly to the bitch. She despised the smile offered in reply. "No, don't wrap it around the blanket. That will just get it soaked through. Just hang the blanket... Oh, never mind."

Nomi hugged herself at the reprieve of rain upon her, and Lea resisted the urge to smash her fuken head in. *Calm yourself.*

"Has your useless mate stirred yet today?" asked Wynn from behind, and Lea jumped in fright. She hadn't heard him walk up. He moved like a wraith these days. People suffered horrors in different ways, and Wynn struggled with the burden of having taken a life. Unlike her, Wynn wasn't born for killing. He might wake one morning and find himself better suited. He might also wake up and discover himself to be twice the man he should be. More likely, he would wake up some morning and discover himself too far from the right path. His path.

"He's still sleeping... getting stronger," Lea said, shrugging. Her eyes were on the other female.

"How is the fever?"

She looked into his eyes and Wynn saw the strength in hers. Saw the kindness, too. A good mate, a good Cull—everything he had not endured.

"The fever never took serious hold," Lea said, sipping her cofe.

"Any day now," Wynn offered quietly, breaking his gaze from the stunning female to look to the forest beyond. *It's time to face the horror.*

"Aye."

"Aye." He never felt comfortable around Lea. He had always believed she looked through him and was disappointed with what she discovered. Lillium whispered in her ears, no doubt. It should have bothered him more, but he was tired these days. *So fuken tired.* Trying to live up to the mantle of elite Alpha was a weight too great for his slim frame. He regretted the choice of step that had brought him over. It was his attempt at seeing to his friend's mate in his absence. It wasn't much. It was all he could do. Really, what words could he offer? Her worry was a soulmate's agony. To the rest of the camp, well, it was something else entirely. Most waited for the one warrior with godlike tendencies. The archetypal Alpha male. He had led them into certain devastation and pulled impossible victory from the fires of darkness. His body had burned for such acts, and he had taken every piercing arrow like a god of war.

And she's just as fierce.

What could he say, anyway?

"I shall leave you two ladies be," he offered, bowing and walking back towards the clustered trees separating his reason from anguish. He wouldn't meet the eyes of any soldier wandering through the camp. These few hardened Wolves had stood when their vile comrades fled, but still, Wolves couldn't be trusted. More than that, they might spot his fragility. The world had turned, and Wynn felt alone among courteous enemies.

The slippery mud gave way to the crunch of vegetation as he stepped through the treeline, away from the smothering stench of their settled camp. He breathed in deep and enjoyed the sweet, cool fragrances of the forest. *Savour this fleeting moment.* Careful to stay upon the path without cowering, he climbed the far slope, and the uneasiness in his stomach began. Same as before. Still, he climbed and reached the summit overlooking the battlefield where the Hunt had first known defeat.

You're doing better than usual.

As it did every morning, his stomach churned violently, and Wynn was grateful he'd eaten nothing. A shrewder move on his part. Reaching the top, he gasped as the memories were brought to life anew, so to speak. The bodies lay where they had fallen. *Butchered.* All of them, except for those who'd surrendered to Erroh. Wynn remembered this too. The fear on their faces as Erroh tore them apart. Fighting through fire; striking arrows from the air. *Casual decapitations.* The Hunt had fallen to their knees in fear before the one they called a god.

Despite the trauma, Wynn laughed aloud and some nervousness left his quivering body. Did the captured Hunt know this shrivelling wretch standing out over the battlefield had once defeated the god they feared? Did that make him a god? Did it make him a slayer of gods? He liked that. Erroh had promised him another opportunity. Sometimes styles made fights, and Wynn wondered might he have the measure of the superior swordsman?

That's what happens when you spend a year sparring with your mate.

Wynn often wondered whether, if Lillium and he had

sparred a little more, might their relationship have taken a better turn? He rubbed the stitching at his shoulder where her arrow had felled him. The wound still stung. Some pain was welcome. Taking a seat against a large boulder overlooking the nightmare, he stared at the many bodies below. His first victims still lay in the rain, slowly rotting and feasted on by carrion birds. *Godspeed, you beasts. Remove the evidence.* It was barbaric to leave them where they lay, but this was war and the Hunt deserved little respect in typical warfare. It would be a foolish Master General who sent an emissary with word of dead comrades. The Hunt were barbaric bastards. They'd take the message and the messenger's head.

He looked to the sky, seeing little break in the rain. Closing his eyes against the gentle, spattering hiss, he thought about his sins. He did so for a time, and it was a pleasant part of his routine.

She was quieter than he, yet he sensed her approach. While he faltered in melancholic silence, others faltered in divine grandness.

"Fuk. I can smell them from up here," Lillium muttered from her place among the undergrowth, before revealing herself to him. His eyes lingered on the bow in her hand; he looked to form a joke at her expense and thought better of it. A fine move on his part. They could speak politely, but jests were not yet welcome. They were strangers that had shared a bed. That time had passed. *Kissed our last.* In other ways, though, they were still bonded. They were the last of the Rangers. Two loyal sufferers under a diminished Master General. That was something, she supposed. *Not a lot.*

He nodded his head in agreement, and she saw the paleness on his clean-shaven face. Still, he'd made it farther than he did most mornings. Only a week more and he'd be able to stare his victims in the rotting eye sockets. Maybe then he'd find his nerve. A broken Ranger was the last thing this war needed; there was much killing to come.

"Enough to turn anyone's stomach," she said, meeting his tired eyes. Again, he nodded and said nothing. Perhaps he was fighting another bout of nausea. She'd seen and heard him retching every morning. Best to leave him to his musings. "We all struggle with death, Wynn. You aren't alone."

"Aye. I wonder will I ever endure dreams of warmth after these trying days."

She laughed wonderfully, for his words amused her greatly. Likely because the fool believed them. He did not know the world for what it was; he was still a wide-eyed child, believing himself capable of great things. He was not Erroh, nor Lea, either, for greatness touched them.

"You believe you will survive this war?"

"…"

She laughed again, kinder though, as though the child had whispered belief in the actions of the absent gods and proclaimed their existence. "You believe I will?"

"Aye, Lillium, I do."

"Oh, my lover, we will both die in the days ahead," she mocked, spinning her bow absently in her hand before turning to walk along the precipice of the slope to gaze fondly at the ruined field of death below. Turning back around, her tone softened. "But who's to say we won't die like barbarians with a thousand victims at our feet?"

She bowed and slipped through the green with an eye to the battlefield, enjoying the memories. There were no Hunt around for miles, but they couldn't rest on their laurels. Lillium enjoyed her patrols. Walking was pleasant; walking cleared the mind. She had seen the darker side of humanity in the form of a vile male. She had lived beyond. What was a little killing after that trauma, anyway? So, she walked, hated, and slowly felt a little better about herself. Nearing the burned-out cart that had almost taken Nomi's life, she listened to the forest for movements beyond. Like Wynn, she had a fine enough ear for tracking. Give her a few months and she would best her former mate in this art, too. Perhaps she could earn herself a fine station in the days to come, filling in where the old Ranger Garrick had once commanded.

Providing Magnus has the will to rebuild the Rangers.

"He will," she whispered, grimacing and stopping mid-step. Something beyond caught her attention. Probably nothing, but something to seek, something to hone her skills with. Her fingers tingled. Death was in the air, and that was alright. She would die well, but she would kill better. A fine outlook to keep in mind. Clearing the treeline and marching briskly towards the distant sound, she hopped over fallen bodies as though they weren't there. Looking back, she saw the speck of Wynn watching on from the rock and wondered if her brazen stroll across the battlefield might instil a little nerve in him. A warrior with nerve was a finer thing to gaze upon than a wretched, fragile whelp, claiming unfairness for their lot in life over brushing themselves off and getting on with it.

The world is unfair.
We are all in it together.
Stop glorifying weakness.
Do fuken better with what you are given.

She sighed aloud and disappeared into the forest, her former mate a distant memory. She followed the path and the tracks and the many stains. Stopping briefly where she'd fought smoke and terror and screaming and horror and come upon the battered and ruined Erroh. The bloodstains were faded now. She'd screamed when she'd found his shattered form still smouldering and the arrows still embedded in his armour and his pale skin. He'd taken every blow and suffered for it. Her screams had alerted the healer. She had screamed more than Lea in those first moments. Lea was tougher, and Lillium, well, she was learning. Biting her lip, she knelt on the wet ground and listened for the noise. The rain turned from respectable downpour to heavy deluge. Still, the rumble was prevalent. *Nearer.* She knew that rumble, too. Grinning, she took off swiftly, her body screaming at the sudden outburst, but pain could be controlled. Exhaustion tenfold more. She hunted the sound, and it was a wonderful distraction from morose thoughts.

Running through the endless green, she caught sight of the cart trundling loudly along, pulled by two exhausted horses. She recognised the driver and smiled at her keen ear. This was life now; she was grateful for it. A life hunting; a life killing. There were worse things.

She liked Wrek, though she did not understand why. After her attack, she'd suspected she'd fear any male gaze, but he had kind eyes. *Killer eyes too.* He carried himself honourably. He wore his regrets deep, and any secrets a little deeper. She had little issue with secrets, for they were all outcasts now. Did she not harbour her own secret? Did she not hide it as well? More than that, she sensed no threat from him. *Even out here, where nobody would hear.*

Above the cart she found a ledge to scamper along like a rodent on a harbour dock. She was swift; she was silent; she was Alpha female. The cart bounced loudly with the treasure of the many sine barrels loaded into it, and Lillium fought her own giddiness. Sometimes, pessimistic imaginings were fine company. Sometimes a girl just wanted to play. For a few feet more, she raced the unwitting driver before leaping from above.

Flying.

The attacker shook Wrek from his seat and he almost fell below the trundling wheels. While he careened precariously, she swayed with the cart's jolting rhythm and found footing between the barrels as though upon a barge swaying delicately, leaving Spark City harbour. He swung at her. For that was what wily warriors of the road did when assaulted by foolish bandits. *Don't they know who they attack?* A flash of beige and ponytailed hair brought the first stirrings of memory, but it was a small matter. She spun away, taking the glancing blow as though patted by a friend, and resisted no counter strike. "What the fuk?" he shouted, realising it to be the Alpha Lillium. She held out her arms on either side, maintaining her balance, and her laugh was almost infectious.

"It was something to do," she admitted, appearing contrite yet wholly impressed with herself for taking him by surprise. Had he not bragged one too many times that few were brave enough to take his cart while delivering the precious alcohol?

Touché, Alphaline.

"I could have killed you." He tried to sound annoyed, but her laughter broke through, brought a smile and all. He laughed. It was a rare thing to see her smile. She'd watched all her comrades die. Endured horror in the days after. A lesser legend would have crumpled, but she remained regal and strong. Now she appeared happy. What was a skipped beat or two when recovering from trauma? "Or you could have killed me with fright."

"Just keeping you alert. Brave thing, carting these riches across the wastes," she said sheepishly, but her eyes were alight. Her breaths were deep and laboured, and he wondered how long she'd chased him before announcing herself so spectacularly. Jest or no, it was complacency on his part not to notice a hunter.

Lesson learned.

Gripping the reins of the oblivious mounts, he recovered his seat and she sat next to him as they neared the camp.

"The last of the barrels?" she asked, wiping at a few mud patches on her beige outfit. Hardly a functional colour to don in the green, but he knew better than to suggest she surrender her uniform. Not even if he'd desired to see her out of it. Which he didn't. *Not really.* Truthfully, there was someone far more wounded he cared for. He'd hold his tongue on the removing of her clothes too.

"Enough to keep the wheels turning for quite a time," he said, bringing the beasts back to the centre of the path.

"Unless the healer gets thirsty," she muttered, eyeing the swift ground underneath. Wrek snorted. Levity and a jest. The girl was doing better.

"How is our sleeping cub?" he asked, pulling the beasts down through a winding slope towards their camp. With his heart settled, he could allow himself a moment to think. To think of how dreadful a turn his and everyone else's life had taken these last few weeks. It was a nasty thing thieving from a widow, but needs must. Had Mea been in her farm when he stole in to recover the last few barrels, they might have shared words, but really, he was happier to pilfer them in the middle of the night without enduring horrific conversations about her fallen mate.

She hasn't even a body to bury.

Wrek was a brave enough fiend, but he'd been happy to see no lights on in their farm. He'd left one barrel behind, and the distillery too. When better days returned, they would be quite a treasure. If Sigi was stupid enough to seek his wares, well, Mea was likely to vent her anguish on the unfortunate collectors.

"He'll be well rested when he wakes." Her words were unyielding. Typical Alpha. Too stubborn to accept that Erroh might never wake. Without warning, Lillium slipped from her seat down to the muddy ground below and began jogging alongside without missing a beat.

"You drive this cart like a child. I'll be quicker by foot." She leapt to the ledge above and pulled herself into the concealing green once more, and within a breath she was lost to the woodland. Further typical Alphaline behaviour. Truthfully, he no longer believed the superstitions surrounding them. Aye, it was an impressive feat to leap onto a moving cart so casually, but as Emir would loudly and rather drunkenly proclaim, they were still human—just a little better at it.

A few of his Wolf brethren cheered at his arrival, yet none offered to help. It was far too early in the morning, and the aroma of the delicious, coma-inducing beverage would leave many a stomach truly sickened. He leapt down onto the muddy ground and shook the rain from his long, shaggy hair. A fresh collection of droplets immediately replaced their fallen comrades. A horrible morning altogether. He would be glad to see its end. Undoing the clasp at the cart's rear, he pulled one of the massive barrels closer to the edge, before easing it carefully to the ground below.

"Do you need a hand?"

Wrek spun around at the sound of the voice and was met with boisterous laughter. The eyes of the bald young man standing in front of him showed little humour and less warmth.

. . .

Doran held his ruined hand up to the bouncer, laughing more. His hand's effectiveness was lost to him forever, but he still took breath where his comrades did not. Humour allowed him to manage his anguish. It was all he could do. At least he could still swing a weapon in battle. That was all that would matter. Despite the pain, he took hold and placed the barrel on the ground.

"I'd give an arm or a leg for a bit of help, friend," Wrek countered, and Doran laughed loudly. They were not friends, but perhaps they were beyond the petty loathing they'd had for each other before the world turned upon itself.

"We could always arrange that," Aymon said, appearing beside Doran. He eyed Wrek with even less warmth than Doran, but such expressions were hardly unusual. Aymon was a decent if angry young Alpha male, slowly coming to terms with his sexuality. He was Doran's best friend, so shit like that didn't matter. What mattered was having his back in a society disapproving of lifestyles beyond simple breeding. Aye, Doran understood the importance of strengthening the bloodlines of their race and rebuilding for the generations to come, but some things couldn't always fit into the right boxes. People knew this; few spoke up. Still, for all the difficulties faced, it wasn't Aymon who spent his nights alone. As they began unloading the barrels Doran caught sight of the goddess Lillium marching by, removing the bow from her back as she went. He loved her walk and enjoyed it for a few moments before returning to task with the barrels.

The trio spent a half-hour emptying the barrels from cart to storage, and then Wrek rolled the last one across to Aymon. "For the help. Share it with the men," Wrek said, and Aymon nodded in appreciation. "Don't let Emir see it. He thinks he has a claim to every drop of alcohol in this place."

Doran's ruined fingers itched and he scratched at them

with his working thumb. He still remembered the agony as Emir had torn at his ruined injury for hours on end. What movement he had now was down to the drunken wretch's ability. Like Wrek, he was no friend, but fuk it, he was an appreciated comrade.

"Appreciate the generosity, friend," Aymon said, standing close to Wrek. Similarly well built, neither would retreat from a fight. There was no love lost. However, there could be respect. Who knew the simple act of suicidal charging into death could ease tensions between rival factions?

History did.

They rolled the barrel across the camp and, dimly, Doran remembered a similar action in the rain before everything in the world went to the fires.

"A gift for the Master General, perhaps?" Aymon mocked, tapping the barrel and the name etched into it, and Doran cursed under his breath. "Aye, perhaps in poor taste," he added, thinking of his words.

You think?

After swiftly draining a bottle together, they left the barrel in their tent for later before wandering back through the camp to speak with their leader. They were not Rangers, but they were not Wolves either. Their army's mass retreat before swinging a blow in anger had seen to that. They wore black, for they had nothing else. Not even a banner. They were, however, generals in whatever this outfit was, and serving Magnus was the only act they could think of that would earn them any honour. All thanks to the great betrayer Sigi.

"Master General, sir," Aymon said, once they found themselves outside the largest tent in the camp. Within, Doran could hear the low growl of Magnus's fierce war-hounds. With a gentle hiss, the dogs were silenced, and he granted them entry, with a growl far deeper than any magnificent hound's.

"I have no more need of gifts, gentlemen," the old Ranger said, looking at the clear bottle they'd offered. Nevertheless, he placed it upon his desk. Doran couldn't help notice the pain in his features with every movement he made. Taking an arrow to the knee ended most people's warmongering, but it was the following battle that had earned him this near ruin.

"Master General, sir, we can come back later, if you need to rest a little more," the bald Alpha offered, and Magnus dismissed the notion with a curt shake of the head, taking the reports from the young man's hands. A quick glance told the usual tale of southern activities. "Another day with no movement. It's as if they are leaderless," Doran offered, and Magnus nodded slowly. He hated the silence, hated the inaction too, but what else was there for now? Until the southerners declared their next intention, all this wretched camp could do was rest and recover what injuries they could. Plans were afoot, unlikely vengeance was in the air, but they were a battered beast and only a fool went marching out into war with fifty or sixty warriors, hardened and elite though they were. The city still had an army. He just needed to take control of them. To "persuade" them to see sense.

"You think we should ride out and attack them?" Magnus asked, eyeing both Wolves. He could see the anger still festered deep within. He could put that anger towards some fine devastation.

"Perhaps a few of us could unsettle them," Aymon said coldly, and Magnus approved.

"Aye, but not just yet, gentlemen. Go see to your comrades," Magnus said, and with a deep bow, both Alphas left him to his quiet thoughts. He stretched his knee painfully, and blood dripped down his leg. Cursing, he inspected the wound with a careful touch. He'd torn free his bandaging as he'd slept. A common occurrence when dreaming of wrapping his arthritic fingers around the throat of some unworthy brute. Or worse, a worthy one. Without Elise to wake him from stirring nightmares, his wounds suffered his traumas. Emir was going to lose his head when he saw the damage, and Magnus's attempts at re-wrapping the bandaging were unlikely to help matters.

He felt older than he had the day before. He did every day. He missed Elise dearly, and he never stopped worrying. When last they'd spoken, her breath had been a wet gasp. He regretted the letter he'd sent to the city, but there was little else he could do. Better to hear the bitter truth from him than through hushed whispers once the Black Guard marched guiltily home. They were her Rangers too. His only worry was her enduring the harsh ride to mourn the loss with him.

She's not that foolish.

Even for Erroh.

He almost let out a cry, but as swiftly as his lament arose, he locked it away in a cage, deep down. "Erroh will wake soon." Speaking aloud helped, because sometimes his thoughts went to horrible places. *Like losing both your mate and your son on the same day.* He touched the edge of his wooden desk and cursed his thoughts. "They will live through this," he declared, and again, words spoken aloud felt better. "Fuk it," he growled, climbing to his feet. Best the Wolves see their master constantly, lest they stage a coup out of boredom alone.

Stretching painfully and finding a step that hurt least, he wandered out into the waking camp and was hit anew by his losses. All camps were the same; this battered, wretched army was no different. He didn't know all the names of the Wolves; he wondered, would he ever? Like one whose heart had been torn apart by a cruel lover, he wondered, could he ever open himself to that horror again? He'd lost warriors before, entire battalions throughout the Faction Wars, but losing his Rangers upon a field of betrayal was something else entirely. He had never imagined himself becoming one of those broken warriors, drunk in whatever tavern would accommodate them, regaling any who would listen with heartbreaking tales. *Did I tell you about the epic of the treacherous Wolves?* That was no life for any legend. Better he die in battle. His knee creaked as he walked, a humbling metal creak at that. The brace did its job just fine but also gnawed at his better judgement that he would not die in battle, would never don the Clieve again, either. They all followed him. These Wolves had no calling and no city to protect anymore. They had no leader, so they followed the last man standing. One-legged as he was.

If only Erroh were able to step into my boots.

Marching through the camp, he held the pain in and remained jovial even when he caught sight of his daughter-in-law tending to the captive. His act of imprisoning the girl was probably a cruelty on his part, but a necessary one. She didn't belong with those who'd tortured her, but she wouldn't last long walking free. She was the enemy. Chains would suit her just fine. *For now.* Feeling the breeze at his neck and the rain seeping through his hair, he felt a fresh pang of shame. Still, it was a small matter. It was all he could do. Had she not afforded similar luxuries to his son?

"How is the sleeping cub?" he asked when he reached the girls. Lillium bowed as only a Ranger could, while Lea shrugged. He smiled despite the slight. There was a fire to her. Perhaps she didn't approve of his treatment of prisoners.

Another unimportant matter. She was family. Family could shrug all they wanted.

"Erroh is looking better today," she said, after a moment's pause.

"That is good to know, little one. He's strong, like his mother."

A few more moments passed and Lea finally addressed him. Her eyes were less cruel than usual, but still hard, as though allowing emotion to enter her thoughts might cause her to crack. "How is your knee, Fa... Magnus?"

He offered a smile and shrugged. There was a flicker of a smile on her lips. He dared a hand on her shoulder and squeezed it before searching for escape. But not before staring at the wretched blonde staring up at them, pretending she did not hate them; pretending she did not fear them; pretending she would not slit his throat in a moment's notice.

Nomi didn't know what words they spoke, but that never stopped them from speaking with her. Mostly they spoke at her. Right into her face. Shouting. Spitting. Not the enlightened race her one for life had spoken of. *No, he is not yours, remember?* She remembered. And oh, it hurt. She was no longer impressive. No longer a brave warrior either. She had no place in the world. Not anymore. Her people called her the great betrayer. Uden had condemned her using those words. Whenever she closed her eyes, she remembered the horrors. The whispered hissings from those of her kind as they'd tortured her, demanded she realise. How could anyone see the light with thick bruises around their eyes? She had known her value as a gift. Months in chains, earning her place in her god's good graces. So much pain, and at the end, with a beating she thought she'd never survive, she'd finally given up and listened to their hatred. Believed it too.

As the flames had come around her, she'd accepted them willingly. So ended the unimportant life of Nomi the mediocre. Until her Erroh had saved her. *No, not mine.* When smoke took her breath and fire scorched her skin, he had torn the Hunt apart and pulled her from the fires. Or at least, that's what she remembered. She had not seen him since, and her only friend was this goddess.

Pulling the cloak around her, she huddled up against the wooden post, listening to the three impressive warriors speak of things unrelated to her. For days now she listened, searching for any meaning behind each guttural sound that rolled awkwardly off her lips whenever she whispered them alone. It was something to do while fighting off sorrow and unknown fear. The chains clinked gently and the three jailors looked down at her. Being scrutinised in silence brought forth her hidden agonies, and she fought the urge to cry out, to weep, to beg for mercy and freedom. She would not do that, however, for were she to cry, she might never stop. Instead, she dipped her head and ignored their silence and thought again of Erroh saving her.

Without warning, a disturbance from the entrance of the encampment drew their attention. A rider in black had emerged from the Arth's endless green, and she almost smiled at their ways. Erroh claimed many things, but his people had still not mastered the art of courier birds. Wars could be lost and won on such actions.

The beautiful girl with black hair and stunning features began speaking frantically, and Nomi suspected this to be Liiiia, though she wore no yellow dress, so who could know for certain? She would not ask either. *Not until Erroh appears.* The rider rode down through the camp, shouting

24

incomprehensibly, and Nomi squirmed beneath her bedding. *Show no fear, like Erroh showed no fear.* She allowed herself a gentle shaking of her body and little more.

The rider, clad in heavy black armour, stopped at the older warrior, bowing deeply and passing across a missive. Though injured, he was still a force. Any fool could see that, and Nomi suspected he was the leader of this wretched little outfit. Within a few moments, the leader began shouting at the rider and Nomi squirmed beneath her damp bedding again. She knew the terror of an angry tyrant. They were primal roars. Gripping the smaller rider, he shook him aggressively. Adding to Nomi's confusion, the taller female cursed loudly, a wonderful word Nomi remembered from her Erroh's teachings. Stabbing her sword into the wet ground, she roared to the sky above. For a few terrible moments the crowd gathered, and only the goddess, perhaps called Liiiia, remained calm, though Nomi could see her fight her own rage, even as she spoke evenly with their leader and the young rider he was assaulting. For a few outbursts more, the four captors argued, shouted, hissed and cursed before, finally, the old bearded warrior halted his aggression and fell still. But not before taking the younger man's shoulder and muttering apologetic nonsense that Nomi couldn't decipher.

To his credit, the young rider nodded and appeared to forgive the attack, until some other commotion brought the entire camp to a deathly silence. All scuffles were still. All steps were held. Every head turned to a large tent and the diminutive man standing at its entrance. She remembered the healer distastefully. He was a drunkard; he could barely stand upright and she did not trust his wandering hands. *Never without my permission.*

His unimpressive tone barely carried in the wind, and Nomi found herself more interested in how the entire camp was hanging on his every word. Suddenly, Liiiia leapt down in front of her, leaning in close, and Nomi could see the beauty in her features. She'd been that close to her before. Right after the fires. She was a deity and Nomi was a ruin. The beautiful girl spoke quickly, and Nomi did not know what to say or how to say it. She kept talking loudly, and the world was silent around her. *I'm sorry, exquisite girl. I wish I could help you, but I've no fuken idea what you are saying.*

"*Something incomprehensible.*"

"*Something Erroh! Incomprehensible.*"

Then Liiiia was away from her and running towards the little aggressive healer, and Nomi was left yet again, alone and cold.

2

LEGEND

Elise never remembered it raining so much in the city, but these last few days had been torrential. Closing her eyes, she remembered the heat of Samara and nothing else. She remembered the better days in her youth as well. For there were many. Resting her bare feet in the mud, she felt the gentle reverberations of her doom stir ever nearer. Thumping inevitability. The rain fell around her, like the deluge of tears she'd now shed for days. She cursed the rain and hoped the sun shone on her last day.

Oh, Magnus.

Her simple question, two and a half decades before, had brought about the change of the world. A simple few words as they shared silken sheets between bouts of guilty, stolen pleasures. He had replied to her simple question with a simple answer: "Yes. I do want to start a war." They had been magnificent. Elise of Samara and Magnus of the Savage Isles. The kings of the Four Factions never had a chance. Not apart; not together, either.

My love forever to you.

Elise closed her eyes and dropped her head in silent prayer to the gods. She would die, and her perfect mate, Magnus, would not be by her side. Perhaps this was a good thing. Better he learn of her fate surrounded by enough warriors far from the city. He would understand her actions. Understand the mercy she would show, too. *Just a scrape inflicted. Hardly a grievous wound.*

She gripped the ruined letter in her hand and caressed his delicate scribblings once more. For an unruly savage, he had a golden touch with ink. She kissed the parchment and clenched it to her chest. Her own message was safe in the rider's pouch. By dawn, it would be in Magnus's hands.

Thump.

Closer now. She could see the mass of movement marching the path in quiet shame and she truly hated them. Returning home after a battle fought dishonourably. Grinding her teeth, she felt her heart quicken. The thin metal dual-bladed halberd in her grip felt impossibly light, and with one end stabbed into the muddy ground, she leant on it for support. She liked to think such a weapon was more impressive than the legendary Clieve, and she had a strong enough argument. Her weapon was dignified; graceful and ruthless. A female liked these types of things. Some might argue that her mate's weapons were more impressive. Her thousand victims would argue differently. She ran her finger along the oiled blade and loved it ever so. How many times had she spun this beast of a weapon above her head and charged forward as a goddess of death? *A legend.*

Thump.

The marching Wolves were upon the path where wastes turned to civilisation. *Welcome home, you fuken bastards.* Anger was a gift, and hers was a boundless, fiery rage. She gripped the blade and cursed her weakened body. There

28

needed to be recompense for their actions. Better hers than Magnus's unforgiving charge; better he remain innocent of ghastly actions, too. She'd counted the numbers; she knew her ability and accepted that she was a faded legend destined to die in the rain, surrounded by vile cowards, this very day.

Thump, thump.

The ground shook more, and any birds taking shelter in their nests took to the rain-filled skies, for they knew murder in the air. Elise took a deep breath. An arduous task on the finest of days. She could feel Emir's concoction performing its task. She'd timed it nicely. She always had more breath after treatment. Kissing the note from Magnus that told of the Ranger's fall, she cast it into the wind. It floated delightfully in the breeze until it met a cruel death under the leading foot of the approaching line of Wolves. How fitting, she thought bitterly, and hated a little more. She'd never felt alone like she did right now. At least Lexi wouldn't see it unfold. Her heart broke in that moment. There was no fine death, but this was finer than most. By her own hand, dealing the last round with no pieces of worth.

Thump, thump, thump.

So close. She could see their grim expressions. A line of black, walking four abreast, in their hundreds upon her path. Her fuken path. Each of them in a twenty-man garrison. All really fuken quiet, walking bravely home. *Home.* She missed her home. Her actual home. Elise shook the rain from her hair and glanced back at the daunting shadow of her old home.

Her thin body shivered in the cold, with adrenalin, with fear too and all too swiftly, her chest tightened. She knew well it was her body retaliating to inevitable demise. The body cared little for honour, for justice. For fuken vengeance.

Thump, thump, thump, thump.

She scrunched her bare feet in the mud to calm herself.

They marched on and finally set eyes upon her, standing in the middle of their path with blade in hand. She coughed heavily and felt a little air stream down into her aching lungs. She lifted her weapon, *Tilla's Ire*, and rested it against her forehead. One more prayer to the absent gods. She did not want to die gasping for air.

Falling to her knees, she gasped pathetically, like a feeble cub in the presence of a god. To them, she appeared diminished, without threat, but they were no fools. Warily, the first line of Wolves approached and parted without breaking step. They knew their shame and few looked her way, lest she look into their soul and discover the true measure of each man. They did not raise their weapons, but as they walked around her, they all cast uneasy glances at the double-ended blade, standing proudly, as tall as any marching man. She did not stir, and the rain ceased its downpour. If Magnus stood where she stood now, the blood would never end. He would tear them apart for their immoralities, and he would never stop until each victim lay dead. It would be a fine, costly sight to behold, and she could almost taste pure revenge on her luscious lips. But killing them all was too great a price. They were still an army. Vile and cowardly, but an army.

The absent gods granted her one delicate moment. The clouds parted suddenly and warmer rays shone down upon her before closing back over and the land grew cooler again.

They did not brush against her as they parted. It wasn't their place to smudge her stunning beige uniform. They hung their heads and passed in silence. The hush was unnerving. She took in their dull, repetitive drumbeat as each foot marched in unison and embraced it. *No laughter or jests, you vile murderers?* Not even songs to lighten the mood. The Wolves had come home.

The wretches along the wall watched in equal silence.

They felt the betrayal. Many had lost loved ones in the Rangers' last stand. Some others knew the shame of a loved one's betrayal. *They are still the happier, though.* All it had taken was the minor matter of the Primary's assassination to turn the entire world on its head.

The first of the Wolves passed the freshly-erected barricade near the entrance of the city, built swiftly, carelessly, to keep the wretches in line. Elise gasped again, letting her weapon waver and slip to the mud beside her.

Dane hesitated as he walked past her. He looked to say a few worthless words, but the anger in her suggested he continue his coward's march. *Fine leader of the Black Guard.* He deserved to die most of all, but not today. The city would need him, were the Hunt to lay siege. It wasn't only about retaliation; it was about restraint and control, and Dane's death would cause more damage than justice.

The last line of cowardly Wolves passed her by. They thought her a broken little Alphaline, all wheezing and spittle and little else. Her breath steadied. With the smell of eucalyptus in her nose, she pulled her blade from the mud and pulled herself to her feet. Lifting the magnificent piece above her head, she spun it in a terrifying arc, building momentum, finding her feet one last time.

Goodbye Magnus. I'll wait for you. Goodbye, Erroh and Lexi. Take your time.

The Wolves had their backs to her. She wondered, could they hear the dying screams of her beautiful Rangers as they fought and fell beneath insurmountable odds?

They would have won.

They should have won.

Fuk them.

Elise held her weak breath and spun the blade. Faster and faster, her arms answered her will until they were a blur, and, one last time, she became a goddess of war. She took a step towards the unaware cowards. She took it fast. As she did the next step. Soon after, she was sprinting. The first strike upon the four unsuspecting Wolves was devastating; unprotected necks were torn open in her first motion.

Easy.

She might not have been so ruthlessly efficient if they had not been walking so closely together, but it was another gift from the absent gods. She was Elise of Samara, mated to Magnus, and she had been killing long before most of them could walk. Storming forward like an enraged Valkyrie of ancient races, she waded into them, finishing the next gathering of unaware betrayers and the group after that, her blade spinning and stabbing and cutting and slaying. Grandly, too. She lost count of her victims—those who died; those who would live and speak of her last march. She counted only the steps she took, the swings she delivered.

The screams from behind alerted those ahead, but too late to save them from meeting the blade. A terrible last vision in a worthless life.

The damage she inflicted was only a taste of what Magnus would do. After the war. But for now, she delivered unto them a portentous warning of things to come.

She had every justification to kill them all, yet with her twentieth strike she fell away from her assault, and the world came alive with the true toll her unexpected attack had taken. The blood streamed along the ground and tainted her bare feet. The screams from the dying were a symphony to savour, and she would savour it as the darkness took hold.

Alive until the end.

She released her breath and retreated slowly back from the recovering army as the terrible truth dawned upon those still taking desperate breath and those turning around to the horror inflicted by one diminutive female.

Wait until you see what my boys can do.

An injured brute gripped at her ankle. With a voice filled with hatred, he roared for his brothers to slay her.

"Silence, coward," she whispered, thrusting the tip of her blade through his mouth. It wedged into the ground beneath him and, backing away, she enjoyed his squealing. *Tilla's Ire* remained upright as his body fell still, and a small part of her hunger for vengeance was sated.

He was her last victim. Screaming in horror, the Wolves drew their blades and formed up around her. She spread her arms wide, inviting them on. Daring them with her glare to strike her down. Oh, she felt their anguish as their brothers died at her feet, for there were many and she loved it so. As a shocked pack, they surrounded her, waving blades, hammers, and axes of many sizes. None dared to strike her down. Perhaps they understood her rights, regardless of her repulsive actions. The moment froze, the screams grew louder and she roared at them.

"I'm waiting, cowards." Fine words, on a breath taken with clear lungs. All it took was a little killing. Slowly, she dropped to a knee to entice them more, but she would not bow. Dipping her head, she presented her neck. Swift decapitation would hurt less. "One little swipe and knock my pretty head free."

"Chain her," cried Dane, breaking through the circle of aggrieved Wolves.

Chain me?

They fell around her, binding her arms roughly, and she offered little resistance even as they hauled her to her feet and began leading her away as though she were a mutt from the wastes. Her body ached, her breath was lost, but she strutted.

Stopping only once to face down Dane. She stared right into his soul and found little within.

He, however, looked right into her tragic, beautiful eyes and saw nothing but eternal passion, desperate to free itself and wage a terrible doom upon all those worthy of it.

3

RECOVERY

Erroh woke up to the sound of his own voice conversing with Emir. Whatever words he spoke were impassioned and lost to him; Emir nodded his head before suddenly disappearing and Erroh found himself pinned in place, staring into nothing.

He remembered pain. Arrows. Some burning too. Taking a laboured breath, he felt fresh stabbings shoot through his chest. *Stop breathing, idiot.* A fine suggestion. He held his aching breath and then released it slowly through gritted teeth. This caused greater pain, so he gave that up right quick. Just take the pain, he told himself. Wasn't much of a plan. His mind was a torrent of visions. Of memories. Of traumas. He knew he'd slept, but felt impossibly tired. How long had it been? Days? Weeks? Hours? *No, not hours.* He took another breath; took the pain too. His fingers tingled as he did.

Control it.

Horror suddenly tore at his mind, terrifying and all-encompassing. He gasped and almost wailed, but clung to his nerve. Leaned on it. The waking world was a nightmare.

What the fuk is happening?

"Am I alive?" he called out, but his lips never moved. He'd moaned and imagined the rest. He looked to a piece of fabric in the sheeting roof above. He focused on it as though it were an anchor in a storm. He wasn't certain anchoring in a storm was a good idea, but he clung onto that anchor nonetheless.

Wait, what?

He tried to shake his head and focus. Above him was grey. It flapped gently, like a tent in the wind. Trying to rise, he rediscovered his limbs were bound fast. *Oh, yeah.* So too was his head. *Chains.* His heart sank. A prison break came to mind and, with it, clarity. Not a lot. For a terrible moment he worried he was back in Samara; back in the city; *back in prison.* He couldn't fight his way out either. Couldn't flee upon a gallant steed as clawing hands reached for him. He suddenly feared claw-like hands reaching for him, so he inhaled sharply, flinched and sought coherency. *Fuken chains again.*

His fingers were wet, so he focused on that sensation. Better that than the agony of everywhere else. Peering closely, he saw the scarring and he hissed. It might have been a moan.

Burning.

He remembered blonde hair and a pyre. A female burning. *Aireys burning alive in the night?*

"Oh no, no, no, no," he cried, fighting the panic, forgetting to take careful breaths and squirming in his bindings. He felt weight in his chest. The world spun. He knew he was dying.

Be still and control the pain.

No, fuk that.

He thought of burning pyres, of fearless Aireys, of caring Nomi, of that poor little fuk, Mish, believer of demented things. He remembered gifts and a battle and everyone he loved in great peril. He remembered Oren and then he remembered everything else after that, and his body shuddered because it, too, remembered things. Mostly pain. Oh, the terrible pain of Emir working on his injuries while Erroh howled and cried until insanity took his consciousness.

Everyone died.

"Lea," he cried, and it was no imagined moan. His voice was haggard and broken, but a voice nonetheless. That terror took hold more fiercely now. Fiercer than restraints. *What if Lea perished?* He roared in agony like a beast mid-slaughter. Outside, there came the thumping of footsteps. They sounded like panicked heartbeats and his mind sharpened. He was not imprisoned; he was merely recovering. He called for her again, fearing terrible things. Visions of her watching over him offered no relief; he'd take this pain tenfold to know her safe. "LEA!"

"I'm here, my beo," she cried, bringing light into the room. She always brought light. He almost wept with relief. She was beautiful; she was beaming. He fought his restraints again. Leaning in, she kissed his forehead, laid her hand across his chest, calming his struggles. After a moment, he quieted.

"You are hurt," he whispered of the graze marring her perfect chin. Everything around her was unfocused, but she was clear like crystal water. And this was good.

A few tears fell from her eyes, but she smiled. "Don't worry, Erroh. I'll survive this wound," she said, gazing at the bandaging covering his chest. *To cover all that cutting and stitching.* He heard more people, but his eyes were on Lea alone. He felt wretched hands remove his head's bindings, and movement returned. With it came jagged shards of pain. Blinking the haze from his eyes, he focused on voices filling the room. Friendly, familiar—and unwelcome. He tried to face them, but the world spun. Letting his head drop to the pillow, he took deep breaths, wincing at the pain.

Many voices.

"Erroh."

"Oh, wow, Erroh."

"You are awake, brother!"

"Oh, thank fuk, Erroh!"

He tried to smile, to acknowledge them, but Emir's voice rose louder than anyone else's. "You've seen he's alive. Leave him be." Fine words that *were* welcome.

The voices took it badly. There was dissent.

Again, Emir's voice was louder. "Oh, for fuk's sake... Will everyone stop bothering him..."

The voices wanted to stay; wanted to talk at once. Erroh managed a smile, realising his friends had survived.

"I know you want to see him, Lillium, but the dream syrup must run its course..."

"No, Lea. He doesn't need more for the pain..."

"You don't need any for yourself, Wynn. It won't help a sick stomach... No, it's not fun to use, Wrek..."

"What do you mean? How would I know?"

"All of you out, now! Yes, you, and especially you!" There were further outbursts, but Emir won out. With all but one.

"No need to glare, Lea. I didn't mean you."

Sleep was calling once more, and Erroh tried desperately to fight it, but Wynn's grinning face filled his vision. "Welcome back, you outrageous bastard," he said, bowing. His grin turned to a grimace as the insistent healer ushered him away before Erroh had the strength to reply.

"Not as fuked," the behemoth Wrek mocked, not too unkindly. Erroh almost called him Quig. Almost, but not

quite. He felt lighter than before. Less burdened by Keri.
Nothing like killing to ease the weight. The big man patted
his shoulder and it hurt slightly.

"We need to see him, Emir," Lillium demanded, leaning
over him. Kissing him once upon the lips. Her eyes burned
with excitement and relief. With a fire too. A good look to
her. "Rest now, Hero of Keri," she whispered, before hugging
Lea with equal relief.

One more stepped forward. He did so with complete
authority. "About time you came back, little cub," Magnus
whispered, placing his rugged hand across Erroh's forehead.
"My boy." His eyes were warm, but tragedy swam upon their
surface. More so than before.

"Thank you, Father." Erroh tried to raise his head but, as
though some wonderful serum of hope flooded through his
body, his worries, his panic, collapsed away to the calling of
sleep.

"Calm yourself, Erroh. There is little you can do but
heal," Magnus whispered, stroking his hair as though proud.
Perhaps he was. Perhaps they were equal now. Perhaps there
were miles left to walk.

"I'll be well enough," Erroh gasped, closing his eyes, and
his father stepped away.

She placed the rag back over his forehead and began securing
him as the visitors left. *He should be dead.* With bindings
holding him fast, she smiled despite the nausea in her
stomach. It was cruel keeping him restrained, but it had been
no simple arrow to the back. Behind her, she could sense
Emir's apprehension. His relief. His worry too. His work was
incomplete.

"I'll dress his wounds again," he said, and she shook her

head. She had tears to shed. Tears of relief. She was tired of him making her cry.

"I can do it," she whispered, sitting beside her sleeping, broken beo.

———

"Nomi is burning!" His cry tore her from her slumber. And slowly, Lea rose from her cot. Stumbling with candle in hand, she returned brightness to the gloom. He squirmed in the flickering flame's light and she felt perspiration on his brow. It felt like the frozen south again.

I will not take beaten behaviour again.

"Erroh?"

"Is that you, Lea?" he muttered feebly, and she hated that tone.

"I'm right here."

"My mind is a blur."

"It's the dream syrup."

"I remember burning. I was saving Nomi."

"She didn't burn."

His eyes closed once more. "That's wonderful," he said, sighing dreamily before falling back asleep.

———

It was night; it might have been dawn. Who knew in this delirium? Tasting a salty flavour, he swallowed and thought it a strange feeling. A ladle touched his lips and he accepted the tasty gift. *Food from a goddess.* Distantly, he heard her voice; it was lovely. It gave simple orders, which he followed. Suddenly his vision cleared and he saw her, loved her.

"You're eating more every day, my love," she said,

spooning another mouthful of warmth into his mouth. It might have been stew. Or boiled eye of mad god. He hated stew, but she bade him eat, so he ate.

"I feel stronger today," he lied. Truthfully, he was in agony, but somehow it seemed important she think him improving; think him fighting.

"No, you don't."

"No, I really don't."

She mashed some potato and gave it to him, and as he swallowed, he realised the restraints.

"Easy, Erroh," she whispered, and he smiled. He wanted to impress her. To shun the icy sanctuary without thought. To fight.

"Pain or not, I want to get out of bed."

She liked this. He could see it in her smile. He fought sleep and remembered the potency of dream syrup. He struggled again in the restraints; he remembered his friends visiting. *Another dream?*

"It hasn't yet been two weeks, my beautiful idiot." She stroked his grizzled cheek. He wanted her to shave him. When he could enjoy it more. "Stay resting."

"You'll rip the stitching," came a voice. Grouchy and stern. Sounded like the healer. Carefully, Erroh eased his head back and took in the room from a lopsided angle. A difficult thing with such swimming thoughts. He watched an upside-down Emir examining a glass jar at his little desk. Lined up behind him were rows of healers' jars on a freestanding shelf. Emir's lips moved absently as he counted, and then he scribbled the number into a little notepad. Erroh lay back and watched the unimpressive legend take stock. It was something to do.

Emir spoke suddenly and broke the trance. "You'll be able to walk in a week," he muttered, looking up from his notes, daring a smile. He poured a glass of green nastiness before adding a generous amount of salt and stirred rapidly. Holding the glass over a candle, he let it bubble. Daring a mouthful, he swallowed and immediately began silently retching. Once he'd caught his breath, he scribbled some more notes. He looked pleased with whatever he'd discovered.

"In another week, I'll be running," Erroh said.

"Soon enough, we'll all be running," Emir muttered in bitter agreement.

———

He couldn't remember them removing the last restraint, only that the pain was immense when he woke. It was worth it for the faint lucidity. Once more he attempted to rise and met pain. *Take it.* Carefully, he held up his injured fingers and shuddered; they were cracked and seeping. They glistened in the dimness, and he remembered foreign fingers massaging wretched, gelatinous substances deep into the scorched brown leathery surface. Strangely, he discovered he could form fists easily enough and felt a thousand times better. *I can still fight.*

His chest, however, was mutilated. He could see the ruin from the arrows in all their ugly glory. The gashes from every glancing blow. Whatever parts weren't bandaged or stitched were bruised a terrible purple. How do I still live? he wondered.

"Aye, you'll have some attractive scarring, brother, but the absent god blessed you upon the battle," Emir called from his desk. His shirt was a different colour. The concoctions an entirely different mixture. Time passed differently when one was healing. When held firm. When in the dark.

"I can't wait to test your stitching, my beo," Lea said

from somewhere, but Erroh's ruined hand had fallen to his injuries. He fingered the ugly indents in his skin and thought himself ghastly. Like some wild boar with a misshapen tusk had used him for sport. His stitches screamed with every touch. He couldn't help himself.

"Look what they did to me, Lea."

She appeared before him, taking his face in her hands, kissing him delicately lest he break. "You will scar like a legend. You will earn more, my love."

Fine words, though they sounded hollow. He thought of a cage, he thought of snow. He bit the inside of his mouth. *Fuk that.*

When she broke away, Emir waited with the foul liquid. "For the pain," he offered.

"Will it get me walking any sooner?" Erroh asked desperately, and fought the anguish in his tone. He coughed. It hurt. He desired the liquid. *Delicious delirium.* Aye, Erroh knew the hold it could take. Emir had threatened him long ago when Lea was struck down. He'd remembered her moaning forlornly as the last of it had slipped from her system. He really fuken wanted it.

"It will make the time pass quicker."

"How much have I had?" Erroh's eyes focused on the creamy substance. He couldn't smell it but decided it would be like drowning in honey milk.

"There was a lot of blood. A lot of cutting. A lot of sleeping required."

"How much, Emir?"

"One would say enough."

"I need no more," he whispered, staring down at his scars again before covering up and feeling miserable. He knew the torment to come, but he was determined. "Please don't offer it to me again. I can take the pain," he hissed, staring longingly at the syrup as it wavered close to his lips.

Just one for the road.

The healer nodded warily before returning the wonderfully vile fluid to a jar and hiding it back among the rest of his concoctions.

"You're so brave, and so fuken stupid," Lea whispered, placing a belt down beside his face for when the pain became too much. He was but one bite away from taking it quietly. He thought it a fine move on her part. Deep down, a cage shattered to nothing.

"I'm godly," he mocked.

———

The crowd's singing woke him for what felt like the thousandth time that day. That week? He waited for the resurgence of pain that usually followed his waking and found instead a dull embrace of discomfort. He was getting better. It brought little joy and less relief. He longed for the syrup and he felt low again. The restraints held him fast and he swallowed a curse. *Alone in the dark and chained.* He felt the dream syrup's absence heavily now, and his mouth watered. To throw up, or drink deeply the bliss he foolishly denied himself?

One more hit for the dark.

Immediately he shook that thought away. There was pain, but another agony was boredom. When not spending his time engaged in delicate conversation with Lea or Emir, he slept. He'd slept more than he ever had in prison, and in sleep he'd found further recovery. Further strength, too. Despite the itch for relief. Despite the monotony. Despite the surging torrents of pain. He fought the restraints and sighed in defeat. He knew he was closer to healing. He dedicated every moment until then to Uden. He had gifts. He would start with Oren's head. A fine first offering.

"Fuken dark," he said aloud, listening again to the music. He wanted to smile, but in his mind, everyone was celebrating life, victory, even the very fact of walking around, and he lay in the dark alone.

They are probably drinking the finest sine.

"To Erroh," he whispered, and craved something biting for his throat. Something beyond the tepid water that Emir insisted be his only beverage. Something to celebrate growing recovery. Footsteps neared, and he braced himself for company. They would light a candle, and his mood would improve. He concentrated on the ropes on his wrists, which were as inflamed and itchy as his hands. Painful memories of his hands were fading now. Soon enough, his chest might follow. The footsteps went by and he sighed. What did he expect? Lea had been with him every day. What harm was there in her enjoying cheer? He forced a smile and knew better.

"Hello?" he said into the darkness.

Nothing.

"Is there anybody there?" More nothing. The only sources of light were the crackling red embers in the stove fire. Ever constant, allowing enough warmth for healing. Maybe if someone stoked them, there would be interesting shadows to ease the stillness. He laughed and thought it a wonderful sensation. Boredom was his newest complaint. Beyond, they sang loudly, and there were stirrings of innocent violence and controlled mayhem. All in the spirit of fine times. Emir would be swinging at the nearest opponent by now. He tried not to be bitter.

Without warning, Lillium stumbled drunkenly through the

door of the tent. Or else just clumsily. She stopped and regained her balance. He heard her curse the dark as she glided to the fire and stoked the flames violently. Godlike fingers of shadow moved across his vision, and he almost laughed again.

"Lillium?" he said.

"Oh, fuk me. I'm sorry for waking you, Erroh," she mumbled, lighting a candle. Through the opened tent flap, the cheers rose. The candle passed over his head and she sat down nearby. He could smell the alcohol on her. On her breath, down her shirt, too. She didn't seem to care either. This too was a good look to her.

"Where is everybody?" he croaked, pulling at the restraints absently. She swiftly began undoing the bindings.

"Mood was low. Wrek organised a little gathering." She pulled his right hand free and he yelped. "Oh, fuk, I'm sorry." Her words were slurred but light. A rare thing from her. Ruination was a good thing. As was tearing her mate's heart to shreds. *Wynn had it coming, though, didn't he?* She attacked the second knot delicately and eased the ropes apart without causing much pain.

"I would kill for a drink," he said, sitting up carefully. Though initially severe, the pain swiftly disappeared. He decided to sit up more often.

Lillium smiled, pulling a large tankard from her belt like a thief approaching a fence. "To make up for waking and torturing you," she said, unscrewing the cap.

It burned as he drank, and it was glorious. Swallowing, he coughed painfully. Some went up his nose and this too was glorious. This felt like being alive. Pain and all.

"How are you?" she asked, drinking a measure herself. She coughed less, and Erroh wondered why it was easier to drink violent brews the drunker you became.

"I'm feeling fierce," he joked, dropping the sheets and showing the ruined chest.

"Scars are a beautiful thing," she said, examining his stitching. She almost reached for him and caught herself. "Ooh, Erroh; I think you need to cover up. I just might do something foolish."

"Aye. I am quite the catch, if you'll remember. This has just made me more alluring."

To this she said nothing. She merely drew her eyes from his chest and stared at him. He remembered her cruel tongue. Remembered her anger. Remembered her regal authority. This battered warrior in front of him appeared a thousand times more interesting.

"Thanks for the drink," he offered, and she smiled. "And the company, too. I feel more awake today." She also smiled at this.

"Lea never let you out of her sight. Even when she was walking among the gathering, her eyes never left the tent. I said I'd watch you awhile. I'm so sorry I woke you."

At this he smiled. "I doubt Lea would have brought me alcohol. I'm grateful, Lillium, truly I am." He looked around, searching for conversation. "So, what happened to the blue hair? It was stunning," he said, and she froze. He could see her sorrow in the flickering flame. He wasn't sure what he'd said. Surely it was no small matter for a female to change her hair so drastically.

"That stuck-up bitch with the blue hair is no longer me." Her voice was loud, assured. She held a few strands of her long brown hair. "Harder to see in the wastes." She played with the strands, lost to thoughts not meant for him. "I was stunning, though, wasn't I?"

"Aye, but brown is nice," he offered, and she laughed.

"I'll take it." Whatever sorrowful thoughts she'd endured

were lost in the moment. "I really am sorry for disturbing you."

As he drank again, there came a crash from somewhere outside, and both Alphalines jumped. Erroh felt a protective hand place itself across his chest, and he saw her other draw into a fist. Within a breath of hearing the loud cheer to go along with whatever clumsiness had occurred, she drew her hand away swiftly.

"You make a great guardian," he joked, and she nodded drunkenly, so he offered her the tankard.

"Not too much. Any more and I'm likely to say all manner of apologetic words of the Cull," she said. He thought them fine words, and she shrugged. "Sorry for waking you. Sorry for touching you. I was startled, is all."

"Are you alright?"

She shrugged again. "Some noises remind me of the nights of riots in the city," she said, and he reached out and touched her shaking hands. He didn't know why. It was something to do.

"It was a bad time," he whispered.

"For others, far worse," she hissed with venom, squeezing his hands in return. He didn't react to the sudden eruption of pain. After a moment she appeared to realise.

"Ah, shit, Erroh—I'm sorry. I'm so sorry for everything."

"Like waking me?"

"Aye, that too. I'm drunk."

"Come on, let's drink away before Emir comes back and kills me for trying to enjoy myself," he said. She laughed loudly and the air in the room became lighter. It felt as though some unspoken thing had passed between them, something he couldn't quite put his finger on. Her eyes seemed more settled than before. Maybe it was inebriation on both their parts. Two shots of sine were enough. *Better than dream syrup.*

———

"I said monitor him. I never said get him drunk," shouted Lea, appearing at the doorway two rounds later. Lillium hung her head, but couldn't stop sniggering at Erroh's tale of the foolish brute, an attractive sword and some blatant cheating.

"Sorry, my love. I am a dangerous influence," he slurred as smoothly as he could. He hadn't noticed the volume of the crowd had dropped to an inaudible murmur. It was later than he thought.

"We will speak of this later," Lea scolded, grabbing the tankard from Lillium. A moment later she was filling three goblets from Emir's collection of breakable things. It was a gathering, was it not? Even in a healer's tent. "I'm the foolish one, allowing Lillium in here to charm my defenceless mate," she mocked.

"Another round and I'd have charmed him into bed. Oh, wait—never mind."

Both females laughed, and Erroh reached for his mate.

"I feel stronger, beo. I might try to walk a few steps tomorrow," he declared, gesturing for a hug. He received both hug and kiss.

"I shall take my leave before your love sickens me," Lillium said, climbing unsteadily to her feet.

"No, no, Lillium, you haven't earned an escape just yet," Lea decided. "Not until we've run dry. Besides, we will need to sacrifice someone to take Emir's wrath."

"I have a use, it would appear."

———

It was Erroh who outlasted them all. Perhaps it was the weeks of sleeping that had prepared him for such an event. Lillium had fallen asleep first, and Lea a short time after. They sat hunched over him on each side, and Erroh thought such a vision was amusing. With the effects of sine dulling his senses, he lay back in his cot, leaving the bindings where they lay. He closed his eyes for a few moments and was rudely woken by a loud, mocking healer.

"Wynn will kill you," Emir growled, stealing the fullest glass. As he did, he tapped both females on the head with a judgemental finger. Lea stirred and squinted her eyes against the morning sun shining through the open flap. She cursed it loudly, and Lillium rose with a start, reaching for a blade from an absent scabbard before realising there was no threat. No weapon, either.

"Nothing can kill Erroh. He is blessed by absent gods," she declared, stumbling from her seat to unsteady feet. "The dark brings horror. Fuk the dark." She stared at the sun, taking it in. "Light is far better," she murmured, grabbing at her hair, yawning.

"I think you enjoyed the gathering as much as I did, Lillium," Emir muttered, eyeing Erroh's wounds. Erroh could see a little swelling over his upper lip. He'd split his knuckle too. *A good night at the Sickle.*

"I did, I had beautiful company. I love you both," she whispered, kissing Erroh once upon the lips. She attempted the same assault on Lea, but her friend was already crawling into her cot.

"Don't I get a kiss?" Emir asked, feigning hurt.

"You are not Alpha. Why would I bother with a lowerline?"

Before he could counter, she leapt upon him, kissing him roughly on the lips, before shoving him away. "I prefer kissing Erroh, but you are fine," she said, shrugging. Her eyes were alight with mischief and a little drunken wildness. "I think I'll walk the perimeter before sleep." With that she was gone, her drunken steps focused and assured.

"Perhaps Wynn will kill us both," Erroh said as she left.

Emir shook his head. Embarrassed at her affection, jesting as it was. "Aye, you weren't the one who asked for the kiss, though. I'm more dead than you."

"Was Lillium kissing my mate again?" Lea muttered from her place beneath the covers. If she was threatened, nothing sounded in her muffled tones.

Though sleep called and the rested stirrings of a hangover were drawing ever near, Erroh slid his legs from the coverings and draped them down along its side. "I think it's time to get up," he whispered, and within a moment Lea was free of her own cot, looking as fresh as the day.

"Get him a crutch," she demanded, and Emir wasted no moment.

"I've rested enough. There are things to be done."

"Aye," Lea agreed. "And events to learn of."

Erroh didn't like that tone. Not one little bit.

———

It was the thick bandaging Emir had insisted upon that made Erroh struggle to breathe, but the healer would allow nothing else. Carefully, and held in place by constrictive wrappings, Erroh shuffled from his prison. He wore no boots, instead enjoying the feel of damp firmament beneath his feet. The camp was unchanged these last few weeks. It was more vibrant, though the stench of bodies was thicker when he moved away from the veneer of eucalyptus he'd grown accustomed to.

His allies of the Black watched him with unblinking eyes. When last he'd charged, he'd been a god of foolish vengeance. Now, he appeared a broken warrior, leaning on a wooden crutch and a doting mate, wavering in the early morning's breeze. *Not for long.*

"I can walk alone, my beo." he whispered, but when she stepped away, his body wavered slightly. He stumbled until his body remembered a skill he couldn't remember learning. The simple act of balance. *Don't fall in the mud, idiot*, he warned himself, and somehow stayed upright. "This feels good," he said through gritted teeth. His head still spun, but he found every step coming easier. Soon he was marching, and Lea was beside him the entire way. Until they walked behind the healer's tent and he came face to face with Nomi.

Chains in the cold.

Chains in the dark.

He suddenly realised he'd heard the chains every day. He'd never imagined it was her struggling in her holdings. He could feel the anger rise, and he allowed it to surface. His hands became fists, and nothing else in the world mattered but the waif in captivity.

Lea gripped his shoulder. "Be calm, Erroh."

Nomi was huddled up against a solitary post, and Erroh knew her coverings couldn't possibly stave off the elements. He spun on Lea. "How could you allow this treatment?"

Lea's eyes narrowed. "Not here, Erroh." He shrugged away her hand and almost stumbled. Her eyes narrowed more. "We need to speak with Magnus."

He tried to reach the sleeping girl, but Lea took hold again. Not for support, but for restraining. *Like chains.* In anger, he felt his strength return. Felt his mind clear. His thoughts were cold.

4

EALIS

Her name was Ealis, and Alder believed her the most enchanting creature to walk the south. She had trapped him like a spider in a frozen web, and he was never happier. Swiftly, they darted through the quiet streets of Conlon. Only the moon watched with a condemning glare, every step they took. For they were careful. Ealis gripped his hands tightly, and he wondered if this was love and smiled against the bitter air. It was lust. Perhaps something beyond, but that was how love blossomed. Love came from more, from trusting, too. Mostly, it came from acts.

Love and trust.

He knew this, because he listened when others spoke of greater, elusive things. Wonderful things he wasn't familiar with. A good listener was a gift to this world; they inherited wisdom. Those who inherited kingly things were wiser to listen and learn before taking the throne. Alder was not ready for such grandness. Not yet.

"Swift, my dear," he whispered, dragging her from one darkened pathway to another. She followed without word.

She knew the danger, too. Followers of forbidden things knew well to listen for threat. Every step they took was an affront to the night's silence. He was taller, his steps heavier. Hers were delicate and silent. Like a dancer's.

Halting for a momentary reprieve against the pace, they took shelter beneath the shadows of a tall building. He listened to her gasping breath and smiled. He knew that gasp well. Daring a glance at her eyes, they sparkled in the night. She was just as terrified as most others upon this first step, and he wanted to embrace her, comfort her. Bed her again, too. She had been nervous, gentle, magnificent.

"How far?" she asked, and he stroked her porcelain cheek. It was paler than most southerners'. She hid well from the sun. Her life ahead would require such nocturnal acts. He smiled again. One for life was a beautiful thing.

"A few more steps, Ealis."

"That's good to know," she whispered. He could hear the worry. She sensed a trap, and that was fine. All southerners fearing Uden's blessed condemnation expected a trap for acts of sacrilege. Aye, Alder had taken a risk trusting her with words suggesting subtle disdain for Uden, but Ealis's trust in his reassuring sedition was downright reckless.

I could be leading you into doom, my dear.

"Don't worry, they will wait for you. They will wait for me, too," he said kindly, and she squeezed his hand. They were late, but Alder's position among them allowed such things. Princes arrived when they needed to. He spun her around and she twirled magnificently into his arms, giggling, despite the threat of watching eyes. Those stunning eyes could dominate gods and set any man's heart to skip out of time.

. . .

Ealis kissed her man fervently. She knew he was a good man. Kind, hopeful and passionate about the world. This world, shaped as Uden the Woodin Man desired. Their lips parted and she thought about their wild furrowing. He was a generous lover. So few of the brutes among their people attacked her body with such attentiveness. Perhaps such emotion and devotion could only come from a solitary mate.

Such a frightening and intriguing notion.

She caressed his clean-shaven cheeks and allowed him to drag her farther down the eerily empty streets. She ran perfectly in time with each one of his powerful strides. Such things might have mattered to another, but to Ealis it was simple timing and undeserving of careless thoughts. Breaking Uden's curfew was a dangerous game ever since his march had begun. Secluded congregating, outspoken dissension— the penalties were severe. People spoke of his paranoia and whispered of fallibility to his actions. Perhaps his eyesight suffered; perhaps those needing the spark of revolution were gathering their flints. Alder was one such man. A leader of many, too. Stifling her better self, Ealis had hung on his every word in the smoky tavern that first night. She'd lost herself in his eyes and his smile. Sitting down with the man who could strike out from the depths of a god's belly was intoxicating. He was beautiful, courageous and so very dangerous. He would lead them all as he led Ealis tonight, and the south would shake from his actions. But Ealis was no leader. At least not anymore. She would lead once again.

"I could kiss you all night," he whispered suddenly, stopping by an old doorway and knocking lightly. Three light taps. She'd have preferred one less or one more, but such things didn't really bother her. "Such a wonderful kisser," he added, and oh, she longed to kiss him too, for Ealis was spun a fine tale and she wanted to believe. Wanted to rebel, wanted to follow her heart. Wonderfully, he kissed her, and she felt a craving deep down. Something beyond primal furrowing. *Something godly.*

He broke away and knocked again, and she looked up and down the eerie street for unwanted patrols. How cruel for a stumbling band of curs to happen upon their little midnight dalliance and ruin a perfectly set plan. She absently counted a hundred similar doorways on either side for a few moments before suppressing that desire. She was impressed with the anonymity of the insignificant door. That's how little southern rebellions remained as secretive as they did. Even in the stronghold of a god's domain. She approved.

"Not just kissing, but other things too," she whispered, biting her lip. He brought out different desire in her. His vigour and strength of will were intoxicating. She loved these moments. When she felt like herself. Her real self. Her oldest self. Feeling like this was a life well lived.

The door opened, and she followed him into their world. Despite herself, she was anxious. She would trust in Alder, though. He would keep her safe. She took his hand and squeezed it again. She hoped he would return the gesture, but he did not. Instead, he pulled her swiftly through the barren house as though he were leading an unwilling beast to slaughter. For no beast wanted to die. And no beast expected its end, and she thought this a strange thing.

"Come, Ealis," he insisted, and she couldn't but follow him. The house was not furnished for living a southern life. Most rooms were bare but for thick, drawn curtains hiding the world from what lay within. Few candles hung from the walls, and no carpets relieved the biting cold. The only constant decoration were endless barrels of unopened alcohol, lined up like soldiers as they passed. She could have counted

them, but Ealis cared little for such things. Their feet echoed
a different melody of loneliness now as they walked through
a long corridor towards a grand room of lavish golden rugs,
silver silk curtains and majestic grandness. Like an outlawed
king's transitory court. Alder looked back to kiss her hand
and she knew, deep down, she had chosen him well. She
bowed, for the light burned her eyes. She took a few deep,
calming breaths and listened to the buzz of excitement as it
spun sparks of energy in the air itself. Around her were
mutterings of a loyal gathering, but it was one voice that rose
above them all. It was old and pompous and regal.

"Ah, Alder. Is this the girl?"

In the centre of a grand room unbefitting such a barren
house, and beneath the glorious light of a candle chandelier,
an old man stood waiting. Beside her, Alder bowed deeply.
The crinkled face was covered in grey hair, but his eyes were
fierce. He wasn't as tall as Alder, but she could see the
resemblance immediately.

"This is Ealis." Alder sounded proud, and she smiled, and
he stroked her hair, and she strove to control her unsettled
emotions. *How many children has he sired in honour of the
god Uden?* she wondered. *Countless, and he desires
something more.* She imagined briefly what a child born of
such impressive bloodlines might be and caught her smile.
His jaw, her eyes. *Perfect.*

She knew he meant to give her a child. He'd pledged to
her as much, told her that humankind, regardless of race or
region, wasn't meant to flitter from lover to lover. "Breeding
like beasts," he'd said, and she'd smiled at such words. He
called their communion blessed. "We have the rest of our
lives to know each other, Ealis. This is the way," he'd said,
and from then she'd known her path, and it was fascinating.

His father stepped from the light and beckoned them

closer with an open, welcoming hand. "Tell me—her beauty is not the only reason you trust her, I assume?" he said, though not unkindly. Merely cautiously. And rightly so. The leader of the southern resistance stepped forward and embraced his son, and Ealis stood quietly, hugging her long heavy cloak of warmth and concealment. The south was cold. It always had been to her. No matter the clothing she wore or the logs on the fire, she was eternally frozen to the bone. She suddenly missed the warmth of the north. She wanted to taste the air where her breath didn't sting.

"No, it isn't," Alder said, laughing. He offered Ealis a wink, and she tried to return the gesture. As usual, she could not master the art and caught the grimace she made.

Ealis wasn't alone in the room, and she wasn't the only newcomer, either. *Comfort in growing numbers.* At least a dozen acolytes stood waiting and watching, gathered in clusters and sharing hushed mutterings of dissent and disgust. She couldn't hear their words, but she felt their burning, nervous eyes upon her. And why not? She was beautiful, a goddess among them, and deep down she wanted to count them aloud. Most wore the smug expression that came with a southerner's instinctive rebelliousness, but a few others shared the same uncertain expression as Ealis.

First time meeting royalty.

She imagined the gift Uden would place upon the man who delivered this meeting place to him upon a platter. *Or a mad god's platter,* as Alder was inclined to say. And she suddenly wondered if one of these acolytes was an assassin, sent with blade and wrath to deliver a god's message. She felt a shiver run down her back. She felt a stranger in this room. A stranger chosen. In her words, in her actions, in her lineage, she was different. These waiting acolytes were of old blood, from before the shattering of the Factions. The remnants of the older families slain by Uden, during his brutal climb to godliness. They hadn't believed in him then; they didn't believe in him now. They were only the beginnings of gathered defiance and little else, but great fires started with the smallest sparks.

"I must take part in a performance," Alder whispered, gesturing to a small stool near the doorway. There was preaching in the air and Alder would play his part. She knew this because she knew everything about her lover. He liked to talk and trust, and she liked to listen and learn. Giving her a delicate kiss, he bowed and made his way through the gathering to join his father upon a foot-high stage at the top of the room. Hardly impressive, but enough for nobility when speaking to their flock. The gathered crowd took seats for themselves as though in prayer, and Ealis leaned back against the wall, watching and learning.

Waiting, too.

When the old man spoke, his tones were stern, yet still charming. There was a familiarity to him. Like a father of a nation. She glanced around and all others listened as if he were a high priest echoing the Woodin Man's words and laws. He was preaching, but he was no god. No matter how eloquent he was.

"Thank you, my dearest brothers and sisters, for coming here tonight. I know how difficult it is to remain unnoticed these worrying days." He took a kingly breath and smiled. "I would also like to thank our comrades from the 'deep north' for providing this venue tonight." There was a little laughter. A few of the audience members held glasses in their hands. Using bandits from the deep north explained the barrels. It also explained the ease in which these meetings had occurred without discovery. If you needed concealment in any of the Four Factions, you used a bandit's trail. Ealis thought this very interesting.

Bandits can be tracked like a Raven upon a rock.

She thought back to their agreed meeting place outside the city gates. Alder had insisted they meet where no watching eyes were present. Twisting and turning through the labyrinth of streets and dark alleys for miles had ensured no enemy pursued. This was not the resistance in its entirety, but among the dozen gathered there were its staunchest and most dangerous followers. There was risk in so many meeting under one roof, but revolutions had to suffer precarious steps when lighting the way for the rest to follow. Alder had said as much. Ealis understood.

"There is still no word of the northerner they call Erroh. Every day without word serves us well," he announced, and many heads nodded. As did Ealis's. "My voice is faint, but it can still travel far," the old man said, and more agreed. Ealis thought he had a fine, loud voice. She shuffled in her seat and her cloak caught sharply on her dagger's hilt. It was a simple dagger and far less impressive than the glimmering, jewel-encrusted swords hanging from the waists of most attendees. She thought it symbolic of the distance between them. A lesser girl might have been intimidated, but Ealis had the support of Alder as companion.

"Speak of Erroh with those pining for our people's older ways," the old man continued. "Speak of him as a symbol and speak with awe. Many need a god. He can be that empty god. At least for a time. Use him to our advantage, for he is our spark," he declared to an enraptured audience. "Uden is a great man. But he is an evil man. No man or woman should rule a people as he has. Any man from another land should never rule at all. As he marches north, we have this moment to reclaim what is ours. Tonight, ride back to your people, to your clans, and gather your words and spread them across this land. Speak our people's language. Speak of their need for gods." He took a breath and wiped a little spittle from his mouth. His eyes were blazing and impressive, and Ealis wasn't surprised he had come to such power beneath the distracted eye of her god.

"Uden delivered unto Erroh his dead lover, Nomi of the south," the old man proclaimed. "She was the beautiful goddess who stole his heart and virtue. Uden took their child's life and delivered it upon a platter, along with his swords of destruction, so when they meet in the city, they will be equally matched." The crowd knew some of this. Ealis's understanding was a little tainted. It was a small matter; it was a good tale to spread. "Upon the walls of Spark City, the fire god will tear Uden apart." The crowd nodded, for it was an epic tale. Alder's father's tone softened. "Tell your kin that scripture will be fulfilled. That prophesy will come to pass. Make them believe. Spread this whisper, and listen to it grow to a godly shout."

A few people cheered in agreement. These were not the ramblings of a broken old war hero, after all, and they were not the ill-informed zealots Uden believed them to be. They were enlightened, and they were dangerous. Ealis had come to the right place. She smiled serenely and listened on, all the while stretching her godly, perfect body. Alder nodded every few moments as his father spoke, and she thought him beautiful.

"I am old, as are many of you," the old man whispered, peering past his royal subjects to the glorious girl with the incredible eyes sitting alone at the back of the room. "It warms me to know that others will continue this struggle," he added, placing his hand on his son's shoulder. "Back in your homes, many of you have kin of your own. They are the enlightened youth, and their numbers will multiply, and, someday, they will walk as free southerners once more. There will be blood and strife. There will also be love. Unions between our people, not out of duty, but out of love and companionship. Now, please come here, little one. You, my dear, are part of our future," the old man said kindly, and reached out for Ealis. "All our loved ones are."

Ealis thought him a great man; a strong leader and a decorated war hero. He was kingly, and, above all, he was a good man. Like his son. With so many bodies in the room it became suddenly warm, and she felt like removing her cloak, but she wanted to listen more to the calming few words. He beckoned again, and she wanted to shy away from his radiance. She could feel the stirring, the clawing. Closer now. Coming to the surface. She stood up and wondered how many steps it would take to walk to her future father-in-law. "Ealis is such a lovely name," she heard him say, and she obeyed his wishes, counting his words because Ealis was fading away. Her other self was climbing free.

Six words spoken.

"It is short for Borealis," Alder reminded him, from beside him. He locked his eyes on her and she smiled and counted. *Five.* She knew the old man's name to be Inden. She knew him as the last king. She passed through the crowd, undoing her cloak. Button by button. Her breath tightened in anticipation. So close to blood. So close to dying. She knew she might die in the next few breaths and it was beautiful.

"They named you after the southern lights," said the old man.

Seven again.

. . .

He had named her after the southern lights. It was the name
Uden had given her, the night he had first gifted torment.
Born in blood. She could only remember his description of
the sky that night for the memory was lost to darkness. The
sky had shimmered with different ethereal colours, and he
had declared it an omen of her majesty and she had been
honoured. He had doused her in blood that night. Doused her
until she nearly drowned. She still drowned in it every day.
She still suffered the fear and loved it.

Her name was Aurora, and she liked to kill.

The two small crossbows strapped to her armoured thighs
were far easier to conceal than she had expected. She
reached down and snapped them free of their holders and
fired. Why bother to aim? She never missed. Perhaps in the
early days she had suffered such imperfections, but Uden had
relieved her of such frailties, painfully enough. These bows
lacked power compared to most traditional crossbows, but in
a room this small the distance was inconsequential. The first
bolt pierced her lover's eye and continued on through. She
knew how to kill swiftly. She also knew the places on the
body that would drain slowest, allowing a more intimate
taste of murder. Allowing a chance of survival. She knew the
time it took for a slow bleed to run dry. She knew the
screams, too.

They are louder with a second bolt.

She had no interest in saving Alder, and even less in
punishing him any more than she did. She would dearly miss
lying in his arms, exhausted and bested. In that moment,
before he died, she wondered did he realise what had
occurred? She hoped not, though she didn't really know why.
Killing was killing, and betrayal was just as gloriously

bloody. She spared a moment to watch his head crack back against the wall. Already dead, already seeping out blood.

Her second shot struck an older woman in the throat. *Foolish, Aurora.* There were more able-bodied warriors to strike down before attending to the lesser threats. She spun and kicked out at the nearest stunned acolyte, who was too frozen in horror to offer threat. Perhaps he and the dying woman were in love, and watching her grip her throat and send a spray of blood into the warm air was jarring. Her kick took out his nose—shattered it, most likely. She dropped her weapons of choice and reached for the daggers along her waist in one smooth motion. She had many weapons, but sometimes a personal approach was needed. So long had it been since she had spilled blood; daggers felt right.

It took only moments, but she cut through several more before the true screams erupted.

How impressive are the shiny swords now?

Built and born to kill Alphalines. A clustered gathering of heretics, fat on secluded privilege and years of inaction, would offer little problem. She would not be careless, however. She never gave them a chance. Astonishment was her ally, and she played upon their shock. Never slowing, with no regard for her own body, she waded in among them, stabbing mercilessly at plentiful easy targets. Her long hair whipped out in a divine frenzy, for she was a god's assassin and the plan was coming to fruition. They stumbled from their chairs as the horrific realisation overcame them. They leapt to their feet as she murdered them. The crimson spray soaked through her as she struck blow after blow in a perfect, unswerving rhythm. Always in time, always in perfect order. One strike was enough to kill or debilitate before stepping to the next. She moved as he had taught her, a blur of unrivalled fury dancing through the room. Screams of hatred, panic and misery were a melody and she hummed along, a little tune of her own, each note driven by each anguished cry. Her fingers were no longer her own. They were bathed in the red of a god's hatred, and she suddenly remembered a night in the mountains when she was born.

So much blood.

Never enough.

Inexplicably, she lost count of her footsteps and faltered for a moment, retracing her steps in her mind before continuing to count again. In the slight respite, an injured acolyte gathered his wit and charged at her with a sword. He even swung it once before meeting his end. She liked when they fought. Those who fought were the best type of murdered. She cut and thrust through all who challenged until no more came forward, and she whined in agony, drawing near the last man. He fell to his knees, wailing for mercy. She stepped past him. A fine jest on her part: he might have believed his pitiful words had borne fruit. Slowly, she held the blade above his crown before shoving down with her weight behind it; through thinning hair, wrinkled pink skin, bone and the soft meat beneath. He shuddered violently and she held the blade a moment longer, embedded within him, and it was divine. He gasped, his arms flailed and he died, and she tugged the long dagger free, leaving him twitching pathetically before falling still.

Delicious.

The world fell to a stillness and Aurora Borealis stood in the middle of her dripping carnage. All around her was the slow sobbing of her victims as they took their last breaths. In her storm of passion, Inden had been struck down. He lay beside his dead son, one hand resting on his kin's blood-soaked hair. A fine way to die, she thought regretfully. Perhaps it would have been merciful killing both first so that neither would have had to endure the other's passing.

Covered in blood.

All those weeks listening to Alder speak of his love for his people had affected her, despite herself. He had been a wonderful talker; so wise, so hopeful, so open. But she was as skilled at deception and seduction as she was with her crossbows. She had eased her way into their circle, and now she had cut the heads free of the venomous snakes. She wondered if Uden would care about the lengths she'd gone to in order to attain their trust. *Uden sees all.* It wasn't his wrath for the writhing acts that troubled her. It was something else entirely. In those weeks of playing the delicate little Ealis, all wide-eyed and warm and kind and lost, she had felt settled. A strange thing not to wake every morning and desire blood and murder and death.

And oh, they are the grandest things.

Ealis was a very interesting thing.

More interesting than Fyre of the Night?

"Perhaps so," Aurora whispered in the quiet room. Her feet squelched in the puddles of crimson forming into one docile lake of glorious beauty. It reminded her of her birth, for that night she had almost drowned in it. *Drown in it.* Kneeling, she rubbed her fingers through the dead liquid. It was still warm and it settled her shaking mind. Uden had promised her all the blood, and he had just given her a taste of it. *Praise be my first-ever lover.*

In her ear, she heard the slow wheeze of another victim, and she set her eyes upon Inden. Leaving her lake of blood, held fast by stained rugs, she stepped over him to watch him die. A wonderful thing to watch the body run dry. For a terrible moment, she imagined no longer being enamoured with such finality and suppressed that terror for another day. *Why spoil a wondrous moment?*

She avoided the vacant stare of her lover. She took little joy in it and didn't understand why.

I don't regret this.

I don't regret this.

I DON'T REGRET THIS.

Kneeling beside the fallen king, she wiped some blood from Inden's mouth and then brushed away the tears streaming silently down his cheeks. No war hero deserved to die while crying.

"You are a fine assassin," he whispered with bubbling breath, and fresh tears appeared.

Suit yourself, Aurora said in her mind, but Ealis reached out and wiped them again. *Hurry into the darkness*, Aurora whispered. Fine words. A suggestion. A kindness, too. Sometimes the dying fought the wrong fight. Sometimes the better fight was in not releasing the bowels until after death had occurred.

"A fine assassin," he repeated to himself.

"I am more than an assassin," she whispered back. She was a leader of the Hunt and her acts for Uden would return her to his favour. These things mattered. These things explained her cruelty.

"We are all so much more in this life," he whispered, and she appreciated it. She smiled and nodded in agreement.

"Uden has no place for you in Valhal," she said, and though she did not know why, she stroked his cheek and left her hand upon him. "Do you fear where you will next tread?"

"As you kneel over me, I will show no fear," he said defiantly, coughing up fresh blood all over her hand. He needs every droplet, she thought, wiping her blade on her leg. Better a clean blade for a kingly task.

"Close your eyes, last king of the south, and I will ease your passing," she said. "Go to Alder."

Although not in Valhal.

"I will take no gift."

"I'm sorry you suffer," she said, fighting the awkwardness of casual conversation and waiting for beauty to occur.

Covered in blood.

He almost smiled. Instead, he sneered. "I'm sorry my boy loved you so." It was a curse and fuk him, but it stung her and she did not know why. "I'm sorry you believe in what you do, vile girl. This suffering I endure is nothing compared to our people's enslavement."

He argued upon death's door. She was impressed. She was patient too. She lost the need to count.

"Our people are not enslaved, not anymore."

This time he did smile and filled it with such hate she wanted to run her fingers through his hair fondly. Perhaps Ealis might have endured a pleasant few words with him before inevitability raised its head from the deepest recesses of chains, blood and anguish. That might have been nice.

"Oh, you are wrong, Ealis. Our people are enslaved. By a maniacal fiend, perverted by ancient scrolls." He shuddered, spitting again, and more blood warmed her ruined fingers. She wanted to lick them clean. "A fool believing them prophesy."

You leave my beautiful god alone, old king. She reached for her dagger. One slice and she would be free of this massacre. "The scrolls are prophetic and he is godly and I love him more than your wretched dead son," she said, and the lie stung as much as his condemning hate. "I'm sorry," Ealis whispered. She felt like wailing, yet held firm.

"I have read the scrolls too," he gasped, for his breath was

failing, and this shook her. *Who lied in their last breaths?*
Blood surrounded her, covered her, and she almost cried out
in ecstasy, and revulsion too. She placed her hand against the
wound along his side where she'd spun and plunged deep. A
king's last words should be spoken. "I read them without a
demented eye. I read them with an eye seeking knowledge.
There are no prophesies, child. There are only old tales
warning us of our own failures."

"Only a king, not a god," she whispered in his dying ear,
and his eyes were glazing over now, looking to something
beyond. Perhaps Alder was calling him. Perhaps his son
already knew the way to go.

"Give me a burial worthy of a king, so my ashes might
rest in the wind," he gasped, gripping Ealis's hand as fear
finally stole his nerve. She nodded, but he had already passed
into the darkness, and she was a king slayer.

And so much more. Leaning across the dead man, she
kissed Alder one last time.

Why the fuk did you do that?

Shaking her head free of foolish actions, Aurora
recovered her weapons and fallen cloak. It was a bitter,
treacherous night, and she could need both for the ride ahead.

"Rest, my liege. Thy will shall be done," she declared to
watching ghosts. She knew what to do. She had known the
moment she walked into this house of blasphemy. She rolled
a barrel into the meeting room, flipped its lid, and allowed the
clear brew to mix with the red on the floor. The fumes were
intoxicating. A fine vintage, no doubt. Taking a breath, she
allowed herself a moment to marvel at her work. Hardly as
difficult as razing a defiant town of bandits, or slaying a few
households of Alphalines.

Countless Alphaline households.

Last of all, she looked back at Inden and his beautiful son

Alder, and it stung dreadfully. "I'm sorry." Two gaping, frozen mouths replied with silence, and she bowed, before taking a candle and setting alight a piece of parchment. She held it aloft for a few moments as it caught fire. It warmed her damp hands and she dropped it to the ground. Within a breath, the flames grew in the rugs and she stepped away from the pyre. A fitting and traditional burial. Worthy of a king, worthy of a tainted woman who had given birth. *All hail Uden.*

Aurora closed the door behind her and walked out into the night, licking the stains from her fingers. She did not need to be wary of meeting a patrol any longer. Her task was complete. At least in this region.

Erroh.

She counted her steps and muttered his name aloud a few times. Practicing her tongue. For she would need it for games and play.

"Air-oh, Ee-row… Era-oh."

Fuken whatever.

This beast Erroh was the catalyst of everything, and she very much had a keen eye upon him. She needed to meet this boy for herself and, aye, if it transpired, she would end up watching the light in his eyes burn out. That was fine. Such an act would displease her god, and that was fine too. She would watch her god's wrath as he smote her with powerful hands, and it would be beautiful. To kill a king was no small matter. To meet a false god with crossbow raised. Oh, that was divinity.

Her steps were controlled, but soon the cold became too much for her. She broke into a run and dashed through the streets until she reached the gates, and then kept running. She wouldn't stop her charge until she reached warmer lands. Traversing the Arth alone was fine times. Being this close to the threat of freezing alive or being torn apart by savage bandits was a marvellous thought to amuse her upon the way.

The guards watched her from their little guard tower as she passed through the gates. Within a breath, she became lost to the darkness in the wood beyond. *Just a girl out for a midnight stroll.* If they followed, she heard no crunching of snow behind her. A better thing for them. She'd had enough exertions that day.

"Hello, little beastie," she whispered, discovering her doomed mount where she'd left it. It stomped unhappily in the snow, and she undid the reins from around the tree, soothing it as she did. "Be still, my pet. We will soon race more swiftly than even your heart can take. Then will you be so angry with me for leaving you in the cold?"

"You are right, Aurora Borealis. I am the bad type of horse."

"That's alright, horse," she said, patting the massive beast's mane, four times along each side. She climbed aloft and brought it through the trees, away from Conlon. She turned at the highest slope overlooking the city to view it one last time. The city had taken on an eerie glow. She could see the smoke rising above the growing flames, which lit the icy darkness and turned it to a city of light. They rose, spread, caught and destroyed. *A hundred houses each way.* Aurora sat atop her mount and watched her true devastation take form. How many still lived in the city? Certainly not enough to quench the flames. She wondered how many of her people were burning. Innocent people?

"Fuk."

King slayer, god hunter and now city killer. It had been an interesting night. Ealis recoiled; Aurora tilted her head. She couldn't see from this distance, but she imagined little victims running through the streets, their bodies in flames.

Woken from their slumber of fiery nightmares to something so much worse. *Little insects screaming their last words.* "Make them kingly," she said to the wind.

Life was extinguished so quickly. It was beautiful, in a way.

She turned her mount towards the frozen wilderness and the calling of the Arth.

5

OUTRAGE

The tent was as far from his father's usual quarters as he'd ever seen it. Usually, Magnus lived a life of neat meticulousness, but this was something else entirely. Crumpled scrolls lay strewn across his desk and the ground beyond; half-eaten platters of food covered every raised surface. Strips of ripped crimson-coloured bandaging lay in mounds in the far corner, where a bin might have sat at one time. But it was the battered and torn maps lying carelessly throughout the tent that shook Erroh most. Those maps were his father's pride in warfare. *That's not like him at all,* thought Erroh, forgetting his rage for a breath. Magnus sat behind his desk, hunched as though broken. The stench of disinfectant permeating the air was strongest here, and Erroh winced.

"Why is Nomi chained?" A fine question. He'd worked on it the last few steps. His father looked up and gestured to a boiling pot of cofe sitting upon the lit stove in the corner. Erroh shook his head and immediately regretted it. *Oh, the mistakes we make when enraged.* He leaned against his father's desk for support but took no seat when offered. It was the principle of the matter.

"It pleases me to see you up and about, showing passion," Magnus said in a tired voice. Losing his Rangers had diminished him. It meant little, though. What mattered was the girl. At least in this moment.

"Answer me, Father!"

Magnus did not answer. At least not straight away. Instead, he sighed. Long ago, it would have affected Erroh. Now it just infuriated him.

"Oh, Erroh, sit down," whispered Lea. Perhaps she sensed the fury in him. He glared at her as though betrayed, and she did not blink. Instead, she took his hand, attempting to bend him to her will.

"I have lain on my back for far too long. I wish to stand." There was a threat to his voice, and Magnus shrugged and she released his hand. He'd pay for that later. That was a problem for later.

"She is a captive like the rest. She goes nowhere," the Master General said.

Erroh slammed his fist down upon the desk and almost fell over. "You saw what they did to her!" His voice carried beyond their privacy and Magnus ground his teeth.

"Be still, Erroh. It is not your mate you speak of with such fury, but an untrustworthy southern jailor."

Erroh didn't want to be silenced. He wanted to scream his outrage and find a few barrels to kick over and possibly some Wolves to punch. Instead, he bit his tongue and took the seat. Lea placed her hand back down on his shoulder. She held him fast.

"The Master General cannot release her. Not if he wants to keep leadership. She is the enemy."

"They chained her, punished her, and tried to burn her alive."

Magnus leaned across the desk. "You really trust the girl that much?" Erroh didn't like that tone. Not one little bit. Lea's fingers tightened for a moment. "You think she's no spy?"

"I would bet my life on it," Erroh hissed, and Lea removed her hand. He thought he heard a sigh; it could have been his imagination. His own guilt.

"The Wolves need strength, and my leadership must be infallible. She is a casualty of war, regardless of her actions towards you," he said in a tone suggesting Erroh should let matters rest. He spoke as though he were no broken old warrior leading a pack of venomous Wolves, pretending to be an army. "You have a mate. Respect her," he added, and Erroh heard the sigh from behind him again.

"This has nothing to do with Lea," snarled Erroh, climbing to his feet. *Enough of this sitting down shit.* "Release Nomi, Master General, sir," Erroh said, loud enough for any passing Wolves to hear.

"I will not," roared Magnus, slamming his fist down. It was more impressive than Erroh's outburst. He'd had years to master the art. The desk shuddered under the assault but did not falter. He stood up just so he could look down on his cub and meet Erroh's own stubborn glare. Two immovable objects, unwilling to concede any matter. For that was how master and apprentice were inclined to behave when they were equals. The world became still. Magnus blinked first, shaking his head in annoyance. "The girl is safer where she is. It is all we can do for her," he mumbled, sitting back down on his seat. "At least for now."

"It isn't right."

"In this, aye, you are correct. But we are barely holding

on here, Erroh. As you've slept, things have taken a turn. Look outside at the wretchedness. We splintered few are all that remain of a resistance to the marching south." His face darkened. "We have few allies left in the city."

"But all she has done for me…" Erroh protested weakly. Again, behind him, he heard a sigh. *Definitely a sigh.*

"Whatever she has done means little to them. Few of us are in our right minds these days, Erroh. If she walks free, someone is likely to do something foolish. You should look beyond your own nose."

"Chained like a dog."

He rubbed his eyes. "Away from the rest of the mutts."

He had more to say, but Lea interrupted him. "You need to tell him, Magnus. It isn't right," she said quietly.

Erroh looked around. "Tell me what?" Those words never heralded merry times. "Tell me what?"

Magnus nodded his head. He tapped the desk a few times as though summoning the will to speak aloud, and Erroh felt a coldness overcome him. Cool enough to temper the fire in him. "Your mother could not allow the Wolves' betrayal to go unpunished." His face was pale; Erroh hadn't realised just how pale it had been until now. The coldness became grim, freezing terror. "She took it upon herself to repay them in blood," Magnus said, and Erroh's heart dropped.

The room spun. "Tell me what happened!" he demanded, already knowing.

Dead, dead.

While I slept.

Lea did not sigh now. She took hold of Erroh as Magnus relayed the tale of Elise's downfall. He spoke with pride, regret and deepest anger.

All Erroh heard were the words "chained" and "alive."

"We do not know what her fate will be, only that she is as

tough as old leather," Magnus said, finishing, and Erroh could see the fatherly attempts at deceiving. Being left to rot away, chained in darkness, was no legend's fitting demise. The terrible anger returned, though for a different reason altogether and tenfold the magnitude. Nomi was Nomi, but Elise was a queen. He desired to rise from his seat, to climb upon a hate-filled mount and charge through the city, injuries be damned. *And allow it to burn while I'm at it.*

"Even after weeks?"

"She is alive. Protected. For how long is another matter." Magnus slid a letter across the table. "Things have changed in the city. Word reaching us passes through many hands first."

Erroh read the letter a few times, each time discerning what he could from the language used. He did not know the female well. Did not know her intentions, either. Mostly, he understood her through the words of a healer. It really depended on the day, he supposed.

My Dearest Wrek.

It's not the same since you left. Everything has changed.

Many of the Black Guard miss you in the city. I do.

Little Linn is breathing steadily, though I seem to give her twice the dosage these days.

Perhaps, if you see Stefan in your travels, you might ask after the recipe.

I know we parted badly, but some things are more important than hate.

Like haste.

I would welcome you with open arms, my love.

For I am so alone.

And the steps we made together are not so easily hidden anymore.

If I could, I would speak openly of my love for you and what fears I endure, but words would not do justice to my terror.

Fear not, though, my beautiful Wrek, for as difficult as things have become, Lexi is here by my side. I keep my eyes on her at all times. She's just like her mother.

I will protect her as long as I have power.

Oh, my beautiful Wrek, come back to me, if only to speak as lovers do and endure wonderful acts for us alone.

Come for me, please.

—Roja.

Lea was the one who'd always favoured solving riddles. For Erroh, it was a gathering of ill-fitting thoughts from a broken soul. Or a smart Alpha female keeping the Wolves at bay. *But can we trust her?*

"I'm a little slower in thought this morning," Erroh said. He understood she cared for Lexi and perhaps Elise. She needed Emir's wonderful eucalyptus remedy. Everything else was confusing. He skimmed through it again. *No, still fuken lost.*

"Have you read this?" he asked, passing the letter to Lea. She nodded, yet read it once more.

"We will know more when Wrek returns. He is certain his hand in the jailbreak has remained undiscovered. He will speak with his... lover, and he has ensured us he has the skills to put in place a more secure means of communication. The city is perilous now. I'm not sure any of our Wolfen comrades are safe to return to Spark, either," Magnus said. Erroh could see how lost he was. Lost, and hiding it beneath the guise of authority.

"Why do you not ride in yourself, Father?"

Magnus snorted. An unexpected reaction, for certain. "Finally, we see eye to eye. I even made it to my horse before some shrewder advisor suggested I was behaving like a child." He nodded grudgingly to the goddess standing behind Erroh. "She might have a point. I'm not sure I'd have shown the same restraint Elise showed to any bastard wearing Wolf clothing."

"Not sure they'd have shown the restraint they showed her to you, either," Lea said.

His laughter fell silent. "Aye, that may be so. A fine lesson in suffering for the masses. Though I fear for Elise, I trust Roja to keep our family safe."

Erroh shrugged at Magnus's subtle point. It didn't mean matters would rest. It meant matters would rest for now. No false allegiance to the Wolves would stop him from freeing Nomi. Fuk their grievances. However, he understood his father would not be convinced otherwise.

"So, what do we do now?" Erroh asked, and Magnus looked to one of his battered maps.

"I'm returning home to gather what forces I can."

"East?"

"Farther."

Erroh couldn't believe it. "To the Savage Isles?" It was no vast distance like charging to the south and back, but it was a journey never taken lightly. Especially for Magnus. Especially with the clans up in arms.

"Spark City will fall long before you return, Father," Erroh hissed, and Magnus nodded in agreement.

"Spark City fell the moment the Rangers were betrayed. I do this to save those beyond its grey walls," he said coldly. "In my absence, the Wolves will need a leader. They are broken and scared, but they can become a significant force."

I will not lead these fuks under any condition.

"I'm choosing Aymon."

Maybe that condition.

Lea's sigh of disappointment matched her mate's thoughts on the matter. Aymon was not to be trusted. He muttered a curse under his breath. *Should have stayed in bed with the two girls. Much finer times.*

Magnus eyed him disdainfully. Erroh knew that look all too well. He'd seen it every time he'd lain ruined on the ground and Magnus stood above him without a scratch. "I see you disagree with my choice?"

"It's your leadership to choose… sir."

"You think you should lead them?"

Erroh didn't like that tone at all either. "I think there are finer candidates to Aymon."

"Such as?"

"Wynn should lead. Was he not your choice before the arena?"

Erroh knew him to be an excellent swordsman and the son of a fine enough veteran. There were worse things, really. Erroh would take orders from a brother of the dark.

"Wynn hasn't the brutality to lead."

"You say that as if it's a bad thing," snapped Lea.

"Very well. He is too weak for such a role," hissed Magnus, addressing Lea. "Do you suggest Lillium is capable?" Magnus added.

Perhaps.

"Erroh should lead us," Lea said. "If you can't see that, Master General, you are either blinded by fatherly duty or, worse, afraid of the whispers of fatherly nepotism." Fine words that Erroh didn't wish to hear in that moment. *Someone else. Anyone else. Maybe even Lillium.*

"Bah! Erroh is no leader. Fierce as he is," Magnus countered, and Lea sighed loudly this time.

"The Black Guard followed him to victory once. They will follow him again. You saw but a glimpse of his greatness, Master General."

Again, Magnus laughed. "The first thing Erroh would do as leader would be to free the southern girl before telling the Wolves to fuk off."

A valid assumption.

"I need a man who will never question his actions, no matter the consequences, while I sail. Erroh would suit his own needs."

"You are fuken right, he would," she screamed, stepping forward and kicking the desk fiercely. Despite her size, she was ferocious.

"Save your anger for who deserves it, little miss. Direct it at matters closer to home," warned Magnus, and Lea's eyes narrowed. Erroh knew that dangerous glare. Magnus was about to learn it, too.

"I'll waste my anger on whatever matter I fuken choose… Legend." She did not shout. She murmured, but such was the coldness in her voice that Erroh almost reached for her, lest she reach out and strike down her father-in-law. That might not improve the camp's mood.

Magnus must have noticed it too. His eyes softened. "Forgive me. That was rude."

"Speak to me as a warrior or as family; never both at the same time," she said in that same bitter tone.

He smiled, bowing. "Very well, Lea. As a warrior, I will defy you for a second time on important matters. I will not choose Erroh on your word. I will choose upon my own eyes. Upon my own thoughts."

"Then this conversation is over," she snapped, stepping away from Magnus. Erroh followed, though without as much vigour.

———

"Where are we going?" Erroh called, and she slowed for him. Her mind was reeling from many things.

"It's time to make Nomi's day that little bit brighter," she said, not daring to look at him. She had feared this since he had wakened. It was a petty jealousy, but jealousy nonetheless. Lillium's flirtation was one thing, but they could not trust this little fuken whore.

My Erroh, nobody else's.

"Do you want to speak with her alone, or would you like me by your side?" she asked. It was a test. There was only one reply. There would be further tests, and she would keep score.

He shrugged but said nothing, and she thought it a terrible reply. "I'll never have you leave my side," he said after a few moments, trying to find the words. *Better.*

Before they faced the captive, Erroh turned to her. "What did he mean by defying you?" Erroh asked.

"You think I allowed Nomi to be chained so easily?" she muttered. "I put up a greater fight," she added smugly.

6

AWKWARD CONVERSATIONS

E rroh limped slowly forward, his strength suddenly deserting him. From outrage, from overexertion. Even from a fuken hangover. His heart hammered at the sight of her. The debt he'd assumed lost was now returned to him.

Get her out of the chains.

"Nomi, it's me, Erroh."

She flinched at his presence, her eyes wide and lost. Hardly a great sign. Her chains clinked gently and he resisted the urge to reach for her. She was terrified, and there was little he could do. Huddled up against her post with a blanket and cloak wrapped around her, she was pathetic. He could see the bruising had all but disappeared, but there was no denying she was fractured. He was close to her now, no more than a couple of feet from her, and she squeaked in disbelief, in agony, and tried to pull away from him. The chain holding her caused her to gasp pathetically, and Erroh was heartbroken for her.

Despite his own pain, he dropped to his knees in front of her and did little more. It was all he could do, really, and he tried desperately not to notice the cutting breeze as he knelt in

83

the mud. He'd claimed his people were more enlightened than hers. Not so much now.

I'm so, so sorry.

Had he expected anything different? Aye, he had expected her to fall upon him, uttering grateful wails, murmuring her undying love for him and her eternal relief at his survival. He thought he'd feel a little relief himself, but this went beyond burgeoning affection. He loved her for what she'd done, but now, the trauma she suffered was just that little bit of extra guilt to carry.

Beside them, Lea leaned against a wagon, attempting to appear relaxed about this grand meeting. She folded her arms, grinding her teeth as she did. Instead of looking at her beo and his whore from the south, she amused herself by picking at a splinter in her hand. Her foot throbbed and she wanted to scream in Erroh's face. A wonderful morning indeed. She saw the panic in Nomi's face. It improved her mood ever so. Her watch was over. It was Erroh's turn. She wasn't sure this was the smarter move on her part, but she'd spoken her mind on the matter more than once. There came a point where she needed to trust her mate's word. His behaviour too. As for that blonde bitch? Well, Lea would deal with that matter should the need come.

Lea's hands felt colder than usual. A trick of the mind, no doubt. Every morning she would sit and share a steaming mug of cofe with the prisoner. It wasn't a lot, but Nomi appreciated it. Some routines were going to change.

Nomi's chains clinked loudly and she shook uncontrollably, and Lea felt the stirrings of concern for the pathetic creature but shrugged it away. That was just habit from looking over the girl these past few weeks, and besides, she had a fine splinter to focus on.

"No," Nomi hissed, climbing under her coverings. A few Wolves walked by and stared at the little gathering with distaste. Lea imagined them wondering just who this southern female was. Very little happened here, and it was something different to talk about. Most believed she was Erroh's concubine from the south and that the child had been his son. If that were true? Well, that would be some wild misunderstandings as to how reproduction occurred. With a flick of her head, she sent them on their way. Let them think whatever they wanted as long as they understood Lea was still the queen.

Eventually, when inaction got the better of him, Erroh reached for her blankets and pulled gently. Not enough to hurt; just enough to pull them from her grasp. Nomi, who had calmed ever so, screamed in fresh terror and Lea sighed at his foolishness. *Small steps, idiot.*

Nomi howled a few incomprehensible words over and over, and Lea thought about sitting down to calm her. Lea despised the girl and her obvious beauty; loathed the kind smile she sometimes offered; reviled her warm mutterings attempting communication. The bitch was endearing, and Lea wanted to punish her for it. Oh, if she just had a rock and no witnesses, that would be fine.

What is this dreadful trick?

Nomi hid her head from the vision of a demon. A demon in beautiful skin. She had caught some affliction of the body. No small surprise in these conditions. These last few days her mind had wandered further than ever before, and now, seeing

Erroh come for her was a cruel move on her mind's part. It had finally betrayed her, just when she thought she could take no more. She took a deep breath and felt the liquid gurgle deep within. The wind lashed her face and she felt truly miserable. She hadn't slept a full night in weeks, and her sanity suffered as much as her breathing through a wet chest. She wondered if she was asleep this very moment, or had she finally died during the night, slain by the beasts wearing black armour? For every night, they drew closer. Waiting for her to let down her guard before they choked the life out of her or slit her throat. She had grown accustomed to their foreign-tongued jeering and the moistness of their spittle as they passed. She had learned to ignore other torments, but it was the silent watchers that unnerved her most. They would not speak, only stare as if deciding on her fate, late at night while others slept. Each time, she met their stares and challenged them in silence. It was enough to send them on their way. At least so far.

"Nomi, me, Erroh."

No, it's not. Where's my guardian?

She struggled again and looked to her only comrade and called for her. Albeit delicately. "Liiiia." The goddess stood away from her barrel, and for a moment Nomi thought she would come and take away the demon but Liiiia never came. That wasn't like her at all. This was most certainly a demonic dream.

Or this is death.

Her mind stirred up further hopeful horrors, and she fought the desire to answer him. To embrace him and weep in his arms. They fed her, gave her a blanket and little else. She'd hoped for more. Maybe she'd just expected more. She'd dreamed of Erroh, but these were just foolish thoughts from a dying sacrifice. She was now resigned to her fate. He had not saved her, and he had not saved Mish, either.

"Erroh!"

This demon of fire, for that is what her people called him, sounded frustrated now, and this pleased her. Why go out like a whelp? She gasped, and her breathing was difficult. Who knew a little dampness would settle itself in her lungs and refuse to let go? She had not started coughing, but that would come. At least with a fever she'd imagine herself to be warmer than she was. She looked back to her keeper, hoping that, even in a dream, she might offer a warm beverage, but the beautiful girl carried nothing.

Is this better than the torment of the Woodin Man's holding?

Being tied to a cart with a rag over her eyes had sent her almost mad. She'd imagined Erroh beside her many a moment, and those moments were all she had. She'd enjoyed countless lovers, but only Erroh stirred her mind. Just thinking of him made her braver. But his warmth was imaginary; it wasn't real then, and it wasn't real now. It was unfair to dream like this, so she shunned this temptation for what it was: insanity, a god's cruelty, or else death.

"Nomi," the demon whispered, and she could only sob pathetically, for she was lost.

"No one's pet," he hissed, and something deep within her stirred. She wiped her tears, gathered what breath she could and looked beyond her delirium.

Is this real?

Is this real?

She looked beyond the dizzy vision, beyond the haze. She looked past the beautiful warrior kneeling in front of her and beheld his flaws. He was thin. He was battered. He was unimpressive, and her heart beat a hopeful flutter. *Please, be real.*

"Nomi's pet," she whispered, and he nodded, and she saw

his fire and her mind reeled and after so long, she began to believe. A spark at first. "Ero?"

"Aye." She reached for him and he did not pull away. He felt real, and she never wanted to sleep again or ever wake again. She held him and the tears kept flowing.

She couldn't stop crying, and she nearly smiled. Instead, she gripped him tighter and listened to his breath catch as she squeezed tightly. He was broken, as he'd always been, and he was beautiful and he was here to save her. He would save her, this time. And then she kissed him for the first time since the day they'd parted. One delicate moment of attachment to support her faith that he lived.

And then she remembered her keeper. And her place in the world. And her crime.

It was a loving kiss, but it was not a kiss for lovers. It was all he would ever offer her, and she would expect little else. He pulled away gently, and she did not fight it. Her one for life held her against his chest and whispered sweet words of gibberish. She almost fell asleep in the sudden calming of the world, but she raged against it despite her drowsiness.

Lea really wanted that rock as she eyed Nomi in silence. Erroh looked back pathetically with an "I didn't mean that to happen" expression, and she formed two fists and hid them behind her crossed arms. They were there, though, just waiting to strike. She knew it was the blonde female's doing, but he would earn some payment for allowing it happen.

"Liiiia?" Nomi asked, gesturing to her keeper. The last thing Lea wanted was to be in striking distance, but despite that, and taking care to conceal her festering hatred, Lea sat down beside Erroh. She would not look him in the eyes. She could only seethe in silence and stare ahead at the pathetic

creature she'd kept alive these past few weeks. She wondered
what the word "whore" was in her language.

Probably "Nomi."

The last of her goodwill had left her the moment her lips
had met his. Tensing as tight as a cart's rope, she feigned a
smile. They would never be friends. Ever. But she would play
her part until they were rid of her. She muttered ugly words,
and Lea held her gaze. *Look into my eyes and see my
detestation, you stupid bitch*, Lea thought, and kept it to
herself.

"She says thank you for caring for her," Erroh said,
releasing Nomi from his embrace before leaning up against
Lea. It was a paltry gesture, but she appreciated it. Best let
Nomi know exactly how things were.

"Tell her I'm grateful to her that I have you now," Lea
said courteously. Still, she would not look from Nomi's eyes
lest the first to break contact might lose ground. Nomi must
have played a similar game, for she never looked away,
either. Was she challenging her? Or else just stupid enough to
think Lea liked looking at her? *Small matter. Fuk off, Nomi.*

Erroh translated happily, in the same tone a foolish cub
would use when blissfully unaware of the threat looming.
Nomi asked something that sounded annoying, and he
nodded, and Nomi offered Lea the most disarming smile
imaginable.

You only kissed her the once, Erroh, yeah?

Without any warning or regard for the hatred Lea felt for
her, Nomi reached out and embraced her tightly. In her ear,
Lea heard excited mutterings in guttural tones.

Don't hit her. Don't fuken hit her.

At least not yet.

"She likes you," Erroh whispered.

"Tell her to get off me."

89

"She keeps calling you 'pretty girl,'" he added. "Or, at least I think that's what she is saying," Erroh muttered, grabbing his head. "I feel lightheaded. Too much shouting, moving… getting kissed." He looked at Lea hopefully. Were it not for Lea's anger, she might have appreciated his wit. As it was, she wanted very much to throttle him. Hard to, though, with a southern prisoner strangling the life out of her with hugs.

On top of all things, the female was annoyingly skilled at embracing. She was also stronger than Lea had thought. She might take some punch, she thought.

Her chains clinked loudly but she would not budge, and Lea bit her tongue in frustration, trying to calm herself. Nomi finally broke the embrace but continued talking. Erroh tried to translate, starting each sentence and falling quiet again as he tried to understand. It was a small matter. Lea understood something beyond words. This close, she suddenly saw beyond her own eyes what horrors the girl had endured. She warmed to her again for a moment. For a moment.

"Liiiia… something, something…"

"What did she say?" Lea asked, but Nomi's sudden scream shattered the moment as Erroh collapsed in the mud, gasping. His bandaging had come loose and crimson was leaking out all over the ground. Lea could see where his stitching had ripped. Too much exertion. She was as angry with herself as she was with the southerner. Roughly, Lea pulled him to his feet.

"Whisht," she hissed, silencing Nomi, who shook as though a demon had suddenly attacked her. "Don't make a fuken scene." Allowing him to rest on her shoulder, she supported him as they shuffled back to the healer's tent, wary that the Black Guard might see his weakness. If he were to lead them, he would need to be imperious. "Take the pain,

Erroh," she demanded of him, and he whimpered, coughed, and nodded his head.

"Taking it."

"I'll get you back to bed."

"Will you come too? I have a few other afflictions to tend to."

"Want me to pretend I'm a southern whelp, in need of some rescuing?" She'd meant it as a joke, but her tone suggested otherwise. He had but a moment to say he had no intention of desiring Nomi. It was another test. The day was young and, injured or not, he would be wise to keep his wits about him.

"Um... no. But you might tell her I'm fine once I'm back in bed." It was a fair enough reply.

"Aye, the poor thing looked terrified," Lea said, as they reached the tent. "Poor little whelp."

I'll be giving her a reason to be terrified if she doesn't fall in line.

With Erroh wrapped up in bed under the watchful eye of a disapproving healer, Lea returned to Nomi.

"Something, Erroh, something?" the prisoner whimpered.

"Erroh is fine."

"Erroh?" she repeated, widening her beautiful southern eyes, searching for any type of understanding.

"Is fine." Lea forced a smile. It was a good smile. She was quite skilled at such an act.

Nomi thought on this for a few moments, her stupid face scrunched up in concentration. "Erroh... ees... ff-ine." She smiled hopefully, and fuk her, but that smile was a weapon. Lea nodded.

"Liiiia... um..." began the girl, as she did most mornings, then burbled out a lot of random mutterings, as though she were engaging in conversation with a sister. Lea said little. Today was no different. "I… wiell… um…"

"You know, I'll likely kill you," Lea said, interrupting. She smiled warmly and Nomi smiled in reply as she struggled to translate Lea's threat.

7

A LESSER PRISON

"I've been to every tavern twice over the last few days. I still can't find him," muttered Wrek. He tried to hide his irritability, but it was late in the evening. She knew he wanted to be free of the city and its growing unease.

"He's always in the Pig in the Hole tavern," Roja said quietly. She felt tired. More tired than ever before. A tiredness born from a city's heavy weight and a female's guilt. She held Wrek's hand for all to see, for those hidden few most likely watching from the shadows. Those who would protect her. And as quickly strike her down. All for the price of a soldier's weekly wage. "He met with Silvia in chambers earlier. He usually ends up there in the hours after." She whispered this last, her eyes in the darkness looking left to right and in between. *Just two young lovers out in the city. Nothing to see here.*

She wondered if Dia had ever endured such rising panic. Was this just a Primary's daily affliction? She was no Primary, nor would she ever be one. She was more likely to end up in chains or banished or hanging from a tree. Sometimes a girl knew the changing of the wind or the stumbling click of a machine, right before it became rightly fuked and things felt rightly fuked.

Wrek sighed, and she felt his frustration. "Fine," he told her. "I'll search one more time, but if I can't find him, you need to take care of these matters." He, too, whispered; perhaps he'd caught the shadow of a watching guard. They would likely favour him above her anyway. He, also, was sensing the change in the wind. He wasn't interested in staying in Spark City a moment longer than was needed.

Take me with you. "Trust me, it's the only place they'll serve him," she muttered, bowing to leave. As she did, he embraced her as lovers and how pretend lovers were inclined to do. She knew his words before he said them. "Is there anything, anything at all you want me to pass on to him?"

She felt Wrek embrace her tightly. Real affection from a good man. She didn't want him to let go. She didn't want to face the loneliness again. Mostly, she wanted another outcast to be embracing her. And oh, how she wanted it to be him warming her against the bitter breeze tonight. "Nothing at all," she hissed, her anger, her horror, her instinct taking over. Better to leave matters be, she thought. Easier to forget too.

"Safe trip, my love," she bade him wistfully, kissing the spy on the cheek. He turned and left her outside the tower gates, and she felt fresh desolation, as though a real love had just departed. When his echoes had disappeared in the low hiss of the wind in an unfriendly city, she felt satisfied that she'd played the part of heartbroken soulmate long enough. Hugging herself against the chill, she marched through the open gates.

Two Wolves standing each side watched her as she passed. "Another lover for the Primary-in-waiting," one of them muttered. He leant against a long pike and stared through her when she looked back. Only a few weeks ago, she wouldn't have stood for such insolence, but now she had little choice.

"Poor Wrek. She'll tire of him as well soon enough," the other added.

It was a precarious thing to be this unstable in a crumbling city. She held no power, yet had no other path to take. The whispers were growing about her involvement with the breakout, too. She'd been so careful. Just not as careful as Wrek, she thought bitterly, and cursed her pettiness. It was a good thing no one knew of his involvement. He still had clout in the city; he still had the ability to walk through the whispering world undetected. *Aye, poor Wrek indeed.*

Keeping her head held high as best she could, Roja slipped away from their disrespect without further insults. They had lost their way since Dia had died. Forgotten the threat she still posed. Tearing them apart with her bare hands might make her feel better in the moment, but such a cathartic act might not be taken too kindly in the tower of the Wolves. With the door slamming shut behind her, she fell back against it and gasped aloud.

I do not know what to do.

I have no allies left in the city.

The Wolves are coming. The fuken Wolves are coming.

I need you, Dia.

She formed a fist and almost put it through the darkened door frame. She'd struck it once as a young female. That was when she'd learned the art of control for the first time. Truthfully, she didn't care about the insults whispered her way about her sexual appetites. She'd had an enjoyable youth, discovering herself and her indulgences. She very much doubted she was alone in such adventures, either.

"Come on, Roja," she whispered. "Fight this." Her stomach ached nauseously in two separate places. Too much stress. Too many betrayals. Maybe it was more than a sick belly. Her nerves were taut and ready to snap. As though defying the spirit of her grandmother, she took to the stairs of the tower at pace. *When one is lost, one should fuken run.* She reached the second level and continued on upwards. Her chest was heaving, each breath agony, and she didn't care. Her feet thumped the ground heavily and she cared for this even less. Let them hear the Primary running. Everything else had fallen to shit—why should this matter?

She reached the next level of the building and kept running. Sometimes she missed the outdoors. The feel of soft ground underfoot and the sound of silence of the wastes. The floorboards creaked loudly as she gathered pace, and her mind almost cleared. Higher and higher the redhead charged until, finally, she reached the highest point in the city. She allowed herself a moment to catch her breath at the top of the stairs and leaned against the banister, panting. She smiled briefly, thinking of Dia's reaction to such a spectacle.

"I bet you ran something fierce in your day," she whispered.

Wiping some long strands of burning red hair from her forehead, she composed herself for her two guests. They would desire word of the city and beyond. Few places were safe these days, but her sanctuary was a haven for the threatened, the reviled, the dying. A prison, where she was jailor. She removed the key from her pocket and walked the last few feet as dignity dictated. Turning the key, she slipped in quietly.

The smell of home cooking almost brought tears to her eyes. Maybe it was the onions Elise was slicing. She was having one of her better days. The legend sat on her bed in the corner with a plate resting upon her lap. She was absently spinning the little knife in her fingers, counting the slices in front, grinding her teeth, and Roja knew she'd walked in on another argument between her and her more impressive jailor. Impressive because not even the Wolves would dare go against her. At least not yet. And when they did, she would win. She *was* Alpha.

"Whisht Elise, and don't be annoying me," Mea hissed from the far end of the room. Roja could see her struggle with the three pots as they bubbled all around her. Her face was drawn, her expression lost, but she held herself as though nothing bothered her. She was a Primary-in-waiting. Far more impressive than the waif who struggled to control a pack of feisty mutts. With steam and mayhem threatening to overcome her, she added salt to each pot. More than she needed. It was good that she was cooking. Good that her focus was beyond her terrible ire.

She was as incensed as Elise.

"Mydame, talk some sense into her. She won't listen to me," Mea cried, bowing deeply to Roja. She looked as though she might hug her but resisted the urge. Mea rarely showed much emotion. Roja wondered had she ever. She'd certainly not known the Alpha too long before everything had turned upon its head. *Well enough that you enlisted her to steal the city from your grasp with one impassioned speech.* Aye, she had done all that, and she had been amazing, and Roja felt awkward accepting such reverence. She bowed in reply and caught sight of the redness in the older female's eyes. So stunning and tragic.

Elise, however, had little issue with sharing warmth. Despite her weakness, she wrapped Roja in powerful arms as she knelt in front of her. Roja stiffened. Any gesture of kindness was likely to bring her to weeping ruin.

"As if anyone listens to me in this city, let alone either one of you. Whatever war you battle among each other is no matter to me," Roja said, releasing herself from the warmth of the embrace. The onions Elise sliced were potent indeed.

"I am a fuken poison to you," Elise said, and Roja rolled her eyes at the usual argument. "I'm dragging both of you down."

"Everything will settle, Elise," Mea snapped. She added some salt, tasted, and was thoroughly disgusted with whatever she had prepared. She slid the pots to the cooler edge of the stove and sealed them beneath heavy lids. "And we will wait with you until they do."

"There is no blowing over of this. I need to be placed in chains. The Wolves will only remain calm for so long."

Elise spun her onion knife absently, and Mea snatched the plate of thinly cut pieces from her grasp. She knew better than to take the little blade, though. That would need to be offered. One never took an Alphaline's blade. No matter the need.

Roja searched the stove for a brewed pot of cofe and was distraught to discover it cold in the sink. She thought about the late hour and the calling of sleep. She told herself it wasn't too late to brew a pot. The shattered moon outside, glistening down, was lying about the hour.

"You are the closest thing to family I have left, Elise," Roja muttered, unaware of how inaccurate that was.

"Family shouldn't sacrifice each other," Elise countered, growing impatient. She looked ready to explode in a manner befitting a goddess. "I killed a fuk-load of the bastards. There's no returning from that, and besides…" she whined before falling silent, thinking darker thoughts. A moment later, she spoke again. "Every day you keep me locked in here is another day your grip on this city is lessened, Roja."

She spoke the Primary-in-waiting's name but looked to Mea as she did. Her actions spoke loudly enough. They all thought the same thing.

I'm already fuked, but Mea is not yet tainted.

"The city is slipping from any Alphaline's grasp, anyway," muttered Roja. "Has been since the curfew was declared in Samara." Spoken aloud, her words were heavy. She hadn't announced the curfew, but it was enforced by the Wolves anyway. Leashed to a new master with ideas above his station. Sigi ruled the city; he thought he ruled the fuken world. He didn't at all.

"Take them back. Take the city back, child," Mea said. She reached to Roja and gripped her shoulder. *Don't be nice to me.*

"'Primary' is a dying title in this world. A king is climbing upon the throne," Roja whispered. Her words were heavier than anything else spoken, for they all felt the changing of the guard, as she did. Elise's blade spun swiftly as she lost herself in her thoughts. No doubt she was wishing she had her halberd returned to her, wishing she had the strength to wield it fiercely as she escaped this city. Roja very much wanted to join her on their imaginary escape.

"What fine conversation this is," Mea growled, offering some of the bubbling mess to Roja in a bowl. It was the spiciest stew she'd ever tasted, and despite there not being enough salt, she began to spoon it into her mouth greedily. The throbbing pains in her stomach began to fade beneath the meal, and it was divine.

"I told you I could make a fine stew without meat," Mea said proudly, and immediately Roja halted her spoon in mid-air. She inspecting the chunks for familiar dark morsels, then tasted again tentatively. No meat? Had her lack of wealth and power reflected so poorly on their supplies? Would she be heading out at dawn with bow and arrow in search of proper sustenance? She swallowed the mouthful and cursed her enjoyment.

"Give me steak, any day," muttered Elise, accepting a bowl for herself and adding a dollop of butter. She glanced at Mea with a glint in her eyes. Waiting for the counter-argument. Sometimes legends just needed to fuk with each other to pass the time. Sometimes they leant on each other in the dark and kept each other afloat.

"Or anything that puts up a fight," Roja added, grinning.

"Well, the lands are dryer of good hunting these days, but we have plenty of vegetables, so shut your fuken mouths. A true warrior of the wastes makes do with what they have."

"Yeah, well, if I have to live off vegetables for more than a day, I'll happily take a few arrows to the stomach." Too late, she realised her misstep. "Sorry, Elise. I didn't mean it."

"My cub lives. That's all that matters. Probably because he's on a diet of steak." She smiled sadly behind the jest, and Roja once more admired her strength. All around her were goddesses, and she couldn't hold her head above the tide. *Get me free of Samara.*

Despite her pleas, Roja would not allow her return to the dungeon. Dragging her from the glorified crypt had been difficult enough, so fierce had her protestations been. But neither Mea nor Roja could be denied. She was a renowned elder and of the highest line. Few had argued openly, but there was ill will. There would be a trial at some point, but the laws of the city were clouded on such a matter, for Elise's justice was justified. The Wolves had betrayed her. Had betrayed the city. Dane had as much right to be in chains as the goddess herself.

Such was the law of Samara. As long as a Primary ruled.

"I just wish you'd save yourselves."

Mea offered another ladle-full of meatless ambrosia. "Jeroen never left Magnus to die. So how could I do anything differently?" She swallowed hard, and Roja saw the heartbreak. The maddening grief at unspoken words. Worse than that: final words, spoken in anger. Well, Roja understood that part, but she had not experienced Mea's love, nor experienced the devastation of losing her love.

Elise climbed to her feet and took Mea in her powerful grip. "You are a credit to that man. If it pleases you, I will not argue this point again," she whispered.

"Any word from below in the streets?" asked Mea, changing the subject skilfully. Her eyes glistened, but she began coughing to shed the veneer of grieving widow.

"The streets are quiet," Roja cursed.

"Would he meet with you?" Mea asked, and Roja shook her head.

"I keep knocking." The redhead reached for a bottle of wine on the counter. She popped the cork and reached for the glasses. There was no need to ask. All would join her. These were not times to be sober. "Fuken Sigi."

"Fuken Wolves."

"Fuken City."

8

PIG IN THE HOLE

Wrek left Roja at the gates and continued on his way, fuming at the late hour. He was hungry and tired, and his mood was dour. He ran their fleeting conversation through his mind and regretted not speaking more for Emir, or speaking more with her, but the crushing guilt he endured took his words and judgement. In every endeavour he'd ever attempted, he'd failed. This was no different. His attempts to help the wretches had inadvertently ruined the city. He'd reached for his own rising star and shattered like the moon.

Sighing in the desolate night air, he put his hands in his pockets and trudged down through the city. Most keeping curfew knew him well enough not to stop him as he marched through each sector. He had no curfew pass, nor would he spend a single piece on such a barbaric form of freedom. If the Wolves between checkpoints had issue, well, he wasn't above taking out his mood with a few swift-fisted arguments. If Elise could butcher a few dozen and be treated like royalty, he could knock out a few teeth. He sighed again and cursed his foolish thoughts. He would do no such thing, for he was one of the few able to walk unmolested through the city these bitterly cold nights. Magnus had given him tasks, and fuk it if he wasn't going to play his part for as long as he could.

Won't cleanse your sins, though, will it? He had many a sin upon him. Not just from Spark, either. On nights like this, he missed his seat in Adawan. A simpler, royal life— provided he kept his archaic principles to himself. He'd once believed coming to the city might solidify his beliefs, but it hadn't. He'd grown more in love with helping everybody. *Absolutely everybody.* He wondered would his Adawan brother have a change of heart were he to know this. Probably not. Swords had been drawn. Blood spilled. He still had a price on his head.

He muttered a curse under his breath. The darkness and abandoned streets of a bustling city brought back unwanted memories, and he quickened his pace, shaking the memories from his mind. He could see the glow of warmth behind shut windows as he passed. People within, praying to their absent gods, drinking their sine, obeying the law, waiting for other people greater than themselves to save the day. To stop the war. Poor fools. When the fires of the south struck them down, would they still be convinced their choices were wise, their faith in others well placed?

"Fuken Sigi," he muttered to the wind. The city was following his will, and sliding towards doom because of it. He couldn't have recognised the tyrant back then, but it was all too obvious now. *And I the fool for putting him in this place.* Oh, Sigi, what happened to you? he wondered. He hoped that when his former companion met his end, it would be swift, for no man who had committed deeds of such betrayal was destined for a long life. He'd reached his star, all right, and it had burned his soul away to nothing. At least Wrek had the mind to regret his wretched actions.

He neared the Pig in the Hole tavern and cursed its

clientele within, those entitled few who were rich enough to buy their way out of the curfew. Sigi was getting paid for the honour of allowing them to walk through the city. A shrewd, bastardly order. Why wasn't he surprised? Around the tavern there were scattered merry groups dispersing for the night. He scanned each group for his target and found little success. It was unlikely Stefan of the hovels was among the boisterous patrons anyway. They were smiling, laughing, joking. That wasn't Stefan at all. Not anymore. The Pig was more lavish than all the others. Lavish, and quite spacious, to be precise. Far more souls could drink merrily under its roof, and for the third night in a row Wrek walked to the bar to see if his quarry was present.

Her eyes lit up when she saw him, but she tried not show it. Lara checked her hair and completely forgot the order she had just taken. Before Wrek could reach the counter, she plucked two fresh pints of ale from a long line of bubbling, settling glasses and walked through the crowd, ignoring the grievances of customers and barmen alike.

"He's sitting alone at the end," she whispered in Wrek's ear. His beard grazed her cheek as she pulled away, and shivers ran up her back. She called him a friend and little more. How long had it taken Quig to notice her? It didn't matter. What mattered was he eventually had. His was the warmest heart she'd ever known, and he would not have wanted her to pine for him forever. She told herself this every day. It was a mantra. It was a prayer. It was therapy, as Emir had suggested. Wrek had once reminded her of her wonderful giant, but now she could barely see the resemblance. Perhaps it was their warm hearts she found so familiar? Quig had been outgoing and trusting, but Wrek was far from this. Different was sometimes good.

He loved her in that outfit. Just snug enough to hold and display all the right features, and secure enough to not drag some drunk's inner brute to the surface. It was harder when he wasn't working nights with her. He desired Lara yet knew her pain, her anguish. He would wait. Otherwise, he'd have to tell Emir, and Emir would kill him. Wrek feared few things in this world, but a fuming Emir was an unpredictable thing. Also, he feared losing Emir's friendship above all else.

"Thank you, my lady," he said, receiving both glasses before spinning away from her. He could feel her eyes on him as he walked through the crowd, and it stung him. Best she not be led on by him any more than she already had. Easier for both. He could never match up to the tales he'd heard of himself. He wasn't a strong enough man to carry her burdens, either. Oh, he would want to, but Wrek was never able to hold precarious, beautiful things for very long before they shattered and broke. She deserved better than what he offered. She deserved the entire fuken city. And? Well, his meagre funds were running dry. He dared a glance back, and their eyes met. She smiled, and he cursed his immaturity.

Humming to herself, Lara returned to her duties. She knew Wrek's game, and it was wonderfully predictable. Honourable even. She knew Emir had warned him off, spoken of her fragility, and the healer was right. Beneath her smile lay deep sorrow. However, among this mayhem, among this roar of the crowd, she felt alive, felt herself. Felt like the first night of Puk every fuken night. Such things could shatter, but also sustain a fragile vessel such as she was. She chose something more: she chose strength. She slept alone these nights; not even imagining Emir was in the room next to hers would rouse her from her sleep, either. She could have said this to Emir, but her wretched companion was lost to her forever. She took the pain and bit into it.

She glided through the crowd as though swimming in a bitter river's current. She stayed afloat, and it was natural. In her ears they howled their orders, and she smiled and took them, as though recalling her own name. Born to serve for coin was no terrible vocation. Good enough for her parents, good enough for her. Snaking through the crowd, an overly friendly hand slid across her rear, taking a grip and sliding to her hips. Laughter in her ear and a few crude, jesting words followed. She felt the terror and crushed it. All part of the recovery. Before she could stop herself, her fist interrupted the assault and the patron fell back in his seat. His comrades' loud roars of approval were welcome, and Lara knew she would be well tipped by that table for the rest of the night. Still, though.

"Once more and I'll ban the lot of you from every fuken tavern in this city," she hissed, and the laughter settled. She smiled, waving away the sting in her hand. "So, you boys had better play nice from here on in."

This was her place in the world, and she would face it with grim determination. No longer would she freeze at a stranger's unwanted touch. No longer would she fall silent as she struggled with the world's cruelty. She'd seen worse suffering these past few weeks, and she had risen above it. She ran this tavern in the great betrayer's absence, and she ran it like an elder Alphaline would the city.

"My most sincere apologies," the offender muttered, growing red. She tugged his cheek playfully and winked. *All forgiven, but do not forget your place.*

As for Wrek? Well, he would demand a strong female by his side, and until he saw her as such, she would be right here, waiting. It was something to do.

———

"Where the fuk have you been hiding?" hissed Wrek, taking a seat by the leader of the most reviled society in Samara. Stefan looked up from his near-empty glass of flat ale and smiled half-heartedly.

"I haven't moved far, friend. I've been here, I've been there," muttered Stefan. He nodded in appreciation as the pint was slid in front of him.

"Not too difficult for one such as yourself, or me, for that matter," suggested Wrek, sipping from his own drink. The brew was bitter. Wonderfully so. Sigi's master brewers were creating quite the concoctions. He took another sip. His mood had improved since he'd seen Lara, found Stefan, and started drinking in a tavern.

"No."

"What?"

"Just, fuken no."

The wretched speaker eyed him coldly, and Wrek saw the pain. It meant little. Everyone was in pain these days. Unless you were a sine merchant from the wastes, with ideas above your station. "All I am saying is you and me are blessed with an ability to slip through different parts of the city without drawing much attention to ourselves."

"Wrek, you come to us all the time with suggestions, and everything goes wrong. I'm not Emir. I don't give a fuk about anyone." He ran his tongue through the gap in his teeth, took a moment to clumsily push some loose strands of grimy hair behind his ear with a bandaged hand. The bandage looked as old as the injury. He probably needed a skilled healer to take a look at it. "Not anymore."

"Ah, whisht. Course you care."

He shook his head and, apparently losing the taste for company, slid the pint back to Wrek. "Well, even if I do, I'm about a day from being removed from my position."

"That'll never happen. You are protected by Roja; by Silvia, too."

Without warning, Stefan slammed his better fist down upon the table. The glasses shook, but Wrek shot his hands out to steady the calamity waiting to happen. "Look around, Wrek. Nobody wants me to speak for them. I'm just adding to their misery. Silvia will scream down everything I suggest, just for the bitterness of it."

"I need you in your position a little longer. These are bad times, Stefan, but you are valuable. Even if they can't see it." Wrek's face darkened; he leaned in closer. "Especially if they can't see it." He slid the ale back to his comrade. "Emir vouched for you." This wasn't pure truth, but it most certainly was no lie.

It had the desired effect. "Ugh… What do you need from me, apart from humbling myself at the feet of a fuken bitch?"

Wrek could see how close he was to cracking. Such was the effect of dealing with Silvia, he supposed. And losing his only comrade. "I need a voice to speak and relay." As he spoke, his eyes moved across the tavern crowd. They searched for enemies, for troublemakers, for interesting things. He caught sight of Lara and his gaze lingered. She was laughing with one of the female servers. Even in the hum of voices, it stood out.

"You already have a few voices to call upon," Stefan argued, catching him staring at the pretty girl.

"Not all have access to Roja. At least with good reason."

"She doesn't attend meetings in chambers anymore."

"If you summon her with word, she will do as you ask."

"Well, everyone already suspects me of conspiring with the Outcasts. Perhaps spying will earn me a little favour with the absent gods." He shook his head. "Until someone shoves a blade through my head down some alley."

"That's the spirit, brother. I knew there was a reason Emir spoke so highly of you."

Stefan shrugged indifferently and drank deeply from his pint. As he did, he raised a finger to grab a servant's attention. The ale dribbled down his chin and onto his grubby shirt. He wiped his mouth with his bandaged hand and belched loudly. "He and I are alike," Stefan mocked, and Wrek realised he sat with a truly broken spirit.

"You both have wonderful taste in female companionship," Wrek said.

Stefan didn't bother answering. Fuk it, but Silvia had hurt him. *More than losing the use of a desperate hand, too.* He had spent long enough after the Primary's assassination forming the words he'd hoped would earn her favour once more. Fine words, with an apology and all, though his part in the terrible events was through no fault of his own. He'd even found a respectable way to say that, too. The words had been left unspoken when his numerous attempts to meet with her were rebuffed. Soon, though, he had learned of her actions through whispered mutterings, for whenever someone has despicable news about an unfaithful lover, it is usually shared. Stefan was no different, and it had struck fiercely. In truth, she had behaved no differently, no worse than he had while he'd been a king in a little forgotten town. Perhaps it was a balance between things in this world. Shit fell on everybody. This time he was simply on the receiving end of things. The absent gods knew he had played and tormented, and only now did he understand the bitter glances he received from spurned bed-mates. When they had finally spoken in chambers under the guise of politics, Silvia had offered no words of her own. Nor an apology either. Just a swift reminder of what a wretch he was and what a queen she was.

Stefan eyed the grubby bandage and wondered about the ruination beneath its surface. It might be healing nicely despite the pain, or else rotting away to nothing, which explained the pain. He missed Emir and he missed direction. Sometimes he missed being naïve and arrogant, too. He most certainly missed pretending he was important. That was bliss. Most of all, he missed not realising his wretched place in the world. Sometimes understanding was a terribly humbling thing.

"Here you are, gentlemen," Lara said, placing two glasses in front of them. Her eyes were glistening, and Stefan remembered her from Keri during the last Puk. She'd looked at Quig the same way that night and commanded the crowd like her parents did. Just like she did now.

"Thank you, Lara," he said, looking at the table. She was the greatest regret in his life, and he had many. *How does one apologise for causing the loss of an entire family?*

He fumbled in his pocket for a coin to tip her. It was all he could do. Wrek could pay the full bill for the alcohol, though. She caught his arm swiftly before he dropped the coin onto her tray. Her eyes broke away from Wrek to stare into his. They lacked the maliciousness he deserved.

"Your money is no good here. Remember that, brother," she whispered, and her eyes were kind, and he was so pathetic.

"I need to do something," he whispered. "For all your trouble." He gestured to the bar and the distance as though a great march had been taken. "If I could pay more, I would pay tenfold." His voice faltered and faded to nothing. He slumped in his chair. "I'm so sorry."

"Whisht, Stefan," she said cupping his grizzled cheeks in her warm, worn hands. "You and I are comrades of the road, comrades in blood." There was no anger in her eyes. It had to be there. Fuken *had* to be there, he thought. Perhaps it hid beneath the kindness. "All you and Emir have done for us, for me." She stroked his cheek as though caressing an infant, and Stefan couldn't help but feel lighter. "Good men, looking after everyone else, never wondering after themselves. Some of us notice these things. Some of us offer a free drink because we've nothing else to give."

With that, she released him from the absolving embrace, kissed his ruined hand, and, glancing once more at Wrek, slipped back through the crowd. Within a breath she was laughing along with another patron, and Stefan was left shaking and feeling a little better about himself.

"Not everybody appears to hate you," Wrek muttered, sipping his drink as any jealous brute might do when sitting with their love's rival. Stefan almost laughed. Almost cried too.

"I needed that. A man could take a dagger's blade far better, knowing some of his sins were a little less than before. Knowing some people cared."

"Aye."

"She will miss you when you leave," Stefan said, and found himself smiling. Wrek shrugged as if it were a small matter, and Stefan did what he'd never done in his life before: offered advice to another on the subject of courting a lady.

"Before you leave, kiss her. At least once. I have seen her in love before. Perhaps I'm seeing it again."

This time Wrek did smile. "You think Emir would allow me to put my grubby hands all over the fragile little waif?" He shrugged again. "He'd be right to kill me as well."

With the rush of the crowd, the melody of the players, the smell of the atmosphere, and the conversation about trivial things like love and desire, it almost felt like a drunken night in a tavern with a friend amidst peacetime. He'd no idea how much he'd missed his only friend until this moment. With responsibility weighing him down, he had been left behind.

"Be damned what Emir thinks. I love him as a brother, but he's a fuken idiot. His advice on matters of the heart is historically terrible." Distantly, Lara's outlandish laugh filled the room and Stefan smiled. "Lara is stronger than both you and me combined. Kiss the girl."

"I'm not that type of gentleman," Wrek countered, standing up. The hour was late and he was ready to tackle the road, it would appear. And Stefan? Well, Stefan was going to sit and think of the matters discussed. He was to pass words between Outcast and allies. What could possibly go wrong?

"Look, Mayor, can I trust you to the task?"

"You have my word, friend."

Bowing, Wrek slid through the crowd, leaving behind a half-finished pint that Stefan swiftly poured into his own. Everyone in the city was drinking alcohol these days. *Nothing else to do while waiting to die.* Stefan knew his name was etched upon a brute's blade. Most people in the city probably thought as much about themselves, too. He watched the bubbles in the clear glass, and then he watched Lara stop Wrek at the door and whisper something to him. Wrek smiled, nodding, before whispering something right back.

"Breaking her heart with word of leaving, aren't you?"

Stefan said to himself. Suddenly, Lara reached up and kissed Wrek on the lips and didn't stop for a handful of breaths. Before he could recover his composure or hide the stupid grin on his face, she pushed him out the door and spun around to return to her duties. Stefan couldn't help but notice the smile on her face, and it warmed him further. *Stronger than either of us.*

"Emir is going to fuken kill you," he muttered, certain now of the behemoth's fate.

9

BAD FEELINGS

"Just because you're able to move freely, doesn't mean you're ready," gasped Lea, spinning her sparring swords as he stalked her. Her breathing was laboured, sweat covered her body and her hairpins had come loose during this melee, allowing thick strands to hinder her view ever so. She was exhausted and nowhere near as sharp as she could be. Nevertheless, her eyes were blazing and she felt alive. "My love," she added, striking out at him before he could find a foothold in this fight's round. Their blades clattered loudly in the bustling camp's dawn, but few noticed them as they circled each other in the arena. Every day the sessions lasted longer.

"I'm better than yesterday," Erroh wheezed, as she battered through his defence once more and snapped a strike across the bridge of his nose.

"Perhaps in another week, you'll feel even better."

He dropped his guard and looked down at the damp mud, breathing heavily. She could see the weight on his shoulders. Could see the desire to delay. Who knew what might occur in another wasted week of inaction? The marching southerners might finally appear on the horizon; the scattered brutes encamped throughout the region might form up looking for a fight. The Wolves of the city might come hunting some Outcast scapegoats. Perhaps this urgency accounted for his need to take action. Once a hero, always an idiot. Her hero, nobody else's. "It must be done."

"It should be me," she argued, knowing his reply and fuming for it.

He snorted in reply, and she didn't like the tone of that snort. Not one little bit. She raised her blades eagerly. Injuries or not, she would make him pay. This was how it was, and this was how it always would be.

They fought a few scuffles more without either one breaking the other's defence.

"You can't beat him," he hissed suddenly, and she drew back.

"I'm better than him," she countered, attacking methodically from both sides. He took a blow to the chest but ignored the barrage and waited for his moment to counter and demonstrate his point.

"That doesn't matter."

While a scattered few watched the legends, one pair of eyes watched eagerly: Nomi of the south. Nomi the forsaken. She stretched the knot in her neck and adjusted herself against her post, searching for comfort. She was always a breath from relief, yet never quite able to find the position. The chain around her neck saw to that. It clinked against the post every time she coughed; her more aggressive heaving caused her to gasp. It was nothing, she told herself. Just that her body was slow to recover after months of abuse. The biting wind made the tarp erected around her flap wildly, but she remained warm. Her whole body was warm. Burning to the touch. Sitting around, wrapped in swaddling, was no place for any child or beast.

She watched the beautiful creatures tearing at each other with such ferocity, and she craved passion like that. She took a deep breath and listened to the gurgle in her chest. Too much fluid down there. If they allowed her a reprieve from the chain, she might take a wander to find some healing herbs. She knew Erroh would free her if he could. She knew he intended to, for he was beautiful, he was kind, he was perfect. They broke again, muttering words at each other as though battling, and she craved to understand such a connection. She watched them every morning and then again at dusk. Her only friends. They screamed and smiled and laughed and drew blood and it was magnificent. *They* were magnificent, and she, well, she was but their pet. But she would become more.

Erroh said something, and Lea cursed him loudly. Oh, how Nomi enjoyed watching them together. Seeing them as themselves alone and not as her constant guardians, sitting near, offering food, water, and that wonderful steaming cofe that ran through her body a little too quickly. What conversation they shared with her was broken and laced with frustration. Nomi tried her best, but still the words would not come easily. Perhaps it was the chain. Perhaps it was the sleeplessness; perhaps it was her burdened chest. She swallowed and her throat stung unmercifully. Coughing deeply like a battle horn, she gagged on her own mucus before a few tendrils of air crept deep into her heavily laden lungs. She shivered as the breeze caught her blonde hair, and she reached for the brush. Lea had given it as a gift, though as the pretty lady had passed her the item, Nomi had failed to find the words to thank her. All she could offer were a few mumbled grunts and a smile. She trusted Lea. She hoped Lea trusted her. That would be nice. Easier to love Erroh that way.

"Aye, Lea, I know you are better. You cannot beat him," Erroh gasped, as Lea displayed her ability by knocking one of his blades free of his grip. A fine manoeuvre even if he hadn't had such a weak grip. He was exhausted, yet exhilarated. Today, he felt more himself than ever; he had even endured the weight of attempting a very stupid thing, all in the name of it being the right fuken thing to be doing. She moved in to deliver the killing blow and he shot out his hand, taking a full grip of her long hair.

Don't.

He did. He pulled fiercely, dragging her low, and she could only go with him. He thought of the river for a breath and quelled the guilt. She was like him. She learned through pain. She swung, for she was fierce, and he clattered her awkward strikes away, and then, leaping upon her as though in an embrace, he knocked her painfully to the ground. Though they fell clumsily, he cushioned her fall as best he could. He was kind like that. He pinned her down and she gazed in fury up at him.

"A little play?" she asked through gritted teeth.

"Aye, that sounds lovely, though perhaps not in front of everyone."

"Just the little southern girl," she hissed, and Erroh offered an apologetic smile. For the lesson concerning the tactics, he remembered his father's teachings. In a fair fight, she could take the legend easily enough. Erroh too, but it would be no fair fight, and Erroh understood his father's tactics better than anyone else in the world.

Suddenly, Lea slipped a hand free and grabbed at his face, driving her nails into his flesh and drawing blood ever so. Her eyes were calm and he could see the killer behind them, and it was impressive. He snapped at her hand, biting deep into the offending limb, and she drew away, her eyes wide with understanding and resentment.

With her fight silently conceded, he released her grip, yet he did not move away. "He will find a way to win. His kind always do." He kissed her before climbing free of her warmth and helping her to her feet.

"Are you not exactly like him?" she whispered, wrapping her arms around his neck as though she were about to flip him upside down into a river. Her meaning was clear: she was Alpha female. Hear her fuken roar. *What river, indeed?*

"Me? Well, I'm something else entirely." Grinning, Erroh stared across to his adversaries, who were sparring in a small ring of their own. It was evident Doran was getting over the unfortunate injury to his hand. His fist was an intimidating knot of leather strappings lined with studs and menace. His better hand held a sparring sword, and he pummelled at Aymon's guard as though he were driving a stubborn post into stony ground.

"I want to know everything of warfare," Lea said, clearly upset at the advantage Erroh held over her, and he smiled. Only a fool believed that nasty tactics in a fight to the death were dishonourable.

"Pull hair if it presents itself," he said, and she grinned as she slid her hairpins back into place.

"And cut my hair to a thimble's length in the meantime."

At this, he spun around. "We don't jest about your hair, ever," he warned, still smiling, before taking her hand and becoming serious once more. He could smell the fresh layer of sweat on her body. On his own, too. Her face was marred and cut from many blows. Her chest heaved as she struggled to catch her breath after the hour of heavy sparring, and he had never thought her more perfect. He had never believed himself luckier to have her as his mate. He stroked her grubby cheek. "This is my fight, Lea. Please support me."

"I'll follow you to the ends of the world, my beo. As long as you don't leave me behind," she pledged, kissing him. It was a good pledge.

"I'll never leave you behind." This too was a good pledge.

They watched the two Alphas spar for a little while longer before returning to their tent, which stood next to Nomi's post. Placing it there had been all Erroh could do in solidarity with the captive, short of breaking her chains in complete defiance of his father.

Erroh's body ached, but he was pleased with his improvement. He had grown even stronger in the last week. Once the wounds began to hold, there would be no stopping his progress. No stopping his intensity, either. Whatever Uden had imagined would come from the gifts, it had given Erroh a fire these past few weeks. It had been agonizingly slow the first few days after leaving Emir's tent, but now he felt almost like himself again. Out of habit, he removed his shirt as he strode towards the tent. Too much grime, sweat and blood still clung to the fabric.

"Erroh," Lea muttered harshly, kicking the discarded shirt into a corner before spinning on him furiously. "Decorum." She looked out behind him and he realised his error. Though Nomi was subtle, there was no denying that she was looking upon his chest in the afternoon sun.

"Oh, shit. Sorry."

She pulled the flap of the tent shut and took hold of him, her eyes still burning with fight. More sparring? He went to kiss her, but was shoved away fiercely onto the bed. In a flash, she was upon him. "Oh, it's been, too long," she growled, and bit his shoulder. He reached for her, kissing and tasting and loving, and suddenly the fatigue in his body had disappeared. She slapped his hand playfully before sitting atop him. He was pinned down and conceded the scuffle. Frowning, she kissed him once and slapped away a second groping assault.

"Not here, beo."

He sat up to kiss her again and, with fingers like talons, she scraped down his back. Not enough to draw blood, but enough to draw a gasp. *Perfect.*

"Very much here," he argued, and thought it a convincing argument. She laughed, shaking her head. "I'll be real quiet, Lea. Real quiet." Spinning her, he took control and pinned her back down, much to her delight. War brought out the best in them. War between them both even more.

"You really do arouse my quickened heart with your poetry," she mocked, and he felt like losing his mind in desire. Instead, he laughed and kissed her.

"And when have we ever been quiet?"

"Besides, don't you have a fight to pick?" She wrapped her legs around his waist and squeezed. She'd done some fine walking with those muscular, slender legs. He gasped again, and she pulled him to his side and ran her fingers down his ruined chest as though aroused by such devastation. Perhaps she was. Perhaps they were driven by darker things than most couples. Perhaps that was a wonderful, enlightening thing. Perhaps it was fine to find desire in the extraordinary. Her smile reassured him, regardless.

"Ah, why drag me in here and torment me so? You

wanted me to wait a week. Perhaps a week of constant furrowing is all I need to keep me distracted." He slipped away from her warmth to sit on the cot's edge, and she laughed at his torment. She reached out and tugged at his hair and giggled again.

"Couldn't help myself, what with Nomi setting her eyes upon you. A girl must mark her territory, you know," she whispered. Her fingers moved to his back. She stroked it up and down a few times, her voice a little dreamy as though in a trance. The delicate rattle of a chain came from outside, and he looked to the faint silhouette of their captive against the post a few feet away. Nomi adjusted the blankets around her and lay down, and Erroh saw a flicker of anger flash across Lea's face. Just for a moment and that was fine. She had little to fear from Nomi, but Lea had earned her right to dislike the girl when the mood took her.

"It is time so," Erroh whispered, more to himself. "Magnus's rage will be unfathomable."

"Aye. That is the cost of the chosen path, Erroh."

Erroh stood from the comforts of the bed and his mate. She roused herself behind him. She thought ill of his plans, yet supported him regardless. Still, her voice was a comfort as it warned its last.

"Regardless of what happens, everything is about to change."

He nodded, pulling away to grab a fresh shirt. *Need to look my best when I shake the world.*

"Everything that happens from here will be my making," he said quietly.

"I'm allowing this insanity. It's our making. It's time to step into our legend."

He stepped from his tent, with Lea following behind. He had pledged to Nomi that he would free her. With every anxious step he took, he drew nearer honouring that pledge. This was what kept his nerve. He'd given his word to Nomi that she would be freed. But as he stepped toward the Master General's tent, he hesitated. Behind him, Lea sighed.

"We've come this far," she whispered. Fine words indeed.

"Father, we must speak," Erroh demanded, stepping onto hostile territory. Magnus was not alone. At his side, Emir smiled for a moment before reading the grim expressions on the faces of father and son. He stepped away from his patient to reach for his bag.

"Um… your knee is healing nicely, Magnus," he stammered. "You might even avoid a limp as well." He bowed to leave, and Magnus held him with a raised hand.

"It might be a tarp, but you could have knocked," Magnus growled at the newcomers, sensing a threat. "Why do you never knock?"

Lea slapped the tent a few times.

"I beg you grant me what I wish," Erroh said, standing at attention in front of the Master General, who carefully stood from his desk to meet his eyes. Probably to look through his soul as well.

"Oh, that shit again." Magnus leant back on the desk, lifting his knee a few times. The ancient crystals within the bone crackled loudly, as did the leather strappings on his brace. Erroh could see the pain in the great man's aged features and sensed the magnitude of his actions to come. "I will not free her, Erroh. Though you may continue to beg."

"I beg for nothing."

"I have greater issues, Erroh." A fine counter to a pathetic request. His father was carrying the weight of the world upon a weak knee, and though he was suited for the task, inaction was bringing no reward upon them.

"You must have heard her coughing. Nomi is dying."

"Ah—she has a slight fever," Magnus said, waving his hand dismissively. "The tent you've erected around her does the job."

Erroh looked to Emir furiously. "I know other soldiers have suffered similar coughing afflictions. I'm just disappointed you refuse to treat her, brother." He spat the last word out, and Emir held his gaze. And why not? Nomi was one of the soldiers who had sacked his town, killed his friends. *Put Aireys to the fire.* Still, though, he was better than negligence. "Your time could be better spent looking her over, instead of glancing at a stationary subject," Erroh hissed, challenging his friend and mocking his father all in the same moment.

What am I doing?

"Let Emir decide how badly she needs treatment," Lea said.

Magnus shook his head. "Do not send Emir out to tend to your concubine and find little wrong with her." He bent his knee one last time and placed his hand on Erroh's shoulder as though he hadn't just insulted him and his mate in the same breath. Erroh felt the anger, yet did not shrug from his father's grasp. Why warn him of a tempest? "The medicines are for those with more pressing issue. She caught a chill is all, little cub." He squeezed Erroh's shoulder as though he were talking to a pathetic child in need of reassurance. "If it gets worse, we'll move her into the healer's tent." The squeeze turned to a pat and Erroh formed a fist.

"Sir, you are wrong," Lea hissed. Erroh could sense the burgeoning fury stirring at the suggestion of Erroh enjoying other females. It was as though Magnus didn't know what to say to women at all.

"Was this your idea, Lea? Whispering in his ear about challenging my orders?" The old Ranger growled and folded his arms for petulant effect. "So soon into a coupling and already you need a little blonde to spice up your play between silk and straw?"

Erroh punched Magnus. It was a fine punch, worthy of any apprentice toward an overly aggressive master. This was not the first time the two had come to blows, but it was certainly the most satisfying on the younger Alpha's part.

Despite his dodgy knee, Magnus did not fall. Magnus would never fall. He wasn't built like that, and neither were his kin. The old Ranger stumbled, though, and his head whipped to the side and he gripped the desk for support.

Lea stepped forward and laid a hand smoothly across her man's chest. Erroh did not move, not even to look at the damage to his knuckles. The taunt had been repaid in full. Even Magnus could have little argument there. The old man spat a globule of blood onto the dirty floor and nodded his acknowledgement of the strike.

"You've been working on your right."

"Free her," Erroh said coldly.

"Lea, keep your pup on a leash," Magnus hissed, straightening and standing over his son. A daunting sight even during peace. "Lest I geld him myself."

"Free her!" roared Erroh.

"I will not!!" Magnus roared louder.

Emir had seen enough. He tried to step through the tent flap.

This time it was Erroh who held him steady, one hand raised. "Master General, sir, I have two witnesses here. I challenge you for leadership," he said coldly.

Magnus blinked and allowed a little blood to flow unhindered. He grinned dangerously, as though playing a masterful stroke in a game of chance. As though seeing his son for the first time and approving of a little defiance.

"As you wish, Erroh of Keri."

10

DANCING ACROSS THE ARTH

H er name was Aurora, and she liked to make good time when racing across the Arth. Chasing her comrades. Attempting to pass them by. To catch up on all she'd missed. To play while waiting for Uden, her god, to come find her. Her hood whipped out behind her as she drove her mount forward. The bite in the wind was long gone, and she took wonderful deep breaths and tasted the warm season all around. She loved this region.

Born in blood on a freezing night. Cold ever since. She looked forward to the day she died. Looked forward to the tearing carnage that would rip her limbs free. Make her blood spill out on everything. Maybe by an axe. *Wonderful.* She hoped it would be somewhere in these lands, where skin could be free from bindings and chains. Oh, to have the feel of a warm season's sun upon her skin as it was flayed from her body.

"Hush now, little delicious," she cried, slowing her horse to a canter at a crossroad in the route ahead. The beast whinnied and gasped, and she tutted at its insolence. "There's plenty more of your kind about, should it come to that," she

warned, reaching for her saddlebags. Pulling her eerie map
from within, she held it carefully in the wind. These
crossroads were massive, dating back to the ancient times.
Cracked, aye, but eternal until now. *Nothing is eternal, not
even Uden.* Shaking her head, she ran her finger down along
the crinkled paper. She was certain of the route, for she had
memorised it—it had been just like counting numbers—but
best take no chances. Not where killing was concerned.

The wind caught the map suddenly and almost ripped her
gift away into the sky. She almost allowed it to happen.
Almost. She tracked her route towards the destroyed town.
On impulse, she held the map upside down. It seemed right to
do so. Even if it wasn't right at all. Sometimes she couldn't
help herself, and sometimes such thoughts hurt her mind.
Perhaps the gift Uden had given her long ago was just a cruel
jest on his part. For he knew her affliction all too well; he
preyed upon it, and she loved him for it. To punish her mind,
she flipped the map back to its intended angle and burned the
vision into her mind, and it hurt like losing count.

"North is no," she cursed, spitting at the ground. *Fuk you,
ground.* After a breath she spat once more.

Even.

Nicer.

Despising her penchant for self-torment, she returned the
map to her saddlebag and brought her horse forward. Beyond
the crossroads, the water streamed along violently; the ground
underfoot was beaten from frequent use. Though not so much
this last year. She walked the last mile and it was godly. She
listened hopefully for the world to reveal its secrets and
hidden threats, but tragically, she was the only one wandering
this path this sunny day. She passed the first whitewashed
house and imagined a life in a place like this. Without
warning, she felt a terrible pain shoot through her chest. She

almost expected to see an arrow protruding through her skin, and a bloom of blood, but instead felt the agony disappear as quickly as it had come.

Born in blood on a freezing cold night.

She left the faded, whitewashed house and its abandoned barn behind her and continued on towards the town of blasphemy. Her mount's hooves were wonderfully loud, and she listened beyond their eerie clatter for any stumbling movement in any building around her. A loose step, a shut curtain. A click of an archer's crossbow.

Oh, please let me hear that majestic click and the silent whistle after.

And then a thunk.

Nothing stirred. No bolt shot through her eye, killing her instantly, and Aurora felt lesser for it. She could feel the ghosts of the dead as she drew near, and her stomach churned at the thought of her own demons, which had followed her around since her birth. *Ever since I first cut flesh.* She hadn't enjoyed it, but oh, how she revelled in such practices now. Death was her gift to this life, wonderfully destructive as it was.

It was a gift, given by him, for him. She aimed to please. And loved every murder.

Except Alder's.

Suddenly Aurora dropped to her knees, clutching her stomach. She saw his dead face, eyes agape, staring at her, through her, and it cut deep. Beautiful Alder. Idealistic and trusting. A fine lover and a warm soul. Ealis howled for the loss, while Aurora fixed her hair.

Stop it, stop it, stop it.

She'd pushed herself too hard, she reassured herself, touching the dry, dusty ground beneath her. She took a deep breath, thought of killing a few fat wretches, and grinned at memories of carnage. "Killer of Alphas," she whispered, and they were stirring words.

Her feet were silent as they touched the cobblestones, and the huntress imagined she was being observed. She walked quietly towards the abandoned town, each step taken in perfect unison with those of the mount beside her. A rhythmic sound of order. It took her six hundred steps to reach the very centre of the town, where she could feel eyes burning into her back. She already knew her hunter, but made no move to strike out. The attack would come in time, and she would spill some blood.

Why do you need to spill blood, Aurora? a voice in her mind asked, and she grimaced.

"Because it's there to be spilled," she whispered to no one in particular—apart from Uden, who saw everything. *Right?* He likely saw her from his marching throne a thousand miles behind her, or a few hundred in front. She couldn't see anything at all. Couldn't see if he'd hastened his journey. Couldn't see if every finger had gathered and they had begun their charge.

Hopefully, not yet.

She walked through the centre of the town and waited for the little cat to catch up with her. She pulled her crossbow from her thigh and cocked the arrow into place with a satisfying click. She loved this process. To savour the moment before it passed. It wasn't cruel; it was something to do. The cat ran along the edge of the street, dipping and ducking through every crawl space it could find, shadowing the deadly assassin. It showed little fear, only curiosity, and Aurora respected its agility and grace. Such a delicate form for such a vicious creature. It was almost a shame. She allowed the reins of her mount to fall from her grasp, and it ambled away slowly in search of water and sustenance. Aurora knelt down on one knee and aimed at her next victim as it drew closer. She did not blink, and she did not allow the gentle wind playing with the loose strands in her hair to distract her in any way.

"What is the point of this?" whispered Ealis to the wind.

"Meow," replied the little black and white cat hopefully, and then abandoned its last hiding place and walked closer to its human predator. Close enough to be strangled. "Meow," it repeated with a little more enthusiasm, before rubbing its face against the tip of the arrow. Aurora hadn't been expecting conversation.

She walked the streets of the town, calming her heartbeat and fighting the stirrings of awe and wonder. This town was historic, and she felt its deathly energy. Oh, she loved it here. She could almost sense the false god's presence. He who'd once lived and breathed in this town and torn the world of the Hunt apart while defending it.

This was Keri, and this was part of her pilgrimage.

"It's beautiful, isn't it, Killer?" she whispered, braving a touch of the mural. The cat didn't seem very interested, though; it sat quietly watching a butterfly a few feet away. Ealis rubbed her fingers along the colourful wall of paint and stepped back again in wonder. "Yes, very beautiful."

"Meow."

Such a sight, she thought, looking at the figures immortalised forever. What divine artist, with such delicate and caring hands, had painted this piece? Whoever they were, they humbled her. She remembered painting, in her old life. Or else in a dream. *Of Fyre of the Night.* Delicate flicks of a brush, the right shading in the eyes, mixing carefully until perfect crimson revealed itself.

So much blood.

No more art.

She brushed the mural with her other hand, because such things were important, before stepping away for one final look. She already knew the story it told. She knew it was an act of sacrilege, but still, she could not bring herself to destroy such work, even if it covered his words. How great a sin would it be to allow such a piece to remain? she wondered. Not as great as burning down an entire city.

"Doomed for such a sin," she said, sighing. Killer replied by leaping upon the butterfly with unmerciful proficiency. It wasn't much of a meal. "And for the sin of defiance," she added, thinking of how she would deliver the body of Erroh to Uden. Without the eyes, of course. Those she would feast upon, and she would be part of scripture. She wondered would Uden slit her throat or take to strangling her. Hopefully the former. It was a terrible thing being strangled and waking up after. Better to know for certain. Far more satisfying as the darkness came.

As long as the pain ends.

Looking across the battlefield and the remnants of the great defence, she cursed Oren loudly. This town, for all its beauty and natural concealment, was simply a quaint unimpressive town and little more. "I would have taken it easily enough," she mused, looking around. She missed the finger of Hunt she'd led for too fleeting a time. The biting wind blew her hair back once more as Aurora walked through the gap. She could feel it strongest here. His energy. The charred ground still offered a suggestion of what had occurred here, and the violence took her breath away. Oh, she wanted to kill him so fuken badly.

"And everyone around him, for good measure." Sometimes it wasn't about the slitting of the throat. Sometimes it was about the journey there. And sometimes, with the throat so close, it was best to prolong the wait, for that was godly.

"Meow."

She ran her hands across each grave in turn and wondered about the deeds of the slain. She closed her eyes and listened to the wind and could see the flames. She imagined the great towering spikes and the shrieks of the dying. The piercing cries, the clash of steel on steel and steel on bone. So much blood, earned with honour and grace, and she wanted to be here on that final day. On the first day, too.

"No woman deserved to burn, Killer," she said, for she knew the tale well. "Not at all." Any warrior standing in defiance deserved a greater honour. When she had led the women to be burned, she had taken little pleasure in their screams as the flames overcame them. She suspected many of her people had felt the same.

Killer looked at her, and with its eyes asked what she would have done with the captive.

Aurora knelt down and rubbed the cat's fur once, twice. *Perfect.* "I would have offered the warrior girl a chance to fight once more." She tapped her dagger. "Then I would have slit her fuken throat and drenched myself." Only then would she have set the pyre alight and allowed her comrades to toast the victory.

And then what, Aurora? What would you do as the dead burned to ash? Killer asked, licking its paw and reaching up behind its ear.

Aurora watched the beast for a moment before shrugging guiltily. She didn't like the cat's accusations. "I'd have furrowed the nearest warrior, of course," she hissed to the beast.

Just any man?

"Fine. I'd have furrowed with Erroh. Until he cried for mercy," she screamed, storming away from her inquisitor. "Fuk you! You're just a cat!" she shouted back before disappearing back through the gap.

She made a little fire in the centre of the town and laid her blanket out along the hard ground and stared up at the clear sky above. She did not wish to sleep under a roof tonight. She never wanted to sleep under a roof. The freedom of the Arth always called. She had spent far too much of her life in a cage. She would not willingly sleep in one now. Aurora craved the night air, always, and the taste of meat upon her lips. Ealis, less so. When the land around her had turned to complete darkness except for the shattered sphere above, the cat returned to her and brought with it a gift of apology for its intrusive questions. "You've been hunting, Killer?"

"Meow," replied the black and white cat, dropping the dead rat near the fire. It lay down and pawed the ruined creature to entice at least one more escape attempt. Alas, the bloodied rodent had passed into the darkness already, and eventually Killer lost all interest and began licking the traces of blood from its paws.

A gift for woman beast.

"Thank you," Aurora said, picking up the gift for closer inspection. She appreciated the gesture deeply. As a fellow hunter, she knew all too well the trials involved in a fine chase. Even finding a fresh track took skill and perseverance. Her thoughts flashed to her former lover, Alder. She had hunted his scent swiftly and eventually taken the kill as she had been created to do, all hail Uden. Aurora tore the rat in half and lanced the upper part onto a small dagger and held it over the flame. Just enough to warm the meat, not enough to dry up the blood. That was the best part. She threw the tail end to her pet, who pounced at it. After a few moments both deadly killers sat in companionable silence, crunching the little bones and swallowing with satisfaction, and the argument was forgotten.

A cool wind from the mountains above blew down on them, and Aurora pulled her blanket around her. As if it were the most natural thing in the world, Killer climbed onto the lap of the girl and lay down.

"That's not comfortable for me at all," hissed the human beast crossly, and the cat adjusted itself a few times before settling itself as awkwardly as possible.

"Please get off me."

"Purr."

"Please?" Aurora toyed with the idea of strangling the creature, but instead found herself stroking the cat along the back of its head.

"Goodbye, Killer," she whispered, climbing atop her horse after a fine night's sleep. The finest since she'd murdered a king. The cat sat by the last embers of the fire, unmoved by its guest's departure. It was a sunny morning, and there was a fresh hunt in the air.

"Meow," said the cat finally, stretching leisurely. It turned its back and walked away to find a warmer spot to laze.

"I would love to stay, but I've been promised an ocean of blood," Aurora called back to her little friend. The animal disappeared around a corner, and both Aurora and Ealis missed it ever so. Aurora wondered if she had liked cats in another life, before Uden had brought her into this world with such violence; or maybe she was simply drawn to a creature born to kill. Or one that *liked* to kill.

"Be more like Killer," she spat, kicking the mount forward and leaving the cat's territory forever. She gripped the reins and enjoyed the freedom of the Arth once more. She enjoyed making good time. Good time begets good times.

"Time to kill," she said laughing, and bit her bottom lip delightfully at her wit.

"Time to pick up his scent."

"Time to find a track."

"Time to hurt a god," she whispered, and then repeated her words in a heavy northern accent. As she rode, she hissed them under her breath repeatedly and pushed herself forward. It became her mantra.

11

THE LEGEND OF TYE

"I have come here to kill someone. Who will accept my challenge?"

Tye crashed through the tavern door, leaving it swinging wildly behind him. A few nearby patrons stared up in alarm and then relief as he staggered drunkenly by, seeking different prey. Perhaps they believed him childish, or foolish; perhaps they did not look beyond his glazed eyes. Their fear likely returned when he brandished his longsword and swung it in a wide arc above his head. Though his mind was awash with agony and anger, he consoled himself with thoughts of amusing the masses with his antics, for he felt witty this fine night. People liked to laugh. Especially pretty females. And the more Alpha the female, the better. They also liked passion, strength and fearlessness.

"Are there any spineless Wolves in here?" He wavered, gathered himself, fought a burp. "Any brave enough to face little old me in a simple duel to the death?" His words silenced the watching, wary crowd. He spun the sword once more and returned it to his scabbard. "Did the true warriors die with the Rangers?" Slowly, he looked around the bar in search of murderous camaraderie or female companionship. Whichever, really. "Aw, come on," he wheedled. "I want to kill something." The crowd must have finally understood the precariousness of a devastated young Alpha male without a master to keep him in line. They dropped their eyes despite the growing scene, and he smiled dangerously.

Come on and start shit.

Nobody stood to challenge him, so he made his way through the tavern seeking adventure and foolishness. He stumbled against a table, whose occupants went deathly still. He bowed in apology and almost fell over himself, before stealing a mug of ale from one of the patrons without as much as a second glance and then stumbling off into the crowd. A trio of musicians continued playing regardless, and he ground his teeth. If he couldn't silence a group of bards, he hadn't made a grand enough entrance at all. He wondered about charging them with fists flailing. Each player looked bored and hardened. They'd likely seen their own share of incidents throughout their careers. Best not start something with them, he thought. So, he started on a wall.

"Fuk ya," he roared, draining his stolen tankard, burping, and throwing his ill-fated mug at the wall as though it were a condemning group of females in a brutal Cull. Like any good mug afflicted with such a terrible turn of events, it shattered into a hundred shards all over a betting table.

"Tye, you little shit! Calm down or I'll have you barred," Lara cried, marching through the crowd as though she were a disapproving mother. Despite himself, he stepped back, and she stood in his way, arms folded, furious. She might have tapped her foot. He hoped she didn't tap her foot. He'd be rightly fuked then.

"Sorry," he whispered, looking at her chest. It was a fine chest. She was a fine female, and he, well, he was a hot-blooded male close to falling apart. "Sorry," he announced, louder this time. He offered a shrug, looked at her chest again and grinned. "You look beautiful tonight, Lara."

"I look beautiful every night," she countered, tapping her foot. Around them, the tavern resumed service. Once Lara became involved, it was as calming as Wrek's threatening eye. If you pissed off Lara, every tavern in the city knew your name and what level of barring you'd brought upon yourself. Her foot ceased its tapping. Her face warmed, and he was smitten. At least for tonight. "Right. Settle yourself. No more barbaric behaviour, and I'll get you a pint," she said softly, and behaving sounded like the finest idea in the world.

"That would be lovely," he said with a bow, and almost fell over again. "I miss Wrek. I haven't seen him much at all," he said, hoping to draw her into conversation.

"Whisht, little one. He comes and goes," she whispered, pointing to a secluded corner. Her meaning was clear: *Drink up and shut up about Wrek and the Outcasts.* He missed the massive bouncer. Wrek was a fantastic sparring partner. Like so few others, when he spoke to Tye, he looked him in the eye as though he were a man.

"I don't think he's ever coming back," Tye muttered as she guided him away from the nervous patrons. For just a moment, he spotted such deep sorrow in her beaming face that he almost apologised again. He knew Wrek had feelings for her. Wrek wasn't a man to talk of such things, but Tye listened to everything around him. She coughed once, flicked her long blonde hair behind her ear and returned a devastating smile.

"He'll be back. There are unfinished things that he and I must speak of." She offered a devious wink. She was convincing and kind, and he almost believed her, except Jeroen had said he'd be back, too, and now he was dead.

No, he's alive. Chained and waiting.
Somewhere.

He shook his sorrow away. Trusted the childish imaginings of his father surviving countless blows from sharpened things and emerging from the bloody wastes with open arms and wounds, and many stories to tell. Any moment now, Tye reassured himself, and enjoyed the lie. Better to lie than succumb to grief like his mother, he supposed. Though her succumbing wasn't a matter of wailing to the darkness. Her succumbing was something else entirely. She was obsessed with saving Elise, and the fuken city too. Charging him to stand guard over the abandoned Ranger camp was hardly a task worthy of a young Alphaline, and certainly not the act of a mother protecting a grieving son. The rage that stirred within him was growing steadily with every passing day.

Lara slipped behind the bar and smoothly poured a pint of ale. Within a breath, she slid it along the bar and it settled in front of him. He looked at his hands and the dried scabs forming around each knuckle. It had been only a minor disagreement between two parties near the hovel's entrance the night before. Only a few punches thrown each way. There was sure to be another argument soon enough. It wouldn't end well, now that he carried a blade. A gift from his mother, because he was the Alpha male in the house now and a lesser child for it. Grabbing his drink, he wobbled over to the farthest table, where a game of cards was in progress. He had little desire to sit alone in the corner, despite what the appealing Lara had suggested. Besides, there wasn't anything else to do in this place. Pickings were slim in the Hole tonight, be they females or fights.

"Are we playing a few hands, then?" he slurred. The four men stared quietly among themselves but said little and offered less invitation. He muttered a few threats in disgust and staggered away through the damp and smoky room. He eventually ended up at the table he'd attacked with a glass a little while earlier. They sat motionless, regarding him warily, each holding a few cards in their hands. He decided they were friends. They really weren't. "You are friends with the Outcast Erroh, aren't you?" he shouted suddenly, and this time a few faces turned toward him.

Excellent.

Was it something I said?

"He is no friend of mine," a blond wretch replied. Tye believed his name was Stefan, but he couldn't be certain. Whatever his name was, he looked positively shocked at hearing Erroh's name shouted. Perhaps he was afraid of getting mugged. *Don't worry. Tye will protect you.*

"No, no. I know you. You are the mayor of the wretches or some shit. You have your ear to the ground. Where is he hiding? There are plenty of Wolves we could kill together. Tell Erroh that Tye wants to speak with him. You can do that, can't you?" He patted the red-faced Stefan on the back. "Of course you can." Only then did Tye notice Stefan's company.

Talent at the table.

His spinning mind sobered for a moment out of necessity. Just long enough to take in the three females sitting at the table, all holding cards in their hands.

Two of the females, evidently residents of the city, wore matching dresses; one was blue and black, the other gold and white. The oldest of the three was clad in alluring dark leather. Her eyes were incredible. They blinked beautifully and focused on the pretty Stefan. Perhaps she was smitten.

"I am not friends with the betrayer," said Stefan loudly, running his fingers nervously through his matted blond hair.

"May he fall from the walls themselves and know a bloody end."

"I'm out," muttered the girl in gold and white. She flipped her cards away disdainfully and stood up from the table. In one fluid motion, she swept past the dangerous Alpha with barely a look and disappeared into the crowd.

"It appears there is a place free," Tye declared, and sat down before any of his new comrades could argue.

"Fuk off," Lexi hissed. Her hands shook in anger. She was pissed, and this night was getting worse. She watched Celeste disappear into the night and fumed at the interruption. She knew Tye. Well, knew *of* him, and thought little of the man despite what Mea might argue. Just another hormonal young Alpha male, sniffing around, looking to start trouble when the world was in the balance. *I'm sorry your father died. How about you honour him?*

She formed a fist and began counting.

One, two, fuken three.

"Oh, wait, hang on," Tye slurred. "I've seen you around the Ranger camp. Before... well, before they got slaughtered. You are Erroh's sister? Hello, I am Tye." He lifted the small glass left by the departed girl and smelled the contents. "Wine," he muttered, downing the remains.

Lexi leaned across the table, really close so no one would hear. "Listen, little Tye," she said softly. "Your mother will hear of this." What had started as a few whispered words between herself, Celeste and Stefan had turned to something far more precarious. It was one thing having this beautiful stranger just waltzing in and charming Stefan; it was another thing altogether having to contend with fuken Tye. All she desired was a few quiet words with Stefan to pass on some words from Roja, after which she might have a few drinks, enjoy a song or two before heading back up to the tower and crushing responsibility.

"I don't care," he snapped, slamming his fist down on the table. His empty mug rolled from his hand and toppled off the edge. Before it smashed, Stefan's charming companion shot out a hand and caught the offending mug before it too met a Tye-inspired end. She placed it upright and sighed deeply, watching Stefan squirm beneath her gaze, Tye's outburst, and the many watching eyes.

"Sorry," Tye said, feeling a little embarrassed for his actions. The look he received from Lexi suggested no amount of apology would earn her favour this night. He held up his hand and nodded his head. Aye, he knew better than to aggravate a young female of the city. Had he not learned that from his hero? It was a small matter. He sighed and waited for his mind to settle, for his better judgement to rise above the terrible sadness he felt. He waited for a few breaths more and felt nothing. So, he looked away from the perfectly reasonable beauty of Lexi and gazed upon the older, more stunning female, dressed in black leather and mystery. She had eyes that had been sculpted by the gods themselves, absent or no.

A few slow notes began to ring out once more, and revellers grabbed their prospective mates' hands and took to the centre of the room. Surprisingly, Stefan stood up and held out his hand to Lexi, who took it immediately. The female in leather raised an eyebrow and sat back in disappointment as her quarry led his partner in a few gentle steps, bestowing delicate sweet whisperings upon her in the gentle sway of music. The alluring older girl with godly eyes and perfect face didn't bother to look at Tye once. So, he searched for fine words to win her attention. Any type of words. Words to make her like him, because no one else in the world seemed to. He reached across and stole Stefan's glass. It was sine, and there was plenty left.

"My name is Tye," he told her. "I am son of one of the greatest warriors ever to live—Jeroen. I think he's dead, though." She turned and faced him, and he was mesmerised by her beauty. "He was a brave Ranger. He was slain protecting the warmonger, Magnus."

"That's really sad, Tye," she whispered, and her heavy northern voice was melodic and ethereal. A voice created by gods too, no doubt. Beautiful and strangely unnatural. As though something more lay beneath. He could listen to that voice all night. "Please, little one, tell me of this Jeroen. Tell me everything about him," she added, raising her hand for a fresh round, and Tye felt charmed and attended to.

"As long as you tell me your name, my dear," he urged her gently, and she dazzled him with a smile and told him.

12

CLASH OF GODS

E rroh closed his eyes and allowed the rays of the sun to warm his skin. He could never remember the exact day of the season. Lea would know if he asked. She was always scribbling her thoughts in her own leather-bound book. Keeping track of days, events, their very lives. He wondered what she'd write about today.

Fuk, fuk, fuk.

What am I doing?

"You seem somewhat lonely over there, little cub," Magnus called from across the arena. His father appeared relaxed. A strange thing, considering his throne was being challenged. Perhaps the few days had allowed him to become used to the idea. Perhaps he was proud of his son. Perhaps he knew he would win, even with a dodgy knee.

Perhaps.

"Oh, I'm fine. I'm at peace with my own company," Erroh countered. He *did* feel terribly alone, though, ever since he'd challenged for the title. Standing out among the watching crowd was a reminder of how unpopular he was.

Alone, and surrounded by allies who wish me dead.

Since the challenge had become known, Magnus had become the most popular man in the wastes. Every Wolf was here, and they stared through the contender. That was no surprise. The apprehensive peace they'd brokered for the old Ranger was already in jeopardy. *Ruined by an Outcast, as well.* Each Wolf stood in his finest armour, fighting ready, lest the challenge erupt into bloody civil war. They should have known better.

This will all end in tears.

Avoiding the condemning glares from the warriors, Erroh looked to the ground. If he could give a good reason why he had challenged, he would. As it was, though, he'd had no choice. He had little interest in leadership. He wasn't built for such things. Not anymore. He was not cruel enough to lead, and he certainly hadn't the will to choose the fate of so many soldiers under his command. He'd led an army before—and led them all to a glorious doom. He had no taste left for it. It amazed him that his father had the strength to lead after the massacre of his Rangers.

He's better than me.

"Any peace is a good thing, Erroh. It's a lonely place up here," Magnus said. He spun his sword absently on the dry, wood-chipped ground of the arena, then clenched and released the pommel a few times and ground his teeth loudly, giving the appearance of a fierce man in complete control. It was a skill Erroh had yet to master.

"Lonely to be a leader, all right," he added, before beginning his routine. He did so slowly, and Erroh could see the ploy. The games had already begun. Erroh could see the powerful muscles still toned in readiness. Though he was old, Erroh had never seen him more dominant. *Because today, it matters.* He'd seen that power in an older warrior once before and lost that fight, too. Erroh trusted his ability, his speed, his sharpness. His youth. All impressive things, but Magnus carried more tricks in his arthritic fingers than Erroh could ever know. He knew war; he knew battle; he knew how to win. Erroh knew some of these things too. It would come down to nerve and nastiness, no doubt. Which one was willing to take the more savage step? Erroh was willing to bet it would be his father.

Magnus reached for his shield and cracked it loudly against his sword. They made a satisfying noise; a fine pair of weapons, worthy of this contest. Magnus tested the weight of the shield and knocked its dull edge against the sharpened blade once more. The sword had a fine balance—all the better for tearing the skin from his son, no doubt. It was his second finest sword. Erroh carried his favourite. At least there was that.

"It's almost time, little one. Pick your blades," Magnus growled, all warmth swiftly fading away.

Erroh turned to his loyal comrades. All two of them. Lillium stepped forward, holding his blades. She had assisted him all day, and Erroh was grateful. She wore her finest Ranger armour as if in defiance of this black sea behind them. It wasn't much, but he appreciated it.

Magnus was still her Master General, but she'd chosen a different path. She didn't face Magnus as she whispered in Erroh's ear. "Remember to turn him towards his right. He's weaker there." Her eyes flickered to Erroh's ruined chest as he stripped his garments free in preparation.

"I can't turn to either side myself," he mocked lightly, touched the stitching and grimaced at the tearing to come. Healthy, he'd have fancied his luck against his father. Less so, now. He'd swung his blade a few times and felt little pain. It would come. After that, it was a matter of surviving long enough to tear his father open first.

"Do what you must to win," whispered Lea, embracing him. "Because we are completely fuked if you don't." She grinned, and Erroh felt better. She had a way with words. It was a wonderful way. Even if they were fuked if he lost.

"I'll do my best."

"That's never enough, Erroh. Do better."

"He'll never forgive us," whispered Wynn to his brother. They shared neither father nor mother, but their bond in the darkness was unbreakable. *Mostly.* Brothers stood beside brothers. Especially in arguments with their fathers. Except for now.

"What he's doing is wrong," muttered Emir, drinking from his shaking mug. He looked as guilty as Wynn felt.

"I know it's wrong. You didn't think I had words with him?" Wynn said, stepping forward to receive the shirt of the Master General. The legend looked old. Older than Wynn had ever seen him. He still looked hardened, though, and ready for all challengers.

Can't we all just sit down and talk this one through? Visions of being thrown through a shack wall sprang to mind, and Wynn almost smiled at the memory. Magnus solved most matters with violence. So far, it had worked for him.

"It's always about a girl," whispered Emir. "And I'll be the one stitching everyone up after."

"You know she's more than that," Wynn growled, and stood back at the edge as the legend walked into the centre of the sparring arena to await battle. Wynn caught sight of Lillium attending to her duties and ignored the guilt. Wynn had been certain to stand with the old guard, until he had seen Lillium marching with Erroh. *Lea's doing, no doubt.* Seeing her pledge to Erroh was just another way to lessen the pain, he supposed. Lessen the pain and allow simple anger to fester and grow. Anger was truly a gift, especially when those you respected strayed from the path. Fuked everything up for everyone else.

She pledges herself to another as swiftly as she forsook me and Magnus.

Emir exhaled, tapping with battered boots the crunchy ground of the arena's edge as though it were the most interesting thing in the world. "Aye, I know she's more than that, but it's easier to betray him thinking this way." He shrugged as though it were a small matter, but Wynn could hear the torment at play.

"War is no place for sentiment," suggested Wrek from beside them. His words were cold and resolute. He threw his hat into the ring with the Wolves most days. And he'd been outspoken about his feeling that a ripple could cause devastation to an already fractured army. "I'm sure it would thrill Roja to hear that the only unit interested in defending the city is tearing itself apart from the inside."

He spat the last few words, and Wynn agreed. The world was falling apart, and the two fiercest fighters were about to kill each other. "I like Erroh, I really do. He has style, and that spinning sword shit is impressive, but if he wins, we are rightly fuked. He'll hold a hollow throne, for a brief period."

That was a fine point, too.

"Erroh is the leader of bitches!" screamed a voice. A few laughs followed, but Magnus spun around on his good knee and battered the offending brute down with a dangerous and silent stare.

Aymon finished the job by hissing his own warning, and the rest of the crowd fell silent. Whispers about the uncertainty of his future leadership had spread throughout the camp these last few days, but Wynn thought little of them. He was born for violence and little more. He doubted Magnus would place that cur in such an elevated position. At least not for quite a while. There were better options. Wynn, for one. Truthfully, Wynn would be next to throw his sword into the ring were Aymon or Doran elevated above him. He could beat either of them; he was certain of it.

"Calm yourself, Erroh," Lea insisted. Her face was stony. She'd jested to put him at ease, but now it was time to suck in the doubt and get the task done. She kissed him on the cheek and took her place by the edge of the arena.

"I will try," he said, accepting the blades from Lillium. "At least I have some people believing in me." He laughed and spun the blades in each hand. Their weight felt right. He almost forgot the pain. Almost forgot that his opponent was kin, had taught him much of what he knew, had the beating of him.

"Everyone is waiting for you, hero," Lillium whispered, kissing him delicately across the lips before bowing. She looked towards the crowd, towards her former mate, and Erroh almost laughed. Were they in the dark, in need of camaraderie, her slightly dry lips could have been a fine source of jesting. Swiftly, she took her place beside Lea, her face confident and trusting.

Their fates were in the wind now. The entire world's was. "This fight was inevitable," Erroh said, looking to his father. Searching for apprehension; searching for a tell; searching for anything, really. He found nothing there.

"Erroh, line of Elise, I accept your challenge," mocked Magnus, raising his sword and shield. He flexed his muscles and stared at his prey. His breathing was quick and controlled. As always, in front of the crowd he donned the skin of a killer. In front of Erroh, too. Something in his eyes, or his stance, or the way he grinned dangerously. A magnificent and terrifying sight.

He fears this as much as I do.

He has to.

Doesn't he?

But Magnus showed no fear at all. As Erroh drew near, he snarled like a beast whose leadership had been challenged by a young insignificant pup. Erroh looked to his father with calm reverence. Magnus looked to him as a little apprentice shit.

I've got this.

There was blood in the air, and Magnus had a taste for it; Erroh thought again of Uden and felt a cough form in his chest. He took a deep breath and ignored the itch on his arm. He would not kill today. He would *try* not to kill today. It was a contest of blood, not to the death. A small blessing considering the few warriors the factions called upon. Stepping nearer, Erroh raised his dual blades and fell deadly still. If there was one thing he remembered from that terrible night, it was throwing away an advantage to a boisterous first charge.

"To the blood, so," Magnus said.

"To the blood."

Magnus's eyes were like a predator's. He watched for any flicker of muscle or a shuffle of feet before an unending onslaught, and Erroh denied him anything. They'd sparred a thousand times, yet not once had Magnus instigated the first attack.

The surrounding silence did not last. A few Black Guards became giddy and starting cheering, calling on Magnus to strike Erroh down, to put him in his place, to win the day for the heroes. The nervous mutterings filtered through the crowd, and the noise rose. No brave leader dared silence them this time, though. All eyes and all concentration were locked on the two devastating creatures standing in the sparring arena. Close enough to reach out and touch. With a blade.

Erroh wanted to charge forward, lead the fight, take advantage where he could, but he made no move. Instead, he held himself perfectly still, allowing Magnus first step. Around them, the crowd grew louder, and it was an infectious, unwanted thing. Their cheers became chants for war and blood. And punishment too. His, mostly, and oh, how he wanted to quieten them. Still, he'd stood with a hostile crowd many times before and learned the value in defying their desires. Let them curse him; let them fall silent swiftly, too.

Staring at his father's cold, unforgiving eyes, he felt his fears grow in face of the brutes' chanting. He'd carried the guilt these past few days, and the weight of his actions suddenly pressed him down even further. He'd believed that, the moment he stepped into the arena, he'd feel like himself again, but his limbs felt heavy.

I've made a huge mistake.

His heart hammered, and he allowed it. Allowed the adrenaline to fill him with the urge to flee. To attack, too. He wondered if his father saw this fear in his eyes. A small matter.

I've been here before upon a mountain in the cold.

Moments passed and the crowd grew restless and uncertain. The burning of the early afternoon heat became too much for some, and the chanting and excitement died away in the face of this silent battle of wills. This contest between master and apprentice that they had no part of. As swiftly as the cheering began, it tapered away, and that was just fine for

Erroh. In doing nothing, he had struck the first blow against Magnus, but there would need to be more.

And then the silence erupted in a roar, and Erroh wished his first blow had mattered.

Erroh knew his father's terrifying speed better than any living warrior, but even he was unprepared as Magnus sped across the dusty arena waving his shield wildly.

I have this.

It was a fine shield. Heavy and wooden, with a few attractive scars and a nice puck at its centre. It filled Erroh's vision. The shield wasn't the threat, however. It was merely a distraction. The attack came from the right, and Erroh leapt away, parrying the sword's strike before Magnus dashed his senses from him. The shield followed through anyway, and it just about missed.

Erroh retreated away, and the crowd's roar returned. Magnus chased after him, swinging easy, devastating combinations with blade and shield, and Erroh's fear thundered through his body, taking his nerve.

I don't have this at all.

He kept coming. His arms were like a hurricane, sweeping nearer, probing and battering, all the while sending the blocking Erroh backwards. For a moment Erroh felt like a little cub scurrying beneath his father's imposing ferocity, fighting not for victory, but for survival.

I remember this feeling.

He tried to counter, to stop the nearing weapons, but his body would not react as he desired. A memory of Lea enquiring what it was to be the son of Magnus returned to his mind mid-devastating block, and he almost smiled.

This is what it fuken feels like.

Get the horses ready. We are going to be fleeing.

It wasn't just the world that slowed, but Erroh with it. He

fled back across the arena, all the while dodging and ducking the massive form of his father, and he knew he could lose this battle in the first few breaths alone. It was humbling. This too was familiar.

Again, the cough grew, and he imagined this force of nature atop a mountain in the frozen south; imagined he would have ground any false god to nothing and brought peace to the world there and then. That cough became a cage.

"I'll get you," Magnus yelled to the delight of the crowd, lunging forward only to strike air.

Probably, agreed Erroh, but held off the attack. Twisting his body to meet the next clattering strikes, he felt himself diminish to nothing beneath a tempest.

In his ears, they cheered anew. They saw the moment coming, and Erroh hated them. Batting away the shield, he nearly met the tip of a strike as Magnus tried to kill him, and fury overcame him.

What the fuk, Dad?

Meeting the next attack, Erroh spun furiously, swinging his blades in a desperate attempt at striking a win. "Aaaaaagh," he howled, nearing unprotected flesh and missing dreadfully. In a rage he ducked to the side and struck fiercely, the haze of war blinding his caution. As Vengeance struck his father's wooden shield, he plunged deep with Mercy and felt the burning tear of a wound being struck upon him.

Vanquished.

It was sudden; it was horrifying, and it took the fight from him. He fell away from the battle and faced no second telling blow, for the fight was already over. Erroh collapsed in the dust. The crowd cheered excitedly, and the challenger knew: he had tasted defeat. On all fours and with the jeering in his ears, he tried to catch his breath, all the while watching as a little growing line of crimson, just above his navel, spread out and dripped onto the ground below. "That's not good," he muttered.

Though he desired the world to swallow him with his shame, he climbed to his feet to meet his vanquisher. Erroh was distraught. He had not fought to his level. There were fewer bitter tastes he'd ever endured.

So much for heroism.

He still held his weapons in his hands, although each tip shook slightly. His injury was but a slight tear, but as with most wounds, the pain was immense. He looked across to his father, who was being helped to his feet by one of his former generals. The legend had a deep gash of his own across his chest. It looked as serious as his own.

Interesting.

"No winner. They struck the blow in the same breath," howled Wynn above the screams of the crowd. Hearing this proclamation, Magnus's eyes sharpened, and he pulled away from his assistant's helpful grasp and charged once more.

"Until a yield," he roared, and Erroh understood the change in rules. The first to give up or fall was a fairer contest, and one Erroh was happy to play. A moment before, he had tasted crushing defeat, but from nowhere, the gods had gifted him a second swing of the blade. Another deal of cards. Another way for his father to thrash the senses from him. But he'd still take that bet.

Be more, Erroh, a voice in his mind insisted, and it was a fine point. He met the challenge head on and was driven back into the crowd by a crushing blow from the massive shield of his master.

Be more, Erroh. Be a bit of Lea, too.

Magnus followed in with a second strike and nearly took the head off a watching Wolf as his apprentice rolled away, leaving a little stream of blood and dust behind him. The angry pain burned through him as blood mixed with sandy wood chippings, but he kept rolling and leapt to his feet to meet the next strike. It arrived swiftly enough, and Erroh was knocked further back by the great shield, out of the arena altogether. He crashed over a table and debris scattered everywhere.

"He's a bit shit for a hero," a voice cried, and the others laughed and he hated them and he was fighting his father and he was losing and he was failing Nomi and it wasn't fair.

The air was filled with rapturous howls and screams for blood, and Magnus's roar rose above them all. He leapt over the remains of the table and struck at his son without thinking, but his chin met a welcoming foot and the impact sent him reeling wide. The crowd moved with the wild opponents, a perfect circle in motion, surrounding them, but wary and excited and entertained.

Fuk, fuk, fukety, fuk fuk. It wasn't the most helpful thought; it was something to do while both combatants circled each other. Through the gathering, Erroh caught sight of Lea and he almost reached for her. Asked her to take over. Asked her for suggestions on how to defeat this behemoth.

He didn't have time to do any of these things, for Magnus was upon him again, trying desperately to batter his son into oblivion. As he ducked beneath another nasty, deceiving shield swipe, he caught sight of her again. She was tranquil despite the surrounding horror, and this was strangely comforting. Perhaps it took more than this to rattle her nerves. Perhaps she knew Erroh always found victory. *Well, sometimes.*

The world slowed, and further memories rushed in, of that horrible night upon the mountain when he'd failed the entire world. As that southern crowd had screamed in his ear and he'd battered back an impossibly tough opponent, he'd never felt so alone. Yet he had never been alone, had he? Lea had been with him. Aye, at the bottom of the mountain freezing her posterior to nothing, but she had been there. And she'd always be there as long as he continued to fight.

"I'm fine, Lea," he said, spinning away from Magnus's next strike. It seemed important in that moment that she knew he was alright. He met the next blade strike easily and struck his guard directly against the puck head of the shield, fiercely enough to dent it. The clank echoed loudly, and then there was another clank as it slipped from Magnus's grip and clattered away to the edge of the crowd. Erroh retreated a few steps back, spinning both his blades coolly as though he hadn't just spent most of the fight being battered.

"Do you yield yet, Father?"

It was a perfectly petulant remark, and Magnus hesitated as though he'd been struck. Erroh wondered if he was remembering a few heated skirmishes from years before. Before walking the road. *Before fuken destiny and all that.*

One blade against two meant little to the master warmonger, though. He merely set his footing differently, placed both hands on the grip and charged at Erroh with a different array of strikes. The clinking clatter of the three blades reverberated once more, around the camp and beyond. Joined with the roar of the crowd, it might have resembled the cries of the great machines of the ancients, and birds took flight in sudden instinctive terror.

Within a few breaths, Erroh found a peacefulness amidst the storm of swords. He was built for this. Standing against a master was exactly where he needed to be. His body worked unconsciously against Magnus's strikes, and suddenly his body no longer behaved as though it were broken. Aye, he felt the rip of stitching, felt the nicking strikes of careless parries and blocks, but he took them as though they were nothing.

For the first time in months, he no longer feared Uden. More than that, he desired another round with the fuker.

Magnus must have sensed this, for his strikes lessened and he drew away, panting heavily, and Erroh allowed him a moment. To charge upon him now would be walking into a spider's lair. The only thing scarier than defending against the attacks of a legendary master was attacking the same master, who was perhaps feigning exhaustion. Carefully, Magnus stepped into the battle again. Each strike was focused now, and Erroh's arms squealed under the barrage. It was exhausting, but Erroh felt the change in the wind.

The fight turned. Only Lea could see it. She bit her lip, the first sign of emotion and excitement appearing across her face. She could see the exhaustion in both the combatants, but Magnus's injury was deeper. How strange, she mused, that often it wasn't the failure of will that led to defeat but the fragility of the body. His blows were becoming fiercer as exhaustion overcame him, and he was godly. An injured beast was more dangerous than ever. She could see Erroh maintaining his strategy. He was calmer now and flowed within the fight. It was as if he were fighting her in the solitude of the wastes. She knew Erroh would take his time, could grind his master down.

Father and son moved through the camp in a terrible dance, never separating too far from each other, attacking and countering, cutting and slicing, waiting for the other to collapse. Finally, they came together violently one last time. There was a clash of steel, and Erroh leapt back to await the next assault. Lea's heart lurched in her chest. Perhaps it was an error on her man's part, allowing complacency to slip into his form. Magnus lowered his blade to catch his breath and Erroh followed suit. It was a simple manoeuvre that should have earned nothing but death in war, but this was master and apprentice, and everything was allowed. Even mercy.

Magnus dropped his sword and jumped forward.

A terrible, genius ruse. Had he thought of it himself, he would have attempted the same lunacy. It was a simple enough choice: kill the legend or get beaten up. He never had a chance.

Magnus landed on top of him, felling him painfully. His head bounded off the ground and he almost lost consciousness there and then, but the clattering of his fallen blades stirred the last of the fight in him. His father sat atop his chest, and Erroh knew it was the end. There was grunting, and then there were punches threshing him. Pinned by the terrible weight, he ducked his head left and right, but the punches were unrelenting.

This is what I get for complacency.

The world shook and darkened, and for a moment, Erroh regretted not striking out at the boulder before it crushed him to pieces. The shaking of the world turned to a shrill ringing in his ears, and all he could hear was the dull thump of each strike from his father.

"Yield, Erroh," screamed Magnus, and it sounded an appealing life decision. He half-nodded dejectedly. The assault stopped, and Magnus leaned in close to hear his apprentice's desperate, wheezing whisper. The crowd fell to silence so all could hear, and Erroh head-butted his father across the bridge of his nose.

Sorry, Dad.

Erroh slipped his knee free and drove it into the lower back of his stunned father and knocked the brute free of his chest. Groggily and absently checking for missing teeth, Erroh climbed to his feet to a chorus of hate-filled cries, and fuk them, but they didn't help with the disorientation. He searched for a sword and leaned on it as though it were a crutch, and his body was slow, oh so slow. The crowd cheered, and he thought this terribly strange until two powerful arms closed in around his chest.

"Fuken yield, will ya?"

"You'll have to kill me," Erroh cried, fighting the grip. The world was spinning; blurred faces sneered while others leapt away. Swinging an elbow behind him, he fought away from the grip and, with ears ringing and the darkened world calling, he stumbled around the crowd, trying to shake away the inrushing darkness.

"Aye, that seems most probable," warned Magnus from somewhere far away. Suddenly he charged at him once more. He did not punch his son this time, though; instead, he gripped his throat and squeezed.

Panic.

Complete panic. And some terror, too.

It all overcame him, and Erroh fell one last time. His father fell with him. Both struck the dusty ground painfully, but neither relinquished the deathly embrace. Erroh tried to scream, but the air was torn from his throat. He gagged as the iron grip tightened around his neck, slowly killing him. Still, he tried, for Nomi's life depended on it. He gripped his murderer's wrists and tried to pull them free, but Magnus's hold remained. All he could see was the burning gaze from a warrior's eyes. All thoughts of competition were lost, and self-preservation took hold.

"Tap out," hissed his master, each word rasping in the blood from his broken nose.

It was a fine suggestion, but Erroh couldn't think. All he could feel was death and darkness moments away. He thought of Lea, then wondered would he feel the joy of breathing ever again? He couldn't even remember why he was fighting this battle, and the world went silent as the beast pinned him further and squeezed relentlessly.

He could see panicked faces crowding around his vanquisher, but he could not see his mate. He didn't want to die, but he knew he could not yield. He wasn't built like that. His body shook of its own volition and he felt the urge to relieve himself. It was only a matter of time. He could never give in, and neither could Magnus. Just another tale to add to the legend. Ferocious enough to kill his own son, rather than allow the reins of control to lessen. That was what influential leaders were made of. Erroh was no influential leader. He was something else entirely.

"Give up," roared Magnus. Less with hatred, more with desperate heartbreak. Erroh could see tears stream from his father's eyes, and he dropped his hand weakly to tap out. It touched against some heavy bandaging on the way, and Erroh didn't hesitate. He dug his fingers into the bandaged wound around the stitching and squeezed a little. There was a piercing scream.

Air. Beautiful air, for an entire breath as Magnus eased his grip, and Erroh gasped wonderfully. However, Magnus swiftly took hold again and Erroh was returned to the torment.

"Yield, damn you."

"Fuk… off… Father."

Erroh bent his knees again, this time wrapping his legs tightly around his prey so that there was no escape. And again, Magnus screamed. He did not release his grip this time. He held on as only a true legend could, and Erroh answered by delivering far more pain than any man could take. Magnus took the pain. For longer than he should have.

Nothing else mattered but the agony. Wrapped in a terrible battle of wills, which neither man could lose, they tortured each other with the unspoken agreement that neither would let go until the other had submitted. Erroh, with tears of his own, fought the darkening world, and he squeezed tighter until his father leaned across as if he were nothing more than one of his many victims and stared into his soul.

"There will be no mercy today," his father said without words, and Erroh believed him.

Until Magnus, betrayed by his own body, which sought a release from such suffering, collapsed unconscious and released Erroh as victor.

He lay in the dirt, gasping for air. Magnus lay beside him for a moment until a thousand eager hands pulled the warriors free of each other's grasp. He could see the blue sky above him and a sea of eager faces. He shook his head, and somewhere among the stench of stale alcohol, sweat and the road, he smelled her aroma.

Lea's arms were suddenly around him, and he heard her hissing and threatening all the Wolves away from her property, and the world finally returned to itself. She poured water down his throat, which he nearly drowned in, but by the time he'd spluttered the unwanted fluid from his lungs, he was already climbing to his feet as leader of the wretched legion.

Lillium propped him up, while Emir saw to helping Magnus wake to this new world.

The healer shouted for all to step away, and they treated

his words with reverence. Using Wrek and Aymon as support, the great man climbed to his unsteady feet once more.

With relief, Erroh watched Magnus shaking his head groggily. He looked as damaged as Erroh felt; the tear in his chest was sealed with dried blood and chippings, but a thin stream of blood flowed from his kneecap and Erroh silently begged the gods that his father not be lame.

Magnus edged forward and reached for his son. For a horrible moment Erroh almost deflected the attack, but then he felt the great, powerful arms wrap around him in a fatherly embrace. He felt the weight of the big man as he leant on him, and Erroh hugged him back.

"You were lucky today, my boy," he roared. He broke the embrace but left an arm on his son's shoulder.

"Aye, lucky," agreed Erroh. He'd take lucky, any season of the year.

"Leaders need to be lucky," Magnus shouted, before addressing the crowd. "He has bested your leader and proven himself capable. I will follow his commands, as will you." It was his final order to a dejected crowd before turning to allow an incredibly unhappy healer to attend to his wounds.

13

BOREDOM

Her name was Aurora, and she had a lovely singing voice.

"That number thirteen is unlucky for some, but not for me… um… Going to the city, to get me a family." She sang loudly above the thunder of her mount, and she made excellent time. She always made excellent time on horseback. Until she ran the beast into the ground and it slipped into the darkness. Such irritations were unavoidable, but she ate well every night it happened.

Her stomach grumbled. Only one horse had fallen since she'd fled from the great Conlon bonfire. And none since the town of Erroh. It was quite the accomplishment.

Aurora desired speed, but Ealis favoured no meat and slowed the beast to a swift trot, allowing it to settle its heavy breathing. She could take her time. It was only a few days' ride to Samara, and her heart was just bursting in anticipation. She loved the green, but oh, the thoughts of a city of grey, all stuffed with pumping bodies and wondrous fluid, made her mouth water.

"Going to the city. She'll open her gates for little old me," she sang again, enjoying the melody, if not the correct words. She enjoyed how common words rolled off her tongue. She loved her native language, its harsh aggression, even when speaking kinder sentiments. The common speak in the rest of the world was quite divine, though, and she had mastered it flawlessly, as though she'd spoken it in another life. She knew there were accents, but she kept hers neutral. Words were prettier this way.

Like pulling fluttering parts off...

"... flowers," Ealis whispered, glancing back at the distant horizon. How far behind was her love? she wondered. What life was he delivering to this world as he did? she also wondered. A beautiful deity like him needed entertainment on the march. There was only so much to see. Only so much to do. Apart from relearning how to walk. To see. To kill.

She licked her lips and counted absently the many fingers of her god's race that she'd passed upon her journey. All for her after the first attack.

If that is what I desire.

She desired an ocean of blood.

"Patience, girl," she whispered, choosing her common speak carefully. "Patience for Aurora." She would be patient, for these things took time. The greatest army scattered throughout the Four Factions had taken a long time assembling. All gathering and growing into one unstoppable force. Marching to Uden's heartbeat. It was beautiful, and it was so fuken frustrating. The bigger the army, the slower the shuffle.

"Soon," Aurora said aloud, looking to the horizon in front of her. Somewhere beyond lay her army to come—after Oren failed. Oh, she desired Oren to fail so much that it pained her.

And if Oren earns success?

She might kneel in his glory. She could lie with him.

Maybe slit his throat after and take what was hers, anyway. Who knew? The possibilities were endless. She spat and enjoyed the warmth in the air for a few moments, until a gentle rumble of movement from a valley beyond drew her from her crimson thoughts.

Another finger marching cheerily towards bloodshed, she thought happily. *So many marching.* Her knuckles whitened with frustration at being denied a battle, but Uden desired her beside him when the real southern march tore the fuken city apart. When they drew Erroh out and thrashed him to nothing.

Unless I kill him first?

This was the longest she'd been away from Uden. She missed her tormenter. She desired his touch, his strength. His ability to take her breath away. He loved her. He would never stop punishing her. She would spend the rest of her life being punished by him. Like a beast.

Without escape.

No escape.

Ealis suddenly wavered atop the horse and nearly fell. Her head felt dizzy, and she gripped the saddle for support. It was the heat. It must have been the heat. Aurora shook dark visions from her sight and reached for her tankard, thinking pretty thoughts of chains and blood and sacrifice.

Delicious.

"Going to the city, to get me a family," she sang defiantly, and poured the water over her head. Cooling, refreshing and comforting. Immediately, she felt better and flicked the clinging strands of black hair from her face. She felt cool drops run down her sweat-laden back, and it felt almost like the coldness of her home. She shivered and took a few deep breaths. Then she kicked her beast forward aggressively to ride the last of the uncertainty away.

———

Bored. She teased herself in the saddle as the afternoon drew on. Just a quick look, she kept telling herself, and it became a mantra in her mind that was too much. *Just a little scratch for curiosity.* She knew she shouldn't have found any great interest in the first wave's preparations, but she couldn't help herself. It was an entire army to gaze at before the savagery.

Sometimes, a girl just needed a little entertainment.

Sometimes, a girl just missed her little cat.

Discovering the gathering of Uden's forces was tragically no tricky matter, nor did it occupy her mind as she'd hoped. The only skill was in avoiding the gaze from the wandering finger as it, too, followed the signs. She wanted to be part of the reunion when they joined up. Easier to observe, and easier to avoid the attention of Oren. Should she not present herself to him?

Eventually, the dull drone of a few thousand bodies working away at their duties carried to her on the wind, and she embarked on those last steps eagerly. As did the marching finger who, buoyed on by the end of the march, increased their pace.

She'd almost forgotten the sounds of divine warmongering. The collective chorus of anxious mounts, wandering warriors, families, friends, followers, all waiting for death, seeking murder. And always by a river's edge. She almost smiled. She believed in many things, but fear of sudden flames, like the ones that had brought the ancients to ruin, was no mere belief. Everything could burn, and if it did, she would watch the fire erupt around her and she would weep with joy.

Because I would be dead.

Where two rivers met, she came upon Oren's gathering of

soldiers and she smiled. Perhaps he had just played to his army of believers. If so, it was a fine manoeuvre. An army was an army; this army was impressive enough. Like any gathering of fingers would be, she imagined.

Larger.

As the wandering finger marched ahead to meet their new comrades, she brought her horse forward, emerged from the treeline and announced herself openly. She had no banner, nor did she wear their southern attire. An arrow through her eye, into her brain, by her own people would have been a delightful end to her glorious life. She'd have liked to die that way. Or else hanged. Or else flailed. Or else decapitated. Or else drowned. Or else trampled by a thousand angry mounts. Or else eaten real fuken slowly by a fat girl during a festival.

She did not, however, desire to be poisoned.

Nor did she want to be asleep when death came. That was no way for any warrior to leave.

Unless they'd spent themselves with a god or goddess, and then it was beautiful.

As long as she died.

As long as I die.

Then I'll never be bored again.

No arrow struck her down, though, and a young Rider rode out to receive her. Or else kill her. Or else try to. Her head spun as she eyed him curiously. His chin was weak, but he had the excellent sense to hide it behind a fledgling beard. Nothing could conceal his lifeless eyes, however. It was never just about looks, though. It was usually about nerve and strength. Especially in the hands, as they took hold of delicate Ealis. Weak jaw, but a Rider's strength, she noticed.

"Are you alone?" he growled, attempting to circle her. She pulled her own mount around to match his pace.

Unblinking, she stared him down and waited for him to prove her wrong. If he did, he would sleep sated tonight.

"Who are you?" He chose southern speak. Were she to offer anything else, there would be blood. A little blood staved off boredom easily enough. She held the moment, wondering would he draw his sword. How far would she allow him to? Was there an archer watching? Had the arrow already taken flight?

He drew his sword. It looked heavy in his grasp. That was a shame.

"Where is Oren?" she replied, pulling her godly pendant from beneath her clothing. It was recognisable enough that he bowed pathetically, and she dismissed him before he could answer. It was no matter where Oren was, really, or whether or not she should speak with him. What mattered was walking through the camp of lost souls and enjoying the taste of Oren's fear and trepidation. Such things were ambrosia.

Oren had done well for himself, considering his many sins. His greatest sin had been delivering the false god to the domain of Uden; to allow himself to be used in the fiend's escape was sacrilege. Better that he had died avenging his master's grievous wound. Instead, he had had the honour of testing the north's defences. She walked her beast through the ranks of soldiers as they greeted their new comrades and welcomed them into their collective. Jests and mocks were exchanged loudly between old friends and new brothers. She wondered where her own beloved finger rested their heads these days. They were family to her. Family she could happily order to death.

This felt wonderful, she thought, walking dreamily through the masses, taking in the morning sun and the energy of commotion. The braying, baying and barking of the beasts filled the air as they were shepherded down near the river to graze. The day was young; there was marching to be done. No tarps to be erected alongside the already full fields of similar little hovels. No sly rest earned upon greetings. For swords were being sharpened and oiled, heavy armour was being donned loudly, and Aurora felt dizzy again with loneliness. She wanted her family back.

My army.

She touched some of the warriors as she walked by. Not enough that they'd ever notice. Just enough to feel a thrill. Their movement was mesmerising. The feel of the heavy leathered armour was deliciously reassuring. She switched the reins to her left hand and tipped a few more warriors with her right. No one took any notice as she walked amongst them. New arrivals and coming battles occupied their minds. It felt like soon. There was something in the air. She heard scouts claim they'd seen the glow of the City of Light already, and she thought this most pleasing.

"Why are you here?" Oren said. He stood behind her. "You don't belong here, Aurora. To the fires with you."

It was a dangerous move on his part. He knew her skill and was aware of the threat she posed. Of the boredom she needed to ease. A greater thinker might have taken this moment to surround her. Lance her a few times with unforgiving poles. Jagged poles. She smiled her most devastating smile and bowed theatrically while maintaining eye contact with him.

"I'm just going to the city, to get me a family," she purred. It had the desired effect. As did most of her words. He stopped in his tracks, completely perplexed by her explanation. Then he reached for his blade, and a few watching soldiers followed suit. Aurora laughed in delight and revealed the weapons under her cloak. She did it as indifferently as she could. Little point in creating a scene on the eve of battle. Revealing the two little crossbows yet making no move to grab them was a good start. However, if he tried taking them, there would be words exchanged and she would end up leading the first wave after all.

She had forgotten what a nice jawline he had. His nose was a little different, though. She didn't like different. Suddenly, she couldn't stop looking at his nose. Someone had broken it rather viciously. She wanted to break it too.

"Going to the city? What does that mean?" he asked, and sniffed with his broken nose.

Ask about the nose. Do it, do it, do it.

She stepped forward and offered open hands. "Calm down, beautiful Oren. We are all friends here. Uden has no wish to see you bled dry." His companions bought the ruse and stood down. Perhaps they knew actual power when it spoke. "Neither do I," Ealis added, raising her hands in mock submissiveness before bowing deeply. Oren knew she rarely lied.

Slowly, he saved his own life and bowed in return. It was the smarter move on his part. "Have you come to join our fight?" he asked suspiciously, sheathing his blade. With a nod, he sent the rest of his companions away to tend to duties for the march ahead. Their ears were not worthy of her attention, it would appear. No matter.

"After you have offered the gifts, I am to assist you," she said. It wasn't a complete lie. If he led his army well enough, there was forgiveness. Uden was a compassionate deity.

A cold chill ran down her back. Suddenly, something at the back of her neck pricked at her senses. She always knew when eager eyes were upon her, and strangely, among a gathering of so many, she knew dangerous eyes were upon her. Not Oren's.

Uden?

"The gifts," Oren said quietly, as though he had little belief in such honoured things.

"May I see them?" she asked seductively, and stepped close to him. Far too close. Her faint smell of fresh sweat and journey mixed with delicious honey oils was sure to intoxicate any hot-blooded comrade. She wore her aroma well, and she caught him inhaling her deeply. She could see him imagining her writhing body next to his. On top of him. Under him. *Who wouldn't desire a god's lover?*

"As you wish, Aurora," he said, pushing her away. Aye, he knew the dangers of her in so many ways. She spun, giggling at his brute strength, and almost toppled over the remnants of a campfire. She caught herself and twirled gracefully on one toe to face him again. All in one perfect manoeuvre. Her eyes sparkled, and she saw his desire rear itself. She thought about leaping upon him this very moment. If only to shake his nerve. If only to scratch an itch. If only to condemn him to certain death at Uden's hand.

"Oh, I suddenly wish many things from you, Oren," she declared loudly, for all to hear. For all to report back to Uden.

Less bored.

She bit her lower lip and looked incredible. Resting her hands on hips, she waited for him and he denied her.

"Enough of this foolishness, woman." He folded his arms, and she grimaced before shrugging her disappointment away. "Follow me," he growled, leading her into his tent.

She lost any lingering interest in him the moment he placed the blades down in front of her. She fell to her knees and hated them as tools of a demon. They were beautiful, though, and licking her fingertips clean of mud, she dared to caress each blade, all the while silently cursing them to failure and bluntness.

"Do you wish to see the child's head?" he asked quietly.

Outside, the entire army moved as one, stripping the tents and herding the beasts, feeding the mounts and donning the last helmet and sword, but Aurora would not be rushed. Nor would she consent to see a horror as wretched as the head of the child.

Ealis shook her head and wondered if, deep down, where all her demons feared to tread, there was still a person in there, clawing at her with guilt, with foolish thoughts of surviving the coming days.

Her stunning eyes glazed over in ecstasy as she examined each blade lovingly. She favoured the heavier one. Her fingers tapped carefully along its edge. The delicate taps were in perfect rhythm, and she felt shivers run up her spine into her mind. She brought the blade close to her face. She ran its edge along her neck and hissed wonderfully as it sliced the skin.

"These are godly weapons," she whispered. It might have been a prayer to her god. "Fine gifts," she sighed, pulling the blade away. She wiped the few drops of blood away lest they corrode the perfect finish, and after a painful moment of want, she slid the weapon back into its scabbard. It slid in perfectly. It was the little things that made her days brighter. "Where is his lover?" she asked, and Oren, bemused by her desires for beautiful things, simply pointed outside to a cart trundling by. A huge tarp covered a figure as it trundled along.

"Marching," he said, grinning at his wit.

"Is she dead?" Ealis asked, stepping away from his hospitality into the mass of movement and noise. The heavy rumbling of the carts was almost deafening.

"Near enough now."

"Keep her alive. Better she die in front of Erroh." What a sight that could be, to see his lover burn alive in front of his helpless eyes. A fine torment from Uden. Her lover was capable of such cruel things. Oh, she missed him.

"I've been courteous. Tell me, what are you doing here, Aurora, if not to slit my throat on the eve of battle?" the general asked.

"Amusing myself while I await my god." Her eyes passed from the surrounding movement to a thin line of trees at the peak of a valley opposite. She felt that prickly itch again. She rolled some saliva around her mouth and swallowed.

"Shall I release a bird to inform him of your arrival?"

"Save your pigeon." She lost interest in her Hunt comrades and stared into the green. Something caught her attention: a flicker of movement. If she were to spy on a wandering army's march, it was the place she'd have chosen. *Interesting.* She might have something to do after all.

"What do you see?" he asked.

"Nothing concerning you, General." It was no lie. Oren would likely have scouts out traversing the Arth himself, but a skilled spy in this lush part of the world could easily elude capture. This close to the city, it would be foolish not to think someone took notes. Why spend time and energy on fruitless tasks, seeking them out, when there were plenty of things for every hand to task themselves with already?

Everyone had something to do, except for Aurora Borealis.

"Will you fight with us, then?" Oren asked.

She shook her head and smiled wonderfully. "This is not my fight. Not yet."

She removed her pack from her horse and cut the saddle and reins free. She slapped the beast, and it thundered off forever from her sight.

"I have no time for your games, Aurora. Do whatever you feel you must," he hissed, and she liked his tone. She liked a little frustration. A little fight. He had a terrible nose, but no fool would deny his strong, callused hands.

"I feel like hunting some skulking beast," she whispered to herself, and walked with the rest of the marching soldiers while Oren climbed onto his own horse and prepared to lead them into victory.

Though they walked in the same direction, it was not long before Aurora broke away from her brethren. As they marched in thunderous unity through the entrance of a rich green valley, she slipped swiftly beneath the cover of the nearest treeline. Her heart beat excitedly and her dazzling eyes scanned the ground. She did not run; there was all the time in the world. She aimed to spend much of that time at task. In a few hastily taken breaths, only the hunt occupied her thoughts. Her mind was calm, focused. She sought entertainment.

14

PRODIGAL DAUGHTER

R oja never knew where her love for cartography came from, save that it was a passion. More than that, she believed herself skilled at both creating and reading maps. Understanding and deciphering the lay of the land upon cloth or paper was a wonderful passion of hers. Her dazzling mind understood distances and scales, mountains and river scribblings, as if they were a language she was fluent in. They reminded her of her size and true worth in this eternal world. It was something to focus on when everything else was hazy.

Running her fingers along a path and creating different routes brought her imagination to life. It made her unconsciously smile. Consciously, too. It was safer to imagine journeys in her little haven than to venture out towards adventure. For all the miles she traversed with her eyes and fingers, to walk the road was something else entirely. Something she was far from skilled at.

"It's just a map," muttered Mea quietly, straining the tea to its strongest and placing a steaming cup by the bedside of the sleeping prisoner. Elise's breathing had settled, but the deathly rattle in each exhale echoed around the room. She was deteriorating. There would be no healing of Elise. They could all feel it.

Concentrate on the map instead.

Aye, it was only a map. Bought at the market stalls for quite a price the morning before. She could walk the markets these days for a short time, accompanied by a few sisters. It was her only taste of freedom in the imprisoned palace she ruled. Were she not so rushed, she might have argued about the maps' value a little longer. She might have argued that the blood along the edging had deflated the price somewhat. The blood was fresh. However, the pieces were passed across to grateful hands, and the intriguing and unsettling map had become her own. Aye, it was a map, and she hated it. "It's an ancient map, ancient." She ran her fingers along a path. So many miles. So very accurate. All to scale. All setting the world on its head.

Magnus could have used this.

It was coated in a strange, smooth varnish, like a clear wax applied to toughen. All to outlast time, she supposed. Each crease in this precious piece was older than she was. Older than the city, probably. And the strangely printed words were in a language she'd never encountered. Yet familiar.

An ancient faction?

For a piece so old, it was in excellent condition. The little dots of brown were unsettling. Some were browner than others. She recognised a few in familiar places—regions inhabited by higher-lined families. She also noticed a few settlements.

Who the fuk knows where Raven Rock is, yet doesn't know the path to Adawan?

Ignoring the ominous little dots above each strange name, she ran her finger along the path towards Samara and she imagined the journey. She blinked and spun the ancient piece around on her desk. It hurt less to look at it upside down. Memorising the different points, she spun it back around. A few hastily-scribed notes fell to the ground in her frenzy, but she didn't care.

"At least the name Samara is correct. It's just everything else that's fuked." How strange that a few little scribbles, immaculately drawn, could cause such unease.

"It's a small matter. It's just a trick piece to pull in eager fools," suggested Mea. She didn't like the map either. She'd glanced at it with Roja first and hadn't looked at it since.

Roja, however, knew the advantage to such a piece. If it were accurate, this little gem might cut travel time tenfold across the Four Factions. "I think there are settlements still out here," Roja whispered, warily. She pointed to three spots along one of her own hand-drawn maps and then adjusted the spots more accurately along the large parchment in front of her. In the first few years Dia would have kept notes of nearly all settlements, but it was impossible to keep track of society as it grew outwards into a vast, open world. If Samara did not know of such places, perhaps the Hunt had not discovered them either. It was worth the effort. Even if it was a walk into hostile territory. "We aren't as alone as I thought."

A loud knock on the old sanctuary door caused Lexi to shoot up out of her bedding. Elise stirred in her exhausted slumber; her delicate arms were still wrapped around her daughter, as they had been when she'd fallen unconscious.

"It's alright, little one," Roja said. It wasn't alright at all. Every day brought more mutterings of discontent. Every day brought the fear of a lynch mob breaching their haven, seeking a little retribution. Every knock could be the end of times.

Would they knock?

She wanted to fall still. To hide. To forbid anyone

entering their little haven. But the fear of not knowing was worse. Gliding to the door, she settled her fluttering heart and calmed herself. Mea stood behind her with sword in hand as Roja's fingers hesitated over the lock.

There was something in the air. Something beyond the wretched stench of sweet eucalyptus and dying, imprisoned legend. Even in the few moments walking through the market, Roja could see the condemning eyes watching her. Though no one dared say it to her, there were whispers. The loudest suggested an incoming trial.

Not only for Elise, either.

The Black Guard had begun their investigations of the Outcasts' escape. And they were voicing their theories loudly. It seemed to Roja they'd spoken to everyone involved, apart from her. She was no fool. When they came for her, they would have undisputable proof. Some unseen bastard catching sight of red hair in the tunnels. Some fuker with eager ears listening to the words she spoke with Magnus under the guise of strategies.

They know. I'm dead.

Troubling events were occurring throughout her city, and she was powerless to do a thing about it. Every day there was a new law, written by a black-gloved bastard and his bastard accomplice. A better Primary-in-waiting might have stood firm, but with every fleeting day, she became weaker. It was the gallows erected near the entrance gates that sent shivers down her spine. The dark brown wood had been cut and varnished in love by the finest carpenter. Were she to hang, it would really bring out her eyes. She used to pray for sanity, for safety, for escape. Now she prayed only that they would leave Linn alone when they came for her.

It was all her fault.

And Tye's.

There came another knock, and she caught the gasp in her throat.

Roja turned the key. The lock clicked heavily, and she slipped the bolt back into place. The door swung open, and she met her oldest friend, standing in perfect white, wearing her most sincere smile.

"I bring interesting news," Silvia declared, embracing her Primary-in-waiting before stepping inside and closing the door behind her. She bowed to Mea and casually tipped the blade away from her face before taking the nearest seat. It was Lexi's seat. This she knew. Even in tough times, it was nice to keep some things simple. Lexi seemed unperturbed by her actions. She sat at the side of the bed, stroking her mother's hair. Her eyes were bloodshot, but there were no tears daring to escape. She stared at Silvia with unreserved hatred. Another comforting, familiar sight.

"Where have you been?" Roja muttered, trying and failing to disguise the contempt she felt. Silvia was the eye of the city's mood. This was no time to be blind.

"Certainly not listening to Stefan's complaints in chambers," she said, grinning. "I have better things to do." Roja knew that tone. She only played that tone when she was toying with her prey. *Or up to no good.* She smiled brilliantly, but her eyes showed little warmth. Stefan really meant little to her.

About as much as Emir does to you?

Silvia eyed the stove, searching for steaming beverages, but found none. Shrugging, she offered Roja a genuine smile and, despite herself, Roja softened.

"Sigi and I have spoken," Silvia said, as Mea sheathed her blade before taking a seat beside the dying fire.

"What does that fuken traitor have to say?" growled Roja,

wondering why he had spoken with Silvia and not her. What had Silvia done that afforded her such prestige?

As if realising she no longer walked the streets as her glorious self, Silvia dropped her head and lost the lively tone most knew her for. She took a deep breath. "I will always support you, but things have changed, Mydame. Sigi has the full allegiance of your Black Guard. Only a small number remain loyal to the Primary and the city."

Roja knew all this.

As did the city.

"Some of them don't want another Primary elected." She took a moment and looked at the floor, unable to meet Roja's eyes. "Most of them." Her voice broke.

Mea sighed and Lexi placed her head in her hands. With no seated Primary, the world was open to utter chaos.

Further chaos.

What right did he have?

Mea was sceptical. "So, the elusive Sigi just happened upon speaking with you?"

"People appreciated my actions at the trial." It had been a wonderful performance, fuelled by anguish and grief. She had behaved as any Primary-in-waiting should have, and that had not gone unnoticed by the false leader of the city, it would appear. "It is Dane who poisons Sigi's ear, but I have convinced Sigi to speak with you."

"Convinced?" asked Lexi, and Roja knew that tone. They were all thinking it, but only Lexi would infer it. Silvia shrugged. Some females believed in love. Some wanted something else.

"Aye, Sigi and I are on good terms."

So much for Stefan.

"Slut," whispered Lexi. It was a rather loud whisper. Silvia did not react to the ruse. Perhaps seeing her with her dying mother had earned her a brief reprieve. Losing Dia was catastrophic. Losing Elise, the most famous Alphaline of the city, would take the wind from every sister in the city.

Even Silvia.

"I pledge to you that Sigi is open to a shared leadership. Should the city not be ruled equally?" There was a desperation in her words, yet still Roja was troubled. Even when Silvia took her shaking hand in hers.

"He has swiftly learned the price of mishandling the city. He does not know the city's intricacies as you do, however; but he knows the anarchy that would befall us if the city were to remain without a leader. He wishes to speak with you, and he has a plan for the southerners." It was a fine speech, and though Silvia was always out for herself, Roja knew the goodness in her.

"A plan?" asked Mea evenly. Her hatred for the man burned deep. Far deeper than she let on, but Roja knew. Only her fists took the strain. They were clenched for battle. Her eyes remained cold, her mind open to Silvia's empty words.

"He believes a peace can be brokered."

"Does he, now?"

Lexi stood up. "Roro… Erroh said they would accept no peace." Her emotions and distrust showed proudly in her features.

If Roro said it, then it is true.

Silvia smiled sadly and kissed Roja's hands. There were tears in her eyes. "Staying in this locked room while the world turns is madness." More tears came; Roja hadn't seen her this upset in her life. "Elise deserves protecting, but no Wolf will come for her. I have been your friend for almost two decades, and I come now with a means to save us all." She turned to the room. Even to Lexi. "Sigi is an ally, but he needs support. Dane is a step away from proclaiming himself

leader. Our people demand leadership, Roja. It must be you."
She bowed deeply to Lexi and to Mea after. If she lied, it was
deceit for the ages. "All the sisters will follow you, Roja. We
will unite under your banner, and the rest of the city *will*
follow." At this she wept quietly. And why wouldn't she?
She'd walked these streets freely these few weeks with eyes
wide open. She had seen what Roja couldn't in one swift
march.

"The Wolves should know their place," whispered Roja.
She sounded almost like herself. Like a hound, Sigi had
thrown a scrap from his table and she aimed to take it.

"And you, Mea. Sigi also wishes to speak with you," she
mumbled. Another tear rolled down her flawless face, and she
smiled to hide the deep sorrow. "He knows what Tye did."
The room became colder in that moment. "He wants to offer
help." This she whispered, lest the doorway beyond had ears.
"He wishes to go against Dane."

"Sigi can go fuk himself," Mea hissed. She looked ready
to swing. And why not? Was Mea not more deserving of
wrath than all of them?

Silvia nodded. A shrewd move. She had more to say. "He
would never expect your forgiveness, but he *can* save your
son," she pledged, as if she spoke memorised words given to
her by a regretful lover.

For a moment Mea, ever close to breaking, rose from her
anguish and nodded her head. If Sigi called, she too would
reply.

"When?" asked Roja.

"To avoid the gaze of Dane or his many sets of eyes, he
will meet you in the chambers of the Cull, at midnight
tonight."

"We can't leave her unguarded," Lexi said. As if to
underscore Elise's fragility, the legend wheezed dreadfully.

It was a fine point. It would be a bold move to storm the chambers, but there was little sense in mocking fate. Before Roja or Mea could withdraw their acceptance, Silvia did something unusual. She dropped to her knee in front of Lexi. It even looked genuine.

"If you'll have me, I would be honoured to stay at your mother's side until they return," she whispered, before taking Lexi's hand and kissing it as a pledge of her honour. "I will be at your service. I yield to your line, Lexi, line of Magnus and Elise."

It was a good pledge.

15

AFTER THE VIOLENCE

"Everything is alright."

His words reassured her, but she dared not get too excited or even vaguely reassured. His grasp of her language was unpredictable at the best of times. The room was a dream; she wasn't certain what was real or delirium. Her fever had her in its clutches, and to stop the room spinning, she gripped the fresh bedsheets around her naked chest.

"Be still, Nomi," he whispered, and none of it felt real. She could not settle; she could not believe, no matter what her Erroh had promised. No, not her Erroh at all. That honour belonged to the beautiful Liiiia.

There was less wind in this cosy little tent. It smelled better, too. She recognised eucalyptus and bitter alcohol, mostly. There were other spices at play, but her sense of smell was far from refined. Nomi's vision was blurred in this light, but her hearing had not failed her. It was all she could count on. The crackle of the little flames as a fresh clutch of twigs met their doom was soothing. It hypnotised her, like his wonderful voice. The voice had mumbled about leadership change. She'd watched in horror as the two colossuses tore each other apart. She wondered had it been a dream. Family did not behave like that. Then again, she knew little beyond the southern ways.

Perhaps tearing apart those you love most was *love.*

A wet rag was placed across her forehead, and a hand squeezed its icy contents down her brow. She shivered violently and her mind cleared ever so. For a moment she believed herself by the post, slowly dying in the rain. But this was no dream. It was her mind gifting pleasant thoughts as she faded away. She preferred the illusion of a warm bed.

"You not need hit him," Erroh said, and she grasped his words and the clarity. Who had she hit? Had they hit her first?

Oh, wait.

Of course she had needed to hit him. Did Erroh not know her at all? She released her grip on her bedsheets and quickly buttoned up her blouse underneath.

That is why I hit him.

Only she would choose who touched her naked skin. Healer or no. She would have allowed Erroh do it. All he had to do was ask.

His mate.

Her fingers stung. It was a small price to pay when sending a message. Her vision caught the blurred figure standing back, away from Erroh. The figure appeared embarrassed, apologetic, and deeply angry, all in the same motion. He also wobbled slightly. He might have had a fever, too.

"Not a pet," she whispered, and found herself short of breath. She gasped, trying to pull air into her phlegm-filled chest. She'd taken worse. She was no delicate little thing. And then she coughed and sounded like she was underwater.

This is happening.

The healer placed a glass to her lips, and she knocked it

away. Could the idiot not see her drowning as it was? What benefit could more water possibly offer?

Stupid northerners.

He'd said something about her being part of them now. Whatever that meant. Perhaps it meant she was a northerner now too. Did that make her stupid, too? Should she take the water and throw herself into their ways? She should behave like these northerners, or else find herself cast aside, left for dead, hammered like a hound to a post.

"No, you are nobody's pet," Erroh said, stroking her hair, and she smiled despite herself. She almost moaned in ecstasy. But she played no seductive game of wits. Erroh belonged to Liiiia.

Erroh belongs to Liiiia.

His touch still tormented her. Even just his stroking her hair. She thought on love for a moment and it warmed her. She loved being in love. Even if he was with another—a nice northern girl, at that. A girl willing to give him children too, no doubt. Despite her fatigue and the spinning room, she reached for his hand. She'd missed him so much. She would always miss him. That was her cross to bear. It was a small matter.

"Something vaguely incomprehensible," muttered the shape. It might have been an apology.

"You trust Emir. He is brother to me and he fine healer," whispered Erroh in terrible southern tongue. He did not stop stroking her hair, and she loved him for it. Loved him in silence, too.

Another cross to bear. They had once nailed her to a cross; she was no admirer.

"He has busy hands," she warned, and fought a yawn. Sleep was nice. Nicer here in a warm tent than out in the chilly breeze. It was strange that the warmer the days, the more she'd shivered.

"Aye, he does, but let him treat you. For me, Nomi."

Anything, my love.

"For you," she whispered, falling asleep to the sound of her rattling chest.

Emir wiped the blood from his nose. She did not break it, which was good fortune. The half-dead bitch swung like Quig. If he hadn't turned with the strike, she would have removed a front tooth. He was skilled at rolling with punches. All children of that dead town learned that skill quickly, or else they lost their smiles early enough in life. *Usually during the first night of the Puk.*

A terrible pang of sorrow struck him, swiftly followed by rage. He held his breath and counted to ten before looking at the sleeping girl.

"I suppose I had that coming," he said. Perhaps he should have offered her a drink and a few wisecracking jests before trying to remove her clothing.

Didn't work for Roja, either.

In Samara, he was the semi-famous healer of the hovels, mayor of a forgotten people, but to her, he was a drunken thug grasping her chest. Aye, he hated everything about her, but he'd had it coming.

She would not die. It would take a few days, but the girl hadn't been in the harsh weather long enough for infection to strangle the life from her. If he'd seen to her sooner, she might not be in this state at all, he thought guiltily.

Fuken bitch.

He believed himself a good man, but Nomi had disabused

him of that notion. If he had truly wanted to help her, he would have. For whatever affections or loyalty Erroh had for the stunning blonde, Emir was not as quick to forgive her crimes. They were no longer chained in the dark. Easier to follow his heart now, but that heart was broken, shattered, unforgiving.

She was the enemy. She was a murderer. Perhaps she had taken the life of someone he'd known. Being a good man suggested rising above this loathing, but he'd embraced prejudice because it fuken suited him. Emir had accepted Magnus's orders not to heal her. Emir had not informed Magnus of her worsening condition either. They were crimes, but Emir felt little remorse.

And if she died?

It never came to that. He had ordered him to attend to her now and, strangely, he would attend to her—as it should be.

I will not let the bitch die.

"The serum will knock her out for a time," Emir whispered, lest he wake her in the first few precarious moments. He could see the grim look on his brother's face. "I'm sorry for standing at Magnus's side." Each word sounded pathetic when spoken aloud. He'd betrayed the one man he owed everything to. How could he ever apologise enough?

"It was the right move," muttered Erroh, shrugging, though he wouldn't meet his eyes.

"Aye, it was."

That apology seemed dangerously easy to accomplish.

"I would have stood at Magnus's side, as well."

Emir wondered what it was to be in Erroh's boots this day. Toppling your legendary father and jeopardising everything, just to save a pretty female from the cold. *Should have treated her sooner to avoid this mess.*

"This is war. Little point in sentimentality," Erroh said,

sounding a little like the leader they trusted him to become. It was a good start.

"That's fine, but I still feel shit, brother."

Erroh faced him now, his eyes cold and hard. He reached out to Emir and gripped his shoulder tightly. "Can I trust you, brother? To follow me? To follow orders?"

Trust? That was an interesting word. Aye, Erroh could trust him. If it took a lifetime, Emir would show how trustworthy he was. He didn't expect his lifetime to have many miles left to walk, anyway.

"I give you my word: I will earn your trust." This time it was Emir who spoke coldly. "However, I will always speak my mind." Sometimes when speaking of delicate, treacherous things, Emir forgot what to do with his hands. He struggled to remain still on the best of days, but sharing words like this made his struggle even worse. He turned to the sleeping prisoner. *No, not prisoner. Not anymore.*

Removing a little jar from his shelf, he smeared some eucalyptus remedy over her upper lip. The fumes were overpowering, but certain to take effect, even in slight measures. If Erroh wanted trust, Emir would begin with healing Nomi. He considered applying some to her chest, but thought better. He'd wait until she was awake and lucid. Her argument had been convincing.

"I would expect nothing else, Emir." There was almost a tone of approval to his words, although perhaps that was some rare optimism on Emir's part. "Tell me, if you could choose again, which edge would you stand on?"

"I would still choose Magnus."

"And you would still be justified," Erroh said, grinning.

"I suppose I'm no longer able to complain about your skills in the arena, am I?"

"No, Emir, you simply disagreed with a challenger's

stance. My debt is not repaid." At this, Erroh's face brightened. Perhaps in that moment, he understood the steps taken by Emir up to now. All Emir could do was turn away, wiping the healing sludge from his fingers.

"Here I was thinking I'd been a terrible friend. But enough of this humbling shit. Let me look at those injuries," he joked, lifting Erroh's shirt to view the ruination beneath. The damage to the stitching wasn't nearly as serious as he'd feared, and even less than Magnus's injuries. *Human, just better at it.* Perhaps he'd one day discover how Erroh could suffer pain in silence and take so much more. He imagined it would involve the breaking of bones.

"Ouch! Will you stop?" Erroh hissed as Emir poked at the tearing stitches. "At least, pour me one of those first," he added, and Emir followed his orders. *Good to be the king.*

"Well, you're probably not going to bleed yourself dry," Emir said.

"It would be a shame were I to miss my coronation."

They clinked glasses and drank. And uncomfortable words were forgotten.

"Will you watch over her tonight?" Erroh asked.

"She will be fine, and no Wolf would dare enter my tent without my blessing," Emir countered, and it was a fair point. Emir would have been a more popular choice to lead. Even if his leadership would inevitably lead them into death. They did not like him, but they revered him as though he were Magnus himself. Out in the wastes, a healer capable of tearing a soul from death was a healer to be honoured. No brute wanted to carry his ire should they end up under his knife. "But I'll stay until I know she's settled. I won't look at her chest again. Not unless she's awake," Emir pledged, sitting down by the fire. He removed a little battered journal and a pencil from a small desk and poured himself a healthy measure of alcohol. "I have medicinal things to think on anyway," he said, and Erroh smiled bitterly, for he knew Emir still sought a cure for heavy lung.

That's the cost of pledging to Magnus.

Nomi coughed up some phlegm in her sleep, and Emir wiped it away unconsciously before downing a mouthful of violent clear fluid as if it were water on a sunny day, and Erroh smiled. Wretched and shaking, but good hands. "If I had all the fuken salt in the fuken world, I'd be fuken polished," he muttered to himself. Even though Erroh stood beside him, Emir was already lost to the dizzying world of his mind, battling the darkness of death. With only alcohol to keep him afloat.

"Thank you, brother," he whispered, and Emir nodded absently.

His stomach turned as he left the tent. Maybe it was the tepid alcohol sloshing around a stomach rich with bile. Perhaps it was the violence of the day catching up on his battered frame. Or maybe it was the company. That was it. Fuk the company he drank with tonight.

The night was quiet. Quiet was a fine recipe for a terrible gathering. They were present. All of his loyal supporters. Loyal, and forced to kneel at his will, and revelling far too responsibly. They clustered around little fires throughout the camp, all muttering anti-Erroh propaganda, no doubt. All waiting for a coup to erupt.

He understood tradition, and it mattered at these events. They needed a fine night of revelry to pull some camaraderie between warring factions.

The silence was ominous.

Every set of eyes that fell on Erroh as he walked among them hinted at disgust. He searched with desperate eyes for a friendly face, but found only suspicious, blank gazes.

A little more drunkenness is all that's needed.

Perhaps they agreed, for each mug was filled and drained, but there was no passion to the merriment. No manic sprint to find inebriation swiftest.

They clinked half-heartedly amongst themselves in a united show of defiance. He was not their leader, nor would they ever accept his rule. He walked through them and nodded uncomfortably to each warrior who stepped out of his path. The fresh stitching stung slightly with each motion, and the nausea worsened the further he walked. Oh, he considered hiding away until the morning when, bleary-eyed and slow-witted, they might accept his voice more easily. Might even hold off outright dissent for a few days. He knew better. To show any fear was an invitation to trouble. A leader held his head up high, commanded respect without a word. He'd been a leader before. There was a simple knack to it.

That's something Magnus would say.

Whoever had arranged tonight's gathering had done a fine job. Long torches were lanced into the ground surrounding the camp, their warmth and light adding to the dozen small campfires lit to stave off the growing darkness. Barrels were rolled and tapped for fine times, and tables were laid out with finely cooked meats and buttered vegetables. To the casual onlooker it was quite the gathering, but Erroh could see there was no joy; no camaraderie. They were attending. They were not happy about it. Miles above, shards of rock tore across the sky and burned up like violent explosions of celebration in honour of the new resistance leader. It was a perfect setting for a memorable gathering, gifted by the absent gods, yet no warrior embraced it.

Crack a joke?

He almost sniggered at that thought. Instead, he sought Magnus, to commiserate and deliver some unwanted orders. That wasn't the only person he needed to speak with. There was also the small matter of addressing his new army. Maybe Magnus could also advise him on that.

He heard his own feet crunch on the ground, and truly, the silence was a dreadful thing. If he knew which warrior played an instrument, he might command them to entertain. Magnus would know. Perhaps he'd ask.

It wasn't Magnus he saw first.

Lea sat against a barrel of ale in the centre of the camp. A little fire was burning away in front of her. Not enough to offer any actual warmth, but enough to cook the slices of honey bread lanced neatly over the flickering flames. She always burned the bread to a crisp. It was a habit she'd formed out in the wastes. Erroh preferred his bread lightly toasted, with the slightest hint of butter spread evenly across the surface with meticulous care. She lathered her own carelessly and added far too much jam or honey whenever they were on hand.

On toasting bread, they differed, but on many other things they were in harmony. Such things as life and love. She sipped at a cool ale and watched the food within the flames. *Not nearly charred enough.*

Though the mood was dour, she was having a fine time indeed. Drinking at the watching Wolves was a wonderful way of killing time. She considered it a fine game. So far, she was winning and becoming wonderfully lightheaded. And why not? Her mate was king.

Sipping at her mug aggressively, she silently dared any brute to let loose a casual jest. Just something about Erroh or herself. *Anything.* She clenched her fist and thought wonderfully violent thoughts. There were examples to be made among their comrades, and she suspected a definitive altercation would lay to rest the doubts of who the Alpha hound was in this tribe.

Or the Alpha bitch.

They'll call me that.

She had little issue with this title. It rang true with her. As did the taste of violence. It was on her lips tonight. Watching her mate battle had been intoxicating. Such violence was terrifying and beautiful. Familiar and liberating.

There was more to leading than violence, of course, but she did not fear his rule. Nor did she fear for him as he ruled. He would lead well. She would walk by his side every step of the way, ensuring that he did. As she always had before. As she always would. Just her.

Nobody else, apart from the whore.

She swallowed badly and spat into the fire. Trust little Nomi to take her mood again. Nomi would walk with them a while. A short while. She would need protecting for a time before they released her back into the wild. Lea would hold her tongue for as long as it took. Or until she could take no more. It was the right move. It was the only move on her part.

"Fuken whore," she whispered. The crowd waited, watching her. Her eyes fell upon the loudest table among the hushed merrymakers. Tonight had much to do with Aymon and Doran's behaviour. She'd tried to speak with her old comrade Azel, but like the rest, he answered loudest to those two. She was not jealous. Love could make anyone lose their better senses.

As could the denying of love.

If Aymon's quiet coldness unsettled her, it was the trouble-making Doran she feared most; he'd be most likely to start some shit. Both thugs were drinking heartily. Ale was ale. When they'd had their share, there would be arguments, well-constructed arguments involving leadership. Things would get heated.

"My beo," Erroh said suddenly, and snapped her from her thoughts. She tipped a little of her sine into his empty mug as he knelt beside her. It was a fine move on her part. It earned her a kiss on the cheek. She might desire added payment in the early hours of the next morning, somewhere out in the forest. Somewhere with no prying eyes.

"How is she?" Lea asked evenly, doing all she could to disguise the ill feelings storming like a tempest through her tranquil body.

"Emir says that she'll recover," Erroh said.

Wonderful. So, we won't be burying her beside the child.

"And how is Emir?" At last, her irritation spilled out. It was fine being annoyed at him. Showing contempt for Nomi was something else entirely.

Stupid name, too.

"We spoke, and all is well."

"Did he grovel?"

"I'd have no Keri man grovel," Erroh countered, and it was a fair point, so she sipped her drink quietly and tried recovering her mood. "It's quite the boisterous gathering," he muttered, and his words carried in the wind. He winced and shuffled his feet nervously. She chuckled to herself.

"You are the centre of attention, my beo. I'm quite certain you'll add some life to the party." He laughed at this, and it too carried in the wind. The low mutterings fell silent and all around them, the revellers watched.

"Did I mention I'll need a second general in command?" he joked delicately, and she shook her head.

"You know my thoughts on this matter. I will take no orders from you; I need no rank to know my value and place in this war. It will be by your side," she whispered. She knew she'd have been a fine general; a better leader, too. However, a coupled pair could never truly respect the chain of command. Not if they were to enjoy a life together after the war. She turned the bread, and a few crumbs fell to a fiery death in the little flames. "Stop wasting the night. You know who your second is. Go to task; prepare everyone."

"Would you walk with me?"

"No, Erroh. You hold the crown. I need no part in these conversations. I'll be here waiting for you."

"As you always are."

"Always."

16

THE TALE OF THE WITCH, THE RANGER AND A CONSTANT FEELING OF PLEASURE

Garrick the Ranger was going to die. He was not going to die alone, but he *was* going to die soon. Until that time, however, Garrick was going to share his humble bedding with a strange woman. An exquisite woman with extraordinary eyes, a godly figure, and a vile soul infused with depthless cruelty.

He called her a witch. She didn't seem to like the title at all.

The old dying soldier stirred in his sheets and lamented this moment of clarity. He could feel the change in the wind, and the breeze sent shivers through him. She'd pulled him down to the river again and bathed his wounds.

The wounds she herself had inflicted.

Why did she bother with such things? No amount of scrubbing could clean the poison from the infection. Still, she tended to him and he hated her.

He watched her now, for he could not crawl away. To hide. To die in fuken peace. For she would not leave him to the natural act. She busied herself with her nightly tasks and were he not so miserable, he might have found her behaviour intriguing. She was broken, her mind a ruin of trauma and horror. He'd seen broken fiends and heroes before, but she was something else entirely. Were he stronger, he might have tried to get through to her humanity.

The last few drips of the freezing-cold water fell from his head, and he heard the scrape of his cruel witch fighting with the flint to create a spark. She counted to ten each time and squeaked in pleasure when the sparks flew and took hold of the kindling.

He'd helped improve her fire-lighting techniques with a few croaky words. It was something to do, something to distract. She'd listened and learned quickly. Even as he lay here dying, he could still teach a few tricks of the wild. Teaching a girl to light a quicker flame had been a small price to pay for earning her favour in the first few days since she'd tracked him.

She'd cut into him a lot less after that.

"I'm getting superb at this," Aurora Borealis boasted delightfully. Her voice resembled that of an eager, excitable child rather than the efficient killer he knew her to be. How did he know she was such an efficient killer? Because she had told him. She liked to talk. Every word sounded more like a confession, though. He was wise to listen with compassion and kindness when she spoke of brutal things. Aye, she spoke to Garrick, but he suspected she spoke more to herself.

Poor little witch. Uden really fuked you up, didn't he?

"You should be able to catch the spark in three strikes," he said. He even pulled himself up from his bedding to aid his scrutiny of her fire. She'd added enough dry twigs to catch, and the wooden spit was perfectly erected over the little burning circle. The rocks she'd gathered would allow few sparks to escape and made the blaze easy enough to conceal at a moment's notice. Such a fire was likely to give fine heat with minimal smoke. The witch had done well. Her original technique was adequate, but now, she behaved like a master fire starter.

"Yes, yes, I'll get better," she pledged, slipping a few more twigs into her flickering creation. Not too many. Just enough to keep the flame constant. She liked constant things. Spending the last few days with this older man had been a fine constant indeed.

"You did well, Witch," the dying man whispered. She grimaced and bit her cheek. She did not like that term. It was a term beneath her divine station, and besides, witches were not beautiful. *She* was beautiful. She wanted to scream at Garrick every time he called her that. She was wiser than that, though. Even in the deep forest, secluded from the world, loud outbursts could end this wonderful constant. If it were her people who discovered this little camp of the dying, they would probably slay the Ranger before she could fully explain the merits of keeping this one alive. Then she'd have to kill them. She had use for the Ranger.

Ranger. She liked the word. It rolled off her tongue. It sounded like something bigger than herself. It sounded significant and ominous. All she knew was that Garrick was one of them, and whoever these Rangers were, they were fine warriors indeed. They were probably all dead by now. He disagreed. She liked that.

The witch stroked his hair and placed her hand across his forehead. He knew he was burning up, despite the icy breeze. The fire was welcoming, though. He wondered would this be his last night in this world before he crept quietly into the darkness to join his fallen brothers and sisters? How many had he outlived? Too many to count. What if Magnus greeted him first?

His stomach turned. *No, legends are never slain.* They just disappeared into their tales. Magnus would be no different. They would not speak of Garrick's great passing, though. It was a small yet painful matter. No kin to keep his name alive, and his undervalued skill as a scout was not what such tales were filled with. He took a breath and fought the tears. In the last week since his injury had occurred and the horrors she had forced him to endure, he had not broken. He would not break now because of instinctive fears of the soul. All must die. Some died better than others. He had lived well. He would die well.

Aurora removed the blade from her satchel, and the dying Ranger flinched. He was right to be afraid. It was an impressive knife. The handle was wrapped in dark leather; it matched her outfit, although it was more that her outfit matched the weapon. It was more than a weapon. It was one of the many gifts Uden had bestowed upon her. It was the first gift, given to her on the night of her birth many years ago.

Born in blood.

She ran her finger along its jagged edge and smiled as it cut a fine slit into her skin. Just enough to sting. Sometimes pain was beautiful. It could remind her of Uden's love whenever she strayed from his path. How many stings had she gifted herself, after she'd burned the city of Conlon?

She tipped the blade twice from side to side and spun it in her fingers. Garrick's eyes watched her every move. He had dying eyes. She didn't want him to die.

. . .

"Will you tear me apart one last time?" the old Ranger asked, all authority gone from his voice. He didn't care how he sounded. He was afraid of Aurora Borealis of the south. It wasn't just because she'd picked up his scent and tracked him down, for such a feat was enough to cause fear in any man. It was because of the pain she had inflicted upon him in the first few days of their time together.

She smiled brilliantly, and his heart palpitated—a final surge of adrenalin to catapult him from his bed so he could tear her throat open. He adjusted his sitting position pathetically. Why bathe him, just to spill blood all over his nice clean body? She was a fuken maniac, and he didn't want to die with her cutting into him again. If only he'd the strength to take his own life.

She kissed him on the lips gently and smiled her finest smile to allay his fears. She supposed it was only natural he should fear the wonderful blade. She spun it again and took out a few potatoes. Slicing the largest into thin strips, Ealis laid the pieces on a little plate and began kneading each one with a few drops of oil. She lanced them over the perfectly prepared flames and scattered salt into the delicacy as it began to cook. Some liked to wait until the potatoes were done before adding salt, but she differed on that method. She liked them her way. While she waited for them to soften, she stroked his clean-shaven cheek. She enjoyed shaving him. It brought them closer, despite their opposing views on the demise of the Arth. He didn't remember her cleaning the loose hairs from his chin. It had been something to do while he'd struggled with consciousness. She saw it as repayment.

It is only fair. The first night, she had tortured him beyond what most men could endure. She'd *had* to. Time was not on either of their sides, for the smell of death had seeped heavily from his wretched form. She stroked his chin again and admired its strength once more. *Old but strong.* She would have desired him greatly a few years before.

He relaxed. This was a good thing. She wanted him to relax. Her Garrick had fought heroically, but it was time to let the darkness overcome him. It was beautiful.

Oh, she had hissed, spat and sliced, and he had screamed, howled and eventually asked for mercy. All into the rag she'd stuffed into his mouth. When the pain had pulled him from consciousness, she'd sat atop his naked and bloody chest and watched the drips of blood soak into her clothing. He was a brave man. Braver than most she'd known. She'd inspected his battered form and discovered the unstoppable infection running from his leg wound. She'd stitched the deeper cuts and tried to burn out the decay and eventually dragged him down the slope, through dense forest and into a little cleansing stream. She'd almost expected a man of his strength to recover from a little touch of healing, but alas, she hadn't enough skill. She'd kept him alive a little longer, though. When he'd awoken, she'd interrogated him further. His resolve was greater than any pain she could inflict.

She'd given up long before she'd pushed him to unconsciousness. It was the kinder act on her part. On the third night, she had felt miserable as her blade slit open his stitching and she'd added a few grains of salt to the wound. He'd stared into her eyes and silently told her he would never break.

On the fourth day, she'd left him alone. She'd dragged him to the water and bathed him, yet spent no time reopening wounds or spitting curses at him. The wind had taken hold and nearly blown the life from them both. She'd struggled to light a fire that night. He had offered a critique from his deathbed, and it was sound.

"Thank you," she'd whispered begrudgingly, while they huddled around the catching fire. She'd put her blade away and hadn't tortured him since. She hadn't needed to. When the fever took further hold of him as he slept, he had spoken freely of many things. It was apparent that even the strongest of minds were unprepared to counter the effects of an infection's delirium.

I wish he'd called me angel again.

He'd spoken of the history of his people, and she'd eagerly listened. His gravelly voice had spoken of wondrous things and it had moved her. She had felt his love for many things unknown to her, yet strangely familiar.

He had spoken of Erroh; he had spoken of the false god's childhood, and she had learned of his terrifying ability, and this too was beautiful.

She had stroked the dying man's hair and allowed him to speak of the city with warmth. The lights still mesmerised him, he told her, and urged her to visit Samara to see for herself. She had promised she would. He spoke, and she cared for him.

Sudden moments of clarity would come upon him and he would cease his words suddenly mid-sentence. No amount of whispered insistences or displays of affection could make him continue. But as the nights continued, she had learned all she needed to know. Every time he spoke, Aurora had scraped the stubborn stubble from his skin. He preferred it that way.

When the moment came that she had to kill him, she had hesitated. He had been awake, yet his mind had been lost to frenzy. Days had passed and still she'd had little idea of the battle's outcome. She was consumed with her Garrick. He'd told her his Rangers would be in the front line. She'd hoped they were victorious. It would be a perfect excuse to assume control of the second wave with as little argument as possible. She also wanted the honour of facing these fine Rangers in battle.

Garrick would want her to see their skill, no doubt. She hoped they'd won victory for Garrick's sake at least.

She tried to rationalise slaughtering the older man as he lay helpless. His blood would be warm and worthy of bathing in. She told herself this repeatedly. It should have been enough. *He deserves to pass in peace.* Yet still, she could not bring herself to say goodbye.

Death was beautiful, but Garrick's was not.

Interesting.

"Thank you, Witch," whispered Garrick, taking the cooked piece of potato into his mouth and chewing gratefully. A fine last meal. He could feel the darkness right at his back. It wasn't just the breeze.

She looked down in mild irritation, and it caused him a spark of delight. It was the little things. She nestled in beside him and pulled the blankets over both of them. Had he the strength to choke her, he would have tried. It would have been an ultimate act worthy of a hero. This beautiful creature would have a say in the coming war. What manner of chaos was she to create in the name of Uden the Woodin Man?

Killing her was essential. It was the only thing to do. Such thoughts were soul destroying. He had little strength for murder. Did he want to share a deathbed with her for the rest of eternity were he successful? He smiled to himself morbidly. He knew her well enough to realise that she would have enjoyed the act. She was fuken terrifying that way.

"I think I'm finished," he whispered to the world, and to his bed-mate too. He supposed they were good last words, not that anybody of note would ever hear them. He ignored sentimental thoughts for the Rangers. This death was for him alone. His march was done and his fealty to his brethren was done. He was simply done.

She stared at him for a moment as though contemplating dreadful things, and then she dipped her head under the sheets delicately. After a moment of confusion and then alarm, he discovered her last gift for him. He tried to move and fight, but her fingers undid the clasp in his buckle all too seductively. He had no will to stop her.

She freed him of his undergarments, and he gasped loudly. She was skilled at such things. She kissed, tickled and played wonderfully, and his body reacted accordingly. It didn't matter the attraction for him, or his age, for he had at least double the years she did. All that mattered was the connection. She couldn't breathe properly beneath the sheets, but that was only a hindrance in this moment.

He deserved her gifts. For fear of suffocation, she finally pulled the coverings from her steadily-moving head and took deep breaths through her nostrils. She would not stop. She would never stop. Not until she sated him. He said nothing, but she could feel his desire. She had tortured him, but this was a fine apology.

This makes it right.

Eventually his breathing changed, and he embraced her act. Perhaps it was the sudden cold or the calling of death. She gave her soul to him and hoped he could offer redemption for her. She wasn't a bad person. He wasn't, either. They were just on different sides of this war. Perhaps in another life, they could have been friends. It was not love; it was something else entirely. Something she needed, and possibly something he did as well.

A memory of a lost lover?

A last reminder of his virility?

Whatever it was, he finally acknowledged her act. She felt him ready to climax. *A divine goddess always knows these things.* A horrible thought occurred to her: that he might not have wanted her touch. That she'd taken him against his will. What type of beast was she?

She paused, but his weak hands suddenly tightened around the sides of her throat. She wondered was he going to squeeze the life from her. Uden behaved similarly and rarely killed her. At least not during this activity.

Garrick's hands caressed her cheeks and then reached up and gripped her long black hair. He was stronger than she thought, and she moaned in ecstasy. He enjoyed her. There was redemption to be had. He gripped the back of her head and climaxed. He groaned loudly, and she matched him. She did not stop until she knew he was a spent force. Finally, his grip relaxed and his arms rested back in the bedding, the last of his energy depleted. She sat up and watched him. The first smile she'd ever seen cross his face warmed her deeply.

A fine gift.

"Thank you, Witch," he whispered, closing his eyes.

She allowed him to sleep and decided he used that vile term endearingly. She nestled in beside him and closed her eyes. It seemed like the thing to do. The wind blew, but the fire stayed alight. He'd trained her well in such a short time.

After midnight, his breathing became laboured, enough so that it woke her from her dreams of green fields and family.

He coughed, and his eyes were glazed. She knew he was slipping further away.

"May I have some water, Aurora?" he asked coherently. She leapt up to grab the tankard immediately. She liked how he'd asked for it. She'd liked his tone. The wind caught her hair, and she felt it pierce through her bones. A long night ahead. Best to keep warm. Throwing a log over the embers, she slipped back under the covers and undid the clasp on the tankard.

"Here, my beautiful Ranger, drink this," she whispered, holding the water to his lips.

He did not drink, and she realised why. His body suddenly became heavy in her grip and his eyes closed over. He took a breath, and then no more. Garrick the defiant Ranger died in her arms, and Aurora Borealis suddenly felt very alone in the world.

17

ALL BAD THINGS

The two Alpha females strode quietly down the corridors. Each of their steps was determined; neither wanted to share her silent fears, but every step made it harder to ignore. Roja led the charge; Mea offered her support a step behind. This would be no casual meeting of elder leaders. There would be no discussions to clear the air. It was a trap. It had to be.

Away from the safety of the sanctuary, where a platoon of Black Guard would fear to tread, the idea of a secret meeting with Sigi held water. However, in the arena of the Cull, both Alphas felt the naivety of a swift decision playing uneasily on their minds.

"I trust Silvia; I do," whispered Roja. It was a peculiar thing to say. She just needed to fill the silence with hopeful words and to reassure herself of her friend's character. Surely her oldest friend would never betray her? Aye, they'd taken different steps, but betrayal was something else entirely.

"I have a bad feeling about this," Mea said, gripping the younger girl's shoulder. It wasn't a gesture of retreat; Mea would do anything to clear her son's name. A mother would walk through fire and sacrifice her own life for a child. *Even for false hope.* If Roja faltered, Mea would march on through. She was just reminding Roja that she was not alone. Two warrior Alphalines were better than one. Roja felt better. "I have a bad feeling about everything these days. Perhaps he offers peace and an escape from this nightmare."

"Perhaps we can work together," agreed Roja, and neither woman sounded convinced.

Stopping outside a familiar door, they took a breath. Typical, they would meet from a lower ground without grandness, but a Primary did what a Primary had to. Elise might argue that they had lost the city the moment the Wolves betrayed the Rangers, but Roja still believed in the dream.

"This will be fine."

"Aye, it will."

They stepped through the familiar door.

Roja had rarely stepped foot below the balcony of the Cull and immediately realised the daunting, claustrophobic atmosphere. It wasn't a small room, yet it gave that impression. The dim lights in the ground were barely enough to penetrate the enveloping blackness. The air was so cold, it made breathing uncomfortable. She hated this room, or what she could sense of it from this rung of the ladder. A masterful move by Dia, conducting business from here.

The door slammed loudly behind Mea, startling them both. The echo reverberated into the rafters and Roja thought about her Cull.

I made my choice just fine.

Finer times, indeed—when she'd felt so young and had viewed life with mischief and simplicity. She could have chosen Erroh easily enough. Nobody would have argued. Even Lea might not have challenged. They would have been a fine coupling. Perhaps things would have been different.

Until I saw Emir again.

Still, how was she to know that no more willing Alphas, eager to claim their prize, would venture to Samara since that day? What had become of the world's youth? Fewer and fewer eligible males had walked the road in the last handful of years. This generation was already dying out. The Hunt need not have marched. The world was doing their task for them.

She thought of Lexi's miserable face when she'd discovered that Roja had stepped away. She thought of her grandmother's silence as well. Her heart had not skipped a beat. She'd craved something else. Someone else. She'd always craved someone else.

Well, this is helping.

She recalled her act of mercy for her lover in this room, and its ramifications, and it stirred the flames of anger once more. Fuk him, she screamed in her mind.

Fuk him. Fuk him.

"Fuk him."

Fuk him.

"What did you say?" whispered Mea from somewhere behind.

"Nothing," she said, staring up at the figures hidden in the darkened balcony. She needed to be a leader. She needed to be a fierce warrior. She needed to be the queen bitch of the city. Only then might she survive this meeting.

"I'm delighted you agreed to meet with us," announced Sigi from above. His voice was kind and welcoming, as though he were standing behind a bar counter, eager to invite a patron to spend all their pieces. A fine skill, considering the company. He leaned against the podium. He did not look as impressive as Dia did when she'd spoken down upon most of her victims, though.

Oh, no.

He hadn't bothered to dress for the grand occasion. He wore simple white garments, yet he wore them well in this light. Loose enough to cover the suggestion of a rich man's belly, and tight enough to give the impression that he was capable, despite his age. He could have been Silvia's father.

This cannot be.

Dane, leader of the Black Guard, stood beside the innkeeper. He wore fine armour with medals glimmering upon it, and looked as impressive as always. It clinked quietly as he adjusted his stance. He appeared at ease.

Ambushed.

Roja eyed the door. Unconsciously, she took a step back, out from under from the balcony above. A step closer to Mea. *Safety in numbers.* Above them, a few Wolves entered the room as well. Their armour was less impressive than Dane's, but imposing enough. Their footsteps were careless and loud; there was no need to be graceful. The females had walked willingly into the trap.

Silvia?

"It is always a pleasure, old friend," Mea said warmly, as though she wouldn't tear his throat out were she given a moment alone with him. Stepping beside Roja, she flashed her warmest smile and allowed little alarm to show on her face. It was all she could do as she realised their predicament.

Betrayed.

How could Silvia lie to her? Roja screamed in her mind. Her body shook. She'd given everything to the girl. They were the closest of friends. No, they were more than that. *Sisters.* Aye, they'd distanced themselves more recently, but that was common enough after tragedy, wasn't it? She couldn't breathe. She heard Mea speak and saw her bow to the brutes standing above. She couldn't bow. Couldn't hold her head proudly, either. She was falling apart, and they were trapped and it was all a fuken nightmare. How much more could she take before her heart shattered? she wondered.

A little more, it would appear. Summoning her will, she bowed too, then waited for their possible captors to return the gesture. They offered no such courtesy, and Roja imagined the world beneath her feet cracking open. A few more breaths and it would swallow her up. Good riddance to a life wasted.

Dane gripped the banister with armoured gloves. He'd come to this room for battle. As had the four armoured brutes on either side of them. It wouldn't be a fair fight. "We wish to speak with your son, Tye," he groused.

"As do I," agreed Mea. She stood forward and shook her head in annoyance. If she was scared about walking into death and leaving Elise and Lexi at the mercy of a betrayer, she didn't show it. In the faint light, Roja could see the older female's breath steaming in the cold. Perhaps her own shaking was just the cold, then. She needed to speak, but something made her hold her tongue. She hated this room. All bad things happened in this room. "I've not seen my cub since the incident." Her voice was firm. The tone was almost enough to shake the redhead from her stupor of fear. Almost. But not quite.

"The *incident*," muttered Sigi. It was the mildest word she could have chosen. Far too delicate for such a crime. Some would have called it murder. Others would have called it multiple murders.

"He's no little cub; he's a fuken brute," shouted Dane. His roar echoed around the dark room and into the hidden rafters above. It was an unexpected outburst, but he was within his rights. Aye, there was a significant amount of justice due to little Tye. He leaned over the balcony and met Mea's eyes. He did not wish to have mere words with Tye. He had finer ideas altogether, and she knew it. He probably knew how protective a mother could be.

"He fled with a woman that night. That is all we know," offered Roja. It wasn't much of a voice, but she found it.

"You can't reach him?" asked Sigi.

"Not at all," lied Mea.

———

Lexi watched Silvia shuffle around the room. She couldn't settle in her seat for more than a few moments before standing up and stretching. After that, she walked to the window, taking in the city as night drew in. She ruffled her blonde hair and stared at the cooking hob for a few moments as though she had many things on her mind. Knowing her as Lexi did, she hadn't.

"Will I make tea?" asked Silvia.

"Keep your voice down," hissed Lexi. Elise's breathing was terrible. Each breath was a laboured rattle, counting down to her very last. When she slept, she improved somewhat. That silly bitch needed to quieten rightly. *Still, though.* "I would take some tea." Silvia was here to protect her mother. She deserved respect. Not much. But some. They were comrades in arms for now. They hated each other, but nasty things were afoot in the city. And tea sounded good.

"As you wish," Silvia whispered.

Lexi couldn't but worry how events were unfolding within the Cull. She was no fool, despite Roja's best attempts at keeping the worst things from her. She knew protecting Elise was but one problem Roja faced. Her "innocence" about the breakout was coming into question. The suggestions had reached her sisters and spread like wildfire throughout their tower. They always said there must be some truth to the whispers and oh, they liked to talk. *They. They* liked to listen to their own pathetic outrage as it grew and ruined. *And made everything worse for the rest of us.*

They liked to lie too. She'd conspired to assassinate Dia. She'd orchestrated a riot. *A fuken riot.* It was easy to join a mugging when you followed your pathetic pack unquestioningly. Easier to remain guiltless when you had nothing but vileness to spread. Those trolls had been the first fuks to scatter. Those who brought nothing of value to this wretched life.

And made worse for the rest of us.

While the beasts whispered among themselves, Roja went to war with the true enemy. They would never even know her greater deeds. Not even if Roja gripped this anarchy by the scruff of the neck and dragged the city up from its knees. Because war was coming and *they* welcomed it. Perhaps, when the enemy was at the gates, rationality might return. Lexi thought it more likely they would present Roja upon a spit as a welcoming gift and call it enlightenment.

"They've arrived by now," said Silvia, drawing Lexi from her frustrated thoughts. She felt the tension too. A bead of sweat rolled down her forehead, and she wiped it away. Looking around absently, humming a song under her breath, she put the kettle on the hob. It was something to do with restless hands, no doubt. It was a precarious thing dancing between leaders. If Silvia played her part in brokering talks, it was an impressive thing.

"Thank you for staying with us," whispered Lexi.

Silvia nodded and sniffed the air. She inhaled and grimaced.

"I can't breathe in here with the stench," she whispered, and muttered something about Emir. Before Lexi could stop her, she opened the far window and leant out, breathing deeply.

"Close the window. The heavy stench helps her breathe." There must have been a steel to her voice, as Silvia slammed it shut. With a sheepish nod, she took her seat once more. A moment later she stood back up and checked the kettle over the flame.

"I'm sorry—I didn't mean to," Silvia said.

"You haven't been here. You weren't aware."

"I've been trying my best with my duties."

Lexi softened her tone. "It's a troublesome time for all of us. We do what we can."

"I think the tea is nearly ready."

"That's good to know."

"Which mug is yours?"

"That one there… Thank you."

It was the most cordial conversation Lexi had ever had with her. The world was turning on its head. They sat in silence a little while longer, listening to the wheezing drone of a dying legend.

And then they heard something else.

It started as a gentle vibration, like a gathering of females stalking the corridors in the after-hours, when Primaries slept and the city with them. Such things occurred frequently. It was late; there were always things for sisters to talk about. Neither Lexi nor Silvia paid it much mind until the delicate hum became something more. Beyond the oak door, they heard footsteps, now rushing upwards. Heavy. Alarming.

"What is that?" hissed Lexi.

"It's probably nothing."

From somewhere down the corridor, the noise grew in volume. More like a charging army with menace and vengeance on their minds than a flock of young deities seeking gossip and sweet cakes. Each heavy footstep reverberated with the sounds of fresh steel and leather.

"Oh no," screamed Lexi, dropping her mug.

"They've come for me," Elise hissed, leaping from her bed instinctively. Suddenly the feeble, dying woman seemed to fall away, replaced by the graceful goddess she had once been. She still had fight in her.

The thundering of boots halted outside the door. Lexi managed one panicked breath before the hammering began, a loud voice calling out between each barrage. Threats, curses. Warnings. Dust shook from the hinges and the frame creaked under the abuse. The Black Guard were here and there was little they could do.

"What happened to Mea and Roja?" croaked Elise, donning her clothing. She wavered, and Lexi thought her too weak for this.

"I'm sorry. I'm sorry—I didn't know this would happen!" screamed Silvia, her eyes never leaving the door. A heavy boot joined in with the hammering. They had come for blood. "I didn't know. It's not my fault." Her voice quivered. She tore her eyes away from the doorway and scanned the room desperately. "We can fight," she cried. "We are Alphalines. They wouldn't dare strike us down."

"We will not fight," hissed Elise. She held onto the bed for support, her eyes terrified but defiant. Knowing and accepting. The hammering continued. A constant, rhythmic drumming. It matched the palpating beat in Lexi's chest. She wanted to scream. To hide beneath some blankets until the bad people went away. She also wanted a weapon to defend her mother, but it was with the absent gods now.

"Open the door," commanded Elise.

———

"Leave the matter of Tye to itself," Roja said, feigning confidence. She thought she sounded impressive, considering the threat. Tye was lost now. As lost as the Outcasts. If Dane wanted to send a few warriors out into hostile territory, he was free to do so. She held Sigi's gaze in one desperate attempt to maintain control. She tried to stare into his soul as Dia had always done. A fine skill to learn. The glorified innkeeper looked indifferent, playing her words over in his mind.

"The rightful leader of Samara is slain," growled Dane. Sigi nodded in agreement.

Sigi cleared his throat. "I offer myself to keep our city open and running," he said, feigning a smile. They made a fine partnership, and it disgusted Roja. They feasted upon the trough of entitlements as though it were theirs to gorge upon. They had brought the city to its fuken knees. To watch it burn, no doubt. "I hold this torch until a stronger candidate can step forward," he added.

This time, Dane agreed. "Aye, a more suitable candidate. There are further inquiries regarding our blessed Primary's murder and the subsequent escape of your lover." His words resonated with their entourage. Each brute gripped his sheathed sword a little tighter and stared down at Roja directly.

Do we string up the bitch now?

The leader of the Wolves stared into Roja's eyes, and she knew the weight in his words. This was no simple suggestion of free elections. This was intent. The threat was real. Suddenly the queen bitch of the city felt alone in the world. She tried to answer, but the sounds fell away to nothing but a loud gasp in her throat. She cleared her throat to counter more confidently, but he cut her off.

"In fact, Roja, we have learned many things these last few days that leave us worried indeed."

Roja felt the walls closing in. She'd known this would happen. *I could have fled.* The city demanded justice, and who better to become the scapegoat than the most despised lost girl in the city?

Surely her sisters in the tower would stand by her?

Surely Dane was not stupid enough to kill her without a trial?

All strength and defiance left her again. The room spun; she felt so very cold. Was this how she would end? Alone in the dark in chains?

Roja wasn't alone, though. She stood beside a female capable of true greatness. Though perhaps not for favourable reasons.

"A candidate, Sigi? You desire a more suitable candidate?" Mea called out. She nodded her head in agreement for all to see and then clapped a few times for effect. Each clap was infectious, and others began to join in until the room rang with the sound. Sigi wasn't certain what he'd said that had brought such applause, but he was visibly pleased.

"You are right to seek fair elections for the Primary's seat, my dear friend," Mea continued. When she spoke, she treated them all as equals. When she spoke, it was hard not to listen. When she spoke while fighting for her life, she spoke magnificently. "Who could argue with any appointment voted by this city?" she said in agreement, and stepped away from her sister. In this light, it was easy to miss the delicate touch she bestowed upon Roja's shoulder, silently reminding her of their solidarity, before addressing the true power in this room. "Such an election among the elite of Samara would go a long way towards settling the ill feelings we have all shared since the turning of events," she said, almost wistfully.

Sigi nodded in agreement. *This sounds grand indeed.*

Dane was less enthusiastic but offered little argument. He gestured to a Wolf, giving some unspoken order. The lieutenant immediately disappeared into the darkness.

Mea's words were strong and offered an alternative to a coup d'état. There were far too many variables to taking Roja into custody while she still held power. Aye, a lynching would be popular among the Black Guard, but there was another force to keep in mind: The Alphaline females of this great city were terrified and hiding behind locked doors, hurting over Dia's violent murder, but they still had teeth and they still had claws. A wiser cub might not be so hasty to tear into another of their kind without justification. Let the females choose their voice and their new mother. If they chose Roja, little would change, but at least it would give them a little more time to build a stronger case against her.

"But… I…" croaked Roja, allowing the realisation to overcome her. Mea shot her a look. In this dim light it was hard to see her terrified expression, but Roja caught it and caught her argument.

Play to the audience and escape this performance.

"I am sorry if the scale of this position has been too much for me," she admitted carefully. "I know now the importance of the city's voice, and if the people choose someone better suited to the role, then I can only praise your foresight, gentlemen," she pronounced regally through gritted teeth. She offered a bow, which Sigi instinctively returned.

A good sign.

Somewhere behind them, the lock clicked delicately, and both females felt the weight of this travesty of a meeting leave them. Neither dared to move, though, until they were granted full dismissal. They had stepped into this room defiant and ready for battle. All too quickly, they had learned a lesson in political manoeuvrings and of their lack of value among the Wolves.

From the darkness, a young recruit dressed in oversized armour slithered in and took his place by the Master of the Black. An errand boy having only recently come of age, he whispered words to an eager listener.

"There is one other matter before you leave," said Dane. The messenger stepped over to Sigi and shared the words with him; Sigi smiled and nodded, and Roja knew what was coming. She had been completely outmanoeuvred. This city was no place for decent people anymore. Perhaps it never had been.

————

"No. Fuk this. We will fight, Mother."

It didn't matter; there were insurmountable odds. It didn't matter at all. Her mother was in harm's way. She alone knew where the one blade in the room rested. Roja had instructed her of its concealment, were the need to arise, when they had first brought Elise to this haven. Swiftly, she released the sword from its sheathed resting place behind the prisoner's bed and held it aloft. It was a fine sword. It had a simple, leather-wrapped hilt with a small enough cross guard that just felt right in her hand. Roja loved the piece.

On instinct, she spun the sword in a wide arc and faced the doorway in warrior stance. Her skill in warfare had developed much like her mother's. Unlike Erroh's defence, she chose offence. It felt only natural attacking. When the Wolves came through the oak doorway, she would spill blood. It was what Magnus would have expected.

"I fear no Wolf," she cried, as though she stood upon a battlefield and she were the fiercest fighter in the Four Factions. Though trapped, they weren't without their own advantages. It wasn't the largest room; it was comfortable enough to seat four or five sisters sharing camaraderie, melancholy, and a fresh brew of cofe. Small enough that, with any luck and a significant amount of skill, they could hold the entrance for a few assaults. Erroh had claimed defending was all about delaying the inevitable, gaining what time they could in awful circumstances. Perhaps they could earn enough time to give the brutes pause. Time enough for Mea and Roja's return. Time enough, perhaps, for her sisters to gather and wage war? She had never killed, but it was in her blood. She would kill them at the doorway; that would slow those charging behind and allow she and her sisters to gain a few moments of time.

Elise had no intention of fighting for her life. "I will not let you die for me," she cried, louder than any hammering. She stumbled forward as she did, her air-deprived body betraying her when she needed it most. "Not like this," she gasped, and dropped to a knee. She eyed the sword and, for a moment, Lexi thought she might take it and add one further legend to the tale of Elise. Instead, she just gasped and died a little more, and Lexi tightened her grip.

Silvia knew her part in these events. She allowed herself a brief sense of pride that she knew her little nemesis so well these many years, especially when the silver glint of steel appeared in her hand and murderous intent marred her stupid face. *Of course, the legends' daughter would not allow the Wolves to claim their prize without further bloodshed.*

The world slowed for Silvia and she embraced the

sensation. The thunderous hammering became little more than a loud crack. The frantic disagreement between mother and daughter was nothing more than delicate, disputed words. Whatever they decided would be irrelevant, because Lady Silvia of Samara was about to declare her allegiance to the victors of this war.

It needs to be done.

If Lexi struck out at the Black Guards, it would not be long before they sliced her little head free of its neck. Then what of the legend, Elise? Then what hope of diplomacy? How then could they control the wrath of Magnus?

She took a breath in the heavy-aired room. The door shifted in its frame, and Silvia was centred in the storm.

I can save everyone.

She looked back to the little fire that had brewed a thousand and one beverages for herself and Roja these past few years. It wasn't a tale of Roja's she remembered, but one from a beautiful boy. A beautiful boy she could have loved. She remembered his lamenting tale about a fireplace, about shameful behaviour by a drunken champion in a little dead town. *Poor, pretty Stefan.* Amidst the horror and the fear, her stomach churned in a pang of regret for her former lover. She reached for the poker. In the hands of a capable Alpha, it made a fight fairer.

"I'm with you, Lexi," cried Silvia, and stepped behind the little bitch to contend with her arguing, legendary mother. It was a tactical decision. The wild threats and curses grew in volume with each heave at the door. A scream of breaking wood filled the air. Elise, pleading for her daughter to hold fast, did not notice Silvia raise her poker. Lexi did not either.

Silvia had little desire to kill Elise, for she was a city legend. Nevertheless, she struck the older female across her chest. A swift strike with enough venom to neutralise.

Though it left a bitter taste in her mouth, it was necessary.
Silvia could not overpower such a warrior, regardless of her
condition. She turned on Lexi as Elise fell silently backwards
into her bed, limp and lifeless.

You traitorous bitch.

Lexi spun around in dismay and watched her mother fall
helplessly. She was too weak. She couldn't survive this. It
was murder, and all she saw was rage. A furnace of rage that
splintered her mind with grief. There would be rivers of tears
to come, but not until she bled the blonde bitch dry. She leapt
forward and sliced the simple blade down towards Silvia's
head. Lexi had not yet come of age; she knew well her skill
was less than her betrayer's, yet she she felt certain that
passionate hatred would win out. She was wrong.

Silvia dipped her head and spun away from the strike with
arrogant grace. Before the younger girl could follow through,
there was a flash of blonde hair and a blur, and then an
explosion across her chin from a sturdy poker. At least it
wasn't hot. Through a dizzying haze, she stumbled forward as
Silvia stalked her.

A betrayer and a killer.

She felt powerful arms grip her wrists and twist. So much
pain, yet she knew the discipline of controlling pain. Had her
father not taught her the importance of controlling pain?
Erroh had certainly learned. She heard a snap and wondered
was it her arm or her own memory?

Take it and survive.

Silvia's terrible strength belied her delicate appearance. She
manhandled the beaten child as if she were little more than a

doll. The blow across the chin had shaken Lexi and ended all resistance. It was a shame she'd hit her so hard. She hoped Lexi would not forget this little lesson. All those jests, through all those years. She had not forgotten. The sword fell from her grip and Silvia bent the youngster further. Using all her weight, she twisted Lexi's elbow towards the floor, using the poker as leverage. The girl did not scream, but it was a small matter. Elise was incapacitated. In a moment, her daughter would be too. Roja would never forgive her, but Roja would be dead in a few days. There was nothing Silvia could do about that. She'd argued until the hour was late for clemency, but Roja's sins were too many. Orchestrating the Outcasts' escape was unforgivable.

One more thrust and she heard a loud snap. This time the young girl did scream—more a horrified yelp, in truth—before falling silent once more and gasping through her tears. Silvia released her, and as a couple of mercenaries fell through the shattered door, Lexi tumbled to the floor, clutching her ruined arm. Silvia grimaced at the protruding shards of bone peering out through bloody skin where the girl's elbow was supposed to bend. The rest of her arm hung limply on the floor.

To her credit, Lexi climbed gamely to her feet and sought Silvia again. Silvia allowed her a few steps before stepping out of the path of the girl's weak strikes, spinning the child away and shoving her at the wall.

Too hard.

There was a sickening, deathly thud, and Lexi crashed lifelessly against a bookcase, bringing it down upon her. Leaving the unmoving girl among the rubble of wooden shelving and tattered books, Silvia turned to the mercenaries. "Let Dane know: it is done." She brushed a few strands of hair from her face and smiled dazzlingly at the leader of the bodyguards.

"I shouldn't have doubted you at all, my dear," the ponytailed brute said, grinning.

"Well, you hardly gave me any time at all," she said, enjoying the exhilaration of battle. "Take Elise to the cart… carefully," Silvia said. She prodded the broken form of Lexi with her foot and saw no threat. "Leave the young one to bleed away in the corner," she said, sliding past the tall man and grazing his chest with her hand as she passed, before stepping out into the hallway.

"As you wish, Mydame." At this, she smiled. A brutal, terrible and necessary deed done. What could stop her rising star now? What could stop her saving the entire city?

18

HIS WILL BE DONE

Garrick's grave was an exact six feet long and three feet across, overlooking a deep valley. Her blistered hands, torn asunder by hard labour with unsuitable tools, spilled crimson into the soil where he lay and it brought a smile to her face. They would be connected forever through blood. Part of her would be with him always. He would not be alone in his eternal sleep. Four feet down, she measured and made smooth the bottom of the trench, for it mattered that his bones be comfortable. She added a thin layer of leaves for his bed and rolled up a small blanket to prop up his head. He might have liked that.

When the first handful of soil was dropped across his pale face, she cried for him and for herself. When the grave was filled, she scraped his name and his station onto a rock and placed it at the head of the mound. She did not know why she did this, only that she never wanted to forget him.

Only then did she continue on her way.

In the late afternoon, Aurora captured a mount. A change in the wind, or another hunter, sent five frantic horses charging her way. She took it as an unlikely gift from her god and ran with them, avoiding their powerful bodies, their crushing hooves, leaping over fallen logs and thick prickly bushes, until a loose set of reins dangled close enough to grab.

Perfect.

After a few struggles, she leapt and pulled herself onto the saddle and began calming her prize. The rest of the horses charged deeper into the green while she brought her own to a stop. Desperate to embrace a new master, the mount bowed to her will almost immediately and accepted the charge she demanded. This wondrous beast was built for human contact. The Arth was beautiful and vast, but it was unfamiliar to their simple minds.

It was not the first mount she had come upon this morning; she had seen at least twenty of the beasts running in small, terrified groups through the quiet, endless forest. Terrified and skittish, and all without masters. Something was terribly wrong, and Aurora could smell blood in the air.

She broke through the heavy cover of the trees and out into the warm sunshine, and immediately felt better about herself. Aurora Borealis wiped unwanted tears from her face and gripped the horse's reins tighter. It was a southern war horse, and it still had the taint of battle along its side where an arrow had pierced it. Whatever had become of the unwanted projectile was a mystery, but she suspected a few days of the horse's running wild through the dense forest had something to do with that. The other streaks of dried blood covering its saddle belonged to its Rider. Whoever had fought atop this animal had met a grisly end. It was a bad omen for her people.

My people.

She missed her Garrick. She had not known him long. Usually she was assured in herself. Usually, she loved her god and little else. Usually, she liked to count things. Usually, she liked the killing.

Ignoring her worry and her tears of loss, she followed the tracks in search of Oren's army, for she had many questions to ask of him. Out in the sunshine with the warmth on her face, she was supposed to let go of foolish, lamenting thoughts, but a terrible empty sorrow had engulfed her since his passing. She was of the Hunt. Garrick had been a Ranger, the enemy, part of the tainted.

She mourned him.

"What have I become?" she moaned to the Arth as though it were a friend. Bringing her horse to a stop alongside a hedge, she frantically wiped the dampness from her cheeks as though tending to an open wound.

I cut him apart.

Because that's what I do.

Because I am godly.

Because I was born that way.

In blood.

One beautiful night.

From somewhere over the next hill, the dull murmur of a settled army and a terrible anger took her attention.

"Stupid old man."

My sweet friend.

She patted the horse absently and thought of the king she had slain, of his loving son, and then of her last act with a dying man. *Everyone dies in the end.* Normally such thoughts brought a wonderful sense of emptiness and desire, but since she'd dug that perfect grave, she just felt lonely. This was the longest she'd ever been alone. The longest she'd been without Uden's blessed gaze or the warmth of her wandering comrades. She couldn't remember ever feeling this lonely.

Not in this life.

Not in this life.

Not in this fuken life, Fyre.

Fyre?

This loneliness felt familiar, and Aurora felt something on the tip of her tongue, some bitter taste, and saw in her mind's eye a blurred image of a different Arth. Of a different road. Something else, something locked deep inside her, drowned by blood and pain and chains and ruin.

In Uden I trust.

She fought the tide of memory as it surfaced, as he'd ordered her to. For looking deeper within would be little Aurora's end.

There is such beauty in the kill, her mind told her, and it sounded like her lover. It was a command. A way of life. Of death, too. She could taste Uden. She could feel his godliness upon her and she was so scared. So fuken scared of saying the wrong thing.

Please him.

"Uden?" she whispered through quivering lips. She could feel her pain leave her, could almost feel his powerful grip embrace her. It was wonderful, and the tears subsided.

Think of the blood, Aurora.

"Born in it." He was near; he had to be. She shook her head as if in a trance and felt the sunlight warm her face. In times of need and loss of faith, he came to her. Only her. He allowed her to kill; he gifted her death and victims, and her head spun with desire for him.

Silly Aurora, all alone in the Arth and making friends with the enemy.

His will was pure, and she was his instrument of war. Her eyes burned brightly once more, and she kicked her mindless beast forward towards whatever army Oren was keeping for her.

———

"I would have expected you to have far greater worries on your mind than my eyes, Oren," said Aurora. She broke a piece of bread from the full loaf in front of her and took a measured bite. She was counting her words again. *Seventeen.*

"I meant little offence," the battered warrior said quietly, reaching for a goblet of foul-smelling liquid. His eyes met those of his second-in-command nervously as he did. He dined with a reaper of fates. She almost grinned. Instead, she counted the words he'd used. Four. This was good. Nice, short, even. She liked those types of sentences.

A fine spread lay out in front of them. Not the glorious feast of victory she would have expected, but impressive nonetheless. Three slabs of sizzling meats and an assortment of steaming vegetables covered the makeshift table. *A meal fit for a goddess.* Once, she might have considered such a spread indulgent and wasteful, but the stocks of provisions were full with so few mouths to feed. Normally, Aurora desired only meat. Today, she desired vegetables. Anything without blood, but slathered in butter and salt.

She felt more herself again. Seeing the remains of the army would shake anyone from their stupor. *From my sacrilege.* Her eyes no longer stung from surrendered, morbid sorrow. Her memory no longer whispered of a different life. She remembered her place in the world. It was right here at this table, scaring Oren.

Good Aurora. She enjoyed her god's whispers in her mind. Whenever she strayed, it was his voice she heard, his calming tones settling the worries until she was ready to be herself again. It was acceptable to stray, sometimes. He swore he'd always welcome her back. *And Garrick?* She forced a mouthful down her throat. She took a breath and reminded herself that Garrick was dead. Weakened by her blade. It was as beautiful as blood. She rubbed at her eyes again. She couldn't even remember crying. It was probably just dust in her eyes from his grave. His perfect grave.

"I care little for apologies, Oren," she hissed. She didn't bother acknowledging the young general seated beside her quarry. When she needed to speak with him, she would do so. She could feel Oren taking her in, and she allowed him to. Let him fear as long as needed. It was more fun this way. Looking out to the ruined camp, she began absently counting the small tents that had been erected, and he stifled a cough as he drank from his mug. There were far fewer than before; they had smashed the city's resistance in spectacular fashion. The only failure was the dreadful loss of their Riders. There were always eager young killers ready to forsake the slow march and join the great charge, but those things took time. Time. It was all about time now.

"Tell me again," she said easily. He outranked her, but everyone at the table knew who controlled the world. He took the request as the order that it was. When she asked to hear a tale a second time, the details of the truth emerged more smoothly. She was patient. She had all the time in the Arth.

Sighing, he spoke once more of how he had stolen victory from an unlikely scenario, and she concealed her disgust with a curt nod of agreement. She was again dismayed at hearing of the champion he had captured to face Uden, but she swallowed this with another chunk of bread. And then he told her of the numbers he'd lost when delivering the gifts to Erroh.

"Tell me once again how you attempted… and failed to kill the false god?" she asked. "And why you went against Uden's wishes trying to kill him?" she added, losing count of her words and not being too troubled about it. She was busy counting other things. Like the pathetic remnants of his army. The usual comforting stench of the march was now mixed with the acrid aroma of antiseptic, blood and melancholy. They were still dying, some of them. She could hear their moans in the morning air. Sometimes hearing the agony of comrades was more devastating than a failed assault.

Oren should have delivered the gifts with a handful of expendable soldiers. But he'd marched with nearly a full regiment, and they had been decimated by a foe one-fourth their size. Decimated and still dwindling.

Beyond the odours of meats and vegetables, she could also smell the dead. They had not yet rotted; that would come in time. There were too many. She had skill in digging graves; perhaps she could help. Her mind was uneasy with questions. Had she wanted a dominant victory? Had she wanted the Rangers to be defeated without scoring a telling blow? Had Oren done enough to save himself? Had he done enough to deny her leadership?

From his description of the battle, they had slain the beige heroes for standing their ground when all others had fled. It was hardly the act of a masterful tactician, yet Oren made it seem as much. Most leaders took credit when there was little to be had. Uden had probably watched the battle, for he saw all. Even with one eye. Whatever her actions, they would be done in his name.

Right?

"We delivered the gifts under a banner of peace. Erroh was displeased and struck us unawares," he said, leaning back in his chair, feigning assuredness in himself.

"Unawares?"

In a field?

His glass was empty, so she refilled it. Beside him, his young general declined her steady hand. She poured anyway.

232

"What did you expect to happen?" she asked. It was a fine question. "Did you all just turn your backs and plod away?" That too was an excellent question.

"I expected honour." He pushed his goblet away in disgust. "I already told you this." He looked ready to flee this table. To flee this entire camp. She stared at him with eyes that made men lose the run of themselves, and he began talking again like a good pet.

"Erroh charged forward recklessly with his army." He leant forward. He hadn't leant forward the last time. "Tell me, Aurora, what type of general allows his warriors to charge so recklessly? We came under peace, but no truce was accepted."

"Were I there, things might have differed."

"You would be dead, so," he muttered under his breath, and she thought of chains and blood and colours in the sky and some fiend of fury gutting her with a cleaver, and she bit her upper lip and imagined it all over again.

"Don't promise unlikely things," she hissed, throwing her bread down on her plate. The meal was over. She decided as much and stood suddenly. Both generals stood with her and awaited her judgement. "Show me the captive," she ordered, as if it were she who led this army. Again, neither man dared argue. The younger general stepped forward to lead the way, while Oren accompanied the second most deadly female in the world.

"What's your name again?"

Four.

"It's Camerin…" Camerin said, as they marched down through the camp. She had not decided on him yet. He recoiled like a beast to be hunted, but he had a fine walk. "Um… Aurora."

Four.

Or three and a half.

Four words were better.

"You call me General," she snapped.

"As you wish, General."

Four again.

He might have fled, but he said all the right things in the right way.

"I have my eyes on you, little Camerin," she said warmly and saw the horror on his face. This pleased her greatly.

Every member of the Hunt stepped out of her path, recognising her importance from the pendant dangling against her chest. The walk through the unimpressive camp did not take long. When they came upon the captured warrior, she was truly horrified.

"This is no way to keep him," she spat, seeing the battered form lying in the mud. His injuries had been cleaned and bandaged, but that was the only kindness they'd offered him. A steel chain was running through a vast hole in his palm, and his skin was slowly healing over it. The rest of the chain wrapped around his waist and held him in place. They had tethered him to a wooden post in the ground and left him shirtless and covered in mud. Aurora was dismayed at his treatment, though she did not know why.

Treated worse than Garrick?

Through the caked mud and dried blood on his bearded face, she could see his defiance. She could also see his burning eyes. He was not beaten at all. He was waiting for his moment. And he would have his moment. He emanated alluring energy, raw and powerful, and he stared right through her.

Kneeling down beside him in the mud, she whispered in his native tongue, real quiet like. "I have a secret." He did not stir. He was trying to trick her. *Silly Ranger.* She was no threat. "Tell me your name, Ranger, and I'll tell you my secret," she whispered, licking his ear as she did.

He was better-looking than Garrick, younger as well, but such things didn't matter. She noticed Oren lean in closer to hear what her hushed words were. She hissed him away and smiled dazzlingly to the prisoner. It had little effect, and again she was impressed with the measure of the man. Most this close to a death sentence craved any comforts they could get. Even a few sweet words from a sweet goddess.

"Go fuk yourself, Witch," he growled, and for good measure, spat a mixture of saliva and blood at her. She flinched at his words, but not the act. Instead, she wiped his mouth kindly and then she cleaned her own. He was wonderfully familiar.

"Please don't call me that. Call me Aurora, instead," she insisted, remembering the perfect grave. Her nails still had some dirt trapped beneath from the digging. That was fine. She'd left a little of herself with him; it was nice having a little of him in return. The prisoner muttered something profane, but he referred to her by her god's given name. "Do you know a Ranger called Garrick?" she asked, crossing her legs and sitting down in front of him. He was strong enough to choke her. Or beat the wretched life from her perfect body, if he wanted to. A few strikes to her throat. A few fingers through her glorious eyes. *Like an arrow.* Her companions would allow it, too.

Kill me, Ranger.

For the love of your absent gods, fuken kill me and be done with me.

Kill me. Kill me. Kill me.

But he did not choose this moment to exact a little revenge for his capture. She stroked the captive's cheek, and he recoiled at her touch, but not before she saw the faint recognition in his eyes at the old scout's name. They had been brothers in arms. She saw fear as well. Fear that Garrick had betrayed them all. Such a thought horrified Aurora. "He passed from this world peacefully, and in the arms of someone who cared deeply for him," she said, and felt her voice nearly break. Nearly, but not quite.

"A good way," the prisoner mumbled.

"He gave no secret nor betrayed a single one of your brothers or sisters before he died," she promised, and stroked his long hair absently. He shivered from cold, and Aurora felt the need to slip away. He was a reminder of beautiful, worldly things. She had other things to do. She leaned in close enough that only he could ever possibly hear, and she told him her secret. It was a wonderful secret. He nodded and smiled that he understood, and she pulled away.

"Jeroen," he whispered.

"Clean him up, dress him and give him proper shelter," she growled at Camerin who nodded that it would be done. "Have him at his best when Uden the Woodin Man arrives," she added, as if her words needed an explanation. They didn't. Her tone commanded respect. She was a born leader, though she had never believed it herself. Her family in the finger had followed her without question, for there was no one else with such a skill at charging. She suspected it was their fear of showing any appearance of cowardice in her eyes, and that was fine.

"A few days' ride to Samara?" she asked quietly, pointing towards the horizon, and Camerin nodded. *Excellent.* It was time to go to the city; she had things to see. Or whatever the lyric was.

"Walk me to my mount. There are a few worrying things

we must discuss before I leave," she said, sighing. The relieved Oren followed like a good little hound, eager to keep her appeased before she departed, and even more eager to see the back of her as she disappeared into the city lights. Camerin shared his sense of relief, though he wore his enthusiasm a little less obviously.

"Uden will not be happy at the loss of such numbers, though I find it difficult to believe he did not foresee such events occurring," she said quietly when she reached her mount. She removed her small dagger from its scabbard along her shapely hips and sniggered when Oren recoiled at its appearance.

"Do I scare you, Oren?"

"Not at all."

She slid the blade through the straps holding the beast's saddlebags and began cutting. It would be best not to show up in the city bearing the signs of southern leather. It would be more difficult to disguise the beast she rode, but such enormous animals weren't completely rare in this part of the world.

"I'm sure once he hears the full truth, he will be understanding and merciful," the leader of the shattered first wave argued, and she nodded thoughtfully.

"He is vengeful, and he is great, and yes, he is merciful," she agreed, as though she were one of his most devoted zealots. Perhaps that was what she was.

"Come on," she growled. The stubborn leather wouldn't break fully under her assault, and she tugged without success.

"May I?" asked Oren, stepping in to assist her. Gentleman to the last. He gripped the saddlebags, and they fell away easily enough. No problem.

As he stood there with his hands full of a heavy mount's leather, Aurora moved as if the world had slowed to a stop and all time bent to her will. Then, like she had done countless times before, she sliced her dagger across the throat of her victim, delivering onto him a mortal blow. His eyes opened in shock and then horror as the realisation came upon him. He blinked a few times and fell to his knees, the saddlebags tumbling down beside his dying body. He struggled to cover the deep slice, but it was too wide. Far too wide. He knew Aurora did not err when assassinating a target. The blood streamed out from his throat and Oren slumped forward.

"Do not avenge him," she warned the horrified Camerin, who stood behind her. She bent to one knee and leaned in to watch the beautiful act of death take place. She would not bury him. She had other plans. "Do you see this, Camerin? He had a weak heart. The blood should have drained from him," she whispered deliriously, and Camerin threw up. It was a small matter. Not every man was required to share her taste for blood and death and torment. They only needed to kill when asked.

Members of the Hunt stood stock-still around them, frozen in shock and disbelief, as their leader was slain casually in front of their eyes. There had been no fanfare or great proclamations to warn them, just a sudden shuffle and then silent gasps and panicked whispers that spread out through the ranks. None took up a blade or tried to help, for the next in line had allowed this. If Camerin was happy to allow this attractive female to slit their leader's throat, then so were they.

It was not the first changing of the guard they had witnessed, nor, they suspected, would it be the last. Oren's eyes rolled, and he gave up trying to stem the flow of blood. He flapped his arms at her, but she swatted his attempts away dismissively.

It's time to step into the dark, Oren. Your story is done.

"You are now my first general, Camerin, and you command in my absence," she whispered, then leaned forward and touched the dying man's throat. The blood was gloriously warm, but there was no sign of the flow ceasing. A very weak heart. "I shall be absent for a time."

"I have a strong heart," he said coldly, and Aurora immediately liked the young warrior after all. She turned and smiled her satisfaction. He looked terrified.

"Conceal this army so they are not open to any counterattack. I will find you when it is time. Do not engage the northerners until The Woodin Man arrives."

She shoved the mostly lifeless body of Oren to the ground. He gave a wet, croaking moan. Aurora looked over at the watching Jeroen and nodded. He had not told on her. It had been a wonderful secret. Perhaps she would share more with him at a later time. Perhaps they could be friends? Perhaps he would tell her more about the Rangers.

"I will do as you wish, General," Camerin replied, wiping the bile from his mouth.

"That's all I ask," Aurora said warmly, as she removed a rope from the fallen saddlebags and wrapped it tightly around Oren's feet. He managed another dull groan, and she knew he hadn't long left in this world. She tied the rope to her mount's saddle and climbed up. It was Uden's will.

"And you, my general, what are your plans?" the shaken second-in-command asked, his eyes still locked on the dying form of his former comrade.

She sniffed the air in disgust and looked again at the remains of a once powerful army. "There is nothing to do but wait for the next wave, and I'm not one to cease a charge," she said, and shrugged. It was true. There was no need for war yet. From what she had learned, the city was not inclined to bring the fight to her people. Except for the false god, that is. "I wish to find and meet this Erroh, and I like a fine hunt."

She kicked her mount along its ribs and left the general to do her bidding. The horse huffed from the extra weight it dragged behind it, but she was relentless in driving the beast on. As Uden had asked of her, she had drained Oren of his blood and his life. At some point early in the ride, he died quietly, but she'd pledged to spread his blood for miles and so she did exactly that. Finally, looking back one last time, she cut the rope and prepared to leave the body to begin its decay in the blistering sun.

His will be done.

Last of all, Aurora stripped from herself all signs of her heritage, leaving them beside the faceless body before turning towards the city. It was time to make new friends, and Ealis was very skilled at this.

19

TORCH

"How is your knee?" Erroh asked, topping up the goblet in front of his seated master. Magnus needed no refill, but it was something to do with unsteady hands seeking stillness. Magnus reclined leisurely in his chair by the fire. His outstretched leg was the only sign of discomfort, and even that appeared to give him little worry.

Scratching at the fresh bandaging, he eyed his son. "Emir was not pleased." Erroh grinned, imagining the cacophony of torrid abuse emitted by the diminutive healer. No soul could withstand one of Emir's tirades. "He said I'll need to be on these cursed things for a few months," Magnus said, pointing disdainfully at the crutches and brace discarded in the corner. "Now is not the time for shuffling. I'll be walking in a week, limp or no."

"Aye, he wasn't pleased with me, either." Erroh had more to say, but fell silent. He sat looking around his father's tent, searching for words to reduce the unease. His relationship with his father was like most other relationships, he supposed. Especially those between master and apprentice. There was warmth and there was conflict, although few shared an actual skirmish as brutal as they had. It was one thing to offer praise in the company of tired soldiers in need of leadership. It was another thing to do it in quiet seclusion. Their brutal bout might well have severed their bond.

He would have killed me.

Without adrenalin pumping and weariness overcoming their shattered bodies, it was easier to sit back and allow feelings of resentment to swallow the soul.

"There's a little sting to it," Magnus said, rubbing at the ruined kneecap. He groaned lightly, and Erroh could see the strain of such an injury. Erroh remembered his lessons in controlling pain. Somehow it was harder seeing his father endure his own teachings. Most others might well be howling for the finest dream syrups or begging for unconsciousness.

I'm sorry, Dad. I had no other choice.

He suddenly wanted to refill the glass all over again. It wasn't how a leader should behave.

"I am sor—"

Magnus cut him off. "It wasn't very fatherly of me, my choking you," he said quickly. His face was flushed. With embarrassment? With shame? "Don't tell Elise. She'll finish me." He smiled sadly. "And she'd be in her rights, too." It was a fine apology. It was how leaders apologised.

"Imagine what she'd do to me if she heard what I did."

This time Magnus smiled properly. "What do you mean "if"? Oh, little one, I'll be telling your mother exactly what you did… You are so dead."

"I'm surprised you had a such firm grip with those gnarled fingers," Erroh mocked, clinking his goblet against the full glass to coax his father into merriment. Also.

I forgive you, Father.

"Your scrawny neck was too easy a target."

I forgive you too, son.

Magnus downed the glass in one and allowed Erroh to refill it. This Erroh did happily, at the cost of a few lost drips. They met their end in the dirt. Such travesties occurred in war. Not every drip made it. Especially with a young pourer, unsure of every manoeuvre. Unsure of their own abilities. Sometimes tragic sacrifices were made so the larger measure of wine could be shared for the benefit of the party. Sometimes, people threw that fuken glass at the wall, and the party really kicked off.

Erroh refilled his own glass but hovered over the goblet's crimson surface and twisted away the last few drops. *Lesson learned. To the victor, the spoils*.

"What are your plans?" asked Magnus. It was a fair question, and unnerving coming from the legend.

"I do not know."

Magnus sighed and nodded his head thoughtfully, as if he were about to gift sage advice. This was never a good sign. Erroh recognised this from years of kneeling at his throne. He was about to receive a lengthy dissertation from one of the world's brilliant thinkers on why he was the definition of a fool, and it would be a fair assessment.

"I had no plan, either. There isn't much to know of those we face. After so long tracking them, learning their ways, the most I have learned is they do not attack a settlement twice." Erroh thought this notion interesting. "Each town that was sacked was likely sought by a finger that knew of its existence. Their movements suggest they never return to a sacked town, or that another wandering horde marches through after." He shook his head, and Erroh wondered how long he'd thought on this matter. "Perhaps they like survivors knowing their vile messages, spreading it through the wastes. Perhaps with so many to kill, they are simply managing their resources."

Erroh leaned forward. "A shrewd coward might take sanctuary in a raised town. A resistance could be born within the belly of the beast. Tell me, Father, do you know this for certain?"

Magnus shook his head, and only then did Erroh see the relief in his father's face. "I have been wrong about a great many things." There was little behind those tired eyes. He'd seen that look on his father before, the night he had come upon him and learned of the Rangers' fate. "I accepted the role of these unwanted soldiers, but truly, I have lost my spirit, Erroh. I have no army, I have no Clieve, I have no Elise, I haven't even the full use of my legs. I am only a symbol now." He reached out and took Erroh's hand. His fingers touched the scars for a moment. "When they found you, Erroh, I broke. Now, I am crushed and unable to gather myself for war."

Erroh wanted to embrace his father, to tear the empty horror from him. He had earned a reprieve from having to watch more of his soldiers butchered. There were limits to what any warrior could take. He was a legend, but still only human.

"Are we doomed?" asked Erroh quietly, lest there be eager ears listening outside the gently flapping tarp. He fought the desolation and the fear stirring in his stomach. Suddenly, he felt his age, and with it a deep sense of solitude. Somehow, he'd believed in his father's shrewd strategies. In his steely nerve. Despite everything, he'd been certain there were ways to stem the tide. He wanted to vomit. He had a drink instead.

"There is always a chance of victory," Magnus said. And something in his tone suggested truth. Erroh would need to learn that tone. Lying to doomed warriors would be a lot easier.

"I will find a way," Erroh said, more to himself, as if hearing the words would lend them further weight. Perhaps he should have said them louder, for he felt no better. He would have preferred ignorance.

Magnus leaned forward. "You showed genius in Keri. You used the terrain to your advantage like few ever could. You saw things no others would have, and earned success that was impossible. It was a tiny spot on a map with little strategic significance, but the consequences have changed the world, Erroh."

"It was a doomed defence. We fell because it fuken rained. How genius was that?" Erroh countered, thinking of his lost brothers on that terrible slope. *All for nothing.* "When the fires were lit, we should have fled. I should have ordered a retreat."

The absent gods thought differently. And they knew things he didn't.

He wasn't to know that the Hunt, enraged and vengeful for such losses, would have hunted them down and slaughtered them out in the open. He wasn't to know that they would have caught the scent of the rest of the fleeing town and followed, out of principle alone. How could he know these things? He was no god, though every day more zealots became believers.

In Erroh, we rise.
Through the burning of the light.
In the dark, he guides our step.
Immortal, he is the way.
Lead us, our lord.
And we will follow.

. . .

"I doubt myself, Erroh, but I do not doubt you," Magnus argued.

"And now I'm the leader of these rejects," Erroh countered. "I should probably find a better name for them," he added after a moment. They were far worse than mere rejects. They were all outcasts. Hated and hunted by the city they tried to protect.

"You're already thinking like a leader."

Erroh nodded and began forming a plan. A simple plan that would never work. It began by topping up the two goblets. He did not spill a drop. His hands had fallen steady. Perhaps knowing his father's fears had settled them.

"I cannot win this war, but I will always offer an ear," Magnus said. "Make no other move beyond surrounding yourself with strong generals to start. Not friends: those who challenge you." He nodded to the tent beyond. "You think Aymon and Doran are comrades I enjoy whiling away the hours with? Oh no. Those fuks challenge me on everything. You could do worse than trusting them, even if you despise each other. Listen to your generals and there will be no poor decisions, just unfavourable outcomes," he pledged, and Erroh nodded in appreciation.

"You make it sound simple."

Magnus smiled. He wasn't finished.

"Be ruthless without ever becoming cruel, although sometimes cruelty is unavoidable."

"You must never hesitate. But you must know the cost of being unprepared."

"You may have to kill those you hold dearest, just to earn an advantage." Erroh didn't like that suggestion.

"When the battle is lost, know it is lost."

"Above all else," the master whispered, leaning forward to take his son's hand, "never stop learning."

Erroh was terrified, but he knew that without Magnus leading them, there was no one better to accept the crown. If he survived an assassination attempt by one of the Wolves tonight, the possibilities were endless. It was time to don his warrior's skin and make some painful decisions.

After a time, Magnus brokered the question. A fine question, too. "What will you have me do, Erroh... Master General, sir?"

"Little has changed. You must travel to the Savage Isles and remind them of your claim," the new Master General replied. It was no plan, but it was something. Besides, time in the saddle might be what he needed. Little steps could still carry him miles.

"Though it will be no simple task, I wish to bring Elise and only two or three guardians," Magnus said quietly, and Erroh's heart dropped. Of course, he desired his mate by his side at her end, but a rushed charge across the wastes would be a dreadful, punishing end.

"Do not give the city further reason to exile our forces. She is safe under Roja's watchful eye, Father. No, you will travel without her." It was a dreadful few words, and Erroh hated sharing them with him. So began the cruelty of Erroh the Inept. He looked away from his father's shattered eyes lest he break down himself. Magnus had every right to be with Elise when she took her last breath. Erroh had denied him that right by banishing him to the other side of the world to gather some uneasy allies.

"Why would you punish me?" whispered Magnus, his voice wavering between anguish and wrath.

Because I still hope Elise will live.

"We need swiftness, Father."

Erroh shifted his feet, and the old desk creaked loudly under the stress of his weight. It was something to do while breaking his father's heart, while robbing him of being there at the end. Silent tears fell from Magnus's eyes, and he wiped them away silently. He did not argue any further, and he did not challenge his new Master General, but Erroh knew the cruelty of his decision.

"As you wish," he said, and each word was a struggle.

"I give you my word: we will liberate her from the city. For now, though, she is safest in the custody of Roja and Mea and Lexi. We must have hope," Erroh said, knowing the deceit in his words.

"Hope?" challenged Magnus, anger rising to the surface. "Know this, Erroh: Elise will pass into the darkness without me by her side. Without me tending to her burial. Don't talk to me about fuken hope."

"Aye, hope," countered Erroh, knowing the sin could never be forgiven. They might have said more, but Lillium appeared inside the tent. She appeared to have words to say, but saw Magnus's face and turned away.

"Apologies," she said. "I was looking to speak with Erroh."

"And you will, but can you find Wynn for me? I have need of him," Erroh said. She raised an eyebrow. Perhaps the whispers about who would be second-in-command had already begun to stir. Two young Alphas leading the fight against the Hunt was a fine start.

"Wynn as second-in-command?" spat Magnus. "I suppose that makes some sense. He needs a little further moulding." Magnus shook his head, and Erroh wanted the ground to swallow him up. He had torn his father apart twice in one day. No jests would erase this grief, though. Magnus must have seen the anguish in his son's face. His disgust softened to mere anger. "Promise me you will free Elise from Samara."

"I give you my word."

"Do that, and you and I will be well," his father pledged. He looked around the dreary, dark room as though seeing it for the first time. There were only a few burning candles staving off the night. He took an unlit candle and passed it across to his son.

"It's a little too dark for my liking in here. Will you light the rest before you leave?" he whispered.

20

IT'S BEGINNING TO LOOK A LOT LIKE TROUBLE

This was exactly how Aurora liked it to be. Right here, in this moment, with dangers surrounding her. Most others would collapse under the stress. She revelled in it. Sitting this close to the flames was just how she liked to warm herself, and oh, it felt like she was burning her skin right off. It was a marvellous distraction.

She nodded her head, smiling sadly as the little cub called Tye told her everything about his father, the Ranger Jeroen.

"It's no common name," he'd replied drunkenly when asked to repeat the name a second time. And then a third. She'd almost squeaked in excitement. Another card to her deck. Another secret for her ears.

As the last drips of Stefan's stolen beverage disappeared down the drunken child's throat, Ealis paid for a fresh round and leaned in to hear more of these fallen Rangers. Her new companion was full of information, and oh, to hear the tale told from another side was so very interesting. But her eyes never left the two figures sharing an uncomfortable waltz upon the dance floor. As much as she enjoyed the little one's drunken antics, she would not lose sight of her quarry tonight.

———

When Ealis saw Samara for the first time, she thought it love at first sight. With her god's whispered suggestion, she'd dreamed of it many times, but nothing had prepared her for the vision it was. Its walls stretched up into the sky forever, and she knew no mere army could ever shatter them. Uden would find a way, though. The city might hold an army at bay, but she had slipped through without too many problems, with only a delicate swish of her hair and a suggestive wink. With an exploratory caress on unprotected elbow skin and wonderfully whispered lies. She had slid into the city as if she were royalty, leaving a charmed gate guard behind. It was unlikely the guard had believed her advances were genuine, but when the prettiest little thing played at allurement, it made a fine break from the mundanities of the day.

And besides, what possible harm could a little angel like her do within? The gods might have held their breath, knowing what was coming.

A steady counting of her own footsteps helped her to control the terror of walking into the belly of their enemy's stronghold as she slipped inconspicuously through the hushed city streets. She kept her dazzling eyes to the ground as best as she could, but by her hundredth step, the attraction of the wonders became far too much. She took it all in. She became drunk on it and she wanted more. It felt like home and she loved it.

To burn?

The acrid smell of waste, sweat and grime was intoxicating. So familiar, so perfectly familiar. It was like the scent of her army marching, and she felt tears in her eyes once more. Joyous tears, though. Welcome tears, more than she'd shed for the fallen Ranger Garrick. Because he was old, and he had meant nothing to her.

More than you shed for Alder?

Shut up, shut up, shut up.

The energy in the people was like nothing she'd ever experienced. They were so much more vibrant than those who walked the drab, cold streets of Conlon. *Or ran through them like burning fireflies.* The sun shone on her flawless face, and she swept through each section of the three factions' capitol as if she were one of their citizens marching to her death. She'd been happy, and had allowed herself a few hours to memorise its beauty for when the day came that she would stalk the alleyways, weapons raised, spilling rivers of blood. Many would die and she would play her part.

Welcome to Samara. Wipe your feet.

———

"Maybe he does indeed live," Ealis agreed suddenly, stopping the young Alpha male mid-sentence. She was glad she'd never appeared at Tye's family's door and murdered everyone within, like many of their kind before. She could barely remember the names. Murder like that was distasteful. She could see that now. Perhaps she'd always seen that. Better late than never, she supposed. Truthfully, she'd murdered a lot of Alphaline families. Fathers and sons. Mothers, daughters. Brothers, sisters and any in between.

Babies?

Delighted that those days were long behind her, Aurora watched him swallow a sob and fight a drunken lament. Agreeing with his unlikely hope might have been construed as kindness, and she'd almost brought him to tears. *Interesting.* She was far more amused by his drunken boasting and the slew of information he was offering. She smiled and stretched her arms out wide and leaned back magnificently, allowing him a finer sight of things hot-blooded adolescent males desired. It was enough to distract him from his misery, and after he took a moment to sip his new drink, he began his tale of how his father had moulded Erroh's ferocious technique.

This was interesting as well.

———

Aurora had never seen so many obvious candidates, but for all the victims she targeted, few held many coins on their person. Money, it would appear, was not terribly plentiful in this magnificent city. She wasn't sure when in her life she'd learned to pickpocket, only that lifting treasures was as natural as breathing to her.

She walked beside her mark and aimed for one bulging pocket. Just one, and nothing more. She would count the rhythm and the steps and match them perfectly. Stalking through the crowd, she was invisible and swift. Keeping her beautiful eyes skywards, she seemed lost in wonderful thoughts—before one quick strike and a prayer for success. In the moments when her stealth let her down and the man in question noticed something amiss, a quick stumble into his arms and a girlish giggle at her clumsiness were more than enough to complete the transaction. They bent to her will. It was her eyes; it was always her eyes, and they all smiled happily, never knowing their own gullibility. She liked men. And their predictability. It was no sin to favour such things.

It had taken almost a day to solicit enough money and to find a beaten old tavern manager willing to rent her a tiny box of a room. It wasn't anything spectacular: straw, sheets and a sturdy lock on the door, in a basement away from prying eyes. To have afforded a grander room would have meant many more hours pickpocketing throughout the marketplace.

To hunt a false god was no straightforward task. Knowing his whereabouts in a city this big would have been easy enough, but worrying things were in the wind. Slipping through the streets, engaging in conversation with whoever would listen, she went to task charming out the whereabouts of the elusive Outcast Erroh. People liked to talk, liked to share the latest truth, and she was a perfect companion, if only for a few moments. She stayed just long enough to learn an unfamiliar name or discover a new clue, then disappeared swiftly enough to be a mere pleasant, faded memory of an attractive young woman. She became a wraith, stalking the inns and markets, searching and gorging herself on knowledge. She took it all in. It was quite easy, she found, with so much animated fear burning through their minds. Intoxicating and delicious. They did not worship Erroh at all. He was an Outcast, living on the run and reviled by all.

Very fuken interesting.

———

"Erroh learned some of his technique from my father," continued Tye, and Ealis giggled in reply. He liked this and smiled. He liked the exotic lady in black leather. She offered him her time without mocking him. She was kind. He could see it deep down inside her, behind those stunning eyes that caused uneasy feelings in his stomach. She was mysterious.

Of course he would tell her all about his father. He would tell her everything she wanted to hear, as long as she listened. She favoured Stefan, but a cub could dream, he supposed. Besides, another female preoccupied Stefan tonight.

"What did Erroh learn?" she asked, playing with her hair absently. Her eyes were narrowed, watching Stefan and Lexi as the last note was played. Tye knew this was no dance. Many people did.

Those with eager eyes.

Lexi was untouchable in the city. Magnus's line had seen to that. It would take more than a few hushed words to dare challenge her honour, but Stefan was something else entirely. Almost everyone vilified him this side of the great wall. Everyone suspected he passed words between the city and the pariahs responsible for the assassination and the prison escape after. Some even suggested he had been the second person to aid Lea that night. That he was from Keri didn't help, either.

Few Samarans had liked anybody from Keri since the riots. Beatings and lynchings had become commonplace for those wretches, as if they hadn't seen enough horrors already.

Tye shrugged to himself and snapped out of his daze. *Fuk them.* It wasn't his problem.

"He showed him the finer merits of two blades," Tye whispered, but Stefan was sauntering back to the table and her eyes were locked upon him.

———

Aurora learned a great deal about Spark City. She learned of the growing tension with the Primary-in-waiting, Roja. They called her the bitch of the city. Some hinted at a coup. Uden favoured Roja leading the city, though Aurora never knew why. If matters were afoot, he might not be best pleased with different leadership.

It hadn't taken more than a few days of accusatory glances and curses to lead her to the smoky, unwelcoming tavern called The Pig in the Hole to seek the daughter of the legendary Magnus, or else the wretched, broken mayor from the little dead down of Keri.

The girl was tough, pretty enough and sure of herself. She carried herself with cautious dignity, and Ealis swiftly gathered that simply charming friendship from her would take a lifetime. To gather any *useful* information from this girl would have required many slices with her blade and perhaps even the severing of a limb. Such a task would not please her god. When Uden came for the false god, he would be furious to know that Erroh's ire would not be directed solely at him. Especially after the care he'd taken with those thoughtful gifts. So, she allowed Lexi to live and felt fine about it. It would be worth a little dying tearing Erroh apart, but not at all worth it for an insignificant child.

Nobody would miss Stefan, though. Following him had convinced her as much. She knew of his disappearances into the Arth some nights, away from the safety of the city, and of how he would return a few days later to resume his life of misery in this stunning sanctuary.

Just who paid for the drinks?

The wiser tactic would have been to follow in silence as she had for Lexi, but he offered a different type of game and Aurora did like to enjoy herself. So, when she could take no more silent observing, she had presented herself in all her glory and taken a seat opposite him in a little smoky tavern and flashed her warmest smile and fluttered her perfect eyes. He'd looked up from his bubbling ale uninterestingly and not returned the gesture.

"I'm waiting for someone," he had mumbled. She wasn't used to this lack of attention at all. It was fantastic. She liked him already and decided her knife was probably the way forward. She removed her cloak and slung it behind her chair.

She felt less restricted in just her leather. He didn't appear to care. This was no problem.

"Can I wait too?" Ealis had asked, running her finger along an old dent in the wooden table that separated them. There were plenty of seats this close to the flames in the middle of a fine hunt, where irregular occurrences were welcome and words were counted a little less.

21

WORDS BETWEEN KILLERS

L illium's steps were near silent. Nothing more than a few crackling leaves rustled underfoot as she glided through the dark forest. She felt at ease in the silent green nothing. *Hunting.* There was little test to her skills tonight; she knew where he'd be. He always chose the same spot: on a quiet, secluded, moss-covered rock, overlooking the scene of devastation.

Same old, predictable Wynn.

There were plenty more nights to mope. Tonight belonged to the new Master General. And to Wynn as well.

She stole in close to him. Close enough that she could reach out and touch his arm through the low-hanging branches. Though she would not. If he noticed her, he showed nothing, and she wondered if he was already drunk. She caught the smell of her own perfume in the wind and rolled her eyes. If he couldn't hear her, he should smell her. Usually, she had no time for perfumes and paint, but tonight, she honoured Erroh.

She watched him, the thrill of her concealment overcoming her need to disturb. She could see his face in the moonlight. His eyes looked hollow against his pale skin. The only signs were the laboured blinks of his eyes, which were youthful and aged in the same moment. He was on the rock, but truly, he was in battle, killing for the first time. Some people struggled. Some never woke from the nightmare. Others became quiet in their very essence. Some became less than that. She knew this because Magnus had told her as he'd held her after her first victim.

Killer.

And how was she coming to terms with her own sins? She was doing just fine.

Glorious killer.

She stepped from the treeline and waited. Perhaps their last kiss had taken some of his instincts. Perhaps he thought himself half a man. Perhaps bedding another woman would return something to him, like outlandish pride and youthful arrogance. Things she'd found most attractive about him once. Sometimes the girl liked a sturdy, assured man. Even if she could take him in a fight. Lillium *could* take him in a fight.

Perhaps, in becoming Erroh's first general, his nerve would return. That would be nice.

For the war effort.

"I don't feel as dizzy when I stare at the body anymore," he said. His voice was low, even in the surrounding silence. His gaze rested upon the battlefield where the Hunt had been slaughtered mercilessly in one terrifying drive.

That gift of a day.

Somewhere out among the debris of shields, blades, arrows and limbs was a broken young brute from the south, slowly decomposing back into the earth. Oh, if she could have coaxed the carrion birds to task, she would have. He looked at that body now as if it could forgive him, somehow.

He's dead, Wynn. Let it go.

She rolled her eyes but concealed her irritation. "That's fine progress," she whispered.

"Maybe it's just the dark that makes it easier."

He didn't like the dark anymore? Well, she could relate. Bad things happened in the dark. He carried no goblet or mug in his hands, though she could smell the alcohol from him. Courage for visiting the body, she thought. Whatever his reasons, he had left the gathering when he was needed most. It was time to raise a toast to the new Master General.

The silence from the camp of wounded Wolves was deafening. She wondered how long it would take for one too many celebratory ales to be drained and the true resentment of Erroh to rear its terrible head. There was blood in the air tonight, and Wynn was wasting his responsibilities, enduring needless issues.

Tonight, you stand. Tomorrow you can brood.

They would need numbers this night. Swords as well. She had a bow and all. "Maybe you're coming to terms with murder. This would be good."

She cursed herself for her choice of words. That was her own guilt spilling over, she supposed. She'd never known her first victim's name. She never would. Nor would she care. He had been the lowest type of scum; he'd deserved to die, but it was still murder. She was a murderer and she would not hide from it.

I am Alpha.

She could see an argument forming in his demeanour. His hunched shoulders. His irritated scowl. He was waiting for her to say the wrong thing. He wrapped his long cloak around him and shuddered against a phantom cold. The night was clear and fresh, with little chance of a cutting breeze. He did not want her here.

"Erroh is looking for you," she said, and rolled her eyes again as he shrugged. Somehow, he took her alliance to Erroh personally. *Of course he does.*

She caught sight of his jaw in the moonlight and was reminded of his beauty. Skilled, young and attractive. And capable of murder. There were worse choices for a mate. There were better ones, too. And sometimes, one had no choice. Even in a Cull.

"Erroh is a good friend. However, his winning will lead us astray." He faced her for the first time, his anger covering his grief. "Do you regret the choice you made, dooming this resistance?"

She almost struck out at him. He didn't know what she had endured during the riots; it was the only thing that forgave such temerity. He'd never know her anguish while she'd stood with Erroh against Magnus. Nor would she ever tell him. He had no right to know. She loved Magnus dearly and trusted him unreservedly. Speaking with him after the defeat had been one of the hardest things she'd ever done. Receiving his forgiveness was a debt she could never repay.

"I faced Magnus. I explained my part. It was a small matter." It wasn't. He didn't need to know that.

"Brave girl," he hissed.

"Watch your fuken mouth, Wynn. You aren't the second-in-command yet." She stepped forward challengingly. It was instinct, and probably the last time duty would allow. "I don't regret any of my choices, nor who I stood with. Nor will I hide out here in the dark looking at decaying corpses. They're dead. Everything dies. Live with it." In her anger, a little droplet of spittle hit his face. He wiped it away in disgust.

"Erroh should not be leading us. He is unprepared for such a position. You know this as I do. We need experience to get us through this war alive." It was a safe argument and one she disagreed with. It wasn't Magnus; the Wolves had followed him into war without a moment's hesitation. Even set alight, with arrows embedded in him, he had continued on single-mindedly. That was the leadership this war needed.

Poor, idealistic Wynn.

She cupped his face in her hands and looked at him. "I don't want to die, my lover, but do you believe we will live through the days ahead?" She laughed, and it felt wonderful to reveal her agony, her grimness, her liberating acceptance. "That's not our fate, nor will it ever be. We're here to kill them all, Wynn." She almost placed her forehead against his so that he might understand her passion. "And we will kill them all. Until we die at their hands." He pulled away, but she would not relent. Sometimes a little cub could hang out around a rock. Sometimes they needed the truth. "Why not ask Magnus who he believes should lead?" she said.

"Why don't you fuk right off?"

"Why not ask him of his strategy? Of his hopes for success?" He stared at her as though she had lost her mind this terrible day. She wanted to tell him she'd lost it the night the city fell. And when she'd found it again, it was beaten and changed. "Did you not listen to Erroh's accounts from the south? Did you not listen to his accounts of Keri? Magnus knows we can't win. He knows every one of us is doomed."

"Shut up, Lillium," he cried, and he was pathetic, and she saw the terror in his face. His mind was younger than his age. He'd slept in silk sheets all his life. He struggled in the mud where rocks made suitable head-rests. He was too raw for the unfairness of life. Of the world. But it wasn't too late to tear those silken sheets apart and weave them into a rope so he could pull himself free. Or else a noose.

"I love Magnus because, knowing this, he still fights. So that's all we can do now, my little, lost Wynn." He shook his head; his hand became a fist. She liked the fight in him. If he struck her now, well, their bond couldn't be any more shattered than it already was. A fine bout of fists might serve them both. "We form up around Erroh, Wynn. We tear into the fukers for as long as we can. So, rouse yourself, and speak with him," she said again, and this time he finally understood the prominent position he was to be elevated to. They were friends, but more than that, they were comrades, and Erroh would need Wynn's effort. He nodded and said nothing more. "You would have led the Rangers well; you will lead this Outcast army well."

People only remembered the heroes of tales, and a first general was a thankless role. That said, Lillium understood its importance just fine. There was no voice louder than the first general's. Were she not so angry with Wynn, she might have enjoyed the pride she felt for him. He would grow into the part, just as she had grown into a soldier.

"Let's return now before celebrations take a turn, Wynn."

Wynn shrugged and turned back to look out at the body in the darkness as though it might climb to its feet without his watch. "I'll be along in a while," he whispered, and she knew it as a lie.

22

THE DEADLIEST GIRL IN THE WORLD

A t the centre of the gathering Lea sat alone, and she was perfectly happy about it. With only a little fire and a tapped barrel of alcohol to keep her company, she rested with crossed knees, appearing as relaxed as any Master General's mate could be. She placed the last of her bread over the crackling flames and watched in satisfaction as it burned away to a crisp. She was quite happy to sit by her fire and eat all of the bread until the night had passed. Knowing there were drinks to be consumed gave her the excuse to overindulge. She'd learned a long time ago in Keri that an empty stomach and a tense gathering were more than enough to make for interesting times.

Her eyes never left two deadly brutes a few feet away, drinking to the unfortunate health of herself and her mate. She was queen, but he was the target. After the king fell, well, they'd come for her. However, she would stand beside the king… and… he would not fall… because…*Wait? What?* She looked at her mug. How much had she drunk? *Who cares? I'm royalty now.*

"To a court of doomed cutthroats," she whispered to the fire. "To Magnus and Elise, too," she added, dribbling some sine over the flames. Erroh had dethroned a legend and now stood to inherit the title. And she would be the new Elise.

No problem.

And Nomi?

Fuk her.

"A paid debt," she whispered, and thought fondly on this. She caught sight of the calluses on her hand and frowned. She had risen to elite status in warfare, and she had no one left to tell. She wondered would her father have cared. Probably not. She tried to imagine him smiling, but his face was lost to her. Her mother's was easier to recall. She wondered did she even care anymore. What would her nervous dead mother, all burnt to ash, think of her now? She had once been little Lea of Spark City, scrambling among the lowest rungs in a ladder of entitlements, perfectly destined for very little. Now she walked through the wastes with resolute steps, hand in hand with her true love, challenging the entire world to a fight and fancying her chances.

How far she had come.

How far she still had to walk.

She thought of running through the snow, weeping in terror. Of burning houses and a wild brute's devilish green eyes. She thought of kindness, and she thought of the dark. She looked at the scar on her hand from her homestead and spat into the fire.

I am Queen, now.

She lifted the goblet to her lips and drank heartily. If no one was going to celebrate her mate's rise to power, then she would. And she would do it grandly. She might even offer a drink to the southern whore. Maybe little Nomi would drown in her generosity. She felt her mood turning and fought it. *Fuk you, Nomi.* She allowed herself to hate Nomi for a few breaths more. She was free; it was the right thing to do. Hopefully she'd fuk off away from Erroh. That would be nice. Some sine spilled down her blouse, and rage nearly overcame her.

Fuk you, glass.

Nomi played the part of the helpless damsel spectacularly well. Neither Lea nor Erroh could afford such a luxury. *Not anymore.* There was nothing wrong with being helpless, but not bothering to try was pathetic. There came a moment when everyone needed to tighten their boots for the coming storm. No exceptions.

Sometimes, she worried for Nomi gasping pathetically in the cold air, fighting tears of frustration. Sometimes, she warmed to her pathetic gratitude when Lea offered her nothing more than a hot beverage and another dry blanket. Sometimes she lamented the torments Nomi had faced in the long march north.

Sometimes.

Today she hated the witch from the south.

———

"I decided to join this fine gathering, boisterous as it is," muttered Emir from behind her. Sitting down, he stole the bread from the flames as though he were a starving hound pilfering a bone from a master's plate. She didn't want it anymore, but she still glared at him. He smiled away, oblivious to the threat, and her glare softened. "This will keep me going for another dozen rounds."

"You drink too much," she said, though not unkindly. He

could do anything he wanted in this camp. His value was too great, sober or inebriated. In fact, many argued the alcohol seemed to hone his skills at healing that little bit more. There were two other camp healers; there might as well have been ten, and still they wouldn't come close to the miracles he performed.

"I'm no drunkard. I'm just superb at drinking."

He eyed the other goblet she'd poured in anticipation of Erroh's return. She ignored him, but he kept staring until eventually his silent charm weakened her resolve. Slowly, she slid the goblet across the barrel in his direction. It was a gesture of forgiveness, and they both knew it. She knew his shame, and if Erroh was quick in forgiving him, well, she could be, too.

"Keep practicing," she said as he drank, and she wondered how he kept hold of his mind, when everything good he'd ever known had been torn brutally from his grasp. His soul had taken more punishment than she could fathom. Perhaps his soul was depthless. Perhaps he really didn't drink enough. She had known him before life had taken its horrific grip on him, and she knew him now, when he could barely keep afloat. Few saw him as he really was. *Apart from Aireys.* She'd seen his greatness. She'd loved him for it, though it had taken her a lifetime to act on it. Roja had seen it too.

Aireys had betrayed him by dying in Keri. And Roja? Well, her justified betrayal was something else entirely.

"This is a shit gathering. Nobody has beaten me up yet," he shouted, as if challenging the world. He was always challenging the world. So was Lea, but she kept that to herself and she kept herself quiet as she did. Easier to succeed when everyone gazed at your prominent mate, anyway. This was how she'd always preferred things. Little Lea of the city, rising up, above it all. She laughed despite herself. Emir was not much different to her in shunning impressiveness. But more than that, he was a welcome distraction from her bitter thoughts tonight. A distraction while waiting for chaos to erupt.

"I promise, I'll take a swing at you later, Emir," she said, allowing herself to calm. This felt like no Rangers' party. Yet here they were, the toast of the hour.

"Better you than those two fukers over there. Up to no good, I'm telling you." He watched Aymon and Doran as she had. They were in muted conversation, surrounded by their bonded comrades.

"Shouldn't you be monitoring our liberated sister?" she asked, keeping her voice low lest vengeful, eager ears might hear. Nomi would be a suitable scapegoat should the mood in the camp worsen.

Emir hopped up and stood next to a table of Wolves. "I should be, but these Wolf fuks won't do anything," he said, stealing an unguarded chunk of meat from an unsuspecting Wolf. The victim in this horrific attack merely growled to himself, waved the healer away and continued with his quiet revelry, albeit a little hungrier. Nobody wanted to fuk with the healer. "These nice brutes stood when the battle was lost. They have honour beneath the hatred. When I thought on the matter a little more, it occurred to me that had they aimed to hurt her, they would have already." He looked at the table of Wolves. To the table beyond. To all of them around. His complimentary words might as well have been a pledge on their behalf. There was truth to them. Many a time she'd seen a chained hound growling and snapping at another, only to lessen their aggression once the chains were removed. Sometimes it was about the barking.

"You ran out of alcohol, didn't you?" she whispered.

"I did," he said, sitting down near the barrel.

"Looking for a fight?"

"I really am."

From the darkness, Lillium emerged from the trees empty-handed and Lea's head dropped. It would have been better if they had spoken about the first general. From Lillium's mouth, Lea knew Wynn struggled with taking a life. With her own eyes, Lea saw his disappointment in Erroh's promotion.

Toughen up.

She caught sight of Doran staring at Lillium as she walked, and she smirked. She still remembered his desperate attempts at charming Lillium in the last gathering. Lillium, despite her nastiness, had not cut short his willingness and instead had humoured him longer than needed.

Truthfully, when he wasn't attacking Erroh, Doran had a quick sense of humour. Such things mattered in war. Lillium glanced his way, and he immediately dropped his eyes and laughed at some jest another had made, as though he hadn't noticed her. It was a skilled manoeuvre, one he'd no doubt used before when unable to strike up a conversation with a pretty young girl. Lillium continued walking on obliviously, and Lea shook her head.

Never look away first.

At that very moment, Erroh emerged from his father's tent with the great man in tow. Erroh marched forward proudly, his shadow catching the flames behind him and casting a great shadow forward. This was a fine sight indeed, thought Lea, and gestured for her king to join them.

"So, Wynn couldn't make it?" Erroh asked, and Lillium hesitated for an embarrassed moment before shaking her head.

"He'll be along soon enough. He said he would," she

offered, though the words sounded hollow. When the new Master General called, it was wise to reply with haste.

"It's a small matter," Lea said after a moment. Such conversations could be had another time.

"So, what now?" Lillium asked, and Lea felt nervous stirrings in her stomach that reminded her of the quiet before battle. The surrounding silence had become contagious, and slowly the rest of the camp fell to a hush. Jokes and stories petered out, and the world held its breath. They were all here, and they were waiting for Erroh to address them. Was this a new beginning? Or the end of the city's chances of holding the line? They were paltry numbers, but significant resistances often began with a trickle down a mountainside. Although sometimes there was just a steep fall.

Lea edged closer to her mate. Not for comfort or support, though. If there was a fight, she would be near him. This was an oath she was becoming better at keeping.

"I think you should say something impressive to your new army," whispered Magnus, gripping his son's shoulder. Taking a stand beside his vanquisher was a fine show of support, even if he himself was supported by two long oaken crutches.

"I suppose so," Erroh muttered, glancing at Lea. She tapped the grip on her sword ostentatiously. He would step into the Wolves' den alone, but if they showed teeth, he wouldn't be alone for very long. Lea passed her half-full goblet to her father-in-law, who took it gladly with a bow. There were no apologies needed within family. Sometimes all it took was a gesture of generosity.

"We have his back," whispered Lillium to Lea, pushing her best friend playfully. She was relaxed, but her eyes burned with fire. She was ashamed of Wynn. Though her hands were clear of him, some bonds just couldn't be severed cleanly.

"Especially me," agreed Emir, who lay on his back beside the fire, drinking flawlessly from his mug as though it were a skill he'd practiced all his life. "Let us hope for the benefit of this gathering that he minces his words."

23

MASTER GENERAL'S GAMBIT

Erroh's footsteps felt like the loudest sound in the camp, such was the silence surrounding him. War was in the wind. So was diplomacy. He wondered, was this his life now? He understood the traumas of a political life, and he thought of nothing worse than having to manoeuvre between factions, keeping his wits, surrendering his beliefs for amicable solutions. Some found little issue with such things as long as pieces lined their pocket. To Erroh, though, it was an affront to the natural way of things. It was a bitter thing needing to apologise for rising to power, yet here he was.

They did not cajole him nor mutter unsavoury things under their breaths. They knew their place, for now. They were his subjects, nervous and reeling and ready to be led. Until they made an inevitable play for his seat. They did not stand as he approached. Merely dropping their meat and ale was all the respect they would offer. It was a start. Every Wolf watched their actions intently. For this short walk, though, he was king. He was also usurper.

Take the throne; I only wanted the girl.

He dared not look back at Lea a second time. She was his

strength, and without her, he was nothing. When fires burned around him, there was no one he would prefer beside him, and she *would* be beside him.

Always.

He stopped at their table and inhaled deeply. He thought about the art of cards and mastering a weak hand. And also playing a strong hand. The difference was all in the mind. Erroh was happy playing a weak hand. The longer a player remained, the more certain it was that the bets and the deals would eventually come his way. These fukers looked like they had more calls to make.

"We need to have words," he hissed. The steel in his voice was thinly disguised. If they'd seen the nervousness in his walk, they heard nothing in his words. Doran gestured with his ruined hand to a place at their table.

Sit with us, little Master General. Speak your worries to your loyal warriors.

It was a tempting offer.

Aymon did not stir. He stared intently and made no offer of hospitality. It was a good, menacing look for him. They'd need that hardness.

"Some words should be best spoken away from such boisterous celebrations," Erroh quipped.

No, thanks. We'll talk on less hostile ground.

Doran chuckled, but Aymon was unimpressed with wit. "Take a seat. Our brethren can enjoy their merriment out of earshot." He was not ready to surrender anything to the new Master General. A bad omen.

"I will not have so many fine warriors unseated for such a trivial matter as a few quiet words," he countered loudly for all to hear. They had thrown the gauntlet down, and it did not intimidate Erroh. There was a knack to this political battle of wits. It involved smooth, silver-tongued compliments. Pledges of unlikely things and gifts. Aye, plenty of gifts.

He leaned in close enough that few could hear, his eyes unblinking, his hushed tones firm. "Walk with me, now."

A few moments passed, and Doran rose first. He grinned as though it were all in jest and he were merely playing along, but he'd faced Erroh at his finest and his worst. He knew the measure of his opponent. "Sure, if I had taken a beating like you did, walking would help ease the pain alright," he said, and a few Wolves laughed. "As you wish, sir," he added, stepping up from the table. Strangely, even though he held that grin, he sounded almost courteous.

Aymon shifted in his seat before he, too, stood up and towered over the cub. He ground his teeth in resentment and Erroh smiled. It was all he could do. Both Wolves reached for their weapons and strapped them on their backs.

"You will not need them," said Erroh, gesturing to his own lack of weapons. Probably not the best idea to be without a weapon this night, but safer than tempting heated words to become more.

"A Ranger asking us to a quiet place without weapons? Oh, I think they're needed."

I'm not technically a Ranger.

It was a fair point, and he ignored the feeling of dread as he led them away from the security of Magnus's gaze into the darkness. Some words needed no listeners; a tarp's privacy was not trustworthy.

It was a simple walk down a well-beaten path, towards a little stream in the middle of a small, open dale, hidden from everyone in the deep green. A tranquil place, away from the movement of many. He needed to be honest, and he needed them to understand, and he really fuken needed them to prove his father right.

They faced each other in the dim glow of the moonlight, as if they were clandestine fiends planning a great revolution to better all of humankind. Three youthful males, terrified for their lives, searching for any escape from the desperate times they found themselves in.

Erroh kept his hands behind his back. It was the most confident gesture he could manage while they stared right through him. Erroh spoke first, and they had the excellent sense to listen.

"The Wolves are yours to command," he said quietly. It was a strong opening move and, from their surprised expressions, the correct one as well. "These men will follow you without question."

"What do you mean, ours to command?" Aymon said suspiciously, crossing his arms like a man who'd never received a gift in his life.

"So, we go to war, while you disappear off into history with your southern concubine?" Doran said. His tone was less respectful than before. "Typical Keri coward." Now his tone was downright nasty.

"You really think I would flee?" hissed Erroh, his anger at the taunt overcoming him. He stepped forward challengingly, like a beast ready to pounce. It was instinct. He didn't expect both men to take a step back as they followed instincts of their own.

Interesting.

"I think you should explain your words," growled Aymon. Aye, he'd taken a step back, but if there was a melee, he would put up a fight. *Good.* Erroh was counting on this. Erroh was no politician at all, but this really was like cards. He knew what to bet when playing a strong hand. Or when a weak hand was played with a weaker bet. Or when Lea made a weak bet after showing her weak hand to the entire table. Or when a brute just went and slammed a massive sword down on the entire table.

"These broken Wolves need leaders capable of turning them into something more," he said, still watching their every gesture. "You can turn them into something great." That was it. That was all he had planned. Simple. It really needed to work.

They said nothing for a few moments, as though choosing their bet, deciding whether to fold or possibly cheat. He had given them more than they'd have expected. A shrewd player would want the cards revealed.

"What would you have us do?" asked Aymon finally.

"Train them as your masters trained you."

"They are not Alphas," said Doran, but he looked intrigued. He rubbed his ruined hand as he spoke. "We are no masters, either."

"There is no time for instruction," hissed Aymon. This too was a fair point. There was no time left at all.

Despite their misgivings, they had not yet folded. Erroh softened, for his words were truthful and cutting. "We do not fight for Spark City anymore. What becomes of Samara is down to the cowering army behind her walls. Perhaps she will hold. Perhaps she will beat them back. Perhaps she will burn to the ground. Fuk it, perhaps she will broker a peace. Regardless, it will not be our fight, brothers. The moment you stood as they fled, your pledge to the city ended. We few are Outcasts."

"Some more than others," Doran added.

"Aye, that is true. You have expert knowledge to impart to these men. They could be a fierce unit of wild killers," he said.

"Why not you?" asked Aymon.

"They will not follow me like they would you. At least not yet," Erroh said.

"What will become of you?" Aymon asked, and Doran nodded.

It was probably time to reveal some of his thoughts, few as they were. "I think it best that I and a few of the city's most reviled citizens slip away from Samara's gaze."

They both nodded in agreement. It was the first time all three had agreed on any matter.

I'd make a wonderful king.

"You *will* answer to me. You will keep truthful your actions. When we turn to fight, you will march with me." He stepped forward, grabbing them both by a shoulder. "I have met both of you in combat but never attained victory. For this, you have my complete respect. We might never be friends. That does not mean we cannot be comrades. I offer you my leadership and I offer you a place at my war council, for the time to take up arms and shed blood is upon us all. You and the Wolves will be an instrument of death. You will have a say in the days ahead. Your eyes will be on my strategy. Your voices will be as loud as Wynn's. This I pledge to you as brothers of conflict. I give you the opportunity to build an elite unit, vicious enough to take the fight to the Hunt. You herded them into battle twice and they followed you. They are hardened and skilled as it is. Imagine the mayhem you can achieve with a little time to sharpen them like blades." It was a good speech and Doran grinned, liking the thoughts of mayhem.

"And you will hide and wait in the meantime?" Aymon asked quietly. There was no malice like before. He appreciated what he was hearing.

Erroh shook his head and then looked around at the tall trees surrounding them. He would not hide and wait for the

Hunt. "They have dared to invade our lands, and now many of them walk freely, as if there can be no reckoning for such a deed."

His eyes narrowed to slits, and the full loathing for his captors rose to the surface. He did not scream his hatred for them, though. Instead, his voice took on an unnaturally bitter tone. "I aim to give them something to regret," the Master General said. It didn't matter that he barely had a plan of action.

"All very silver-tongued, and all, but tell me, what happens if we turn our backs on such a fancy notion?" Aymon asked, but his voice lacked the threat of his words. If he was betting, it was a weak offer. The cards were already on show. Erroh could also see the fear in his eyes. It matched his own. They were all just young little cubs thrust into a violent world. They had grabbed onto Magnus for leadership when all had seemed lost. Now, they would do the same with Erroh. Magnus had shown little fear, so they had believed. They hated Magnus, but they would have followed. They also wanted to believe in Erroh.

"If you would not accept my rank, I would probably have to kill you both before you staged a coup, though I would be fuked trying to find better warriors than you for the task." He shrugged his shoulders and knew he sounded terrifying.

"Aye, probably," agreed Aymon lightly.

"You have my fealty, Master General sir," said Doran quietly, and dropped to his knee.

"We will train them, sir," agreed Aymon, dropping to his knee at the same moment.

"No. You will never kneel in my presence, comrades," Erroh said, taking both their hands and pulling them to their feet. Strangely, Aymon bowed and Doran shook Erroh's shoulder as though they had been friends for a decade.

"Drinks are on me, Hero of Keri," Doran said. He laughed and marched off into the darkness.

Aymon remained a moment longer. "Tell me this, Erroh. Do you believe in all the antiquated rules of the city?" Erroh knew what he referred to; it was a strange thing for Aymon to bring up.

"I think love is love," he said, and Aymon nodded. That seemed to please him, and he walked away towards the party.

———

After the two men had gone, Erroh sat down over the stream to clear his head and calm his beating heart. He only needed a moment to settle himself. So much had happened this day; the night was young. He heard a delicate rustle in the trees nearby but did not stir. He already knew who it would be. "I wanted to be alone to speak with them," he said loudly, dipping his feet into the freezing water.

"I know," said Lea, breaking through the branches. The need for stealth had passed. She set Baby aside and sat down beside him as her accomplice broke through the undergrowth behind her.

"It wasn't my idea," she argued, nodding to a guilty-looking Lillium.

"Some of us weren't convinced of the better intentions of those two," she said, placing an arrow back in its quiver. "So… you gave them the Wolves… Didn't even think about giving them to me?" she mocked, though her attention was drawn back to the camp. There was growing noise and the sound of arguments. Apparently, word of Aymon and Doran's acquiescence to the new Master General was not going down well. Or else Emir was attempting to start the party all by himself. Either way, Erroh didn't want to think about it.

"I gave them what they wanted. That type of love can be harnessed for violent things."

One primal roar rose above all the rest. It was the sound of a legend.

"I think it's time to leave," said Lea, climbing to her feet, but Erroh was already up and running. Something in that scream was recognisable. Something terrible had happened. He thought about his mother.

He thought about Lexi.

24

THE TOURIST

Ealis smiled and played with her drink as adorably as she could. This turned out to be quite adorable indeed. Her hands shook as if she were nervous, and her eyes fluttered alluringly. She was putting on quite the display for her stubborn mark—and he *was* being incredibly stubborn. It was a small matter; he would reveal the location of the false god eventually. Ealis would earn his trust. Aurora would reap the reward.

"I am new to the city," she said, tapping her glass delicately. It was a fine alcohol. Clear and bitter, like fire going down her throat. This brew was the city's lifeblood—another useful thing she'd learned while skipping through the cobblestone streets pickpocketing fortunes, forgetting to count her steps. She loved Spark; she preferred the chase.

"I am too," Stefan countered indifferently. He looked around the crowded inn. The band had not taken the stage. Once they did, the mood inside would rise. She'd seen it happen every night she was here. The pretty blonde innkeeper was busy lighting the candles in each room corner, and she found them pleasing. The little glass bulbs of sparking daylight hanging throughout the room unsettled her ever so, but candles were just fine.

"It's the most beautiful place I've ever seen," she said, watching her mark. Always learning. Always adapting to his mood. She liked the art of silent language. The body told many stories different to the words that were spoken. This one wore his emotion openly. It was almost something to cherish, to welcome.

"You need to see more of the world."

"Would you show me?" she cooed, leaning across to stroke his hand gently. He didn't flinch away from her touch. This was something to work with. His slightly clenched teeth suggested indifference.

Interesting.

"I'm sure you would have little difficulty finding yourself company," he said, pulling his wrist away gently.

"Oh," she replied meekly. She studied his movements, his facial expressions, listened to his very essence and ever so slowly figured him out. She loved this part of the game. She loved to test the waters and see which of her behaviours sank, floated or skimmed eternally.

He's not Alder.

He's different.

Stefan was prettier than most. She liked pretty little things, and sometimes she liked to rip apart pretty little things. It made them prettier. He tried to hide his pain behind indifference, but he might as well have screamed it. His long blond hair was dishevelled and knotted. She was certain she could see a twig entwined within those locks. His chin was covered in stubble, with uneven tufts from a careless razor. His worn clothes were faded, and he smelled of the city. He probably had a pleasant smile under all that sorrow, even with

the gap in his teeth. A girl could tell these things. She pledged
to see him smile just once, before she slit his throat.

No, not the throat.

She would cut his heart out. Yes. That was something to
look forward to. "Your friend is late," she said, avoiding
another silent moment before they became too comfortable.
He replied with a shrug and a sip of his ale. Somewhere in
between he sighed, and she frowned. He was trickier than
most. Searching for words to cut through his shield, Aurora
counted the cracks in the old wooden table they shared. There
were a great many to count. It would be a fine waste of her
time. Ealis swiftly drew her eyes away from reassuring
things.

And then he changed completely. He looked past Ealis,
and for a moment, a flood of wretched misery overcame him.

Aurora did not glance behind her to understand what had
brought such emotion to the surface. Instead, she studied his
distress and learned what she could in a breath of time.
Without warning, he calmed, and Aurora saw this as a
deceptive veneer. Suddenly, a stunning blonde appeared at
their table. Stefan tried, blessings upon his broken heart, to
hide his feelings even more with the Alpha female present,
and Ealis almost reached for his hand.

"Hello, my dear Stefan," the newcomer said, and Aurora
did not like that tone at all. She never trusted blondes.
Especially when they smiled. There were likely better first
meetings to happen in the Arth.

Stefan said nothing. His words caught in his throat, and
Aurora fought the urge to comfort him again and to grab that
blonde bitch by the head and slam it off the table, just once.

"Who is this strange-looking creature?" Bitch asked.
Aurora thought again about slamming her head off the table a

couple of times. Blonde and blood were a wonderful combination. She knew this from her birth.

"My name is Ealis," Ealis said, bowing as though this Alpha female from the City of Light was a thing to respect. Truthfully, though, she was a beauty. Her eyes were alive with wretchedness. Her smile was as real as her unnaturally painted lips. Stefan must have adored her. Ealis had a bigger obstacle to overcome than she first thought. The Alpha resonated power, and Aurora played her submissive part perfectly. She hadn't killed an Alpha in quite some time.

"I don't really care," she whispered.

Aurora wondered would crimson sit well on such a flawless white dress. *No, you strangle a bitch like that.* The blonde reached out and gently tugged the black strands of Aurora's long black hair as if toying with a plaything.

"You have strange eyes," muttered the bitch. and pushed Ealis's hair behind her ears to take a closer look.

Strangle her and listen to her gasp.

The girl stared through her, and Aurora blinked as though facing the sun.

"Leave her alone, Silvia," growled Stefan, pushing her away.

My hero.

Interesting.

Silvia caught his wrist and pulled him across the table in one fluid motion before slamming his arm down against the surface. The two glasses of perfect clear alcohol and ale toppled and spilled all over Ealis, who squeaked in apparent fright. Silvia twisted Stefan's fingers until he yelped. "You never touch me again, you vile brute," she hissed, and Aurora watched with grim interest. Her sudden show of strength was impressive.

Suddenly, she released him and stepped away as if

nothing had happened. A few drops of delicious crimson escaped from his open bandaging onto the table. He pulled his ruined hand away and dropped it under the table as if its appearance disgusted him.

Injuries are beautiful.

"Leave him alone," whispered Aurora, fighting the urge to stroke his arm a third time in a feeble act of comfort. She found pleasure in the spilling of blood and all manner of torture, but Silvia's actions were unnecessarily cruel. Any fool could see he was broken. What sport was in this?

When she produced her knife, she wouldn't be unnecessarily nasty. She would do what was needed. She would never humiliate him. It was war, and he would be a prisoner. It would be fine.

The river of alcohol continued to stream over the table's edge into the lap of Ealis. With his less ruined limb, Stefan tried to stem the flow. His sleeve made a dull scraping, sloshing sound that was as pitiful as he was. He looked as though he would shed tears, such was his humiliation.

Aurora wasn't sure why she took Silvia's cruelty so personally. She pledged that before Stefan died, she would tell him of her plans to remove Silvia's heart as well. *Just because.* Maybe she could hold them side by side. See which one was more misshapen. See if they fitted perfectly together. *Oh yes.* Aurora was looking forward to meeting Silvia alone sometime.

"Pathetic," sneered Silvia. She turned to leave, but stopped in her tracks.

Two women, unlikely allies, stood behind her. Their entrance into the tavern had been completely unnoticed. One female was dressed in gold and white, and the other wore a matching dress of blue and black. Ealis thought the gold and white to be the nicer outfit, though they wore them well.

Ealis recognised Alexis immediately. She knew quite a lot about the girl. She even knew that she only liked to be called Lexi. She did not recognise her companion, though. It was a small matter. Ealis's eyes were upon the young girl. She emanated power, just as Ealis imagined her older brother would, and this was most pleasing. As was the chance of speaking to her face to face in a dimly-lit tavern as opposed to merely stalking her in the bright sunshine.

She looked like she wanted a fight.

"What's your fuken problem?" Lexi hissed.

Aurora caught sight of the young tavern keeper watching with wary eyes. She'd just finished pouring a glass of sine for a willing patron, but before he could reach for it, she snatched it back and downed it in one. After a moment, she slid a fresh glass across to him. Her eyes never left Lexi or Silvia. Tavern keepers could sense a storm rising like a beast out in the Arth.

Out in the wastes.

"Watch yourself, little one," Silvia said slowly, before offering the younger girl a dazzling smile. "Say hello to your brother for me," she added before spinning away from the table, and Aurora's heart skipped a beat ever so.

"Someone needs to knock that bitch out," said Lexi, loud enough that everybody in the tavern heard. Including Silvia, who hesitated momentarily at the door. "Maybe break a fuken bone or two, while they're at it." She sat down in an empty chair against the wall and glared at Ealis.

Aurora really didn't like that glare, not one little bit. "Do I know you?" The girl's eyes were slits of concentration. Aurora knew she was a skilled hunter, but even in a crowd, a false god's kin might have sharper senses. She thought about lying. Ealis took over. Ealis knew best.

"If you've walked the city in the last few days, I'm sure

you've seen me wandering around. It's so big. I keep getting lost… I'm sorry—Hello. I'm Ealis."

"Who the fuk is this?" Lexi growled as her companion sat down opposite her, completing the gathering at the table.

"Hello… Um… My name is Ealis."

"You are so rude, Lexi. Hello, Ealis. My name is Celeste," her companion said. She too was an Alphaline. Her dark brown hair was bushy, unkempt and wild. She had a plain face with sharp features; she hid her attractiveness well enough. *This girl thinks little of herself.*

"She and I were just having a quiet drink," Stefan mumbled, and Ealis desired to embrace him. There was nothing more striking than a fierce boy, brought to his knees by hardship. He was still shaking with shame and anger. Though it could have been pain. He wiped the last of the alcohol away as if it could somehow redeem him for being such a pathetic wretch, and he fascinated Aurora.

"I don't know her," warned Lexi. "I am not pleased with this, Stefan."

"If you have words, let's share words," he said, calling for another round of drinks. "The first thing to learn of Samara, Ealis, is knowing your fuken place when an Alphaline speaks."

"I'm so sorry. Do you want me to leave?" Ealis said. She almost whimpered, but that would have been too much. There was a cold grandeur to Lexi that wasn't to be tested. The type of girl who saw through the finest ruses.

For a terrible moment Aurora wondered if she shouldn't have simply taken a seat nearby instead of making a direct move on Stefan. How freely might words have reached her ears then?

No, this is more fun.

Stay the course.

She'd come to the right place after all. All those whispers and suggestions from suspicious citizens and treacherous Wolves had borne fruit. She allowed herself a smug smile and thought about a river of blood. Erroh's blood. Or else making a friend of him and delivering him to her true lover, when the time came. Such wonderful thoughts.

"I vouch for her," said Stefan.

"Oh, wonderful. Because vouching for someone has never gone wrong," Lexi countered, accepting the drink as it was placed in front of her.

25

TAKING FLIGHT

R oja knew this bitter taste in her mouth. She knew it far too well: the unbridled flavour of fear. Fear so rich it grasped and clawed at her chest and threatened to tear her apart as she gasped for air. Fear that caused her heart to hammer wildly out of time and scream in her ear to take flight and leave this city behind. This fear had whispered in her ears for weeks, but now it was given a full voice and she was almost ready to listen.

She couldn't breathe, yet still she ran up through the dimly-lit halls of the Alphaline's tower. Mea ran ahead of her. Despite being the elder of the two, she showed little sign of slowing. Perhaps it was the panic driving her forward. Dia would not have approved of running at this late hour, especially with this lack of grace and dignity.

Roja heard Mea curse under her breath, though it might have been a prayer to the gods. Any joy of escaping the chamber of the Cull was lost the moment the heavy door slammed behind them. His words still rang in her mind: "We've taken Elise."

They'd been fooled into believing this meeting was honourable.

We foolish wretches.

Roja should have known disaster loomed like a massive army, hardened with war, bent on their complete annihilation. Hindsight truly was a beautiful thing.

"Nearly there," hissed the older Alphaline, more to herself. She took the steps three at a time. Roja heard her dress rip as she took a leap of her own. Her legs felt liberated despite their heavy weight. At the top of the dark stairs, they could see the doorway and a flickering glow from a dying light. Someone had left the door open.

"No!" screamed Mea, eying the shattered panel along the arch where a perfectly solid door had once stood. It was almost too much to take.

Be strong for the next few moments.

Mea stumbled in the darkness and almost fell through the sanctuary's ruined doorway.

Roja followed, her chest tight from running, from terror. Only then did the true nightmare reveal itself. Clutching the still body of Lexi was little Linn. Huddled among fallen books and rubble, it was all she could do.

"Elise is gone," Mea gasped at the far end. "Oh no," she cried, only then seeing the ruin of Lexi and her weeping protector.

"I must see to her," Roja gasped, prying the girl's arms apart.

"No one came. They heard the screams," Linn whimpered.

"It's okay, little one. You did well."

"Silvia…"

"I know, little one."

Roja did not fall apart like she had when Dia was struck

down. Perhaps she was growing as a person. Gently, she moved the weeping child away from her first little sister and towards Mea. Mea's motherly instincts took hold; she fell to her knees beside Linn and embraced the young child.

"It'll be okay, little one. Roja and Mea are here now. Stop your crying," Mea whispered gently, stroking her hair. Her tone was serene, but her eyes were frantic and wild. She hugged the child and feared the worst. She too could see the pool of blood beneath the deathly still body.

"It's okay, my Lexi," whispered Roja, feeling for a pulse. Just to be certain. And then her eyes widened: the girl had a pulse, strong and steady. Roja felt around her head and touched the massive bump above her forehead. "She's just knocked out," she whispered, giddy with relief. Then she saw the young female's shattered elbow and her stomach turned. *No time for that*, she told herself. The weeks of walking with Emir through the hovels came back to her in a rush, and, tearing away a strip of fabric from her dress, she wrapped the wound until a proper healer could attend to the girl.

"It was Silvia. It was Silvia," whimpered Linn again, and Mea hugged her tightly.

"We know, little one. We know. You must tell no one," Mea whispered. And it was fine advice. Who knew what she might still do?

I'll kill that fucking bitch for this act.

Roja took hold of Lexi as Linn had, and wept for a few breaths. Then, she rocked the girl gently, for that is what any older sister of the city would do for one they cherished above all else.

"You need to wake," she said. The girl did not stir.

"You still need to tidy your room." This might as well have been a greeting between them.

"I'm sick of you stealing my booze." She smiled as she said this.

"Stop beating up the boys or they'll never want your attention." That line always provoked a reaction.

"Wait until Magnus hears about you and Celeste smoking that weed in the alley." That threat she would not fear, alas. Roja would never tell on her.

"You need to wake up right now, or I'll kill you." That threat she meant.

The girl stirred and grimaced, hearing a familiar voice, but she did not wake. It was a small matter. What mattered was getting her out of the city.

Mea released Linn and wiped the tears away from her cheeks. She placed her hands on the child and spoke as if giving an order to a recruit.

"Go to Lexi's room and fill a sack with some of her clothes and anything she holds dear, including her journal… Make sure you bring her journal."

She released the child and smiled at Linn's nod of understanding. The child must have learned the art of fleeing from homes already.

"Be swift," Roja said, as the child, grateful for distraction and action too, darted away into the darkness.

Mea knelt down beside Roja. "You and Lexi must leave the Spark."

———

Near dawn, as the city of Samara slept peacefully, one fragile, broken figure walked through the streets, wide awake despite her exhaustion. Her heart was heavy. It might have been shattered. Roja hated fleeing the city like this, but Mea was right.

With her hood over her head, hiding the fiery red hair, she allowed herself one last gaze around her home. One last time to take in the towers, the streets and the massive walls sheltering her from the road's nightmares. Last of all, she eyed the cursed tower of the Wolves. She swallowed her hatred and lamented for Elise. Were she more impressive, none of this would have happened. Were she in any way popular within her own tower, she might have stormed theirs with her warring sisters. They would have been enough. Regardless, there would be repercussions for tonight's sins. Magnus would shed rivers of crimson for their transgression.

Her eyes caught a movement in the tower's highest window, a flicker moving across the window of the unlit room. A moment later a bird flew from the darkness, and with bloodshot eyes she watched it soar silently out over the walls, and then it was gone forever. It looked like a pigeon. She'd always hated those stupid creatures.

The Primary-in-waiting walked on towards the front gates. The sun was rising and rain was in the air. The threat was against Lexi and Roja alone. Linn had not cried as Roja had whispered into her ear a pledge of distant devotion. Where she was going, Linn could not follow. She had hoped for a smile, a kiss, an embrace. She had received a scorn and little more. The child's family had left her before. This was life, and this was familiar. She would become a strong Alpha female.

Roja wiped away her tears again and neared the gates. It was easier leaving the city than entering it. As she slipped by the guards, she dared not meet their eyes. There was no notice to arrest her, but the daring attack on her sanctuary was a declaration of their intentions. Mea's quick thinking in the Cull had earned her a grace period, just wide enough to escape. Come tomorrow, though, she expected many charges involving the jailbreak and the assassination of her grandmother to be made public knowledge. It wasn't fair.

She wept again, and a lamenting moan escaped her lips as she passed through. The guards heard, but they paid little notice. Many cried in the city these days. Better inside the gates than out, though.

She met Mea at the abandoned Rangers' camp. They had pillaged all tents and supplies since its one sentry had disappeared. All that remained was the beaten ground of a few hundred brave but very dead soldiers. A few empty crates and barrels that hinted at better times, and the ashes of the fires that had kept them warm at night.

Mea stood in silence beside her cart, lost in terrible thoughts as she looked at the site. Her arm stroked the horse absently, and she did not hear Roja approach.

"How has it come to this?" Roja asked, and Mea turned to embrace her friend.

"Through many dark deeds, sister. Committed by fiends without conscience."

Wasn't that always the way?

Roja turned away from the cart to watch the city lights fade as the dawn took hold. She couldn't do this. To actually face the road was scarier than fighting the tide with the Black Guard. She could gain support. Stand for the position. Retake her place, even though she was terrified. Dia would have wanted that. She would do it for Linn.

"You won't last another week," whispered Mea, reading the intention in her face.

"Aye," Roja agreed miserably. "Make sure Linn is protected."

"It's one thing for Silvia to make an attempt against you and Lexi, but Linn will be protected by those left behind, and we are fierce." They were fine words, and they reassured

Roja ever so. Her one gift to this world was ensuring Linn's future. She had not come of age; nothing would threaten her. Even Uden's child could probably walk those hallowed halls unprotected were she delivered to the city. This was the way. Always would be.

Lexi stirred in her bedding in the cart, lost in between consciousness and sleep. When she finally woke, her eyes were dull, and she was far too amiable for Roja's liking.

"Get on the road, Roja. I'll send word when I know of Elise," Mea insisted. She looked to the sky, grimacing. It would be no comfortable ride in a downpour, but rain was in the wind. Turning her back to Samara, she climbed aboard.

"Be safe, Mea. Be careful, and be brutal."

"I am truly alone now, sister," Mea said, and the tears streamed from her eyes.

It was almost too much. This misery she called a life had torn every joy from her . She tried desperately not to cry, but the anguish was too much.

None of this is fair.

It was Mea who recovered first. Kissing Roja's hand, she stepped away from the cart. "May the road rise to meet you."

"May the wind be at your back."

Roja pulled on the horse's reins and drove the beast forward. She did not look back at the gates. It would have shattered her resolve. Nobody in the city noticed the quiet figure drive the cart slowly away from the great walls, and they never noticed it disappear into the wastes.

26

LEGENDS

L exi sat atop the cart crying softly. The unexpected reunion with her father had been too much for her, and Roja had strayed from Magnus's line of sight lest he turn his wrath on her. There was only so much she could take. She wanted to find a quiet corner where no eyes condemned her and just die a little more. She had not been ready for his explosive outburst, though she should have been. She couldn't see a friendly face among the watching pack.

She wanted to go home.

She had no home.

She had no other place to go.

"Leave him be," suggested Erroh to the surrounding crowd and the few Wolves attempting to restrain him. They took the reprieve, for the legend roared loud enough that Uden himself might have heard him. He attacked a defenceless barrel with feet and fists, his injuries hindering him only a little. Everyone waited for the storm to blow itself out, but nobody dared to get in its path. It was probably the finer manoeuvre on their part.

"I'm sorry," Roja cried to the snarling brute as he drove

his fist down through the lid of the wooden barrel a third time. After so much abuse, it finally cracked. He punched it again and his fist went right through. He hissed and pulled his bloodied hand away. He screamed again before falling to his knees in despair. "I'm so very sorry." Her words sounded hollow. She could understand their disgust. She wanted that dark corner really badly.

The Black Guards knelt, as he did. None of them met his eyes; his disgust with them was as clear as his anger. These were the Wolves of old. For a moment she felt less alone. However, they looked to Magnus and not her. It was telling.

"It's not your fault," said Erroh, appearing beside her. She could see the turmoil in him. Each word was a struggle. Perhaps because they were false.

It's all my fault.

To her horror, Emir rushed past her. He did not acknowledge her or announce himself. Carrying his healer's bag, he sidestepped Magnus and leapt up to the cart to tend to Lexi. Seeing him in his wretched glory was all too much for Roja. She felt lightheaded, as though she were about to fall away from this world. Her vision spun sickeningly. Leaning against the cart she'd driven to the campsite, she tried desperately to catch her breath and concentrate on anything but the anguish threatening to swallow her whole. She was diminished to nothing; she'd delivered her precious cargo. She had nothing left. She felt her chest tighten. Felt the taste of dreadful things. Nothing in the world would ever be good again.

Somehow, she did not faint. She watched Emir tend to Lexi, and it was calming.

Reassuring.

"Minor concussion is all," he muttered. The surrounding crowd took this moment to take an easier breath. "Follow my fingers, little one." He waved a hand in front of her, and she followed it with her eyes. Roja noticed they were less glazed over than before. Emir's very presence was healing. She hated loving him.

She hated him.

"Get her a drink," shouted Magnus, collapsing on top of the vanquished barrel. His hand streamed blood, but he didn't seem to pay any attention. Who knew broken fingers meant so little to him?

A Primary need never engage in such barbaric rites of passage.

With his rage spent for now, his fatherly instincts took over, and Roja watched him dote over his daughter and felt like crying all over again. She had let him down, had let them all down.

Almost every Wolf reached for a goblet for the injured girl, and Roja smiled sadly. Wynn was swiftest. Appearing from nowhere, he leapt atop the cart and knelt down beside Lexi. He held out a glass of sine and she poured it down her throat. The burning liquid had the desired effect. She coughed loudly, and he laughed, and then she laughed too.

"Don't tell your brother," he said, eyeing Erroh with a grin, and she laughed again.

Emir took the goblet from her and, checking to see it was empty, began to work on her injuries. "One more, please," he shouted, turning to Wynn. "Stay here. I'll have need of you."

Roja had never felt as beaten as this. She couldn't stop quivering, and she wondered if it were shock, fatigue or cold. Her stomach rumbled with a sickly hunger. Her body was wound like a wet roll of linen. Two days of driving the cart without sleep had taken its toll. When the road became too much for Lexi, they had rested, but Roja had not been able to settle, no matter the tiredness. The fear of hearing city riders in pursuit had kept her alert. So she had pushed the beasts forward, and now she had arrived in a sanctuary. Perhaps she would sleep now. She had done her best. She was not hardened like these warriors; she was soft and privileged, and she had gone far too long without refreshing her training. It was a common enough thing for Alpha females. It was no excuse.

Now that she was here, she'd no more plans.

Did I expect a warm welcome?

Open arms and a warm, silk-sheeted bed?

Truthfully, she had hoped for something more than segregation. She would have taken a few bows of greeting. Maybe even a few words of reassurance.

Maybe just a slice of bread and some warmed butter if possible.

She stayed by the cart and shivered for a while. It was something to do while she figured out what to do with whatever remained of her life. She could not stay among these warriors. She could see their hatred. They could see hers. Come morning, after a few hours' sleep and maybe a few slices of bread, she would disappear into the green. She still recalled enough lessons on walking the road from her youth. Who needed warmth, friendship and love? She'd had all of those things; each one had led her to desolation.

"I'm sorry, Lexi," muttered Emir miserably and nodded for Wynn to give her more sine. The girl wept freely but still drank the numbing alcohol. She rested her head on Wynn's shoulder and groaned once more in agony. With her good hand, she gripped the edge of the cart for support, and Roja thought her so fuken brave. Emir unwrapped the elbow's bandaging and dropped the blood-soaked rags to the ground beneath. She saw him recoil at the injuries, then saw his disgust rearrange itself into his healing gaze as he planned how best to repair them. That was the man she'd loved. For so long.

I hate you.

"They took her unlawfully. There will be a reckoning," Erroh roared so all would hear. He had vengeance on his mind and he was not afraid to share it. He looked around challengingly to his newly-gained warriors and met little resistance. "Blood has been spilled for lesser actions."

Aymon and Doran held his gaze and nodded their heads in agreement. It was the closest thing to deference they could offer. He had taken a step with them, but they were not willing to drop everything for him. That was fine. These things took time.

Lea stood beside him, her eyes burning with a similar anger. Not just for her mother-in-law, but for the actions against her kind. Her sister. She was Lea of the road, but also Lea of the Spark. "They broke the old laws in taking her. So, when we find her, there will be no crime," she roared, and no one dared argue. Not when the queen spoke. More nodded in agreement, and this pleased Erroh. He needed to swallow his hatred and act like a leader. Every part of him wanted to rage like his father, but nothing had changed. The moment had passed. The barrel was broken.

"Wynn, carry her to the tent," Erroh ordered, and for a moment Wynn eyed him curiously. It was only a moment's hesitation, and Erroh almost cursed his friend. Instead, he played his part. "And don't give her any more to drink. She's too much like me." He offered a grin. A Master General's grin. A grin suggesting that, even as the world fell around him, he was in complete control.

The ruse worked, and Wynn tucked her up in his arms and

dropped to the ground. All the time whispering sweet consolations, and the young girl was immediately enamoured with the ponytailed fuk. *If nothing else, he makes a fine distraction for her this horrid night.*

The crowd shuffled, unsure of what to do, and Erroh smiled to the gathering.

"It's far too quiet here," he announced, and there was muted response. He caught Magnus staring at him, and for a moment he hesitated. His father nodded approval. The night needed to continue. The torch needed to pass. The Wolves needed to meet their new Master General. Nothing else mattered. Not even devastation.

Besides, they cannot afford to allow Elise to die in their care.

They will lose every fuken Alpha in the world.

They will lose the city more swiftly than they took it.

"If there's to be a celebration, there should be music and drunken singing and much messy revelry," he roared, and Aymon and Doran cheered in reply. They too would play their part. Erroh felt a little better. Only a Primary would condemn Elise to die, and he doubted any female in the city had the nerve to put the living legend to death.

Much to Erroh's liking, Doran signalled for instruments and entertainment. In the time it took to crack open a new barrel, the first melodies rose into the night and everyone felt more at ease. The musicians were not greatly skilled with their weapons of choice, but as they gathered, the rest formed a little circle around them, clapping and stamping in time. Swiftly, the music found its way into the heavens, where the gods nodded approval of their own.

Erroh walked among his small army. He calmed his beating heart and tried desperately not to think of his weak mother, chained and gasping for air. Aymon offered him his goblet as he passed, and Erroh took the drink and the gift of respect and bowed in appreciation. Both had played a part in forging a truce among all. To their credit, their word was worth more than he'd assumed.

Divided we burn. Together we stir some shit.

As usual, he missed Lea's company, her quiet reassurances at these gatherings, but he walked alone through the camp, for he was to be the figure most recognised tonight. As he lost himself in hopeless thoughts of intricate and simplistic plans alike, his steps led him back to Emir's tent. It was important that he spoke with Wynn, despite recent events. He slipped inside, leaving his goblet behind.

Magnus was at Lexi's bedside. "Remember your training, little one," he insisted as he held her goblet for her. She was busy struggling with the pain as Emir set the bones in place. Wynn stood deathly still, unsure of how to help, and Erroh walked up beside him. The only sign that he was aware of his friend was a deep sigh. Perhaps he was just upset for the girl.

"I'm sorry, Lexi," whispered Emir in between her gentle sobs. There was anguish to his voice, odd for one so experienced in horrors.

"She's fine," growled Magnus, and offered her the goblet again.

"Remember your training," said Erroh. Magnus was right, cruel as it sounded.

Wynn leaned into her face and smiled charmingly. "Take the pain." It was a gentle order, and she took a deep, anguished breath. Emir tugged at a piece of loose flesh and she gasped. She stared at the three warriors above her and nodded that she would not scream again. Magnus would have insisted she endure the foulest of training. A good thing. It made for an easier time now. Alphalines, through discipline, understood the value of thinking clearly when pain was almost too much to bear.

Almost.

Erroh remembered his own childhood and shivered despite himself. It had been easier for him to take pain, to recognise and control it, when he had been younger. Why was it that, as people grew older, pain became more difficult to deal with? Perhaps Erroh would have been destined for a similar fate to Lexi's. Problem was, he spent most of his time in pain. He didn't like pain, but he fuken took it better than most.

Control.

Lexi stared away to nothing above her and held her strap of leather in her teeth. Erroh knew well that dreaded taste, and he could see the terrible, reflexive grimaces every time Emir went to task, and his heart broke for her. He placed her elbow out straight and she gasped and bit and took it. The moment passed and, removing the strap from her mouth, Magnus poured more sine down her throat.

"Not in front of Erroh," she jested gamely, and Erroh smiled with pride in his young sister. She was already becoming twice the warrior he had been at her age.

"Even Master Generals make shitty decisions," Magnus said, offering the strap again.

She was so brave.

She took the pain.

Controlled it.

Eventually, Emir smiled and stroked her forehead. "Nearly finished," he whispered, and the girl nodded. Perspiration dripped down her face, but she did not cry out. Emir wrapped her elbow, bracing the arm out straight in a plinth. As he tied the last knot and the pain finally subsided, she passed out. Magnus wiped her forehead with a cloth, and

Erroh imagined the legend had felt every wrench of pain in his daughter's face.

"Fine job, healer," Magnus whispered.

"She's strong," muttered Emir, unsure what to do with the compliment, so he checked the bump on her head again and seemed satisfied with it. "Human," he muttered thoughtfully. "Just better at it."

"Thank you for helping her, Wynn," Erroh said, gripping Wynn's shoulder tightly. "We need to speak now," he said, leading the young warrior away from the sleeping female.

"As you wish, sir," Wynn said.

They walked out into the cool night air, away from the stuffy, claustrophobic aromas of Emir's healing tent. Wynn was first to speak, though. He spun on Erroh and gripped his collar. "The world is falling apart and you steal leadership for a southern wench." His voice was low and Erroh spun away from his grasp.

"Not here."

"Are you afraid I might cause a scene, ruin the unstable balance of this charade?" Still, he did not shout, but the disappointment he'd shown in Erroh's choice to challenge was now lost to the fury of Erroh's victory.

"Not here."

If he'd avoided bloodshed with two snarling beasts, surely he could avoid a confrontation with a friend he considered closer than most.

"I will not walk from this place, Erroh. If you have words to share, share them here among your brethren," muttered Wynn, and Erroh held a sharp retort on his tongue. Little point in aggravating his brother more than was needed. He took this moment as preparation. When war came and emotions were volatile, it was best to keep as steady as a barge on the Great Mother. Erroh could see Lillium marching

over now, her eyes casting daggers upon Wynn. Erroh held up
his hand to hold her charge.

I have this.

"You have every right to feel aggrieved, friend, but know
your place when I order," Erroh said. As he did, he smiled for
anyone watching.

"I will follow you into fire, Erroh. You have my word on
this, but I can't agree with what you've done, humane as your
reasons are. Allow me this silence," Wynn said, gripping
Erroh's shoulder. He too played a part out of friendship—or
out of respect?

"Will you not walk with me, brother?" Erroh begged.
This was not the last conversation for this wretched night.

"Not tonight, Erroh," Wynn said, dropping his head, and
Erroh refused to blame him or feel himself denied support at
every corner turned. Honour and pride and all things driven
into young warriors motivated Wynn. Fine teachings, but a
wise warrior would bend when left with no further
opportunities. "With friends like me, eh?" Wynn muttered,
turning away towards the forest.

"So we are still friends," the Master General called
after him.

"We'll always be friends, brother. Doesn't mean we will
always see things the same way," Wynn called back, and
disappeared into the darkness before Erroh could mount any
further argument.

"I'll speak with him," said Lillium, stealing up as casually
as she could.

A few feet away, Lea was busy burning some toast and
downing her drink as though nothing had occurred. If she'd
heard anything, she showed little interest. Her eyes were lost
in the flames, her thoughts a thousand miles from here.

"He is just taking the aftermath of the battle badly," Lillium assured him.

"Aye," agreed Erroh. Justified or no, it was on Wynn's stubborn head. He very much doubted their next meeting would go any better.

"He will come around. He needs some time. He is improving, he's just… hurting." She shuffled her feet, unsure of what to say, and Erroh almost laughed.

"You still care for him."

"I am responsible for many of his actions," she countered swiftly. "But I'll probably always care for him. He is a good man. An idiot without a clue, to be sure, but a good man."

Erroh sniggered. "I agree, Lillium. Ease your worry. It wasn't for my benefit I spoke with him. It was for his. I don't think ill of him for his struggles. Nor do I condemn him for his slight. We are learning our way. Mistakes are made, forgiveness is gifted, and loyalty is a precious thing." He folded his arms and watched the black forest into which his friend had vanished. By the time he returned, it would be too late to spare his feelings. Erroh was quickly learning how politically minded a leader needed to be. "So, Lillium, goddess from the Cull, she who tore me apart so easily every wretched day I faced you." This time she sniggered. "Why did you stand with me?"

As they spoke, Lea slipped away from her battered barrel with some freshly-burnt toast lathered with butter and honey. She had things to do. She didn't need to be around them. The Wolves parted as she passed. A few nodded in deference, and she returned the gesture where needed. Erroh had calmed the storm despite the waves of discord. Who knew? Perhaps Emir might not get his wish for violence this night. She wasn't certain everything was well, but the mood had lightened. At one point the musicians had broken into the first bars of Spark City's melody, and the jeering had been rather entertaining.

She stopped below Wrek, who was busy pouring from a tapped barrel, and took a glass of sine and made her way back through the crowd. Someone else needed something tonight. It took a queen to notice these things, and Lea would be no docile, regal fool, dressed in all things green and offering empty words to thoughtless listeners. She was a girl of action. She had more than enough enemies on the horizon, anyway.

Roja busied herself with her meagre belongings in the cart. It was something to do while fighting desolation. As she searched through damp sacks in search of a fresh blanket, her loneliness knew no bounds. She'd waited and watched the flickering torches as the great gathering returned to its revelry, and nobody had come for her and that had been fine. They had offered her nothing but the darkness, and so she took those lonely moments as gifts and died a little inside. It hurt less than she'd expected.

Nobody came.

They had the look of beaten men, and she recognised a few from her finer days as leader-in-waiting. They had tasted war since, were tragically wiser for it, and they no longer needed to show deference. She tried not to be insulted. A few sang along with the cheerful music, and she almost remembered what it was like to sit in a tavern singing along with Silvia, excited for the foolish games in the night ahead.

Moments of nervousness became an hour, and the last of her panicked energy left her. So, with no one caring to watch, she climbed back into the cart, where she could hang her head with a little more privacy.

Immediately, she felt the bitter bite of the wind at her back, and she wondered about sitting near one of the lit fires to settle her shaking bones. She'd behave; she wouldn't even say a word.

She was not welcome here. She never would be. She was an Outcast, and she was to spend her life alone. She entertained thoughts of stepping forward into the light like she had done when she was walking the city, of becoming the tough, heartless bitch her grandmother had built her to be. Had she stayed that tough, she might still be in power, but her heart had allowed Emir to betray her, innocent as it had been.

Do not think of him now.

"You look terrible," said Lea, climbing up onto the cart as gracefully as a queen could after so many drinks. She was mastering the art of drunkenness, like her mate. Roja smiled weakly. She was too tired to offer a rebuke, and besides, Lea looked incredible. Were she to offer a snide remark, well, the battle would hardly be in her favour.

"I do, Lea. I really do. It was a long trip."

Lea had spent most of her life despising this bitch, yet seeing her crushed like this gave her less pleasure than she would have liked. She had come here bearing gifts, but it was also fine to remind her nemesis who had the power. She passed the bread across without a word, and Roja took it. But before she could take a bite, she began to weep, and Lea was unprepared for this.

"Thank you, Lea."

"I think you probably need this more," she said, passing the fresh glass of sine into her shivering hands.

Roja tried to wipe her tears away before looking up, but they kept flowing. After a moment, she chuckled pathetically. "I'm not able to endure gestures of kindness."

"We're all in the same dreadfulness now, Roja," Lea said awkwardly. This was no sport at all. More than that, Lea suffered for her. Lea called out to a young Wolf stumbling by. It was time to discover just how influential she was. "Roja needs a tent. Gather a few of you to erect one as quickly as you can," she ordered. It was just like a good game of cards, played by Erroh.

"Aye, Mydame," he replied without breaking drunken stride, and Lea smiled despite herself. He sought out some unwilling comrades, passed on Lea's orders in a hushed tone, and they went to task. "And put it up near Magnus's tent," she called.

"I never cry," Roja whimpered, and hid her weakness in clasped hands. In that moment, Lea forgot most of the nastiness the female had delivered upon her. This was not Roja, she knew. She was broken. She had nothing in the world. And Lea was no longer a timid little shrew scurrying around the city, taking whatever shit they threw her way.

Miles walked since then.

Lea put her arm on her shoulder. It was all she could do. The road was tough, and Roja was quickly learning this. Drinking helped. She'd learn that as well.

"You are safe with us Outcasts, now."

———

Lillium shuffled her feet nervously once more, and he was happy to wait. Why didn't Wynn just stop and speak with him? she thought miserably. Why couldn't he just toughen up and accept responsibility for once in his fuken life? There was only so much she could do. He had shamed her, and shamed himself. It entitled her to walk away, yet she still found herself unable to leave him to his wretchedness. He was capable of great things. This she knew with all her shattered heart. And she would try to pull him from his wretchedness until she saw nothing left in him. He could have stood with Erroh. He *should* have stood with Erroh. It was just another display of his narrow-mindedness, turning his back on him.

Like I did.

"It was right standing with you," she said. "I honour Magnus, but I would follow you."

"I'm grateful for that," he said.

"You will be a fine leader, Erroh," she said, and he smiled. He hadn't smiled enough in the Cull. It wouldn't have mattered, because some things mattered more than love. She had regrets in this world, but she did not regret that he hadn't smiled more. She was happy with her station. How many people could say this?

"A fine leader will need strong generals to call upon," he said, and she nodded in agreement. Her face was calm, untroubled, but her heart flickered in excitement. She knew his intentions now. No, she suspected his intentions, and it was exciting.

Part of his war council?

She'd presumed he would reserve that for Magnus, Aymon, Doran, Wynn and Lea.

Please, Erroh, you beautiful young male. Go on.

As her excitement surged, she tried her best to hide her enthusiasm. It would be an honour to fight with him. She'd listened to the tales, and she'd seen with her own eyes that he was built for war. She'd followed him into battle, and they'd earned an incredible victory. She wanted more.

"It would be an honour to be called upon," she said, before she could catch the words in her mouth.

Fuk.

He raised an eyebrow, and a smirk appeared across his lips.

Fuk, fuk, fuk.

"You think I'm considering you to be one of my generals?" he asked lightly, and her stomach turned as she realised her assumption had been premature. Perhaps he had other plans for her. Fine; she would still serve. She'd never felt more alive than when she was serving the Rangers. She knew her place in life. "You served Magnus well, but you are not suitable for such a position," he said, and she was crestfallen, and she smiled weakly and nodded.

"Aye, sir. Sorry, sir," she offered, clasping her hands behind her back. She didn't care about being embarrassed at saying the wrong thing. She was above such childish things.

For a terrible moment she wondered if this was because of her behaviour in their Cull. She held that thought for a moment, and it steeled her. That was fair. She had been cruel. It didn't matter her reasoning or how much it tore at her. It was a fair attack. She would still fight, though. She would earn her place, eventually.

He sighed and dropped his head apologetically. "I wanted to speak with Wynn before I spoke with you. For courtesy alone."

"No matter what you decide, Wynn will answer your call, Master General, sir," she insisted. Her former mate would open his eyes soon enough. He was disillusioned, that was all. He had a childish adoration for Magnus. She'd quickly learned this on their first ill-fated journey through the wastes. His pain at seeing the great man humbled had blinded him to what exactly had humbled him. Aye, Erroh was probably going to lead them to a grisly death, but what a journey for those walking it with him. She wanted to be part of it.

"He was never my choice," Erroh said, placing his hand on her shoulder. She held steady. She thought she'd recoil at being touched, but she was strong. Strong enough to take rejection well.

"Do you see how each Wolf straightens up as you pass?" Erroh asked quietly. He grinned, and his voice was calm and kind. "Aye, you are exquisite, and men are forever tempted, but I suspect it is more your abilities they fear and respect. Even Aymon… and Doran."

She had noticed. She had assumed it was quiet respect they offered for her being one of two surviving Rangers. She had done what any Ranger would do. Lived and killed.

"You are a leader, Lillium. Wynn is not. At least not yet."

"I would have no problem taking orders from Wynn," she offered weakly, desperate to fight for the cause. In Wynn's case, she could help mould him into something great. It would just take a little time. She was so focused on arguing Wynn's case, she never noticed what Erroh was saying.

"The first general only takes orders from me, Lillium," he explained.

She didn't get it.

"I want you to be first general," he said.

She didn't quite understand what he meant.

"If you would stand with me," he asked.

She finally realised what he was saying. It was a delicate moment, and her body trembled in shock. "I accept," she whispered, and felt the need to throw up, or cry, or else break into manic laughter. Whatever came first. She leaned in and met his lips with her own. She couldn't say for certain why, but she needed to touch him. It was suddenly very important that he knew how grateful she was. They would be forever connected, and emotion got the better of her. A kiss was far more apt than a formal handshake. It was no kiss shared between passionate lovers, though. It never had been. It was something else. It was probably not the proper action of a first general, but he didn't seem to mind. Regardless, she stepped back and dropped to one knee and bowed her head.

"It will be an honour to ride with you, Erroh, line of Magnus, line of Elise," she pledged.

"It will be a tough ride," he pledged in return.

Behind them, the improvised band broke into a rendition of "Tale of the Brigand," and Erroh stood upon the doomed wall and surveyed the insurmountable numbers before him. Trying desperately not to take it as an omen, he led his new second-in-command through the crowd to celebrate with his mate and their new guest. Humming along with the tune, he thought of fallen legends and the legacy of a tiny band of lunatics and their minor act of defiance that had grown into legend.

27

GOOD NIGHT AT THE PIG IN THE HOLE

S tefan smiled despite himself. He hadn't felt relaxation like this in a lifetime. A lifetime when he'd worn the crown of champion. It was no special night, but there was a chaotic familiarity that roused his good mood. If this continued, he might break into a laughing fit. He was good at laughing, if he recalled. He was capable of boisterous outbursts and a few knee slaps and all. It was a long time since he'd found merriment in anything.

It had been weeks, too, since he'd enjoyed conversation with anyone in the city. The snide remarks and nasty accusations about his traitorous blood were growing in number, and they were crushing him. More than once he'd received spittle to the face as he passed an innocuous gathering; fists would be next. They knew him. They hated him. They had a point.

Fuken they.

He wasn't strong enough for passing words between the Outcast army and Roja. He was a solitary cog in a twisted machine, rolling them all towards doom. He had expected tonight to be no different when Lexi had come brazenly to

him with word of nothing again. This was the lull before the
tempest. Magnus had no word on the Hunt. Lexi had no
word on the mood of the city. Everyone knew nothing would
change until the southerners attacked. Yet still, he was
forced to meet openly to keep the chains of communication
oiled.

Nothing, nothing, fuken nothing.

"Safer to be seen in the taverns," Lexi had insisted.

Aye, for her.

The little witch hadn't stayed long beyond his pledge for
Aurora, beyond Tye's appearance. With nothing else to do,
they had become a trio of Outcasts in themselves. At least for
the night. Which had not finished.

He walked behind the figures and enjoyed their
foolishness. It was closer to dawn than midnight now, and
barely a soul walked the city streets. Fatigue plagued his
every step. It was a small price to pay. Sleep would find him
when it needed to. Their footsteps echoed loudly through the
little walkways, but it was the raucous singing that probably
woke most of the sleeping citizens as the trio stumbled home.

Home.

"I have the finest bread and cheese to share," shouted Tye
as loudly as he could into the swaying ear of his beautiful
companion. She was still singing the third verse of the Spark
City ballad, nodding in complete agreement. Cheese and
bread was a magnificent idea, it would appear. Ealis stumbled
under the young cub's weight as he spun her around.

"I would love cake," she said, giggling, and squeezed the
young Alpha warmly.

"I have the finest cake," promised Tye.

"And we need some more wine," she decided, turning
back to Stefan and giggling some more. This giggle was for
him alone. She was gentle and soulful, but there was a

devilish desire in her eyes he was interested to explore. *Such wonderful eyes.*

"I have the finest wine," declared Tye, the solitary guardian of the Rangers' forgotten post.

"Hurry, Stefan," roared Ealis, laughing. "There are fine times ahead."

"If you aren't careful, I will steal her away as effectively as you did Lea," Tye shouted, and Stefan smiled. He probably shouldn't have told them the story of the first night of Puk, but he'd felt compelled to reveal a tale after Tye's humbling admission of his first meeting with Erroh, the Hero of Keri. It was that sort of night, and besides, Ealis had hung on to every word he'd offered.

"Going to the city, going to get me a family," Ealis sang terribly, and this time he did laugh, though not enough to throw her off her performance. The sine had been kind to her warm personality. The longer the night went on, the more she appeared to say the correct thing. He'd dismissed her as a delicate wretch seeking a few additional supplies from his privileged place. Soon enough, though, he'd seen the pride in her. She was not the type of girl to beg for anything. He liked that.

Tye joined in with the singing, desperately trying to impress the pretty girl. A decade in difference between their ages wasn't nearly enough of a deterrent for him. Stefan could see how he moved with her, watching her sway, staring into her eyes, looking at her luscious lips, touching her arm more than needed.

Drunk and unprepared.

All good things.

She treated him with little more than gentleness, and this too gave Stefan pause for thought. Her interest in listening to the young cub was simply kindness. Any fool could see the agony he carried, even when *not* mentioning his fallen father. When he *was* mentioning his fallen father, she stared into his soul and brought tears to his eyes. Stefan had never known his father or mother, but listening to the tales of Jeroen was a strangely bonding thing.

When Tye spoke coldly of his mother, Stefan thought this a tragic thing. Ealis did too, and swayed him away from wrath, back towards Erroh, back towards Jeroen, back towards the fallen Rangers.

"Oh, come on Stefan. Come sing with us," Ealis cried, and reached drunkenly for his hand. She smiled the smile he'd known most of his life. The wanton, inviting smile of a girl enamoured. Oh, how he'd taken for granted such gestures all these worthless years. Believing he would always be champion, always be among lovers, always be a soulless husk, unsure of and unprepared for the entire world. In most ways, he did not miss that fool. That cruel waste of a wretch. He liked nothing about himself now, but at least his eyes were open. They would be open when they closed for the last time.

"I am the best singer," Tye declared, and turned to Stefan with bleary eyes. "Why don't I ever get the pretty girl?"

"Because you set your sights on pretty girls," Stefan countered, and dared a broken-toothed smile at Ealis. "I seek goddesses alone," he said, wincing at his unoriginal wooing words.

Ealis held his gaze for a moment. Perhaps she saw through his charm; perhaps she was that type of girl. Perhaps it was something else. "Would that make you a god, Stefan?" she asked, watching him with calculating eyes. It was delicate humour, a little flirtation, yet something in those eyes demanded truth. It was likely her kind soul, open to love and warmth and everything beautiful.

"I am but a man, Ealis. A wretched man with nothing to

offer. When I see a goddess standing in front of me, I tell her so, and hope she does not smite me down with a flick of her will." He didn't know why he said that, but as he spoke, he felt an emptiness come upon him. Instead of allowing the emptiness to swallow him up, he fought it. He offered her his broken smile again, and it matched hers.

"Fuk's sake," Tye muttered. "That type of shit is exactly why I don't get the girl."

A little further on, Tye tripped and fell against the wall beneath the last arch of the city, and Ealis caught him before he knocked himself senseless. "Aw, thank you. I think you are great. You have pretty eyes. I love you so fuken much," he declared drunkenly.

"You're so sweet. I love you too, little one," she cooed. Suddenly, the young cub crumpled forward and collapsed onto the ground. He moaned loudly as the goddess knelt down beside him, stroking his cheek.

Ealis was drunk. She couldn't remember the last time she had been this drunk, but for tonight, she had no intention of allowing her mind to steal away such fine times. Tye was a minor disaster, and she was fond of him. He was destined for greatness. She could always tell these things. His unrefined fierceness was delightful and terrifying. He cared little for what anybody thought of him. She'd seen him challenge a roomful of seasoned drunkards to a fight to the death, and she'd seen the room look away. She'd found the sensitive part hidden beneath equally impressive. A wild warrior like him could be twisted to become elite indeed. Perhaps that's what happened with most legends, she supposed.

Same age as Fyre of Night.

She felt an instinct to care for him and, despite herself, didn't want this night to end.

"Let's carry him home," she whispered. Her little Tye. Her beautiful, wretched companion nodded and lifted the semi-unconscious child to his feet, slipping an arm under his shoulder. She took the other side, and the trio shuffled out through the gates towards camp. The gates did not slam loudly behind them, as was usual. She felt that strange sensation of someone watching her, yet pushed it away.

No more hunting, tonight.

No more blood.

"I have no place to sleep tonight," she whispered, knowing they would soon furrow in whatever bed he took her to. She'd seen the hovels, smelled the stench. Still, sweat was sweat. The Rangers' camp was empty, however, with each flapping tent a reminder of the betrayal they had suffered. She would have preferred an abandoned tent; that would have been just fine.

Reaching across, she ran her finger playfully down Stefan's chin and bit her lower lip. Men melted under such gestures.

"I'm sure little Tye would be happy to keep you warm," he mocked.

"Oh, he wouldn't want to give his gift to little old me. There will be plenty of little Alpha-ettes all eager to fall for him."

"Humble goddess," he whispered, and she liked that. She would make him whisper it in her ear as he emptied himself in her. And when she cut into his chest.

No, no, no, not tonight.

"There's enough bedding in the Rangers' camp," he said, and she smiled.

"Will you stay with me tonight?"

"If there's wine, certainly."

"And cake," she reminded him.

"Aye, the finest cake as well."

———

Earlier, word had spread swiftly among those who desired retribution, and tonight they sought it. Seeing Tye and Stefan sitting at the same table had been too tempting an opportunity to break a few bones and send the message—to Stefan for his disloyalty to the city, and to Tye? Well, for nothing more than his threat, his allegiance to the Rangers. Elise might be safe in the tower somewhere, but these two fuks deserved a beating. Six Wolves without banner or armour, but with serious intent, set themselves the task of justice.

They thought it incredible fortune when the tavern was cleared and all but three drunkards remained inside. While the regular patrons were shunted home, these wretched bastards were offered an unentitled lock-in. There were only so many rounds in any drinker, however, and the Wolves were patient beasts.

When they finally emerged, the trio were easy to follow; the streets were empty. Perfect mugging conditions. And doing the deed beyond the city gates would make it nice and legal as well, should the beating take a nasty turn. When they scrambled past the hovels, the watchers couldn't believe their luck. Free of the gates and with the guards happy to look the other way, they stole down after the unwitting drunks until the Rangers' camp neared. When the female tended to the drunken lout as he threw up in a bush, they fell upon Stefan with sober efficiency.

———

The youth's stomach eruptions were louder than the footsteps in the dry, dusty ground, but a flicker of movement gave Stefan just enough time to meet the attack. His Keri reflexes served him well. He caught his assailant's wrist and struck once, trying to knock the club away. His assailant fell back, only for another blow to take him from the side.

More than one.

Ribs cracking, he fell to the ground. "Run," he gasped, and took a kick to the head from another.

Three murderers?

His vision blurred, and he tried to rise, knowing the next few moments could be his last. Hands grabbed at him, but he swung instinctively at his attackers. He broke from their grasp and slithered away pathetically.

At least five.

I die tonight.

No trial. No last words. No furrowing with Ealis.

"Leave him alone," screamed Tye, stumbling from the bushes. Though barely conscious, he still spoiled for a fight. He just didn't expect to meet six heavyset Wolves, armed with clubs and malice, beating the life out of his new friend and love rival. Ignoring Stefan's warning, he charged forward. Six men against one little cub. It was hardly fair. He pulled his sword from its scabbard and attacked. "I'll kill every last one of you."

The girl called Ealis stood frozen as he leapt into war with trembling hands, dizzy vision and vomit down his vest.

The leader of the mob grinned and spun away from the traitor to meet the child's inebriated attack. He swung wide with his club and probably expected to feel the satisfying crunch of broken bone and shattered cartilage, but Tye was a blur.

He did not think. He only reacted. It was the Alphaline in him. He ducked under the blow and thrust his sword forward. It went through the heart, as his father had trained him. He could hear Jeroen's voice in his mind: "How many times must I tell you, Tye—when a brute has armour, always aim for the chink at the neck or the groin. Aim for the heart if there is leather or cloth." It was a fine strike, and his father would have been proud as his foe fell to the ground and Tye took one step closer to becoming a legend. Then, turning to tear the rest of them apart, he received an unexpected club to the face.

No legend just yet.

He fell backwards, swinging his blade instinctively, and it slipped from his grasp. As he fell, he saw it nearly impale the watching Ealis. He would have apologised, but the ground struck him fiercely and he knew this was the end.

"He's dead. The little shit killed him. Oh no, oh no!" someone screamed, and Tye tried to shake his senses awake, but his mind was a blur of drunken ache.

This is no way to die.

"Kill him," someone cried, and hearing such a thing only made his inability to rise that little bit worse.

I'll take care of this, whispered Aurora to Ealis, and Ealis thought it a fine plan. She reached down and picked up the blade. It had a nice balance to it.

You leave my boys alone.

. . .

Stefan tried to rise. He had witnessed the murder and knew Tye had doomed them all. Their attackers left him for a moment to fall upon the child. He could have dragged himself to the water, dropped in and found salvation in escape, but he reached for the dead man's club.

He wouldn't leave them. There were finer ways to die; he would never run from war again. He gripped the weapon with his good hand and tried to rise. His leg buckled and searing pain ripped through his back. He tried again, and this time he climbed to his feet. Whatever useless presence he brought to the battle, he would still try. By the time he rose, the melee was already finished.

She was panting heavily and blood had soaked her through to the skin. She still held the sword in her hand, but her expression was blank. *In shock, no doubt.* The surrounding carnage offered little clue as to what exactly had happened. Many of their eyes were still open, their faces contorted in grimaces of pain and shock. Streams of blood filled the path at her feet, and Stefan swore he was staring at a demon from one of Jeremiah's gospels.

Their bodies were everywhere. Broken, torn and finished. One Wolf held his chest where she had pierced him. His head still shook in fear as his bowels released and his dying moan filled the night air. She stepped forward and casually pushed the tip of the blade through the man's eye socket.

"I crept up on them," she whispered, and her blade shook. Then the rest of her body followed. "I crept up on them because they were going to kill you and Tye," she said, louder now, and tears flowed down her cheeks. "I crept up on them, and I think I killed them," she wailed, falling to her knees, her hands splashing in a fresh pool of crimson. "I didn't mean to." She eyed Stefan in panic, desperate for forgiveness, but he could not say a word.

"Thank you," muttered Tye. His head was pouring blood, and he lay among the rest of the dead bodies. The brutes had turned on the child. Blinded by vengeance, they had focused only on Tye and allowed Aurora to attack them. It was lucky, and she had taken her chance and saved all their lives.

"I'm sorry," she screamed, and her cry was piercing and primal. She stared at the warm blood on her hands. On her dress. In her hair.

"We must flee this horror," hissed Stefan, reaching down to help the shaking girl to her feet. They would hang for these crimes. There would be no trial. Six Black Guards had died this night, and nothing would save them. It was pure murder, regardless of the fact they'd been defending themselves. He'd seen how the law worked in this city. He would attend no arena.

"We must go to the authorities. We were defending ourselves," she said, her voice little more than a gasping choke. "It was a justified kill."

"No. We have to leave, now," growled Stefan. After a moment, she nodded.

"Together?" whispered Tye, staring at his bloody sword as though suddenly realising the weight of his actions.

Why did you draw your sword, boy?

He wiped it on his shirt and knelt down and kissed the forehead of his first victim. He said a silent prayer to the absent gods. "Killing differs from how I'd imagined it would be. It was easier," he whispered pathetically, and Stefan's anger faded somewhat. He was wild, boisterous, tactless, but he was still a child.

Aye, little one. Death is easy to accomplish and harder to live with.

"We will flee together, this very moment," Stefan said with steel in his voice. He was a broken wretch, but he'd been broken for a long time. These two waifs had only just fallen into this miserable hole.

———

With the sun coming up, Stefan shielded his eyes and led the two murderers away from the terrible scene, determined to find them a sanctuary. His duty to Spark was broken in this moment. Another Mayor of Keri was fallen to ruin.

Tye marched behind him. Unsure of what to do about his spinning thoughts, he sought consolation in silence. A rare thing for him.

Aurora, behind them both, licked away the taste of fresh kill from her lips and allowed herself a restrained and satisfied smile of the Hunt.

28

THE ONE-EYED GOD AND THE FYRE OF NIGHT

B *ored.* Uden's feet crunched gently in the melting snow. He relished the sound and the sensation as he did; while he could. There weren't many more miles left before the perfect white would be replaced with warmer browns, forgiving greens, and cruel yellows. He missed the sight of his frozen breath. These evenings it was barely visible in front of his face. This was not like the beautiful cold of the southern lands.

The south.

That wasn't its proper title at all, but he knew better than speak aloud an entire world's inaccuracy.

The entire world.

He smirked at that inaccuracy too. Everything was skewed, lost in time, but Uden the Woodin Man knew it all. Such a burden to have a deep well of knowledge and none worthy to hear its endless secrets. He shrugged absently, stretched his neck muscles and let his heavy leather boots carry him over the slushy ground. These were godly thoughts for him alone.

The murmur of ten thousand soldiers filled the

surrounding air, and he loved its melody. Line after line of camped warriors flanked his stroll through the battlements, yet none dared approach him. Engage him. Delay him. They knew their place in the world. They knew punishment. His warriors dropped to a knee or sat down completely as he passed. A tidal wave of fealty, and it pleased him. They knew the law of the march. When Uden walked, no man could stand in his presence. A shrewd order, given by Gemmil, and it certainly sent out the right message. *In Uden we trust. In Uden we walk through the fire.* Any man who approached the god without leave was quickly struck down and his head mounted on a pike to remind and educate. A shrewd tactic, indeed.

His presence now, flanked by three of his most trusted enforcers as he marched down through the great war machine of cavalry, livestock, and massive carts, certainly ensured the rules were enforced. A younger Uden wouldn't have allowed himself to be accompanied. A younger Uden would have taken any threat as the challenge it was. Alas, he was too precious for such things now. So, he made a safer march. A less interesting one, too, filled with training regimes to account for infirmities.

"So bored," he muttered to himself.

He hated the waiting. Great tales were told of heroic warfare and blood and honour and death, but few tales were glorious when recounting the mundanities of a slow march. Yet a slow march was necessary when leading the second wave. A younger Uden might have resisted better sense and begun his grand advance towards the city, but the city was not ready to fall and Uden was not yet ready to raise a sword as he had before.

He who hesitates might be lost.

He shook that thought away as swiftly as it emerged. It

was many weeks since they had made camp in this valley, awaiting word of Oren. Aye, it was disappointing not to lead the attack, but he was too important to be taken by a stray arrow or a careless charge in a well-fought battle.

I am not ready to face the false one.

A god never marched unless victories were assured. A thousand miles from here, his fingers worked their brutality enough as it was, terrorising the wretched settlers and driving them towards Samara. Gathering them all together. It was a finer way to scour the tainted from this world.

In the meantime, Oren would do his task, and it would weaken the city's twisted heart.

Absently, Uden touched the patch covering the deep hole in his head. He'd taken to pushing it inwards, an unsavoury habit. A human habit at that. He couldn't help himself. It was a strange thing to push into nothingness. Losing his eye had been inevitable, just as the false god's challenge had been. He'd seen it before it occurred. Read it in scripture.

"The dreams, the dreams, the terrible dreams. And the Woodin Man knew of this day," he whispered.

His dreams were of wrath and fire, all within a blizzard of sorrow.

Godly things lost in snow.

Flexing his shoulders back, he took pleasure in the satisfying clicks of powerful muscles drawn to movement. Too much walking and not enough exercise had affected him. As much as he wanted to traverse the paths at pace, allowing miles to fall beneath his powerful sprint, exercise for its own sake was an unseemly action.

"Bored," he growled to himself again, his tones loud and harsh in the evening air. One of his guardians glanced at him and then, realising the statement was for Uden himself, looked away immediately and watched the soldiers dropping to their knees. *Safer that way.* Uden was not above battering a guard to death for failing to bow at the right moment. A guard would deserve such treatment.

He passed a long wicker basket attached to a small cart. It was the length of a man, with small openings, and the god ran his fingers along its edge as he passed. The cage thrashed and shook from the assault, and the carrier pigeons inside howled their annoyance as they flapped their wings. He smiled at the lack of understanding the rest of the world had for these beautiful creatures. They saw them as vermin, and, at desperate times, a distasteful delicacy. It took only a few diligent keepers, a few safe havens and a little knowledge from the ages to realise their full importance and essential advantages.

"Hello, little ones," he whispered, and thought them beautiful. Every day, another one returned from a faraway region. Every day, he learned more about what they marched towards.

And the North thinks I hesitate indolently here.

He closed his eye for a moment as he walked. He feared no stumble, for he was graceful, and listening to the camp was a settling thing. His magnificent army grew larger and larger. Every day, he learned of more settlements that had been scattered and sacked and stripped clean of tainted blood. Every day his hunters slaughtered in his name, and the dead were the objects of his holy wrath. He felt little for the innocent, especially the life-giving women. He only cared that they burned, that they be brought to ash for their sins. To carry life and have it taken away was a cruelty beyond all others. It was a kindness on his part.

The innocent ones were betrayed and bloodied.
The beautiful were struck down.
And the Woodin Man knew of this day.

"It was said at the end of the world there would be a terrible hurting, but at the end would come a light," he whispered in prayer. No guardian glanced his way, and this pleased him.

Opening his eyes, he sniffed the familiar air, and he hesitated. Looking across the lands, he realised that he knew this region. He felt stinging revulsion for it.

All dead, all lost.

It was a human thing to lament, and he spat his frustration on the ground.

Bored and bitter was an unpleasant combination.

"At least this evening, it will be different," he declared loudly, and his watching guardians had the grace to nod in agreement. Gemmil's word had quickened his step. Some of this boredom would end tonight. Tonight, he would gift life once more. Was a god not capable of such feats? Was it not his obligation to bring life forth?

His body was old, yet his godliness was in its youth. He had not mastered the act of creation, but all gods failed at first. Some even needed a day's rest. His was a more personal design, anyway. He was down with the lesser, moulding the world to its betterment. With every act of divinity, he honed his delicate skill. He had not yet created the perfect being. That would come.

"I hope it will be a girl," he said, and they followed his godly march in silence. They probably hoped so too.

Who would argue with me?

He passed the last tent, and the ground opened up ahead to a secluded area, for chosen eyes only. A place of holiness, where a god could see the first steps of birth. He passed a cluster of trees and stepped into a clear glade of mud and worship. Waiting for him in a large circle were a gathering of worthy warriors. They remained still and patient, their armour reflecting the light from their torches and casting eerie shadows into the forest. It almost felt like home.

I need a girl.

Of those warriors present, only a few, those generals he'd elevated highest within his court, carried weapons. Aye, perhaps one might choose to stake their claim upon his throne, but Uden was a gambling sort. Sometimes it eased the boredom. He would bet no fool would shatter what he'd built. At least not yet.

Within the circle stood a group of terrified little cubs, and he eyed them all and favoured the tall girl standing among her chained comrades. There was strength in her stance. A glimmer in her eye. She had beautiful eyes, and beautiful eyes enchanted him. More so these chilly nights. He missed his Aurora most. She had not been the first of his creations, nor would she be the greatest.

He walked towards the makeshift arena, this time with eyes unblinking. He wanted to savour every step. The ground was dryer where they stood. A layer of sawdust and salt had been spread here, and it allowed a finer grip than the rest of the camp. *Excellent.* It would be a shame if the winner attainted the prize through the lottery of bad footing.

The line parted as he neared, and he dismissed his guardians to stand with the crowd. He desired no protection for such a brutal event. If he were to witness barbaric bloodshed and horror, he desired to feel its threat in his mind, in his very bones. It made the moment sweeter.

The sun was nearing its setting, and the surrounding white was turning a deathly black. He preferred sunset to dawn. Sunset was beauty, and night was divine. Dawn was the birth of a day unproven. It was rare that birth was beautiful. Birth led to death.

Death.

The flickering flames growing in the dark brought back the memory of Fyre.

Oh, Fyre of the Night—you called yourself.

If Aurora was his triumph, then Fyre was the goddess whose death had paved the way for such success. Fyre had challenged him. Such strength, such courage, and she had fought for her soul until the very last moment, until he had finally killed her on that terrible, beautiful night.

Beautiful, dead daughters.

It had been necessary. Fyre had been his greatest moment, until she had closed her beautiful eyes and never opened them again. Necessary and terrible.

"We are quite eager this evening," announced Gemmil, the glee in his voice clear. He was a true bastard, and Uden loved him for it. His diminutive frame suggested a diminished waif, and he played that part to any who gazed upon him until he no longer needed to. Even Aurora feared his grace. He was no deity, but he was a man. A fierce one, at that, and it was nights like this that sated Gemmil's savagery, much as they did Uden's.

A few warriors grinned in anticipation. Whispered jokes and hushed wagers were offered, and he allowed them their release. Few had witnessed a contest like this before; however, they knew its importance. Only the highest generals of Uden's army were ever invited to attend.

"This is pleasing," the Woodin Man replied evenly. His casual tones were still louder than most of the voices raised. He stood taller than any of his generals, and age had done little to diminish his power. Though he refused to run through the encampment, he maintained nightly silent routines in his tent: arm push-ups, chest crunches and whatever other archaic exercises he could do in silence until the sweat streamed down his muscled frame. He still had not lost the body he'd called upon these last two decades since the Faction Wars. Perhaps there were a few extra lines creeping into his features, but that was the human in him. He *would* conquer old age. His wall of scripture did not allude to such miraculous things; however, the knowledge was out there. He would find it. Immortality came to those patient few, not to false a god who waged war on a city brim-full of defiance.

He eyed the reluctant combatants with curiosity and stared at the raven-haired girl again. She had not come of age, but she would soon. She shivered from fear, but her beautiful eyes were composed.

I want those eyes.

Each of the nine combatants knew their role in the skirmish ahead. Six nubile girls and three young boys, all from separate parts of this region of the Arth. All from separate destroyed settlements. They were strangers. They held no allegiance to each other once they struck a blow.

A sturdy young cub with dark hair eyed Uden. He shook like the rest, but his tremors were from a fiery rage of hatred. As a guard unlocked his restraints and those of his rivals, Uden almost expected him to charge forward and attack his conqueror.

One normally did.

Beside the threatening boy stood two younger males. Nervous and still, they watched the rest of the girls and each other uncertainly. As the chains were unlocked and fell to the ground beneath them, the crowd's mutterings increased in volume.

Aimee's favourite colour was green. The darkest type of green. A green that was comfortable among the many shades of the road. Easier to hide in the green. This, they had taught her to embrace. She hadn't had enough training. She was the tallest girl, but she'd never been more scared than in that moment. Actually, that wasn't true. Watching her bandit clan fight for their lives upon the walls as the brutes tore them apart had been more terrifying. As scared as she was now, it paled compared to watching those she loved fall savagely. She'd been unable to move, let alone flee at the end. She'd just screamed for the gods to wreak an awful vengeance. Her prayers, as usual, had gone unanswered.

Gemma was the heaviest of the girls. She knew this because, all her life, they had taunted her for her eating. She saw little problem with this. Her family were wealthier than most, and she'd eaten well. And while her stomach was wide, her strength matched her size. There were no weapons at hand. She would earn her prize with her strength. She swallowed her fear and waited for the inevitable. Growing up, she'd always favoured the colour of the night, the purest black the eye could see. Occasionally, she had painted her lips this colour. Sometimes above her eyes as well. It was another reason she had not been popular among the rest of the children in her village.

"We will not do this," growled the young cub menacingly, and stepped towards the god. Such defiance. Remarkable in one so young, Uden thought, enjoying the predictability of the moment. They knew the coming dance of horror. There was simply no other choice. The child behaved as though he could not draw a blade. Could not plunge it deep. Could not save his own life. *Foolish northerner.* From the age of walking, all humans were old enough to kill.

. . .

The boy did not charge. He was wise enough to know the crossbows would tear his body apart long before he took even three steps in anger. He merely stood as his father would have, many years before, as a warrior in the Faction Wars. Proud, despite terror. His father was dead now, slain by relentless brutes. His fate would likely be the same, but he would not die in vain. He would die honourably.

Becki stood beside Gemma and held her bladder as best she could. She had shared a few words with the heavyset girl in the hours before, when they had all learned of this terrible event. They had promised the reward of life to the victor, but she knew she would die in this arena. Her skills were inadequate, and she had little experience in taking a life. Tears streamed down her pretty little cheeks, and she begged the gods for a swift step into the darkness. She hoped her family waited for her there. She missed her room, her now-shattered sanctuary. The beautiful pink dress her mother had made for her was ripped and faded after so many weeks walking in chains. Its delicate weaving had been painstakingly created in love. Her mother had chosen the colour well. It had always been her favourite.

Ella grimaced at the fresh abrasions at her wrists and stood away from her opponents. The marks were bright red where the skin was rubbed away. Usually, the vibrant colour provoked pleasure whenever she looked upon it, but as she twisted her arms painfully around to look more closely at the cracks in her skin, she felt nothing but rage. She was older than the rest, but appeared much younger. She had come of age a season before, and she dearly wanted many seasons more. They all did. She *would* kill, if that's what it took to live. She was numb after all she had seen, but she had survived horrors before and she would survive again. Despite her quivering hands, her fingers had the strength to choke the life from the other females. It was the brute, thoughtless strength of the males that concerned her most.

"You will do this, or you will all die," hissed Gemmil loudly. This was hardly the time for further demonstrations of rebelliousness. The young cub had stated his grievances many times already, and Gemmil had nodded and listened. There was nothing else to say. A smart young cub would silence himself and get to striking down his opponents.

Kara stood beside the two silent boys and hid behind her bushy hair. Her hands shook and her quivering shoulders betrayed the tears she shed freely. *This isn't real.* She refused to believe what was happening. This was all a horrible dream, and she was soon to wake. *They aren't dead.* She couldn't be alone. She had to wake up soon, though this dream had lasted weeks. It couldn't be real. No man was so cruel as to turn chained companions against each other like this. She would not fight. She would wake up in her own bed any moment and laugh this nightmare away. She closed her eyes and thought of the deep blue sea. Its serene colour calmed her in moments of despair. Her short lifetime of living with such a view was as far from this horrible, endless white as she could ever be. She imagined the warmth of an afternoon on her face, her sister beside her as they giggled and hunted crabs. She wanted to wake up. She desperately wanted to wake up.

Mikayla watched Uden and thought about making a fruitless run towards their keeper as the chains fell away. She had tied her light blonde hair back in a ponytail, and she was ready to stand beside the tall young cub fighting for their souls. He was brave and beautiful, and she desperately wanted him to know this before the end. She wasn't brave. She'd never been brave enough to escape her unhappy life with a bastard, abusive father and a wretched, broken stepmother. She'd also never been brave enough to speak to a boy. She held her tongue and prepared herself for what was to come. She never knew that her favourite colour was yellow. She never would. It had never occurred to her to think about it.

The crowd shouted. They wanted blood. They had waited long, and their thirst for blood was growing every day. They were a warring nation. They always had been. This encampment was bad for the mind; bad for the soul. Uden had gifted them barbaric slaughter between heathen children. For a few, it left an unpleasant taste in the mouth. For the rest, it was scripture. Something to enjoy. Something to wager on.

"Begin," growled Uden loudly, his voice harsh and threatening. It was a warning to the defiant youth standing before him. He held the young boy's gaze and waited for the nine to tear each other apart. It would be brutal, magnificent, and from the ashes of horror, a new life would emerge. The child would only then begin the painful process of their true birth, and Uden would show them the way. He hoped it was a girl.

. . .

"We will not," shouted the defiant young boy. He raised his arm and pointed to the god condemningly. He was ready to die, but he was ready to die with his hands around the throat of their leader. A finer way to die. His father would be proud.

No other combatant moved. They hoped for anything but the inevitable. They stood and waited for their apparent leader to act. It was all they could do. One boy behind him cried. He was the smallest. The youngest, too. There came the stench of fresh urine, and the defiant, outspoken boy stepped forward in challenge, daring this vile bald brute to meet him in conquest.

"Kill the boys," whispered Uden. He blinked languidly, as if uttering those damning words caused him no strain at all. There were many clicks and a collective whistle of torn air.

The brave cub never felt the arrow pierce through his vest and into his heart. Nor did he feel the second arrow as it pierced his stomach. The two arrows that flew through his skull mercifully ended his life, before the shock of Uden's words could make sense to him. He fell to his knees but did not fall over. He just slumped, as if praying to his murderer. The arrows clung cruelly to his body as his soul stepped into the proud arms of his father.

They slew both remaining boys with equal efficiency and swiftness. Their bodies fell into the dirt as their shattered hearts beat their last. The surviving girls screamed and leapt away from the fallen. There were tears and hysterics, but none of them attacked. They had not fallen to darkness. At least not yet.

The point was made wonderfully. It *would* be a girl. A god knew these things. A god made things like this happen.

"You will begin," repeated Uden, his voice rising over the howls of the crowd as they roared and jeered the bodies of the fallen youths. The combatants had received one warning: there would be no more. Still, they froze in their places, staring at the dead bodies as they spilled their blood into the dirt. Food for carrion birds, and little more.

Kara moved first. She fell to her knees and began sobbing uncontrollably. It spurred Aimee into action. Between Aimee and the crying girl was the stooped body of their fallen speaker. She leapt forward and tore an arrow from the corpse, allowing it to finally fall to the ground.

"I'm so sorry," she screamed, and struck the kneeling Kara through the neck with the weapon. The terrified girl tried to fend her off, but her killer stabbed a second time. It was enough, and her screams became loudest just before they broke off altogether.

It was Ella who attacked Gemma first. The sudden flash of brutality had stirred her as well. She had no weapon, so threw punch after punch at the larger girl. Seeing the advantage of eliminating the largest and most deadly of opponents, Becki turned and joined Ella in her vicious assault on Gemma. It was nothing personal, but the heavy girl's eyes were wide with shock and betrayal. They kicked and punched her in perfect rhythm, like a team of elite warriors striking down a bear.

. . .

Mikayla tore an arrow from the dead body of one boy and sprinted into the centre of the arena to meet the graceful form of Aimee, the shaken murderess. The crowd held their collective breath in between raucous screams for blood. The god had promised entertainment. The god had delivered.

Uden stepped into the arena to watch the murder unfold. His eye darted madly among the three who were embroiled in a desperate last struggle and the two aggressive girls as they stabbed and cut at each other with their blood-streaked arrows. He still favoured the tallest girl. When she came of age, he would favour her even more. She would be beautiful. She would be grand. She would be a goddess.

He stepped closer, waiting for the killing blow. The screams were music he'd not heard in a deity's life. *Melodies to dance to.* That was something Aurora would say. Were any of these females as strong as Fyre, or as brutal as Aurora? He would find out. This was only the first bloody step.

As Gemma fell in a bloody mess on the ground, Becki stepped forward to step on her neck. She couldn't stop the shrieks escaping her own throat as she did. She was no killer, but it was all she could do. She had split her crimson hands open, and pulsating pain shot through her fingers. Her throat was raw. She was sorry for attacking the girl, but she didn't want to die.

Before Becki could kill the heavyset girl lying motionless in the dirt, Ella turned on her comrade-in-arms. It was a clever tactic, and Uden smiled as he caught the brutal change of allegiance. Ella swung at Becki as hard as she could. The smaller girl stumbled forward and tripped up on Gemma's feet. In her last ever act, she fell forwards and tried to gain her balance, but Ella struck her again and knocked her to the ground. She spat the dry dirt from her mouth and tried to rise. Dirt clung to the track lines of her tears. Fresh streams flowed from her tired eyes, and then Ella stood over her and began to stamp down.

Mikayla had all the natural ability to become a sublime warrior when she came of age. She was strong and incredibly fast. She swung and missed again with the bolt's tip and spat blood from her mouth. Her lungs were heavy and an invisible claw gripped at her chest, tearing her asunder. Aimee danced away from her, waiting for her to die. The bolt Aimee had held now lay nestled deep in her chest. Mikayla tried again to pull the bolt's head free and failed. Her slippery, blood-soaked fingers could not grip the impossibly thin piece of wood. As skilled or as great a warrior as she might one day have become, Aimee was better. Mikayla collapsed to the ground. She hacked and tried to suck in some air before drowning in her own blood. None of the combatants noticed her death. Aimee was already rounding up on Ella.

Aimee had another crossbow bolt in her hand, liberated from a nearby body. Hearing her own heavy panting over the roar of the watching crowd caused her a moment's delay. *Best take a moment to gather my breath.*

· · ·

Ella pulled her foot away from what remained of Becki's head. The body had long since ceased its twitching. She hadn't been able to stop herself, even when her opponent became nothing but a savage mess in the middle of a fuken nightmare. It was her first ever kill. It had been easier than she'd expected. She turned around to another opponent and found her vanquisher instead. The girl raised the crossbow bolt and drove it through Ella's vest, through skin, through muscle and through organs. Its searing pain almost took her sanity.

Aimee snapped the thin wood and leaned away from Ella's desperate counter-strikes. Ella's knees crumpled, but she did not fall. She gasped, and the horror struck Aimee anew. Instead of finishing her, she took the girl's waving hands as they sought life like a drowning sailor's in the middle of a tempest. Aimee held her in her arms and they both cried as the smaller girl's life slipped away.

"I'm sorry, friend," Aimee whispered. She did not see the flicker of movement behind her. She missed Uden gliding across the arena, eager to see the last moments. She only wanted to beg her victim for forgiveness. "I'm sorry," she said again, and felt her opponent become terribly heavy. "Please, I'm sorry," she screamed, and she was alone. "Please, answer me." The dead girl's head fell forward onto her shoulder, then drooped to one side.

Aimee released her grip and lowered the body into the dirt. She was champion. She would live. The crowd still screamed as though the competition continued. All the others had fallen around her. A terrible thought struck her: Perhaps the ultimate victor was slain by their leader. Perhaps that was what they all waited for. She could feel his massive presence up behind her now, and she gave up. She had no more will. She was tainted. Her path into the darkness would be blocked. She dropped her shoulders and listened to the noise all around her.

The heavy form of Gemma stirred in the dirt. The girl drew a wet breath and grasped her moment with both hands, despite her grievous injuries. She'd watched through battered eyes as the last few innocents had turned to sinners and slaughterers. She had heard the anguish in Aimee's pleas for forgiveness. She stood slowly up in the river of blood and the dead, gained her unsteady feet, shuffled forward and then fell upon the unsuspecting girl. It was almost too easy.

Uden watched with a dissecting eye as the little fat girl choked the life out of his next creation. He stepped closer, picking his way almost delicately through the ruined arena, to experience it more. It had been worth the wait. The skirmish had taken only moments, after months of waiting, but it had been perfect, down to the very last detail. He wiped the saliva from his lips and watched Gemma kill Aimee. He was mesmerised.

If he wanted, he could just end it for the fat little swine now. She had used cunning tactics, and he admired her for it. So many months of selecting the finest candidates for his little venture and now, he was ready to take the first step. A fine way to spend the lonely months of marching.

Aimee watched her killer. It was all she could do. The girl was younger than she, but her weight made this fight unbalanced. She tried to pull the girl's iron grip away from her throat, but after a few attempts and much wasted energy, she surrendered. The girl above her adjusted her knees, pinning both Aimee's arms, and squeezed tighter. Instinct made her kick out, but her legs were heavier than she'd ever felt them before, as though she were stuck in a marsh from her youth. She stopped fighting and watched the battered girl above her press down harder. Beaten, she allowed her last tears to flow down her cheeks.

"It is fine," Aimee whispered to her vanquisher through breathless gasps, as the dark of the night took her vision. The girl was only doing what was needed. It was horrible for all of them. It was the worst way to die. She felt her bladder prepare to release, but mostly she felt the call of the dark and the unending pressure. And then the grip loosened suddenly, and Aimee's vision cleared. Gemma's face wore an expression of fright and shock. She stared past her victim and her hands shook as she released her grip completely.

"Come, little one. The fight is done," a terrible voice whispered to Aimee, and the crowd fell to silence. It was a terrible reassuring voice. It sounded as if it loved her. A warm, wet haze splattered across her face, and then the weight of the heavy girl removed itself from her chest.

Gemma tried to stop the slit from opening any more, but the blade sliced across her throat again. He pushed her to the ground, and she flopped in the dirt, trying to stop the bleeding. It wasn't fair. She had won. The massive figure had cheated her of life.

It wasn't fair; she had won.

It wasn't fair.

Gemma closed her eyes, and the pain and the shock

subsided. It wasn't fair. She saw nothing but the beauty of black. The black of darkness. She stopped seeing anything at all. She had won.

Uden sheathed the blade and picked up the battered young girl from the little pool of blood and held her in his arms. It was his right to intervene. It was his right as a god. He moved the world with his thoughts. He created with his love and his movements. She had been his preferred choice, and she would become something greater than this little broken soul that she was now. He kissed her grubby forehead fondly and carried her from the arena of the dead. The sated generals bowed and fell to their knees as he passed. His guards flanked him on either side. Gemmil followed a few steps behind.

He would be bored no more.

29

HOT AS HELL

"Well, we can't just leave the bastards here to die. Problem is, we don't have enough supplies to feed them and us another week," Doran argued, as he had for most of the meeting so far. It was a fine point, Erroh conceded. They *were* a fuken problem.

It was no small matter to fuk up the first grand generals' gathering, but Erroh had found a way. He'd intended it to be a few awkward conversations with those whose voices he trusted, a few words as they found their feet, but it had turned into something else entirely. It had turned to shit.

Perhaps calling the assembly at the crack of dawn after a heavy night celebrating had been foolishness, but he feared they would be lethargic once they settled into the march. Feared wasting a moment longer than needed. They needed to go their separate ways. He feared that the Hunt would come searching the day they decided to depart this camp. It was irrational, unlikely, but Erroh's paranoia couldn't be contained. So, despite himself, he had summoned those who stood beside him now.

He'd chosen to hold the gathering outdoors, where the

rest of the camp could see the actions of allies. It was no lavish event, though. They sat around a simple table, just large enough for ten weary warriors, in the centre of the camp. But he hadn't counted on the heat of a blazing morning. To quote a dead man, it was "as hot as hell." It played around in his mind and he liked the term. Made him sad, too. It *was* as hot as hell, and the heat was adding to the misery of the worst hangover he'd ever endured. His mouth was dry. He wanted to spit away the taste of early morning, but he hadn't drunk enough water to form the spittle.

The night before had been long, and conversation had kept him up later than he'd intended. More than that, his foolish hope of setting their grand resistance on its first steps had kept his tired mind from proper rest. He sighed and fought the urge to throw up the bile churning in his stomach. Lea stood beside him now. She appeared as though she'd slept a dozen hours in silken sheets, waking every few to drain a pint of water in between. He rubbed his head and suppressed a moan. It would be noon before the pain ebbed away. That's when the real exhaustion would kick in.

By then, dreadful things could be afoot.

Could be.

She, too, found this meeting unpleasant. He could see it in her eyes, her clenched jaw. To distract herself, she concentrated on the unsettling map, spread out across the long table for all to see, for all to question. Her eyes scanned the ancient piece as though it were art, or gold, or a good hand in cards. Such things were rare to her, he imagined. She ran her finger along a black line leading to the city, and he watched her in a daze. She ground her teeth, and he understood her apprehension. An accurate map cut right through the hours lost in the saddle. An accurate map belonging to the southern army and its army sites was a glorious thing indeed.

And Roja doubted her value to this resistance.

Across from her, Doran rubbed his bleary eyes. Like Erroh, he appeared worse for wear. Uneasy allies or no, he had outlasted most of the others and was paying dearly for it.

From where Erroh stood, he could look down at the southern prisoners. They stared at him. Perhaps they knew Erroh's plight.

Hard building a resistance with a shackle dragging you down.

Aymon, beside him, shook his head in annoyance. "You think the answer is killing them in cold blood, Doran?"

"I never said that. I merely pointed out the problem."

Let's not speak of murder.

Aymon shook his head. "Well, that's how nasty things begin: while pointing out a problem." At the table of generals, there was a cool breeze. Even if it was hot as hell.

Emir didn't seem to belong at this gathering. Nor did he seem to desire to be at this gathering. He looked worse than any of the others, and given how much he'd drunk, it was hardly a surprise. He wavered more than normal. His mumblings suggested he was still drunk. As did his bloodshot eyes. Perhaps he was. "That fuken map is unsettling me," he muttered, looking away from the parchment and sipping at his cofe before glancing back at it with renewed courage. "If it matters, I don't think we should kill them, either," he added. The effort of speaking took a lot out of him, and for a moment Erroh regretted inviting him to the table. He scribbled Aymon's last few words onto the sheets in front of him and his own after. How anyone could discern the notes was anybody's guess, but it seemed important they have a record for posterity. For the generations to come.

So that our vanquishers might understand their victims more.

Magnus appeared as fresh as the day. He too couldn't keep his eyes from the map, and it didn't surprise Erroh. How long had he agonised over accurate maps to the Four Factions? Some might say he was obsessed. As much as it unsettled Erroh, it seemed to focus Magnus ever so. Earlier, he'd discovered him attempting to copy the impressive piece in his tent, his hands a blur of excited scrawls and sketchings. He'd even begun copying the ancient letterings. Perhaps he had been attempting to resurrect the language through cartography. Perhaps he wanted to understand the words of the ancients more. Who knew what languages had once existed? Though Magnus still wore his gaunt, defeated gaze, there was a spark when he looked at the inverted map. "Well, they will not join our fight," he said. Most agreed, but it needed to be said.

Erroh didn't like how swiftly the table was getting away from his grasp. All were eager players, playing at being gods to the wretches. He didn't like the change in the wind.

Wynn's mood was no better than it had been the previous night. Spared the agony of a wonderful night's revelry, he was annoyingly spry for this early call. His words were short and bitter. "They cannot be trusted," he growled. Upon learning of Lillium's promotion, he'd bowed deeply and said little more. Perhaps he'd understood the strength of the female. Perhaps he'd been relieved to have little say. Either way, he'd answered the summons without argument and accepted his own lesser promotion with a wry grin. That was a marginal victory in winning over this broken war council, Erroh supposed. Or else he was simply bringing closer a swift downfall in the guise of a slighted friend.

"Aye," Lillium agreed, her eyes upon the gathering of

southern prisoners at the far end of the camp. "Though distasteful, killing them is the only way of assuring our concealment." She had pledged she would always speak her mind, and Erroh appreciated her pledge. Perhaps not at this very moment, though. He was no butcher. Despite the southerners' sins, they had offered a surrender, believing themselves among honourable opponents.

Just like the towns?

Just like Jeremiah?

"See where pointing out problems gets us, Doran," muttered Aymon.

"Well, she's not wrong," Doran offered sheepishly, as though regretting his leading argument. His eyes were upon the scribblings of Emir. It was all on record. "There must be another way."

Erroh sought rational thinking. He felt the stirring of panic grow.

Wrek spoke next with a voice of reason. Like Wynn, he'd drunk little the night before. He'd spent longer ensuring everyone else kept their noses clean, kept the mood light. He'd been the last general Erroh had sat and spoken with. They'd raised a glass, shared a few words, and both men understood the importance of communication. He had taken the appointment with an easy nod of the head, and Erroh had been grateful. They'd spoken of tactics and warfare, and Wrek had spoken openly of humanitarian things. It hadn't taken Erroh long to realise the brilliance to the humble man.

"It's wrong to slaughter those who have offered surrender," Wrek said, and there was steel in his tone. He challenged any to argue; his unflinching eyes met those of his comrades and cut through them. Sometimes casual, terrible discussions were not a casual thing at all. "Has anyone asked their intentions? Has anyone questioned their loyalty?" He shook his head as though speaking to children. "We charged them, and many surrendered easily enough. Perhaps the southerners aren't all answering to Uden's call."

"Of course they will say they will join us," Lea said, "You can't trust a fuken word any southerner says."

Especially the blonde ones.

"Have you seen the way they gaze at our Master General?" Emir asked, still writing. His hand was a blur as he recorded his own thoughts on the matter.

Erroh had, indeed, seen how the southerners gazed upon him and found it disturbing. They all watched him whenever he walked past. Some blessed themselves as though they were zealots of another age. Little lost lambs, searching for something more. Forty contrite members of the Hunt awaiting their fate.

He'd intended to open a vote on an insignificant matter and go along with the deciding vote, regardless of personal issue. It would be good for morale and reaffirm their confidence that their voices counted. But this was something else entirely.

He would call a vote on their fate, he decided. Whether he honoured the result would be another thing.

He looked at the redhead standing quietly beside Lea. She'd said little. No longer did she give the appearance of the fiery queen bitch from the Cull. The city had not been kind to her, it seemed. Was it kind to anyone? She had many sins to answer for, but she'd earned favour by caring for Elise and Lexi. The fact of her having assisted in their escape was no small matter, either. She still had a spark in her eyes, even though she looked jaded and worn. It had been Lea's suggestion to invite her to the council, and although the suggestion had surprised Erroh, it was a sound recommendation. Roja knew the city, the taste of politics. Only a fool would ignore her voice.

"What of sending them to the city as prisoners of war?" Emir offered. It was a fine suggestion.

"And who would bring them?" Doran asked. A fine counter. "Not sure what reception the Wolves would get when we showed up with our forty-strong problems. A fine honourable suggestion, Healer, but an impossibility."

"They'd likely just hang them from the market gallows by day's end," whispered Roja.

"Including their keepers," muttered Emir.

"They wouldn't hang me," Wrek countered.

"I'll take them," growled Magnus. "I've been meaning to visit the city."

Erroh held his hand up. "I would like to hear how each of you would vote on the matter," he said, wiping the beads of sweat from his forehead and regretting this gathering even more. Only a fool would delay longer than needed. Knowing his father's hesitation spurred him on to make a decision. *Make a strategy. Fuken get them moving.* Besides, he wasn't sure Magnus had been joking about going to the city. "If I choose for them to die, it will be today. If we show mercy, well, we will address that problem later on."

He played his hands and hoped the deal came up right. There were nods of agreement, but nobody wished to begin the terrible decision. So Erroh looked to Lea.

"Mercy or murder?" he asked her quietly.

"Mercy," she said, and looked to the next.

"Murder," said Wynn. His fingers tapped the map. He looked as though he wasn't certain of his decision.

"Aye, murder," agreed Lillium. She clenched her jaw, perhaps understanding the true weight of her vote.

"Murder," growled Magnus.

"Mercy," sighed Aymon, eyeing his closest friend.

"I… um… Murder," Doran said. "We must think of the greater matters." It was what any leader would say.

"Mercy," whispered Wrek in disgust.

After a few moments, Roja said, "Murder."

Nobody said anything.

"We are waiting, Healer," Lea finally said, quietly. He stopped scribbling.

"I can't condone murder like this. I vote mercy," Emir bellowed.

"And I, too, choose mercy," agreed Erroh.

"Too many voices at this table," Magnus said, spitting at the ground in annoyance. He'd argued against so many. His point was made. Too many voices. Not enough listeners.

Erroh, however, was relieved at the outcome. "The council is locked. I will make the final decision: we will release the captives," he said. Nobody argued. The decision to take such a brutal slaughter from their hands was welcome, though Doran ground his foot in the dry dirt. Aymon slapped his shoulder, and he grinned instinctively. Aye, it was the right decision—and a terrible first vote at a fragile council.

Truthfully, this vote had merely sped up the events to come. Magnus should have moved their camp long before now. The surrounding forests could conceal any number of enemy scouts. He glanced at his father again and felt his stomach turn ever so. Magnus was not the legend they needed right now.

"We move the Wolves' camp deeper into the green," he announced. "We release the wretched Hunt to this wretched place." This too was met with agreement. "If they gather up under Uden's march? Well, what difference could forty fighters do among such numbers, anyway?" That's what it came down to, Erroh thought coldly. Numbers on both sides.

He had delivered forty warriors back to the enemy, but really, he'd saved them all from the horror of a massacre.

With the crushing weight of forty souls no longer in their hands, the council spoke more easily than before. There were plans to be made, and Erroh's order to upturn the camp was met with more positivity than he'd expected. It had been a place of slow recovery and had perhaps allowed for a taste of bonding between uneasy allies, but that moment had passed. The time for separating the spurned from the downright reviled had arrived.

There were only the finer details to arrange.

"We waste the healer by letting him wander the road with you Outcasts. We need him with us," argued Aymon. They'd already covered this, but he wasn't quite ready to let the matter drop. And why not? Wasn't that how supplies and weapons were shared between allies? Begrudgingly? Through bitter argument?

Beside him, Doran nodded his bald head. They were completely right in their desire to keep Emir with them when the two parties separated. They had the superior numbers, and there were likely to be many injuries incurred by their brothers once the brutal training began.

"Aye, you do, but it cannot be helped," Lillium countered before Erroh could say anything. He recognised that tone; he'd heard it in the Cull many a time. Hard to argue with it.

"Do I get a say in my fate?" asked Emir.

"Aye, as long as it is not with the Wolves," said Wynn, clasping his shoulder gently.

"He will come to no harm under our watch," argued Doran.

"We spoke of this before, Doran," Lea said. "Little point in severing your ties with Samara over a drunken wretch like him," she added. "Better he stay with us outcast few."

"Stupid name," mumbled Emir, tapping his finger on the paper. "It makes greater sense that I disappear into the wastes for a time."

If Erroh didn't know better, he might have seen a glimmer in his friend's eye. Perhaps having his fate taken out of his own hands was welcome. Perhaps Emir wanted time away from wretches and responsibility. Tending to the wretches in the ruin of the hovels was where he belonged, of course, but every man had a breaking point. Maybe a little time in the delicate silence of the wastes was exactly what he needed. Erroh looked at his father and thought similar thoughts about him, as well.

"At some point we might need the city, and it won't help you to be housing the most wanted fugitive of all. Besides, you have a few healers as it is," Erroh said, and Doran nodded his concession. As much as they needed a skilled healer for bandaging wounds and treating bruises, the ramifications were too costly.

"We *will* need him for where we are going," Lillium said quietly.

They spoke for an hour more, and to Erroh it was a strange thing. Their words and actions became defiant—not against Erroh, but against their coming vanquishers. With the first vote offered and disagreed upon, each member of the council found their own voice. When one spoke, all nine listened, and it felt natural. More than that, advice was offered—and offered with respect.

The road ahead would be daunting and terrifying, especially considering how insignificant a force they were. Their chances of living out the year were slim. As they spoke and made futile plans about where to camp, how to communicate, how to fuken release the enemy, there came upon them all the same realisation Erroh had long accepted.

They were going to die. Every single one of them. That was the way of this life. What mattered was succumbing with flailing fist, with fire in the eye and teeth gritted in defiance. The world was over; their actions belonged to the absent gods alone. Yet even humbled and without a path, they had earned their part in the tale to come.

Erroh tapped the table. He spoke clearly, for he'd been here before with grim, defiant and positively doomed warriors. "I took twenty peasants and held a line against an impossible enemy in a little town. Imagine what we can do as an army." His voice rose from a whisper to a growl; he was fierce. Nobody noticed his finger touch Lea's own under the table. A secret message, just for her. He'd never been alone. She knew that all too well. But she liked the reminder. She also liked his bravado.

"We alone face the oncoming tide. We stand here and make plans that determine the rest of history. Hear my words, warriors, and think on them," he warned, getting to his feet, stepping back, and squaring his shoulders. Any suggestion that he was the wrong man to lead this hopeless fight was quickly forgotten. Erroh could see Magnus nod in approval. "You know what you have to do, so get to it," he ordered, and struck the table fiercely. Within a breath, Lea did the same. Wynn right after. Soon after, they all followed, each one resilient and defiant. The hot-as-hell morning peace seemed to fall away now at the birth of a tradition.

"Dismissed," he said, and the table scattered immediately. Each general, tasked with their duties, was eager to escape the heat. All except Emir. He hastily finished the last of his notes and handed them to his Master General.

"Am I free to ride into the green forever?" he asked.

"You're going to miss all the fun, brother," Erroh countered, rubbing his eyes in the glare.

"All the death, you mean."

"Aye, plenty of death, but at least you'll have family around," Erroh said, rolling up the map delicately.

"I don't have any family," said the healer. But there was levity to his usually miserable tone. He seemed almost embarrassed. He would always have family in Erroh and Wynn.

"Roja forgot this. Can you give it to her now?" the Master General said sternly, passing the map to his brother of the dark. Roja was good for Emir, even if she was only a target on which to focus his annoyance. "Or perhaps give it to her while we're out on the road?" he added, shrugging his shoulders.

"Ah, for fuk's sake," Emir muttered, snatching the priceless map and shuffling away to gather up his belongings for the march ahead.

So concluded the first and last generals' meeting in this camp. Erroh wondered would they ever meet again in similar numbers, and doubted it.

"That went well," Lea said, stretching in the morning sun. "It's as hot as hell," she added, and he smiled.

"Come on. We have plenty to do if we are to seek out and kill Uden before the city burns."

"Sounds like a plan, my beo."

30

SIMPLE PLAN

"Don't let anyone see your hands shake," whispered Lea, bringing her mount alongside Erroh's magnificent beast. His mare wasn't enjoying this leisurely ride any more than its rider was; Erroh could tell these things. He'd never cared deeply for Highwind, and the beast reviled him outright. She and Shera had had several owners since they'd marched to Keri under Emir's watch, and only an act of the gods or a case of nasty serendipity had brought her back to him. Still, she was fast, and fast was reason enough to endure her aggression.

"It's not good for morale. Keep them steady," she added, and Erroh thought it fine advice. His hands had been shaking since his father had set out. They hadn't stopped even when the few outcast, unwanted wretches had followed a few days after.

———

As Magnus packed his few horses and climbed aboard his chosen mount, dawn was just beginning to break. Only Erroh stood with him now at the edge of the camp, and it was a terrible departure. Erroh had hoped there would be words shared before the end, but Magnus's face was stern and resolute.

Unforgiving.

And Erroh? Well, he never knew what to say to his master at the best of times. He would never see him again. There was something in his walk, in his demeanour, in Erroh's fuken gut. Magnus knew it too. That was the cost of the betrayal his master felt, and that was fine. Anger was a gift, and where he walked, there was nothing like a little anger to keep firm his charge.

"Let's go," Magnus hissed, and his hounds bounded up from their lazing far more swiftly than any right-minded warrior would at this time of the morning. They ran on ahead, for they knew this part of the march well. They were the enthusiastic ones.

"May the wind be at your back, Father," Erroh said at last. There was nothing else to say. He would not beg for forgiveness, would not suggest things would be fine once they met again. For that would have been a lie. They'd separated like this before, of course. Years before. That had been a source of pride for both master and apprentice. This was something entirely different. This was goodbye forever.

But for whom?

The absent gods had an idea.

"Goodbye, Erroh."

Magnus kicked his horse and charged away from the camp's light, leading his pack of horses out into the still night. For a moment, Erroh wanted to run after him, to call out. To tell him how much he loved him. To embrace him one last time. To savour their last shared moment.

But he didn't. For that wasn't what a Master General did

after condemning his father, his master, his idol to banishment. The echo of hooves disappeared, and Erroh felt a terrible hollowness.

––––––

"It's just the tiredness," he whispered, and Lea knew it was a lie.

"Well, I still don't like seeing it," she said, ducking under a low branch as she cantered along.

Ancient oaks and birches closed in around them as the wastes became greener. Darker. Safer. The trees creaked in the wind. Endless rows of brown and green leaves, wilting and breathing on all sides, were usually all Erroh needed to calm himself. But he found no peace this hazy afternoon. Gripping the reins tightly, he tried to settle his quaking hands.

They'll settle when I'm dead.

And when Uden's head has rolled free.

Lea liked this quiet, even though her body felt a ruin. She had not slept well, and the last thing she desired was a ride deep into the forest seeking a bandit's domain. It hadn't gone well the previous time. Everything had changed since then. The city cared for her, as much as it did for those of Raven Rock. Perhaps they would find willing allies. Perhaps they would find a haven from the harsh wind. For a few nights, at least.

Riding beside Erroh brought alive her desires for a life of silence with her beo, within the green. She wondered absently about forgoing all responsibilities and creeping away into obscurity with her mate in tow, and she smiled. She wasn't destined for a silent life.

Still, she liked seeing him in the saddle. Fighting his

mount, his mood, his own unease. The wastes were a good look to him. It's where she'd loved him first. Aye, everything was rightly fuked, but she was happier now than she'd been in months. This was home; this was life. She did not fear the days to come like he did, for she knew herself blessed by the absent gods. More than that, she felt herself blessed with her own ingenuity. She no longer feared her life. She embraced it.

"Dammit, Erroh. Grip your reins tighter and let them see nothing," she hissed, and he muttered a curse in reply. They led a line of terrified young warriors; the least he could do was look impressive. Glancing behind her, she saw that they appeared as lost as their tracks in the dust. She grinned, thinking of how nervous she herself had once been. Not anymore; not after the fuken south. It was difficult fearing unknown things after months of that life.

"Maybe I should lead," she mocked, and he laughed and his hands gripped the leather straps again. Highwind whinnied as though ready to charge, but he dampened her enthusiasm swiftly enough. The pace would be slow until they found their feet. A few days is all, she told herself.

They would adapt too. Some quicker than others. They were only as skilled as their weakest comrades. It would help if they could look at Erroh with unwavering trust. She would whisper in his ear until he no longer needed her. And then, well, then she could argue her feeling more openly.

"You want to lead? You'd have us out looking for flowers for your hat," he jested.

"Ribbons, Erroh. It was ribbons I desired for my hat. Get it right. You underestimate the importance of ribbons… and flowers in a battle. I mean, you could always win, but then again, you could always win with style." She grinned, and for a moment it was just them. Alone. In the wastes.

Perfect.

. . .

Behind them, Lillium watched the line of trees on both sides, her keen eyes searching for movement as her mount followed the procession instinctively. With the thicket this dense, she knew it unlikely they'd meet a wandering finger this far in. However, there were always scouts. Her fingers twitched. She enjoyed the quiet, but she craved vengeance. She always would. She had little intention of seeking death, but she was comfortable enough in its presence. And when they found southern battalions? Well, she fancied her chances in the melee to come.

She looked ahead to Roja's cart and the unimpressive figure of Wynn riding alongside. She was glad he'd joined them, despite his disappointing attitude. He behaved without banner or ambition. A far cry from the cub she'd first known. He might have flourished among the Wolves, but she had her doubts. Though his face still carried the same hollow, pale complexion, his eyes were more alive than before. He watched the path as though reading a scroll. Few were better trackers than he. Such a skill was invaluable. She wondered about reminding him of this, but thought better of complimenting him. Let that be Erroh's gift.

Stretching, she accidentally released her mount's reins, and they fell down along the beast's side and rubbed against her thigh. Absently, she thought of the dark, of the fallen city and the crack of a dead man's shattered teeth. As quickly as the miserable thought came upon her, she shook it from her mind and grabbed the reins and hoped nobody had taken any notice.

. . .

Wrek brought his beast up beside Emir as he neared the two leading Alphalines. Since leaving the camp of the outcast Black Guards earlier that day, he'd lamented his decision. He had been given a choice, as they all had: to march towards death a little wiser, or dig in with the rest of the Wolves attempting to batter together an effective army. Though Aymon and Doran had less issue with him than before, he no longer desired to march with his adopted brethren. Besides, he still wasn't certain the city was unaware of his hand in the jailbreak.

Having been offered no real choice was little consolation now as the sun set, and the saddle hurt his rear. He didn't want to die, but he wasn't entirely convinced of the great hunt Erroh was attempting. He was quite certain it *would* be the death of him. He was a mere man, among elite Alphas. As was Emir, but the behemoth knew that the wretched healer's shadow was larger than them all combined. He just tried not to show it.

"Hey, Erroh, what's with your hands? Are you doubting yourself already?" Emir asked, drinking deeply from his water tankard.

Wrek had never seen a man relish water so completely—until a familiar aroma struck his nostrils. Moving alongside, he snatched the flask from Emir and drank a mouthful of his own, before offering some to Erroh and Lea in turn. He did not know Erroh well, yet he considered him a friend. They had shed blood together, and Wrek did not take such things lightly. Wrek had been part of the mass frenzy when swords had clashed in anger. Erroh had charged an army alone, and many warriors who cared little for him as a man had followed his foolish charge anyway. There was something about him. Maybe it was his walk. Maybe it was the effect of the tales, sonnets and songs sung about one so young. Whatever it was, he commanded respect without ever trying.

His plan had a poetic foolishness to it.

Find Uden the Woodin Man.

Kill him.

No problem.

The matter of the massive army Uden called upon didn't seem to worry Erroh in the slightest, so Wrek didn't push the matter. For now, Wrek would listen to the Master General's orders. Better that than simply waiting for Uden to crush them all, he supposed. If truth be told, Wrek wasn't sure why Erroh valued him or trusted him for such a task, but a chance at saving the world from unspeakable losses was impossible to ignore.

Wrek's greater unease came from their destination. He wasn't sure how far his name carried in the underground's wind anymore. Raven Rock was a town he had rarely visited. And certainly not since his fall from Adawan. He'd heard, through whispers, of a low price upon his head. A small matter, as every decent runner earned a price upon their head at some point. It was when the price grew to a substantial, more appetising amount that a runner worried more. Such things were easier to avoid in a tiny tavern, or when lording it over Spark City, or even when one was an Outcast in the wastes, surrounded by Wolfen companions. But walking into the beast's belly was just poking a bear. Still, it might be nice being around his kind again. Especially if they didn't want to stick a knife in his back.

Lea wiped her mouth and tossed the bottle of sine back to Emir, who almost fell from his beast as he reached to reclaim his treasure. He downed another mouthful in celebration of this victory and fell back towards the rear of the procession, alongside the cart of the broken and the needy. He wrapped the reins of his horse along its edge before dropping to the muddy ground below and then leaping gracefully onto the slow-moving wooden machine. He did this as if he'd spent a lifetime in constant motion, leading a long caravan of refugees wandering the road.

Maybe half a lifetime. At least he wasn't in charge. Now and then he reminded himself of this, and it was wonderful.

He tended to Nomi first. She flinched at his touch, and he sighed and shook his head in frustration. "I won't touch you there," he said, feeling her forehead for further sign of fever. She was an extra load in the cart, and the pace was slower. The sooner she could ride, the better. "See? I'm not all that bad."

Roja did not bother to look his way, and he repaid the gesture in kind. Lexi watched on anxiously. She knew he would set upon her soon enough. She still would not cry out. An impressive thing.

"Will you need me?" asked Wynn, gesturing to Lexi, and Emir shook his head.

"I can take the pain," Lexi argued. Emir couldn't help notice her straighten up as Wynn gazed at her. She was ever so smitten with the ponytailed fuk, and Emir was going to have quite a laugh at Erroh's expense once he brought this to his friend's attention.

Wynn offered her a smile, and then looked above the canopy to the setting sun before kicking his beast forward. Emir watched him as he came up beside Erroh. He also watched Wrek and Lea drop a little further back, finding sudden interest in a clump of trees on their left, a fallen log on their right.

Emir smiled. He'd seen behaviour like this on the march

many times. The politics of conversation within the saddle was a precarious thing. Was he himself not doing his best to ignore the beaten gaze of the gorgeous redhead a few feet away?

"You need to take this," he said to Nomi, and she stared at him in dumb silence. Holding a little jar, he mimicked a rubbing gesture at her chest, beneath her nose. At all the places needed, really. She nodded and grabbed it from him, her cold eyes never breaking from his. "You are welcome."

Southern bitch.

Erroh stared at Wynn in silence. He would not speak first. Any friend who behaved as Wynn had needed to say the first words. His hands still shook, though the shot of sine helped calm him. Hours in the saddle had not returned to him nearly enough serenity, though.

Eventually, when the silence became agony, Erroh almost broke; almost told him to fuk off and watch their rear. Almost, but not quite.

"We are making good time," Wynn said. A fine opening gambit. He sighed as Erroh said nothing. This close, in the fading light, Erroh could see how worn he was. Whatever energy he'd shown at the council gathering was long gone. He looked like he hadn't slept in weeks. His face was deathly pale and set in a tight grimace. His hair was unusually greasy and tied up carelessly in a ponytail. He had looked better in the hellish prison cell, when their bond had been forged. Maybe it had just been the light. "I can feel the cut in the wind, and those clouds ahead don't look terribly inviting." He was trying. Fuk him, but he was trying.

"You think we should make camp?" Erroh asked carefully. He really was pale.

"Aye, Erroh, I do."

The Master General nodded and looked ahead. There were no obvious breaks in the treeline; any place was good. Distancing themselves from the Black Guard was essential, and the slow pace was agonising. He absently patted Highwind in apology. The horse snorted as she denied it. She was raring to sprint onwards. This slow pace likely reminded her how little she liked him. And he her.

"Another mile," Erroh said, and winced inwardly. It sounded too much like an order. He wasn't entirely sure barking out orders to the slighted young Alpha was the best of ideas.

"Aye, sir," muttered Wynn, and tapped at something metal hanging down the side of his beast. It looked to be a large piece of heavy steel, unskilfully smelted. It resembled a strange shield, though such a piece would not stand up to many strikes. It was southern, and Erroh almost asked about it but kept silent.

Such an uncomfortable silence.

Fanned by his agitation, Erroh's anger at Wynn's behaviour grew. He counted a few numbers in his head and thought about finer things, like yellow dresses and wet cloaks in unsuitable campsites.

When he could take no more of the rhythmic sound of tapping, he spoke again. "At least it's dry. We'll have little difficulty setting a fire."

"Nothing like a fire to keep away the dark," agreed Wynn grimly, and then smiled. They'd come through the dark. It would be wise to remember that.

"Oh, I don't mind the dark at all," lied Erroh, shuddering. His mouth suddenly became dry at the thought. Wynn instinctively reached for a water can of his own and drank deeply. Aye, they both remembered all too well.

"Will you ride ahead and find us a grand spot to rest for the night?" the Master General asked.

"Aye, sir, I'll do my best," the ponytailed Alpha said. He drank once more and offered the tankard to Erroh.

"You're the best tracker here, Wynn. I trust you."

Wynn nodded his head in thought. He looked like he had words to offer. Thoughts to share. Perhaps grievances to air. "I'll find us a pleasant spot with a fine view," he mocked, before kicking his beast forward and disappearing into the deep green.

Erroh's frustrated mount snorted in disgust as the beast charged away. "Ah, don't start with me, Highwind," he grumbled.

———

True to his word, Wynn located a fine spot, surrounded by tightly clustered trees and protected from harsh winds by a little slope that broke up the flat of the land. There was suitable grass for the tired beasts to graze, and a thin stream from which to refill their tankards. He had set a small campfire to light in the centre of a wide-open space for when they arrived, and it was most welcome.

"Not a splendid view," muttered Erroh, clapping his brother on the back. It was a fine spot. They would be safe for the night. Wynn, in reply, almost smiled again before turning and preparing his bedding.

Small steps, Wynn.

"I thought you said that camping near a water source was an invitation for the Hunt to discover us," Wrek pointed out, cupping his hands in the cool, flowing water and washing the dust of the day from his beard.

"They stick to rivers. A stream will be fine," Lea said. "I

learned that one swiftly enough," she added, untacking her horse before brushing it down. Her eyes were upon Nomi, climbing down gingerly from Roja's cart. If looks could kill.

"So, we should be free to wander the road, as long as we stay away from rivers," said Emir, holding his water canister above his head and trying to drain the last few drops of... water.

"That's part of the plan," said Lea and nuzzled Shera, who replied in kind. Their bond had been unbroken since an arrow had almost torn her rider apart.

"It'll never work," decided Emir.

"You don't believe in looking on the bright side, do you, Healer?" Wrek laughed and stuck his head under the water.

"I just keep my eyes on the middle... and... um... He's not listening. He's drowning himself instead of listening to my deep thoughts."

————

There was brief conversation within the group as the light faded and turned to darkness. They ate sparingly; there was little game to be had. Usually, once they settled at a long-term camp, there was plenty of time to enjoy the thrill of the hunt. Lea above all missed unleashing Baby on her unsuspecting meals. She slid her finger along the bow's arch and pledged that she would soon let many arrows loose. She chewed some dried, salted meat and missed fresh kill a little more. She studied Erroh. His hands shook less. Small steps taken with Wynn had helped, but her man carried a substantial burden.

She thought of his prowess and smiled despite herself. She felt a primal longing to drag him into the dark woods and explain once more just how impressed she was with him, as her mate for life. Instead, she broke off a piece of salted meat and lifted it to his lips. She dared a quick kiss on his cheek before getting to her feet, hauling him upright and dragging his limping form towards a clearing at the edge of the camp. He knew her movements, and he groaned at the thought. Leaving him where he stood, she went back and pulled the heavy chest from the cart, then dragged it loudly across the ground.

He sighed dejectedly and argued about his stitchings. But she would have none of it. Soon enough, they both began stretching as the others lazed and prepared themselves for a well-earned sleep. She flipped open the chest and took from the dozen sets inside.

"Come tear me apart," she challenged, offering the weapons.

"Not in front of everyone," he mocked.

The crack of the blades was all too familiar, and she danced around him, attacking madly. She held nothing back, her hair flailing wildly in the growing breeze, her perfect form twisting in a blur, her arms periodically striking terrifying combinations. She was the finest of elites.

And Erroh, well, he was a little less graceful. Though he did what he could to avoid tearing his stitching, she offered no mercy. Within moments, he was stumbling back from her strikes, grunting as each of his defensive forms was tested a little more than he would have preferred. Onwards they danced through the camp, now watched with great interest by an attentive audience and a few crows above.

With no boundaries to their sparring ring, Erroh frequently crashed and stumbled against some innocent spectator too slow to step out of the way. These accidents brought great amusement to the rest and added to the shared entertainment.

Eventually, when he could take no more abuse, Erroh

collapsed on the dry ground and pleaded for no more punishment, and she allowed him a reprieve. After a few jests at his inadequacies with the blade, she bowed and walked to the centre of the camp.

"If you ride with Erroh? You fight," she declared, before removing a few more blades from the chest. She tossed a set to Lillium and solitary blades to Wynn, Emir and Wrek. After a moment, she threw a wooden blade down at the feet of Roja. Her too.

"I recommend each of you stretch," she said, wiping sweat from her forehead.

"Winner stays on," she announced, and waited for her next challenger. After a few moments, Lillium shrugged and tested both blades. Then, spinning them slowly, like she'd seen Erroh and Lea do, she met Lea in the centre. Stripping down to her vest, she bowed to her future vanquisher.

"This is going to hurt, isn't it?" she said, then laughed and attacked wildly. She slashed left and right a few times and met a steady wall of defence before spinning away to catch her breath. It was in this moment that Lea unleashed her full ability on her friend and battered through her defence mercilessly. Within a flash, Lillium was in the dirt, nursing a nasty bruise across her cheek, but the fire of competition burned in her eyes.

"Aye, this will hurt a lot," said Lea, laughing and looking across her audience, eyeing each of her future victims in turn as a beast would its prey. Erroh leaned back beside a nervous-looking Emir and warmed his hands on the fire contentedly.

"I know it should terrify me, but there are worse things to gaze upon as the night closes in," Emir whispered, watching the females engage in a fresh bout of aggression. Blinking as little as he could, he reached across and opened a fresh bottle of sine, but before he could sample the fresh brew, Erroh snatched the bottle from him.

"Fuken typical males," muttered Roja from behind them.

He remembered a younger, waif-like Lea rediscovering the wastes for the first time. "Best of luck, Mydame," he called as she stepped into the invisible arena. She did not spin her blade; she merely tested the weight and stretched her long legs a few times. Emir held off his outrage at his stolen bottle for that part.

"Maybe you should be sober. You might last longer," Erroh whispered to the silent wretch, who lost a little more interest as the two goddesses went to war.

With the first camp settled and sleep calling after some fine entertainment, Erroh finally felt a little lighter. It suddenly didn't matter how much he missed his father. It didn't matter how much he feared for his mother's health. It didn't matter how enraged he was at the injuries incurred by his little sister. It didn't matter that he was helpless in so many terrible things.

What mattered was the hunt.

Somewhere out on the road, Uden the Woodin Man was marching on Samara, and though the mad god believed himself infallible, Erroh was hunting him and he had the measure of him.

He watched as Roja collapsed in a battered, bruised and blissfully exhilarated mess, and Wynn stepped forward only to meet the same fate. The loud, familiar clatter of aggression was reassuring, and Erroh joined in with the rest of the onlookers as they mocked, jested and jeered at the combatants.

. . .

Eventually, Lillium sat down beside her Master General and nursed her wounds with a shot of Emir's remedy. Erroh began stretching, wincing at his own bruises, and she watched eagerly and made an oath to improve herself. Some pain was a good thing.

"Today was a good day, Erroh," she whispered, and drank deeply before offering it to Wrek.

"Aye. May we have many more," Erroh replied, watching with pride as his perfect mate destroyed all who stood before her.

31

THE WRETCHED REDHEAD

The fire at the centre of the clearing warmed the air. The last few nights had carried an icy breeze, and Emir feared the season was changing early. Some nights in this region were so cold that a wind could steal an unprepared man's life, and the following morning, his corpse would be nearly cooked in the sun's heat. It was a fine camp, though. The grass was lush enough that the mounts wouldn't complain.

Even fuken Highwind.

Wynn was finding his feet marking their route, and so far, their path these last few days had carried them through enemy territory without sign or trace of a brute. It made it easier to believe they might come upon a permanent haven, somewhere to properly prepare for their hunt.

Emir, for his part, had never been more terrified in his life. He wasn't used to experiencing terror, yet it held him in an icy grip. He was wretched, and wretched things deserved to die, yet still, these last few days, he'd been almost overcome with fear.

What is it I fear more than death?

On the far side of the camp, away from the fire's warmth, he watched Roja stretch, and her beauty was staggering, and oh, he hated her for it. She lived this march detached from the gathered group, always a few lengths behind the nearest comrade. Always offering fewer words than pleasant conversation required. Always a few smiles short of good cheer. She spun her body gracefully as she countered invisible foes, but to Emir she appeared to be dancing, and he wanted to spin with her as though they were together in a tavern in a city of light.

Maybe trip her up a few times while he was at it.

"You've been staring at her all day long. I think you should talk to her," Erroh said, drawing him away from the task at hand. "Or at least allow me to rest," he mocked.

"Sorry. I was just thinking of Lea in that dress—*out* of that dress," Emir countered, then returned to the task of changing the dressing across his chest. Erroh didn't even react, and Emir worried after his wits. "It's more fun when you threaten to beat me with a rock," he muttered, and this time Erroh smiled. *Success.*

"Am I still a ruin?"

"Getting better every day." There would be some heavy scarring, and Emir thought it unlikely these wounds would be the only ones Erroh would suffer in the days ahead. It was a fruitless task being a healer to a pack of warmongering Alphas. He took Erroh's scorched hands and examined them. These were healing nicely. However, just like his chest, there would be souvenirs. Erroh clenched his jaw but said nothing of Emir's probing. "Do they still hurt?"

"Not as much."

Emir tapped the skin with fingernails in need of a shearing. He heard Erroh gasp and hold his breath as he tested the skin for infection or weakness.

"Would you tell me if it did?"

"Not at all."

"Fuken Alphas. Can't show weakness or restraint."

A few feet away, Roja twisted her neck and closed her eyes, and he watched her again. She wobbled slightly but gripped the edge of her cart instinctively, and before anyone could notice, she straightened out.

He almost called out to her, to tell her she wasn't as alone as she felt she was. She shook her head and her hair flowed out magnificently, and he tried to ignore any stirrings. She was beautiful. Oh, she was so beautiful, and she hated him with all her might. A fine, glorious hatred, and he knew if he called out to her, she would recoil. Then he would too.

These wretched few Outcasts upon this march were all suffering traumas. Some upon the skin, but most deep in their souls. He could treat physical afflictions with no bother, but the soul was something else entirely. There was nothing worse than time in the saddle brooding over unpleasant things. If truth be told, there had been a strangeness to Erroh these last few days, and it unnerved Emir. He'd seen the same distant gaze long ago in the great betrayer's eyes, though Cass had been drowning in an ocean of madness. This strangeness of Erroh's was only a glistening river. Perhaps it was the trauma of war. Had they not suffered similar horrors in Keri together? Erroh had things like foolish honour and naïve gallantry to keep his path assured.

Still, though.

"It's perfectly acceptable to tell me how much pain you are in. In your body, in your thoughts," he said, catching Erroh's eyes and holding them in a serious gaze. He wished he'd said such things to Cass. Wished he'd pushed further into the man's horrors and sought the sinking man before he drowned.

"Fine words from a man like you. Oh—she's looking over at you, now," Erroh countered sharply, and Emir shrugged. *No, she isn't.* He wrapped the gauze and tugged it tightly before poking at the covering until the Alpha yelped. "She saw that."

"The sparring sessions are slowing your recovery, Erroh," he scolded, already knowing the futility of the argument. "And some of us cannot keep the pace."

"You just don't want to practice, Healer," Erroh laughed, sliding his vest back over his head and covering his injured chest. Emir had seen no one as tired as he. He always looked close to death, but since becoming the Master General and deciding that Uden was his responsibility to kill, he'd appeared to grow old overnight. His face was gaunt and pale, even after days in the burning sun. His shoulders were slumped despite the strength in his walk. Always first to rise, last to settle. Never resting long in the hours between. As though showing weakness would bring catastrophe upon them all.

"Well, I fight my war with needle and thread, potions and bandages. Blood and ruin, too. I could use the time in between to drink," Emir countered. It was true; he craved a reprieve from the daily abuse Erroh's mate inflicted upon them all. He thought he'd endured the pain of the march until he'd marched with Alphalines, all energetic with hormones and pride and a desperate desire to prove themselves. Also, he really didn't want to fuken practice.

"All of us fight, Emir. Best we have a healer capable of inflicting devastation, should the moment arise."

Emir knew this already. "Aye, but do you really expect me to ride into battle with you?"

"I expect you to kill as many of your vanquishers as you can before you fall," he replied, a little too casually.

"If I fall."

"When we all fall."

"A fine point, I suppose," muttered Emir. He turned and caught sight of the impressive form of Wrek receiving a beating in the middle of their camp. *Winner stays on?* The law of the nightly skirmishes. Whoever thought that was a good idea? Emir thought bitterly. He'd always believed himself a decent enough fighter, or at least average for any wanderer of the road, but for four fuken nights in a row, Lea had humiliated him with her swordplay. Oh, he didn't mind the embarrassment. Just the welts and bruises and the incessant challenge of avoiding throwing up in the arena. It would be an interesting choice of tactic, he supposed.

He wasn't alone in his humbling. That was something, at least. Each member of their group took turns getting battered by Lea. Even Erroh suffered under her relentless dance. Though admittedly, he took his beatings well.

As did Wynn.

On the second night, Wynn had disarmed one of her blades with a shield strike. Buoyed on by victory, he'd lashed out to score a killing blow, only to have his blade twisted in his grasp and ripped from him. She'd danced away as he'd fallen to his knees, holding his thumb, which had been hanging at an odd angle. Before Emir could help set it back into place, the ponytailed Alphaline had gripped the digit and popped it back into place himself before picking his weapons back up.

"Taking the pain," he'd growled under his breath, and said nothing more as he raised his weapons to face her once more. Lea had allowed him the reprieve of a few deep breaths before ending the fight swiftly. The last blow had been a rap across his injured thumb. He had not cried out. This had pleased the watching crowd.

Now, as Wrek fell, there was a polite applause for him. He stood there wiping a bloody nose and laughing at the attention, and Emir though of Quig in the festival's time. *Better times.* He thought he'd been miserable in those days in Keri. Oh, to spend a moment with that bitter fool and smack him a few times, so he might better appreciate the fleeting moments he never took as happiness.

He wondered if another version of him in the days ahead could sit down beside him this very moment. Perhaps thrash him a few times and demand he remember these days as the finer ones. Especially with what was to come.

Days and nights of screaming to come.

Emir shuddered. "It could be worse, I suppose."

"Tell me this: how is Nomi? Is she fit to ride?"

"She seems well enough. If you like, I'll insist she climb a horse."

"The lighter the cart, the quicker we'll go. I'll trust you on the matter," Erroh said, but his face darkened. He kicked at some dirt on the ground. "Um… I don't know if you've noticed, but Roja is looking exhausted."

"She should rest, so," Emir countered.

"It's a healer's calling to see to those in need of help," Erroh said, and it sounded like an order.

"Well, I *have* to train," Emir countered as he recovered his pair of sparring blades from his pack. He eyed his opponent, who had taken a knee to gather her breath. She had beaten four already, but Wrek had lasted longer than normal. "Besides, it's Lea who looks tired," he whispered, more to himself.

"Tired? This is only the beginning, friend. Wait until we are sparring twice a day."

Emir spun on him. "What a terrible thing to suggest."

"Though you can still earn a reprieve seeing to Roja," Erroh offered.

So tired. So tired that forming words in her mind was a struggle. But regardless of her exhaustion, Roja was still limber. She touched her toes one last time before worrying what to do next. What would distract her? These moments were the worst. Being out of the saddle, sitting and being silent, was an invitation to lamentation.

Beside her, a mount nickered, and she pulled a thick brush from the back of the cart.

Perfect distraction.

Gently, she smoothed out the beast's mane and brushed at its chestnut coat. There was a comfort to manual labour. Focusing her mind on the simple art of brushing made it easier to ignore the crushing misery. She despised feeling this disconsolate, but it was all she had left. What hope for happiness was there, when nothing but hatred remained? And she had quite the hate to give. All too soon, she finished tending to the beast and left it to its grazing.

"Prettiest of the other mounts," she whispered, and returned to the cart, seeking further distraction. Of all the great tragedies that had befallen her, it was the sleepless nights that took her fight. Aye, there were moments near dawn, when the camp was quietest, that her mind finally settled and she earned an hour here or an hour there. Just enough to keep her from full madness. Still, however she tried, she could not sleep a proper night.

The fighting was a release. That was something. Every day, she came alive during the violence like she were a young cub again, honing her craft. Learning her fierceness. She could take the stinging pain and the humbling defeats delivered upon her by Lea. She could become better. She was built to be better.

She had fought last this evening, and she cursed her luck. She might have fought sooner and exhausted herself enough to slip away to slumber while watching the others compete. That was fine distraction too.

Oh, to close her eyes and dream incoherently once more. To fly above orange clouds and run naked through a forest of spoons and tankards. To wake up and feel refreshed and willing to grab the light the rest of her companions clung to. The light of belief and love and warmth and sweetness and joy. All those things she'd taken for granted, along with Dia's reassurances, whenever she'd feared for her people. For the world. For herself. She wanted to join their naïve bravery.

She'd tried calming her heart rate and thinking of little more than the surrounding silence, but it was silence that screamed so loudly in her ears. Lying among so many quiet bodies, listening to their dreams and their fretful mutterings, was no replacement for the hum of Samara, that wonderful lullaby of her long-ago life.

Roja closed her eyes and stretched again. She could feel the tears coming once more. She couldn't take breaking down again. Not with everyone around to judge her weakness. She shook her head and allowed her hair to cover her shame. Her vision went dark, and she felt herself waver slightly. Despite her tiredness, her reflexes served her well.

She missed her silken sheets like a child. She could take the horror of the road if she could just lie in silk bedding. Its touch was reassuring. It was home. What was a girl to do? She sighed again and listened to Wrek's groans as Lea battered him further.

Lea was no longer the little shrew, stumbling through the shadowy corridors of their tower. Always cowering. Always behind Lillium. Roja wondered if Lea noticed the way Lillium stared at Erroh. Lea's suspicious gaze was turned on Nomi alone, no doubt. It was hard not to notice the venomous glances she offered the weak southern female. Lea probably didn't know Nomi stared at her just as much, when her gaze wasn't on Erroh.

Roja grabbed the bridge of her nose and squeezed it until there was relief. It was the closest thing to sleep she would get for many hours, she was certain, as she waited for darkness to overcome her. So many hours to think tragic thoughts about her life and companions.

"You look terrible," said Emir, startling her from her miserable reverie. He stepped close to her and stared right through her into her soul. She looked away instinctively and fought the urge to vomit. She'd fought that fight since the first morning of insomnia.

So tired.

"Oh, fuk off, Emir," she hissed, turning from him. He declined her suggestion and stepped around to stare into her eyes again. Not as a friend, and not as anything more than a friend. She knew that searching gaze. She tucked her hair behind her ears and didn't know why. Nor why, despite her exhaustion, she was still glad to have applied paint to her eyes, dark as they already were.

He brushed aside a loose strand from her brow and leaned in closer before steadying her head by cradling it in place. She allowed him to do it. She was tired, and this distracted her. She could smell his breath, tinged with alcohol and cofe and, somewhere beneath, some barely cooked meat, and her stomach turned. Shivers ran down her spine from his touch, and she never wanted his grubby, unworthy hands to let go. Still, though, she stared right back into those caring, broken eyes and tried desperately not to scream.

Just once with spittle and all.

"Easy, woman. I'm not trying to kiss you," he hissed, placing his hand across her brow. With a dissatisfied curse, he drew away and sat staring at her for a few more wretched breaths.

"What do you want?" she growled, pushing him away. She hated those shivers. They had no business tormenting her like this. Settling her fluttering heart. Causing this strange stillness.

"I want a better life."

"Well, fuk off and find it somewhere else, so," she snapped, but did not move. For as much as he unsettled her, he was also a man of healing. She desired relief from this torment; she just didn't want *him* to help her. Or else she didn't want *him* to know she wanted help, or else she wanted *him* to help her, without wanting him to know she wanted *him* to help. Most of all, she wanted him. No, she wanted sleep. That's what she wanted, she realised, and flinched.

"Oh, if I could. All paths lead me back to helping all the miserable, cruel witches and desolate, vile bastards in the end," he whispered, and she thought it a strange thing to be condemned so gently. She leant away from him, rested against the cart and exhaled.

He just waited.

"I'm tired," she said after a short time. Speaking these words aloud brought forth how deep her ruin was. She was broken and lost and she couldn't find her way back towards the light. If he understood this from these few words, he showed no sign. And how could he? He simply stared at her, and she wondered how deep his hatred for her might be. "I haven't slept in four nights now," she said, grimacing at having admitted weakness to him.

Beyond, she caught sight of Lea spinning her blade as

Wrek collapsed down beside Wynn and drank heartily from a bottle of cursed brew. Oh, she wanted to steal away from sobriety until the darkness washed over her, but no matter what beverages she consumed, nothing helped with her plight.

"Your time, friend," Lea called to her now, pointing to Roja's sword leaning against one wheel of the cart.

Wretched distraction.

Roja shook the tiredness away, offered a weak smile and reached for the blade. So exhausted.

"Not tonight, Lea," Emir said, knocking the blade out of Roja's hands.

"Everyone fights," Roja growled. She reached again for the sword, but Lea swept it away from her grasp.

"Why not tonight?" Lea asked Emir.

"Just not tonight," he said, bowing slightly, and Roja thought it a weak argument.

"As you wish, Emir." Lea returned the sword to its place. As she did, she stepped forward and clasped Roja's shoulder gently. Just for a moment. It might have been a gesture. It might have been her way to balance as she returned the blade. It was something.

Emir watched Lillium leap giddily into battle for a second time that night to try for the crown, and he shook his head in disgust. "Fuken Alphalines. They can't just take the rest of the night to recover," he grumbled, watching Lea meet Lillium's first strike. Within a breath, they were engaged in a fierce contest with the rest watching on. All but two.

"Well, I like the fighting," Roja scoffed, and he almost smiled, until he saw how badly her hands shook. Worse than Erroh's, and with good reason too.

"Of course you do, Alpha female," he said. He rummaged in the cart for his little sack of remedies. Grunting under his breath in frustration, he finally found what he sought. Taking out a little leather pouch, he grasped her hand and led her away from the gathering. She followed obediently, and he knew from this that she was truly in a poor condition. He stopped by her bedding, bundled the blankets swiftly under his arm, and led her out through the darkness to a quiet little spot away from prying eyes and eager ears.

"Is this where you try to ravage me?" she mocked, though she did not draw away. She knew the measure of him, knew he would be horrified at such a thought. The clatter of swords faded away behind the forest's hum, though the fire's light could be seen through the rows of trees. Though close, they were very much alone, and here he dropped her bedding onto the mossy ground.

"Let's try to settle you in a place where you won't be disturbed," he whispered, sitting down beside the blankets and smoothing them out.

She sat down opposite him, crossed her legs and stared at the fire a lifetime away. "These blankets do little more than block out the breeze," she said, poking at her bedding as though it had caused her great offence.

Was this how Cass had fallen into darkness? he wondered. Did it start with a few sleepless nights? "Have you ever struggled to sleep like this?" he asked, doing his best to speak as though she were a patient and not a girl he both adored and reviled. But mostly adored. He sounded smug, he realised. He could hear it in his tone. It was a small matter.

"Only when Dia…" She dropped her head.

"And it passed?" This he said less smugly. There was even compassion in his tones. He fought his sorrow. Fought it

hard, and treated her as a patient to be repaired. Easier
that way.

"Aye, after a day or so," she said, and sighed, and she was
pathetic and he wanted to take her in his arms and hug her
until the agony flittered away like a harmless invitation
offered by a careless fool.

"A day or so is fine," he said, scratching his head. "Are
you drinking more cofe than normal?" he asked. To this she
replied with silence. He could read her easily enough. *I
haven't slept, so I drink jumping juice to really set myself a
challenge, you fuken idiot.*

"When I first left Keri, it was with a broken heart and a
heavy load of responsibilities to weigh me down," he said,
allowing himself a moment to miss Aireys and ache for her.
He sighed again and opened the pouch. A sweet aroma of
natural things filled the air. "For three days I couldn't sleep,
and it led me down a dark road," he admitted.

"A dark road?"

"A man without sleep can't think straight on any matters,
even matters of death," he said, wiping his eyes. Just in case.
Kissing thoughts of Aireys away for the moment, he turned
his attention to the pouch and inhaled its contents.

"I half expected something with a eucalyptus smell," she
jested.

"It's my only potion," he said, laughing. She knew the
truth as well as he did. Everything went down better with
eucal tree mixed in.

Not everything.

"While I'll always say that sine is the finest cure for
everything, I found that this little plant took great care of me
when I needed it most," he said, offering the pouch.

"You're suggesting I smoke tobacco weed?"

"What else do you I think I mix into my concoctions," he

countered, feigning insult. He reached in and took out a few dry flakes and held them in his fingers.

"I'm not taking that shit," she hissed, smacking his hand away. The flakes took flight and disappeared into the darkness.

He thought about shattered eggs.

"I'm really sorry. I'm really, really sorry," she said, reaching for the lost flakes on the pine needle ground. To find them would be near impossible.

He caught her scrambling hand. He dared a gentle squeeze, and she trembled in reply. "Most people can't sleep because their minds are wild with thoughts." She listened, and he was grateful. "The flakes will calm your mind." She nodded, and he thought about kissing her. "I have stronger medicines, ones that smell of eucalyptus and everything. Medicines that will send you to sleep right away, but I don't like to prescribe potent brews, unless I have to." He heard his kind tones and thought them unfamiliar. He took a few flakes for himself and popped them into his mouth and began chewing. After a moment, she held out her hand, and he placed a healthy clump of the wondrous medicine on her upturned palm.

This'll fuk her up nicely.

He removed the flask from his jacket and passed it across to her. "It's the last of my supply. I've never known such fear," he said, watching her drink and wash down the chewed weed. She spluttered and swallowed, then passed the bottle back. She smiled at his woeful words and appeared more like the goddess he loved.

Aye, fuken love.

"Thank you, Emir."

"Maybe you should put your head down a while."

"It's safer near the fire, surrounded by friends," she

suddenly said dreamily, as the effects of the drug and the alcohol crept into her voice. He smiled, sat back on the soft patch of ground, and yawned.

"I'll stay nearby," he whispered, allowing the full exertions of the day to overcome him. It might also have been the medicines.

"Why are you doing this?" she said. It was a fine question.

"Because you needed to sleep." It was a finer answer.

"You could have let me suffer in silence like everyone else," she whispered, and lay back in the bedding. The grimace on her face softened slightly.

"Everyone is suffering Roja, but tonight I tend to you." He adjusted his sitting position beside her, leaned across and took her flowing hair in his hands. *A healer's tasks are never done.*

"Please stop," she whispered, as he stroked his fingers along her scalp, squeezing and massaging. She sighed with pleasure. She raised her hands to pull his hands away, but moaned as though in a lover's quiet embrace. Her arms fell to her side, and she smiled in relief.

"Sparks in my head, in my mind, in my body," she whimpered, and he continued on as her protests fell away to silent weeping.

"I need to hate you," she said weakly, and tears flowed from her eyes like rivers. He said nothing but continued to rub his fingers along the top of her head, down along her neck, and she allowed him without argument.

"We can spend all our energy hating each other in the morning," he promised, and fought fresh tears of his own. Better nobody saw this.

"Until the morning, so," she whispered, and fell silent.

He did not know how long he remained massaging her

head, only that he never stopped until she was in a heavy sleep. With her breathing deep yet peaceful, he slid his fingers away and wrapped her blanket around her shoulders. She did not stir.

As quietly as he could in the dark, he slipped back to camp and recovered his own bedding and then, taking a few moments to threaten death upon any who woke her before dawn, made his way back to her. He laid one more blanket upon her before making a little bed for himself beside her. He didn't know why he did this.

Come the morning he expected screaming and violence. It wouldn't be the first time she had woken up beside him and knocked him out cold. It would never hurt more than it had hurt then. She would never hurt him again.

She rolled over in her sleep and rested against his shoulder; she sighed magnificently and snored for a few moments before returning into a deep, peaceful sleep. She'd have his rear come the morning, but it was a small matter. As were his own feelings of betrayal and anger, stirred by an enemy in a red dress. Nothing else mattered, though, when a good person was screaming out for help.

However, he was running out of sine. *That* was a fuken worry.

32

CARRY ME WELL AND I WILL SHIELD
YOU ALWAYS

Erroh watched his little group of doomed generals busying themselves with packing up and preparing for the day's ride. They were in brighter cheer than when first they'd left the relative safety of the Wolves' camp. The fresh air was obviously doing them no manner of damage at all. They still carried their worries openly, but the calling of the green was good for the soul. Good for the hunters in them.

He stretched as he waited for Roja. There was a bite in the morning air, and he could see his breath steaming out in front of him. He wished he'd taken a second mug of hot cofe before preparing to leave, but the road was calling. It was a strange thing to believe himself destined for great things, yet Erroh couldn't help feeling he was in the absent gods' grace.

I'm coming for you, Uden.

"I will find you," he whispered into the bitter morning air. He whispered this pledge every morning. It was becoming part of his routine. Just a moment alone with the Woodin Man, all personal-like. It was a good mantra, and a better pledge.

Roja carried a steaming mug of her own and sipped from

it carefully as she made her way through the departing camp. In her other hand was the unnerving map. She bowed and placed the ancient piece of history on the ground. She straightened it out with her arms and spilled a few drips down along its side.

"Thank you, Roja," Erroh said, kneeling down beside her to study the piece. His eyes darted across the unfamiliar words and names and general directions. Such a map was invaluable to their success in remaining concealed while traversing hostile territory. If only he knew where to begin.

As if reading his confusion, she leaned across and pointed to a design indicating a segment of lowland surrounded by forest. "We're somewhere here."

Erroh noticed her hands still shook, just like his had. Less than before, but enough for concern. He would insist Emir continue his treatments. Whatever they were exactly. He dropped his own map down beside Roja's and tried not to count the glaring differences between the two. There were some similarities, to be sure, but he needed to look closely to see them.

"Many rivers in these parts," he muttered, following the faded blue lines with his fingers. They seemed to run wildly everywhere. He knew there would be plenty of Uden's fingers to march each route as well; the last thing he desired was wasting time tracking. He felt dizzy with the thought of it all. The pit of his stomach turned, and he felt the doubt growing. Roja just sipped her cofe.

"Aye, there are," she agreed, and inhaled the fumes before sipping again. She ran her fingers along a peculiar-looking marking. It was certainly a path of travel, but it was printed in heavier black ink than the rest: a long, winding streak across the page with slight dashes running through like a thousand X's joined as one. "If you really want to reach Raven Rock, there are worse routes to travel," she suggested, tapping the page absently.

"You disagree with marching to it?"

She coughed and drank again. An untrusting Master General might think she was forming a lie in her mind. "It's a town at odds with Spark. They will welcome some of us. Others, less so." It mostly sounded like the truth. Mostly.

"There are fewer settlements around it," he said, examining the map. "Only one small river, and depthless surrounding forest. But it's the best chance we have at finding sanctuary, perhaps even comrades in arms. I've made my decision," he reminded her. It was Roja who'd suggested Raven Rock first, yet still, she appeared less than enthusiastic about making it their first stop. As he stared back and forth between the two maps, he was reassured once more of his decision. His war council's decision. Only Wrek had argued against it, but they had outnumbered him.

"You look better rested than before," Erroh said, and her face flushed. She had slept long beyond dawn and no one had woken her. They had set out later than usual, and it was her fault.

"I'll be no further hindrance on this journey. I'm sorry I slept so long."

"Emir's orders. I've never known him to be wrong," Erroh said, smiling, and a faint smile threatened to crack through her glum expression in return. He would fight Emir's fight for him, even if the fool didn't want it. Even with the anger between them. Everyone knew they burned for each other. "He still loves you. It might be better if you two thrash out your differences and…" Erroh knew little of female ways, but he knew from her expression that falling silent was the better tactic for him right now.

She snorted and sipped her cofe. "He loved a dead girl from Keri." It was a fine point.

"Aireys was a dear friend. An amazing person," whispered Erroh, and the red-headed girl sighed a perfect "Of course she was" sigh.

"When I die, maybe he'll think more fondly of me," she countered.

"Aye, probably," Erroh agreed, and she laughed. A hearty laugh. He wasn't sure if he'd ever heard her laugh before. A fine laugh indeed.

"That's not the correct response, Master General."

"Every response is correct when spoken by the Master General."

She wiped her eyes. "I really didn't give you nearly enough of a chance in the Cull," she said, grinning.

"You loved me from the first moment you saw me," he mocked.

"No, just Emir. Many years ago." She drained her cofe and looked back at the map. "But I am no child anymore, and he, well, he is a wretched brute unworthy of forgiveness."

"Perhaps there is redemption, down the road," he whispered.

"Perhaps, Master General," she said, gathering her map up and walking away. It was the most genial conversation they'd ever shared. He still did not know her well. A few days before, she'd appeared shattered and lost. Now she appeared merely lost. And what were foolish endeavours against insurmountable odds, if not a lantern in a stormy night?

He re-joined the rest of his comrades. "Still marching south," he declared, and they nodded and began gathering the last of their belongings before setting out. They did so swiftly and without argument. His voice carried across the camp and it sounded confident. Perhaps he too was learning to find himself again in the wastes.

Marches like these, he knew, were rarely swift, but they were littered with excitement and memorable moments. Mostly, it was a matter of controlling wandering thoughts, all the while fighting boredom and looking at the sky above. There had been a lot of looking to the sky above, and there would be more of it. He glanced up and tasted the air.

The sky was filled with thick, bulbous clouds, spreading their heavy, grey veneer and blotting out the blue of the sky. There was still a glittering sheen from a stubborn sun attempting to break through, but rain was in the wind. It would be a miserable day in the saddle.

———

"Do you need me to say something, or should it be you?" asked Lea from atop her mount. She pointed to the edge of the camp, a peculiar, anxious smile on her face. Her mate nodded reluctantly. Emir was releasing Nomi from her bedding in the cart. Because of his inability to communicate with the southerner, or else his contemptuous attitude towards her, his explanations about how to ride a horse were clearly getting lost in translation.

"Apparently, she's not willing to ride with us," said Lea.

"Maybe she's still unwell." Erroh didn't want to defend her yet.

"Emir said she is well enough," countered Lea.

"No," Nomi growled at the healer, and dropped the reins in disgust. She stepped back from the mount, but stroked its head before she did, muttering curses under her breath.

"I don't know what you mean," he argued, and picked up the reins for the third time. "I don't care what you mean, either." He threw the leather-bound straps at her. They missed and bounced back against the chestnut mount's head.

"Nomi no ride mount!" she roared in reply. She pushed him away and climbed back into the cart, frustration and irritation showing in her every move.

Lea sighed. "What is she growling about? I can't understand a word she says in that guttural tongue of hers."

"He probably went for her chest again," Erroh said, struggling to keep a straight face.

"Well, you had better calm this revolt," she said, gripping the reins on her mount a little tighter.

"As you wish," he said, taking her hand and kissing it before walking his useless horse across the camp to the feuding pair. He was swiftly learning that showing Lea affection before speaking with Nomi made life a little easier. He would likely need to learn other such tactics when dealing with this band of exiles. This gathering of opinionated warriors would push his leadership skills to the limit. Alphas just never played well together, did they?

Except in war.

Problem was, they were not warring yet. These were the tedious days before the bloodshed, when fear and frustration made the very air explosive.

Lillium brought her own mount alongside Lea as Erroh walked away.

"Do you trust her?" the first general asked quietly.

"Until the end of the world," muttered Lea evenly.

"She has eyes for Erroh," noted Lillium. Lea snorted and looked at her closest friend for a moment before shrugging nonchalantly.

"I notice these things," she said evenly. "I owe her a debt, which I will someday repay, in some form or other."

"Still, a female like that should be watched," whispered Lillium.

"It is not your concern, Lilli. I trust Erroh," she said, beckoning Lillium follow her to the front of the line. "Best we keep our eyes on things that matter, like the road ahead."

Seeing Erroh approach, Emir raised his hands in annoyance. "You wanted me to make sure she was healthy enough to ride? Well, she's healthy enough to ride," he growled, and held out the reins for Erroh. *Your problem now, friend.*

"No!" shouted Nomi defiantly from atop the cart. She folded her arms and muttered a few curse words at the healer under her breath. Erroh translated, and Emir appeared intrigued by the descriptions.

"Why not?" Erroh asked her in terrible southern tongue.

"Riders, Nomi, not Nomi," she said, and he wasn't sure he translated it correctly in his mind. She stared at him, her eyes full of hope. She always stared at him with such kind and warm eyes; it was a little unsettling. She was like a child, searching for reassurance—or a skilled player, playing the delicate waif as she plotted mayhem.

"Not worthy of mount, only. Riders. Finest of our kind," she said, and he smiled, and she smiled immediately in reply. "Only finest of us," she added in his native tongue, and rubbed the mount once more. "I can drive cart," she suggested. "Cart good."

Though it made adequate entertainment, the rest of the companions rode out into the dark forest, leaving them to their impasse.

Emir shook his head and walked off, muttering something

about a "southern witch," and climbed atop his mount. He did not meet the eyes of the approaching Roja, and she did not acknowledge him. It was a fine agreement, it would appear. She slipped past Erroh and climbed atop the cart to her rightful place in the driving seat.

"Come down," Erroh said to Nomi, offering his hand. Nomi took it and dropped to the ground as the cart rolled off, leaving Erroh alone with her. She didn't appear to mind.

"Why not cart?" she asked.

"Not sick. Time to ride," he offered, and hoped his words were correct. "Take mount. Worthy," he added, offering the reins.

"No."

"One of us," he said as the gathered camp disappeared in a line, leaving them to their standoff.

"Cannot ride," she said, and he now saw the fear in her eyes.

Now, why would a girl reviled by her people still follow their ways?

Resolutely, he answered her fear with cold strength. If she was to survive with them, there was no place for extra weight, extra trouble. She would ride with them or they would leave her behind. Even if it tore him apart.

He held out the reins once more. She did not take them; she stared beyond him as the others left them.

"Scared," she whimpered in his own tongue.

He nodded and waited.

"Please, Erroh," she cried.

He tried to find the words in her language.

"It is gentle beast, carry you far," he promised, hating himself. It was a horse. They were unpredictable at the best of times. "Alone…" he said and pointed at the ground, "or with family," he added, pointing at their group in the distance and hoping she understood his meaning clearly this time.

He climbed up onto his black mount, pointed to the chestnut horse, and waited for her to follow suit. He reached over and laid a hand across the brown horse's rear to keep it calm and listened to the last of the noise from their travelling party as they disappeared into the wastes. *Come on, Nomi. Hurry. Lea will not be thrilled to leave us alone for too long.*

She did not stir; instead, she stared into the horse's eyes and whispered a brief prayer to the animal. Erroh couldn't hear the words, but it sounded like she was attempting to broker a deal with it.

"Carry me well and I will shield you, always," she whispered, kissing the beast. He almost laughed. Mounts were mounts. Unpredictable and unreliable. He himself rode upon a magnificent beast but trusted it as far as it could throw him.

Taking a few deep breaths, she put her foot in the stirrups and pulled herself up. With some gentle help, she climbed atop its back and finally sat up in the saddle.

"Very high," she groaned, and wavered as if dizzy. The mount stepped sideways and whickered in annoyance. Nomi squealed in alarm and tugged the reins. The horse spun around and she squealed again and Erroh laughed loudly.

"Gently, whisht," said Erroh, and Nomi brought the beast backwards. She squealed for a third time and the horse reared. Somehow, she held firm and leaned forward with the animal and remained seated. She screamed a little more but eased her grip on the reins.

"Can't," Nomi pleaded, and the horse answered her call by spinning around once more. Erroh said nothing. He watched on and remembered his first ride on a horse. It had gone a lot worse than what he saw now. He'd fallen the first time, if he recalled.

Eventually the beast calmed and stepped forward tentatively. Nomi took the reins again, then reached up and rubbed its head. It nodded a few times and, tugging the reins gently, she squeaked as the beast started walking toward the break in the trees.

"Well done, Nomi," Erroh called, bringing his beast alongside her own. For just a moment she smiled in victory, and even ducked under a low-hanging branch in their way.

"Scared," she said again, watching the path ahead. Aye, he could see the fear, and the excitement too. Far ahead in the distance, their companions' horses were making better time, and she copied Erroh's gentle kicks to increase her own mount's pace.

Lea rode out from behind the cover of the trees and watched them now.

"Liiiia," cried Nomi in delight as she went by, with a proud "Look what I can do!" expression upon her face. Lea nodded and feigned a smile as the girl urged her horse to a trot and moved on.

Only once did Nomi sway in the saddle, and Erroh felt proud of his leadership. He was fixing matters like a legend, and he was still only a few days into this miserable term as grand-champion-hero-legend of the Four Factions.

"Did you think she would bat her eyelids and we would run away together?" he asked her with a gentle smile, and reached for her hand again. She dodged it easily enough.

"You would probably have had to run away slowly," countered Lea, shrugging.

"Oh, leave her alone. I thought she did well," he said, reaching for her hand a second time. This time she allowed it, and he held it to his brow and squeezed.

"We'll make better time without her weight on the cart. She really is heavy."

"I love you, Lea. I will never love another," he pledged.

"I know you love me. It's just that you wouldn't mind furrowing her a little bit. Just to be sure."

"I am a man. I like to be thorough. You could watch and everything."

She eyed him dangerously. He could only jest so much before the hammer of her wrath came crashing down upon him. He suddenly feared their combat to come this evening.

"Besides, you'll always come searching for me," he said, and her eyes narrowed.

"Not if you left me," she whispered, and he smiled. "Come on, let's catch up with them," she said, kissing his hand.

"No, let us stay here a few moments and enjoy the silence together, my love," he said.

They sat atop their horses and listened to little else but the call of the road and each other's breathing, imagining they were out in the middle of nowhere, holding hands with all the time in the world. When the clouds above them opened up and the first fall of rain struck them, they turned their mounts and followed their doomed companions through the forest towards an incredible sanctuary that they would call home.

33

LEADING BY EXAMPLE

This was misery. Wet misery. The type of wet earned only through nearly drowning your mate in a river, or by sitting upon a mount throughout a tempest. The rain cracked loudly on his hood and battered him. He felt every drop seep through the fabric, and he knew he was not alone in this misery. His place at the front of this march was the harshest, but he refused to be beaten. He would lead by example, even if it was fuken miserable. Two days and as many nights of rain they'd endured, and there was no sign of it letting up. This afternoon, however, was brutal.

"It's too fierce," he heard someone behind him cry out. It might have been Wrek, and he agreed. Still, with aching fingers, he gripped the reins tighter and kept going. The idea of stopping and waiting out the rain, letting themselves get dry, was appealing, but if they stopped for shelter now, who knew how long they would waste.

Take the rain. Make up for lost time.

We've already come so far as it is.

"It's just low cloud," Erroh called back, wrapping his soaked scarf around his throat. It offered little comfort, but for a moment the harsh wind was lessened. He enjoyed that moment. It was the highlight of his day's ride. He pulled on the reins gently as his mount slowed above a steep drop in the path. The path had become a little grey stream of gathered rainwater flowing down the slope. He hadn't realised the angle of the valley, and he cursed his carelessness.

Too busy making good time to check the road ahead.

Through streams of drips upon his hood, he peered down the slope to the bottom of the valley and cursed aloud. It was at least a fifty- or sixty-foot descent, on a steep angle. It would be a long slide for any mount without steady footing. For a moment he considered resting, or attempting another route, but it was late in the day, the hedging too thick and clustered around them.

"We need to slow ourselves here," he shouted, trying to conceal his frustration. How many precarious rises and drops had they traversed these last few days? Many, but this slope was the worst. Behind, his companions gathered up around him, their grumblings and dark opinions filling the air and not helping matters. A frustrating day's march was becoming a right fuken nightmare.

"This is a mistake," a voice groused.

"At least at the bottom there will be more cover," another voice countered, and before an impromptu war council could begin, Erroh brought Highwind forward slowly, leaning back in the saddle as the mount stepped through the gushing, flowing water and began making his way down.

"Easy, girl," he hissed, grinding his teeth. The slope was a menace to gaze upon, but descending it was even worse. He felt every muscle of his mount's powerful legs ease down and drive into the ground, searching for surefootedness. What a dreadful way to end a legend, he thought warily as Highwind slid a half foot but kept herself in control.

And then the ground gave way completely and Highwind lurched forward.

Fuk, fuk, fuk.

He heard screams behind him. Curses, too. Mostly he heard his own gasps as he fought the unfortunate beast's slide. He pulled left, but the stupid mount did little more than turn her head with the order. The world sped up on either side, and Erroh clung to the horse as it slid further down the valley. Behind him, the cacophony of terrified voices filled the air, and he was helpless to reply. To tell them he was fine. To reassure them he wasn't scared.

To convince them that everything was alright.

Stupid way to die.

Unable to counter his mount's panicked stubbornness, he relinquished control and waited. His vision blurred from the rain and mud as it splashed into his face. He ducked down behind the massive horse's head and waited and prepared himself for the sudden devastating halt to the fall.

Sliding.

Spinning.

More sliding.

The rush of wind and rain lessened; the panicked voices, too. Though it felt like an eternity had passed, he knew it was just moments. Then his pace slowed. He heard Highwind's panicked whinnying lessen. A few wet moments after that, they slid to a graceful stop at the bottom of the slope.

No problem.

Fighting the urge to contain his morning cofe, he tried to calm his thundering heart. It was a terrible thing to rely on a beast like Highwind to carry him to safety, yet here he was, in the creature's debt. Only then did he realise mud covered her rear completely where she'd slid in a sitting position.

"Sitting helped?" he mocked, patting her.

Highwind walked forward, nosing for grass on the valley floor as if nothing had happened. Above, Lea was inching down the slope, holding the reins in her hands and urging her horse slowly and far more carefully. She was pissed at him. He could see it, even from here. By the time she reached the bottom of the valley, Wrek was already walking his own mount down the path taken by the furious young Alphaline.

"Stupid," she growled, slapping him across the cheek. Then she leapt on him and hugged him tightly.

"I'm sorry," he muttered, touching the sharp pain with his hand.

"You're too reckless," she whispered, kissing his stinging cheek.

"I was always in control. Highwind was just clumsy in her step," he said. He patted the beast a second time and allowed it to graze. Truthfully, his nerve was shaken, and leading or not, he was not ready to climb back in the saddle. And besides, it was pelting down.

"No, my beo," she warned, holding him to her once more. She was freezing to the touch. Far colder than he, yet she appeared far more at ease. "You need to be smarter in everything you do."

Criticism from his mate stung above all else. He took her words in and nodded sheepishly. "I'll do better," he pledged. "For you," he whispered, and wiped a small blotch of mud from her chin.

Roja watched on as the rest of the horses were led down the steep valley wall. She flicked some strands of hair from her face and cursed the weather. Not as colourfully as Lexi had, but still impressive. It was a fine way of passing time. Eventually, only the sound of rain and running water filled her ears. This would not end well, she thought, staring down the steep incline while those around her went to task securing the cart. She thought about arguing for a delay, but those clouds were unyielding and she'd already delayed them long enough. It was a strange thing to march so willingly towards doom, but, until they reached Raven Rock, there could be no next step.

Raven Rock.

She feared their reaction upon arriving. But it was a necessary sanctuary, and she was tired of the road, as it was. All of them were. The rain brought out the worst moods in most people, and they were no different. Sleeping rough only to be rewarded by a rain-drenched trudge was no way of keeping spirits high.

"Slow," Nomi said from beside her, and patted the rear of the cart-horse. She pointed down the incline and made a spinning motion with her finger. She might have made a crashing sound; Roja couldn't be sure.

Sage advice, idiot.

There was something untrustworthy about the female. "Aye," muttered Roja, feigning a smile, before flicking the rain from her face again. She missed silken warmth.

"Tight and slow," Nomi added helpfully and gripped the ropes along the horse's back that attached the beast to the wooden machine. She tugged, and there was little give. She nodded to herself. "Good... harness?" She tested it once more and smiled. "Horse strong. No fall, and slow good," she said with a tongue unfamiliar to twisting itself around their language. Before Roja could answer with further indifference, the female spun around and knelt down to watch Wrek and Lillium tighten the rope at the back.

· · ·

Nomi loved the rain. She loved it because it had helped her to earn some favour these last two days. The first evening, when the rain fell and the orders to erect tents were met with half-hearted efforts, Nomi had taken it upon herself to help her new comrades; it had won them over nicely. Watching the biting wind catch the sheets as they drove stakes into the ground carelessly had been almost painful for her. So many loose knots and sloppy measurements would have doomed this merry little group of wanderers during the first cold front in the south.

It had taken her mere moments to erect her own canvas cover and truss its base securely. Erroh and Liiiia's cover was next to hers, and though their cover was adequate, without thinking she took the support rope and repositioned it to allow better wind cover. When she finished, she smiled and attempted to return to her own bedding. Before she could, though, Liiiia had stepped forward and pointed to the rest of the soaked wanderers, each struggling with their cover.

"Will you help?" asked Liiiia, and Nomi had smiled at the pretty lady and bowed. Liiiia's approval would serve her very well.

One after the other, she'd set the rest of the shelters in place, and the rain had drenched her. She could sense the group's thinly-veiled anger towards her, and understood some of their dark mutterings, but she had bowed to each one in turn, as etiquette demanded and moved on to the next task.

Only the healer had refused her help, apparently preferring to sleep with wind blasting through his measly tent all night. But when they set down again the following evening and she'd walked among them offering assistance once more, he had grudgingly allowed her to step in and seal up any drafts.

Only Erroh and Liiiia's tent was sturdy enough the second

night, though the rest had made valiant efforts. A desire to learn was the finest trait in any person's repertoire. It was just like the sparring, she thought. Each night, she'd watched the wanderers learn the art of the blade, and oh, how she wanted to join them. They were graceful and fierce, and improving in leaps and bounds. Hers was an entirely different type of warfare altogether, however. She wanted to fight Liiiia.

That would be wonderful.

Kneeling down beside the cart's rear, Nomi approved silently of the knot tied by the big one named Wrek. He wrenched one end with his powerful hands and tested the give once more. It would not slip, even in this downpour.

"Good," she whispered favourably, and moved to the thin tree around which they'd wrapped the other end of the rope. Lillium and Emir were pulling the end through and securing it as tightly as they could. Not tight enough. Nomi could see the give and shook her head.

"No good. Cart slide, kill Roja," she admonished, pulling the weather-beaten threads from Lillium's grasp and wrapping them once more around the tree. Touching the bark and kicking the trunk, she reconsidered. The knot would hold, but the tree's roots were young and brittle. "Um… no… use bigger tree," she suggested. Truthfully, she enjoyed helping them with their task. It felt almost like home. Every member of the finger, working together to travel that extra mile.

"Witch," muttered Emir, shoving her away and almost knocking her from her feet. She took the slight with a flicker of anger before shrugging and leaving them to it. Probably better for morale she did. She was fairly certain she could take him if it came to blows. She eyed the tree once more and gave up. They likely knew this region better than she did anyway.

. . .

When preparation was complete, the party gathered around the cart. Roja could read the nervousness in their faces, and it instilled little confidence in her. Still, she was determined to earn her place within this group. Slowly, they edged the heavy cart towards the slope and Roja offered a prayer up to the absent gods; were they bothered on this dreadful afternoon? She gripped the reins and brought her mount to the edge. The rope attached to its rear was merely a precaution were the horse to slip like Erroh's had. She would not be as careless taking the same path. She looked to the sky and wished for the rain to cease.

"Lead the way, when you like," called Erroh, and took his place near the tree. He took a length of rope and dug his feet into the muddy ground. Wrek stood beside him and knelt low for better balance. Lillium stood closest to the cart, where she wrapped the long rope around her arm, ready to feed it out as they moved. Nomi took the horse's bridle and stroked the beast's mane, while Lea and Emir stood on each side, ready to holler out instructions.

It was a simple plan.

The heavy cart embedded itself in the loose surface and found grip. Slowly, Roja shook the reins and urged the beast forward. *No problem.* Within a few feet, her view changed as the cart rolled forward and began its steady decline. It felt more like a mountain from this angle. Behind her, the rope rose into the air as Lillium allowed it to tighten slightly. The three kept the rope steady without slowing the horse's progress.

"First slight drop," warned Lea, just as the cart bounced precariously forward, but again after a moment it found its grip and trundled on. The mount cried out with this unusual strain, but her legs were strong. Stronger than most. She was built not for war or blinding speed, but for heavy lifting. Or heavier pulling. She was far more sure-footed than most, and as her hooves dug into the ground, she obeyed her master, even with the heavy load bumping into her rear every few steps. Led by Nomi, the beast was calm enough.

About a quarter of the way down, just as they believed that the effort would be worth it, Lea slipped in the mud and the ground beneath her fell away. She reached out and gripped the massive wheel beside her, but her footing betrayed her completely and she fell away from the cart.

Her slip became a dreadful slide. More than that, it was face first. Blinded by the mud, she twisted and flung her arms out. A thin sapling saved her and stopped her fall. Erroh was supposed to be the clumsy one, she thought to herself as she climbed to her feet. Her entire front was covered in a heavy layer of brown mud. Wiping her face to regain a hint of dignity, she spat the taste of road from her mouth. There would be jests at her expense. Erroh would have a few as well, when next they sat alone. He would be merciless too. It was she who had slipped on the slope, after all her warnings to him.

There really was nothing worse than been corrected by your love.

Maybe burning pyres or drowning in rivers.

The first to lose his composure was Wrek, who boomed laughter from the top of the slope. Soon the rest of the group was guffawing helplessly, all except for Nomi, who strained to keep her balance at the front. She'd watched Lea fall and had marvelled at her reflexes, even when she was blinded. A few moments later, she found herself in the same position as the ground underneath her gave way completely. She fell forward and released her hold on the horse. The horse reared and then slid on the unsteady ground. Miraculously, it recovered its footing, but not before the cart lurched forward and then twisted dangerously sideways. The sudden turn caught them all unaware, and Lillium almost had her arm torn from its socket. She screamed in frustrated agony and wrenched herself free, and the cart twisted further, pulling Wrek and Erroh with it. The rope whipped up tightly and the cart's full weight pulled down against it.

It was a fine rope. Sturdy and tightly wound, capable of supporting terrific weight even in an emergency, the stallholder had promised Roja. In this moment, he was proven right. In the same transaction, he had presented her with a strange, upside-down map, bought from a tavern keeper whose guest had "disappeared mysteriously without paying her dues." Roja was glad now that she'd begrudgingly agreed the few additional pieces that morning.

Unfortunately, though the rope and knot held firm, the tree did not. With a loud groan of breaking wood, the roots were ripped free of the mud. The cart lurched again, and the tree was dragged free completely.

Roja fell from her seat as the world spun, but she did not fall free of the cart. Instead, she fell into it and somehow regained her footing. Someone is about to die, she thought. The world turned again. Her horse was dragged a few feet. In her ears she heard screaming. Not just her own.

Far below, she saw Lexi covering her eyes in terror, and then Emir was beside her, trying to pull her away from her lurching vehicle. Suddenly Nomi appeared below her, sliding towards the mount. Dodging the cart's deadly wheels, she reached for the horse's bridle as it fought the weight of its load.

The hooves trampled all around Nomi, and inevitably, one stamped down on her palm, shattering bones. Horrific, burning pain brought tears to her eyes, but on instinct, she twisted out of the beast's way and climbed to her feet, screaming in agony and fright. Beside her, the cart continued to drag the struggling mount down the slope. With her good hand, she grabbed the straps and tried to steady the animal, pulling and screaming at it to fight the weight. That's how they did it in the south in worse conditions.

"Jump free," screamed Emir, gripping Roja and attempting to save her as they veered forward. At any moment, the pull of natural order was likely to overturn them all and send them tumbling to the bottom of the hill in a battered mess of blood and broken bones. She fought him and attempted to drive the beast forward to counter the turn, but nothing happened. She saw Nomi drag at the beast, but the horse fought the direction and reared once more.

"Cut the beast free," screamed Wrek, sliding down towards them, his voice cutting over all the others. "Cut it free now!" he bellowed, reaching the cart just as Lillium grabbed at the wheels, hoping to ease the deadly weight.

"No!" yelled Erroh from behind.

"The horse can hold it," cried Lea, trying to climb back up to her comrades.

"No," shouted Nomi, finally understanding as Emir reached down and lifted one blade from its scabbard on Lillium's back. Lillium howled at his thievery and tried to climb into the cart to stop him. The cart jerked forward as the horse fought the weight and nature itself. Nomi dragged the beast by its mane and screamed in pain and terror and triumph as, at last, the cart careened one final time and levelled out and the beast caught its footing.

"Cut it, Emir!" shouted Lexi, who began scrambling up from the valley basin.

"Don't fuken touch it," roared Erroh, grabbing the cart to weigh it down. Lea climbed up beside him and followed suit.

"You'll kill us all! Cut the beast free, and let this cursed cart fall," shouted Wrek from beside the Alphas, but he too held the cart to stop the deadly slide.

"I can hold it," hissed Roja, knocking Emir away with her elbow. Gripping the reins, she yelled at the beast to obey her. Then she was flying.

It was all Emir could do. Wrek was right. He was no master of the road, but the horse could not support the weight. The cart was about to overturn, taking everyone with it. The world shunted again, and he reacted. He didn't mean to punch Roja so hard, but the crack of his fist against her chin was loud enough that he heard it above the explosion of surrounding noise. She fell from the cart into the soft mud with a heavy thud. Her senses dazed, she tried to rise and stumble back up, but the cart was already gone. So was her horse.

"Cut the beast free," screamed Lexi, now halfway up the slope.

Emir couldn't think. He stumbled to the back of the horse where the strappings were tightest. The blade was sharp; he knew this because Lillium sharpened it every night. It was just one of her many unnerving habits. Emir was grateful for her routine in this moment, though. He heard their voices all around him, desperate and all-knowing and yelling almost as one.

"We can hold the beast."

"Cut the ropes."

"Do it, Emir."

"Don't do it, brother."

"Do it."

"Don't."

"Emir."

"Oh fuk…"

He slid the perfect blade along the leather straps and cut. Within a few attempts, the leather came free, and he quickly cut into the second strap. On his second strike, the band snapped free, and the horse, freed of its crippling load, lurched forward.

The cart immediately bucked and lifted into the air. Before they could be dragged with it, the trio released their grip and fell as one back onto the ground, their momentum carrying them forward. The cart overturned and spun wildly, just ahead of them. Tents and bedding and supplies spilled out into the air. White and clean turned to brown in moments. Food was crushed and ruined; essentials devastated. Erroh, Lea and Wrek rolled through the debris and kept going.

The mount knocked Nomi to the ground as it broke free of its harness and charged free across the steep hillside. It was wild-eyed, grateful for its sudden release. It struck her battered hand once more as it rushed past, and she screamed. Unable to stop herself, she rolled down after the others, clumsily thrashing against the ground as if she were a rag doll thrown by a child.

Before the cart flipped, Emir leapt clear and reached Roja. She looked concussed, and he felt guilty. His fingers stung from the strike. He didn't notice the rope whipping past them both.

Lillium did. She left her sword where it lay and leapt at Roja and the foolish Emir with all her might. She knocked the two out of the way of the oncoming tree, as the cart dragged it down the treacherous slope at terrifying speed. Deadly, twisting roots whipped past her face, thin branches grabbed out at her hair and she ducked and rolled beyond their reach, down towards the bottom with Emir and Roja. Spinning too forcefully to stop themselves, they rolled painfully to the bottom of the valley, crashing through bushes, branches and debris along the way.

The valley filled with the noise of agony, shock and anger. As the cart crashed to a stop at the bottom, the rain lessened its roar to a wet whisper. A few moments after that, it ceased completely. To most, this was a portent of positive things. To the battered comrades, it was a typical example of wretched luck.

When he was certain the painful spinning and slipping had finally ended, Wrek was first to climb to his feet. His haste was brought on by the bile in his mouth and his need to get rid of it. He wasn't the only one to throw up either. In a few bitter breaths, he made a ruin of the bush he'd chosen for the nasty deed. "Is everyone alive?" he croaked from a kneeling position. Wiping some stray bile from his beard, he began counting those who still moved. A terrible thing, indeed. He seethed at this turn of events but held his temper in check. He doubted he was the only one who was furious.

. . .

Looking up at the ruined supplies strewn all along the slope, Erroh's heart dropped and with it, most of his hope. Lillium patted him on the back and he watched her climb back up through the mud in search of her sword. He tried not to show his anguish, but the world felt too big for him. Looking to the break in the weather, he cursed the burning sphere trying to break through the cloud and take the cutting wind from their shivering bodies. Then he cursed the absent gods for casting such misfortune on them for their entertainment. Then he cursed himself for not delaying a little longer.

Emir went to task with the whimpering Nomi. Unlike the Alphalines, she gasped openly with her pain. Her fingers shook, and he rummaged through the remains of the cart for his medical bag. He recovered bandages and a few plinths and sat beside the girl from the south and carefully made a little support for her smashed fingers. It was all he could do. A little tear rolled down her cheek, and he looked away in disgust at himself for enjoying her anguish.

It was Roja who felt most aggrieved. Before Emir could finish his treatment of the injured southern whore, she stormed forward. "Look what you did!" She gripped him by the collar and swung him around and pointed him to the ruined supplies all up and down the slope. "Look what your stupidity caused!" She took to shaking him now. He did not react; he merely allowed himself be handled like an animal. A useless animal. That was how most people saw him.

"He did what he thought was right, girl. Leave him be," warned Wrek, climbing to unsteady feet. He knew that look; he'd seen that expression. On all of their faces. They were likely to murder the lad. Or at least batter him a little. Emir likely recognised their glares as well. Wrek's anger, however, was not directed at a solitary player in this drama. His was focused at the director alone.

"It was your stupid idea to cut the beast free," hissed Lillium, slipping back down the hill with a muddy blade in her hands. She wiped it on her vest and strode towards the wretched healer with murderous intent.

"It needed to be done," challenged Lexi, stepping in front of Lillium, holding her one good arm out to halt the charge. The sun broke through, but there was a storm brewing at the valley floor.

"Move yourself, little one," warned Lillium, not unkindly, stepping away from the younger Alphaline. "My fight is not with you," she said, staring ahead to the healer, who was brooding in his soulmate's angry arms.

"I saved us," shouted Emir, pushing Roja away.

"Calm yourself," said Lea, and stepped between the girls lest they both attack Emir. She placed her hands on Lillium's shoulders and held her in place. "Be a leader," she whispered.

"I just want to hit him once," growled Lillium.

"Oh, fuk off, Ranger," Emir spat, wiping some mud from his lips and flicking it onto the ground.

"We all need to be calm. We all made mistakes," shouted Lea to the group at large. There was something in the air. Easier to see it in the sun's light. The frustration of days was about to erupt.

"Lea is right," shouted Wrek. "We made mistakes."

"Something, something… mistake," Nomi hissed as she held her hand. She muttered something else incomprehensible. "Saved life, horse." She frowned and tried to form her words. "Healer, Emir, save," she offered.

"I need no defending from you, witch," Emir snapped.

Erroh wanted to crawl away into a hole and hide. Maybe he could dig one wide enough for himself and Lea. He could get a few branches of trees for cover and everything. It would be so much nicer than feeling this low; thinking these thoughts. He felt like no leader. The colossal task facing him had never seemed so far away. He wanted to seek out and kill the leader of a nation? He couldn't even get a fuken horse down a slope. He looked at his comrades, each more dishevelled than the next. Mud covered their bodies; their clothing was soaked through with the rain. They were battered and bruised and bleeding, and he'd made the decisions that had brought them to this.

"Enough," he roared, and the order reverberated around the valley. The argument fell silent, and all eyes turned to him. "All this is my fault," he shouted. "So, stop spitting your venom at Emir." No one disagreed, but they still looked less inclined to mug him than Emir. It was something, at least. More than that, they appeared to listen. "Emir, Lea, climb back up and recover whatever you can," he ordered. Lea nodded immediately and after a moment, Emir dropped his head and followed. Roja spat some mud at his feet as he passed by, muttering something about "still having the mount under control," but Emir did not acknowledge her. He just dug his feet into the mud and climbed. "Roja and Wrek, go round up all the horses and set them to graze for the evening." It was only afternoon. There would be no further marching today.

"Aye, as you say," agreed Wrek, and bowed to Roja.

"Let's go find your fine horse," he offered to the fiery redhead. It was an attempt at easing tensions. Whatever her feelings, she followed him into the green, seeking hoof prints.

"Lexi, set a fire for the night," Erroh snapped at her, as only a disapproving brother could. She shouldn't have climbed the incline in the middle of the chaos. But that was his fault as well. Dragging her into the wastes was putting her in harm's way. It would be wise to monitor her.

Lillium stood with her muddy sword in hand; he could see that her anger was still roaring. She wiped at the blade absently, and Erroh took one of her filthy hands in his. "When everything calms down, have words with Emir," her Master General whispered. "He does not understand the significance of a blade. Had he known, well, he might still have taken it from you, anyway. It's the healer in him," Erroh said quietly and released his grip on her. "We need to keep it together for now," he said with finality, and she nodded her reluctant agreement.

"I will say nothing for now," she pledged, eying the wretched figure as he scrambled miserably up the steep incline to search through the wreckage of his own making. After a moment, she nodded. "I'll just punch him a couple of times," she said, grinning.

"Just not in the face. We'll never hear the end of it. In the meantime, will you assist Lea and the idiot?"

"As you wish," she said, grinning again before climbing back up the slope.

Only Nomi remained. Carefully climbing through the wreckage of the cart, she began pulling out some tents and bedding that had not met their end on the slope.

"Are you okay?" Erroh asked in her language.

"Nomi strong," the girl replied in his language, holding out her hand to show how she took the pain. The damage was nasty. Her fingers were swollen, but no bones had broken through the skin.

"Poor Nomi," he said, taking her hand, and she held her breath.

"Nomi strong like Liiiia," she whispered as he examined the injury. His own basic knowledge of healing, not to mention a lifetime of clumsiness, reassured him that there was no serious break. She would recover quickly. This was good. She could also ride. This was even better.

"You are very strong," he said in his native tongue. She was learning their words well, he noted. Getting better every day. He released his hold, and she released a delicate gasp.

She missed lying beside him in the freezing cold, not kissing. Before she knew it, he had bowed and walked away. She watched him leave and then turned to the beautiful girl walking along the side of the valley, radiant in the growing afternoon, despite the mud covering her shapely body and ruined hair. Strong, beautiful Liiiia. One for life with Erroh. Nomi sighed and returned to her work by the shattered cart.

As Wynn stepped through the break in the trees a few hours later, alarm overcame him when he saw the makeshift camp in the middle of the valley floor. Everyone sat apart from each other. All stared into the large fire in the centre of the path as it flickered and danced, seeming to mock them all. There was no shortage of fuel. It would burn brightly and for many hours.

"What happened?" he cried.

Nobody stirred but Erroh. Nobody wanted to speak. Nobody wanted to air their grievances. The Master General had taken the blame, but there was still seething anger waiting to surface again.

"We had an accident."

"Is everyone okay?"

"Everyone is fine."

Wynn nodded and looked at the shattered wagon. Riding would be quicker at least. However, their supplies had taken a great hit.

"I may have found something," he said casually. It was nothing big and nothing to be excited about, but certainly something peculiar.

"Can it wait until the morning?" Erroh held his hands out over the burning flame, trying to return some feeling, to banish the numbness he felt. He did not want to hear of "something." All he wanted was a release from this wretched guilt. He also wanted to kill Uden.

"Aye. It's going nowhere," said Wynn, taking a seat down beside Lillium as she oiled her blade with great care and affection.

34

DORAN

It was an ugly thing, and Doran could not look away. And why should he? It was a part of him now. Mutilated, ruined, gelded. He held his lesser hand out in front of him and despised his fortune. It was a dreadful way to begin every morning, but this was part of his routine now. Better to gaze upon this horror in solitude, away from prying eyes, from commiserating comrades. Oh, aye, they bowed as though they were deferential to him, but he could see the pity in their eyes. What good was an Alpha without his preferred hand?

A master of warfare.

He snorted and turned his hand over in the hazy, dreary morning light and as usual saw no improvement. Three working fingers and two stubs where digits should have stretched and gripped and made him whole. His stomach turned, and he fought the queasiness, like he did most mornings.

Take this pain.

He dared a careful sniff where the healer had stitched the stumps over, and grimaced. No sign of rot. Not yet. He had spared him that dreadfulness, at least. He wondered if Emir could have saved more of his fingers. Even if they had no movement. Even if they'd ached every fuken day. He'd have taken them. Perhaps, were Emir inclined, he might have moulded and shaped them into something resembling a fist. That would have been functional.

Here it comes.

Like a gushing spring bubbling over, he felt his horror emerge from deep within and he allowed it. Some days, he did little more than snort as disgust overcame him. Other times he dashed his ruined hand against the nearest solid surface as though to prove himself above agony. Yet other times he cried silent, guilty tears for this wounding. Those were the worst mornings. It was much harder to pull himself together after such raw emotion.

Today, he held his breath and counted to ten in his mind. It was less satisfying than his normal routine, but there was a need for discretion this morning. A little crying or cursing could easily be carried in the wind. It would be hard to deny when he was the only likely candidate. So, no, he held his anguish in silence, bit down deep and swallowed.

Be Doran.

It was fine advice, and it allowed him to endure the day that little bit more. With his less horrifying hand, he rubbed his bald head a few times. The season was changing. Less chance of sunburn these days. Still, there was a sting, and he rubbed harder. He didn't know why; only that a little pain in the morning settled him. As long as he endured it in silence.

"Be Doran," he muttered, and took a breath. "Fuk it, let's do this."

From behind the last remaining tent in the camp marched a less-than-ruined Doran. He was fierce and energetic and determined. He was a master to those lesser brothers, and he would make them fierce, energetic and determined. He would make them warriors.

Walking through the ruin of the camp, he offered a silent goodbye to insignificant things. He did not know why, for he despised this camp. But he had found purpose here; could recall the finer moments now that he was leaving today and never returning.

Goodbye, abandoned galley; I can't seem to remember how much I despised the stews I ate from you.

Goodbye, little ditch on the outskirts. You served admirably as a trench for waste.

Goodbye, burned-out campfire. I once enjoyed a conversation beside you with Lillium as you kept the chill from the mood.

Goodbye, goodbye, just fuken goodbye.

He had a parting gift for their guests, and as it was his last act in this wretched camp, he took no chances that a brother would deny him the gesture. He came upon the barrel, standing alone where once there had stood many similar others. It was full, heavy and discarded. Carefully, he tipped it on its side and began rolling it down through the camp towards the enclosure.

The rains were unkind to any tents left abandoned since his comrades' grand departure. It felt less like a simple abandoned camp now, and more like something that had been destroyed by a terrible tempest. This was only half of the truth, he knew. His feet squelched as he rolled his prize over the Master General's former quarters, and he said a foolish goodbye in his mind as though it had been a place of reverence.

It had not; it had been a beacon in a dark time, but now, he and Aymon were beacons in themselves, and he was rightly fuken scared at this responsibility.

"I can't believe you were serious," muttered Azel, as Doran approached the enclosure where his two friends waited. Azel had donned his finest armour and drawn his sword in preparation.

Beside him, his lover shook his head in agreement. "I never know what you are thinking, brother," Aymon muttered, not unkindly. Aymon was clad in his finest armour also, though his sword was not yet drawn. Who knew such grand gestures could be so precarious? He grinned, and Doran smiled dazzlingly. In these moments he was miles from the whimpering waif hiding behind a flapping tent. He was a master and in complete control.

He stopped the rolling, waved with his ruined hand and allowed them to place the barrel upright.

"We have enough sine as it is. What's the harm in offering a little gift come emancipation? Might slow their pursuit of us. Might even earn their favour for the days ahead. Who knows—perhaps they might even drink from this ungodly brew and find their zealousness tested."

Azel popped the barrel and sniffed the violent aroma within. "It's not too late to go against Erroh's orders." He looked at the cage behind him and the forty-odd prisoners within. The covering above their heads had suffered from the heavy rainfall but mercifully had not collapsed on them. Minor miracles, indeed. "Who would know?" he asked. There was weight in his words. They were the three remaining Wolves among a pack of broken southerners.

"Erroh ordered us to free them," Aymon argued weakly, and Doran knew his unease. Perhaps that was why the trio alone remained. Were unsavoury things to occur, there would be fewer people left to tell the tale. Doran knew how to keep a secret. As did Aymon. Perhaps Azel could remain as tight-lipped as they.

Azel dipped a finger into the sine and drew it out again. His eyes were unusually cold. "I've seen them burn before. It's quite a sight." He sucked the sine from his fingers and eyed Aymon hopefully. "Smells like some fine cooking," he jested when he sensed no agreement.

"Who speaks for you?" Doran called out, standing at the gate to the makeshift cell. It was a slapdash affair of chains and sturdy beams dug deep and tightened. Doran thought it a strange thing that the prisoners had never tried to break out. Perhaps they plotted dastardly acts. Perhaps they enjoyed the northern hospitality. Perhaps they were too frightened to anger their keepers. Whatever the reason, they remained in silence as the Wolves' camp packed up and set out for their new home.

At length, a diminutive man appeared at the gate. His clothes were tattered and ruined, and Doran could smell him from where he stood. Daily bathing was not a service provided in this jail. Doran recognised him: the brazen southerner who had marched into the camp in search of Erroh. He'd appeared so smug and assured waving his white flag then, offering gifts and threats in the same breath.

He'd been the first to wave his white flag again as the Wolves charged through them the following day. He was a wretch, but he still had a glimmer in his eyes. Pride might serve any warrior, even when humbled and crushed. Doran clenched his ruined hand.

"I, speak for... us."

Slowly, Doran slid the key through the beams and gestured to the locked entrance. The prisoner didn't seem to understand. Behind him, the rest of the prisoners climbed to their feet. They'd seen the grand departure. Things were afoot beyond the dismal waiting in the cage.

"You are free."

"…"

Aymon tapped the lock, pointed to the key in his grubby grip. Still nothing.

"Idiots," muttered Azel, stepping away from the doorway, still clutching his sword. "Freedom," he said, raising his voice.

"Me?" the prisoner asked.

"All," said Doran, pointing to the man's comrades, and then indicated the barrel of sine. The prisoner was thoroughly confused, and Doran realised bringing the barrel had complicated matters. "Gift," he added, and the man nodded uncertainly. With the skill of a man who'd drunk a hearty amount of alcohol in his time, Doran reached into the barrel with his working hand, scooped out some sine and drank. "See? Not poison."

"This is a stupid idea," Aymon pointed out.

"Aye, it is," agreed Doran, accepting defeat. "Let's ride. At least they are too confused to attack us, let alone follow us." With a deep bow that anyone would recognise as a gesture of goodwill, Doran turned and led his comrades away from the cage as the heavy click of an unlocking gate filled the morning air.

As they climbed atop their mounts, the captured soldiers emerged slowly from the gate. They stretched; they scratched their heads; they looked around at the abandoned camp in bewilderment. A few dared to sip from the barrel. Their enthusiastic coughs soon filled the air and, despite himself, Doran enjoyed the humanity. They were enemies, but they were all the same species.

Suddenly the diminutive prisoner jogged unsteadily towards him. It was pathetic to see how the man's body betrayed him after so long with no proper exertion. He wavered pitifully and almost fell twice. He called to them, and Doran, wrapping his reins around his lesser hand, held his charge.

"Please… why?"

"Erroh decided you would not die," Aymon replied. Doran could see the grubby streaks of tears down the man's cheeks.

"Erroh? Fire god of Spirk?"

"The god demanded mercy," Aymon called. "All hail Erroh," he cried mockingly, and Doran grinned.

The prisoner did not. He thought this was fantastic news. He cried out to his freed brethren in delight. Doran caught only the word "Erroh." After a moment, the prisoner dropped to a knee, bowing.

"Thank you… All hail Erroh."

Behind him, the rest followed. They bowed, they gave thanks to their emancipators, and then they gave thanks "to the fire god, Erroh."

Soon enough the camp came alive with chanting, and the three Wolves turned their horses and rode away.

"All hail Erroh?" mocked Azel, giggling in delight. On most matters Aymon and Azel agreed, yet Azel's blind devotion to Erroh and Lea was a bone of contention at the best of times. However, even Doran found the humour in Aymon's ill-taken jest.

"That wasn't my intention," muttered Aymon.

"Who knew Aymon was a believer?" mocked Doran.

"I can't wait to tell this story," declared Azel.

"Oh, fuk off, the both of you."

The ride wasn't too long. Some hard hours racing north in the saddle put a safe distance between them and those they had released, those who sought the end of Spark. The path was clear, and they took no rest. Only once they'd left the camp behind did Doran fully understand the weight of responsibility now placed solely upon them. It would be no small task to take battered veterans and turn them into something fierce. It would be a far easier task to fail them completely with ineptitude.

He feared greatly the measure of his own worth.

Aymon appeared perfectly relaxed with this weight, or at least appeared as much. To question him would suggest Doran's own shortcomings, and some truths brought calamity to great partnerships. Aymon had insisted he would deliver ruthless, regimented training with the blade, and though it had stung, particularly where his hand hung, Doran couldn't argue.

Azel had been first to offer instruction in archery, and Doran was grateful for it. For all his jests and coldness, he had known more horror and violence than most. His nerves were iron, and if he could impart such strength to their warriors, it would be indispensable training.

As for Doran, they had charged him with whipping the men into an effective fighting outfit. A life of policing had already hardened them, but warfare was something different indeed. They would need to learn discipline, control and loyalty.

The problem with discipline, however, would be turning on those he loved and beating them down to nothing so he could rebuild them for war. He wasn't sure he had it in him to tear and berate those who'd stood upon the battlefield when all others had fled. Whenever he thought of training, he envisioned the Rangers and the cruelty of their demise. Their discipline alone was a tale of legends, and he did not know how to capture such potency. He feared causing their deaths. Mostly, he feared watching them die.

"I see the torchlights ahead," called Azel as they neared the camp and the fatigue of the ride set in.

Summoning his courage and wit, Doran swallowed his anguish at his mutilation once more and gripped the reins and followed his brothers in towards the camp. The Wolves had set camp two days before, while the trio had remained behind to ensure they had enough time to set up and prepare. But to Doran's dismay, there came no sentry to check their approach.

Farther in, they saw most tents had been erected haphazardly, with the Wolves themselves relaxed and spread out around a huge bonfire, enjoying themselves as though they'd just attained a stunning victory.

The camp was a pathetic thing. Not only were the tents sloppily constructed, they were too far apart. As though they'd earned privacy now. There was no discipline on show, no sign of respect or belief or fuken pride, and Doran was furious. Furious enough to see his own weakness.

"It's too late to fix this shit tonight," muttered Aymon. "Training will be a right struggle tomorrow." He slowed his horse to a walk, and a look of fright replaced his usual confident appearance.

As he had his entire life, Doran never let his best friend be troubled for long. Brothers just never did that, he told himself, and such words infused him.

I have this.

"What do you mean, tomorrow?" Doran roared, dropping from his horse. Around him the gathered army looked up from their idleness and he felt his temper burn wonderfully. He recalled the brutality of his father, the lessons of respect earned and never gifted. The fear and the reward. The leadership.

"What the fuk is this shit?" he cried again. Only then did he realise that a song had been playing; it fell silent now.

A fuken song. In a new camp. Without guards on patrol.

"You, you and fuken you—here, now." He beckoned to the nearest Wolves. "Grab your armour, grab your swords, and get walking the perimeter. Two hundred yards out, all the way around. Come back at dawn.... What the fuk are you waiting for?" He struck one unfortunate soldier across the back of the head. He knew his name. It was Darian. A nice enough man. A bit dim. Fuk you, Darian.

"There will be no further alcohol drunk until I decide it will be," he challenged, and all around the gathering he saw glasses swiftly drained, emptied, hidden.

This pleased him.

"I hope you rested before we came, because I can't see any of you sleeping for the next few days," he roared, and were there a hidden southern finger preparing to attack, such was his ferocity they might have fled for the now.

"What do you need us to do?" Azel whispered, dropping from his horse.

"Leaders rest all they want, though there will be some raised voices this evening," Doran hissed in reply. To the crowd, he roared again. "Where are our tents?"

He glanced at Aymon and accepted the man's simple nod of appreciation. Punching his ruined fist into his hand, Doran went to task beating his brethren into an effective group. Marching through the gathering, he barked out orders, and they were obeyed immediately.

"I'll have this fuken army a thing of beauty before we all die," he called out at last. To his amazement, he received a terrified cheer from his warmongering students.

at the front of the procession. Lillium, however, looking equally ruined, was similarly disinclined to converse, and Lea too fell silent, unwilling to push unwanted words.

They followed the tracks for a few hours, enjoying the warmth from the afternoon sun after the previous few days' rain. Eventually, as dusk set in, Lea noticed a break in the trees a few miles ahead. A few dilapidated structures stood silently along the tracks upon an elevated slope of stone. As they neared, she discovered them to be monstrous metallic structures, as impressive as the skyroad.

The elements of centuries had rusted the steel to nothing, and the wilderness had overtaken what support girders remained. It felt like a tomb as they dipped under its vast entrance. Perhaps this had been a town of some sort, she thought, and held her breath as they walked beneath a massive dome of precarious metal and weed, arching far above. Countless rocks filled the tracks at their feet, making it impossible for the horses to walk safely through at any healthy pace.

"This place is strange and ancient," Lillium muttered, bringing her mount to the side of the tracks. Her voice echoed, and it was unsettling.

They could see more sets of tracks now, branching off from this one in many directions, disappearing into the wastes through equally grand openings. Most were missing strips of metal, while others were covered in rust and looked likely to crumble to brown dust if touched. The path the Outcasts had followed was the only set that was complete, and Lea wondered if the rest had perhaps been sacrificed to keep this one track in working order.

She wondered absently where the other tracks might bring a wanderer, were they blessed to be free of burdens like

35

TRACKS IN THE WASTES

"These are cart tracks?" Lea asked, running her fingers across the cool ridge of steel in the ground. They were a pair, a few feet apart, as smooth as a flawless blade but as dulled as a forgotten relic. Stretching for miles. As Wynn described their function, she shook her head. Speed attainable but only able to move backwards or forwards? It made little sense. As he spoke, he tapped at a long shard of steel hanging down the side of his horse. If Lea didn't know better, she'd have imagined it was a southern shield with all the fur ripped away.

"I didn't travel too far along them, but it's a fine path through unforgiving terrain," Wynn suggested, and continued to tap away absently at the bit of metal. He appeared proud of his find. It was no sky road, but they welcomed any clear path in the wastes.

"A fine discovery," she said, and he smiled.

Each of them took turns walking up and down the unnatural path, hopping between each carefully sculpted piece of wood, measured and placed evenly along the ground.

Two long, endless strips of perfect steel winding out each way into the wilderness. It was a wonder.

"I've seen something like this before, under the city, in the dark," Emir muttered. "With Erroh," he added.

"They were not in the same condition," argued Erroh.

"Smuggling," Wrek said. "Swift movement of delectable things for the city."

"They go all the way to the city..." murmured Roja, and ground her teeth ever so.

Lea ran her fingers through her hair and grimaced as flakes of brown mud fell in front of her face. She was a ruin. All of them were still covered in the light caking of dried mud. Staying clear of any fast-flowing rivers was not without its disadvantages. She was content to live with fewer dangers, but a girl liked to look her best doing so. Her one consolation was that Nomi looked even worse. Deep streaks of brown still covered her perfect little rosy cheeks. She hadn't the grace to at least attempt to clean herself. Typical.

"From where?"

"Raven Rock. I've... seen them. Two or four people stand upon a rolling metal cart and take turns pushing down on opposite levers. They move more swiftly than a racing horse, even with a heavy load." She looked around at the surrounding forest. "How did you think cofe entered Spark in such outrageous amounts?"

"How have the tracks continued to be maintained?" Emir asked. It was a fair question.

"A man could spend a lifetime out here, maintaining these tracks," mused Wrek. "There must be quite the payment for keeping these beasts smooth." He knelt in and ran his fingers through the clusters of weeds growing between each wooden panel. He looked at the wild undergrowth, much higher than the weeds, on either side of the tracks, seemingly trying its

best to reclaim the wastes from the touch of ancient civilisation.

"It wouldn't take a female that long," Roja mocked

"Aye, a fine point. Sometimes I forget I'm among s group. My apologies," Wrek conceded, bowing. He pick the weeds again. "It's been a season or two since these v cut. That's never a great sign." One set of the silver track journeyed towards Samara, and the other went south, the they were headed.

"Nicely done, Wynn. We can follow the tracks for now said Erroh, climbing onto his mount.

"As you say, Erroh," agreed Lea, climbing atop her ow beast. Her agreement spurred the rest to follow without argument, and she was grateful for it. They brought their horses in line and followed Erroh down the ancient pathway

With no cart or supplies slowing them, they made swift time. Their mood was low, but the cursed rain had eased off, at least. Conversation was muted once more in this group, and only Lexi, struggling with this new arrangement, muttered curses from her saddle. Lea rode beside her at first and engaged in what conversation she could. It was strange having a sister. In the march's mundanity, she intended to get to know her.

Perhaps it was the mood or the exhaustion, but Lexi spok little and soon enough Lea left her to her own devices. It was only Roja she spoke with warmly, and Lea wondered if she didn't believe Lea had stolen a better mate away from her brother. It was a small matter that Lea *had* stolen him. It was a beautiful crime. If Lexi was anything like her stubborn brother, it would take a fine amount of time under healthier circumstances before they would share sisterhood. Lea was patient girl.

Leaving Lexi to her vague mutterings, Lea joined Lilliu

responsibility, honour and vengeance. Would they lead to a little farm with crops, a pleasant kitchen and a wonderfully reinforced bed upon which to start a new life, a new family?

She loved these drifting moments of imaginings.

"Look at the size of that monster," Wynn said, drawing her from her thoughts. He pointed at a long, covered cart that could easily have been a tavern upon wheels. Beneath the dust and grime, she could see the faded yellow paint. It sat on rusty wheels of iron, alone upon one stretch of tracks, unable to move a foot either way, and Lea felt a great sadness for such a beast. Those who had come before them had known much. They had lost so much more.

"This is bigger than the ones I've seen before," Wrek said in disbelief. "I see no levers to drive this beast, either. Only seats within."

They passed through the structure in silence, looking this way and that, each thinking their own thoughts about these strange, unnerving things. When they reached the other side and the fading sunlight warmed Lea's face once more, she breathed easier.

A few miles more along the tracks, Erroh discovered a small well with a hand pump. He dropped down from his horse, took hold of the handle, and the rest of the group held their breaths, scarcely daring to hope. Having discovered no nearby river, they had been forced to ration their water. They weren't thirsty yet, but they had all been uneasily aware that that day would come...

The piercing scream of rusted metal filled the air and echoed in the eerie, abandoned place. Instinctively, Erroh stopped pumping and pulled his hand away as if burned. He glanced into the forest beyond, scanning for any movement, any sign of fiends lurking. When nothing stirred, he shrugged and began again, trying desperately to ignore the shrill cry of the water pump.

After a few attempts, a drizzle of brown water dripped through the spout. He kept going, and at last, a comforting gush of cool water spilled from the spout. He immediately dipped his head under and enjoyed the fruits of his labour.

"We're camping here tonight," he declared happily.

———

"After a while, you can't even hear the pump," said Emir, sitting down beside Lillium away from any eager ears. With such a covered area, there was little point huddling in close together, braving the winds.

"I can still hear it just fine," she snapped, and he knew the trouble he was in. He just didn't really understand why.

When asked, Wynn had told him that no fool should ever touch an Alpha's journal or sword without their permission. The fact of Emir's grabbing her blade to cut the cart away, against her wishes and those of many others, was a crime she would make him pay for. "At least she's not staring at me with outright hatred today," he'd joked, bringing his mount forward and leaving Emir the time to plan.

He held a mug of cofe in his grubby hands. Even without milk, it was glorious after the riding. He watched the steam for a moment and felt the slight change in the air. It was becoming a lot cooler at night. He offered her the mug, but she was distracted, watching Erroh and Lea. They had sparring swords in their hands. They kissed once and then broke into terrible violence, the wooden swords clattering loudly in the night.

"I'd prefer to watch the spectacle in silence," she hissed.

"I should probably apologise for taking your sword." He was excellent at apologies. A lifetime of seeking contrition had educated him in these matters. She sighed and watched the stunning Alphalines. "Are we good now?" he asked.

Again, she sighed.

"Aye, I think we're good," he mocked. He knew he was making it worse, but he couldn't help himself. He had offered an apology. It was her own issue if she couldn't accept it.

"It's a lucky thing I'm in debt to you, Healer," she growled, and Emir knew he had her. No problem. Like a fish on a line, he just needed to reel her in.

"Aye, it's a lucky thing, alright," he agreed. "Are we good?" he asked again. She produced her sword and held it out in front of him. The fresh aroma of lacquer struck him. Like every blade owned by an Alpha, it was exquisite. It was far older than any he'd seen and shorter than most, but it suited her. He could see blemishes at its grip and dents on the guard where its wielder had suffered strikes, but down along its grey blade, it was almost flawless. It shimmered in the moonlight, and he felt a pang of guilt for the care she took of it. "I'm really sorry, Lillium," he said, and meant it.

Perhaps she noticed the sincerity in his voice, for she smiled a little and spun it absently, lovingly, before holding it out for him to take. He did not.

"Only take a sword from an Alpha when they offer it," she mumbled.

As you wish.

He took the sword and examined it carefully. It seemed like the thing to do. For all its beauty, though, it was an object of death. He could not love such a thing, like Alphalines apparently did. He ran his finger along its cool surface and then passed it back to its rightful owner.

"What name did you give it?"

"I would consider it rude to ask such a question," she snorted, standing up. "Her name is Lady." She sounded embarrassed.

"It's a fine name," he reassured her. "And the other sword?" he asked.

"That blade has not earned a title yet, perhaps because it doesn't yet feel natural in my left hand," she said, watching Lea spin away from Erroh and lure him into dropping his guard. "I wish to be elite like them."

"Well, I think you are great," he said lightly, and she sniggered.

"Thank you, Healer."

"Are we friends again?"

"Friends?" She thought on this a moment. "Were we ever friends?"

"Oh." He didn't have many friends. Now he had even one fewer than he thought.

"Just because we are gathered in a group, reviled by a doomed city, hunting an impossible foe, does not demand we become bonded."

"Well, I still consider you a friend," he countered, and her stern gaze cracked ever so. She might have even lifted her eyebrow as well. He could tell he was getting through to her.

She cracked her knuckles gently and her neck loudly. "Did you come to apologise, hoping to avoid some recompense?" she asked, standing over him. "You are a decent man, Emir, but I'm no decent girl."

He stood up and raised his arms in submissiveness before offering his chin. "Just one strike?"

. . .

Lillium knew of Emir's history. She'd listened cheerfully before as he'd spoken drunkenly of his life in Keri. She had taken especially great interest in his explicit descriptions of their penchant for fist-fights. The healer was a skilled storyteller: amusing, quick-witted and adding just enough embellishment that the tales were memorable. Having grown up in Keri, he could take punches. Roja could vouch for that. She had heard that tale as well.

Lillium swung at his face, but held her blow as he blinked. Instead of knocking him to the ground, she opened her palm and tapped his cheek gently. He opened his eyes suspiciously and dared a hopeful grin, and fuk him, but he was a charming wretch. Maybe they were friends.

She smiled warmly, and he dropped his guard. She knew she had a dazzling smile and used it when needed. He replied in kind and was about to speak when, still smiling, she shot her foot out and struck him between the legs. A strike all the more devastating because of his unpreparedness. Even more ferocious, for she had summoned all her hatred and grief in the blow. She always thought of that horrible night whenever she struck out. It always made her strike a little more fiercely. His body convulsed, and he fell limply to the ground, and she suddenly wondered if wearing steel boots had been a little too much.

I will not cry out, Emir pledged as the horrible moments passed and the pain grew. Something inside him had exploded. This, he suspected, was not accurate, but it still brought little comfort. He doubted he would ever know comfort again. Writhing in the mud, he pleaded with his will not to betray him. He held his manhood and the rest and moaned as his stomach lurched and he threw up a little bile. He saw Roja laughing silently from across the camp and dug his head into the dirt. He did not want her to see his tears. They streamed freely from his face and he tried to wipe them away, but just ended up leaving muddy tracks on his cheeks.

"Aw, fuk me. I forgot about my boots," Lillium whispered, dropping to her knees beside him.

"I deserved it," he wheezed, curling up in a ball. He didn't know if he deserved it, but he desperately wanted to recover his pride. With every pump of blood, he fought the urge to moan. Years from now, many, many years, he hoped to laugh the way Roja did now. He couldn't blame her. He was a mere wretch among violent Alphalines. He saw that now. They had a different code, a different way of viewing the world. They were a rung, a whole ladder, above him and he accepted that.

"No, Emir, you didn't," she whispered softly, and hugged him before trying to help him rise.

"No. Nope, not a chance. Just leave me here to die… alone," he joked weakly, before sitting up. He looked across to Roja and discovered she had fallen still. If he didn't know better, he might have seen concern on her face. Perhaps for his misfortune, but more likely for his recovery; it had been a brutal kick.

"I won't leave you here, and you won't die alone," Lillium whispered, and though she looked thoroughly uncomfortable, she wrapped him in her powerful arms and hushed him soothingly. "Friends don't do that," she pledged, resting her head on his, and he stared into the darkness all around them. Behind them, the camp returned to its preparations. He heard the hammering of blades and the grunts of effort, the muted conversations as they prepared themselves for the skirmish to come. Neither he nor Lillium moved, and he felt the pain begin to ease away. After a time without either saying another word, he was surprised to feel her tears dripping into his hair, and he dared not ruin this moment by asking of her horrors. At least for now.

36

ADDRESSING THE BEAST IN THE ROOM

Comfortable enough wandering the road now, Erroh and Lea endured each passing day. However, many of their companions showed fatigue from the relentless march. Strangely, though, it was this relentless fatigue that served them well.

There was better cheer than before, and Erroh credited Emir with that. From his seat atop his mount, his brother of the dark loudly offered his thoughts on arbitrary matters and played the part of entertainer to a welcoming audience from dawn until dusk. Gone was the terrified caution of the quiet march, replaced by a desire to stave off the cursed, crippling boredom of silence. Fuk it, he thought: if the Hunt appeared, they were no longer a lowly gathering of wanderers who would flee at the first sign of trouble. No, they would offer quite the fight. The good cheer and camaraderie were well worth the risk they took with conversing and laughing, and Erroh could feel a change in the wind. They rode closer to each other these days. It almost felt like family.

Especially when Emir began rambling.

"I've been thinking," he said now, and somewhere behind, Erroh heard Wrek mutter, "Here we go."

"Hear me out, friends. We need a name for ourselves," the wretched healer declared. There was a glint in his eyes. "All the legendary groups have prominent names, really great ones. What do we have?" he asked his audience. His audience looked back at him in silence. It was a tough crowd.

"Nothing," he said, answering his own question. "We're nothing but worthless outcasts." He spat on the ground for effect.

"I'm still a Ranger," corrected Lillium.

"See, that's a wonderful name," he shouted. "I want us to have a legendary name like the Rangers. A name to strike fear into all who hear it," he explained as though they weren't getting it. "Magnus chose that name well. And think of the Black Guard—they're called the Wolves. How terrifying is that?" he asked. He balanced in his saddle and brought his hands up as though they were claws. "It doesn't even matter that most wolves are grey. That's not the point," he said, and Erroh heard a few chuckles. The man worked his audience well. "Even Uden chose a terrifying name. The Hunt is primal and relentless. To me it sounds like death," he said, giving an exaggerated shudder. Only Nomi peered at him coldly. Any time he went blaspheming about the south, she took offence.

As though she still believes we are tainted curs.

Erroh could see the glee in Emir's eyes as he drew them in with his inane words. He'd believed he would be a right wretched bastard enduring sobriety, yet Emir seemed to have come into his own with his clearer, sharper mind.

"Emir's Legends?" suggested Lea, as seriously as she could, before joining Roja in laughter.

"I love it," agreed Wynn. "There's a certain poetic ring to

443

it that just strikes hard. Like a kick to the groin, I suppose."
There was a burst of laughter, and Emir grimaced good-
naturedly.

Erroh had asked Wynn to ride with the group today
instead of scouting ahead for a campsite. Safety in numbers,
he supposed, and Raven Rock was sure to be near now.
Roja's map suggested as much. Besides, the camaraderie was
doing Wynn no harm at all either, and this was good for
morale. The last couple of days, he'd jested a little more, and
Lillium reacted more positively to him. They had even
engaged in a handful of courteous conversations, as though
they were friends. Who knew a few days of miserable
marching could ease tensions?

Emir continued, unperturbed. "None of you are taking
this seriously. We need a name. A right shiny name with
polish."

"Kick him again, Lillium," Wrek shouted, bringing his
horse forward. He pushed at the healer in the saddle as he
went by, almost knocking him from his seat.

"I think I broke a bone in my foot the last time."

Roja snorted in delight.

"Proof I am talented between the legs," Emir quipped,
and straightened his back a little.

The ground they walked took a steep turn upwards now as
the tracks brought them slowly towards the top of a valley,
and their beasts struggled a little under the incline. Few of the
riders took notice. The teasing was heating up, and Emir was
a fine target this afternoon.

"Aye, Emir, you're quite the sturdy one. Much more
impressive than Wynn," agreed Lillium. There were more
delighted guffaws, and she smiled in triumph. Erroh caught
her embarrassed glance at Wynn, who returned the gaze with

a booming laugh. "You really missed out there, Roja," she added playfully.

Roja laughed aloud, and Erroh knew that the jest had struck gold. "I have no regrets about missing out on any male whose manhood could break bones," she said, taking the mantle and running with it. "As we all know, I am a delicate flower."

"Oh, you missed nothing, Roja," Erroh said, taking over. "When we were in chains, our dear healer was all ready to reveal his talents to the guards, hoping to earn us sustenance."

"That explains why you were half-starved and dying of thirst when we found you!" suggested Wrek.

"It was a trick of the light," argued Emir. "I have nothing to be ashamed of. In fact, in Keri I was a legend," he boasted unsuccessfully, to further peals of laughter.

Lillium turned around to face him. "I think we should decide for ourselves. It's been a long road, and I think we deserve a little entertainment. Pretend we are in the Cull. Come on, Emir—pop it out." She bit her lower lip to keep from laughing. It was an effective tactic.

"I'd like to see his manhood," agreed Lexi, staring at his lap.

"Emir, you will not show your manhood to my sister," warned Erroh. "Alexis, line of Magnus and Elise, you are far too young for this conversation."

"Don't call me that, Roro."

"I have an idea: I think any of us who have been… erm… 'viewed' by Emir in a state of undress should be gifted a little reward," Lea said, and Emir's face faltered. The jesting had suddenly become very precarious.

"Whatever do you mean?" he asked, with the look of a man who knew he shouldn't have asked.

"Is there any female here whose talents have not been seen by our healer?" Lillium asked.

"Oh," said Emir unhappily. "I was worried that was what you meant." He eyed the forest as though considering making a break for it.

"Well, he hasn't seen my chest yet," mumbled Lexi.

"No, nor will he ever," snapped Erroh, staring hard at the healer. He felt like he had had a similar conversation not too long ago.

"But you saw Elise's chest quite a lot," Wynn reminded Emir, before realising his error and immediately bowing in apology to the Master General.

For a breath, Erroh's anguish caught in his chest, and then the moment passed. "Oh, you fuker, don't remind me," he laughed, forgiving his friend easily enough, for that was what a Master General would do.

"Perhaps I am too young for this conversation after all. I don't wish to think of Emir healing my mother," murmured Lexi.

Emir spoke up again, and as always, made things both better and worse. "Wynn, my brother," he intoned, "her breasts are the finest of all that I have ever seen. I look forward to treating them again soon, once we kill that bastard, Uden, save the city and earn our pardons," he proclaimed, bowing to Erroh. Despite his light tone, Erroh knew his words held a certain truth. He knew how dearly Emir cared for Elise. Had he not caught him weeping with worry for her the night they had learned of her abduction? The gathering fell silent for a few moments, thinking of Elise's unknown fate.

Then Lillium piped up again, breaking the tension. "Wait a moment, what's wrong with my breasts?" she asked.

"That's right, Healer. She has wonderful breasts," agreed

Wynn, and shrugged. Lillium glared at him, though not unkindly, and Erroh thought this significant. If they couldn't jest about their failed heartbreaking lives as mates, then just what were they able to jest about?

"I… not understand," Nomi said, looking around and trying to follow the outbursts. Erroh laughed at her confusion and wondered how well she grasped their humour. "Slow… speak… please," she added, and was pleased at the laughter she received.

"He told me I had the finest breasts, as he was cutting the arrow out of my back," muttered Lea, and spat in disgust. "It was a little romantic, I'll admit. I've kept that thought to myself, Erroh. It keeps me warm at night," she added, stroking Erroh's arm playfully. "Now I just feel the right fool for being charmed."

"I was really drunk," admitted Emir. "They were most lovely… in that moment."

"He had to get me drunk, just to see my chest," added Roja, without too much malice.

"At least I made you breakfast," he countered, grinning.

"Oh yes. And I would probably take those eggs right now," she said, looking away. Her face was flushed.

"Nomi, best chest," said Nomi, and held her arms across her own talents. She looked around and smiled as her companions laughed at her. Or with her. Instinctively, she glanced at Erroh and appeared thrilled with his laughter.

"Aye, witch, you have very good breasts," agreed Emir.

"Might I suggest a competition?" asked Wrek. This was met with wild approval from all the males. Alphalines were competitive at the best of times. Sometimes they competed for a mate, sometimes for survival, sometimes for an extra drink on the house. It was a small matter.

"Outstanding suggestion, Wrek," declared Erroh. "As the

rightful leader of this group, I think it only fair that I be the judge. I'll let you know how it goes. Come with me, ladies. Follow me into the forest." He pretended to turn his mount toward the edge of the woods.

Lea slapped him across the arm. "Like you don't have enough female attention as it is," she growled warmly. A fine skill, if truth be told.

"Aye, we can't have him choose," said Wynn. "It wouldn't be fair at all. Erroh will just choose Lea." He coughed importantly, as though he were addressing a congregation as they chose a new king. "I, however, would be a fair and just critic."

Erroh wasn't quite willing to relinquish the task "I don't know, brother. Nomi may set up to be quite the challenge to my darling mate," he insisted.

Oh, Erroh.

"And that is why you sleep alone tonight… my beo," Lea said. He really feared how she'd said that, too. Then she slapped him again, this time a little harder, and the gathering laughed.

"Well, if Wynn is judge, I don't think I'll be showing him any part of my body again," warned Lillium.

They were nearing the top of the valley. Here, the steel was at its shiniest. The weeds a little fewer. The forest a little thinner. There may also have been the sound of a fast-flowing river that none of the travellers could hear above the boisterous laughing and the healing words.

"It's alright, my dear. I remember them well enough to form a healthy and fair score."

"Same with me," agreed Emir. "Usually at night when I'm alone in bed," he added. "I'd love to think of all of you, but alas, I can't remember Roja's at all. I was too drunk to really see them," he admitted sadly. Wynn patted him on the back in understanding. Life was cruel sometimes.

"Well, if Wynn is judging, I will take Lillium's place," said Lexi.

"No, no, you won't... Lexi."

"Fine," she said, sulking.

"Does that mean he'll have to show us his manhood?" asked Lea thoughtfully.

"You will not be showing your manhood to my mate or my sister," roared Erroh.

"Can he show it to your mother?" asked Emir.

"All joking aside, Wynn is perfectly fine where it counts," said Lillium. She shrugged and smiled at Wynn.

The nervous but thoroughly enjoyed laughter continued for a few moments more until suddenly Wynn sat up in his saddle, realisation dawning on his face. "Wait a moment, just how many men have you seen?" he cried, and brought his horse to a stop alongside the beautiful Alphaline.

"Not nearly enough," she said dreamily. "But now that I'm no longer spoken for, I think I'll enjoy the hunt."

"Very well," decided Lea. "I declare that there shall be a full contest among the females, but only after the males endure a similar contest. I think that's only fair." The laughter fell away as the challenge was put forth. "My money is on Wrek. I bet he has a wonderful manhood," she added, and was met with much feminine agreement.

The male Outcasts were unimpressed with the tables being turned so swiftly.

"No, that won't be happening," Wrek declared.

"No, I'd prefer the mystery," Emir agreed.

"No, no, I think that's how friendships end," Wynn decided.

"No, it's far too cold for such a contest anyway," Erroh

decided, speaking as Master General once more. So that made it official.

"Fuk me—look!" Lillium cried, pointing to something up ahead. It was a little town, and it looked quite abandoned. "We've arrived."

"Too late to help," Roja said, her voice catching in her throat, and a coldness overtook Erroh.

They walked their mounts up towards the town in silence. Nearer to the gates they drew to a halt as one, and gazed in shock at the horror that lay before them: abandoned houses, overturned carts, scorched stones, and countless tangled, bloated bodies, lying where they had been struck down.

"This cannot be," whispered Erroh.

Not again.

Oh, please, not again.

37

RAVEN ROCK

A gain. The cheer abruptly died away as the group entered the settlement. Erroh thought of Keri. It was half the size and housed a tenth of the people, but it had shared similar horrors. This town was surrounded by a thick stone wall like Samara's, though nowhere near as high, nowhere near as impenetrable. It stood perhaps fifteen foot, and the roofs of the houses within were visible from the tracks. It appeared the warriors who had stood upon them had held out for as long as they could. He understood their doomed bravery; their terror too.

There was an ancient taste to this place. The massive iron gate was bent and broken through. It rested to one side of the archway where the killers had surged in. Erroh shivered at the thought of the terrible screech it must have made as it failed.

"This can't be," wailed Roja. She stumbled forward, releasing the hold on her mount. No one comforted her, for they were all as anguished as she was. "So many," she cried.

Aye, many.

Even though they knew the horrors to come, nothing could have fully prepared them. They followed the old stone road into the town and began to look about them. Erroh held his stomach as he edged his mount away from the first set of remains lying in the dust. He stared at the grinning skull and held its demented gaze for a moment. The skin had been picked bare long before, and the weather had done the rest. All that remained was dried bone and steel from its armour and weapons. Many months it must have rested here without being disturbed.

I can't take this.

It was all too familiar. Leah walked beside him with head bowed low. He took her hand; her only acknowledgment was a delicate squeeze in return. She was pale, and just like Erroh, she was not seeing this for the first time. He let go of Highwind's bridle and draped his arm around Lea, enveloping her completely. They were in this torment together. It was all he could do.

The town itself had once been beautiful; he could see that. It had lasted many generations, and like Keri, it had fared better than most settlements. Many structures still stood with glass in their windows. However, many others had burned down during the town's last stand.

Wynn unsheathed his sword, and Emir followed suit, taking out a blunt longsword he had no business brandishing with such a stature. Better that than "borrowing" another alpha's blade.

"There's little need for that," Lillium muttered, stepping carefully over a body. It was smaller than Lexi. It would grow no more. Other corpses were strewn in the middle of the street. At least a hundred lost souls. "The killers are long gone."

"We should have saved them," Roja mumbled as tears streamed from her eyes. She dropped to a knee, but few of her companions noticed. They too fought the urge to collapse. "I should have… I… I didn't know."

They spread out in a line as they walked further towards the centre of the town, each lost in their own thoughts as they numbly made their way through the horrors of war and savagery.

There were two roads leading away from either side of the main street, both showing the ancient scorch marks of pyres and heaps of charred bones. Here was where the women had been burned, Wrek knew. He collapsed to his knees, holding his head in anguish.

Eventually Lexi dropped down beside Roja and gripped her as a child would, tears coursing down her cheeks. They held each other for support, and Erroh, watching on, desperately wanted to take the pain from his sister, but he was no absent god, was not capable of compassion.

Nomi shuffled along as though she were stumbling home from a night in a tavern. Her feet echoed loudly in the silence. She, too, released the reins of her horse and walked with the rest, but her face was cold and serene. She'd likely seen this type of horror ten times over, but this time she saw how those left behind were mourning the dead.

"Terrible," she muttered. "I want kill them," she added, and Erroh wondered how deep her sense of shame might be in this moment. "Fuk… Woodin Man."

"I now see the pain you spoke of in Samara," muttered Lillium, placing her hand upon Erroh's shoulder. Her face was pale, and she struggled to keep herself upright as she stood in front of the remains of the pyre.

Wynn walked away, clutching his stomach, and ducked around a corner. Erroh heard him heave up dry nothingness. After a moment, Lillium collapsed against one of the burned-out buildings and threw up herself. Erroh almost smiled; they both took trauma similarly. That was something.

In the centre of the road lay a strange open hole leading down into darkness. Sitting partway across it, like a lid on a steaming pot, was a heavy iron covering. Hoisting the heavy piece out of the way, Erroh looked down and saw nothing but a ladder into deep nothing.

"It is a smuggler's route," Wrek said, watching him. "At least some survived the butchery."

"Where does it lead?" Erroh asked.

"Some distance away from the town gates, I'd think… Such things are handy should the city come a-raiding."

"Raiding?"

"Raven Rock and Spark did not see eye to eye on most matters, especially cofe running."

"Are you proud of this?" Emir barked. There was a coldness Erroh didn't recognise in his friend's words. He was staring at Nomi, who stumbled around in a daze.

Not now, Emir.

"Calm yourself, Emir," Erroh said, sliding the lid back across the hole lest some fool take a nasty fall in the dark.

"I said, are you proud, Nomi?" Emir leapt at her now, shoving her from behind. She stumbled forward from the blow, barely tried to catch herself, and Erroh had no will to calm the assault. If she wanted, she could break him in two.

"Regret," she cried, turning to face him, but she did not strike him. Perhaps she read the genuine anguish on his face and could inflict nothing more upon him.

They were getting on as well.

Emir charged at her, and still she made no move to stop him. "You fuken witch," he roared, and raised his fist to strike her, and Erroh snapped to attention. He ran, but Emir's hand fell back to his side.

"If I struck you, I might never stop," he cried pathetically.

"Calm yourself, Emir," Lea said from behind him. "This is not Nomi's doing."

"I wasn't going to hit her."

"Nomi had no hand in this," Lea told him sharply, lest they suddenly take Alpha matters into their own hands.

————

They attacked their task with grim efficiency. They dug into the soft ground beyond the back gates of the stronghold, in a fine clearing, peaceful and green. Soon the warm afternoon sun turned to a chilly evening, but still they dug the mass grave. It was better not stopping to sleep and then facing this terrible task again upon the morrow; easier to take the exhaustion and keep going. Just one vast grave it would be, in which those brave few would sleep everlastingly.

Erroh dug resolutely, stopping only to wipe the sweat from his brow. It was easier to concentrate on the pain in the back, the blisters on his fingers, than on the soul-destroying labour of laying the dead to rest.

Aye, Erroh had been here before. Once was enough for any man. So, he dug the hole, and so did the rest.

When the shattered moon appeared in the sky above them, Lexi, tasked with preparing a meal, lit a fine fire beneath the archway and hung a stewing pot over the dancing yellow flames. While supplies were low since the incident along the valley's edge, and none of their remaining meats had survived the ravages of time, there were still plenty of vegetables growing in the few fields beyond these walls. After a time, the delicious, rich aroma of salted soup filled the air. It was welcome after the stench of the dead. Erroh counted at least forty bodies wrapped now and ready for sleep. There were twice as many still to be prepared, but until the grisly task was finished, he could not settle his spinning mind.

No one complained. They just dropped their heads and steeled themselves for the misery to come.

———

As they sat down to eat, Emir lowered himself to the ground next to Nomi.

"It's a weak man who strikes a woman," he said quietly and dipped a spoon into his bowl of salty vegetables.

Nomi nodded but said nothing. She was lost in her own turmoil. She scooped some soup into her mouth and ate swiftly, eager to return to her duties. The moments spent resting were no fine times at all. "Healer strike Nomi? Nomi strike harder," she said after a few more mouthfuls, and it was a fine reply.

She was tired. Tired from holding herself together. It stung how little they cared for her; she could see it clearly now that she'd been left alone with the task of wrapping the bodies for burial. Aye, maybe it was her injured hand that stopped her from digging holes, but this work was worthy of the damned. She felt more alone in this moment than when she'd been wandering with her brethren in the Arth. She wondered if Erroh or Liiia would come and talk with her later, or maybe sit with her by the fire. That would be grand. She needed to hear words that had no venom. Though she did not know all the words they spoke to her, she understood their meaning well enough.

"Why do they do this?" Emir asked.

She said nothing for a few breaths and then she told him. "Uden the Woodin Man is god. What he say, must do," she said. Her words were heavy, her accent heavier. "*We* must do," she corrected.

"You could say no," argued Emir, and she shook her head in desperate frustration. How could he ever understand what defying a god truly felt like? How defying her people's way was unnatural. She'd spent long enough in chains during those lonely months to understand the cost of saying no to a god.

"You say no, you die," she said. "Or worse—become Nomi, chained. Burned."

"Aye."

"When Nomi young," she said, pointing to herself.

He nodded.

"Had sister… old."

Again, he nodded.

"Nomi young, can't remember. Blonde, like Nomi. Beautiful, like Nomi."

He nodded once more.

"She say no." She shrugged and raised her hands. She hoped he understood.

He did. There were no words to say.

She smiled and offered him a ladle full of soup. "Emir still hungry?"

"Aye," he said, passing across his bowl. "I'm sorry," he said softly. She looked around at the devastation and the remains of so many innocent victims.

"Nomi sorry too," she said, and kissed him on the cheek.

"Don't let Erroh see you. He'll be jealous," Emir said, and dared a wretched grin.

———

"And so, only two remain," said Wrek, resting his head on his arms and leaning on the shovel. It wasn't the most comfortable he'd ever been, but he'd take any comfort where he could. His shirtless body was aching, and sweat glistened on his skin. In the cold evening, it was just another torment. He wasn't sure where he'd left his shirt, and he certainly would not stop to go shuffling through the dark to find it. Not now, at least. Not until Erroh ceased his relentless task. And until Erroh ended for the day, he would stand with him.

"You should rest," Erroh suggested, seeming to read his mind. He looked as ruined as Wrek felt. That said, they all felt shitty.

"I need to work off my dark mood. I'll stay a little longer," he said. Straightening, he dug out an enormous chunk of grey dirt and tossed it into the massive mound at the grave's edge. "I wish no ill will upon Nomi, but, fuk me, I feel angrier at her than I've felt in many years. No, better I just dig this horrific grave and be done with it."

Erroh smiled and ceased his own onslaught on the defenceless ground. "In my anger, I once struck Nomi. It wasn't my finest moment." He took a few deep breaths. "Anger and grief can cause dreadful mistakes. Trust me, friend, she is one of us. She will *never* betray us."

"I doubt she took it well," said Wrek. "I have no wish to earn her ire. And Emir, well, Emir's likely to come around too. In the meantime, I'll monitor her to make sure nobody clashes with her."

"I'm lucky I survived her wrath. I've seen her take the nose of a brute as impressive as you, Wrek. I think she'll be fine."

Wrek laughed at this and Erroh laughed with him, and there was a glimmer of recognition Wrek tried to grasp and failed. His face darkened.

"Tell me, Wrek. Are you a quick rider?" Erroh asked.

"Aye, like the wind in a gale," Wrek assured him.

"Magnus believes the Hunt never strikes down the same settlement a second time," Erroh said, his eyes distant and thoughtful.

"And what do you think, Master General?"

"I wonder how far the Wolves' camp rests from here."

"A few days. Quicker with Roja's map," Wrek said, already knowing his fate.

Before Erroh could say any more, Lea appeared at the gates carrying a basket. She threw a loaf of honey bread to each of them and handed around a decanter of water before picking up one of the forgotten shovels lying in the wet grass.

"How is the mood at the fire?" Erroh asked between bites, savouring it despite its staleness and its aftertaste of wet mud.

"They're uneasy in this place. Emir is already speaking of ghosts. It enthralled Lillium," she mumbled. "And unnerved her a little. Even I started to get the shivers after a time," she added.

"Is that why you returned without resting, my love?" he asked.

"Aye, Erroh, that's exactly why," she mocked. Then her face darkened as she looked around the group. "These people have had enough time without rest. I shall not finish until every one of them has rested before me," she warned. "We still must eat, however."

They're just about perfect for each other, thought Wrek, and swallowed some more bread before continuing on with his labour. Her words, though simple, were stirring. Like her mate, she was a leader, even if she didn't know it or crave it. He dug into the ground once more and felt fresh pangs of pain surge through him. One more day, he pledged.

Then never again.

"They will need to find ease here. It's a fine place to rest ourselves for the foreseeable future," Wrek told Erroh, dragging a piece of stubborn earth from the ground. "When you see fit, I'll ride out and inform the Wolves."

"Thank you, Wrek," Erroh said, picking up his shovel once more.

No rest until the task was complete.

38

HONOURABLE DUTIES

E rroh patted the dirt until it was flat and then stepped away. Night turned to dawn, then dawn to day and day again into night. His blistered fingers gripped the shovel, and he leaned on its wooden shaft for support, looking upon the massive grave. They deserved individual burials, but such were the numbers that there was no other way. He was weary from rationalising such things. Wearier from digging mass graves.

He was exhausted, and he was not alone. The Outcasts around him had tended to their tasks until sleep deprivation and horror had overcome them. They rested now around the pit, none speaking, none able to dig another foot. Determined to continue leading by example, Erroh stayed until the end. He thought he would weep more, as he had when he'd buried the dead before, but this task had left him simply hollow and more determined than ever to make Uden pay. If he had energy, he might have proclaimed this, but even words seemed exhausting. So he drove his shovel into the dirt over and over again and tended to the last sleeping defender.

He'd promised himself a few hours' sleep, had held onto

that thought like a drowning man clutching a floating twig in a riptide. His work was not yet done.

Only Lea stood beside him. Though she said nothing, her presence was fine company. Her stunning eyes glittered with tears as she stared at the fresh dirt; her head was bowed in sorrowful thoughts. He took a breath and saw the mist appear in front of him. It was a fitting, unsettling thing for this place, this time, and Erroh shivered.

All dead, but at rest.

He wondered if he could hope for a gesture like this when his own time came. Would the southerners find a nice place for his bones? Would they place him in the ground with Lea beside him? That would be something, at least. He could think of worse things than spending eternity beside his mate for life, his mate for all time.

He shivered again, and someone behind him coughed. They were waiting for their great leader's next move.

He could feel their eyes burning through him as they waited for kind and respectful words to comfort them. They knew he made speeches, and aye, he would address them later when their grisly task was complete. It was hard to be poetic now, harder to be a wordsmith. The dead were dead, and he was tired of digging holes. Tired of doing the only honourable thing. Most of them had slept. Most of them had walked away and huddled by the fire when the horrors became too much.

Not Erroh, and not Lea.

He looked at the seated form of Wrek, his head drooping, fighting the call of sleep at the edge of the glade where he'd dropped his spade and sat shaking for a time. He hadn't moved, but his shaking had lessened. He'd lasted almost as long as Erroh and Lea—no small feat when a man was inexperienced with such ghastly duties.

"May they be at peace," said Wynn suddenly. His voice sounded cracked and eerie in the quiet. They were fine words, and Erroh closed his eyes.

"May they know no finer sleep," said Lillium quietly. She sat beside her former mate, her face taut with anger and sorrow.

"May the gods take them," said Emir. If he had anger deep within, he showed nothing now. Nomi nodded beside him. She dared not offer a prayer, and Erroh thought it a fine silence.

"May they never be forgotten," said Roja, folding her arms across her chest. It was part of an old prayer for the dead, uttered in reverent whispers. Erroh was certain no gods were watching him now. Had the gods been watching when this town fell?

Aye, they were, but that was a different tale entirely.

"Aye, never forgotten," agreed Erroh, snapping his eyes open and lifting his shovel behind his neck. So tired, so very tired. "And we will be reminded of them every day, friends," he said, turning to face his little band of warriors. "This will be a fine place to rest our heads, for now," he said, confirming their suspicions. He remembered how well the little town of Cathbar had treated them. Perhaps the fallen town of Raven Rock would be equally healing.

He thought again of Magnus's beliefs that, even in the middle of hostile territory, they might remain concealed. Magnus was mostly right about these things.

Mostly.

With a fresh running water supply a few steps from the main gate, the fields surrounding were ripe and overflowing with different crops. They could eat adequately for quite a time. The wall offered some safety as well. It was that or sleeping out here beyond it, under the stars, wary of every noise.

"From here, we can scout the land, learn everything we can about our enemy. From here, we can find Uden and take his fuken head," he declared. It wasn't much of a speech. It wasn't much of a plan.

"It's a fine place," agreed Wynn, but he looked troubled. "But we came looking for allies. Instead, we take a place at the table of the dead." He looked across at the remains of the once-grand town. "Should we not remain concealed among the green?"

"Hunt not attack settlement twice," Nomi said, and Wynn's eyes narrowed.

"Regardless, look at her walls," Erroh said, "All we need is to reset that gate and we will be fortified within."

"And if they come and lay siege?"

It was a fine point. "This town was built for survival. There is a secret smuggler's tunnel. If we lock the fuken gate, we can escape swiftly if the enemy comes calling."

"I would like to see this tunnel."

"And you will. In fact, I declare you the new master of the tunnel. Will that suffice, O Master of the Tunnel?"

Wynn laughed at this, and Erroh took it as his acceptance of the role.

"Regardless, we will keep an eye out in all directions. Any group wily enough to remain unnoticed as they creep up on us will not have the numbers to trouble us."

"And if they do trouble us, well, we are hardly worthy of calling ourselves legends," Lea said staunchly.

"Well, I for one am happy to stay in this haunted horror of a town," Emir declared. Of all the exhausted Outcasts, he looked the freshest. "Perhaps it would be best for all of us to find a bed and something to eat before we go to task seeking

Uden and killing him a bit," he said, stretching and yawning.

Erroh nodded in agreement. "Rest tonight, and tomorrow we ride out in pairs to get to know the lay of the land. But for now, I need to bathe the smell of death from me." Taking Lea by the hand, he led her from the graveyard towards the fast-running river beyond the town's wall.

He'd expected more arguments on the matter. Perhaps the gruelling ride through the wastes had assisted his cause, he thought grimly. Nothing like a stumble down a hill to tip the scales in favour of a nice little settlement to hide behind.

―――――

He and Lea walked through the undergrowth as if in a dream. By the time they broke through the last line of ferns and stopped at the edge of the river, his mood had improved. It was Lea's presence, he realised. It felt like an age since they'd been alone together. He longed for her, in all ways. To hold, to love, to ravage. Something about death demanded he take hold and never let her go.

"I think you should wade out and see how deep it is in the centre," he told her. "I'll wait here and see if you slip under," he jested. He sat heavily down on the riverbank, summoning the will to drop in and embrace the cold. He removed his shirt and draped it in the steady flow of the water, deep in thought. There had been humour in his words, but also a warning. They did not know this place yet. Who knew the current of this beast? Raven Rock looked a fine place to make their own, but it would be wise to take care and keep a keen eye for strong, unseen currents—in the river and otherwise.

Lea dropped in and squealed in misery as the water tore any warmth from her body. She gripped some reeds and shivered, staring balefully back at her man. He laughed at her unhappiness.

And then he cried.

And then she did, too.

Climbing out of the freezing water, she climbed onto him, her freezing body seeking his warmth. She wrapped her arms around his waist and buried her face in his chest. They held each other and sobbed in silence. For the dead, and for those before. For their fallen friends and more.

At last, spent, he raised his head and ran his fingers through her dark hair. "I'm so scared, my beo," he whispered.

"Never be scared with me beside you," she whispered back.

"What if I lead us all into death?"

"Then it will be a fine death, and we will take many with us," she countered, and somehow, he felt better.

"Some plan I've created," he said unhappily, thinking of his early days with just his beautiful mate at his side. He was sick of this story. Sick and tired of this life of fear and violence. He wanted to enjoy her a while. To walk the road with a beautiful girl and do little else but love her. Was that too much to ask for?

It was, replied the absent gods.

Erroh was far too tired and bitter to hear their suggestion in the wind. He shuddered in the breeze.

"Always tell me your deepest fears and doubts, my love," Lea said. "But stay strong in front of the rest. We need the Hero of Keri. We do not need a little cub."

"What else, my love, so I might take no ill steps?"

"Do not leave me behind. Do not desert me, even for the greater good. We are only you and me. No other." She referred to Keri, and he smiled sadly.

"I give you my word, beo."

Though her words chilled him, she offered a smile, one that told him, no matter what, that she would be with him at his worst moments. When everything around him burned, she would have his back. He pledged in silence to never let her down.

Before he could reply or indeed kiss her, there was a rustling noise behind them in the undergrowth. Suddenly Nomi stumbled awkwardly out through the trees and nearly tripped over them. She had stripped down to her undergarments, and held a soap in one hand and her leather dress in the other. Somehow, she appeared both clumsy and endearing in the same moment. Maybe it was the kind smile she directed at the Alphalines.

"Erroh bathe. Good idea. Nomi bathe," she said excitedly, then dropped her dress by the edge of the river and leapt in without hesitation. Despite her small size, she was skilled at splashing water everywhere, and Lea smiled despite herself as a wave of water soaked both Alphalines.

Nomi went under the surface, nimble as a fish, and rose back up after a few breaths, moaning in pleasure at the cold, bracing refreshment.

"Perfect," she said, kicking up and floating on the surface. Her feet gently paddled with the current, while her hands held the edge of the riverbank, and Lea held her smile.

After a time, Nomi turned and stood with the water at her waist, and eyed Erroh. "No need cry," she said kindly, and smiled dazzlingly at him and Lea. "Erroh fight Keri. Erroh fight Uden. Erroh fight Orrin, save Nomi. Erroh not lose," she explained as best she could. Her complete belief in his ability was strangely reassuring.

"I lost nearly all those battles," Erroh said, averting his eyes from her near-naked form. She waded a little closer, and Erroh felt Lea tense. "But, thank you, Nomi. Maybe we will survive," he joked, and this time he caught Lea's dangerous glare.

"Thank you, Nomi. Fine words," Lea said evenly, and slid away from her mate. Her body shook in the cold, and Erroh knew he should have reached for her.

Nomi dipped the soap and began scrubbing herself, swaying happily in the water as though she had been born in a blizzard. She hummed under her breath, and Lea dropped into the water again and waded out beside her.

"We need privacy for a time," Lea told her, smiling her best "Fuk right off" smile. Erroh knew it well.

"You need play? Oh! Nomi leave." She gave Erroh a strange smile that piqued his curiosity, but having never understood the finer details of the incredible female mind, he left the matter for what it was. She handed Lea the soap, and then pulled herself out of the water and walked further down the riverbank to complete her bathing. Erroh tried not to watch her as she walked away. Lea had the finest walk he'd ever seen or ever wanted to see. But truly, Nomi had a very fine walk too.

"She has a very fine walk," Erroh said, teasing Lea a bit.

"Aye."

"You've a much nicer walk."

"Aye," she said, leaning on the riverbank and watching him closely.

"And I'd much prefer to walk with you, all our lives," he said, leaning over and kissing her hand. Taking a deep breath, he plunged into the water beside her, gasping with shock.

"Aye," the most beautiful girl in the world replied distantly, turning and watching Nomi disappear into the forest.

"Leave her be, Lea. She is no threat."

"I'm not threatened. I'm just pissed that she couldn't

leave us to our private moment. Who knows what we'd have been doing if she hadn't blundered in."

"Well, what's stopping us continuing on now?" he said, nudging her gently. Despite the freezing cold, the many days without Lea's touch were now taking their toll on him.

"She'll probably come back claiming she heard some struggles."

"I'll keep my mouth shut," he countered, drawing her to him and enjoying her warmth as she wrapped her legs around his waist.

"I would hope you won't."

"As you wish," he whispered, and took hold of her roughly. She replied in kind, enjoying his strength. His vigour.

"If she is watching from the bushes... like a depraved whore... let's give her a right impressive show, my love," Lea cried loudly. She leapt upon him like a wild beast, and it was perfect.

39

SETTLING IN

With the worst of the horrors now dealt with, the new inhabitants of Raven Rock found it easier to settle within its rustic beauty. The town had been built by a planner with a keen eye for detail and regiment. It lay in a perfect square. On either side of the main street were a few tall buildings; they were roughly similar in size, built long before the fires and well-maintained like the tracks outside the gates. Four similar structures stood on the next street; the remains of others were visible, likely burned down during the siege. At the far end of the town was another street with similarly burned-out buildings; only two remained standing among the charred debris.

Despite the other signs of war, it was a stunning settlement, and now, without the bodies, it was easier to love this place.

All it needed were a few amenities to make it a place worth loving.

Emir tipped the barrel over, shook the dregs out through the little bunghole, and cursed the gods loudly. He shook it again, and a few more rancid drips of stagnant ale fell onto the floor.

"I've changed my mind about this place," he grumbled, kicking the massive wooden casket, then yelping and clutching his toe. The gods didn't care. "It's a fuken shithole." He rolled the offending barrel away from him and let it clatter loudly against two other empty barrels in the corner.

Fuk you, barrels.

"Some tavern this is," he spat in disgust. "It lacks any charm." He swept an empty bottle off the marble tavern counter and watched it meet a grisly end on the floor. It was a passing pleasure. He needed a drink. *To honour the dead.* Was that too much to ask? He hated the tavern because it had broken his heart. He'd spotted it before they'd finished preparing the dead, and fate had cruelly insisted he imagine the treasures within. It had been all he could do to keep his spirits up while he'd laid each broken body to rest for eternity.

When he'd finally had the opportunity to explore the tavern for himself, he'd felt like a child on his day of birth, with presents set before him. He'd never actually received a gift his entire life, but he imagined it was something akin to this excitement. Now, though, he hated this tavern and its many empty bottles and barrels. He spied a strange little ornament standing upon a shelf, an insignificant figurine that wavered on a spring and bobbled back and forth as he tipped it. "I like this. I will call you, Drew," he said, flicking it a few more times, and the character bobbed for his amusement.

"Ah, it's not so bad," Wrek argued, lighting a candle in the dusty air. "All it needs is a working distillery and a bit of cheer." He kicked at some sawdust on the floor and smiled.

"No establishment should ever have sawdust as a carpet," Emir argued, leaving Drew to bounce away in the darkness alone. It was a fine figurine, but not enough to warm him to this dreary, dry place.

"But those are the ones with the hardest alcohols," Wrek reminded him.

"Well, maybe they're not all bad. Bye, Drew," he called, slipping out of the tavern to search for treasures elsewhere.

———

Roja stormed through the top floor of the deserted house and kicked the bed in frustration. Then she sighed and lamented for a few moments. She held the little lamp out, and its light cast eerie images across the walls. Images of demons and death and guilty regret. She shook the shadowed imaginings from her mind and looked around. This would be her room. She'd searched a half-dozen buildings with a half-dozen bedrooms, and found little success. She was resigned to sleeping in one of these perfectly comfortable beds. She kicked the bed a second time and hurt her toe. Then she sighed again and laid the lamp on the little dresser. This had been a little girl's room. That girl was dead. She had died in the fire, no doubt. She had not fled to Samara. None of the Raven Rock inhabitants had. Better to fight, Roja thought, than come a-begging.

She told herself to keep searching for finer bedding, but her heart wasn't in it anymore. The search was too discouraging. Every room whispered of a lost history. She'd never known these people, never would either, but seeing each abandoned home was tragic.

And here I seek silken sheets.

This was the room she would take. This would be the last

bedroom she took in her life. This thought was settling. It was also terrifying.

She sat on the bed and tested the mattress. It could have been worse, she supposed. The child's cheap glass jewellery lay scattered on the dresser in front of her; her shelves were covered in pictures and toys. The window was covered in a pink sheer veil. It was strange to see delicate things in a town of savages.

She felt a chill run through her as she gazed at the bedding. The duvet and matching pillow were decorated with embroidered flowers and meadows, all created with great skill and at a greater cost. How Linn would have adored this place, she mused, and fought her grief. Crying won't help, she reminded herself, and wondered how much of an adult's life involved such childish actions as crying. She despised crying these days. Better to be angry. Be vengeful. Be impressive.

She fought a fuken tear regardless and lay down in the large bed. It was too large for a solitary Alpha queen bitch female of the city. Too large for a dead child, too.

Dead.

Dead.

Dead.

It was her fault, too, because her dutiful attempts at brokering peace had fallen dismally short.

"Let it go, Roja," she said aloud, and sought sleep. Closing her aching eyes, she tried to clear her mind of guilt-laden things. But no matter how long she tried, sleep eluded her, until eventually, she opened her eyes and stared at the little dead bulb above her. It mocked her and the anger grew.

So very similar to home. The bulb still had life in it. It simply needed nourishment. She wondered if any of her companions had noticed the many strings of lights spread throughout the town and along its walls, as she had. And why wouldn't she? She had had a hand in putting them there.

Fuken dead.

She wondered, could she even remember how to churn the turbines, anyway? She closed her eyes and tried to sleep once more. She vowed to ignore her curiosity until the morning. The turbines could wait. There was safety in darkness.

———

Wynn stepped gracefully, silently, through the dark interior of an empty house. The gloom unnerved him, but he swallowed back his fear. His stomach had settled since they had buried the last body, the pit of nausea replaced by the primal urge of hunger. Still, he shrugged to himself and stepped further through the dark building. Someone outside had lit a fire in the centre of the street, and the fresh flames illuminated his path. He was dizzy from fatigue, and his search for a bed prevailed above all else. Food could wait until the morning.

It was a plain enough house: a few carpets, a few cracked walls, a washing room, a grubby kitchen and a scattering of long-forgotten decorations once owned by the dead. Overall, it would suit him just fine for the now. Beside the stairs was an oak door, sturdy and unassuming. He supposed it was a doorway to the basement below. Instinctively, he turned the knob, but it remained sealed, likely secured with a lock. Another small matter. He released his hold and strolled upstairs in search of bedding. Nothing special; a few sheets would suffice. A pillow, if possible.

Like the rest of the house, the upstairs carried little invitation. A solitary picture he could not make out in the dark decorated the solitary bedroom he found. A small bed stood invitingly by the curtained window, and Wynn dropped heavily into its surprising warmth.

This will do. He liked the town. He liked the idea of settling down with a roof above his head and letting his uneasy stomach rest for a few days. His bed creaked as he rolled over, looking through the dark into the street below. Erroh was talking quietly to Lea. They stared at each other with unbridled adoration and Wynn found himself smiling despite himself. They were love itself, the very definition of it. Wynn sniggered. He was no poet, yet his mind filled with poetic thoughts at the unlikeliest of times, and he wondered if it made him a good man.

A hopeful man. And not a jealous man.

Somewhere nearby he heard footsteps, but took no notice. The buildings were close together; it might well just be someone in the next building, no doubt rummaging for incredible treasures like some salted meat or a bottle of sine. Maybe preparing for a feast in the town centre with those too foolish to attempt sleep.

He almost tapped the glass to signal his presence to the two young Alphalines below. He wanted to join in their good humour, but the world was crushing his soul. A few days' rest would help. A few days of not looking at his own reflection would help him overcome his shame.

He was a murderer. He had taken lives. Aye, in war, but his hands would forever be tainted. He couldn't stand himself. Instead of becoming angry about the horrors that had befallen this town, he'd wanted to shy away into the darkness where he was most at ease and cower from the world.

But Wynn would not do that, would he? Instead, he would face himself every fuken day and live with the disgust he felt in every breath he took. His only light was his friendship with this group. And his eternal love for Lillium. As though mocked by the absent gods, he saw Lillium walk into the centre of the town, and his stomach lurched. It lurched because she looked at Erroh as though she loved him.

She did. She probably always had.

This, he knew.

Wynn did not understand females, but some things were glaringly obvious. Lillium laughed at something Erroh said, and Wynn smiled. He heard the noise in the house again, but his eyes were locked on her. It was probably a cat.

It wasn't a cat.

He loved making Lillium laugh—a rare thing. It was such a wonderful thing to hear her laugh, and Wynn's heart stirred at the memory. It was probably just the exhaustion.

What right did he have to feel jealous towards Erroh? He was from a fine line and destined for greatness. What a weight to carry, having watched so many friends die. What strength the man must have to continue on, now and when he had been chained and alone for an entire season. Erroh was a better man than he.

Again, Wynn felt his usual shame, and then more shame that he was arrogant enough to believe it entitled him to anything. It was arrogance to blame his father for his own mistakes.

"You can have him, Lillium," whispered Wynn. "If he makes you laugh, you can have him." He turned from his mate and her friends and faced the wall. He closed his eyes and adjusted his head on the pillow.

If she took Erroh to her bed, he resolved, he would merely slip into the road forever. Easier that way. He was not naïve enough to believe he'd find no love or companionship again. It just hurt for the now. You can have him, though I'm certain Lea will have something to say about it, he thought, slipping from consciousness.

Uden walked into the room. He took out a blade. He stood over Wynn and grinned. The Alpha leapt from his bed just as the beast charged him. The brute looked like Magnus, though Wynn wasn't sure—he'd never seen the legend. Erroh had described him meticulously over the last few days, but only the size of the man matched Wynn's perception of him. It was a small matter. The Alphaline knew he was about to die.

Uden screamed in his face and one giant hand took Wynn by the throat and the other drove the dagger into Wynn's flesh. He heard the ripping of his own skin. The brute roared and noise exploded around him. A cacophony of drums. Wynn knew the world was ending. He tried to fight, but the dagger drove into him again and again. Screaming, he felt himself falling, and yet the pain had not reached his terrified mind. He fell back in his bed and reached for his sword, but the Woodin Man leapt back on top of him, pinning him, roaring. His voice thundered as he stabbed him one more time, and Wynn died.

Wynn shot up and grabbed his chest in panic. Uden's voice still haunted him, but it wasn't a voice at all. It was a hammering from downstairs and he cursed loudly. The hammering stopped abruptly. He was alive and in the dark. He glanced outside; Lillium and Lea were still talking with the Master General. Everything was fine, though his heart pounded.

Again, he squinted out, to be certain no attackers neared. Nothing had changed. He had slept less than a few breaths, yet it felt like hours.

"Who is that?" he roared into the empty house. A wonderful release of aggression. He felt a lot better about himself and forgot the sudden violence of the dream.

"Oh… is that you, Wynn? I thought someone was being murdered. Lillium's not up there murdering you, is she?"

called a voice sounding remarkably like Emir's from the darkness below. The hammering resumed and then and halted again. "I'm just seeing what's behind this door."

More kicking and hammering, and another abrupt stop.

"Do you have this door's key?" Emir called up.

"No key."

"No problem. I'll be done in a moment," he replied, kicking happily.

Wynn stretched and stumbled out the door and down the stairs. The little candle beside Emir lit his features. He seemed to be smiling dementedly.

"What are you doing, fool? It's too late," Wynn snapped, though truthfully the intrusion was welcome after such a nightmare. The healer merely shrugged and searched for better leverage.

"Who knows what treasures hide behind the one locked door in this town, my friend?" Emir replied, taking a moment to catch his breath. "Did I wake you?" he asked, and leant against the banister as the Alpha slipped by.

"I'm sure there are more closed doors in this settlement," Wynn muttered, eying the door in question. The healer's strategy was flawed. A door was not opened this way. He pushed at the frame. Aye, Emir's incessant kicking had created noise and little more.

"If there are more, I'll attack them with just as much vigour and enthusiasm," Emir declared, and there was a frenzy in his glare. "You never know—there could be a wonderful little distillery hidden behind here," he said, stepping back.

"I have this, brother," Wynn said.

Without warning, he charged the door with his shoulder,

hitting it just above the lock. It held despite the force, and he bounced back and charged a second time without hesitation. With a loud crash, the door swung open. Wynn fell through and then clattered wildly down a set of steps into a pitch-black basement. His reflexes saved him before he could incur any real injury, but not before he earned himself a few bruises. He came to a stop at the bottom and squinted into the gloom.

Emir leapt down after the Alphaline. He shone the candle around and then cried out in amazement. It was a wonderful room, large enough to hold a dozen people comfortably. A collection of copper canisters, pristine pots and other utensils with strange attachments sat on a long table.

"I don't believe it," Wynn cried. It *was* a distillery, a sine distillery, and Emir looked ready to fall to his knees in prayer to the absent gods. "This is mine," the wretched healer gasped. He reached out an arm, grasped a bottle and popped its cork.

Wynn smiled and knew the futility in arguing. "Enjoy your night, Healer. I'll go seek another room."

Emir held out the bottle, grinning. "One for the road?"

———

Roja pulled at the lever, but it held fast. How long had it been since last it was used? She imagined it had been on the last day. Wiping the sweat from her brow, she closed her eyes for a few precious moments. The ghosts of this town would not let her sleep—not yet. But if she exhausted herself further, the sleep would come. For now, she attacked the machine with relish. Childish enthusiasm, to be exact. How much did she remember of these machines, anyway?

More than most.

She greased the lever for a third time and waited. The lantern's beam died as the last of the oil burned away, but it was a small matter. She would work this beast until the light gave out and begin again at dawn. Waiting for the lever to come unstuck, she debated returning to the river and the line of spinning turbines and once more following the route back behind the walls to this building to look for sign of any damage. She pulled the lever again, and this time she felt a little give. She poured the last of the lantern oil into the machine and waited a few breaths more.

She liked this silence. Attacking the workings of these ancient, familiar devices was strangely calming. She could only hold so many thoughts in her fragile mind; mechanisms, however, required little fuss or pondering. This machine was like Samara's. Despite some modifications with its workings, the theory was the same. Turbines on a river made electricity. Electricity lit the world.

And invited everyone from miles around.

She prayed silently to the gods and pulled with both hands as her light finally died. With a heavy clunking noise, the lever slipped down and a great reassuring humming sound filled the room. A few sparks flickered in the bulbs above her, and then grew to small, hopeful glows. A few moments later they took hold, and she yelped in delight and hurried away from the machine, back to her comrades outside in the street. She was not the only one whom sleep evaded this night.

With every step she took, the bulbs took light, following along behind her as though she were a goddess of dawn. Soon, they flashed out in every direction through the town and lit up the night. She giggled with joy and pride, and for a few moments she forgot the last few months of worry and strain and misery.

It almost felt like home again.

———

Erroh lit the kindling and watched it take hold. This would be a better fire, he thought, looking at the previous pyre's scars. If they were to stay here, he didn't want a constant reminder of their terrible fate. So, he had set this fire where the ashes and bone once rested. He muttered a few half-hearted prayers to the absent gods and stepped back as the flames grew. The sudden warmth on his skin felt wonderful, and Erroh felt sleep calling again. He was even more exhausted than he thought possible.

He heard the delicate tap of Lea's feet behind him, and he smiled. "Have you found us a place to rest our heads?" he asked without turning around, and threw a log onto the flames. The massive fire's heat grew. The light took the eeriness from this dead place. Some, but not all.

"Of course, my love," Lea said, wrapping her arms around his waist and resting her head on his shoulder. "I found us the biggest of them all, at the back wall. It has a fine herb patch growing along the side."

"Only the best for us," he replied, leaning against her.

"How do you feel?"

"I feel better, my beo. I feel this place will keep us safe,"

"I feel it too."

Had Erroh or Lea listened to the wind a little more closely, they might have heard the absent gods whisper unsettling things as a great darkness took delicate steps towards them.

40

NIGHT OF HIDDEN TALENTS

They needed something. To merely find bedding and rest their heads after the trying days was simply not enough. The switching on of the lights had brought everyone back onto the main street. Much-needed sleep could wait a little longer. In the electricity's hum there was familiarity for some, a taste of home, even when home wanted you dead. To the rest, it was a reminder of what they fought for. They gathered to gaze at the unnatural light and bathe in its reassuring comfort, ease the fatigue from their bodies, and release desolation from their diminished souls.

And then Emir brought over a few bottles of sine, and the gathering became an event.

Besides the supply of sine they'd discovered in the basement, Wynn had found a six-string locked neatly in its case of leather and wood. He had no exceptional talent with the instrument, but it had a nice weight to it and, when he strummed it gently, many years of practice returned to him in a bittersweet flow of memories. His mother had been a far better player than he, but he tried his best. In the dark, all alone, he sat on a step and tuned the instrument as best he could. When the glowing lights illuminated all around him, he took it as a sign and followed his brother back out into the street.

As they popped corks and cracked uneasy jests, he rolled an empty barrel to the edges of the fire's warmth and sat grandly atop it before beginning to play what familiar pieces he could remember. As it turned out, there were quite a few.

Erroh sat beside Lea and gladly accepted the bottle passed his way. He knew that in the Savage Isles they celebrated the passing of the dead with much revelry, so he allowed himself to smile and enjoy the gathering. Perhaps the dead were watching from the darkness, he thought, taking pleasure in the same good humour. This both unnerved and comforted him. So, he drank to them, and he drank a great deal.

They all did.

Lillium sat next to Wynn as he strummed a few delicate, loose notes on the wooden piece. She watched his fingers intently. "I thought you were lying when you claimed to play the six-string."

He shrugged and continued to send the sweet notes out into the darkness. "I'm able to play a few ditties and little more, Lillium," he said, and, to her pleasure, played a few intricate chords as though it were a small matter. She rocked gently with his playing and Wynn found, to his surprise, that he was pleased by her enjoyment.

Emir, suitably drunk after a few days and far too long, drained another glass of sine as though it were water in the middle of the Adawan wastes. He poured another, clinked it against Lexi's goblet and drained it once more. He, too, had a skill unbeknownst to his comrades, nay, his friends, and he was now drunk enough to embarrass himself. He reached into his pack, rummaged deep within it, through his many remedies, and recovered a little tin whistle. It was rusted at the bottom and worn, but it emitted a fine enough tune when played.

He sat beside Wynn and blew gently on the pipe and completely missed the right key. He ignored the laughter— including his own, for this was the happiest he'd been in an age—before attempting to accompany the ponytailed fuk in a terrible duet once more. The contrasting notes clashed, and the laughter grew in volume.

Healing laughter.

"Keep playing, Emir," Wynn said, and listened for a few moments before nodding along with his awful timing and testing a few notes of his own. His fingers danced across the instrument and kept time and nearly the right key to match Emir's attempts, and to most, they sounded as tight as a tavern troupe. Albeit, not a terribly talented one.

Wrek suddenly began stamping his foot on the ground and striking the wooden box he sat upon, and his fine rhythm kept both musicians in a constant time.

"You never told me you could play, little healer man," cried Roja. She was lying on the ground looking up at the little beacons of light hanging above their heads. Her eyes were lost in the brilliance; a drunken smile touched her lips. Emir thought she was beautiful in that light and looked at the burning fire instead.

"I'd hardly call this playing," he said mid-puff.

"Keep playing, idiot," Wrek hissed.

"Oh, right. Sorry." He was a man of many skills. Blowing air through a metal pipe was barely one of them.

They finished the tune, and Wynn immediately played a

few notes of an ancient crowd-pleaser. He let the notes ring out and eyed Emir.

Fuk it—let's go for it.

It was the first song Emir had ever learned. He'd learned it in the city a lifetime ago, when he'd believed himself capable of great, miraculous accomplishments. All conversation fell silent as the music wove together wonderfully, and both musicians grew more confident as their captivated audience watched on. Wrek's drumming became mesmerising and all of the revellers nodded along, sipping their drinks, sneaking electric glances at those who captivated their thoughts, and slowly remembering what it was not to have the weight of the world upon their shoulders.

By the time the piece reached its crescendo, Emir's lungs had emptied and his chest was aching. Wynn's fingers were bleeding from their assault on the strings, yet they did not miss a beat, for Wrek would not let them.

"Ride on, ride home, with barrel in tow," sang Lexi, the alcohol giving the edge to her confidence. She sang like a goddess of the stage, drawing out each word with strength and a poise that belied her age.

"You brought blood. You brought death. You brought the end," she sang, and the musicians matched her. The night came alive with energy, and not just the electric kind. If the ghosts of this town were present, they would have approved of the performance.

"Oh no, oh no, oh no," everyone sang in reply, the contrasting melodies playing wonderfully against Lexi's tones. Even a thoroughly confused Nomi sang the repeating lines, for they were hardly lyrics written by the absent gods. Anyone could follow along.

Basic, and wonderfully catchy.

Eventually, the song petered out pleasingly and Emir

collapsed in front of the fire to catch his breath. He drank down the nearest glass and thanked the gods again for his good fortune in finding this supply. He took joy in seeing the warm faces around him as they chinked glasses and shared jests and behaved like the youth they were, but his rest was not long enough. Before he could recover, Wynn called for him with a raised eyebrow. There was a crowd to entertain.

They settled on an easier ballad, with just enough of a rhythm that Lillium walked in front of the fire and danced to herself. She hummed along and spun on the warm, hard ground, her feet taking pleasure in movement. Her hair whipped out behind her as she twirled. Now and then, her eyes fell upon Erroh, and then upon Wynn and his fabulous flashing fingers.

There, they lingered a little longer.

Lea quickly joined her and gripped her waist in mock embrace and spun her around. They twirled majestically as if in combat, but their laughter could be heard clearly above the music. Lea was no dancer, but her enthusiasm soon enticed Roja to shake herself from her daze and join the merriment. She clapped and laughed as they pulled her onto the transient dancefloor. They held hands, spun each other in the fire's light and the electric glow, and then, in the next beat, slid up against each other, their perfect bodies embracing the art of allurement and sensuality. No male could keep their eyes from them.

"Come on," shouted Lea, breaking from the embrace and reaching for Wrek's hand. "Erroh will never dance," she slurred, pulling him into the heart of the group of dancing goddesses. He tried to hide his smile. He was only male, after all, and these writhing, wonderful beings surrounding him would stir trees to life. He swayed with them, laughing as all his anguish and remorse was forgotten.

At least for now.

"I'm a fine dancer. I just choose not to," argued Erroh, but Lea didn't hear, for she was far away, spinning in the drunken arms of another man. A moment after that, Wrek's hands were clasping Roja gracefully and Lea was pouring another glass of sine and Erroh felt a lot better about that, until Lillium dragged her back into the little circle to test Erroh's watchfulness.

Looking around, he noticed Nomi gazing at Lea, one eyebrow raised, watching her stumble drunkenly against Lillium and then an innocent barrel. While Erroh found this amusing, Nomi merely watched. Her focused attention was unnerving.

At length, she stood up and joined them on the dance floor. Her head bobbed slightly with the music. Her hips swayed gently. She ran her fingers through her hair, ruffling the dampness from it, and then she slid up close behind Lea, her eyes unblinking and wary like an eagle watching over its next meal.

"Liiia, lucky," the drunken girl from the south said, and placed her hands on Lea's waist. Lea spun in alarm but did not react. She stood glaring at Nomi, who, unprepared for her turn, stopped dancing and stood watching with a clueless grin on her face. Erroh held his breath, worrying an argument might spill out all over the evening's cheer, until Wrek, leading Roja in a waltz, knocked against them.

This spurred Nomi to life. "We dance?" Nomi cried, pulling Lea across to where Erroh sat alone. "For Erroh?" she added, and grabbed Lea's waist once more. Gently, she swayed with the beat, and Erroh saw Lea's eyes narrow.

Oh, fuk.

487

Nomi raised her arms above her head and stepped close to Lea, far too close, and Lea looked ready to ask her to step back. With a fist.

"I don't want to dance," Lea said evenly, and though she smiled, her eyes offered little warmth.

"Aye, but we dance for Erroh," Nomi repeated, and gyrated her hips just enough that her body became the quintessence of temptation.

Erroh thought about separating them, enforcing peace, but still he made no move. Why? Because he was an idiot and wondered if it would be better that they sort their disagreements between themselves. Besides, standing up and standing between them seemed like an awful idea at that moment.

"I will not dance *for* Erroh. I will only dance *with* him," Lea said through gritted teeth. Still, she kept the smile and the blonde girl stepped closer to her.

Nomi giggled seductively, obviously taking great enjoyment in Lea's discomfort. She linked her fingers in those of her quarry and began to sway with the music again. Enticing her to come play. She thrust herself against Lea, her hands releasing their grip and moving to her rear.

Lea shook with anger, and Erroh breathed out a sigh of relief when she slipped away from her dance partner and sat down beside him again. Nomi shrugged and continued swaying in front of Erroh, and suddenly he knew the precariousness of the moment.

"Anyone up for a few hands of cards?" he cried, and incredibly, she kept dancing.

"I'm not impressed, Erroh," Lea hissed in his ear.

"But she's a wonderful dancer."

Oh, Erroh.

He reached for the nearest bottle and poured them both a

glass. It wouldn't matter in the morning if they couldn't remember anything.

Wrek spun Roja a little aggressively now, and the redhead tripped and fell forward into the little gathering of musicians. The music came to an abrupt halt as she knocked Wynn from his barrel. They ended up in a heap of instruments, bottles and jests in the middle of the dance floor, Roja pinning the Alpha to the ground amid laughter and crude suggestions. She climbed off him apologetically and handed him back his six-string. It had survived the attack, and he put it back in its case, holding his aching wrist and fingers.

"No more dance?" cried Nomi in dismay, before collapsing down beside her two favourite people in the world. "Need long dance," she explained, holding out a glass to be refilled. She smiled dazzlingly at Lea. "Next time." And then her smile faltered. "Like home, we dance, music." She shrugged, and Erroh saw the drunken sadness in the gesture.

"You are a wonderful dancer," he said, and oh, Lea's eyes narrowed again.

"Nomi show you dance, good," she said to Lea. "We dance, make him happy...." She searched for a word and muttered under her breath. "One for life, deserve happy." She wobbled a bit and pointed at Lea and then prodded her, though not too unkindly. "Beautiful Liiia, so lucky. So, so lucky."

"You are very fuken lucky too," Lea said, but Nomi wasn't listening. She was still muttering under her breath, staring at the lights around them as she had done frequently since they had been lit. Erroh remembered his own dumfounded reaction to seeing spheres of contained sunshine for the first time.

A lifetime ago.

"I'm the lucky one," Erroh said. He knew he was in

trouble. He wasn't exactly sure why, but he knew Lea was annoyed at him. Some things never changed.

"Not lucky," argued Nomi, patting Erroh's hand dismissively. "Nomi want Erroh, want him one for life. Nomi not alone. All girls want Erroh, one for life," she explained, as if speaking with a child.

Wait, what?

"Not all of us," said Roja, dusting the last of the dirt from her dress. "He's far too heroic for my liking," she said mockingly.

Nomi shook her head. "Roja one for life with Emir," she explained, as though Roja was unaware of this. "Emir… sad… not see," she added, shrugging her shoulders. She wavered now and tried to drink from her empty mug. The gathering fell suddenly quiet at her words. Lea reached out and refilled Nomi's mug. To the brim. That's what friends did.

Nobody said anything. Erroh felt like he had entered the Cull again. Unlike then, though, he said nothing aloud now.

"Emir lost his one for life in Keri," Emir said quietly, putting away his tin whistle. His hands fumbled with the buckle on his bag. They were shaking again. "I'm finished for the night," he declared, and stood up abruptly. "Fuk…"

"Are you okay, Emir?" Erroh asked.

"Aye."

"You are just standing there."

"Aye."

Silence.

He looked around as though seeing this town for the first time. As though seeing the potential in its seclusion. It was a bastion for the wretched. A place to rest their heads and heal their souls. "Can anyone remember where my house is? I seem to have misplaced it." Before anyone could answer, he

wandered away from the fire. He marched towards a tall
building before stopping and changing direction. There were
a few more curses. Then he disappeared.

"I think we, too, might retire," said Roja, lifting a
wobbling Lexi to her feet and leading her off into the night.
Lexi's arguments about more alcohol faded away.

"A fine night, but some bastard has me riding at dawn,"
Wrek jested, before bowing magnificently.

"Aye, and I have to find myself a new bed," Wynn said,
strapping his six-string case onto his back. He was an elite
fighter, yet looked more at ease with the piece than Erroh had
ever seen him. He secured the straps, and Lillium took his
arm. She was wavering drunkenly, and Wynn smiled warily.

"I'll help you find a place to stay," she whispered, loud
enough for all to hear.

"Let's find *you* a bed first… friend," he said awkwardly,
and she batted his shoulder playfully before winking at Erroh.

"I'm not ready to sleep. I wish to hear more music," she
said dreamily, and he led her away.

"But… Lillium want Erroh," whispered Nomi. She still
wore that thoroughly confused expression, and it matched
Erroh's own.

Lea climbed to her feet first. She offered her hand to
Erroh, who, grateful for the offer of peace, accepted it as he
stood. Lea turned and helped Nomi to her feet as well, and
accepted the hug the blonde girl offered.

"Show me this wonderful building," Erroh said as Lea led
him away. Like a good little pup, Nomi followed them,
stumbling and tripping on everything and nothing. *Fuk.*
"Where will you stay tonight?" Erroh asked.

"Near Liiia and Erroh… Safer."

Lea released Erroh's hand but said nothing, and somehow,
he knew he was in trouble again.

. . .

It was a fine building. Taller than the rest, as she had promised. There was a much smaller building alongside. A kinder term might have been shack. Damaged by time and battle, its wooden walls were warped and cracked; few windows held a pane of glass. The roof was lopsided and likely to collapse after the next downpour. Yet Nomi appeared to love it.

"Love dark place," she said, before slipping through the blue-painted wooden doors. "Blue doors," she cried in delight, and they listened to her stumble around for a while. Then a light flickered on, then flicked back off then flicked back on a few more times before darkness and silence fell upon the building.

"Do you think she is okay?" Erroh asked.

"Should she be on your mind right now?"

He knew that tone. He didn't like it. Not one little bit.

"It's tradition to bed on the first night," he argued as they made their way upstairs to the bedroom. He grinned and left his trousers on him, falling into bed beside her. "Let's not anger the gods," he added. He thought it was a compelling argument. It wasn't.

"You're drunk, you whelp," she snapped, turning away from him.

"I'm sorry," he said.

"For what?"

"I don't know."

"Then how can you be sorry?"

"I found a way," he whispered, and slipped under the covers. They were old and smelled of age. They were also the most comfortable coverings he'd ever experienced.

"You left the light on," she hissed, pulling the duvet

around her in protest, and he thought her jealousy charming. "Did you like her dancing for you?"

"Of course," he jested, and, as he nestled in beside her, she allowed him envelop her with his arms.

"I would have preferred both of you dancing," he added, and kissed her ear, fighting an urge to laugh.

His hands slid down her waist. They slipped between her legs and he pulled gently at her trousers. Far too easily, the leggings slipped down.

"Even after the river?" she said wearily.

"Oh, that was a lifetime ago. I have my needs, woman."

She pulled his hair ever so.

"I would have preferred you alone to dance for me," he said, and bit her ear. "I am the lucky one." He pulled her legs free of the unwanted garments and ran his fingers along her thigh. She moaned but crossed her legs and faced him.

"It would be wise for you to remember that, my beo," she warned. He tried to pry her legs apart, and she grinned at his failure. She was in full control.

"I know my place in this world," he whispered.

"It's a fine place," she whispered back. There was a time for violent furrowing, scratching, biting and screaming wildly, and there was also a time for sensual reminders of the bond they shared and the incredible love they had for each other—a love that grew every day. A love that would need to be resilient against the many darker days they knew they would face soon enough.

41

————

LIES IN THE DARK

"You bastard. You absolute fuken bastard," Lillium spat, and fell through the doorway of the building she had claimed as her own, disappearing from Wynn's sight.

"Are you okay?"

There were further outbursts of colourful language, and Wynn stumbled through the doorway after her.

"Leave me be," she hissed from the darkness, and a few steps in he discovered her tumbling towards the stairs leading to the rooms above. There was a solitary light a few floors up, and she appeared to follow it like a moth would a candle. Or an illuminated glass bulb. He wasn't sure if he should leave her be. Or if following her would be any better. He wasn't even certain why she was annoyed at him. He *was* certain she was mad at him, though. He was perceptive that way.

His body ached, and his stomach was queasy. Too much merriment, not enough sleep. Oh, how he wanted sleep. He sipped from the bottle of sine he held. He'd already had more than enough, as had she, but it was a small matter. It was something to do while being unsure of what to do. Emir would have approved, he thought.

"All males are fuken bastards," roared Lillium, halfway up the first flight. She managed a couple of steps more and tripped. Reflexes saved her, and she bounced back to her feet smoothly, feigning gracefulness. A few steps later, she collapsed on a step completely and sprawled out, head against the banister, allowing her hair to drape over the side. A terrible bed. He watched her for a moment and wondered if she wasn't contemplating her life choices. Or holding off throwing up on herself. Perhaps a little of both.

He thought about what he'd said. He remembered saying how much he hated the dark now, after his stay in the cell, and then she just fell apart.

"All of them. All bastards. Well, most men are," she hissed, and wiped her mouth where spittle dribbled free.

He stopped a few steps below her and smiled hopefully. "But not all?"

"Not all," she growled, climbing unsteadily to her feet.

"But I am a bastard." It was an attempt at a jest. He knew he was a bastard. Such things were obvious when they were screamed at a person. Such things were obvious when you thought about it really hard.

"A complete one," she agreed, but some of the anger had left her voice. He leant against the banister and searched for words to soothe her before she had another outburst. He found none; he never did.

"Is Emir a bastard?" he asked, and she smiled drunkenly.

"Emir is a total bastard, but I like him," she slurred, and her head swayed in time with each word she uttered.

"At least I'm not the only bastard." He offered her the bottle, and she drank from it as elegantly as she could, which wasn't very elegant at all. Loose streams of the bitter alcohol flowed down her blouse and spilled onto the floor. Before, Emir would have licked the ground for flavour, but not now, not tonight. She sat down and dropped the bottle through the railing to the floor below, seeming not to notice the piercing noise as it shattered into a million deadly shards.

"I think you have a drinking problem," he jested. It was a common jest, used by his father, all his life. It wasn't hilarious, but it brought a smile to her perfect lips.

"I'm very good at drinking, just like that bastard Emir." She sniggered at her own wit.

Though he made light of her words, they stung, even if they were true. Especially because they were true. He was trying though, every day he was trying, even when the weight of his horrible deeds came upon him, swallowed him up and whispered that relief lay only in death. Even then, he still tried. But nights like this eased the pain. Made him forget his own sense of worthlessness.

She climbed to her feet again and resumed her treacherous climb to the top of the landing. Somewhere beyond, a fine bed was calling. She gripped the banister, and he followed behind.

"I'm unsure of Wrek," she went on. "He has kind eyes, but I imagine he's a bastard as well. All of them are. All males." She reached the landing and swayed and fell against the wall. With shaking knees, she steadied herself and muttered her hatred for the males of the world a little more, and then she muttered about loving them as well.

He stepped beside her and held her shoulder to keep her upright. "When you are behaving normally, Wynn, I hate you less," she whispered, and this stung too. "You looked alive playing the six-string. That spark in your eyes, Wynn. It was beautiful. You looked beautiful… You are so fuken beautiful, and I hate you."

He thought her beautiful and said nothing.

"I think you need to get some sleep, my… um…

Lillium." He looked around the landing. Her bedroom likely lay a few steps past the solitary light.

"So much pain in this wretched place," she whispered, pushing him away. "Where's the bottle? I need a drink, bastard."

"I can never imagine the horrors these people experienced," agreed Wynn, manoeuvring her towards the bedroom. "As for the bottle, it's already in your room, just ahead."

She slid against the wall and he let her walk the last few steps.

"All this death makes me think about life. What would have happened had we conceived?" Her face was pale in the light from the bulbs. She looked shattered. She fell again, and he caught her and eased her through the doorway, towards the nearest bed.

He ignored the question. Every fool knew thoughts of procreation after viewing the dead were a common thing. Primal instincts and all that. Instincts taking over one's better senses, whispering devious suggestions of wonderful furrowing and incredible climaxes with beautiful partners. Aye, he desired Lillium, but that river had been crossed. That right was lost to him forever. For now, his only pleasure would be the gift of putting her safely to bed.

"You saw my weaknesses soon enough, Lillium. Thankfully, we avoided discovering what a terrible father I'd be. I'd have been a worse father than mine was to me," he lied. "A child would have made things worse between us," he added. This, however, was the truth. "Now, please. Tell me more about the world's bastards," he asked. The last few steps were the worst. Her feet barely moved; her weight was heavy in his grasp.

"You are the worst bastard of them all, because you never

saved me that night," she snapped suddenly. Her eyes opened, and she lashed out, striking him across the cheek. The bright room darkened as he stumbled away from her, and as usual, he did not know what had brought forth such hatred. "Fuk you, Wynn," she growled, and he stepped away from her next strike. He'd seen the damage she could do with a kick, and he'd no intention of receiving another similar blow. She leapt towards him suddenly, and the room became tiny. She slapped him fiercely and continued her assault. "I hate you for not being there!" Each slap stung his face, and she did not hold back. Stumbling and screaming, she struck him again and again, and he let her. Something deep down told him to allow her. "Where were you, my beo?" He collapsed under the assault and she was upon him like a rabid wolf. "Where the fuk were you, when I needed you most?"

"I'm sorry," he finally cried, as she pinned him down and sat atop his chest. Finally, unable to take the stinging blows, he blocked her assault. With her strikes suddenly meeting resistance, she gripped his long hair and pulled until he screamed.

She appeared to like this. "It was dark and nobody helped me." He did not fight her hold. He gave up and swallowed the pain. His head was pulled forward and then dragged violently back. He could feel ripping at his scalp, and then, just as he nearly found the will to fight back, there was a merciful halt. He wished he hadn't called out in pain. He deserved this, did he not?

"I'm sorry," he whispered again, and her tears fell onto his cheeks. She released her grip completely, and he sighed in relief. She smoothed out his hair and stroked his cheek a few times as if in apology. He didn't mind; it was better than being battered. The tears kept flowing and falling onto him, but neither made a move.

"I woke during the riots, in the stadium, all alone," she whispered, her voice strong, detached but tragic. "Alone," she repeated. Then she told him what had happened that fateful night. It took a time. He lay there, barely daring to breathe, as she spoke, and his heart broke for her.

"I don't hate you, Wynn," she told him finally, and he merely shook his head in the dark. There were no words. "It was a cruel act, driven by hate, that we kissed our last in the dark," she whispered.

It sounded like an apology, but he did not take it as one. He was not deserving of any apology, for his sins were far worse than he could ever have imagined. His heart was lower than ever before, but he fought against himself. He would show strength, for that is what she demanded of him.

I gave in easily, never knowing the depths of her tragedy.

Her first kill had almost destroyed her, and now he knew the source of her anger at the world—and her strength. She had risen above it. So too would he.

"I don't love you anymore," he lied. It was all he could say. It was a good lie. He would not allow her to carry the guilt for their last kiss in the dark a moment longer. "Though I will always cherish your company and your leadership, and perhaps someday, your friendship." She climbed to her unsteady feet. "I failed you as a mate. I will never fail again, as a companion," he pledged, and helped her into the bed. It was a fine bed, fit for two, and he stepped away.

"Will I leave a light on for you while you sleep?" he asked, wiping her tears from his face. A wonderful change from his own.

"I do not need to sleep," she whispered, and gripped his wrist gently. "I'm sorry for hitting you." Her face turned serious. "Stay with me tonight." He lay down on the floor beside her bed, reached up and kissed her hand.

"I'll stay awhile here," he said.

"No, Wynn. Stay with me tonight," she said, and it sounded like an order.

"As you wish."

He got to his feet and climbed in beside her, the stinging in his cheeks and the thumping pain in his scalp immediately forgotten. Her warmth was comforting and familiar, and only now did he realise how much he had missed it. Her scent, her touch, her everything. Wynn sighed in near completion. Perhaps it was the alcohol.

"You are still a bastard," she whispered, and pressed herself against him. He almost remembered what it was like to be intimate with her. Though he tried, he could not conceal his arousal. And then she kissed him and he loved her with his entire being. Her sudden invasion took him by surprise and, once again, she climbed on top of him. "This means nothing," she warned, and he heard the desire in her voice. Her craving and her drunkenness. Her hand dropped to his belt. It felt like the first night. Desire, fear and excitement.

"I'm far too drunk to perform," he lied, and gently tipped her from his lap. Her head drew away from his and her wonderful lips were no longer his to enjoy. She knew he was lying, and anger flared in her eyes. Was she going to hit him again?

"Of course you are," she said, but she did not lash out.

"Despite your beauty, some things can't be helped," he admitted. It sounded pathetic.

Perfect.

"I am beautiful," she agreed distantly. She lay on her back and stared at the ceiling, each breath a heavy sigh.

"Perhaps if we wait a while…" he suggested, and ran his fingers carefully through her hair. Feeling no resistance from her, he began to massage her head. Emir had sworn on his life that a head massage put anybody to sleep on demand.

"Aye, we could do that," she said dreamily, as his hands caused her body to squirm in delicate pleasure. Within moments, she closed her eyes and fell into a deep sleep. He continued to massage her until he was convinced she would not wake, before slipping from the bed and creeping from the room like a thief in the night, leaving her to wake with the dignity that she deserved. Something he'd never done before.

It wasn't much. It was all he could do.

42

DYSFUNCTIONAL FAMILY LIFE

S he watches him beneath her. His eyes are distant and thoughtful, though his thrusting is methodical and composed. He is no stranger to this act. With each effort, disciplined and rhythmic, she experiences the precise amount of pleasure that he wants to offer. She moans and stares into his eyes and they focus on her. He leans in and bites her lip, but he does so out of necessity. He knows her preference. Another part of his performance to bring her to climax.

He grabs her hair and pulls slightly, and to her dismay, she likes this as much as the bite. He is no god in bed; no legendary beauty, either. His body is too thin, his fingernails a little too long. His taste, a little bitter. She hears him exhale and wonders when the moment will come. Most men would kill or offer remarkable treasures for her gift, yet this blond boy seems annoyingly relaxed whenever he takes her in this act.

Her name was Aurora, and she wasn't entirely sure how she felt about Stefan taking her in bed. As was usual, when she neared climax, so too, did he. Fuker was that capable. If only he offered a little more passion, she thought, allowing herself a cry of fulfilment. A few moments after, he fell away from her and embraced her tightly before falling still. All that remained were their exhausted gasps.

Aurora wondered, would he have shown enthusiasm had she been a stunning blonde bitch with a sharp tongue? Just another reason to kill her, no doubt. She smiled as he slid away from her.

"That was exquisite, my love," Ealis whispered, and he stroked her hair absently as though he'd performed a duty of distaste, his gaze distant and uninterested.

Come back to me, boy.

"You don't love me," he whispered. He stated it as casual truth. Simple conversation among the bedclothes after the mediocre act of love.

She burrowed into his naked, sweat-covered frame and kissed his skin playfully. "Give me a little time, my beautiful Stefan." She flashed her dazzling smile.

He broke the embrace and sat up. "I will not fall for you, my dear Ealis. I'm sorry." She pulled the covers over herself; the chill in the morning air was unwanted now that she was still. "I'm not capable of love."

Ah, the pretentious depth of a broken-hearted poet.

"Oh, Stefan. Don't worry about love. Let us enjoy ourselves and see what occurs," she said, stroking his back. Men always liked that. Even when they were trying to be deep and meaningful, they were annoyingly predictable.

"You are sweet, but I'm no companion of worth."

But Stefan, you are of worth. You know the way to Erroh.

"But Stefan, you are of worth. You just can't see what I can see," she promised. The beaten man turned and offered a smile, the gap in his teeth apparent. She liked that smile. It was real.

Knowing there was little to gain from this conversation,

she whipped the sheets from her and reached for her clothing. Staring at the actual owner's fine dresses hanging in the open wardrobe, she resisted the temptation to steal them and donned her worn leather garments. It was all she had to her name. She hoped the tavern owner made quite the profit from her weapons and accessories. When the city fell, she would enjoy flaying him until he revealed their whereabouts. Mostly, she would enjoy the flaying.

Outside, the morning drizzle had increased to a downpour. This was no place to have hope. It was time to leave, yet still, Stefan had fought her suggestions. Denied her the knowledge of the Wolves' camp. She tied up her hair as he dressed slowly. The hours of furrowing had affected him more than they had her.

He left her sated every time they went to bed. A good thing, too. Better a little furrowing over cutting, and he had wonderfully warm skin.

From warm, wet blood.

She was getting restless here. They'd stayed longer than she'd hoped. Sometimes, knowing Erroh lay only a few feet away was a madness that took hold. Choosing acts of desire to achieve her goals was a most frustrating thing.

Or I could cut him? Then all would be well.

"We are too close to the city. There must be a better place we can seek refuge," she said, counting her words and finding their unevenness displeasing. Tying her boots and glimpsing herself in the mirror, she was reminded of her beauty. And only Stefan appeared unappreciative. Fuk him for his lack of infatuation, she thought, and liked him a little more. Not a lot, but a little.

"Ah, the usual morning argument," he snapped, and she knew his argument well. In this little clearing in the middle of a forest, he had food, water, a bed, and a goddess all willing to please him in any way she desired.

Too comfortable.

Visions of chains and rain and blood and death and horror, so much horror, flashed through her mind. *Take his fingers.* There was a blade concealed beneath the bed for when notions of blood overcame her.

Now?

Maybe now?

Oh, please, maybe now?

She spun around, humming, suddenly giddy despite the gloom, and kissed him on the cheek. They had little issue with writhing against each other, but the intimacy of kissing was uncomfortable. "I say it every day, because every day I'm right," she whispered.

"This is a fine place," he argued. As he did, every day.

"Both Tye and I fear for our lives, my love," she said, blinking as if fighting tears. Just another part to play. The loving bed-mate and the scared damsel. Boys always reacted well to these things. Apart from Uden, that is.

"As do I," he argued.

"Aye, but all they'll do is kill you," she whispered.

He said nothing.

She continued. "The boy is terrified; he hides behind bravado and we lie here pleasing ourselves. You know well where we will find sanctuary, and you deny us a chance." She let a tear roll free for effect.

"I do not know how the outcast Wolves will react when they discover our crimes," he snapped, pulling his trousers on as angrily as possible. A skill he was incapable of accomplishing. She could already see that he was ready to break. His guilt and reasonableness were too much. He did not want them anymore.

"We should have left with Wrek, when we had the chance," she muttered. The behemoth had delivered the coordinates of their haven a few nights before. At the time, Aurora had chosen staying with Tye and Stefan over trailing the big man through the forest. It had been a costly error, and one to rectify should he come wandering by with word of the road and contagious good cheer. "He seemed fond enough of Tye that he'd want to keep him safe."

It was a fine argument. She shrugged and slipped out of the room before he could gather a counter-attack. She didn't know him well after this short time, but she knew he was prone to thinking on serious matters when left alone. He was no great thinker, but he could make sound decisions.

Eventually.

As she slammed the door behind her, she swallowed a frustrated scream. "Oh, Stefan, Stefan, Stefan," she whispered. Her body had not broken him. It should have broken him. It was intriguing and frustrating. Perhaps, in another life, she might have sought meaning behind this. As it was, she tired of waking up beside a mate, eating well, and caring for a child struggling into manhood.

Not that she detested this life. She was fond of her Tye, but being a mother was not something she was taken with. Not while chains and agony and swimming in blood consumed her thoughts.

For now, she accepted that Tye had won her over. He would live through the coming events. Stefan, however? Well, the moment he offered his heart to Aurora, she would enjoy ripping it out. She'd thought a great deal about it, every time he reached climax in her. Every time she felt unappreciated. Every time he behaved as though he was not besotted with her.

I am a goddess.

You are a wretch.
A beautiful wretch.
Fuk.

Aurora imagined a hammer first. A single-handed hammer with a good balance. Just enough for the task. Shattering his ribcage would be most pleasurable, perhaps after a few messy incisions with a sharp blade. He'd still be alive. She would cut through the layers until she could reach right in and tear the still-pumping heart free. *Delicious.* Then he'd be dead. There would be Stefan's blood all over her. It was going to be wonderful.

"Oh, fuk off, Ealis," her wonderful lover roared after her, as she walked through the hallway and out into the farm to face the rainy morning.

Just think on it, my lover.

Aurora walked towards the cub, her boots almost silent despite the wet mud. If he heard her, he did not stir. He was going ever so mad. That was okay. Everyone went a little insane at some point in their lives. She had embraced her insanity the day she was born in blood, in the hands of Uden.

The child's face was scrunched up as he watched the break in the clearing to the north. If they came, they'd come from the north. So, he had sat down here to wait. It was no life for a cub. She almost felt bad for him.

"It's getting heavy, little one," Ealis said, wiping the fresh rain from her hair. He sat by the well, a little stool the only luxury he would allow himself. The animals on this farm were no longer enclosed by fencing or barn. Tye allowed them run free and felt little guilt for it. His mother had abandoned him in Samara, and his father was dead. Who would care for them now? Leave them to their own devices. Some would die, some would thrive, and it was natural.

Like death.

Death.

He understood life and death now. Had since the attack that night. The human body was too weak. It couldn't take much abuse. He'd been aware of this, but seeing the murders had been an eye-opener. Since that night, he'd struggled to close them. So, now, he watched the front gates and waited for inevitable death.

Aye, he could always take to the forests, but truthfully, he was scared. This was all he knew now. This wretched, wonderful farm. "I'm fine, Ealis," he said, facing her.

"Why not take cover in the barn? Watch from there?" She sat down beside him and put her arm around his drenched shoulders. He loved her warmth. He loved her because she was kind to him, protective of him, and he didn't want to leave her. Sometimes, he felt she cared more for him than her lover. That mistake was on her. He liked Stefan. Stefan treated him like a man. No one else treated him that way.

"I can't see the entire farm from there. Better I keep watch right here," he mumbled.

"That's some fine thinking," she agreed, and dropped her head on his shoulder. Unlike Stefan, she treated him like a little one. And that was nice, too.

"I could hear you from here," he said, after a while of comfortable silence.

"I'm sorry," she said awkwardly.

"You are guests in this place. You need never apologise." He had questions, but words failed him. He bit the inside of his cheek and returned to looking at the entrance to his farm.

"You have a question about our play?" she asked, hoping

to save some awkwardness but only adding to it. "I assumed you knew what to do, by your age."

"No, I know what to do. I just wondered… is there more to the world than who you bed?"

She laughed, and he blushed and thought about climbing up the ladder in the barn and continuing his vigil there.

"Furrowing is wonderfully important, little one." She leaned in close, a grin on her perfectly flawless face. "If you hear your lover make the noises we made, then you are doing it correctly. That's important too," she said, pushing him playfully.

He rocked gently on his stool and smiled with her. It was all he could do. "I've lost my right to Cull," he muttered.

"Oh, Tye. You will have all the ladies begging to make noises with you soon enough," she teased, kissing his forehead. And he liked that.

"Thank you, Ealis."

The door opened behind them and Stefan stepped through into the rain. He looked angry with the world, and Ealis tensed. They argued frequently, and Tye found it almost comforting. Like being in a family again.

"Fine, you fuks. We will leave this place," he said, and Ealis's fate lit up with delight.

43

FORCING THE ISSUE

E rroh could hear elevated voices from his slumber, and they drew him to a terrible alertness. He was not panicked, but something was awry. Groggily, he climbed from the bed and dressed, his joints clicking as he did. Oh, he felt weary and used. He had not slept well. He never slept well. He coughed hoarsely and grimaced, tasting the bitterness in his mouth. He wasn't as skilled at drinking alcohol as he had once been. Too much worry to enjoy himself. Too desperate to stop one drink earlier.

He heard the voices again and wandered to the far end of the top floor, out to a balcony overlooking the town's wall, and gazed down to where the sounds of disagreement were coming from. Wiping the sleep from his eyes, he listened to the bickering figures and wondered how best to play this part. Deep down, he knew well he should have insisted Nomi stay on the other side of the settlement, but he was not ready to trust she would remain unharmed there. There were still ill feelings among his companions. Still, there was a naïve competence to her he knew he shouldn't ignore. She was capable. Perhaps a few more days of seeing how she behaved free of her chains would lessen his concern. Things would improve. He was sure of it.

"No, Nomi, I claimed this patch. There are plenty fields for you to weed," Lea said loudly. A growl erupted from Erroh's stomach, loud enough that he expected the girls to stare up at him from the small weed-filled beds of herbs below. They didn't. They were far too deep into negotiations.

Nomi's hands were muddy, and a quarter of the greenery was pulled away; a large heap of dying weeds lay nearby. She'd been busy since dawn, it would appear. "You sleep, and Nomi weed. So, no. *You* take fields, Nomi take here."

"These herbs are mine," Lea said, rubbing her temple.

Nomi stared right back at her. "Not fair." She spat on the ground, her face flushed with anger. "Liiia, can't have everything."

"I can have what is mine."

"Not fair."

"It *is* fair."

Nomi's shoulders slumped, and Erroh felt for her. She really had done a fine job clearing the weeds—no small feat with a ruined hand. "We share?" she asked hopefully.

Realistically, Erroh thought the herb patch was a small matter. The sun was struggling to break through the clouds most days. They wouldn't be arguing about this in a few weeks. They were entering the colder seasons, and there would be far less growth in the freezing rain.

"I will share nothing with you, Southerner." Lea placed her hands on her shapely hips, and Erroh knew that careful tone. She was digging in. Nomi would do right in backing down. "These herbs are the reason I selected this house. This is my fuken patch."

Erroh wondered why she was so upset, but held his tongue. Like bickering sisters, he imagined they probably needed to snap at each other a few more times before they found a balance. Nomi needed to learn; Lea needed to dominate. They would know their places soon enough. Like the previous night, Erroh wondered if getting involved was the right manoeuvre.

"Not fair." Erroh could hear the hurt, could see the growing rage. There was only so much a bullied waif could take before they lashed out.

"If you want another herb patch, I'll help you clear one somewhere else, Nomi. This, however, is mine," Lea said. She offered a smile.

"It… not… fair." Nomi looked around and kicked at the gathered weeds, and Erroh suddenly felt compelled to help. Felt compelled to come between bickering sisters and calm the morning. It was only a patch of herbs; hardly a reason for this. Let them argue on more important things.

"Let her to it, my beo," he called. He offered a smile, a charming and hopeful one at that. He realised his mistake when she shot a look at him deadlier than if Baby was in her hands.

"This is not your place, Erroh. This is between me and Nomi."

Leave this one, Erroh.

"You won't have any time to tend to gardening over these next few days," he said. It was a suggestion, but it sounded more like an order. And she responded.

"Aye, Erroh." She turned on Nomi, and for a moment Erroh was convinced she would attack the girl outright. "It is yours to enjoy, Nomi," she muttered, and plodded out of the herb patch. "Just wanted a place for myself." She stared through him. "Not that it matters."

Idiot.

"Nomi, clean yourself up. We are taking to the wastes,

today," he called down before hurrying back inside to reassure his mate. When he met her on the stairs, he was relieved to see her untroubled. She shrugged and said it was "a small matter" as she slipped past him and began preparing for the ride.

No problem.

————

The two groups separated at the main gate of Raven Rock. Erroh, Lea and Nomi took a beaten path, while Wynn led Lillium and Roja out through the forest.

Settling in was important, but only a fool would continue without knowing the surrounding land. Though they could not travel with any great speed in such denseness, they still managed many miles in a great loop around the secluded town seeking tracks and hunting grounds, and keeping an eye out for possible marching armies containing impossibly powerful deities in human form. It was clear from the amount of overgrowth on the paths, however, that no soul had passed through this town in many months, and at last Erroh relaxed, convinced that no concealed foes were lying in wait. At least for now. When they understood the area better, Wynn would delve further into the green. But not today.

"Liiia and Nomi share patch," Nomi announced suddenly. She seemed very determined. The sun was setting, and they were already on the way home. Nomi's sudden suggestion after so many hours of silence startled him. Lea slowed her horse and brought it alongside Nomi's.

"No need to share anything, Nomi," she said evenly. "Take the patch. I have better things to do." It was a fine speech, but Erroh recognised the fight to come. Perhaps not this evening, but soon he would make a minor mistake and she would leap upon him furiously.

Don't fuk up, Erroh.

"No, Liiia, make time to grow. Nomi and Liiia talk. Friends," the southern girl offered. She sounded sincere. If Lea thought differently, she merely smiled and looked away while stroking her mount's mane. It was something to do instead of hitting her, he supposed. "Insist," argued the blonde delightfully. She gripped Lea's arm and squeezed it affectionately. "Patch friends!"

"That's really kind of you, Nomi. You have a kind heart," Erroh said. He locked his eyes on a high crest off in the distance. "It really is a fine idea." An eagle-eyed Outcast could see for a hundred miles each way from that crest, he imagined.

Wynn will enjoy the climb.

"Thank you, Erroh." Nomi positively bounced in the saddle despite her infirmity. She turned to Lea and winked, and Lea turned to him.

"It's fine, beo. I'll leave her to it," she snapped. Though the reins rested in her lap, both her hands were clenched as though gripping them in a sprint.

"No, I think it would be good for you both."

"So, now I have time for such things?"

I've fuked up already.

The right tactic was to fall silent. Or to support his mate, as she deserved. Erroh, however, was completely clueless about issues involving favouritism and jealousy. He didn't understand that stating Lea could never be replaced was simply not enough where Nomi was concerned. He hadn't the sense to separate them, instead of pushing them together in the hope they'd eventually bond.

As usual, Erroh believed he was doing everything just right.

In his defence, sometimes he was just an idiot.

"Oh, whisht. Just do it, beo," he ordered. He meant it more as a jesting request. Lea, however, didn't see it that way. She sniffed the air. Cleared her throat. Her silence was terrifying. Best have this conversation with you behind closed doors, she said, without saying anything.

I fuked up again.

"Thank you, Erroh," Nomi repeated, grinning, and Lea's teeth clenched as she forced a smile again. There would be blood. Plenty of blood and intense conversations.

"I think I'm done for the day. Best get home, sooner rather than later," Lea said. Then, kicking Shera hard, she galloped back through the darkening woods towards Raven Rock, and Erroh could only follow, feeling like the fool he was.

In the soothing rhythm of hooves on hard ground, Erroh found his thoughts returning to his mate and his casual dismissal of her. It was a small matter, or so he thought, because he was an idiot, and he vouched to make up for it once they set down to sleep. As they led their mounts to a rich enclosure for grazing just outside the town, Nomi walked up beside him, her face thoughtful.

"What is beo?" she asked.

Lea, who was already there, holding the bridle of her horse, sniffed as if she didn't hear. She marched towards the open gate and unbuckled the saddle of her mount and led it through. Nomi followed and Erroh after. When the horses were brushed down for the night, Nomi had still received no answer.

Eventually Erroh answered. "It's a term of endearment between two who care deeply for each other." He spoke in the southern tongue. Now and then he liked to speak the ugly words to keep them fresh in his mind. Who knew when such knowledge would serve his purposes? He was quick enough to switch back to their own tongue, however, once he saw Lea's thoroughly displeased expression.

He remembered a time ago when he'd believed himself capable of a politician's life. Now, though, every word he spoke was as terrifying as walking down a slope in the rain.

"Kind word," Nomi decided, kissing her horse's snout. The beast whinnied, appreciating the attention. "I will clear patch, for Liiia," Nomi decided and, bowing magnificently, she sought the patch to weed.

When she was gone, Lea turned to Erroh, and he knew he was fuked. She stepped in close to him and wrapped her arms around him as if she were truly in love. She was quickly learning the art of keeping up appearances in front of all who followed. "Don't you dare order me around, ever again, as cavalierly as you did today," she whispered coldly.

"I wasn't ordering you around. I was trying to find a way for the two of you to get along," he whispered back, hugging her, but she resisted.

Never good.

"She wants you, Erroh."

"Of course she does," he said, and laughed, kissing her forehead. Silly, paranoid Lea. The girl was trying to be friendly. Had she not said as much?

"She'll come between us." He could see the dismay in her face, and Erroh finally understood: this was fear, not jealousy at all.

"Nothing will ever come between us," he pledged. "Trust me, the girl has a kind heart. She looks at you like a sister. I'm not wrong about this," he reassured her, and she drew away from his warmth. "She is my friend and nothing more."

"You're an idiot, Erroh." She pushed him away. "Why can't you see it? Why can't you believe me?"

"Even if I saw, what could I do?" He reached for her, trying to calm her.

"Banish her." She dropped her head and drew away from him. Whether her disgust was with him or herself, he couldn't tell. Probably with him. For once, it didn't bother him.

He wouldn't banish the girl. "She cared for me for months and sacrificed everything. I will not banish her. Better you become accustomed to her presence, Lea. She is bonded to both of us."

Lea stormed away from him. She'd lost the higher ground and this battle. Rage surged inside her. Erroh was hers. All hers, and nobody else's. Fuk him if he didn't see the threat. She'd wanted to return to her room to compose herself, but her anger drove her away from the settlement's walls and out into the forest. He didn't follow, and that hurt even more. Nomi brought out the worst in her. She stomped gracelessly through the undergrowth, kicking at trees and bushes and anything that dared get in her way. When her rage could carry her no farther, she took a seat on a fallen log, in a little glade far from the town. With no one around to see or hear, she wept, delicate silent tears. She wrapped her arms around her knees and gently rocked. She cried for her mate and his foolishness with the female. She cried for what would befall them. Their powerful bond had been unfairly tested in the year they'd been paired, and she felt this test would be a mile too many.

Then again.

What if she were wrong? she wondered. What if the female did seek just friendship alone? What if she had

nothing to fear and was needlessly being cruel to the girl?
The tears continued to flow, and Lea allowed them. She knew
this familiar loneliness. As Nomi had spent months winning
Erroh over, Lea had spent the same time watching in lonely
horror as she went about it.

Not lucky at all, bitch.

After a time, she heard the others' voices as they returned
home. As much as she wanted to stay hidden, she took a few
calming breaths and wiped her eyes. Within a few steps, her
usual thick veneer had returned, and she resolved to hold her
temper a little longer. A little better, too. Her stomach turned
as soon as she saw them all gathered together. Like the heads
of one great happy family. Emir and Lexi stood proudly
around the cauldron, taking turns stirring the brown broth.
Every few turns, Emir added some salt, while Lexi filled
bowls and passed them to waiting hands. The pleasant smell
reached Lea from the treeline, and it drew her back home.
Not that anybody noticed.

"I'm no cook, but despite that, I'm far better than anyone
here when I'm bothered to try," boasted the wretched healer.
"May I tempt you to some fine Keri delicacies, Lea?" he
called merrily as she neared the great fire.

"Always grateful for a delicacy," she said cheerfully,
forcing deep her anguish. Roja sat with Lillium and Wynn,
blowing at the steaming broth in matching bowls. They
looked a ruin after the day's ride, but they appeared in good
cheer. She imagined she looked just as tired. She certainly felt
it. Her eyes kept returning to two figures seated beside each
other. Her mate nodded a greeting, but he would not meet her
gaze. Nomi sat far too close to him, murmuring to him in her
broken attempts at language, a stupid grin on her stupid,
whorish face.

Lexi poured a steaming helping of food into a wooden

bowl and passed it to Lea, who, doing her best to keep up appearances, smiled and sat down on a barrel opposite her mate and nemesis.

Your move, Erroh.

"I'm not suited to sitting around here, scavenging for supplies and making extravagant meals," decided Emir, taking a seat beside Lea.

"Steaming hot and rich in salt. It eases the pain after a long day," suggested Erroh, spooning broth into his mouth. Nomi passed him a piece of bread, which he took gladly. His eyes flickered to Lea to see if she had seen this act.

She had.

Erroh was too tired this evening to walk carefully around Lea's feelings. He had remained true to her for half a year in this girl's company, yet now, when Nomi tried her best to earn Lea's grace, his mate spurned any approach and snapped at him. He would have been angrier, but he could see the barely-concealed pain in her face. He knew he was wrong. And worse of all, he had hurt her again.

"I'm sorry, Nomi. My companion for this meal has arrived," he said, and sat down beside his mate. If Lea was in any way pleased with this, she showed nothing. She merely slid along the barrel to make room for him.

If Nomi showed any displeasure at this, she showed nothing either. Instead, she offered her last piece of bread to Lea. Erroh sighed inwardly; the way things were going, Lea was likely to think it was part of a plan to make her fat…

Sure enough, Lea rejected the offer. One piece was plenty enough for her.

"I should have left with Wrek this morning," said Emir.

"You were sound asleep," mocked Roja.

"How would you know that?" asked Lea.

"I can hear his snoring from a mile away."

"I'm not built for cooking. Ugh. Fuk me, I see this now," Emir said. "A few days' riding to speak with the Wolves would have been time well spent."

"Then you will be happy to know that at dawn, you will ride out with Nomi and Lillium," said Erroh. It was important that everyone get to know this land. Best to have many eyes out there searching.

"Can we make it noon?" he asked hopefully.

Erroh laughed. Question answered. The healer sipped a mouthful of sine and put the bottle away. "I reckon that's the end of my drinking for the night, so," he lied, and Erroh laughed again.

"How was the ride?" Erroh asked Wynn.

"There were plenty of tracks both new and old throughout the wastes, but nothing nearing us."

"Are you good at climbing ridges?" Erroh asked.

"That I am, Master General," Wynn said.

———

Wynn, too, had spotted the ridge, and were he not enjoying Lillium's company all day, he might have ridden off alone to get a better idea of the surrounding lands. Roja's clumsy presence had put an end to any talk of the previous night's conversations and activities, but when the redhead had disappeared into the forest to relieve herself, Lillium had taken him aside and forced the issue.

"I'm sorry for my stupid, drunken, behaviour, and I'm grateful for your decency," she whispered. She'd kissed his cheek and then walked briskly away as if embarrassed. Before he could reply, she'd spun around to correct herself.

"Not decency. That's not the word I meant to say. It was more than that, Wynn. It was goodness," she said, and bowed.

"What are friends for?" He'd left it at that. He would never show how much her approval pleased him. He had no right being affected by her. Another Alpha male would earn that right. It was easier this way.

———

"Take Roja with you," said the Master General, drawing him from his thoughts. "Lea and I will ride up the river."

"I'm a terrible climber," Roja blurted out. Emir handed across his bottle of sine.

"You can stay on the ground and bring back my body when I fall," suggested Wynn. He felt a shiver go down his back at the jest, but he ignored the sensation. He was learning to accept his certain demise. It was oddly comforting, jesting on the matter. Everyone laughed at his words, and he smiled back. It was nice to bring a smile to their faces. He knew, though, that his death most certainly would not be from falling from a simple mountain crest. Oh, no; he would have a blade shoved through his body. By Uden's hand, no doubt. It would be a fine way to walk into darkness.

When the food was eaten, Erroh walked to the centre of the main street and began stretching.

"Everyone fights each other tonight," he said, once his routine was finished.

It was a fine idea. It was also, incidentally, when everything went wrong.

44

UNNECESSARY VIOLENCE

Whatever infused Lea this night, Erroh struggled to control her storm of swords. She hammered him even harder than normal, and he was no match for her. Each combination cracked loudly against his shaking wooden swords; she was unstoppable, and no one wanted to fight her next. Her body was a blur of aggression and venomous movement, and Erroh retreated under her barrage. Spinning, ducking and dodging, he tried to meet her attacks, but she was far too quick. Thrusting, slashing and riposting, he desperately fought her back, but she was too fierce. She made him pay with painful strikes.

I deserve this.

Retreating was all he could do. His body was unprepared for her ardent violence, and by the third knockdown, he was contemplating yielding for the night. Let someone else endure her ire. If he was capable, he would have given her the victory outright, as a peace offering, but truthfully, giving up wasn't in him. So, he fought on, eager to claim at least one scoring blow.

Soon enough, welts covered his chest, blood trickled

down his nose and he lay on the ground looking up at her. She grinned humourlessly. He would suffer for the sins of Nomi. All was fair in war, he supposed. Picking himself up from the dust, he summoned the energy to face her one more time. They were alone but for the watching Nomi. Her face was a grimace of concentration and anxiousness as Lea tore him asunder. Resting against her knee was a large wooden sparring club. Erroh hadn't even seen her remove it from the chest.

"Do you want to fight after?" Lea called over to her.

"Need practice," said Nomi. She displayed her injured hand, still tightly wrapped in bandaging.

No problem.

"I can spar with her," Erroh said. He didn't want Nomi anywhere near Lea when she was as furious as this. That was how murderous actions occurred. Then again, another part of him was wary of aggravating the already volatile situation.

For a moment, he thought about the less precarious life of wandering the road alone, worrying only about the occasional raised settlement or two along the way. A life of burying the dead and slaying bastard bandits too greedy to see what sat with them.

The before times.

"Winner stays on," Lea explained, as though he'd forgotten. She eyed Nomi like a cat would a rodent. A rodent far too brazen for its own good, seeking a cheese wedge it had no business desiring. "That club looks too heavy for her."

"Hold club fine. No problem," Nomi protested. Perhaps she didn't appreciate the suggestion of the club being too heavy. Or else she tired of Lea's aggression. Whatever the reason, she was prepared to fight, and Erroh was certain she would face his mate's wrath for the deed.

"I suppose I had better win, so," Erroh said to himself.

Getting to his feet, he charged forward suddenly and knocked a sword from Lea's hand before she could steady herself. The weapon flew a distance and crashed up against the door of Emir's new home. Without hesitating, he was upon her, and with pain surging through his battered body, he struck at her from both sides. Screaming his pain into every strike, he pushed her back, but never really troubled her defence. She was reaching her peak as a master, and he was just a little too injured. A little too battered. A little less himself.

A little slow.

He spun away as if frustrated and allowed her to bring the fight back towards him. He moved even more slowly and allowed an enticing break in his defence to show, and to his delight, she took it. Taking a blow across his left arm, he spun his right weapon under her guard, cracked it loudly against her forehead and knocked her to the ground. Nomi squealed in delight. Probably not the right move on her part.

"Well done," Lea mumbled. "You're not as weak as you presented yourself to be." She bowed and picked up her second blade and stood waiting.

"Nothing like a little deceit while I'm trying to keep my pride." He met her at the centre. Perspiration ran down his forehead. Each muscle was strained and tender. His body had taken enough abuse for the day.

She looked pristine.

"It's time to take the rest of your pride," she whispered dangerously. Her eyes were alive and angry, and he knew there would be only one winner. All he could do for Nomi was weaken the storm.

He lasted another bout. Nobody noticed his body crash to the ground amidst the storm of clashing blades. He lay on his back and coughed some blood from his burst lip. Gasping for air, he regretted his attempts to save Nomi a little hurting. Lea flexed her muscles and took a few deep breaths. At least that was something.

"My turn," declared Nomi, lifting the club over her shoulder as though it weighed nothing at all.

"I'm not done yet," gasped Erroh from the dirt. But truly, he was done. He was really done.

"You are done, my beo," said Lea. Her eyes narrowed as she studied the doomed Nomi, who spun her club around impressively. It was a barbaric weapon, lacking the grace of a sword, but she showed ability. Keen ability. Her shapely, slender arms belied the strength needed for exertions. She was impressive, even if Lea would tear her apart in a few exchanges.

"I did not lose."

"Aye, beo, you did."

"Aye, my love, I suppose I did," he conceded, climbing to unsteady feet. The sweat on his hands stung the burns they carried. The wrappings had come loose in the skirmish, and he regretted sending Emir to spar.

"Well fought," she whispered as he stumbled away from the battleground.

"Nomi wait. You catch breath," Nomi said. She limbered up, copying the stretches she'd seen them do before every skirmish. After a few moments, she shook herself and hoisted the club. She pointed it out in front of her opponent and smiled knowingly. "Let's play."

Lea charged immediately. Nomi met the attack, swinging the club more quickly than Lea must have expected. The weapons clashed loudly; the air rang with the shriek of the thin swords and the dull clunk of the hollowed-out club.

To Erroh's relief, Nomi was a good fighter. Not a great fighter, but capable. He watched her turn and twist with each blow. A life in the Hunt had earned her a future in this war.

Back and forth the two women clashed, and for a moment they were evenly matched, until Erroh realised Lea was not fighting with her usual ferocity. In her movements and attacks, there was less intensity than before. He wondered if he'd tired her out after all.

It took only a few moments for Lea to learn that Nomi was a fighter. Her anger subsided as the blonde moved around her, striking out in lumbering, powerful attacks. Better to allow the girl some time holding her own before putting her face in the dirt. As much as Lea wanted to make the bitch pay for her lineage, her behaviour, her fuken presence, Nomi had earned a little grace for stepping into the arena.

The club never stopped swinging, and Lea fell into the moment, ducking and weaving, offering openings for Nomi to counter. It became almost routine, as Nomi tired swiftly. As if she were fatigued, her blows became lazy and desperate. She threw everything into each strike, and Lea stepped up the pace.

Dipping under a wild swing, Lea broke below Nomi's defence and went for a killing blow. A gentle rap across the cheek, just enough to sting and remind. But Nomi was swift. Unnaturally so. Perhaps it was instinct; it was a small matter. Lea swung, and her chin met a fist. Nomi was strong, incredibly strong. Stronger than Lea.

The punch shook her senses, and Lea stumbled back, only to meet the swinging club across the side of her head. She heard the heavy clunk before the pain made her vision darken. The blow echoed around the settlement centre, and heads turned towards them now. In combat, it would have been a killing blow. In sparring, less so. But the humiliation was mortal. Lea wavered. Her eyes became unfocused, and she dropped her weapon. Nomi, aware the battle was over, resisted an unnecessarily cheap strike and stepped away. She wore a fine smile, though.

Lea took a few steps backwards and collapsed in a heap. Erroh immediately ran to her. He took her in his arms and pulled her to him.

I'm fine.

A simple blow to the head couldn't damage much.

Could it?

"My beo?" he whispered.

"You can let go now," she said, rubbing her head. A lump was already forming, and she'd lost to the bitch.

"Sorry, Liiia," cried Nomi, dropping the club and kneeling down beside the beaten girl. She stroked her hair and Lea wanted to tear her apart.

"It's pronounced, Lea."

Emir appeared, healing bag and all. He wasn't alone. They gathered around her, concern on their faces, and she, the champion, was humiliated. Worst of all, by Nomi.

"I'm fine, my friends," she said. Her bottom lip was swelling under Nomi's strike, and she knew she looked a ruin. She wiped the dust from her trousers and tried to rise, but Erroh refused to release her. He held her as tightly as he could, his instincts to preserve and protect now at their highest. It didn't help with her humiliation.

Little Lea of the city.

"I'm fine. Just a little dazed."

Erroh finally let go. Regardless of her anger, his concern was touching. Still, though.

Fuk off, Erroh.

By the time she climbed to her feet, all dizziness had left her, and she'd learned a little more about her vanquisher. She couldn't be underestimated. She also knew that when next they fought, Lea would show her no mercy at all.

"Terrific. Another person I'll be terrified to fight," muttered Emir, touching the edge of Lea's head carefully. "Only a small bump," he told her. "Nothing, really."

"It was a fair fight," Lea offered, and though it stung, she bowed to the delighted Nomi.

"A quick fight," mocked Nomi, grinning before dipping her head in return. Lea bit the inside of her lip and fought the urge to retort. She'd lost fairly. Her emotions had blurred her judgement and caused this embarrassment. She hadn't expected Nomi's injured hand to play any part in the battle. Emir took that moment to inspect the quivering hand of her opponent. Nomi stepped away and gripped one of her fingers. With a grunt, she twisted the misshapen appendage and popped it back into place. Fear shot up through Lea's body. This was the sacrifice Nomi was willing to make, just to best her in a friendly bout of violence. How far would she go to attain a greater prize?

"Well fought, Nomi," Erroh said. Lea could see the relief in his face, but it didn't make her feel any better. Why hadn't he put the blonde in her place that morning? What had he expected to happen? That if he kept pushing them together, they would eventually become friends? Become the closest of friends for always?

Like fuken sisters.

Lillium displayed similar worry. "Are you okay?" she whispered, leading Lea from the gathering. With Lillium, there was complete trust. There was complete sisterhood. The sacrifices they had made for each other throughout their lives reassured her always.

Aye, Lillium, I'm fine. I just need to kill Nomi and I'll be perfect. How are you?

. . .

"Erroh enjoy?" Nomi asked him hopefully. She spun her club as though it were a blade in the hands of a flamboyant Alphaline.

"You did well against a master of the blade," Erroh said, and Lea's humiliation was complete.

"Thank you, my beo," Nomi said loudly, and laughed at her wit.

Lea spun around and caught Nomi's wink at her. "You can't call him that." Her temper was finally plucked one too many times. She was ready to kill the bitch. With her hands, if need be.

"She didn't mean it," Erroh countered, reaching for Lea between their comrades. "She doesn't understand the word."

"What is wrong, Liia?"

"You can't call him beo. You have no right," Lea said. She could feel her temper surge. Felt her fingers form a fist. She couldn't help herself. This was too much. Everyone was watching, and she had lost her chance to crush Nomi.

Too much.

"It just word," hissed Nomi. "Fuken Liia with other word. No." Nomi stormed towards Lea, pointing a finger. Her face was flushed, her words confused and angry. "Nomi patch? No, Nomi... We share patch? No, Nomi. We friends? No Nomi. Liia Lucky? No, no, Nomi." Nomi spat on the ground in disgust. "Remember chains? Liia nice? Nomi not pet. Nomi not chains. Liia not champion, tonight. Nomi champion." She ranted as though her true anguish were suddenly welling out, and Lea despised her.

"Shut up, whore."

"Aye, shut up, Nomi, whore," Nomi mocked. "Not fair. You have everything. Can't own word. Beo beo, fuken beo."

"It's more than just a word," Lea shouted. She pushed Erroh away. He muttered something stupid about "letting it go." She told him to fuk right off. This was a matter for them and them alone.

"Beo, beo… Erroh, beo," Nomi continued, and other voices called for calm.

Lea felt her comrades around her, gently persuading her to let this argument go, but none of it mattered. What mattered was shutting the bitch up. Claiming what was hers.

"Why you hate Nomi?" shouted the hated Nomi. She held out her hands in seeming exasperation. "What Nomi do?" Her nostrils flared, and Lea understood her bravado. Her confidence, too. She was taller than little Lea of the city. "Thought, friend?"

"I wouldn't hate you if you knew your place," shouted Lea. This was it. She'd tried. Oh, she'd tried. She'd done better than most. She'd even believed she could hide her anger for the rest of her days, few as they likely were. But the bitch had to push her, to stretch her nerves to their limit, and Lea could take no more.

"My place, here," cried Nomi. Erroh attempted to stand between the two warring factions, but Lillium grabbed his shoulder.

"She needs to have it out with her. Leave them to it."

Thanks, Lilli.

Lea stepped close. Real fuken close. "Your place was the south."

"In chains?" Nomi pushed her away. Lea resisted the urge to thrash the southern whore. She merely dropped her head and counted.

A last resort to violence.

For the war effort.

For morale.

One, two, three.

"You cannot call Erroh your beo," Lea said, dropping her voice in one last attempt at avoiding thrashing the female against the nearest rock. Nomi saved Erroh, she told herself. "That is reserved for me, and me alone." She forced her hands behind her back and clenched her fists tightly.

Four, five, six.

"Lillium love Erroh. No one mean to Lillium. No one treat like animal."

Seven, eight, nine.

"Shut your fuken mouth, whore," Lillium roared, taking offence at this. Lea didn't even care. She trusted Lillium. She knew Lillium.

"Hey, let's all just calm down. Let's go get that drink," said Wynn, grabbing Emir and Lexi.

"Lillium stare at Erroh all day. Lea say nothing."

"You're a fuken liar," hissed Lillium, though her face was pale.

"Nomi not lie. Nomi see it all," she shouted right back at her.

"Like your false god," countered Lillium.

Nomi muttered something in her savage tongue, and Erroh again stood between the girls.

"Stop it, little cubs," he shouted, loud enough to calm the argument momentarily.

The aggrieved parties fell quiet; the only sound was Lillium's deep breaths of controlled rage. Rage and probable embarrassment.

"As you wish, Master General," Lea said.

"All for you, my beo," declared Nomi. "Sorry… Erroh." She played with her hair as if it were no small matter. Distantly, thunder growled. Its booming call echoed across the valleys and stroked upon Lea's last nerve.

She leapt at Nomi and struck out with her fist. If asked about it later, Lea would admit the fine crack across the unaware female's chin was the most satisfying sound she'd heard in her life. The whore stumbled sideways and Lea struck her once more, this time a nasty blow to her stomach. She fell to her knees and Lea turned and stepped away, resisting the urge to kick her.

"Stop this shit!" Erroh cried, leaping between them. "Stop it!"

Lillium gripped his shoulder. "They need this."

You are fuken right; we need this.

"You hit like northern child," growled Nomi, struggling to her feet.

"Better that than a southern whore," snapped Lea.

"Whore, whore whore, fuken whore," Nomi mocked. And she had a point. Why would a whore have an issue being called a whore?

"Do not test me again, Nomi of the Hunt," Lea warned, and to her quiet pleasure, saw Nomi flinch.

"Not sorry when Lea dies. Keep beo for Nomi," screamed Nomi. Then her eyes widened, and for a moment she appeared to regret what she'd said.

As if she'd just revealed her best-laid plans a little too soon.

"Nomi!" cried Erroh in horror, but Lea was already sprinting at the blonde again, fists raised. Lillium wrapped her arms around Erroh to keep him in place.

"If you get in between this, Lea will not forgive you," she warned him, and he suddenly realised she spoke the truth. This was how Alphas finished arguments. Helpless and horrified, Erroh watched on, seeing everything unfold in terrible slow motion. Every part of his exhausted body screamed to interfere, but Lillium held him fast, her powerful arms wrapping around him.

Nomi grinned under the barrage. This was a fight she could win. She knew Liia had not performed to her best with weapons, and that she had been lucky to win that first round, but this was Nomi's territory now. She would take the pretty girl and defeat her. Perhaps things would change in the camp afterwards.

Nomi took the strikes and struck back just as aggressively. It was not a delicate and graceful dance like sparring. This was something else entirely. They screamed like animals, tearing at each other, searching for blood. Soon enough, they found it.

It was Lea who backed away from the struggle first. Nomi was far stronger than she, and continuing to wrestle with her would end badly. Oh, no. Lea would take this bitch apart, but she would do it like the skilled killer she was. Truthfully, there was no deadlier girl living. Her father would have been proud. Had he ever been given the chance to know her?

She felt the world slow around her, and Lea went to task. Feigning an attempt at grappling with her larger opponent, Lea sidestepped before jabbing the blonde twice in the stomach in quick succession. It was enough to upset her and allow her to get closer, where a devastating hook sent Nomi crashing to the ground. The blonde roared in frustration and hopped back up. She charged forward once more, but Lea merely spun out a kick that caught her in the ribs. Again, Nomi fell to the ground, sliding forward with her own momentum. She squealed in frustration and pain as her fingers ripped, but again she climbed to her feet.

Screaming in rage, she charged down at Lea, eager to envelop her in her powerful arms, but Lea stepped away and drove her fist into Nomi's face three times in quick succession. Disorientated and bleeding from her nose, Nomi staggered forward and met another powerful strike from her vanquisher. At this, she fell to her knees.

"Stop it, Lea," Erroh cried, and distracted, Lea saw him grimace in horror. It meant little.

She realised then that, all around her, her comrades were also calling out for an end to this fight.

"Try to find a better solution."

"Try to find respect."

"To be the bigger person."

"She's done."

Lea didn't believe this fight was done at all. She struck Nomi across the face. And then she struck her again. And again.

"Stop it Lea," Roja cried, and for a moment Lea almost laughed, thinking about Roja, the queen bitch of the city, having the audacity to call for mercy.

A small matter.

"I hate you," Lea hissed as Nomi, bloodied and battered, still tried to get up. Her hands hung limp, but there was still fight in her. Lea almost admired her will, but continued to set about destroying her. Why? Well, because she was beautiful. She struck her again, a wet strike that sent Nomi's head rebounding off the ground.

"End this, Master General," Wynn growled.

"It's over when Lea has taught her a lesson," countered Lillium.

"Of course," mocked Wynn, shaking his head in irritation.

"Fuken Alphas," muttered Emir.

Lea sat atop the barely moving figure now. Nomi struggled, but Lea pinned both her arms to the ground. Rage like nothing she'd ever experienced before blinded her. Her Erroh. Nobody else's. She drove her fist into flesh and Nomi moaned and Lea remembered snow and fire and death and she hated everything. If Nomi died at her hands, her problems would be over.

Some of them, at least.

Erroh would forgive her, eventually.

She struck the blonde whore from the south once more. When she drew away, some strands of blonde, bloodied hair stuck to her fists. She shook them free.

Nobody stopped her.

So she stopped herself.

She held her fist in the air but did not take another piece of vengeance. The still form of Nomi offered little resistance, anyway. She looked dead but for a small globule of blood bubbling from her nose with each breath. She knew letting the girl live would have great ramifications. She just couldn't bring herself to murder her this way.

"Let me see to her," hissed Emir in disgust, pushing Lea aside. He knelt down beside the girl's still form. Her face was a ruin. The swelling had already begun, and it concealed anything attractive about her, and Lea slid off her.

"That was brutal," he said, running his fingers along her battered face.

"She will live," Lea hissed.

"Aye, she will. I doubt she'll be in any shape to dance tonight," he muttered, uncorking a little capsule and holding the lip under the girl's nose.

"She can dance tomorrow," whispered Lea, flexing her blood-soaked fingers.

45

AFTER THE STORM

"**G**et her whatever she needs," Lea said, propping the semi-conscious female up to a sitting position. From here, the beating looked even worse. Nomi muttered something incomprehensible and wavered unsteadily.

"She needs time to come to," Emir hissed. He stared at Lea for a moment before returning to holding the aromatic salts beneath Nomi's nose. After a few wheezing breaths, she swiped at the offending aroma. "Easy, now, little one. Ease yourself."

"Everyone, leave us be," Lea said, and no one moved. All stood in silent, harsh judgement of her. "I said, leave us," she shouted, and reluctantly they took the order. Keeping her eyes on the bloody ruin of Nomi, she heard their footsteps fade away. Nomi moaned under her breath and coughed a globule of phlegm and blood from her mouth into the dirt, and Lea felt her face flush in shame. "Come on, Nomi," Lea whispered, dropping to her knee beside her. She took her hand. It was limp and quivering.

Emir held the bottle of aroma beneath her nose once more, and the girl's eyes flashed open and blinked.

"It's okay, Nomi. It's okay," Lea said, and gently pulled her to her feet. Easier to recover while standing. Better that than sleeping. Nomi stood unsteadily, weaving from side to side. Her dazed stare of confusion was a terrible thing.

I didn't mean to hurt you.

That much.

"The rest of you can leave too." Lea turned and eyed Erroh and Emir.

And Lillium. Lillium was there as well, unable to face Wynn after what had been said. She certainly wasn't looking anywhere near Lea, either. It was a small matter.

Emir passed Lea some cotton, ointment, and fresh bandaging. "Do not strike her again," he warned, and there was a coldness in his tone.

She could have challenged him, such was her mood, but she nodded sheepishly. She had fallen far this evening. She could still fall farther. Satisfied she would not kill Nomi in a more personal setting, Emir grabbed his healer's bag and headed off towards the fire in the centre of the town. Lillium followed.

Lea stared at the bandaging in her hands. She knew that as her comrades gathered at the fire tonight, her assault would be the main topic of conversation. There was no defending what she had done.

Even now, she couldn't remember the fury that had overcome her. She'd endured this fury once before. Her fingers still carried the scarring.

She was left alone now but for Nomi and her mate. She couldn't look at him. Her shame matched her disgust that he'd led her to this cruelty.

"Don't say a word, Erroh, line of Magnus," she warned. "Leave us alone." She finally met his gaze and saw how shaken he was.

"Your hate is terrifying," he said coldly, and it cut through her. Aye, she was filled with hate. Fuk him for only seeing it now. "Come on, let me help," he offered, this time sounding more himself.

Nomi muttered something and then dropped her head as she reached up and felt the bruising on her face. "This is my doing. She is my sin." It didn't matter that it had needed to be done, she thought miserably.

"A fair fight?" he asked, then turned and strode away towards their home. Lea didn't reply. It had been a fair fight, at least to start. And it should have ended sooner. It didn't matter how she felt now. What mattered was her murderous intent.

Shame.

"Come on, I'll take care of you, Nomi," she hushed softly, holding out her hand.

Nomi walked without Lea's help, mostly. Every few steps she stumbled, but Lea was there to steady her. "This way," was all Lea would say as she led her away from the fire. The darkness somehow made it easier to walk with the battered girl. With only the moonlight to guide their way, she couldn't see the devastation she had caused.

Nomi wept, shaking with near-silent sobs. Every pathetic tear that fell down her ruined face made Lea feel worse. Nomi struggled in the darkness, and Lea took firmer hold of her hand.

"Where are we walking?"

"Nearly there, Nomi," Lea promised, as their feet touched the softness of the wastes. She followed the sound of running water and led her helpless little victim through the line of trees. Along the edge of the river they stopped, and Lea bade Nomi sit on the bank.

Without hesitating, Lea dropped into the freezing water

first, and her breath caught tightly in her chest. Nomi just sat miserably, watching her through tiny slits where her eyes used to be. Beautiful eyes that Lea had simply felt like destroying. Where was the pride in cruelty?

"Cold."

"I know it's cold. Better this way."

She took a cloth and soaked it in the water and edged up beside the stricken girl. As gently as she could, she dabbed at her face. She started with the tears. Their streaks were visible through the blood.

Depthless shame.

"I should not have done this," Lea whispered, stopping briefly to see if there were improvements. There weren't. She had ruined her. "I'm sorry." Any apology sounded pathetic considering the devastation she had caused. Nomi said nothing. She winced at her touch, but Lea knew she welcomed the cool cloth against the agony.

"I start fight, you finish," whispered Nomi after a while. Her voice was surprisingly strong and defiant. What else could a southern whore sound like, considering the life she had led? This beating was likely little compared to the daily attacks she'd probably suffered under the hands of the Hunt.

Had Lea really been naïve enough to believe a fine beating was all it would take to remove her as a problem?

What if this show of force had simply horrified Erroh, been the first tragic step towards even unhappier times?

"How do you feel?" Lea asked, wiping some antiseptic into a gash across her eyebrow. She winced herself at the injury. As she dabbed at the wound, a little fresh flow of blood escaped the gap, but she continued on regardless. She took the cloth, held it over the girl's face again.

"Beaten."

"I'm sorry."

"Is small matter. Fair fight," the blonde replied.

Allowing Nomi to hold the soothing rag over her face, Lea hopped out of the water and, taking a brush, began combing the dirt and blood from her hair. Nomi sighed in pleasure as Lea carefully rinsed the ruined, tangled strands.

For a time, they said nothing. They sat side by side on the riverbank, shivering in the cold, until Nomi gently took hold of Lea's hand. "Why hate Nomi?"

Lea didn't want to answer. "I do not hate you," she whispered, and as carefully as she could, untangled a knot from the thick blonde hair. Loath as she was to admit it, the girl's southern locks were stunning, even soaked through and tarnished by blood.

Nomi pointed at her own face. Through the swelling, Lea saw her beautiful eyes. They looked amused. "Friends?" Nomi asked mockingly.

"Perhaps. Friends don't do this," admitted Lea guiltily. Maybe she hated her, just a little.

"Why Lea not attack Lillium?"

"Lillium had an opportunity to have Erroh in the Cull. She chose Wynn instead," explained Lea quietly, in case anyone was listening.

"Bad choice," muttered Nomi after a few moments, searching for the right words. "Happy life with Erroh. Not Wynn," she added, thoughtfully. "Nomi choose Erroh from moment I see," she pointed out.

Lea felt the anger resurface, but she held herself to that river of tranquillity.

"So did I," she said evenly. Then, after a moment, she said, "I don't trust you because you say things about Erroh that you have no right to say."

"You don't trust, so you beat Nomi?"

Lea shrugged in shame. She was an Alphaline; that's how

they lived their lives. Go wild, and think about repercussions after the dust settled.

"Nomi see how you not trust," muttered Nomi. She thought on her next words for a few moments. Whatever she was thinking seemed to take some concentrating. "Nomi speak truth of one for life. Did… um… did… not know, not speak… Not speak of Lillium. Of Erroh?" She sighed. "Nomi speak good. Not perfect."

"We don't speak of things. It hurts here," Lea said, and touched her heart, and Nomi nodded in agreement. Lea thought Nomi understood a little more. Or else she'd just learned the art of deceit. Regardless, this conversation should have happened before the violence, which would define her life from now on, she thought glumly.

Whatever healing was in the water worked wonders on the battered girl. Despite the bruising around her eyes, she looked better than before. She still had her teeth, for one.

She will smile again.

"We should probably return to town," Lea said, climbing to her feet.

"Someday, *Lea* see Nomi for who Nomi is," the battered blonde said. She took Lea's hands. They were shaking. She tried to smile; it looked like it hurt.

"I don't want Lea die," she said. She held the cloth to her face once more. It was something to do.

"I don't want to die either."

She desperately wanted to believe the little waif. She wanted to ignore her gut feeling that Nomi was playing a clever game of strategy and deceit. That said, what proof had Nomi offered that she was anything but this genuine female who'd paid dearly for protecting Erroh?

Surely, they had not staged her captivity in chains, just to garner some sympathy?

Surely, Uden the Woodin Man was not that diabolical?

Though her heart wanted to believe, she knew deep down that Nomi was not one she could trust with her life. If she was outnumbered, injured and moments from death, would Nomi stand with her? No. The bitch would land the first blow.

"Nomi want Erroh," Nomi whispered.

"Aye."

"When we walk south, happiest days of Nomi," the southerner explained. "Never wanted to end, but Erroh love one for life." She gingerly touched the swelling around her lips. "Want Erroh, but Lea have Erroh. Nomi sad." She stared at Lea, choosing her words. Lea hoped they would be better than the ones already spoken. "But happy for Erroh, happy for Lea," she said quietly. She shrugged. "Sad and happy."

"We will never be friends, but we can be sisters," offered Lea carefully.

Nomi suddenly wept again. She stroked Lea's cheek, startling her. "Sister?" It was heartfelt, or else the blonde was a master of manipulation. Despite her trepidation, and pledging to herself to keep a watchful eye, Lea embraced the crying girl quietly. Perhaps, after everything, it would be wise to let go and just believe in her. She would certainly be a lot happier in herself.

As if sensing her unsureness, Nomi broke the embrace and stood back, eyeing her almost playfully through her swollen lids. "Nomi not need patch. Lea take patch," she announced.

"We can share the work, Nomi," Lea said, and saw the girl fail to conceal a smile.

46

BEATEN

He grimaced, placing the cards down on the mossy ground. A bad hand. A terrible deal. Flipping those he could use and discarding those that were unplayable, Magnus went to task playing the game. He didn't know why he bothered. It was something to do instead of spending the night lamenting his shitty lot in life.

He'd come so far, and fallen farther. They said it was good to be the king. It was less good to be deposed and alone, far from home, begging for scraps from an army without an army.

"Fuk," he growled, revealing the ace of queens. In a game of chance, he had struck gold. In this solitary game, it was a deathly card to draw. Returning it to the deck, he began shuffling again. To play this game, the rules demanded no second shuffle. Such was the skill involved. Tonight, he desired no skill. He just desired a win.

Anything.

He drank from his bottle of sine and, despite the sting in his mouth, throat, and belly right after, he drank heartily. It was his fifth drink tonight. It might have been his ninth. Who was counting?

His head ached. He knew this ache too. Looking out at the dark, cloudy night, he could feel the turning of the weather in his head. Any time now, he supposed, dropping a log into the small crackling fire, before throwing down another few cards and attempting to win this game.

"Success," he growled, losing a few more from his deck.

More miles to walk in this game.

He'd believed he'd enjoy these evenings to himself, reclaiming his soul, his will. It couldn't be farther from the truth. When his mind wasn't consumed with thoughts for his taken mate, it was with his children, who'd been forced into a life of awfulness. One he'd presumed could never happen again.

The wind blew in, and he heard a crack of a twig in the distance. He hadn't concealed the fire expertly, and that was fine. He had little fear of any wanderer or bandit venturing near. He welcomed the unease. A younger Magnus would have risen to his feet, donned his armour and raised a blade in cautious preparation. But not now. He needed to gain humbleness once more. Pride was important to a legendary warrior, but it was death to a fallen king willing to barter.

Resting his tired back against a wide trunk, beneath the heavy canopy of the seeping oak, he waited. It was days since he'd seen another soul out on the road. He listened, but those who marched through the forest were skilled in the art of concealment. They came from upwind of where Magnus had set camp. The hounds surrounding him would not smell their scent. At least not yet.

"Come, gather at the fire," he called into the night. His hounds raised their heads as he called out. A few sniffed the air, and he watched them. If they caught a scent, they'd remain alert, wary. If they returned to slumber, it had all been just a sound of the forest. "All are welcome, this weary night."

No reply came, and he returned to his game. Having spent a lifetime rising above doubt, terror, brutality, he was tired now. Tired and still full of needless pride.

He reshuffled and again met little success. So, he shuffled again after that.

He did not favour this journey. He knew what he marched towards, and truly, he was unprepared. He had no faith, either. Too long he'd been away from the Savage Isles, trusting them not to kill each other. He wished Elise was with him now. He could face what was to come, knowing he had her strength to call upon. Now, all he had was his pack of hounds.

The hounds had not dropped their heads. Instead, each fierce beast remained staring into the darkness. Watching, waiting… sniffing. Another snap of a twig upon the ground rose above the fire's crackle. There came around him the delicate hum of a hound's growl, followed swiftly by those of its brothers, Magnus knew for certain now that he was no solitary wanderer out this night.

Above him, a bright flash of lightning lit up the land. He counted under his breath, and by ten, the low rumble of thunder joined the growling of his protectors.

"Whisht," he hissed, and the protective hounds fell silent, and now Magnus heard the slow trudge of creatures marching through the night, no doubt drawn to the light of his campfire. He stripped off a few pieces of fresh boar and placed them across the flames. If he were to be mugged, he would ensure they were well fed. It was the little things.

"I can hear ye coming," he called, and the wanderers slowed. "Hear you slowing your step now, too. You have nothing to fear tonight. Come sit by the fire." It was quite the warm invitation. Beside him rested his sword. His armour, however, was concealed within his saddlebags upon his chosen mount.

Doomed to leave the game incomplete, and therefore lost, he gathered up the cards and pocketed the deck, lest he lose them in a game of wits.

A voice from the night called warily, "We mean you no harm. Call off your pack."

"They're about as vicious as a herd of swine. Come sit by the fire."

They must have trusted him, for two tall wanderers appeared from the darkness and stood near the fire's light. They made no sudden gestures, and the hounds simply watched and waited for Magnus's decision.

Too much death.

Too much pride.

They portrayed themselves as wanderers, yet Magnus recognised them as trouble immediately. They wore armour of steel and leather, far too heavy for such a late-night wander. Upon their arms were black sashes, tightly wrapped. Their weapons were not drawn, but their hands hovered near their grips. Their eyes fell upon Magnus's mounts and the bulging saddlebags.

That'll be the hound armour.

"My name is Joel," one of them said, bowing.

"And I am Levi," the other said. They could have been brothers. Tall, muscular, with bushy beards that matched their long black hair. This close, Magnus could see the dents and scuffs upon their armour. They'd seen their fair share of battle. Never a good sign, when he was outnumbered and older than both their ages combined.

"Wonderful to meet you. My name is Marvel," Magnus said, smiling.

There was a second flash, and he counted to eight before the thunder rolled. A fresh bout of sharp pain pierced his head, and he felt it in his neck. Heavy storm, rolling in real fuken close.

"I just put a few scraps of meat on. Won't you join me?"

"You are most kind for the offer, Marvel. Tell me, why wander on a night like this?" Joel asked, standing over the flames. The fire crackled happily as the fatty juice caught fire and sizzled away to nothing. Only a fool would turn down an offered meal. Or else some bandit fiend, up to no good.

"What makes you think I'm alone?"

"We watched you awhile, is all," Levi whispered. They had not taken their seats. They continued to stare at the saddlebags, no doubt wondering what treasures lay within.

Precious treasure if you are alone on a battlefield and your boys come to your rescue.

Less so, if you are up to some banditry.

Levi slid his crossbow from his back and loaded a bolt. "You are very hospitable."

"Aye," Magnus said, realising he'd wasted the meat on an unwanted invitation. "You feel that brewing of trouble in the wind?"

"Aye, Marvel, we do," Joel said.

Magnus didn't bother to meet the man's eyes. He was too tired to accept the challenge or warn the brute what danger he stirred. "So, how will we do this?"

"You like your hounds?"

"I do."

"Your pack might do some damage."

"I said they're as gentle as a kitten with yarn."

Joel found this funny. He relaxed his stance, and Magnus imagined leaping up and ripping his fuken throat out, before tearing into… into… Levi? Was that his mugger's name?

547

Regardless, he could do it, even with a bad knee. He only needed to stir his desires. To tickle his bastard bloodthirstiness. To want to.

To have pride.

Pride.

The downfall of the honourable.

"You probably wouldn't want to see a few of them slain in front of you," Levi said. It was a fine threat. He wouldn't.

"I wouldn't."

"Then let's keep this robbery all gentle and civil, friend."

Magnus reached down slowly, removed his purse of pieces from his waist, and held it out for the bandit. It wasn't all he had, just most of it. Once he reached the Savage Isles, he'd have no need for pieces.

Joel drew his sword and held it out in front of Magnus's face. "Easy, friend. No need for me to have your pelt."

Seeing the blade drawn, the dogs set up another round of growls that caused the sword's tip to shake ever so. It was one thing mugging a solitary wanderer, but killing even one or two hounds was a brutal act of inhumanity to be avoided. Who knew what the remaining gentle hounds might do if threatened?

"Whisht," warned Magnus, and the dogs fell silent, but all stood. Ready. A thief might have been smart enough to conclude this business swiftly. Despite himself, he was proud of them.

Magnus placed his pouch of pieces upon the weapon's tip and ignored the itch in his sword arm. He had no desire to protect himself; all he desired was beyond his grasp, so why bother caring about such insignificant matters?

"What's your trade?"

"Hound trainer. Preparing them for war," Magnus replied.

"There's no war in the wind," countered Levi.

"I heard different. I heard Spark is rightly fuked," he said.

"Oh, you probably make a fine living training hounds for war and all. Spreading lies in the wind. There's no fuken war. Probably just Alpha fuks finally acting out."

"East doesn't have problems like that," Joel added.

Magnus nodded in agreement. This mugging was going splendidly. "That seems most likely, my good friends. As long as people still buy my hounds, I'll not argue."

Joel looked over at the four mounts. "We'll take your mounts and then we'll be done."

Magnus revealed his bandaged knee, still a ruin after weeks in the saddle. "Please, sir. Take what you want, but leave me my mount," he whimpered. "I'm heading to the coast. I'll never make it without a mount."

There was the perfect amount of pathos in his tone. And why wouldn't there be? He had little left in the world. He did not believe he would see those he loved ever again. So, he used that fuken sorrow and threw it into his begging.

A hard thing swallowing pride.

Sighing, Joel dropped to a knee in front of him. He peered at the sword beside Magnus and, without warning, snatched it from where it lay. "This sword is valuable. Could get rich with this beast."

Magnus dropped his head. It was valuable. He'd killed a king with it and all. "Please, don't take my sword. It was my master's. It is all I have to remember him."

His stomach twisted. A terrible bile churned, and he wondered what could stop him throwing up.

Joel must have had a touch of humanity to him. He replaced the blade in its scabbard and returned it to his victim.

Magnus and his hounds remained silent as the ordeal continued. Dug in against the tree, his body ached more as the storm moved in. He watched dispassionately as the two bandits released all but one of the mounts from their holdings. They rummaged through his saddlebags, spilling the contents out all over the cool ground. A few letters, a pouch of salt, sketching of an accurate world map.

"I thought this far east was mostly free from bandit raids," Magnus said at last, and both brutes laughed.

"Rangers neglecting their duty," Levi said, and for a moment Magnus felt a stirring of anger. A desire to recover the pouch of pieces. To rise.

"Perhaps they've gone to war," Magnus countered, and felt his heart hammer in fury.

Rangers.

"Then you'll be doing some fine business," Joel countered. Above them, there came a flash of lightning, followed swiftly by a roar of thunder, and despite himself, Magnus jumped.

"And with that, fine Marvel, we will depart."

"Unless you'd be interested in selling one or two of your hounds?"

"These mongrels aren't even close to trained," Magnus countered. His temper was rising. He calmed himself as best he could. He might have even started counting. The sooner they lowered their weapons and left him to it, the better. It was no small matter being mugged. It was no smaller matter allowing it, too.

They stood to leave, and Magnus was grateful in part for their lack of greediness.

"It is a dreadful thing to steal from one so old. Apologies, friend," Levi said, bowing.

Magnus counted again. He could only play the decrepit old man for so long.

Take this humiliation.

Control it.

"I wish you safe on your journey, comrades of the road. Stay clear of the north."

Like ashes upon my tongue.

They looked at him for a few breaths more and then disappeared from the camp, the thunder of his horses fading in the night with them. Above him, the rain fell, light at first, but then he felt it in his neck. "Don't worry, my boys," he said to the hounds. "The last of our worries will be armour. Should it come to it, should we all live, I'll have the finest made."

He leaned back against the tree as the rain gathered weight, and he contented himself with watching the deluge give fight to the flames of his little fire. They fought bravely against insurmountable odds. Eventually, the one light in the forest dimmed to nothing, yet Magnus felt little desire to take shelter. Instead, he lay in the dark, listening to the rain as it covered him over, cut through to skin and did its best to tear the life from him.

The last march of Magnus was drawing to a close. He closed his eyes and accepted the cold. His hounds, sensing little threat in the air, gathered up around him and dug in for warmth amongst themselves, treating him both as cover and as a master to be protected and warmed.

As he closed his eyes to sleep among them, he smiled.

47

FUKEN RAIN

Erroh sat at the edge of the platform above the town wall and hated the world, himself, and the weather for a while. Wave after wave of light rain sprayed against his face and soaked him through. It wasn't the freezing rain that caused the misery, nor the driving wind cutting through his cloak. It was desolation. He sipped on a small tankard that contained nothing stronger than water. He should have accepted the offer of Emir's sine, but he knew it would set a bad precedent. It was his turn to do the watch, and even though there was a heavy storm forming above his head, it didn't excuse him from dereliction of duty, as futile a responsibility as this was tonight.

The first drips of water trickled down his back and his body shook ever so. The one part of his body enjoying the rain were his numb hands. *Wonderfully numb.* He looked at them in the radiance of the glowing electrical orbs and smiled ruefully. Though they were terribly scarred by fire, the freezing water eased the pain he sometimes endured. They shook regardless, and a fresh gust of wind set him shaking a little more.

There was cover at the front gate on the far end of the town, but he couldn't avail himself of such luxury the entire night. Walking the perimeter along the wall every few hours was a necessary sacrifice. He looked into the night through the waves of rain, deep into the darkness beyond.

No army hiding in the bushes, waiting for my back to turn.

"Ah, fuk this," he whispered against the wind, before turning back along the wall towards the front gate and the cover on the platform above. It was a little open shack, built into the wall as a watchtower for nights like this. Had he been smarter, he might have set a fire to burn in the old steel barrel inside it for when he returned.

Another oversight on my part.

"There's no one out there," he muttered. Again, his words were lost, but it was a small matter. What mattered was giving himself permission to seek shelter until the rain fuked right off.

Walking, head down against the gusting tempest, he felt terribly alone tonight. Lonely for the world. There seemed to be a terrible stillness in it of late. He felt like the last man alive. Just how many settlements lay in scorched ruin like this, out in the world, he wondered miserably. How many other, more fortuitous towns remained blissfully unaware of the horrors at work? How many fugitives fled inwards towards Samara?

How many made their way to Adawan?

An army's worth by now, perhaps?

He jogged the last few steps and dipped in under the cover of the shelter, immediately seeking a few logs and kindling for the fire barrel. Beneath him the heavy gate creaked, blocking off the wastes from civility. It had taken two full days of manoeuvring and repairing. Were it not for

Wynn's aptitude for steelworks upon the small smith's forge or Roja's talent for the mechanisms, they might well have been hiding behind an open wooden gate, hoping for the best. Erroh understood that the heavy beast was raised and lowered by a chain, like an anchor at sea. A heavy, shrieking lever wound the chain up and dawn, opening and closing the gate as required.

Just like Spark.

"Lonely," he whispered in the darkness, and felt it anew. He and Lea had not spoken in days now, and he was the lesser for it. Recovering a few pieces of dried kindling, he set alight a little flame in the barrel. Something to take away the air's bite. Beside the barrel rested a small box of dry logs. Whoever had stood watch on the town's last night had known the chill, too, it seemed. He offered a respectful nod to the ghosts of this town for leaving behind a little fuel to keep him warm.

"You really fuked up, Roro," Lexi called from below. She wore a heavy cloak wrapped tightly around her. It wavered in the wind, and he saw a small bottle of sine in her injured hand. As carefully as she could, she climbed the nearest ladder and took a seat beside her brother. She hung her feet over the side and sipped from her bottle. At least she was exercising the elbow.

"What did I do now?" He drank his tasteless water. It was bland. Maybe if he'd added some lemon or something.

"I never liked Lea in Samara, but I think she's a fine mate."

She tapped her feet loudly against the wall, her eyes scanning the darkness for friend or foe. Though she was young, injured and heartbroken, she was still a hunter. She would become elite, once she came of age. Once she killed for the first time.

A week had passed since Lea had battered Nomi to a pulp. He knew he had hurt Lea terribly; he wasn't exactly certain how he had hurt her, but he knew he had. He didn't need his younger sister to point it out.

The wind howled, a piercing cry like a phantom beast from a netherworld. A cry like that could fuel any wanderer's paranoia of things taking a terrible turn. "She is more than that to me."

Every night since the disagreement, Lea had slept in a separate bed to his own. He had given up trying to speak of the matter, as her eyes were dangerous and unforgiving whenever he did. So he said nothing, and when she failed to come to him a second night, he had finally taken himself to her room and offered a more sincere apology. He had met a frosty glare as chilling as the wind he sat with tonight. He had tried once; he would try no more.

The days were formal between them. She behaved respectfully to him in front of the rest, but she did not offer a spark of warmth when they were alone. His presence irritated her, and he'd received the message clearly. When she was ready, she would allow him near her. It was only fair, he supposed.

She would come around.

Things weren't that bad.

Are they?

"Well, you fuked it up. Go fix it, now," hissed Lexi, and drank deeply from her bottle.

"You're too young to understand these things, little one—and why are you drinking like that?" he snapped, reaching for the bottle.

With reflexes of any youth holding a fine bottle of alcohol, she snatched it away from his grasp. "Emir gave it to me for the pain." It sounded like a lie. A well-thought out lie.

"Oh."

"It really helps me." She drank deeply again, emphasising her point.

"How long before you can move it properly?"

She shrugged and stretched out her arm. He could see that it pained her, but she held it in. He was proud of her.

"I miss her," Lexi said, watching the dark for a hidden army that had no business out on this wretched night. The fire grew, and she placed her hands against the barrel's side as it warmed them both.

"We will find Mom, after we do all this," he promised.

"She'll be dead." She wiped some rain from her eyes.

"Aye, that could be." He patted her head; he knew no other way to reassure a youthful female. "Have heart, little one. Elise is a legend for a reason."

Lexi nodded miserably, but feigned a smile. She drank again and shivered a little. Erroh suspected it was the drunkenness.

"Not that I hated Lea, or anything," she slurred. "It was actually Lillium whom I hated, but that was only because she was such a total bitch."

Erroh smiled. There was something entertaining about the drunken ramblings of young cubs. And drunk or no, it was nice to talk to her. Truthfully, he wanted to speak with her more of their dreadful circumstances, but every time he tried, she remained closed off. A better brother might have pushed, but he suspected that when she was ready to talk, she would.

Even drunk.

"Would you like some?" She offered him the bottle with a shaky hand. He immediately recoiled and sipped his water, and decided a night off from drinking alcohol was a night well spent. Why? He didn't know. But every other night until a few hours before dawn, he, Wynn and Emir had sat by the flames and drank liberally at each other. It was becoming a wonderful waste of an evening, every evening. It was something to do instead of sitting around and missing their lovers, both former and current.

"I wish you and Roja had become mated for life, but there is nothing we can do about that now," she said.

"I somehow doubt Roja would have found any type of happiness with me. Like her grandmother, she had little love for our family."

"That's not true at all." She pushed him in the shoulder, as any drunk would when making a point. "She likes me."

"I was destined to be with Lea, anyway," Erroh said quietly.

"She's not the girl she was. I think I like her now. Fix this, before you fuk everything up, brother," she whispered. She pulled her feet up and dropped soundlessly to the ground with delicate grace. Injury or not, she had her mother's elegance. When she took to war, she would be formidable.

"I'll do my best," he called down to her. "Go get home to bed," he ordered.

"Not just yet," she said, wobbling unsteadily on her feet, all surefootedness lost in a moment. "I'm drunk enough that I think I'll go hang out with Wynn for a while... I think he's in his room." She laughed and skipped away. And then she was gone, and all he could hear was the faint echo of his drunk younger sister's giggles as she disappeared through the streets of the dead town.

Erroh turned around and wrapped his soaked cloak tighter to halt the wind and felt very lonely in the world once more.

True to its word, a fiercer storm formed and struck the quiet town, long after the last spark had spat from his fire. Roja had turned the lights off, leaving him in darkness and chill and a dash of melancholy.

He shivered and watched his breath form a little wisp of moonlight white in front of him, and once more he considered climbing back down and taking proper shelter for the night. Sitting up against the barrel and enjoying its last embers, he looked out into the night as the thunder grew fierce and the lightning crackled.

He clasped his arms to his chest and ducked his head under his damp cloak to stave off the blowing wind. But that offered little relief. The wind pulled and tugged at him and eventually took his hood for its own, and no amount of wrestling it back did him any good. Eventually he gave up and allowed the garment to flap aggressively against his back while he sat as miserably as before. It was a terrible thing to sit in darkness, thinking on matters. Erroh knew no good would come of it, yet still, he let his mind wander to dark places.

Doubt.

Doubt was a fine thing. It taught a man to tread carefully along a seemingly straight path; it also offered defeat to a fine army with little to do but think about the battle come dawn. But for a scared little cub with a scared little plan, doubt could almost swallow him up whole. He felt like a little lonely cub tonight. He sought reassurance, yet that prideful part of his mind was missing. The part telling him that all would be okay. That he would find a way.

Simple plans that would never work.

They had taken to riding through the wastes every day in search of quarry. Their search, like his battle with the hood, had been futile. There were plenty of tracks spread throughout the miles and miles, but none hinted at a single finger of the Hunt. He felt blind to the world and restless to act. To do anything. Anything at all.

Why does Uden wait before marching on Spark?

A gust thrust itself violently against him and drew him from melancholy. His hair flapped wildly, and far away through the raging howl, he heard something metallic tear and break. This was a healthy storm, all right, he thought bitterly.

I need you tonight, my love.

Whenever he felt his lowest, he thought of Lea. Sometimes, those longing thoughts turned bitter, like quenching thirst with a lemon. He'd done little to disrespect her, apart from suggesting she and Nomi share a patch of herbs. As wretched luck would have it, since the fight Lea and Nomi had been on better terms. He'd listen to them every morning going to work on the herb garden, even as the wet weather closed in.

"Fuken typical," he hissed, and spat into the darkness over the edge of the wall.

I need you always, my love.

He imagined her sleeping, her gentle breath calm and contented, with wrappings of blankets all around her. He imagined himself beside her, and though he tried not to let it, his anger dissipated, replaced by his terrible feeling of loneliness. He missed her so much. He missed her warmth. Her breath upon his neck, her dark strands of hair resting across his chest as she nuzzled him. She was everything to him, and all he had was the storm for company.

Oh, for just a few calming words in his ear, with no one else around to hear. The words of reassurance, to end all doubt. Words only his soulmate could offer. Instead, he sat alone.

Bitch.

I need you tonight.

He held the anger again. Anger was a gift.

He never heard her approach. He was busy wrestling his hood again, trying to wrap it around his frozen face. The last of the rain clouds had blown away, and the shattered moon blazed brightly, but the wind remained. He didn't hear her climb the ladder and steal up behind him. He focused his miserable eyes on vile fiends from beyond the darkness.

"There you are," Lea said, above the roar. He jumped with fright but quickly composed himself. He was Erroh, legend of the road, after all.

He stared at her and nodded. Here he was, indeed. He had been here for quite a while. His heart lightened a little, but only a little.

"It's wild out here," she said, taking a seat beside him. Her dress was soaked through and her hair was wild. Her body shook in the cold. She'd endured the storm looking for him. The thought should have warmed him. Mostly, it did not.

Probably thought I'd hidden in Nomi's shack with her bosom as a pillow.

"It has been all night," he hissed, and regretted it ever so. He wanted to talk it out but couldn't help his mood. She shrugged indifferently, but did not move. That was something.

"It's unlikely there will be anybody creeping up to us, beo. Perhaps it would be better to take shelter for the night." It sounded like a fine idea altogether. Instead, he shrugged. It was probably not the reaction she was looking for. She didn't stir, so he brought the fight to her. It was petty, but this was a relationship.

Also, she'd said 'beo,' but still, he was angry. Angry and in desperate need of her attention.

"You can take shelter wherever you want," he muttered. She sighed and said nothing. And this felt wonderfully familiar. He decided not to push any further. A superb tactician always knew when to hold the charge and wait for the counteroffensive, even one who lacked confidence like he did. He said nothing more and waited for her.

An hour passed, and neither said anything. They merely sat in stony silence, watching the world and slowly freezing to death. Despite it all, it was the best either of them had felt in a good many days.

"The storm is getting worse," she said eventually, and edged herself closer to him.

"Please Lea, go get some sleep. I'll finish the watch alone," he said. He'd surrendered his anger and the foothold. So, too, were the intricacies of relationships.

"I'll stay here," she said quietly.

"With me?" he asked.

"With you," she said.

"I love you."

"Of course you do," she retorted, but he caught her smile before she hid it under the scarf around her neck. He suddenly wanted to kiss that neck. And her lips. And other things. Instead, he shuffled a little closer to her. She appeared to like this. He was skilled with females, after all.

"Please, trust me: there is nothing between Nomi and me," he whispered.

"I know, Erroh, and I trust you. It was never about that."

"What was it about, then?" he asked.

"She needed to understand her place in the world. She needed to understand *my* place in the world." He knew that tone. It was the tone she used right before she battered people to within an inch of their life.

"What can I do?" he asked carefully. He was wary of

angering her again. If she became angry, then he'd get angry. Then another week would pass. They could be dead by then.

"Do better, beo. Do better by me," she warned. It was a fair warning.

"I swear to you, beo," he promised. It was a good oath. She smiled and met his gaze.

"Let's go get some sleep," she suggested, laying her head upon his shoulder.

"Aye, maybe it's time," he admitted, and climbed to his feet. He could see her blue lips in the moonlight and wondered how cold he must look himself. It was a small matter. He would kiss the warmth right back into them. He was taking her to his bed tonight, regardless. Even if he did nothing more than hold her and warm the life back into her. Into them both. He took her hand and led her from the platform down to the ground below and, wrapping his cloak around them both, fought the crossing winds and silently walked her back to their home.

48

FINE WAYS TO EASE TEDIOUS TIMES

R oja laughed and inhaled the smoky substance deeply. She held her breath and her balance atop the beast and exhaled. A pleasingly sweet cloud of white smoke floated around her and she waved it away absently.

Go away, wonderful smoke.

It was a pleasant afternoon, and the company was pleasant. Emir the drunken, wretched healer was her pleasant companion on this ride today, and if truth be told, there was no one else she would rather share it with. Apart from little Linn. Her stomach clenched. Only for a moment, though. She didn't worry about things beyond her grasp as much as usual. Especially when smoking the weed. There was nothing she could do for Linn. The little one remained in Samara. She missed her terribly, even though their bond had barely blossomed. But separation from one so young and frightened was just a part of her culture. A way of life. Her chosen life. Even if life wanted no part of her. She passed the little wrapped bundle of burning weed across to Emir, who took it gladly.

"At least Mom and Dad are no longer fighting," he said

dreamily, and sucked the smoke into his lungs. Taking the weed wasn't at all different from drinking a fine few glasses of sine, but out here in the wastes, drinking for hours atop an unsteady steed was folly indeed. He gripped Highwind's reins as the beast walked carefully down a slope, and she followed, trusting her mount to carry her steadily.

They were following the river home after a long day out in the saddle, seeking phantom threats; there were worse ways to recover the spirit, she supposed. They'd journeyed farther east than was usual. That's what happened when enjoying the company of the ride, she also supposed.

"Aye, it's almost boring now," she agreed, sniggering and wavering in the saddle. No matter how she tried, she couldn't find full balance today. Most days, she would have cared how ridiculous she looked. Today she was perfectly happy rocking like a drunk all the way home.

"I enjoy boring," Emir said.

"Aye, boring."

Every monotonous day, the group separated into pairs and rode out into the wilds to look for signs of the Hunt and its demented leader. Riding for hours in one direction was bad for the soul, but there was little else to Erroh's plan. Was he wrong? Probably not, but that didn't lessen the frustration of a fruitless search. Roja's own hatred for their unseen enemy fell short of her companions', not that her instinct to strike out at the murderers didn't consume many of her waking thoughts.

Just where is the Hunt?

There were scatterings of them, she knew, the remnants of an army who had been given an undeserved victory. She knew there was more to come. Roja remembered the reports. Thousands more. Yet, no grand armada had reached their shores, stepped upon their territory, heralding the end of times.

At least not yet.

"Boring is nice. Boring is quiet," he added, offering the last drag of the medicinal herb. She declined with a dizzying shake of the head, and he flicked it into the streaming water below. There it met a tragic death, and she watched it flow down through the swift rapids and disappear in a haze of white-water rush.

She could have stared at those swift, flowing rapids all fuken day and been wonderfully entertained. She suddenly wished she'd stared at the Great Mother a little more while living in Samara. Wished she'd smoked a little more, too.

"Peaceful," she whispered, and he grunted in reply. She decided it was in agreement.

This was the farthest part of the river they'd ridden. Erroh and Lea had taken off at dawn along the opposite route, while Wynn and his former lover had lost themselves in the thick undergrowth of the less travelled paths. For a week, each of the Outcasts had ridden out with the same comrade. Roja was uncertain how effective her partnership with Emir might be should they come upon trouble, but it was a small matter. She stole another glance at him and thought him fetching atop a mount. One might even forget how wretched and hopeless he was.

I enjoy these times, Emir, she said, though she did not meet his gaze. And he did not meet hers. It took her a moment to realise she hadn't spoken aloud at all.

A fine wander altogether.

He brought Highwind forward, and she snorted in protest. This was not Master at all. She did not like his weight or his grip. It felt unnatural. He moved differently to Master, and she fought the urge to bolt. She liked few things in the world. Master was not one of those things, but Master's grip was at least assured and dominating. She liked this. Her ears pricked up, and she felt the gentle pull sideways from her rider, who was not Master. Far away, she heard them first. A terrible sound she'd heard before, when she had been separated from Master: the low rumble of a slow-moving beast. Was this her fate once more? Had Master left her again? She felt her anger, and she grunted her dissatisfaction. She did not like Master, but she preferred Master to this unsure rider.

"I'm not sure this beast likes me," muttered Emir, bringing the horse alongside Roja.

"Nonsense. She's magnificent. You should be grateful Erroh allowed you to ride her today." She leaned across and stroked the animal's mane. The horse appeared to mutter a curse under its breath.

"She dislikes you as much as she does me," Emir said with a laugh. She liked his dry, drunken humour. It did wonders for their mood. She felt herself sway again, and it was wonderful. Only her legs, clenched tightly against the beast's powerful ribs, kept her upright.

"I think Erroh has little love for her. Would you take the beast if he offered her to you? Better the least effective warrior gets the fastest mount, should the time come to flee. She is like lightning," she pointed out, then fell silent, listening to something in the air. Something low and heavy somewhere up beyond. Through the trees, over a few hills.

Probably nothing.

An insect flew by and distracted her, and she wondered why she could not fly like the buzzing little beast. It found a home in a bright red flower, and Roja tried to remember what had unsettled her a few smoky breaths before.

"I thought I heard something," Emir said, peering into the thick forest. His eyes were glazed over with the effects of the herb. It was a wonderful look to him. Maybe that was the herb taking effect for her, too.

"It was nothing," she whispered, and led them down across the fast-flowing rapids. The scream of water filled the air, further relaxing her. She wondered about dropping in and allowing the current to drag her downstream.

I'd ruin my dress. She stretched magnificently and allowed Emir to gaze drunkenly at her. It was harmless play, something to do among the hazy green and brown and the shimmering blue of the sky. Every day she found it easier to forget the cold grey of the city. Memories of her training returned, and she felt better than she had in an age. Fresh muscles had appeared where fleshy Primary skin had been before, and overall, her body ached less. Aye, her world had fallen apart, but she was enduring it.

Especially when he treated her to some healing.

She felt almost perfect. Her insomnia remained, and it embarrassed her. Ever since she was orphaned during the Faction Wars and delivered to the city in the hands of a legend, she had slept every night in silk, surrounded by four great humming walls. She no longer missed their humming drone or their shadows, but she could not sleep soundly without the comforting feeling of soft, smooth silk against her skin.

She'd confided in Emir of this matter, and he'd only half-heartedly mocked her. Perhaps in those words he'd seen an eventual end to putting her to bed every night and massaging the consciousness from her. There was only so much he could tolerate, she imagined.

Feeling shivers run down her spine, she stole a glance at his chiselled jawline and wondered if he'd allow her to stroke his chin just once. Nothing more, just a touch. Just something to keep her warm at night when he wasn't there to give her *real* shivers and put her to sleep. She was a mere Alphaline, after all. Perhaps she could…

She quickly slapped herself across the cheek. The sting immediately pulled her from her daydreaming, and she brought her beast forward forcefully. It was time to put juvenile cravings away for this afternoon.

He fell behind, lost in his own dim-witted musings, and she ducked under a low-hanging branch leading into a clustered area of the forest. Without the constant growl of the river or the distracting flutters of insects, she heard it clearly.

Not the wind at all.

A low tremor of movement caused by a thousand pairs of boots. A thousand suits of rattling marching armour and a thousand low voices as they marched unawares. She knew it was the Hunt. They couldn't be far away.

I need my mind.

Behind her, she saw Emir slow his mount to listen. They were no more than a valley or two away. She was certain of it. All she could see was the darkness of the trees, heavy in green and brown, broken up in scattered places by thin rays of stubborn sunlight. Carefully, she brought her mount forward.

Oh, fuk, fuk, fuk.

She felt the bile climb in her throat and she fought a retch. Best not make any noise, she thought. Best clear the stupor, too. Her hands shook, and she wondered could Emir hear her heart beating from here. She took a few breaths and allowed the horse to carry her farther in towards the noise's source.

"It's them; it has to be," growled Emir from behind her,

causing her to jump. There was strength in his voice. A
strength earned through bitterness and heartbreak, no doubt.
He brought his beast alongside hers. His eyes were clear and
sharp. He looked less the kind and troubled healer she knew
well, and more like a cold and experienced walker of the
wastes. He looked like a killer. She shouldn't have found this
alluring. But it really was.

Wake up, girl.

He dropped from his beast and tied the reins to a branch
in one swift movement, and she followed suit. Her mind was
betraying her. She knew the shrewder manoeuvre was in
scurrying away without being seen, yet setting eyes upon the
brutes was too powerful a lure. She took a deep, controlled
breath and gripped the pommel of her sword at her waist.
Emir had already slipped an arrow into his crossbow and
loaded it.

"Just in case," he said. He sounded delirious, yet assured
of himself.

"Aye," she whispered in agreement.

*Just in fuken case we stumble drunkenly into their waiting
arms.*

They said nothing for a time. Despite the terror, there
were thrills to the hunt. Moving smoothly through the thick
undergrowth, they sought an invading army, and they did so
as though they'd hunted their entire lives.

She believed her steps were smooth and silent, and
perhaps they were. Perhaps this herb had gifted her skills
beyond her usual capabilities. Perhaps this was a dream, and
she was asleep in the saddle.

So wonderfully tired.

Those they hunted were in transit, she knew, and with
Emir at her heel, she marched through the evergreen of forest,
over rough muddy terrain, passing along inclining and

declining slopes, always listening, always nearing this rumbling wall of sound.

She was Alpha. Hear her silent roar.

He was healer. See his discreet stagger.

She led, and he kept in step with her, his eyes blinking as little as possible, his head moving slightly from side to side. Searching for anything. She admired this greatly.

What have I become that he affects me so easily?

Finally, they passed through one last covering treeline and saw the long, trailing march of an exhausted finger of the Hunt on the other side of the river.

Oh, fukety fuk me.

They dropped to the ground and dug into the mossy soil. Holding their breaths, they watched the rear line of six southern brutes following the deepening river north. Her eyes scanned the rest of the rows at march and, absently, she began counting, but there were too many. Great, massive carts trundled past. Their low, rumbling groan reverberated through her stomach. She had been craving food before, but now she fought the urge to hold her breakfast down.

Emir was tucked in against her, all low and concealed. "There are enough of the fuks," he whispered uneasily. It was a fine point. His eyes burned with hatred. Some fear too.

"They're walking with the river," she whispered, and her voice caught in her throat.

So many.

Too many.

"A lot of breaks in the river between here and Raven Rock," Emir said, reaching into his pocket. He watched the trailing line of savages as they led their livestock along behind the leading pack of foot soldiers. There were hundreds. "They'll continue on towards Samara." He pulled a little sealed bottle from his pocket.

"We need to get ahead of them and warn the rest, just in case," Roja said, studying the terrifying Riders as they brought their horses alongside the carts. Each Rider sent a special shiver of fear down her spine. What numbers could stand against them? She knew of fewer things more intimidating than seeing a group of them charge down their prey upon the battlefield.

She watched them from the relative safety of their hiding place for a few moments more, until a horrific smell filled the air. She shot a glance at Emir and his bottle. As good a time for drunkenness as any, she supposed. Then she realised Emir held one of his bolts, and he was giving it a drink.

"It might not hurt to lead them a merry chase, though," he muttered, climbing to his feet and rubbing the dark, emerald-green liquid along the tip of the crossbow bolt with a grubby rag. He wiped the rag along a second tip, then a third. Then the rest. And then he stepped out into the cold light of day. She couldn't help noticing the fear in his beautiful eyes wither away as he stood defiant. She thought she heard him utter the female's name under his breath as he walked to the edge of the river, raising his crossbow.

Who is stupid enough to challenge an entire army to a fight?

She watched in her stupor and dug her fingers into the ground as Emir went to war without her.

Magnus still held the recipe to the vilest potion in the land. As would Erroh, if he took a moment while lamenting his friend's death to read through his notebook. It would be a terrible legacy to leave behind.

Poison.

Emir was about to commit some dreadful sins. He

intended cruelty on this dizzying day. He gazed at the running water, some thirty feet across, and took hopeful pleasure in its inky darkness. It was quick moving, deep and constant. No Rider would be best pleased to charge recklessly into it—or so he hoped.

"I earn my place in hell. I'm sorry, Aireys."

Shaking his head a couple of times to lose the wonderful dizziness, he held his breath, exhaled as he pulled the trigger, and struck an unsuspecting Rider in the back. He heard the distant thump of metal piercing through leather into flesh. Not deep. Wouldn't matter, though; it was a fitting first strike. A scream erupted, and he looked back to ensure Roja hadn't moved. She had not. This pleased him. She wouldn't be needed for this part. No one would.

Just me and my immoral experiments.

The Rider fell from his horse, snapping the bolt loudly, and he screamed again. His startled comrades turned and reached for their swords, raised their shields and sought the roving army attacking from behind. A few noticed the unimpressive wretch with his crossbow across the river. Fewer noticed him lazily reload the weapon and take aim once more. They gathered up in alarm to gaze upon their attacker as their brethren ahead continued their march, blissfully unaware they were engaged in battle.

He fired once more and struck a soldier in the shoulder. He was no skilled crossbowman, it would appear, but still a pleasing second scream of agony filled the air. The soldiers stood dumb for a moment, seeing one solitary foe with the audacity to bring the fight to them. Perhaps they had not learned the history of the fallen.

I'd love some honey bread right now.

Exhaling again and fighting the bleariness, Emir dropped to one knee, removing another terrible-smelling bolt from his quiver and fired into the mass of death standing on the other side of the river.

That's right, fukers. It's just me.

And I'm winning.

The bolt buried itself in a soldier's throat. The unfortunate warrior yelped silently and struggled to pull the arrow away as she fell to the ground. He imagined she died, but the brutes finally went to war now and blocked his view.

"All hail the Puk!" he roared, sending one more bolt into the gathering of charging, outraged Hunt. They dashed to the edge of the river and then halted, unsure of what to do, so he fired again and somehow sent a bolt through the arm of another.

You marched all this way to die so unexpectedly.

Finally, a Rider charged into the river, and this stirred Roja to move. She leapt from the dirt and charged through the treeline with sword raised. If any Rider dared attack Emir, they would meet her steel and die in blood. It was a simple plan. It would never work.

The Rider's horse stumbled in the sudden pull of the water. It reared and swayed, and the man fell into the icy river. Unable to right himself in the current's pull and his heavy armour, the Rider struggled and fought for breath and then fell still and sank forever.

Roja watched this as though the world had slowed to nothing. She stood with Emir as another two Riders ignored their comrade's fatal fall and charged in, sending plunging waves of water high in the air.

They drove their mounts on, screaming their hatred and guttural warnings of vengeance. Roja stood along the edge of the river and waited eagerly. She'd wondered how she would be in war, but this felt oddly calming, as though all her former masters had been right about her potential for prowess in battle. She thought of Dia and offered a prayer to her grandmother.

Let me be a fine killer.

Ahead of the march, the Hunt reacted far too slowly to the rear assault. Watching their cumbersome, confusing turn far ahead was as beautiful as watching a rainbow while smoking herbs in the saddle. They were tired, they were confident; they carried their faith in a false god.

"Come at me!" Roja roared, as the first Rider forded the river and struggled up the bank towards her, and although he raised his hammer to smash her skull, her speed caught him off guard. She thrust the tip of her blade right through his wrist with terrifying quickness, and he dropped the hammer and fell screaming from his charging mount. He never recovered. Smoothly, she dragged her blade across his neck before kicking him back into the water, where he struggled for a breath and then nothing. And she was a killer.

This feels right.

And fuken terrible.

Her mind discovered a cold clarity. She remembered every lesson with her masters, every suggestion of technique, every criticism for tells in her form. Her mind reeled, thinking of skirmishes with her new comrades, and she gripped her blade. She wanted to flee. She wanted to live through this. Mostly, she wanted to stand with Emir and kill them all.

The second Rider drove his beast out of the river and pulled his blade free of its scabbard. Without taking a breath, she struck out at him with her spinning blade. It was a strange thing to hear a blade pierce flesh. A bolt whizzed past the Rider's dying face and struck down a warrior behind him, and she grinned. They had taken the fight to the Hunt, and it was so easy.

Beyond, she caught sight of a gathering of crossbow wielders preparing, and it pulled her back to sobriety. She heard orders barked out in unfamiliar tones, and she knew the moment of surprise was behind them now.

What am I doing here?

The crossbow wielders were slow in their actions, however, and she took a few steps back from the edge. It was about to take a terrible turn. This, she knew. Like striking a wasps' nest, they'd just invited the curs to swarm. Another Rider reached the edge of the river. He managed a few feet before she clashed blades with him and dealt him a terrible blow. It was easy. Her instincts and superior speed met each of his blows. "We have to go," she screamed at Emir, as she disarmed the Rider and sliced deep into his flesh.

"Just a few more."

The Rider fell at her feet, blood streaming from him. He was dying, and she watched with relish.

They were animals.

So was she.

That was okay.

Her victim reached for his sword in the grass, but she swiped it away and spun around behind him, laying her blade against his neck. Standing behind him, she faced the Hunt and fought her panic.

A terrible anger took her, as it had with Emir. They had come to her land and deprived it of hope. If she were the last Alphaline to stand against their tide of death, she would cut into them until she could no longer swing her blades.

She knocked the helmet from her victim and gripped his hair tightly.

Let them see.

She could hear his grunts of fear and agony. She could hear their braying, disbelieving cries. And she heard her heart again. It hammered wildly and out of time. She felt adrenaline course through her body. She stared upon the charging southerners. Those few who could fire crossbows struggled with their weapons; those who rode terrifying horses struggled with the treacherous crossing, and she thought it was an impressive sight of confusion.

"Look," she demanded, and the Riders did so. She felt Emir step up beside her, his casual manner slowly giving way to terror as he realised his actions. He was so brave, and she loved him.

She slid the sword through the back of her victim's head, holding him upright as he shuddered wildly. There was fresh screaming, and she took each note as a divine piece of music. She pushed again and felt the bone hold against her murderous intent. Mostly she heard the screaming. And so did the Hunt. She pushed one last time, and the sword pierced through, and the screaming intensified and then fell to a terrible silence. She held her sword aloft, the dead man drooping lifelessly from the tip. His useless blood flowed down the blade and warmed her hands.

"Now, it's time to go," shouted Emir, as a volley of bolts flew across and embedded themselves in the ground, in the trees, and in a dead man. She pulled the sword free and kicked the body away in disgust, then screamed in triumph and vengeful rage. A terrible roar of warning to all who would dare to follow. And then her man pulled her from the battlefield and back into the unending forest.

Where things took a terrible turn.

49

CARRY US TO SAFETY, HIGHWIND

I *feel alive. I feel like dying.* Perfect strides. Each step taken with careful swiftness and complete panic. Roja could hear his gasps as he struggled to keep up. Oh, he tried, but she pulled away from him easily. Leaves and branches slapped her face; briars and bushes tore at her dress through to her skin as she frantically led their pursuers through the endless woods. She glided through the green while he fought against his own clumsiness, his heavy boots catching in tree roots, shrubbery and other such obstacles with every step, as they both took part in a terrifying race.

They fought their way through the clustered green, and the wind carried the sound of the aggrieved Riders far behind them, struggling to charge through the clawing, disruptive, protective branches of forest. If they made it to the horses, they'd survive. Out in the open, their northern mounts could outrun the southern warring beasts, she knew. She held this thought in her mind, repeating it every few steps to bolster her courage.

"We could hide," gasped Emir. It was a fine, desperate

plan, and it might just keep them alive if their pursuers were not able trackers.

"No, it has not come to this," she hissed, though her aching lungs argued differently. From behind them, the sudden snapping crack of stubborn undergrowth giving way filled the air as the Riders relinquished caution in favour of desperate pursuit. Slipping under a low-hanging branch, she forced herself to run faster, despite the screaming in her aching limbs. Knowing the route was more difficult for their pursuers kept her encouraged; kept her pushing.

Our mounts will outrun theirs.

Time stood still as they sprinted. Nothing mattered but the desperate retreat, and somehow, Emir stayed within reaching distance of her. She fought agony, despair and terror until, up ahead, she caught sight of their prize.

"Come on," she screamed, snapping through the treeline into the open green, where she almost fell at the hooves of their calmly grazing mounts. She'd never seen a more beautiful sight, and she gave thanks to the absent gods.

Emir appeared a few moments later, looking a ruin. Gasping and hacking, he dropped to his knees and caught his breath. Distantly, she heard their pursuers.

With shaking hands, she tried to untie the knot holding her beast in place. Both horses shuffled irritably. They knew something was amiss. Perhaps it was the scent of blood covering her gown; perhaps it was the invisible roar from within the shaded forest. Highwind cried out in fear and pulled against the ropes. It was time to leave, to escape.

"Calm down, you bitch," hissed Emir through clenched teeth. He yanked the reins and stared into Highwind's eyes. A subtle warning and nothing more. He'd killed enough today. He patted the beast and untied the knot with his other hand as carefully as he could. The Hunt were still coming. Carelessness would not serve them. He was calm despite his terror. The beast dared to rear, but he grabbed at her mane as a second warning. It settled but appeared to seethe in silence.

Beside him, Roja undid her knot at last and clambered atop the horse.

Without warning, Highwind broke away from Emir's grasp. He tried to grab her, but she broke away from his reach.

"No!"

As a parting gift, the magnificent black mare turned and snapped at her rider, nastily biting his shoulder before turning tail and storming away from them.

"Oh, fuk you," he screamed. The Riders roar grew ever closer; they were just a slope or so away now. "Oh… fuk… you," he cried again, and knew his doom. He felt the panic take him then. Felt it clasp hold and grab his insides like a vice. He wanted to run, to hide, to find another fuken horse and flee with his Roja from this terrible moment. Still, despite the horror of his unfortunate circumstances, he regretted nothing but being denied some further killing. A miserable end to a wretched life. He tipped the little sealed bottle in his pocket absently.

I'll kill a few more.

Roja watched the beast race off into nowhere. It was all she could do. She could never catch it atop her own, and were she even able to do that, by the time she returned to Emir, the Hunt would have slain him. Her mount wouldn't carry them both very far either. It was quite simple, really. They were finished.

He is finished, and I am a killer.

"Go, Roja. Get word to the rest," he screamed, climbing to his feet and running from the clearing, all the while loading his crossbow. His voice broke with fright and her heart broke for him. For them both. His weapon shook as he aimed at the oncoming killers, still hidden within the forest. She wanted to leap from her mount, drop and stand with him and face the impossible odds together.

Do it, killer.

"Leave me," he cried, turning away. "I brought this upon us." She knew he had. Fuk her, but she knew this was his fault. The thunder of the Hunt filled their ears, and there was nothing they could do. He ran from her and she screamed. He did not run far, but she saw his plan, flawed as it was. There was a mound of rocks gathered together, all tight and secure beside a steep slope on the far side of the dell. It was only ten feet across and the same in height; a fool with a crossbow might climb among them and earn protection for a few moments longer than they would in the open. She understood now that Emir aimed to kill a few more before he died, and she was a killer and she was in love and none of this was fair.

Stay with him.

He ran in the opposite direction to where Highwind had galloped off. She watched him go, and she loved him, and she had to leave him behind.

Don't do this.

With tears in her eyes, she galloped off after the rogue mount. Unable to offer words. Unable to proclaim her love. Unable to stop this moment so they might spend a thousand more wrapped up in each other's arms. Unable to do anything but turn away from her companion, her lover, her magnificent disaster.

I'm sorry, Emir. I really am.

Her horse sped up, carried her away from threat. Distantly, she could see Highwind galloping along the path, leaving a cloud of dust in her wake. Her own mount matched the pace, and she slapped the beast fiercely, leaned forward and slid her leg over.

Faster.

She only needed to ride a few breaths more, and she'd be clear. *There.* She slipped gracefully from the saddle and dropped smoothly. In the same movement, she slapped the beast a second time as it left her behind, and the horse, liberated from her weight, took off at great speed after Highwind, leaving an impressive trail of dust behind it.

Fuk, fuk, fuk.

She sprinted back to Emir. It was all she could do. She could hear the Hunt coming closer, ever closer, and she wailed with the torment.

Save him.

Emir turned, surprised, and began jogging towards her, his eyes alight. Each plodding step they took seemed slow as death closed in around them. They met along the slope and never stopped running. As they tumbled together down the incline, they embraced as the world spun wildly around them. Holding each other, they rolled and bounced and then crashed at the bottom.

He lay dazed, gasping, but she never allowed him the luxury of catching his breath. There simply wasn't the time. Climbing to her feet, she managed another few feet before she spied salvation. It was a bush. It was a very fine bush, because it was the only bush within sprinting distance in which to conceal themselves. She hauled Emir to his feet, dragged him wheezing behind her and then shoved him into thick green leaves and clusters of prickly stems and dove in a breath after.

She climbed over him and then turned to get a better view of their pursuers. Holding her breath, she strained her eyes until they hurt. She watched and waited and listened to the sound of very bad things as they neared their quarry. So near. So terrifyingly near.

"Don't make a fuken noise," she whispered.

"You should have fled." He lay below her, pushing her flowing hair out of his eyes.

"Whisht, idiot."

She folded her arms upon his chest and rested her head on them. Above, she heard the cracking of branches as the first Rider broke through the treeline, and she imagined Emir standing atop a gathering of rocks, bringing the fight to them in the last few moments of his life. This is better, she told herself as the trampling slowed to a rumbling, as the Riders formed up and sought their attackers.

Please don't look at the shaking bush beneath your noses.

She waited for death as their bobbing heads went to task, seeking tracks.

Look for dust. Look for the fuken dust.

Aggrieved voices filled the air, and her quaking body went deathly still. Her fingers dropped to her weapon's grip, and she planned attacks in her mind. She would take six if good fortune favoured her. Aye, six would be a fine tally before the end.

Mercifully, the Riders took off again. The ground shuddered, and then they were gone, out through another break in the trees in pursuit of a prize unattainable.

She let out her breath and took this as a gift from the absent gods.

It was.

"Wynn would be disgusted with their tracking skills," she hissed as the thundering faded away. And soon enough, the two companions were alone again, with nothing but the echo of Riders and the distant screaming of dying foes.

Emir took her lead and lay in the dirt, breathing as quietly as possible. After a time, he eased her weight from him, and she allowed him.

"Well, that was… anticlimactic. However, I am glad to still be alive," he said, staring up through the canopy of green.

"You should have told me your plan." She hadn't meant to sound as cutting, but there it was.

"I wasn't really thinking. I blame the herbs," he said, reaching out and running his fingers down her face. He showed her the blood on the tips of them. "An interesting look," he whispered.

My victim's gift. She didn't mind how much blood covered her. She would bathe it away later, if she desired. It was a small matter to wear their stain. She'd been stained with blood before. This was better. She nodded thoughtfully and returned to watching the world for movement. She wanted to move, too, but all adrenalin left her. Her body was content to lie here, in a bush in the middle of the wastes, and just wait and hope.

"You should have told me you would not need your horse," he said, and she shrugged. He was indebted to her now. It was the least she could have done, though, having placed him in chains and had a hand in condemning him to death.

Think nothing of it, Emir.

"Because I could have taken it," he muttered under his breath. She rolled her eyes and cursed him quietly, though she knew he was trying to ease the tension. "I'd be halfway home by now."

She laughed, and this appeared to please him.

They lay there a while longer to ensure no further southerners came searching for them. Strangely, the screams in the distance never let up. They echoed through the hills, carried in the wind, and they had a terrible sound, like the screams of a beast in the greatest torment ever known.

He flinched every time a fresh bout of wailing erupted. Perhaps it was one thing to kill and move on, but listening to the afflicted was a torment for a healer like him. Still, though, this was war. Such things were sure to occur. Roja, for her part, didn't appear to mind their anguish at all.

After a time, Roja finally climbed to her feet and beckoned him to follow. This he did with great skill, and they crossed the clearing swiftly to follow the path taken by the mounts. It was possible that, when the beasts finally tired, they would stop to graze. Monitoring the path ahead, they slipped briskly through the cover of the trees and escaped the hostile ground as though they'd never even been there.

They walked for hours in silence, listening for threats and finding none. They took turns leading each other through the forest; they worked well as companions of the road, each smoothly matching the other's steps as though they were lovers moving in perfect rhythm.

Eventually, as the miles passed, she felt a hollow wretchedness take over, as though someone had cut a sliver free from her soul and left her just a little less than before. With it came a terrible sadness for her deeds. She remembered the violence now with a clearer head, without adrenaline and fear and excitement guiding her every move.

After a while, it became too much. "How do you kill so easily?" she asked. She was tired, her body ached, and she'd never known hunger like this. Killing gave one quite the appetite, it would appear.

He didn't answer her question. "You scared the fuk out of me," he said, moving up beside her. His steps were more assured than before. His head was no longer bowed, and his eyes were sharper than normal.

He saw that her face was pale. Her eyes were lost, too. He'd seen that look before, when he'd knelt over a torn-up body. He thought hard for an answer to appease her, strong words to help her through the suffering of having murdered—of becoming a murderer, for this was what he considered himself to be. Ever since he'd taken his first life out on the road, he'd thought of himself as such.

"It's easier when they deserve it," he replied at last. It was the same fine, predictable answer given by every warrior who ever lived when questioned about their bloodlust.

"Aye, they did," she agreed, and he wanted to hold her and take the pain away. To boast that he had thicker skin than she did. Insist that she'd learn this talent too. He wanted to lie and take away the desolation she felt. That's what companions did, when horrors were too much.

He chose truth, instead.

She deserved truth today.

"Let's rest for a time, Roja," he whispered, halting her relentless walk by gently taking her hand and leading her to sit down with him against a fallen log covered in ivy and time. The forest was quiet as night set in, and after many hours, Emir at last felt safe. She sat and nestled against him.

"That was not war. I was wild, and what I did to that Rider was unforgivable," she whispered, looking at her dress, finally acknowledging the ruin it had become.

"It was nothing special," he said, and kissed her tainted hands.

"I am not a good person." Many times in the past, he would have agreed. Now, though, he chose truth instead.

"You are one of the finest people I've ever met," he said, staring into her eyes. He wanted her. Actually, every moment he'd known her, he'd wanted her. In this moment, at her lowest, she reminded him of how much he wanted her. Loved her. As much as someone he had loved before.

"I am the queen bitch of the city."

"And what a fine bitch you were, leading and protecting until you weren't enough of a bitch to stay in power." He smiled, and she ran her fingers absently along his chin, momentarily lost in thought. It was a fine reply.

"How many have died for my actions, though?" she said, and her voice broke.

"Not as many as could have." He was determined to win this battle of words.

"Dia and I disagreed on many things. I live with the consequences."

"What do you mean?"

She gasped and caught her breath, her eyes wide. "I mean so many things, Emir. So many things." She shook a few times, and he did not pry further. Sometimes it was wise to say the needful things. Sometimes it was better to let the wanderer reach the path by their own step.

She got there.

"The town of Raven Rock should never have fallen, never should have stood alone," she cried, and tears slipped from her eyes.

"And we made some of their foes pay for it today," he said, embracing her and resting his forehead against hers. But she wasn't with him. She was distant, lost in thought. He could only wait for her. She said nothing for a while, merely struggling to breathe and understand whatever grief she suffered, and he was patient. He knew the steps would be taken painfully, but they would be taken. And though he realised comforting words offered little, in time the truth would serve her better.

He took a breath and kissed her forehead. "Your sins are nothing to my deeds," he said, wondering how sharply she might judge him. "The ambush was fair, but this was my true crime," he said, reaching down and showing her the little bottle.

"What is it?"

"The screams we heard will last days. Most of my strikes were not fatal, but the poison I placed on each bolt will be fatal, eventually." She looked at him curiously. "It'll turn their blood to fire, and they will scream for every fuken moment until it is over. Each warrior will burn up from the inside tonight, and then the real suffering will begin."

She was horrified and intrigued. She allowed him to continue. And he did, and it was shameful. "There will be no worse death for those I struck down, today. Any man, woman or child struck with this terrible creation will know torment like no other," he said.

"How did you come upon this mixture?" she asked.

"There is certainly no eucalyptus within," he whispered, and this time it was his voice that broke. "I know of so many medicines, it hurts my head. So many afflictions and their awful symptoms run through my mind even as I sleep. Sometimes, though, when seeking elixirs, terrible mistakes are made."

"That's why you left Spark City?"

"How did you know?"

"You were missed."

He didn't know what she meant, but he did not push the matter. He was too busy struggling with the knowledge of his victims' fate. "Aye. I made that vile tonic and left Samara as a foolish child seeking redemption, hiding from my sins."

She drew away from him. "Why carry this tonic with you all these years?"

"I brewed it freshly."

"Why?"

He thought miserably of the gifts he had brought to this world. How Magnus had intended to make fine work of this vile serum. He quoted the big man himself now. "The world is ending. A wave of death is seeking to pull us under. What if every strike still claims lives, still takes the fight from those tending to their dying? Gives them fuken reason to fear when going into battle?"

"You think we should lace each arrow with a drop of your poison?" she asked.

"And every sword," he added, and despised himself.

"So, every strike will inevitably be fatal," she said thoughtfully. He looked at her uneasily. Magnus had worn that same expression when Emir had foolishly told him of his sins.

"Aye. It seems fair." It wasn't fair at all.

"You are a monster, just like me," she said, drawing away from him. She stood and began to walk back towards their home. It was only a few miles through darkness. Her back was straighter, and he wondered if he hadn't finally said the right words. He could take being a monster.

"No, your cruelty is nothing to mine," he said, shrugging, and got to his feet to follow her.

———

They continued their trek through the forest with only their wits and the dim light of the shattered moon to guide them. Emir took the lead, and she followed closely behind, glancing at his rear every few steps. It was something distracting. The brutal act of killing and the fear of death had stirred something in her. A strange type of want. An unusual need to procreate. All manner of interesting things.

"I thought about Aireys's face before I took the first shot, and each one after that," he said, hopping over a small stream and taking her hand as she followed gracefully. He said it casually enough. "Maybe, if it helps, think about Dia next time," he said, turning away from her. There would always be death between them. He was just reminding her of this tragic point.

After a few more steps closer to home, she smiled. "I will, Emir. Thank you."

My beo.

50

THE LONG DARK

"It will be a long night," said Lea, and shrugged, as though it were a small matter. As though the possibility of attack was nothing to fear. Perhaps it wasn't, thought Erroh. Perhaps Uden the Woodin Man was about to march in through the gates tonight and engage them in combat once more. Perhaps they would end the war this very night. She kept her eyes upon the gate, her body taut and ready.

It would be a long night.

"Aye," agreed Erroh, feigning a smile. He wasn't sure how to behave as Master General. He certainly knew not to share his true feelings. Behave as Lea does, he told himself. It was fine advice. He could feel their eager and terrified eyes on him as the exhausted Emir continued his telling of the day's events. All the while, a thin sheen of perspiration formed up on Erroh's body. They didn't need to know that, either.

Roja was as exhausted as Emir. She was stained with blood and mud, her tangled hair was ruined, her face was a deathly pale and her dress was shredded. She shook whenever Emir spoke of their misdeeds. She added little to his words, merely nodding in agreement with some points he made. Still, though, underneath it all, he wondered whether an elite Alphaline was struggling to tear itself free. Or else the queen bitch with her sheltered upbringing was nearing the breaking point.

"You did well, both of you," Erroh said, once Emir's telling of the Highwind saga reached its end. Erroh's face burned with embarrassment. So much for finding her a new owner. Allowing Emir to take the animal out had been unwise, and its behaviour had been disgraceful. He'd let his friend down. He'd let two generals down. That was unforgivable. "I'm sorry about my mount."

Wynn, for his part, thought Emir's misfortune was a marvellous thing. He started laughing, and soon after, Lexi joined him. Even Lillium smiled as she continued sharpening her sword. Like Lea, she kept one eye on the locked gate, an eager expression on her face.

Emir seemed to rally as the audience laughed, and with some encouragement he retold the funnier parts of the tale once more, though with more humour and greater embellishment. When finished, he pointed down towards the stables, where the mount in question was busy grazing. "I will have my revenge," he concluded, grinning. Strangely, he wasn't drinking this evening, and Erroh approved. Easier to be brave with liquid fire running through one's veins. Easier to fuk up when inebriated, too.

"I fuken hate that animal," he muttered.

The beast in question wasn't listening. She was grazing on fresh oats from Master, given to her as a reward for her run. She drank some water from the stable trough and savoured the exhilaration of the day. There had been terrible noise. Her rider had not taken heed, so she had taken care of herself. Sometimes she knew best. She knew Master was happy that she'd led the other horse home with her. There had been a desire for freedom as the miles disappeared under her charge, but in the end, she would always run to Master. Until he didn't need her anymore.

"Will they hunt us?" Lea asked Nomi, who had taken over stirring the brew. The girl was adding more salt than needed, though more salt was always welcome when stirring such a brew. That, and adding every possible herb to the mix in the faint hope of making the vegetable meal edible. That said, these past few days Nomi had improved the mix considerably. Who knew plants could be so tasty? Nomi would have loved some boar to drop in, but the beasts were scarce. A strange thing indeed. She added few more flakes of mint, rolling them a few times in her hand to release the flavours. She rarely added mint to a stew; she preferred it with a little sine. Still, since there was nothing else to do here, she would experiment. Just like Emir experimented with his terrifying poisons.

"Perhaps they will come," she said. "If Nomi's… my finger, I search. But, close to city now. Difficult find in woods, Lea." Truthfully, she was terrified. Something always terrified her. Did she believe the Hunt would seek them out this night? No, not really, but who knew how enraged they might become once they learned of Emir's potions?

What if they come seeking him out?

"Well, the spy thinks we are fine," Emir jested. He winked, and she knew he meant no offence. She was learning the art of camaraderie, the mocking between comrades, and it was delightful. Someday she might make the right jest and not cause Lea to roll her eyes. Lea tried to hide the disdain more these days, but Nomi saw it easily enough.

It was a small matter.

She took a few leaves of a different sweet-smelling herb from her little pouch and tore at them absently before dropping them into the pot and stirring. She tried to remember the name. Lea knew it. It was a tough word to remember, and precarious if overused in any meal. *Tearigan?* Three leaves, just enough.

The aroma filled the air, and her mouth watered. Tipping the pot carefully, she poured the contents into two little bowls and passed them to the killers of her people. It was only fitting she offer them gifts. Neither thanked her. She didn't expect them to, either. Their thoughts were elsewhere.

"Regardless of them hunting us, we can still hunt them just fine," Erroh declared, and this made him feel a little better. Sometimes, lying to oneself made everything better. *Sometimes.* He stood up from the warmth and hoped they couldn't see his shaking hands. He scratched his arm absently. "We will hunt them come dawn. Tonight, though, we take turns watching the walls for attack. We do not drink. Those who need rest, sleep ready by the flames." He looked around the fire at his weary, wary comrades. "Master of the Tunnel, I hope you've ensured a smooth retreat, should we need it."

"I'll climb down and light the torches," Wynn said.

"I think it best we remain without light tonight," Lea said, and Roja went to task shutting the rolling generators down.

They watched the wastes for what remained of the dark as it turned to day. Walking in pairs along the walls, they monitored the darkness beyond. Erroh walked with Roja, for he noticed how unsettled she was. Had he known her better, he might have offered comfort. As it was, he hoped his silent, reassuring strength was enough to help her with her melancholy.

Only Wynn challenged his orders. And truthfully, his wasn't the worst suggestion. Choosing daring over concealment, he requested to patrol the town's perimeter, and though Erroh was unhappy about separating a fierce fighter from the ranks, he trusted his general.

Strapping his bow to his back and a solitary blade around his waist, Wynn tied his boots and lost himself in the lonely, darkened world. Running swiftly, calling upon his lifetime of training, he mounted a solitary defence of the town. He ran a mile deep into the dark forest, then circled back and completed a full lap of their territory, searching for signs of marauding killers. When his search bore no fruit, he took to a knee and caught a breath before rising and venturing a little further in. Again and again, he ran into the night, searching for something. Anything. He found nothing.

He continued to do this as the hours passed. Relief surged through him every time he completed a lap and the moon had moved a little further across the night sky. He found it easier in the dark. Comforting. Not once did he allow the smothering panic to rise to the top. He wondered, would his father be proud of him? Did he care?

At dawn, he jogged one last time around the edge of the town before wearily returning to Raven Rock. Exhaustion weighed him down and the early glare of the sun burned his eyes, but discomfort aside, it had been a night well spent. They opened the gates wide in honour of his glorious return, and he joined the rest of his friends by the fire as they prepared for the Hunt ahead.

All he received from Erroh for his exertions was a casual pat on the back as he walked by. It was greatly appreciated.

Perhaps it was the lack of sleep that distracted them so, or uneasy thoughts of the day ahead. They sat around the fire in the early light of dawn, forcing boiled and salted oats down their throats. Conversation was muted. Surviving the night was one thing; riding into the wastes to set eyes upon the marching group was another thing entirely.

Erroh spooned porridge into his mouth and tried his best to savour the flavour, despite his lack of appetite. The first law of war was never fighting on an empty stomach. The second was running away when the odds favoured the opponent. With exhaustion as his waking companion, it took him a moment to recognise the familiar sound of hooves on the tracks outside the opened front gate.

Erroh swallowed the oat mixture and closed his tired eyes for a few moments. When he opened them, he felt drowsier. He could have slept for an hour or two, but his heart hadn't stopped pumping wildly all night.

No other companion had rested, either. He imagined they were probably feeling the same uneasiness. He shrugged absently and shook the sleepiness from his mind. He climbed to his feet just as they all heard the gentle hoof beats.

"They're here," Lillium cried, reaching for her bow. As one, the rest of the gathering sprang to their feet, frantically gripping weapons and whatever armour was at hand. Curses and panicked cries filled the air, and the casual clip-clopping sound of riders came ever closer.

"Line the wall," Erroh cried, running towards the front

gates to close them back down. He dared a look across as Lea scrambled to the top of the wall, notching an arrow as she did. "Close the gates behind us," he cried, and then Lillium was beside him, ready for battle. Charging out through the gates, he leapt out onto the tracks to meet the charge of their invaders, hoping for only a dozen. Roja followed close behind on his left flank, fear in her eyes but steel in her grimace. Wynn was but a few steps behind her. They were four Alphas armed with shimmering silver swords, facing unknown odds. It was a fine, irresponsible way to start an incredibly long day.

And then the four drew to a halt, lowering their weapons in relief and surprise. Riding casually towards Raven Rock was not the Hunt, but familiar wanderers of the road.

"Calm yourselves. I bring gifts," roared Wrek cheerfully from atop his horse, laughing at the overreaction to friendly reinforcements. He held his hands out in the most disarming gesture he could muster.

51

CLOAKED ENLISTMENT

Celeste wore a gold and white dress, and she wore it well. It matched her brown hair, though it shouldn't have. Doran noticed these things rarely, but this evening, he was perceptive. He remembered her. He wished another had come instead. He was in no mood for awkwardness.

The things I do for the cause.

She played with her hair absently, and her movements hypnotised him. Each tug of a curl sent slight tingles up his spine and into his mind. He couldn't help staring; couldn't stop, either. She'd behaved similarly in their first meeting. He'd said enough to lose her attention that day. He still felt bad about it. Felt bad about what he'd missed out on. Still, though.

Queen bitches of the city with their archaic beliefs.

He liked her chin; it was strong. Such things were underrated, but it was something he appreciated in females. *Well done, Celeste.* Apart from a fine chin, she had an even finer body. A little bit petite, but perfect for him. And the eyes. Oh, the eyes were alluring. They danced like diamond stars in the sky at night.

Did I just think that?

He smiled at his lack of poetry but hid his mouth in his hands. She wasn't really looking at him, anyway. And not enjoying his leering, either.

You liked me once, girl.

She sat opposite him at the grubby tavern table, staring distantly, playing wonderfully with her long brown hair, and she enchanted him.

Please, beautiful goddess, stop the fidgeting soon before I lose my mind.

Patrons packed the inn, yet Alphalines rarely struggled to find a seat. Certainly, none as imposing as Doran or as intriguing as Celeste. Or as impressive as their third companion. A quick glare was usually enough to clear the room. Besides, they knew him well here. He'd caused quite a few disturbances in the walls of this smoke-stained room during the few times he'd visited Samara over the years. It was better to lash out at the lowerlines than take issue with the females, who forbade beautiful, natural things because they believed them ugly, unnatural oddities.

Antiquated, cruel idiots.

It didn't matter out in the wastes, though, where the green trees and shrubs had little issue with his friend finding enjoyable companionship with another male. However, in the humming cold grey, while alone and broken, Doran found it hard not to think of his own selfish desires at the cost of his principles. They were all going to die. It would be nice to know a female's godly touch just once before it happened.

"Did you hear what I said?" Celeste asked. He hadn't. He'd been imagining reciting poetry, being witty enough to entice her to remove her dress. Or just make her smile. That would have been nice, too.

"You said…" He smiled. He remembered smiling like

that at her before. She had been impressed back then, too. He eyed the rest of the patrons for any sign of eager ears, but found none. They were not alone in their gathering. If Celeste was like the stars above, then gazing upon Mea was like staring at the sun. She radiated an energy unlike anything he'd ever seen before. She did not step, either; she floated from one place to the next without sound. Born for the city, born to lead the world. She was inspiring while simultaneously scaring him considerably. Mea was a force, and her rung on the ladder of entitlements was near the top. She was not a female to anger at the best of times.

"I said, do you have issues with the child?"

Oh, that's right. Fuken Tye.

"We will have no issue with the cub, Mea, should he appear at our gates."

"Thank you," Mea said, and sounded as though she hid her true anger beneath geniality. Nasty, controlled tones reserved for a Wolf. He didn't like those types of tones, even when he spoke with a potential Primary. She leaned back and Doran felt the warmth of her glare once more, and its burn. She was a powerful ally and an even more powerful enemy.

She was incredible.

"He's a lucky young cub," warned Doran, holding her gaze as best he could. Sometimes, a brute needed to stare the sun right back down.

She stared through him. It burned even more. "Ensure he remains that way, or my wrath will find you."

Simple words, delicately spoken and terrifying.

"It's not the time to speak of unsavoury matters, Mydame. He honoured your request," Celeste hissed, holding her hand up between them. "Doran, don't look at her like that. She'll put you in the ground."

Doran laughed. He'd always believed himself capable of

a pleasant laugh. "What can I say?" he said loudly enough for all to hear. "Your little shit of a son escaped our clutches. Fled deep east. He's probably reached the Savage Isles by now." It was a fine lie, and one fitting for a politician in the making, struggling with the sins of her Outcast kin. He caught the flicker of sorrow on her face, but it was gone in a breath.

"Thank you," she whispered once more, though a little more warmly this time. He bowed and swallowed his ale. It was warm, and the taste was flat—from too long sitting unloved and untouched, no doubt. He knew that tale well enough.

The hour was early, but he was already tired from the journey here. He didn't want to get comfortable. There was the small matter of the return trip home once business concluded. His few selected boys waited on the room's other side. He didn't want them getting too comfortable, either. A few rounds was all he'd allow. He was anxious to conclude business before the night turned messy, which it no doubt would if word of their arrival reached Dorn.

"Do you have the names?" he asked quietly. This was no matter to be shared with eager listeners. It was the true reason he was in Spark City.

Celeste slid the paper across the table. She would not be the one who would suffer the political backlash of siding with the Outcasts, building an army, so she handled the more precarious parts of this endeavour.

Erroh of the Sweeping Grasslands.

They were speaking highly of this glorious victory, and Mea was taking advantage. The Sweeping Grasslands? He could have sworn it was an insignificant field in the middle of nowhere, but they did not build lore on such titles. The Sweeping Grasslands was now marked on every local map as a place of importance. More than that, the title was doing its part in earning recruits.

Despite himself, he shuddered, remembering the swift attack by lesser numbers under a banner of truce. Rage had motivated them, and led by the wildest Outcast of them all, they'd driven those southern fuks into the ground.

All beautiful and brutal.

Doran lifted the dried parchment and held it up to his eyes. He ran his fingers down through each name, a tactic that eased the problem of each letter dancing wildly across the page, and counted loudly. "Thirty-four is hardly an army," he muttered, counting again.

"It's a fine start," countered Mea. "It will take time."

"How many from Keri?" he asked.

"We didn't accept any from Keri," Mea said quietly, lest the very name of the cursed place raise eyebrows, entice questions.

"We didn't think it wise to seek them out just yet," added Celeste.

He sighed and cursed under his breath. He missed the quiet of the wastes. He missed battering his brothers to a pulp thrice daily. Beating them into line. Dragging discipline from them. Building them into greatness. He'd lived a life unfamiliar with such things as pride, but, seeing their behaviour change and turn as routine took them and drove them towards impressiveness, he couldn't help but feel proud. Of them. Of himself too. Oh Aye, Aymon and Azel worked the finer art of skills and warfare. But Doran was the true master of the camp.

Thirty-four raw recruits would be a fine enough start, he supposed. Still, though, he was ready to invite the wretched from Keri. All was fair in war and discipline.

"It's a fair point," conceded Doran. "Let us start recruiting Keri wretches, men and women both. I expect to see a few names when I return next week." Every single fighter was needed.

"I disagree, Wolf. Those we have gathered will set out towards your camp at dawn," Celeste whispered.

"Always at dawn," he muttered. "Ensure they know the route and carry no map. We don't need that knowledge getting out."

Mea drained her wine and scrutinised the Alphaline. He appeared as lost as she felt, yet his skill at hiding his misgivings was that of a novice. After the dust settled, you worked with whatever remained. Mea worked with Doran. She would have desired more. Still, he was from a good line, and underneath that brutality, his mind was as quick as his strike, despite his infirmity.

Her own infirmity was herself. Her desolate self. She felt dreadfully alone this very evening. Even though she was surrounded by allies, she felt as if the weight of their expectations would overcome and strangle her. Her chest was tight and heavy, and though her face was calm and reassured, each breath she took was a battle. She missed him so.

Fighting a primal wail of agony, she allowed as few thoughts of Jeroen as she could. It was a continuous battle, and in every moment she fought, she desired to shed this responsibility, to disappear and lament him properly. Oh, to fall to her knees and quake and cry and never rise again. To give up this futile fight against this inevitable defeat.

To surrender completely.

But, like Doran, who was so unsuited to his task, yet so

willing to play his part, so too would she bear this terrible weight, for everyone else in this wonderfully flawed city certainly looked at her as if she were up to it. Their gazes burned the back of her head as she passed. Throughout her life, she'd deluded herself that she could pick up wherever Dia left off, but in the harsh light of the day, with her eyes wide open, she believed herself to be no leader.

And what did that say of her followers, with their hopeful naivety? Of those who quietly pledged themselves to her cause, out of earshot of eager ears? Those who proclaimed quietly that she was cut from the right stuff to lead the city and who would scream her name from the highest rooftop once she announced her intention to place her name atop the ladder for consideration.

They were fools. Celeste included. Elise should have taken the throne, not the pretender. Silvia would lead this city into fire. The Hunt were gathering. She suspected terrible deeds were afoot, that the Hunt waited for a new city leader.

Regardless, the city would fall. The betrayal of the Rangers had sealed this tragic certainty.

Jeroen.

"I have things to do," she said, forcing thoughts of her bearded man from her mind. She had things to do and people to see. Whispers to listen to. Betrayals to uncover. And grand schemes of escape to ensure. But first, tonight, she would speak with Seth, the keeper of the archives. Anyone who held a record of every Alphaline in the Four Factions was a man to win over, and she would win him over through charm and grit. She had need of his knowledge, just as the city needed their Alpha strength.

She bowed swiftly to the two young Alphalines and made her way out of the tavern into the cool night air, treading carefully lest anyone see her hurrying and believe she was a ruin. A broken vessel, never to recover. She breathed deeply and disappeared into the night. She'd tried not to notice how quickly the crowd had parted for her, quickly stepping aside and pushing away chairs that blocked her path, as if allowing royalty to pass through. Did they not know? How could they not recognise the strain in her features, in her walk, in every fuken breath she took? She was but a weary widow, struggling in the current to keep her head above water. And the current was growing ever stronger.

"We need the Keri wretches," Doran hissed as the door shut behind the most extraordinary female he'd ever seen. Celeste shot a glance back at him, but said nothing. Her fingers returned to playing with her hair, and he almost sighed.

The path not chosen.

The questions not answered honestly.

"Keri?" she mocked.

"They sing songs of Erroh. They'll want to fight." He puffed out his chest. If they were beasts, it might have been construed as a courting gesture. He'd been no master in the art, though. What did he know? His hand was annoying him. He knew that.

"Such fine songs," she mocked. He liked that, even though he suspected she was mocking him. She grinned. He liked this as well. She kept twirling her hair. The evening could take its time.

"We need bodies," he snarled, and immediately cursed his tone. He wasn't on the training grounds, barking out orders. She smiled and stopped playing with her hair. "I hate them too, but I do not have the luxury to enjoy prejudice."

She sipped her beverage and shrugged indifferently. Of

course she did. She could afford prejudice just fine. "You left without a mate," she blurted out.

Ah, that.

He blinked rapidly. Nobody ever spoke of the Cull. It was certainly something no Alphaline ever talked about, and he grimaced inwardly at the prospect of speaking of it now.

"Perhaps they didn't like what I had to say?"

"Maybe we didn't."

She eyed him. He didn't like that at all.

"Maybe they didn't like what they saw," she muttered, patting his ruined hand. It felt like a gut punch. He blinked a few more times and searched for an equally cutting retort, but all he could do was swallow deeply and wonder how long it would be before they concluded their business.

Until next week.

It wasn't the first time a pretty thing had cut him down. Normally, he could shrug such things off, but in this troubled mood of his, he feared he was becoming a little sensitive. Maybe beating the head of some irritating little drunkard would set him at ease, he thought. Although that would hardly be the act of a fine recruiter, he imagined.

"You have a pretty face," he mumbled, for he was no poet. "I should have said that back then. I should have said other things during those miserable few days."

"But you said nothing of the sort."

"No, I didn't."

"I really wanted you, Doran."

He hadn't expected that. He felt the blood drain from his face, and she laughed at his surprise. "I love this city, but her laws have hurt some I care deeply for," he murmured.

Celeste opened a little pouch of pieces and dropped them nonchalantly on the table. It was enough to pay for another round or two. This was a fine way to spend time together. She leaned back and eyed him with those beautiful, alluring eyes. He gestured to the innkeeper for another round.

"I have questions I would like to ask," she said. She twirled her hair in her fingers once more.

"As you wish."

52

HUNT'S END

Her name was Aurora, and after a very long hunt, she had found her quarry. The last miles had been most precarious, most frustrating. But she had arrived, and it was divine.

All hail Uden.

The trio had set out from the farm that very morning with nothing but enthusiasm and the barest of supplies. It had been wonderful. Tye had led them out through the gates at a giddy trot.

When they had arrived at the Wolves' mediocre camp, Aurora had been underwhelmed and highly entertained. They were so few in numbers, yet they drilled impressively as though their ranks were thousands deep. Stefan had assured them they would be safe within the camp and Aurora had nodded in agreement, all the while wondering if she would meet her glorious doom here among their strangling, bludgeoning hands. They three were killers of their brethren, were they not?

She'd expected a mugging, and the silent intent in the Wolves' eyes as they'd brought their horses through the bustling camp had done nothing to reassure her. Yet something had made them hold their strike. Some unknown watching god, perhaps? Or a decree by some power higher than herself. Or maybe they hadn't seen a girl in so long they were willing to put a little vengeance aside, hoping to win some quiet time with her.

Fools.

Ealis was with Stefan; therefore, Aurora was with Stefan. And if they came at her with vile, depraved intentions, she would not play. She would kill every one of the fukers. Fortunately for all involved, they did not come for her; they did not try to kill any of them, either, which was a pleasant thing.

Truthfully, learning of their actions and the betrayal of the Rangers, she thought these army drudges to be beautiful creatures. They had been honourable enough to fight as cowards had fled around them, yet wily enough to escape with their lives. Bloodthirsty enough to counter-charge under leadership of a false god. But they were no Rangers, so she would not send them too many good wishes in the days ahead, even when a familiar face vowed to escort them all the way to the camp of the false god, Erroh.

———

They brought their horses away from the tracks towards the town of Raven Rock. Aurora's eyes darted wearily from side to side. It was now, more than ever, so very important that she remain careful, and by the love of her god, try not to show her true self to them. Oh, but she wanted to. She wanted to kill each of them and scream as she did, to laugh and bathe in their warmth as their blood seeped away into the soil. Like she had before.

Like chains and blood and agony.

She knew this place. She had known it when people had walked its streets, and defended it bravely. She felt a kinship to this place. She'd taken a gift from here and delivered her to her god.

A lifetime ago, it would appear.

She recognised their welcome all too well, and it was beautiful. They drew their bows, they shouted in terrified defiance, and she watched their murderous intent with great interest.

Excellent.

Beside her, Tye dropped from his horse and ran towards a battered-looking rodent of the road, embracing him. The fiend hugged him back warmly. And then she realised who it was. She hadn't noticed him earlier; now she saw that he was far smaller than they had led her to believe. He carried himself as if he were about to break. It was easy to see the dreadful pain he endured in every movement he made. She'd killed and tortured more than enough to recognise that tired expression he wore, and this false god was one very tired man. It was delicious.

Aurora closed her eyes, and Ealis smiled at all who watched.

"Erroh," cried Tye, hugging him tightly. For once, the young cub was allowing his age to show in his actions, along with the loss he had suffered.

"It is good to see you, little one," Erroh cried, dropping his swords and bowing to the guests.

———

Ealis sat by the fire, eagerly listening to Emir regaling them with the tale of the attack on the Hunt. She smiled nervously, playing the part well. It positively thrilled her to be among them in this guise. To know a loose step could end it all was fantastic. A rewarding thing, too. She wanted to cry out. To tell them of her relief at finding them. To explain the distance she'd travelled. Her heart fluttered wonderfully. She looked around at her deluded comrades and loved her place in the world. It was right here. It was perfect.

She enjoyed the tale, and though Emir spoke little of bravery, his soothing tone as he explained these devastating acts was endearing. She liked an expert killer. He too carried deep reserves of agony and little pride, but there was an unquenchable strength buried deep within him. Something in his eyes she couldn't quite put her finger on.

Should Aurora decide—for the benefit of her Uden, of course—that she needed to strike out at this false god and his blasphemous prophets, she would start with Roja. The girl was weak. Surely Uden wouldn't mind her having a little fun? Two arrows to the chest. Enough to maim, but maim slowly. More pain that way. Lots of blood.

Perfect.

Emir would be next. It would be a simple kill. She'd like to watch those eyes fade to dark. A knife across the throat to fill the ground with a wonderful stream of crimson. She licked her lips. Her hands felt naked as she sat here by the fire in the middle of the day, surrounded by her victims. She wished she had her crossbows.

She looked at the one they called …Wynn? Was that his name? It was a familiar name, though she couldn't be sure from where she knew it. He was working clumsily with a blacksmith's furnace across from the fire. He was struggling with his wares, and he would struggle as she tore into him, too. Something blunt, she thought. Something to crack open that wonderful skull and make him less pretty. Maybe she'd

throw his body into the furnace after and see if it burned
to ash.

Ealis spooned the warm oats into her mouth and enjoyed
the flavour. She'd never eaten such a dish, and it was divine.
Aurora would have preferred boar after the long ride.

So, after Wynn?

Oh, that was easy. She wanted to tear into Lillium. That
girl was a fire. That girl was never far from looking her way,
either, and Aurora loved the threat. She wore her distrust
openly, and Aurora appreciated her honesty. Such things were
important to her. If it happened, it would be a gloriously
brutal fight. *Up close.* If she had time, she might cut on her a
while. See how strong her heart was. Aurora suspected she
had a strong heart. She might even rip Aurora's throat out
during the skirmish.

I would still laugh as you killed me.

Who next, though?

She wondered, did she have the heart to slay the big man,
the one who appeared to be a simpleton? Had she known it
was this town, she might have led them here herself sooner. A
small matter and time well spent. She'd engaged Wrek on the
road and, strangely enough, had found his kindness a curious
thing. Oh, he was a warrior. This, she could tell. Probably
capable of some right bastard behaviour, and that was fine,
too. She imagined him capable of strangling the life out of
her in a heated battle. In that moment, Aurora pledged to
allow him the act, were he to reach her before she shot him
down with a few bolts to that big, kind heart.

I would let you kill me, big man.

As long as you killed me well.

Ealis yawned and eyed the pot absently. Her hunger was
sated, but the desire for flavour was too much. Erroh took her
bowl and refilled it before passing it back across to her. Her

heart hammered wildly. Her vision went dark. Oh, if only her god could see her in this moment, it would be glorious.

"I know Stefan, and I know Tye, but I do not know Ealis," Erroh said, and she smiled nervously.

You will know me.

He looked at Aurora and then through her, without apology. She tipped her head sideways to lure some warmth from him, but he'd already looked away before her charm could work.

She wanted to kill him. She'd wanted to kill him this entire hunt, but now, she wanted to know him better than her god knew him. She wanted to know them all, for they all mattered.

Aurora thought Lexi a fine young thing, destined to squeal under the watchful, salivating gaze of Uden—unless little Tye came to her rescue. They were both similar in age, and Aurora understood that a young boy needed a willing bed-mate. Lexi was a gift Aurora was willing to offer the cub. They would make some fine, sturdy children.

Oh, hurry, Uden my love. Come to the north so we may play.

"If she is to stay, she must earn her place," said Lea evenly.

Earn my place?

With blood?

There were a few agreeing nods, and Aurora looked to the small, unassuming false goddess sitting atop a barrel overlooking the fire. Ealis bowed humbly, still playing at subservience.

Lea the legend of the north. Unknown and unloved by her people.

Well, Aurora knew all about Lea's tale. A lost girl who had

followed her mate all the way to the frozen south to pull him
from an icy river when he was at death's door. A girl who'd
single-handedly slain more of her people than any other warrior,
with her mythical bow and mighty flaming arrows. Aurora
gazed at the weapon resting against Lea's leg. A fine bow,
though nothing special. Perhaps it was how Lea drew it that
made her so impressive. Still, though, Aurora was interested to
see her in full flight. She wanted to know this girl before the end.

Uden would kill Lea. In front of Erroh, if possible. Aurora
wondered, would Uden allow Nomi to watch? Was Nomi not
a god's concubine? Would Aurora be allowed to rip that
blonde girl's hair from her scalp so she might make better use
of the strands? Gloves, perhaps. Nice blonde, golden-locked
gloves for the cold march home. That would be something
too.

Her mind raced, and saliva formed in her mouth. She
could barely control her frenzy.

Calm yourself, girl.

"She can fight," Tye insisted, and Aurora smiled
genuinely for the first time. She loved her little man. She
loved him as much as she loved slitting skin and tearing
muscle from bone. Theirs was a bond that could blossom to
greatness.

Young enough to be born in blood.

"Can she do anything else?" Lea asked evenly.

"What else is there?" asked Tye.

"Everyone here needs to fight," Erroh, the false god, said.
Once again, he looked through her. If he approved of what he
saw, he gave no suggestion. She liked a challenge.

The false god climbed to his feet and walked from his
legendary mate to face Aurora. This close, she could see the
sharply defined muscles through his vest; his was a powerful

build, one that had seen very few seasons yet spoke of experience.

She stood up to face him and wondered if he truly was blessed with the gift of sight. Was he able to see in through her beautiful eyes, right down into her black soul? Could he see her true self? Could he see Aurora Borealis for who she was? She fought the urge to throw away all pretence and just tear his fuken head off right there and then.

He stepped closer. Close enough to stab.

She would die drenched in the blood of the false god and it would be splendid.

Do it, Aurora. Kill him and love it.

Do it.

Uden would not approve.

Neither would Fyre, were she still alive to see it.

Do it.

Closer.

Look at that spark in his eyes.

"I'll do anything required, for I have no place to go," she whispered as Ealis. She shook ever so and tucked her hands behind her back. They rested on the handle of a thin blade with a varnished wooden handle.

"The Hunt destroyed her village. She wants vengeance," said Stefan.

"Then you've come to the right place, Aurora Borealis," Erroh, the false god, said, bowing.

"Please, call me, Ealis," she said sweetly, and returned the gesture with a fine show of respect.

53

TEMPEST

Uden scratched his bald head absently and played with the scraps of food on the plate in front of him. All that remained of his godly meal were a few grapes and some meat juices. Eating tempered the boredom somewhat. There were few things worse than waiting for word of an unstable Spark from those who called themselves allies, yet here he was, forced to delay even longer than he'd expected.

It should have welcomed me by now.

Tonight, the waiting felt cruelly tedious. He sighed, flicking a grape from his plate. It took flight and disappeared into the gloom. A fine death for an insignificant fruit. All deaths were insignificant. Until they mattered. The wind blew at the large ceiling of his tent. It was the second largest of all the tents in their settlement. He watched the roof flutter wildly as the wind caught it.

"Still no word of her," Gemmil said, sitting back to peel his orange. Gemmil was always careful, removing the bitter orange skin in one smooth skinning. Many a time Uden had seen him discard an orange for the simple crime of tearing too soon. Uden respected that attention to detail, that discipline. Even when he was giving unsavoury news.

Where are you, my lunatic lover?

"I imagine she has hidden like a rodent, after the incident in Conlon," Gemmil said, tearing the last of the peel away and breaking off a segment of the orange. He smiled at Uden's unease. Gemmil had earned his place at the table; earned his right to mock Aurora.

He had brought Fyre to Uden.

She had brought Aimee, though.

"She has no reason to fear me. She did her task."

"Aye, my lord, and she did so in quite the blazing flames." He swallowed a well-earned segment and savoured the taste. "Youthful exuberance, I suppose."

Uden laughed, for there was fine humour in his companion. Only with Gemmil could he relax, release himself from the shackles of responsibility and jest and complain and show his human side, meagre as it was. When they were upon the march, the god presented himself as such. A being of divinity, whose every step was an earthquake, each breath a gust of foreboding wind. In that milieu, Gemmil was disciplined and quiet, a disciple of reverence, a bishop of his creed, careful to offer only a whispered suggestion whenever they disagreed on matters.

Here, though, his voice was almost equal. Almost, but not quite.

In here, Gemmil was Gemmil.

A master. A legend.

One might say the greatest.

Uden smiled.

This man inspired everything he'd ever done or dared to do. For that, he would be eternally grateful. Gemmil tore another piece of fruit free but held off the pleasure of tasting it.

"There is nothing about Erroh," he said. Uden looked at him sharply. He'd taken his sweet time revealing this news. Perhaps he feared Uden's anger. That was fair. Uden pushed his plate away. "That little rat will come out of the forest eventually," Gemmil insisted.

"Oh, my friend, what if he cowers away?" He could hear the pleading in his own voice, and it was pathetic. He scratched at the patch over his eye. It wasn't itchy, but it was something to do. Something to calm him. "What if I never get my chance to kill him? What if I wasted so very long learning how to walk with this ailment?"

Without warning, Gemmil flung his orange at Uden. It was a fierce throw, and only reflex saved Uden's pride. He knocked it effortlessly from the air, and Gemmil smiled in approval. *Aye, I have continued my training.* "The time you have delayed has been time spent wisely. However, if Erroh never rears his head, those who speak of him with veneration will lose what feeble faith they have in him." He wiped drops of juice away with a handkerchief, then tucked it back in his breast pocket.

"I want my vengeance," Uden growled.

"You are above such things."

"I want it."

Gemmil sighed and shook his head like a disapproving master. "Very well, Master. We will draw him out."

"If I have to raze the fuken city to the ground, I will."

"Was that not the plan, Master?"

"Aye, but I'll do it in his name."

Gemmil had one more piece of information. He smiled wryly. Uden knew that smile.

"They've removed Roja from her post. She has fled the city in fear of her life," he said casually.

"Can we find her?"

"We will."

"She will not go quietly."

"I would not expect her to."

"The eyes of Spark already seek her out."

"It will be good to see the child again," Uden whispered, and a tear fell from his eye. It was a welcome release, and he felt no shame. "The city will be in turmoil; our whisperers will take full advantage." He closed his eye and sought knowledge. He found nothing but impatience. "I think it is time."

Gemmil stared at him for a few breaths before nodding in agreement. It was time to march the last few hundred miles. It was time to begin the end. "I will send out word for the fingers to gather. I will inform our friends in the city." Gemmil did not need to bow in his presence, but he did so and disappeared out through the tent's entrance.

Uden climbed out of his chair, patting it absently as he did. It was no mere chair; it was a throne, a symbol for his followers to adore, something to remind them of his magnificence. It wasn't the most comfortable seat. Its varnished mahogany was embossed with gold and emeralds; they were dazzling to gaze upon, but he'd have preferred something a little less refined. It was the human in him. Gemmil, however, had insisted upon it, and sometimes Gemmil had a point.

Mulling over the words they'd shared, Uden left his chambers and took the few steps to the largest shelter, which stood alongside his own. Slipping through the two heavy cloth flaps into a dark stuffy walkway where a smaller tent was erected, he held his breath until he became accustomed to the stench.

Gemmil, likely guessing his intentions, had lit the torches earlier, and the air was thick and heavy. *Like a burning home.* Uden could see the smoke billowing upwards, searching for an escape through a few carefully placed hatches into the night sky above. A man could have privacy to do whatever he wished beneath this canopied haven.

A god, too, and Uden would commit godly acts this evening. *Creating life.*

Dipping under the flap, he stepped into the warm room and waited. The small torches hung on each wall of the enclosure. A small gust of wind tried to extinguish their light, but to no avail. The torches merely rocked gently, creating unnatural dancing shadows in this wonderfully unholy place.

It looked less like a tent and more like the chambers of a condemned soul, for this is exactly what it was. The ruined girl hanging from two sturdy lengths of metal chain was the only decoration. To Uden, it was more than enough to make any room extraordinary.

There would be screams tonight. There were always screams. No one would listen, however. Distantly, he heard a hum of noise gathering in intensity as word spread throughout the camp. They had shuffled most of this march. They would stride the last few miles.

Gazing at her, he could only smile. Her eyes were closed, her tangled mess of bloody hair hung limply down in front of her marred face, and Uden thought her so tempting. She wore no clothes, and for a moment, the god of life enjoyed her fragile frame as it hung lifelessly in front of him. The layers of grime, blood, and bruises had done nothing to diminish her beauty. Or the beauty to come.

Not yet.

Not until she gazed upon him with love and devotion and understanding.

Not until she ventured out into the world to do his glorious bidding before returning a godly woman.

"The night you were born, there was the greatest storm of legend," he whispered.

"I don't remember," she said, without looking up. Her voice was cracked and uneven. Not from the many hours of screaming, for those agonising days had long since passed, but from days without water. Oh, how she craved water. But he would not gift her a drop until she had fed.

She hung above the ground, her toes just grazing the surface. Not enough to relive her pain, but enough to tantalise. He put great thought into every action. It was the little things.

He took a step closer. Her stench invaded his senses, but he endured. Soon enough, he would become accustomed.

"What is your name?" he asked, reaching out and taking her chin in his powerful hand. Her hair was still damp with sweat, her cheeks unpleasantly marred by tears and blood.

Are you learning?

"Tempest," she replied automatically. She knew, now, that to utter anything other than the title he had chosen for her would cause swift repercussions and violent reminders. She looked up and stared into his eye, and he saw the fear and the defiance mixed with terrible regret.

Delicious.

He ran his finger down her impossibly smooth skin, beginning at her neck. She had answered well; she deserved his touch. It didn't matter that she recoiled. He ceased at the navel and drew his hand away. She swung gently as he withdrew. The chains clinked slightly, and a fresh drop of blood ran down her left wrist. She sighed. From pain? Frustration? She was learning to control herself. Next time, she would allow him without reacting.

She was a clever girl.

She never stopped learning from her mistakes.

"Did they not call you Aimee?" he asked. His tone was kind and warm and open, and he wanted her to love his voice, his touch, his everything.

She would. It would just take a little time. *Time.* Something he had plenty of. Her face scrunched up. It was hard to learn when he asked questions with no fair answer. These moments amused the Woodin Man.

"Aimee?" she asked. She hadn't lost nearly enough of herself not to recognise her name of birth. At least not yet. Regardless of her confusion, it was the wrong answer, and she knew this even as she said it.

He struck her in the stomach, hard enough to send her rocking back in her holdings. Her skin was so soft. She moaned loudly.

She would not cry, and he was proud. However, tears would come soon enough. It had been three days since he'd fed her.

Three days?

Three visits. Day and night didn't matter to her anymore. All that mattered was her keeper.

"Do you love me, Tempest?" he whispered as she rocked back and forth. They were hushed words, but she flinched as though she'd been shouted at. He could see her flourishing madness. She wanted to kill him. She wanted to die, too. He leaned closer, and the chains clinked loudly. So loud that she flinched again. "Do you?"

Her aptitude for survival was incomparable, greater than any of her predecessors'. Greater than Fyre's will? he wondered. Fyre's proclivity for murder had been exquisite. Would Tempest outdo the success of Aurora, though?

If he willed it, then it would be so. He stroked her hair lovingly. "On the night you were born, there was the greatest storm of legend," he began.

She smelled it before she heard the footsteps, and she knew it was time to eat. Her stomach clenched, and she felt her bladder weaken.

Please, Uden. No more.

Not the boar meat.

Anything but the boar meat.

She heard the clinking of chains releasing, and she prepared herself. There was a sudden jerk, and she dropped. Only memory and reflexes saved her from collapsing. She fell to one knee gracefully, grunting with the effort. He would not like gracelessness. The servant entered the smoky room, and immediately the stench and low air caught in his throat and he coughed. The platter of meat he carried in his hand remained undisturbed.

It still needed a little cooking. It always did. She climbed to her feet despite her suffering. Every muscle in her battered body was strained and rigid and burning. Her head was dizzy and she struggled to raise her arms, so she allowed them to hang lifelessly down by her side.

There was no place for prisoners in the Hunt, apart from those used in contests. Uden, however, had allowed several fit young cubs to live. To serve his will. As she did now. There had been many to harvest during this march. Grateful for the chance to prolong their lives, they gave him their unquestioning loyalty—at least for the short time that he made use of them. They never questioned his motives, for their relationship was mutually beneficial. They had taken her before this march. She wondered when he'd tire of her.

Perhaps tomorrow.

The young man blinked a few times, but kept his head bowed as he presented the plate of meat to Aimee.

To Tempest.

The first few times, she had hidden her shame. Now, though, she had ceased to be bothered by it. Her soul, diminished though it might be now, was all she had left untarnished. She didn't mind them gazing at her nakedness now. It was her gift to distract.

She didn't reach for the food.

She never did.

"That meat needs a little cooking," Uden insisted. "Place it over the flame," he added thoughtfully. It was merely a culinary suggestion. It shouldn't have sounded quite like the threat it did. The servant nodded. Why argue with a monster?

Aimee wavered a little.

Be strong, Tempest. Be strong.

After a few moments, the plate heated at its centre and the three slabs of pink and brown meat sizzled. The aroma soared into the air and for a wonderful moment she could smell its tantalising richness over the stench of her own waste.

"I want to die," she whispered. She'd come too far and done too many vile things to merit redemption. Killing herself should have been easier, but she was broken now. She didn't even have the strength to wish for vengeance upon him. Not anymore. She only wanted silence.

If Uden heard her outburst, he showed only minor irritation. He fixed his eyes on the plate and the sizzling meat.

"Taste the meat. See if it's cooked well enough for her," the god said quietly. He licked his lips in anticipation. She made no move to claim the life-giving meal. That was fine. It was always her choice.

Always. That's what made his lessons so very important. The servant's fate had been settled, ever since he'd stepped foot into the room. He tore a piece from the plate and stuffed it into his mouth with relish. It looked divine, and he tore a second piece as he swallowed the first.

She pleaded with Uden without speaking a word. The tears sprang to her eyes. *Please, by the absent gods, no.*

The absent gods had little power here.

"It's perfect," the servant said, swallowing the unexpected treat. He licked his fingers and savoured his last meal. Uden took a step towards him.

Without warning, Aimee leapt from where she stood and struck out at the unsuspecting boy. Though he was taller than she, she grabbed his short black hair with ease and struck behind his kneecap with her bare foot. He dropped the platter and screamed in pain and sudden terror. It would be kinder for him to die at her hands than face Uden's torments. She had learned this cruel lesson with the many servants who had gone before.

The servant struggled, but her exhausted arms wrapped themselves around his neck tightly. She locked them in securely and squeezed with all her might. He gasped and tried to break the hold, but she forced her body weight down on him. "Easier like this, little one," she whispered, listening to his fading breath. He managed a primal moan as his body betrayed him and he succumbed to her technique.

"Do you love me, Tempest?" roared Uden as she killed for him.

"You will be perfect."

I will be perfect.

"Born in blood."

Born in blood.

The boy closed his eyes, and all fight left him. He kicked once more and fell unconscious. She held him for a few moments more and then finally released her grasp and placed him gently down on the ground.

Uden stroked her cheek. It was awful, and yet better than his wrath. He passed the blade across to her waiting hand. It was an incredible weapon, fit for a deity, no doubt. Evenly balanced, with an unblemished edge. Cutting into skin was no small thing with this perfect tool.

"I want to die," she repeated, taking the sword. It was a fine mantra; this was just another stage to pass through. Her eyes were wet, but the tears did not fall. He stared at her, waiting for them.

"My love, I'm so proud of you."

She lifted the sword without hesitation. Hesitating would incur the god's wrath. She could take another beating, but he would flay the young sleeping man alive in front of her. She couldn't watch another human pass so violently. So cruelly.

It was her mercy. It was all she could do.

And it made him happy.

Making him happy was very important.

She slid the blade across his throat, as Uden expected of her. The blood immediately surged out and ruined the weapon's perfect finish, but things like this couldn't be helped. At least he would know little pain.

"Bathe in it," he suggested, as he always did.

She cupped the warm, streaming fluid in her shaking hands and then placed them against her face.

"There's warmth in death, and it is beautiful," Uden whispered, as one lover to another. She nodded in agreement and allowed her god to take the dead body from her. He lifted the dead boy and held him above her as she reached for the fallen meat lying on the soiled ground. Her stomach clenched in revulsion at her act. She bit into a blood-soaked slice and swallowed methodically.

It was mercy, she told herself.

It was all she could do, she told herself.

After each kill, he allowed her to feed and to cry. He was kind like that. The god held the body over her until the last drop of his blood fell and she had eaten her share.

"Do you love me?" he asked, casually dropping the tool of his teachings in a heap on the ground and taking a second sword from the scabbard at his waist. She sat in the flickering torchlight and wiped her tears away before taking hold of the tarnished weapon.

"Do you love me, Tempest?" he asked again, and stood, awaiting her attack. Every day, whatever wonderful torment he planned brought her ever closer to her god. It was a fine way to occupy his time out in the wastes waiting for word of a false god.

"I want to die," she whispered, though he knew her lie all too well. She was special, was she not? Chosen by him above all others because he saw her will to survive—the will that threatened to betray her now.

"You don't want to die," he said, and she nodded weakly. "The night you were born, there was the greatest storm of legend. It was a beautiful tempest," he said, and charged forward with his sword raised.

54

TOO MANY NAMES

Erroh lay on the grass under the cover of the heavy branches and dared himself to blink. It wasn't like he couldn't still hear the cries if he blinked. He chewed at a twig absently and wiped the sweat from his brow. He inhaled, looking up and down at the enemy's finger.

Screaming.

He blinked. To his left lay Lea, her eyes as cold and calculating as his own. If she knew what to do, she said nothing. She was probably as lost as he was. Beside her, Nomi and Wrek watched on with equal trepidation. On his right were Emir and Roja. They were the quietest. They moved least. Both were lost in their own thoughts, guilty ones most likely.

Farthest from him lay their newest recruits; the unusual girl, Ealis, whose unsettling gaze cut through him, and her lover, who somehow bothered him more.

Emir had pledged that Stefan could be trusted, even in warfare. He had assured him that the irresponsible grand champion from a different life no longer walked the world, and that he was a trustworthy warrior. He was still a brute with wandering fingers, but Emir's pledge was no small pledge. Erroh would trust him for now, even if he found it difficult to meet the man's eyes—mostly because the tall blond dropped his gaze whenever Erroh addressed him. A worrying trait at the best of times.

Too afraid to hold the line, too afraid to meet my eyes.

More screaming.

The enemy had camped where they'd been attacked the afternoon before. They were now watching their brethren die, and those who'd been struck with the tainted bolts of Emir were dying just fine. The screams overlapped each other, creating a relentless song of anguished misery. A wall of death wails. *Like siege horns in a valley.* Some words filtered through now and then. They begged for euthanasia. They begged for relief. It was an unsettling sound, so instead Erroh concentrated on blinking to distract himself. It didn't help.

As they wailed, their comrades went about their business as though this encampment was planned. It sent a shiver down his spine. They talked loudly among themselves and discussed their next steps on the path in front of them. They did this because of the screams. Emir had given the defenders of these lands quite a taste of psychological warfare. It was magnificent, and it was truly dreadful. Erroh understood why Magnus found great value in the wretched healer.

Perhaps, had Emir's imprisonment not occurred, things might have differed for the Rangers.

He heard a faint rustle from behind as two skilled Alphalines moved through the canopy of the wastes in near silence. He glanced over his shoulder as Lillium slid up beside him. Her eyes were wild, but she looked alive and excited. She looked ready to inflict some fine horrors upon them all. She looked ready to stand up like Emir and attack. A tempting suggestion, admittedly, but theirs was not to die in a hail of bolts in the middle of the forest. Theirs was to watch and wait for Uden's forces to appear, and though it was a large gathering of southerners, it was hardly large enough to carry Uden. There would have been more trumpets.

Wynn followed behind Lillium. He took a knee and hid himself behind the trunk of a tree.

"Nothing for miles," he said quietly, wiping sweat from his forehead. "A few tracks where they searched for Emir and Roja, but apart from that, they've stayed on their side of the river." He looked pale and anxious, but better than he had when he'd last gazed at the Hunt's shadow.

"Scared of finding attackers armed with poison," muttered Nomi. She was paler than the rest. Perhaps hearing her former people scream was too much. She held her hands to her ears and jumped every time a fresh cry emerged from the healing tent the victims were lying in.

"You hear that Emir? You've scared an entire army," said Wrek, grimly. It was an attempt at levity, at easing the guilt the young healer was likely feeling.

"Is this what it sounds like to lose a soul?" Emir whispered. He dropped his head in the grass and Erroh patted his back. The wretched healer knew what he needed to do.

Make more.

"I think we have seen and heard enough," Erroh said. Lillium gripped her sword in anticipation. Her eyes flashed dangerously. He shook his head in warning. *Not now*, he said in silence. She pleaded with her eyes.

Just a little killing?

He shook his head again.

Listening for an hour was sufficient. Emir slithered away first. Lea immediately followed, no doubt to ensure he wasn't too shaken. It was brutal, but it was war. He'd done a fine job

ROBERT J POWER

with his concoction, and though it would sting, Erroh would
congratulate him for his actions.

Slowly, all of them slipped away from the chorus of pain,
back to the horses, until only Lillium and Erroh remained.
She still looked ready to bolt, and he wouldn't leave until he
was certain she planned no madness.

She tore a strand of grass and clenched it in her mouth
and chewed. She looked like she lazed in a meadow at the
season's changing without a care in the world. "I could listen
all day," she said coldly, and Erroh edged up beside her. They
were two fine generals, charged with holding the line against
an unstoppable force.

"It's killing Emir."

"Aye, but he can be proud," she countered, spitting some
green mulch back onto the ground. They watched the last
tents collapse as the demoralised workers prepared to march,
and Erroh suddenly remembered chains. Chains and a really
wet cough.

"He's too good a man to be proud," Erroh muttered,
glanced behind him, but Wynn had long since departed. They
were alone with their thoughts and strategies. Lillium
shrugged, and he imagined that seeing her comrades savaged
in front of her eyes allowed such indifference. Still, he wasn't
ready to lose her to an insignificant skirmish. If he lost her in
battle under his charge, he would ensure her death meant
something.

"What do you think of our latest recruits?" he asked.

"Emir and Wrek have vouched for them, so if they're
skilled, we can use them."

"They swear Ealis struck down most of the Wolves
herself."

"And she has pretty eyes," Lillium said, shrugging again.
It was a fine point. It was probably coincidence that the Hunt

had returned into their lives at the same time as the alluring young female. "I wish I had my bow," she said.

"Oh, I think we need to get you away from here," he said, and she smiled. Perhaps she realised her frenzied glare gave her an unsavoury look.

"And these animals?" she asked.

"We can track them any time we want. We monitor their movements, and if a moment presents itself, we tear the fuckers to pieces," he said with relish. It was a simple plan— one of his better ones, in fact. "For now, let's go home and think on interesting matters." Trusting her not to do anything stupid, he finally slipped away from the screams of the dying. He heard her mutter a few curses before following.

————

Her name was Aurora Borealis, and despite herself, she was enjoying her time among the doomed group of Outcasts.

"I hate that name. I think it should be something else," suggested Emir. Though his speech was slurred, he had a point to make, and he was making it. And she smiled.

They were all gathered around the arena, watching Aurora attempt to prove herself worthy of a title as an Outcast. Sweat covered her brow and ran down her back, soaking into her clothes. The welts on her arm stung wonderfully, her stunning black hair was a mess of tangles and untidiness, and she did everything in her power not to giggle in unrestrained delight. She felt drunk on their violence, and it was magnificent.

She spun into the blow and felt the wooden sword crack loudly against her nose as she collapsed forward and fell into the arms of the behemoth, Wrek. He held her easily, as if she were a child, and politely returned her to the arena and the awaiting Alphaline Lillium.

They were all watching her spar, and it was delightful.

She clicked a knot in her neck and immediately fell into an attacking stance. It was a fine act, and she knew they were enthralled with her performance. She nodded, smiled respectfully at the taller girl and waited. Lillium looked anything but tired. This did not bother the deadliest girl in the Arth. Why show all her tricks on first meeting them? Why lay all her cards on the table? Best they see her as a keen little waif, willing to stand with them in their fight.

"We don't need a name," laughed Wynn. His eyes were on Lillium, though he spoke to Emir. He drank quite a lot. As did the rest. Even Aurora felt tipsy. It wasn't the finest sine she had ever had, but it hadn't blinded her. They should have been cautious and quiet, fearful about the Hunt being ever so close, yet they continued on with their routine. They drank heartily, and Aurora thought this was magnificent.

"We are outcasts, nameless. Let it go, Healer," Erroh, the false god, mocked. He watched her as she glided around the arena, and strangely, she wanted to impress him.

Just cut Lillium a little bit.

Just a little blood is all.

"Nameless is a good name," the healer with the godly potion argued, and spilled his non-blinding sine all over himself. She liked Emir for his cruelty. Liked him for his potion, too. She wanted to taste it. She wanted to drain a goblet of it and slip into the night with fire in her veins. Now that was a worthy death.

Lillium met Ealis in the middle of the arena and, after another brief struggle, disarmed her opponent with grace and ease. Ealis had charged in recklessly, and that had ended the engagement. Aurora allowed her wrist to present itself enticingly. The weapon clattered loudly at the feet of Lea, who picked it up and flung it carelessly back to its owner.

"It's a stupid name, Emir. Stop being stupid," mocked Roja, fidgeting with a cracked nail from her earlier skirmish with Lea. She was covered in bruises, and Aurora very much wanted to meet the apparently undisputed champion of Raven Rock in battle.

"You're a stupid name," came the witty reply.

She was losing their interest as a threat, mused Aurora, tying up her hair and acting as though she needed rest. She was having the time of her life at play. This deceit rivalled the pleasure of the hunt, she decided.

As good as the taste of blood.

She took a deep breath and cast a loving gaze at Stefan. He sat cross-legged with a completely dim-witted, proud expression on his face. He didn't seem to care she was losing.

Idiot.

Still, though, this suddenly attentive gaze from him unnerved her so. *Go away, pretty boy, and leave me to plot my disruptions on this perfect little family of tainted souls.* Perhaps he was concerned that she'd leave him for a fresher buck? A younger cub with a finer bloodline?

Such eventualities seemed likely. It wouldn't matter. When everything shifted, her attention was the last thing he would desire. She'd been in his company long enough already, and he would pay for that. She spat in the dirt and controlled her anger and joy at the pain of the swords and the humiliation of defeat in front of Stefan.

Don't you mean humiliation in front of Erroh?
Shut up.

"I have it," Emir declared deliriously. "Emir's Brotherhood," he cried, draining his glass and falling over in a heap. His mood had improved, Aurora thought. She had noticed his doomed comrades working tirelessly to keep his glass full all night. He was certainly better company for it, too.

"That's a noble name," he slurred from his seated position, and despite herself, Lillium held off her attack to laugh at his antics. She wasn't alone in her amusement. The entire group appeared to take great joy in his drunkenness. "Isn't it?"

Ealis thought it a fine name, altogether.

Suddenly, Lillium danced forward, her hair pristine once more despite the effort in her movements. She tore Ealis's defences apart, and Aurora allowed her to. It took all her efforts not to counter, for if she threw herself into the battle, who knew how violent it might become? Still, countering the girl's aggressive combinations with both swords was some excellent learning.

"Why are you holding back?" Lea roared suddenly.

Fuk.

A terrible chill ran down Aurora's spine. Both combatants separated, but neither dropped their guard. Lea had the floor. She stepped forward and an unusual panic rippled through Aurora's body. There was a threat to this girl. Few people could induce terror in Aurora. The accusation should have amused her. Instead, she stepped back.

"I wasn't aware I was," Aurora countered a little too quickly. Lea rattled her. *Complacent? Foolish?* She tried to remember her steps. Had she telegraphed each strike so obviously? Uden had spoken of the group's dedication to the craft of swordplay. She'd naively presumed they were nowhere near her standard. Despite the fear she felt now, she also thought this brilliant.

"You show divine skills in one moment, and the next you are as sloppy as Emir," said Erroh quietly. His tone was condemning. She had never been happier in her entire life. She did not know why.

"I gave her every fuken opening," Lillium said. She rested on one sword, the fatigue finally showing as she took deep breaths. Aurora found this quite interesting, too. Lea, too, had seen through the assassin's ruse, apparently. Suddenly, Aurora felt very much outnumbered and was thrilled about it. If she attacked them as a group, she would fall.

Fuk.

Suddenly, she didn't want to fall tonight.

"You are a master, and yet you pretend you are a novice," hissed Lea, walking into the arena. Ealis's stomach clenched, and she took a second, involuntary step away from the approaching Alphaline. The girl radiated power despite her size, and Aurora very much wanted to choke the life from her. Squeeze until the bitch's eyes popped right out of their sockets. Perhaps she could gift one to Uden, and keep one for herself? Maybe she could keep it in a little jar of brine and look at it on lonely nights when she could not sleep.

She also wanted to listen to the impressive girl's words. The night had taken a sudden dangerous turn. Out of the corner of her eye she saw Tye climb apprehensively to his feet. He had spotted the trouble brewing. Bless him, she thought, and allowed Ealis do the talking.

"You are right," she said, falling to a knee. Her mind raced, searching for words to save herself as the Alphaline stood over her. She knew their tendency to overreact. No Alphaline kill had ever been easy.

"You move with grace, yet sloppily offer Lillium openings," growled Erroh. He remained seated, offering no support to his mate, and Aurora thought this trust in her ability was an interesting thing.

"I'm scared," she said, offering Lea her most disarming,

hopeful smile. "I was thrust into a town of fugitive Alphalines and ordered to spar with one with them, and I confess it took my nerve. I feared facing the wrath of Lillium if I gave everything, so I took the strikes," she said, dropping her head as if the shame were too colossal to bear.

Well done, Ealis.

"I'm really sorry," she whispered, as if she were about to cry. Tye stood up, as did Wrek, but it was Tye who marched up to face Lea. She was so proud of him.

"Is it any surprise?" he growled. "They sought refuge, and you threaten her for trying to be humble when facing daunting odds. Ealis is a good person and a decent fighter. We should be glad of her presence," he said, crossing his arms. It was a fine argument.

"Please, Erroh. Many people conceal their talents," Stefan said. "We've all made mistakes, too." His words affected both Lea and Erroh. They fell silent for a moment, and Aurora wondered had she said enough to save her perfect flesh from a nasty skinning.

"The Fighting Mongooses," Emir shouted, from somewhere on the ground behind them. "That's a glorious name too," he declared. "We are the Fighting Mongooses. That's a polished name, that is."

"That's a stupid name," Lillium sneered, before bowing to her defeated opponent. "Until we spar again," she said, taking a seat beside the drunken wretch. As she did, she tossed her weapons to Lea.

"Come on, Ealis. Show us what you can really bring to the fight," Lea said, offering her hand to the scared waif.

So easy.

———

Wynn violently strummed the six-string with dancing, blurred fingers, striking each note skilfully. Emir could barely keep his drunken body upright. His shoulders were slumped, but his fingers did not fumble the melody as he kept time with his passionate bandmate. The song was fast, and it filled the night. It didn't matter the danger. Any morning they woke could be the day they died, so each night, they lived as best they could. That's what they claimed, and it was wonderful.

Aurora danced with her lover, despite the bruises covering her body. She was drenched in sweat, dust and exhilaration. It wasn't every day she met her better in the arena, and it was something to cherish.

Lea, mate of Erroh, walker of the lonely south, had punished Aurora Borealis, killer of kings, with ruthless efficiency. She'd done so without great effort, as well. They'd stalked each other, yet only one had been the hunter. It had taken Aurora only a few breaths to realise this. Lea was quick. Her shapely body moved as a blur. Every time Aurora struck out, she was already a step away and a step ahead. She was effortless like Uden in her stalking, and the assassin had pushed herself to match her manoeuvres.

Not to best her, but merely to keep pace.

Oh, she had tried her best, but in the end, she had not been able to get the better of the incredible Alphaline. Spitting dirt from her mouth, mixed with a little blood after the umpteenth strike, she'd climbed to shaky feet and faced her conqueror despite genuine exhaustion. She had performed admirably, and the few delicate marks upon Lea's deceptively slender arms were testament to her ability.

No killing strikes.

So, she had struggled on until Lea had finished her. Despite herself, Aurora had been grateful for the respite. The demoness had merely taken a few breaths and then requested that Stefan enter the ring, where he, too, had met the same fate. Albeit far sooner.

Stefan twirled Aurora and led her in the dance like the plucky champion he'd once claimed to be, and she allowed him. She laughed and tried to sing along, but she did not know all the words. He didn't mind at all. He didn't seem to care whether anybody was looking, and she found this endearing.

The energetic song ended, and Emir continued to play on alone. He started a slow ballad, and after a moment Wynn strummed along. After the war, they might be able to make quite the fortune. All they had to do was stay alive and hope the gods rewarded them. Aurora would see to that unspoken prayer.

Aurora rested her head on Stefan's shoulder as he led her in the dance, and wondered how long it would take to bleed him dry once she hung him in the air. Less time than Orin, probably. That would be nice. And then Erroh was standing beside them, his eyes focused on her Stefan.

"I believe it my right to have this dance," the Master General said. He bowed and held his hand out. Stefan stood numb for a few breaths and then, without looking at her, offered her hand to the legend. She should have been offended, but it was too intriguing.

The music continued, and Erroh held her tightly to him. Enough to show his strength, but not enough to make her uncomfortable. One dance wouldn't hurt, would it? Uden wouldn't mind. Would he?

"I'm no dancer," he whispered, and led her through his basic moves. After a few steps she edged herself closer and swayed with him, taking the pull of the music, taking the dance for her own. Up close, he was beautiful. Though he tried to hide it.

"I love to dance," she said, and swayed close to him. The music was soothing to her ear. She knew the words of this song. Dancing was wonderful, like killing. She would happily dance all day and on into night. Uden had never appreciated her grace when she had danced for him.

She could see Stefan standing away, watching quietly. His folded arms were the only sign that he was not enjoying the show. He accepted a goblet Lea offered to him and clinked it against hers, and Aurora suspected there was more to this moment than was apparent.

The false god spun her around, and she turned magnificently with him. This was not blasphemy; this was fine sport. She giggled loudly, and somewhere far away she heard the delicate tones of a young girl singing. It was glorious and wonderful, and Ealis smiled as she committed the moment to memory.

Such beauty happened rarely in a life. She turned to glance at Erroh and, strangely, she saw little desire in his eyes. Though she should have been insulted, she was glad of it. It would make the slaying of his perfect mate, Lea, that little bit more enjoyable.

"Can we trust you?" he asked, pulling her close. His sudden strength was incredible. She'd not imagined him capable with a frame so slight. It was oddly comforting and familiar.

Still, though. He had to die. It was that simple.

"I'll not let you down," she lied deliriously. The music, the alcohol, the part she played—it was all wonderful. She wanted to sing along. She wanted to know these people. She wanted them to believe they knew her. And when they loved her most, she would tear their fuken kidneys out.

"Then you are among friends," whispered Erroh, smiling. He fought the lead back from her and led her across the dusty ground with as much skill as he could muster. She gave him a smile in return to allay any doubts he had regarding her allegiance.

As they danced, she saw Lea grab Stefan's hand and, without asking his permission, led him out to dance alongside them.

"We didn't finish the last dance," Aurora heard her say, and somewhere she heard a wretched healer guffaw.

Though a storm brewed in the sky above, there was little to fear tonight. There would always be storms brewing. Especially the ones that blew hard enough to shake the foundations of the world.

55

THE GIRL LEFT BEHIND

O n the third day, the screaming fell silent, either through Emir's vile fluid or the miserable gift of merciful euthanasia. Any fool could see the effect that the pain and screams and eventual deaths had had upon the morale of the massive travelling family of brutes. They had walked around the camp for days with their heads lowered. Even the cessation of anguish had done little to raise the Hunt's collective mood.

Had they held their heads a little higher or dared to peer deeper into the forest, they very well might have spotted the odd flicker of movement, heard the sound of a snapping twig or seen the glittering eyes of their concealed ambushers as they watched their every move.

The Outcasts worked in little groups. No one could ever observe the enemy alone. Always in groups of two or three, the Outcasts slipped through the trees gathering any intelligence they could. Praying to the absent gods, the army met up with a grander force.

It was something to do.

Days passed, and no longer did the Outcasts quake in

terror when they looked upon these animals. Riders and guards walking the perimeter from dusk all the way through to dawn would never know how closely the enemy watched them. A solitary guard might have been an easy kill, yet the watchers held their strike. It was not fear that halted their instincts, but merely better judgement. They were improving as warriors. All but one.

The girl left behind.

———

She usually did her hair in the morning, first running soap through it and then adding a few styling oils. Her favourite oils were the rose-scented ones, and she took a few moments to breathe in their aroma. Then she would brush her hair as it dried in the breeze. It was something her mother had always done, before she died.

Lexi blinked back a tear and took a few deep inhales. She loved rose. Satisfied that her hair was dried and fabulous, she carelessly tied it up for the frustrating day ahead. Every day was just full of frustration.

Another dawn, another day of boredom.

"Hello," she called out to the silent town, then returned to her task of cleaning out the fire's ashes. Her body hurt from the previous night's sparring. It was the first time Emir had granted her permission to fight. The next step would be the road, and after that, the hunt. She was terrified. Excited too.

Perhaps tomorrow?

She flexed her arm gingerly. It was always stiff in the morning. After a few hours she could move it without discomfort, but, come evening, it throbbed mercilessly. The pain infused her anger. She longed to kill Silvia. Mydame or not, she would see that bitch buried in the ground.

Allowing herself a few moments more to picture imaginative punishments for the witch, she shovelled the last of the glowing embers and ash from the near-dead fire into a small metal bucket and dragged it down to the river. A thankless task, to be sure, but this was her place in the world. She was crippled for now, so Erroh demanded she complete chores as if they were back home.

In the city.

She tipped the ash into the water and watched the coals spit and die and form into long strands of grey as the water took hold and pulled them away. She patted the bottom of the bucket and coughed as the last grey specks fell into the waters below. Then she sat and listened for any sign of threat out on the road. Erroh had charged her to do this after every menial task. Was it a test, or concern? Regardless, she sat and listened and heard nothing more.

She could sense the good cheer slowly returning to the camp. Seeing the enemy had taken their nerves at first. Now, though, they were more relaxed in all their duties and activities. They had simply acclimated to the circumstances, sobering as they were.

Soon she, too, would face that fear. She had not seen blood or taken another's life. She was a cub in these matters. Erroh sought to protect her, but she was of Magnus and Elise's line. Blood and death suited her.

She was supposed to be a legend.

She was certain she would become just that.

She would not die.

She would not fuken die.

She liked Raven Rock. She liked her adopted family, even if they treated her like a child. Respect would come in time, she supposed. It was strange being around intimidating warriors, but her mother would have expected her to rise to the occasion. Learn from them, know them. Earn her right to accept what they were willing to teach. Watch and learn things they did not.

She gazed across at the now-idle furnace and smiled. Wynn was no great blacksmith, but among the burning coals and metal shapings, he hammered away happily. He never showed his work to anyone. He was working hard upon some secret project, and she hoped it was something truly brutal. It wasn't her place to ask him. So, she simply enjoyed the spectacle of him working shirtless. She sighed and shook that vision away.

Stefan, too, was a pretty young thing. He was quieter than all others, and that suited Lexi just fine. She'd shared only a handful of words with him, but he was always deferential in her presence. She appreciated this. It reminded her of when she'd lived in Spark. As the days passed, he'd warmed into the group. Whatever issue he'd had with her brother or adopted sister was lost in the wind now. This was a place of healing, she supposed. She felt her injury gingerly and cursed her vanquisher. She was healing, too.

Lexi had respected Ealis from the beginning. She was strong and spoke warmly with the younger girl whenever they sat down by the flames to eat or sing. Everybody appeared to like her. She, too, spent hours when she could, carving and crafting a weapon of some sort within the small armoury opposite Wynn's forge. Lexi couldn't understand exactly why. There were plenty of weapons as it was. Magnus always said fine warriors made use of anything available. Still, the pretty female with the startlingly beautiful eyes was adamant that she attempt to piece together something a little different. Perhaps it was a fine project to occupy her mind. To stave off fears while waiting for death. She worked hard and showed little fear, ever.

Ealis was fond of Tye. Lexi was not. She could not take his voice. His actions. His fuken walk. She was bitter that Erroh allowed him to ride out to watch the encamped enemy. Hated that he learned from so many masters while she was a fuken cook. It wasn't fair. Fuk Tye.

A gleam of sunlight caught in a clear glass bulb hanging above her head, and her irritation faded in its glimmer. She had seen that Roja was obsessed with the town's lights. Whenever one burned out, she insisted on replacing it straight away. It didn't matter whether there was wind or rain, what time of day it was, or whether or not she was sober. Lexi didn't know why she needed to keep them running, only that she did. She wasn't the same since the attack. Lexi had tried to talk to her about it, but met nothing but the usual stoic Roja, as though Lexi were an inquisitive child. She might have pushed the matter. She never did. People were entitled to their behaviours. At least Roja wasn't alone.

Emir was never far from Roja. They played at being friends, but any fool could see they were besotted with each other. Emir was good for Roja. Truthfully, though, she doubted Roja was good for Emir at all. She brought out the wretchedness in him. Still, that wretchedness was generous where alcohol was concerned. A girl like Lexi found these things important.

Lexi adored Wrek. He was the kindest bastard she'd ever had the pleasure of meeting. Like her, he felt outcast among the Outcasts, and she appreciated that greatly. Never able to sit among his brethren for longer than a couple of days, he lived a precarious sort of life. Forever upon a mount, riding between the two camps, was an exhausting, morale-crushing task. But he never complained, and she learned the art of patience from him.

She walked to the vegetable patch, all the while listening

to the wind for any sound of very bad things. It was a
fortuitous thing that they'd happened upon this bandit town
as the crops came in. Lea was insistent they spend a full day
harvesting the crops and storing them away before they
turned in the soil. But the Outcasts had skilfully avoided the
task for at least a week now. It was only Nomi who offered to
help with harvesting. This offer was not taken up by her
sister-in-law. At least, not yet. Regardless, the southern
female never left Lea's side. Always smiling, always helping
with chores. Once or twice, Lexi had wondered if she were
waiting for a moment to strike Lea unawares, but ultimately,
she doubted this. The blonde female was simply lonely for
friendship, she told herself. Lexi had seen the same behaviour
a dozen times before, in the city among her sisters. Lea had
every right to doubt Nomi, but Lexi trusted her just fine.

Lexi pulled a dozen carrots and twice the number of
potatoes and placed them in a rough sack to be prepared later
in the afternoon, once the flames were relit. Around the
flames was where Erroh and Lillium found themselves most
nights, while the others went about their own duties. The two
were always plotting and planning for attacks that might
never occur. Always staring at various maps, calculating
routes along the roads. Searching for a strategy that would
bring them victory. She had learned through simple
conversation that both Alphas had slipped far closer to the
camped Hunt than the rest had. Close enough to reach out and
pull a wandering southerner into the bushes for an easy kill.

In another life, she imagined Erroh as a scout. Garrick
had always imagined this, too. Every day, Erroh wrote down
all he learned about their enemy, even the most trivial things.
He thought it very important these brutes were creatures of
habit, almost obsessive in their rote actions.

He was searching for some way, any way, to kill them all.

Or at least that was what Lexi believed he did. She also believed this war had fallen to a stalemate. The south had seen the impressive sight of Samara and had second thoughts. And why not? The city was impregnable. Why else had Uden the Woodin Man not yet appeared? She suspected hidden negotiations were in the wind.

She said as much to both generals, who smiled at her instincts and sent her on her way.

Just like Magnus was sent away.

She stemmed her anger, for it would serve her little. She still had issue with Erroh's daring to send Magnus back home to face the savages. She'd begged to go with him, and he'd dismissed her as only a beaten father could. She wished Magnus was here with her now. Sometimes, she wished he had defeated Erroh.

Count.

One, two, three.

Exhaling slowly, she began preparing the carrots in a small kitchen she'd adopted as her own, keeping one ear tuned for any strange sound. Slicing the vegetables with her injuries was trying, but she persevered, now and then stretching her aching elbow against the stitches. She imagined it to be part of her rehabilitation. It was a slow process of returning to the fight, but she would do it. She threw a carrot into the little basin with the rest, saving the onions and garlic until last. It would be stew again tonight. She was a chef of limited skill. At least it was something that she could do to earn her place here, as each day blurred into the next.

Oh, to sit in the saddle among her comrades and find her calling in this world. Find distraction from such humbling boredom. Find a place among the elite.

Perhaps tomorrow he would allow her.

56

GOING TO THE CITY TO GET A FAMILY

T he creaking and rolling of the monstrous carts filled
the night. They filled the day too. Always rolling,
always heralding their march. Beneath their roar, the
drumming march of thousands of soldiers followed. The
clamour of clanking armour added to the thunder. For when a
southern army marched, they marched in preparedness.

At last, the hum of camaraderie filled the lands, a
wonderful sound to the ears of the allies. Excited, energetic,
bloodthirsty. They laughed, they cheered, they counted the
many miles marched in the hours of the day and sometimes
into night and beyond. They sought the City of Light and the
false god within.

Gone was the languid postponement, and although they
had used the pause wisely, they were grateful to their god
now for the gift of war. At such a brisk pace, there was little
time to think of the dark days coming.

One sound was lost beneath the roar of machines: the
fluttering of wings. No less important than armour and
blades, the messenger pigeons had their part to play in this
battle. Released from their cages, a hundred of them took to

the skies now, and they were beautiful and they were eager to reach their homes once more.

The soldiers watched them in awe and saluted their pious journey. And it was pious. For hundreds of miles in every direction they flew, each bearing a final summons to gather and support the cause. They were safer than any Rider would be in these precarious territories. The north did not enjoy every advancement.

There were sacrilegious whispers among the soldiers of Erroh's deeds. Some said he had razed the city of Conlon with fire, and their fury overcame their trepidation. They did not fear for their fallen comrades, for Uden's pledge blessed them: "A life lost in the Hunt is divine. Once the Hunt finishes, those who were lost will return in the new world," quoth the Woodin Man.

They did not fear death. Oh, no; they merely raged at the affront and the actions of a false god.

From his grand cart, Uden watched his gathering southerners, and he smiled. Vengeance was a beautiful thing. His time was at hand. All parts were falling into place. He had the city. He merely had to claim it as his own.

And claim it while standing over the body of the false god, Erroh.

Days became weeks, and the road opened up for them. Such was their pace, they swept past tainted settlements and left them to their ways. *For now.* For what were needless delays when the city called? Every day, the grandest army of the Four Factions grew as fingers, long patiently settled, met them as agreed and marched in union alongside them.

Eventually, when the season had turned from sunny to wet, they reached the territory of Samara. With no army to greet them, they walked the last few miles in eagerness. Thirty thousand strong, they spread out across the lands, enveloping Samara in their shadow.

It began as a few panicked reports from the scouts, and then fear spread quickly throughout the city as whispers of an invasion grew. Only when the southern army appeared on the horizon were the gates locked. In the dead of night, the sound of screaming metal filled the air as the city secured itself against the invaders. And the wretches in the hovels.

They came as one terrifying, thundering pack, and the world held its breath as they set their sights upon the only glowing light in the vast darkness. A mile from Samara, they halted again and set down, spreading out along the Great Mother.

For three days, they made no further move. Faint sounds of the clearing of forest and the setting up of camps were borne in on the wind. They took territory without argument and settled themselves like an honest convoy merely resting in the wastes. Perhaps this was exactly what they presented themselves as. Perhaps this was exactly what they were.

The Wolves went to war casually. They formed a barricade along the front wall of the city, not against the invaders but against the wretches who were desperate to seek salvation within the city walls ahead of any actual siege. Riots broke out during the first few days and nights as they dashed themselves against the unforgiving barriers. Perhaps not all the Wolves relished beating back those desperate few, but they remained diligent in their task.

Some took to the wastes, taking their chances against the elements. Others stayed steadfast at the barriers, believing that when the time came, the city would open its gates. In the end, the barricade held, the gates remained unlocked and, in the shadow of the southern monster, the city fell to an uneasy stillness.

As they waited uneasily for Uden to make a move, whispers spread throughout the city streets and the citizens of Samara feared the best. For anything less was doom.

What secret negotiations were occurring between both armies that held them at a distance?

People believed; people hoped.

And they were wrong.

57

PREJUDICE

Erroh was tense, but he dared not show it. Not when he'd fuked up. Veiled behind the thick green wall of leaves, he watched the Hunt go to task, ever so distracted. Of all days he could have chosen, it had happened today. He considered sending Lexi back to the camp, but showing favouritism would not serve him well. She'd never forgive the embarrassment either.

Beside him, she crouched low in her saddle, looking through the break in the leaves. Her eyes were cold. Far too cold, but they looked controlled. He couldn't remember the feeling of seeing the army for the first time, but he was certain he hadn't been so assured. She was her mother's daughter. He thought about Elise and suppressed the frustration. The rage. The depthless sorrow.

Still no word, sight, or sound of his mother in Samara. He feared the worst. She was dead. He knew she was dead. He'd had no opportunity to save her. To seek her out. To…

Gather yourself.

"I've seen far more encouraging things in my life," Lea hissed from his other side. Her hand gripped Baby in anticipation. There was something in the air. It felt like blood and very bad things, and he'd brought his sister along for the ride.

"Birds," said Nomi, on her horse beside Lea, as if it were a small thing. Seven pigeons flew into the sky above the finger of the Hunt. They flew as one, as if they had leapt from the one nest together. A strange thing indeed, and all members of the Outcasts sat and watched them as they flew overhead.

On the other side of the treeline, the brutes in fur and armour were far too busy hastily gathering themselves to notice the birds or their watchers. It had all been peaceful until the deep bass notes of a horn had rung out, and the desolate, beaten warriors had taken up arms and halted their mundane activities. As one impressive unit, they had gathered their camp and packed up. It was an unsettling thing to gaze upon. Gone were the marks of Emir and Roja's violence, which had caused their idleness these past few weeks. Like a frenzied anthill, the camp buzzed with their excitement.

They've caught a scent.

Uden?

Another town?

The brutes took to the march quickly and efficiently, moving with weapons drawn. Within no time at all, they disappeared from their encampment, leaving only a cloud of dry dust in their wake. Leaving their observers behind.

A hammering boomed hard in Erroh's ears as the southerners faded away, and he realised it was his own heart drumming his panic. He took a few calming breaths and found his nerve. Fright usually passed, replaced by adrenaline. Bloodlust soon followed.

I'm not alone.

Everyone is here for this.

Everyone is terrified.

"They're tracking something," declared Emir. Everybody knew it, but he said it regardless, to bring a certainty to his feelings. There were a few nods of agreement.

"Something big. Riders not charge ahead," Nomi hissed. She had pulled her weapon, a large war hammer with a damaged grip, from behind her back. Its head was heavy and dull, with little decoration. The body was old but strong. She rested it against her leg and waited for orders. Her lower lip quivered.

The rest of them instinctively drew their weapons as well, readying themselves for more than just watching. All except for Aurora. She watched the dust with unemotional eyes and her hands held behind her back. She was obviously too scared to unsheathe her sword.

Think, Erroh. Don't leave the innocent to face the threat alone.

"That's a pursuing charge. I've seen it before," said Wrek coldly. He looked shaken.

Wynn wiped his brow. "Well, fearless leader. Do we follow?"

"Aye we do. Carefully." Erroh gripped the reins. It had been a perfectly normal day watching the Hunt, waiting for some action, hoping to ease Lexi into the task. Now that something had actually occurred, though, he had no clue what to do. No, that wasn't true at all. He knew exactly what to do. He would watch no massacre in silence. He remembered the scared cub he'd been in the first town of Nioe, alone with the dead and the burning pyre, screaming for a challenge. Highwind whinnied in disagreement and stamped her hooves loudly in agitation. He wondered, did she recognise that sound?

"Brother, I need you to get ahead of them," Erroh told Wynn quietly. It was an order.

Wynn nodded. Order accepted.

"I'll ride with him. Better two than one," Lillium said. It sounded like an order, too.

"Why not all?" Lexi challenged.

"I'd like to monitor them," Erroh hissed.

Don't question me, little one.

"Take no chances," Erroh warned them, dismissing the former lovers as he brought his horse away from the treeline's safety. "Ride ahead a while, search for their prize, and wait for us on higher ground," he called, as the rest followed uneasily.

Wynn and Lillium tore up the ground beneath them as they raced into the heavy green, first matching the Hunt's running charge and then overtaking them. They crouched low in their saddles, their thundering movement lost beneath the roar of the march they were following.

Far behind, the Master General followed the clustered, marching brutes. He counted at least three or four hundred warriors with sharpened blades. The Hunt had fewer riders for such forces, and he took it as a small blessing.

A dozen warriors against an army.

No problem.

They seemed to charge forever. They charged with fervour and hunger, and Spark City's Outcasts followed close behind. They never spoke among themselves. They merely followed their Master General in a thin, wary line through the thick foliage, trusting his leadership would not bring doom upon them all.

I have waited for this, he told himself, and couldn't shake the terror stirring deep within him.

————

It was night before Lillium and Wynn reappeared and met up with them upon a steep hill, far from eager eyes, where Erroh had commanded them all to stop and rest. They set down in a clustered little hollow to stretch and eat what scraps of foods they carried. Erroh's entire body ached from the exertion. The day-long strain of pursuing while maintaining a safe distance had been exhausting. Erroh touched his chest to see if his old wounds had opened. It was one thing sparring; it was another riding all day. He shared some dry bread with his mate and sister, all the while suppressing the fear that he was leading his companions to a grisly death.

There's something in the wind.

"They're following tracks made by another nomadic procession," Wynn said. He, too, was exhausted, Erroh saw. They were all feeling the effects. "We would have returned sooner, but we needed to know how fresh the tracks were," he added, dropping carefully to a knee. His eyed glimmered despite the terror. It was a better look to him.

"You both did well. Rest a while," Erroh said.

Of them all, it was only Tye who appeared unreadable. The young cub leaned against a tree, watching the distant line of brutes disappear through the trees. He tapped his foot rhythmically as though he were at the fireside with a song in the air, but apart from that, he appeared tranquil.

Jeroen would be proud.

He hadn't spoken a great deal with Erroh these last few weeks. Instead of engaging in unsavoury discussions, he had offered to patrol the perimeter and had been first to climb atop a horse to watch the Hunt's gathering. Attempts to speak of Jeroen and his heroism were unwelcome, and Erroh honoured Tye's request for silence on the matter. Safer conversation was to be had on the subjects of tactics and swordplay, or the particular intricacies of the opposite sex. These were no straightforward conversations, however, like he'd had at the farm before his Cull, but there were glimmers of the same camaraderie they had once shared. Perhaps it was the consequence of the terrible circumstances they lived in, or the effect of his own position as Master General that made these things awkward. Regardless, though Tye had changed, there was still an unquenchable spark in his eyes. Would Jeroen have wanted him in battle? Erroh wondered, and shuddered.

Probably not.

"Walk with me a moment, Tye," Erroh said to him quietly.

Out of earshot of the others, Erroh turned to the younger man. "Can I trust you?" he asked, when he was certain no eager ears were listening. The youth nodded, though his eyes never left the disappearing brutes. His hatred rivalled Lillium's. Erroh's too.

It's okay, friend. We'll be back following them soon enough.

"If there is fighting, I need you to keep Lexi safe," he whispered, lest the young girl hear and create a problem. "Keep her out of harm's way." He gripped the young man's sturdy shoulder. He wanted to thank him, to embrace him and reassure him that his father's sacrifice meant something. Instead, he merely nodded.

Tye's head dropped, and he looked his age again. "Why not send her away, now?" The last thing Tye desired was responsibility. Erroh could see his bloodlust, and it was unsettling. Had he ever had such a look in his own eyes? Aye, he had.

"Oh, if only I could." He knew that Lexi would prefer dying out here, with her family, over cowering away any season of the year. It wasn't in her to avoid a fight. She was a child with a legendary lineage. "She would leave, for a time, but then..." He left the sentence unfinished.

Tye nodded in frustrated understanding. "Do you have some rope?" he jested bitterly, and Erroh realised the arduous task he'd placed upon the cub. Tye eyed her warily. Hard to control a girl like that.

"I expect her to fight, but stay beside her. She is no killer. Not yet."

"I will stay by her side, no matter what."

"That is all I ask, brother," Erroh said.

After a moment, Tye paled. "We're really going to fight, aren't we?" he asked, all hate giving way to fear. *Good.* Better now than on the field ahead.

"Whomever the Hunt chase will not be left alone to face their fate tonight," Erroh said. "So, aye, we will fight." This would be no sacking of Nioe. No slaughter of Cathbar. Saying it aloud made it real. "If I fall, see to it you and Lexi get word to Aymon and Doran that they continue the fight." Erroh squeezed Tye's shoulder once more, then turned and strode away.

"As you wish, Master General."

Something in the boy's nervous reply brought forth the memories of Keri once more. There was a terribleness to waiting like this, knowing something was in the air. Erroh felt like he stood atop the wall with his doomed comrades once more, and the lyrics of a song played in his mind. He wondered about the fleeing convoy. Wondered about their numbers, too. Wondered if they were aware a desperate horde of brutes had their scent, if they knew the greatest gathering of warriors the world had ever known was intent on pulling their doomed fate from the fires.

It would not be Keri, he told himself.

————

The Hunt lit their torches, and Erroh knew they intended to march all night. Like a machine fuelled by a generator, they would march until they'd nothing left. "How long before they catch the convoy?" he asked, returning to Wynn and Lillium, who sat listening to the sounds of the natural night returning.

"Their tracks suggested only a day or so west," Wynn whispered.

"We should rest for three or four hours and then catch up," Lea said from behind him. She was playing with a piece of moss at her feet. She moulded it into a heap, and then placed her cloak upon it to make a pillow.

"And what if Wynn is wrong?" asked Lillium, though not unkindly.

Wynn sniffed. "I'm not wrong."

"Then we rest," declared Erroh, grateful for Wynn's certainty. His body was battered by the day. The Hunt would march until they were exhausted, he knew. A few hours' sleep might be the difference between the Outcasts delivering a killing blow and taking one.

He tried to find words, but none came. All of them were fine warriors, and each of them was likely to face the enemy soon. They looked uneasy, pensive and incredible, and he wanted to take them all aside, each in turn, and build them ten feet tall before sending them out into battle, but he didn't have the heart to lie to their faces. Some of his comrades were going to die in the coming battle. He'd done his best to protect Lexi, which was all he could do. Life wasn't fair at the worst of times. Without tactics or lay of the land to call upon, he felt helpless before the gods of fate. He had no cards; he had no bet. The pot was real fuken precarious, as well. The smarter move was getting up from the table. Yet here he was, playing cheerfully as though it were a small matter.

Erroh closed his eyes and curled up against Lea, and fell into an uneasy sleep. His companions around him slept, too. All but Roja. She volunteered to take first watch.

They caught up with the Hunt long after dawn. The continuous march had taken its toll in the last few hours and slowed their pace. He gripped the reins of Highwind and followed Wynn through the heavy undergrowth at pace. The taller Alphaline had a knack for navigating through the forest, and they made excellent time. If the Hunt's scouts noticed the line of riders charging past them, they never let on, and indeed allowed them to go on their merry little way. Their tastes were for the fresher tracks beneath their feet. It was only after the sound of death was far behind that Wynn dragged his horse through the trees and followed the fleeing convoy's tracks.

At noon, they finally came upon their quarry. They were in a shallow valley, with clustered trees running up the hills on either side of it.

"Hold," shouted Wrek suddenly, as the Outcasts almost broke from the safety of the forest midway up the valley crest. "I know those flags," he growled, seeing the coloured banners waving lazily in the wind. Their quarry was no longer interested in fleeing, for they had settled themselves in the valley centre, seemingly awaiting their pursuers. A fine place to mount an ambush. Shame there weren't enough soldiers for the task. "That's no fleeing town at all," growled Wrek, steadying his mount as it fought to bolt forward. He leapt to the ground and pulled his beast farther up the slope, careful to keep his hulking mass as low to the ground as possible. On another day it might have been humorous. As it was, it was perfectly reasonable behaviour when hiding from death.

"Oh, fuk me. Get up through the treeline, now," murmured Wynn, dropping and following.

"Were we seen?" hissed Lillium, looking behind her as she, too, dropped to her feet and led her horse up after the rest.

"Their eyes may have been on the valley entrance and not us," said Lea. It sounded reasonable enough, so Erroh accepted it.

There were twenty long carts set up tightly in a circle. Each cart was loaded and reinforced with every scrap of material they had. A desperate blockade for desperate times.

Like Keri's defences.

Many figures stood ready atop the carts. They knew they were being followed, and they knew they couldn't outrun their vanquishers, so they had found the most suitable place to engage the Hunt and dug in.

"Least we know why they aren't marching towards the Spark," Lexi said. A fine point. They would not be welcome, regardless of their desperation.

"Fuken bandits," spat Emir, lifting his crossbow instinctively.

Stefan placed a hand on his shoulder. "Let's not start another fight, brother. At least not yet." It was a fine suggestion.

"I've never seen so many, not even in Raven Rock,"

whispered Roja, following behind the line as they walked their horses up the valley's edge, away from the future battlefield.

"I have," muttered Wrek.

Lea nodded absently. She'd seen as many before. Erroh too.

There were at least a hundred and fifty bandits—men, women, and children. Each wore a black sash around their arm. All that were able held weapons in shaking hands, and Erroh knew this was not a fight they were invited to. They travelled high along the valley's edge and moved past the little blockade without incident, and Erroh's heart beat wildly. Under the cover of trees, they set their mounts out to graze and then set themselves down in the long grass to view the doomed thieves below. They were close enough that they kept their voices low, but far away enough that it would take an attacker a long time to scale the steep incline.

"We'll have a fine view of the slaughter," said Emir in disgust. "I'm not entirely sure who I favour in this battle." He plucked a fine strand of wild grass and chewed it, savouring its sweetness.

"Many bandits are no good at all, but there are some, decent like," Wrek said, stroking his beard nervously.

"There are probably a few good southerners among them," added Wynn.

"Bandits or no, there are children among them," Lea whispered. She held Baby in her hands but it held no arrow. Not yet.

"The enemy of my enemy," said Erroh quietly. He wasn't sure anybody heard him.

"They are savages," suggested Stefan, shrugging. Erroh knew the man's first kill had also been a bandit. Stefan held no love for them after the long march to the city and the horrific losses they'd incurred under their attacks. Regardless, Erroh doubted that Stefan's coldness extended to the children. They *were* bandits, but these brutes were not holding up wanderers of the road or ambushing wary, weary travelling refugees. They were refugees themselves, fearing the oncoming storm and the inevitable slaughter. They were human, too. They just weren't as skilled at appearing so.

On the other wretched hand, they were Spark's enemies. How many below had murdered innocents in better bandit days?

"It is pure murder if we do not help," said Lexi. Her eyes remained focused on the circle below and the little group of children in its centre, as far from danger as possible, hidden behind drinking barrels and sacks of food.

"It's not murder," argued Wynn. "But remaining concealed for the greater good is a dreadful thing."

"Aye, it may not be murder, but that doesn't mean that it's right to leave them," said Tye. He was pale, and he gripped his crossbow tightly. High above them, a low rumble of thunder sounded. The sky had taken on a terrible dreary shade, and rain was coming. It was no day for warfare, for riding, for marching, or for harvesting, either. A smarter fiend might take cover beneath the smallest tree in a large forest and keep a wary eye on the clouds above.

Roja knelt and stared down. "The Hunt can't be allowed to slaughter anymore." It was a fine argument. The people camped in the valley were from the lowest lines, but death was death. Shame was shame, too. "Not again."

"Bandits?" asked Nomi, and Erroh caught Lea rolling her eyes. Choosing his words carefully, he translated as best he could. Nomi nodded as he spoke, and Lea rolled her eyes a second time.

Not now, Lea.

"Can't leave children," cried Nomi. "Can't leave those fight alone." That was exactly how Erroh felt. Problem was strolling on down there, without getting an arrow in the heart the moment they stepped into the encampment. And coming to the brutes' aid? It was likely they'd be mugged for their troubles, or even worse. As for the children? The world stopped when it came to children. Never mind the fact that these youngsters would grow to become killers themselves.

Prejudice.

If no one attempted to climb above their prejudices, how well could the world continue to grow? It was a fine, humbling thought, and Erroh had no issue with changing his mind on matters he was passionate about. Perhaps the world might have been better if people were simply allowed to hold their different beliefs and opinions.

If only.

Only Ealis had little to say. She stared serenely at a crop of wild grass waving in the wind in front of her, ignoring the discussions, the decisions, the threat in the air. She counted the strands under her breath as she plucked them and Erroh found it was an unsettling thing to gaze upon, though he wasn't certain why.

"Have your crossbows ready," he said, in a tone that brooked no argument. "We bide our time."

———

In the hours before the Hunt caught up with the travelling convoy of bandits, the weather took a poorer turn, and as night set in, a thin wave of rain fell. The clouds above groaned and threatened to erupt into a full tempest, and Erroh and his unvanquished Outcasts lay in the cold, damp grass waiting for death. Unsure of what to do except watch.

The bandits with the black sashes kept their heads up and their red flags flying, as if they somehow believed in patriotism and pride. They lit torches to welcome their vile conquerors. It was a final invitation for all to see, and Erroh, despite his own misgivings for their kind, approved of their insolence. Born to a life of thievery and murder, these animals had learned that once an enemy picked up a trail, the end was inevitable. Had they themselves not been the hunters many times before? Was this not their way?

Unlike their victims, though, they would not run and hide. They ran until they could make a stand, and though they were outnumbered two to one, they were ready to meet the attack and their deaths' head on. The children in the base's heart were quiet, huddled together, no doubt praying to their criminal gods. They did not cry out. Surely something like that deserved respect? Acknowledgement? Salvation?

Were it to be a fair fight, Erroh would have had few issues with intervening. Were it a town of innocents, even fewer. As it was, it was his decision as Master General. He would not put the matter to a vote. Would not place such guilt upon his generals.

They heard the rumble an hour before the first of the Hunt erupted from the trees, like a swarm of wasps maddened by smoke and water. They came for blood and they came for death. They came for the end. They did not hesitate, and they did not answer to generals. They merely surged forward with swords raised in weary hands. Their intimidating screams filled the world, and when the great horns sounded, Erroh felt chills run up his spine. He suddenly felt every dead warrior of Keri nearby. Could hear their singing voices against the unending call of ominous pipes. He could almost taste the fine meat they had shared around the fires. And then Erroh, Keri's champion, remembered the last night, when the rain had fallen upon them all.

Are you watching, Quig?

Is Aireys with you?

"Lace the arrows," Erroh ordered. His comrades became a shuffling unit, dabbing their arrow tips, one after the other, in the little bowl of foul poison. Their few muted curses of fear and annoyance soon fell silent as what was happening around them became more than just a philosophical debate. They were Alphalines; they could not run away. And those without the blessed, entitled bloodline? Well, their heroism was something else entirely. Something impressive.

"Is this not why we fight?" growled the Master General. The rumble of foot soldiers grew louder and shook the valley itself. The horns grew louder, but so did the natural world, and the thunder finally roared as the storm broke.

Twenty terrified bandits held their nerve and leapt from their cover, scrambling over the blockaded carts and out into the middle of the grassland. They sprinted towards the soldiers, and then, under orders from one large brute, fell to a knee and loaded their crossbows. In the darkness there was a sudden flicker of movement, and beyond, five or six of the leading line of Hunt fell in the long grass. A terrible first volley. They were hardened bandits, but in the end, fear made even the most assured hands shake.

Regardless of their terror, they never stopped. The Hunt continued their charge, and the bandits reloaded and, as commanded, fired once again. A dozen fell. The second strike had been made with far less nervous fingers.

Better.

"Back," the bandit leader shouted, and they retreated swiftly.

.   .   .

"Magnificent," shouted Wynn, in awe of their bravery and precision.

"Magnificent. But it will not help," said Emir. "The children," he said softly, his coldness forgotten as he realised the massacre to come. The children clung to one heavily-pregnant woman in the centre, and she clung to each of them as if her arms would somehow keep them safer. It was too much. Gripping his crossbow, he stood up and cursed the fiends, and Erroh wondered was Emir imagining the last moments of Aireys and Quig, those final moments he'd been denied. "It's not right," he shouted, and it was a fine outburst.

"Well, you heard him," Erroh cried. "Let's take them out."

Lea fired first. The arrow flew away into the night. It carried high in the wind and then dropped like a stone into the charging army. The warrior she'd struck ran for a few moments before realising he was mortally wounded.

Following her lead, the rest of the comrades picked their targets and fired. After a few moments, they fired again. And then again. Not all hit their mark, but enough did that the bandits began to notice the unexplained deaths of their attackers. From behind their barricade, they fired their own arrows.

"This is easy," Lexi cried in triumphant horror, reloading her crossbow. Her bolt felled a third faceless brute and she smiled grimly. Erroh carried no bow, for his focus was reserved for the battle alone. Besides, he didn't trust his clumsy hands not to poison himself while trying to load an arrow. He was happy to sit this massacre out.

For the now.

"Take the shot, Tye," he whispered from behind the

young cub. He was shaking, as though unprepared to kill. "Don't hesitate. They are swarming," he added with more force. The child needed a master, not kind words. Tye released the bolt into the night. "You missed… Reload," Erroh hissed, and Tye did so, quicker this time. Releasing again, he struck a warrior down, and Erroh was satisfied. "Better," he said, watching the doomed man crawl on all fours from the melee, unaware that the sooner he passed into the night the better. "They took Jeroen," whispered Erroh. It was a cruel tactic to stir the hate in the young man, but he knew that in his place, Magnus would have said those exact words. War was brutal, and Erroh directed his first command with brutality. Tye fired and reloaded without bothering to watch the fate of his previous victim.

Excellent. Well done, soldier.

The great carts rolled slowly into the clearing and halted. Above them, the thunder continued to rumble, like drums calling for the dead, beckoning them home, asking them not to come alone. The Hunt spread out along the barricade, searching for a means of entry. The torches cast an eerie light upon the attackers, and from above, it looked like an escaped nest of angry arachnids crawling all over the barricade.

The Outcasts went to task swiftly and viciously now, firing bolts and arrows from above. It was glorious brutality, and the Hunt suffered dearly in those first few bloody moments.

The bandits held off the first wave. Born into a life of struggle and bloodshed, they dispatched the few attackers who breached the carts with dull efficiency and calm assuredness. They had built the wall soundly, and the Hunt crashed up against it and killed themselves every time they attempted to breach. The southerners were a warring, savage race, but what good was aggressive savagery against such well-trained forces?

Still, though, they were relentless, and they had superior numbers. They had belief and pride, for they hadn't yet heard the first screams of agony from their fallen brothers and sisters far behind them, those unlucky few who now tasted the pain of Emir's potion as it flowed through their veins and set them alight. They charged forward, intent on victory. Any watcher with an eye for war could see the outcome of this battle.

"The bandits will fall, soon enough," predicted Wrek, dropping his head. He had no more arrows left. None of them did.

They had done all they could. The brave defence would fall, and the true horror would follow soon after. Erroh could see the heroic brigands standing atop the carts to stem the tide of the next wave of brutes. They swung and cut and tore into their killers, and screamed and wailed as they did. He remembered Keri again, and it felt bitterly familiar.

Suddenly, lightning cracked down, striking the Hunt's tallest flag, and Ealis fell to her knees as the landscape was lit up bright as noon. Sparks flew down the flag's metal shaft, and an invisible wave of energy exploded outwards, knocking men and women from their feet. It was almost enough to stop the attack.

The fear of electrocution did little to stop their bloodlust. They killed in the name of Uden. With a mighty roar, they drove into the barricades and rocked them under their weight.

"We should move from here, lest the lightning strike closer," declared Lillium uneasily, turning away from the violence. "I wish to see no more."

None of them did.

They could hear the fresh screams now from their victims

as the poison took hold. They climbed onto their mounts, preparing to make a swift and unnoticed escape, but Erroh held back a moment longer. Emir and Lea brought their horses alongside him but said nothing. This was his guilt to carry, and all of them accepted that. Far below them, the Hunt overturned one cart and gained ground at the gap. The bandits desperately battered them back with shields, while others swung hammers and battle axes, hoping to stem the tide.

The breach was too much for one watching child, intent on survival. As the comrades watched from the hillside, she ran, swift as a hare, into the dark.

Her name was Elcass, and she'd always been a swift runner. Her mother had always told her as much, but she couldn't see her anymore. Nor her father. Somewhere out in the madness, they were fighting the monsters. And it terrified her.

She could take no more. A good thief always knew when to use their fleetness of foot. She slipped from her keeper's hand and leapt over the barrel and out through the darkness towards one of the barricades. She was small and slippery. They'd never see her. Crawling under the cart, she crept through a few obstacles of buckets and sacks of clothing. She pushed them aside, and when there was a break in the awful boots and rampaging mounts, she charged out through the darkness. On either side she heard screams of hate and aggression as the monsters ran past her, searching for a way to get at her people. And then she was clear of them.

"I can't watch this," Lea whispered, seeing the child slip free of the Hunt's charge and race towards the slope they stood on. Nor could Erroh, but the Alphaline blood coursing through his body forbade him from looking away. From remaining unmoved.

The defence was a thing of legend, but he knew it was destined to be forgotten like the fall of Raven Rock and countless settlements before. No person would live to tell its tale of bravery. The correct move on the Master General's part would be to step away into the wastes with his comrades. Unfortunately, this was Erroh, and seeing the child fleeing stirred something in his heart.

"The child will die if they spot her," Erroh hissed. His mind spun.

"That she will," agreed Emir. Bandit or no, there was a time and place for hatred. For prejudice too.

"Let's charge, Highwind," cried Erroh. He kicked her forward, and they raced down the steep slope. After a moment, Lea and Emir followed. It was a fine way to die, was it not? He didn't hear the rumble of his companions' mounts as they all followed his lead. He could only see the child, maybe ten seasons old, and hear her sobs of panic as she ran blindly away from the madness.

Down through the trees he raced, leaning forward in his saddle. He dared the beast to stumble, threatened it loudly at every step. Distantly, through the canopy, he saw a few brutes turn and set off in pursuit of the little one. He dug his heels into the horse's flanks as they reached the bottom of the slope and kept racing onwards, towards the melee. For only the second time ever, Highwind did not fight his determination.

Beside him, Lea appeared on Shera, with Emir less than a length behind. He glanced back and caught sight of Wrek, Wynn and Lillium, Stefan and Roja, Tye and Lexi, Aurora and Nomi. One divine group, side by side, storming through the open plains into certain death.

Their deaths are upon my head.

"I'll grab the child," screamed Lea, pulling her horse slightly wide to match the child's frantic sprint. Her voice trailed off as they parted, and Erroh changed course to charge down the girl's assailants. He couldn't hear the pumping of his heart or his better senses screaming to retreat. All he heard was the thunder of hooves and the raging wind in his ears. Somewhere deep down, where he locked away all his hate, a cage was breaking open and the Hero of Keri, the legend of the Sweeping Grasslands, was tearing himself free.

With a primal roar, the Master General announced his arrival on the field of battle, and he announced himself grandly. Gripping his mount with his thighs, he pulled Mercy and Vengeance from behind his head and charged forward.

The lightning struck again, though its target this time was not a proud flag, but one of the great carts as it rolled slowly through the field. A plume of fire blew out of it in a wonderful explosion, sending the attackers scattering for cover as it burned to cinders, and it was an incredible, godly sight.

A third bolt struck another great cart, causing further casualties and triggering pandemonium through the ranks. The smell of burnt flesh filled the night, and once more Erroh, amidst the chaos, remembered Keri.

The land was illuminated now by lightning and fire, and without the cover of darkness, the Hunt could plainly see the thin line of cavalry charging from the edge of the valley, led by a screaming myth known as the false god of fire.

Three of the pursuers fell as the Master General struck. On either side of him, his swords tasted blood, while the razor-sharp hooves of his thundering beast dashed those in front to nothing. All the while he roared, and they fuken heard. Erroh was real, and he brought lightning; he brought fire; he brought a turning of the tide.

. . .

Lea broke away, and as the child neared, she leant across the saddle and reached out. Instinctively, the child reached for salvation. An arrow passed between them, and Lea saw the fear in the girl's eyes.

So close. Don't let them take her now.

She thought of the little girl dead among the heather.

So close.

And then their fingers touched. With a yell of triumph, she wrenched the child up on to her lap, clasping her tightly. As the girl bawled in terror, Lea pulled Shera's head around and galloped back towards the line of Outcasts as they crashed into the Hunt. Nobody noticed her heroism. Then again, few ever did. Hers was the quieter path, even if it was the more impressive.

Erroh screamed with everything he had, in the hopes he could move them with his voice alone. A fine way to die, no doubt. Line upon line he broke through, and the Hunt, with their backs turned, died under his comrades' collective charge. Lightning flashed again and thunder roared, and onwards he led his companions through the wall of black until they reached the gap the bandits tried desperately to seal.

"Clear the way," he roared above the terrible noise. The bandits leapt aside, and the Outcasts cleared the last line and crashed through into a slightly less hostile battleground. Erroh dropped from his mount and ran to the opening to meet the attackers as they recovered from their rear assault. His companions passed him by. He counted them as they did. Had they lost anyone?

Emir, Wynn, Lillium, Roja.

Tye, Lexi, Wrek, Stefan.
Ealis.

Where was Nomi? Where was Lea? He screamed her name in panic, and in the next moment, Lea and Nomi charged through, side by side. Close behind them, the Hunt came on with all they had—an excellent tactic when a line was breached. The Hunt still had fine numbers, did they not? They were not to know they charged straight into the finest gathering of warriors in the Four Factions, who gifted them a fair fight.

The clash of steel and howls of anguish filled the air as the Hunt flooded in through the hole. Erroh met their charge single-handedly, his blades spinning with murderous intent.

Only a hundred to fell?
Still, no problem.

Around him, the bandits renewed their defence, buoyed by the ferocity of their new allies. As Erroh tore into the attackers, they too countered the waves of invaders as they scrambled over the crudely efficient ramparts, meeting the assault with renewed aggression.

Lea and Nomi reached him first, charging into the battle as recklessly as he had, and in a few swings of deadly blades, they cleared enough room to breathe. Ealis charged in, clutching two long daggers in her hands, which she used with sublime skill. Stabbing swiftly, her hands a blur, she then used each of her dying victims as a shield against the next warrior in her way. She swayed among her companions, as though she'd fought with them all their lives.

Beside her, the rest of Emir's Fighting Mongooses brought the fight to the unsuspecting Hunt. They slashed with deadly accuracy, and their victim numbers soon rose.

This was not Keri. This was something far greater.

This was swift; this was violent; this was divine.

. . .

Only Wynn did not join the line of fighters. He moved to their flank and used his talent to pick off the brutes who scaled the carts around the rest of the barricade. It was simple, and it was murder, and it was necessary. He struck out and killed any who attempted to sneak behind the impressive line, and it was he, upon the edge of the defiant blockade, who saw that victory was at hand. Taking a moment to catch his breath with a dozen still bodies at his feet, he was surveying the battlefield in all its glory when another bolt of lightning struck one of the huge carts. As the flames roared skyward, the Hunt stood watching in dumb awe as a ragtag pack of nomads slaughtered their entire army.

Too shocked to blow the horns of retreat, the Hunt mustered their remaining strength and continued to charge aimlessly into the wall of Outcasts, where they swiftly met their end. Those who did manage to retreat fled the ill-fated plain, seeking refuge in the unending forest.

Watching the enemies' numbers dwindle like water down a hole, Wynn almost believed in his comrades' eventual survival. He roared in defiance, and months of horror slipped off his shoulder, leaving him almost lightheaded. Were he to think on this, he might have considered this an exceptional moment in an otherwise wretched life.

The tide of invaders slowed and then became still. The air was filled with screams of the injured and dying. Erroh fell to a knee and tried to gather his breath. He'd never felt so tired. No, that wasn't true. He'd felt this tired before, each time he'd had as many deaths on his shaking hands. Gasping, he looked along the line of his companions. Each one, as still as he, was watching the gap, waiting for the next lamb to be slaughtered; each one wore an old warrior's stare. Their numbers were impressive. Then, somewhere above the cries of agony, he could hear another sound. Far warmer, and primal.

Cheering?

The bandits should have been lamenting their dead, but instead, they celebrated. They roared their defiance. They cheered the strangers who'd rescued them at their hour of need, and Erroh felt the strange sensation of … victory.

Emir moved first. He dropped his sword and ran to his horse to gather his medical supplies. He'd been here before, many times. Bandits or not, he was a healer, and the wounded and dying lay all around the barricade. After a few more breaths, the cheering fell silent, and the world returned to itself. The bandits went about tending to their wounds and rummaging among the dead for trinkets and valuables. This was the road, after all.

Erroh walked in a daze throughout the blood-soaked encampment. His hands shook, still tightly gripping his swords. He wanted to fall to his knees and lament his misery, but it was Nomi who pulled him from his stupor. Her hammer lay against her thigh, its head a deep, wet crimson. She was trying to wipe the little shards of shattered bone from it now with her bare hands. Her head was low, her face pale like death, and her hands shook uncontrollably. He wanted to run to her and comfort her. To be a killer of one's own kind was fine in war, was it not?

Instead, he walked away from her. Lea would not have approved, he thought bitterly—and perhaps a little unfairly.

But as he strode away, back turned, she dropped the weapon and ran to him. Without warning, she grasped onto him, hugging him tightly in the vain hope that he could take the shame from her. All she could do was cry, and he turned and held her as she wept. He was but a man. She cried and moaned a few incomprehensible words until he gently released her. Wiping her eyes, she stepped away and returned to the gruesome task of cleaning her former people's blood from her weapon.

Erroh turned to see the quiet figure of Lea standing among the dead. She, too, appeared jaded. But she was still radiant and beautiful, and his instincts told him to run to her and cradle her tenderly. It was a fine plan, and it didn't work, for as he took a step toward her, an unfamiliar voice full of great threat drew him from his thoughts.

"Thank you, stranger."

58

DESIRE

He introduced himself as Bison. He was a tall, burly, middle-aged brute with short brown hair. His face was impossibly clean shaven, and although his eyes were dull, they flashed with intelligence. He was taller than Erroh, and he stood over him now with arms crossed as though he were impatient with the newcomers. As though gratitude was beneath him. Erroh recognised him as a leader, and he knew that any bandit leader was likely to be impressive, threatening, resolute, no matter what deeds had occurred.

All around him, the bandits sheathed their weapons and began disassembling the barricade as if it were daily routine. There were few tears shed for the departed, nor anger for those who had assailed them. It was merely a way of life and death to them. It was interesting and unsettling to witness.

"My friends call me Erroh."

Bison, playing the part of casual host, invited Erroh and his comrades to sit where the children had cowered at the heart of the gathering among the barrels. Lea and Lillium followed, their eyes as wary and curious as Erroh's. With a subtle gesture, Bison summoned a bottle and two glasses.

These were brought to a makeshift table, where Bison poured two generous measures of dark red wine. He never acknowledged Erroh's companions. This was a table for the males, it would appear.

This is different.

His hands barely shook now, despite the turmoil of battle only moments before, and he lifted one goblet to his lips and drank heartily, as if they were friends enjoying a drink after a day's toil in the fields. "Join me, warrior," he growled.

More torches were lit. The extent of devastation was apparent. The bandits were now methodically heaving the many bodies of the enemy over the barricade, to join their dead brothers and sisters in the crimson-coloured grass. The carts were being repaired and reloaded, and the world continued on with its turning. Erroh sipped the wine before offering the goblet to Lea and then Lillium after. Bison watched him impassively.

Point made.

He knew of the different customs among the wild brutes of the road, but he had no intention of breaking his life's habit merely out of politeness. Women were the primary species in this world. Males were merely physically dominant. In a better world, there could have been balance, but no world was better.

"You bring women to the tables of leaders?" Bison said at length. It was the first gambit in an exchange of nerves. It was not the first time Erroh had faced these animals this way. It wouldn't be the last. Their heroism had earned them grace in the camp. But there was a limit.

"They usually lead the seating," Erroh countered smoothly. No need to irritate the brute needlessly.

He snorted. "Well, each to their own, friend. It would take a lot of persuasion on my part to bow humbly as you do. Still,

I am old. Stuck in my ways," he said after a few moments.
"So pay my prejudices no heed, Alpha." He made a gesture
with his hand across his chest, an old superstitious blessing of
protection from evil. Erroh thought it unusual to see such
practices here. They must have travelled far.

"Aye, I am an Alpha. This close to Samara, you are
certain to see enough of us. Our tables are impressive. All are
equal, and all are welcome."

"Shame I'm not marching to Spark."

All around them, the energetic buzz of activity was
increasing. Erroh's eyes broke away from his host. Aurora
was out on the battlefield with Stefan and Wrek, taking a last
walk through the dead. Dispatching those struck down by
Emir's potion.

What could this battle be called? he wondered. What tales
and songs would spread throughout the land, through the
voices of the thieves and the Hunt?

I waged war and returned with all my allies.

Erroh felt unusually settled. The relief of knowing his
comrades lived to kill another day without carrying serious
injury was a wonderful balm to qualm the battle shakes. He
could smell the blood on himself, though. The full horror of
the skirmish had not struck him yet, but he knew he would
have fresh nightmares after this, each one vivid and bloody
and likely filled with further losses to those he cared about
most. He couldn't remember when he'd stopped having
terrible dreams. Perhaps he'd just become more adept at
forgetting them. Forgetting his sins, too. He'd lost count of
his tally. The ghosts of Keri would be pleased. His soul might
disagree.

Lea and Lillium rolled some barrels closer and took a seat
with Erroh. The few children shuffling behind them,
watching their every move, all scurried away from Bison, lest

they incur some unknown punishment for taking an interest in such an unusual event.

Foreign ways were both terrifying and intriguing to young minds, Erroh knew. Sometimes it was perfectly acceptable to allow them to investigate; other times, it was best to shelter their poor, precious little minds. A fair thing, he supposed. It was not his place to interfere, regardless of his own inclination to allow them to draw in closer. Customs were customs, and he was the outsider here. He believed everyone had a right to their ways and beliefs. He wouldn't condemn and crush the man for being brought up as he was.

That was prejudice, was it not?

The children shuffled away, still gazing at Lexi and Nomi, who had displayed such prowess in battle. It wasn't just the children who stared, either. Some of the older women gazed at them with awe, and Erroh thought that an interesting thing. Sparks had been lit over smaller matters.

It was Roja alone, staring blankly out across the breached wall, whom the children dared address first. Perhaps she looked most approachable. They didn't know her at all.

She knelt down to answer a young girl's questions. The little one was dressed in a shredded outfit comprising of decade-old fabrics strung together with a prayer and a firm piece of thread. She was not alone in her destitution; the other cubs were similarly ragged. Erroh caught Roja's delicate smile, and he wondered if she was appreciating the lives she'd saved for the first time. As the child peppered her with questions, Roja laughed and answered what she could about her hair, her dress, her sword, and Erroh smiled. It was a good look to her.

Winning this battle was a good look to them all.

. . .

"It's a little bitter," muttered Lillium, returning the glass to its place at the centre of the oak barrel. She eyed Bison as though challenging him, and after a moment he called for two more glasses. It wasn't a lot, but it was enough.

They shared few meaningful words for a time until eventually, with tiredness overcoming them all, Bison looked to the ground as though in deep thought. Perhaps he thought of the battle and the losses incurred. Perhaps he thought of a mugging. Perhaps he thought of a suitable reward for the actions the Outcasts had taken. Regardless, it was Emir who disturbed the delicate truce. Having finished tending to the few injured bandits, he took to a little bartering.

"I need them," he called suddenly, and Erroh looked across to see him aloft in a cart, tearing at some sheets of dark red. "It's a fair deal," he added, turning to the aggrieved bandit below who had his hands on them, keeping them from his grasp.

"I said you may have *some*," the nasty-sounding bandit countered. He looked fierce, but there wasn't blood in the air. At least Erroh didn't think so.

"This is some of them."

"That's all of them."

"These four? That's all? Come on? I saved your friend." Emir pulled his treasures free from the rest of the sheets and dropped to the ground.

"It was an arrow to the knee."

"That can kill!"

Bison laughed at the commotion. "Your healer has decided a little retribution is in order for his services. He knows the road well enough."

"He doesn't know his place," Erroh retorted.

"We owe you a debt. We have wine and supplies. Fabric

too, apparently. I suppose you might take your fill and be on your way. And we on ours."

"Your friendship is all I wish this gruesome night, friend."

"You ask a steep price." Bison sniggered and tapped the table a few times. Perhaps a debt unpaid was something to be avoided in this gathering. "You will have it, Alpha, at least for tonight."

Enemy of an enemy.

He pointed carelessly at the deadliest girl in the world. To Erroh, she was the most beautiful girl in the world. "I like this one. I'd like to purchase her." Erroh could see the cold mischief in his eyes. Or else stupidity, thinking a girl like this could be bartered. "Can you cook?"

"I'm a terrible cook," Lea said, and somehow it sounded like a threat.

"You've a fine eye. However, she is spoken for," Erroh growled.

"Fine. What about the redhead?" Lillium snorted at this, before leaning forward to stare right through him. Erroh knew that look; he'd met it in the Cull in better days. "Or this one here? The one staring at me."

"I'm a magnificent cook," warned Lillium.

"We take our leave of you, sir," Erroh offered. He got to his feet and bowed.

He rose, but Bison took his hand, sending him back to his seat. "Ye can't take a jest, can you?" Erroh could see now how he had tested them from the moment they had sat down at the table. How he had manoeuvred them towards serving his greater needs. Apparently, any debt owed by bandits meant little.

"Oh, I can. However, the night is drawing in and I have many miles to walk before dawn."

"And what if I preferred you stay a little while longer and

join us on our merry little wander? For both our benefits." He smiled with everything but his eyes, and Erroh understood the threat. Why allow a dozen warriors to leave their group when a little manoeuvring might earn them additional escorts should another army come a-hunting?

Still, he held onto Erroh's wrist, and Erroh eyed Lea.

Should I?

She shook her head. No need to kill the cur. Not yet. Not until he actually made the threat.

"Friends don't ask such things. We gifted you time enough to slither away from this region. Be satisfied with that reprieve … friend," Erroh said, and gently twisted Bison's hold from him. He could have kept hold, kept twisting and pulled the fuk over the barrel to emphasise his point. Bison might be the bigger hound, but Erroh had the bite. He didn't fear being outnumbered for a second time tonight, either.

"Oh, and our gathering was going so well," Bison mocked, and shook his head as though truly devastated. "I've cut down fiends for less." It was a weak threat. His face flushed, for he knew his cold assuredness meant little among this gathering of warriors. They had impressive numbers and the fight *would* be in their favour should he cry out. But at what bloody cost? Only a fool avoided one slaughter, just to walk straight into another.

"Tell me, who is your second-in-command?" Lea asked quietly. Her fingers played with a little splinter sticking out of the top of the barrel. The brute felt no need to reply, so Erroh explained the distance of his misstep.

"She wonders whom we address, after she slits your throat a handful of breaths from now." Erroh tipped the goblet of wine over on its side. His heart beat and his arm itched, but his face was serene. He no longer desired Bison's hospitality. The wine streamed over the edge of the table and down the front of the bull's lap. There was no greater insult, and everyone was watching.

"I would take some deep breaths," warned Lillium, and it was fine advice. Perhaps Bison's subjects would avenge his death, but the losses would be catastrophic and he would never share their glory. Some fights weren't worth it.

Erroh rose and bowed once more, slowly. "Be safe on your journey, Bison. I will see you in Adawan, someday," he said. Surprise replaced fear on the brute's face at the mention of the sanctuary.

Realising he would suffer no wound and earn no allies to call upon during the last stretch of their journey, Bison bowed in return before chuckling. The Alphalines turned away and, signalling their comrades, strode with deliberate casualness through the ruin of the camp to recover their mounts.

"I've never known such ungrateful bastards," Wrek hissed when they were out of earshot, and Erroh thought it a fine condemnation.

"But they know how to fight," offered Wynn.

"Aye, that's true," Erroh agreed as he climbed into his saddle. Looking back to the big man sitting at the table, he bowed once more and kicked his beast off to begin the long march home. Though he doubted Bison and his band of nomadic warriors would ever come to his aid, they were fighters and worth their weight in salt, were the Hunt ever to crash over the sandy ground onto the green and dust oasis of Adawan. He sincerely doubted Adawan's leader Ulrik, and Bison would take a step back in leadership, but it was no matter. Whichever bastard earned their place commanding them would have a brutal if undisciplined little army under their watch. That was good for the war. He just hadn't figured out how to take advantage.

Yet.

———

They monitored the surrounding forest, seeking fleeing Hunt, but found little reward. Without the distraction of a slow-marching army to trail, they reached home swiftly enough. Only Lexi seemed distant on the ride, but Roja rode beside her, offering words of reassurance. And this pleased Erroh. If he couldn't comfort the girl, better Roja carry that burden. Aye, Erroh still raged that she had followed him into war, but Tye had stood with her as he'd been instructed. More than that, she had performed admirably. She was bred from thick-skinned warriors. She would wail, she would regret, and she would kill again when needed.

Eventually, the familiar walls welcomed them. Exhausted and worn, the Outcasts returned home victorious. Erroh believed the mood would be disconsolate after such terrible violence. He imagined tears, regret and venomous accusations. He imagined derision for his leadership, and the suggestion of dissent among the ranks. He expected anger. But to his surprise, instead of revolt, he received accolades, kindness and friendship.

All of his companions were uplifted by the night's events, harrowing though they had been. They were built for war, after all. The battle had been a timely distraction from their main cause, but one that had borne fruit. Killing ate at the soul but killing had served them well this night.

Despite the terrible fatigue, Erroh relit the logs in the centre of the town. Though it was closer to dawn than midnight now, Roja set the electric lights to life. She did so in celebration, and Erroh would not argue the point. Tonight, they could do whatever the fuk they wanted. They were heroes, legends, champions, killers.

The companions each took turns soaking themselves in

the river, bathing their bodies and garments clean of human blood and cleansing their minds of the night's dark deeds. Somehow, the cool water made it easier to rise above melancholy.

Erroh was the last to venture to the river. The world felt deathly still now. Despite the water's bitter cold, he leapt straight in, ducking a weary head beneath the surface. He did not laze or swim. Instead, watching his breath in the air, he furiously scrubbed his body free of the mud, sweat and dried blood, and remembered Keri.

You were with me, Quig and Aireys.
Weren't you?
They were.

When he climbed free of the freezing river and donned fresh attire, he found the guilt and the feeling of a tainted body had lessened. This was war; this was his life. He had made a pledge and he would keep it faithfully.

They all sat around the roaring fire, finding its warmth far more comforting than usual. They devoured strips of salted vegetables from their provisions, for their hunger was fierce. They sipped red wine in honour of the lives they had taken. It was Raven Rock wine and a fitting tribute for those who had fallen. He attempted to talk with Tye and Lexi again, but found no words. Instead, he offered each of them a warm embrace and a reassuring whisper that they had performed admirably, that their parents would have been proud. They took the painful compliment well, and it was enough.

Perhaps they were better killers than he was?

He might have shared further words with those needing reassurances, but he was empty. Spent. Satisfied. There were worse ways to end the evening.

. . .

Her name was Aurora, and she was almost sated. She gazed at Stefan and believed him a little taller than before. It was something she couldn't quite put her finger on. In the weeks she'd known him, she had learned all she could to please him. He'd always carried something beneath those pretty eyes. Some dark shame he refused to speak of. She wondered, was it a penchant for strangling cats? She hoped not. That would be strange. She did not know why. Beneath the warm glow of the crackling fire, surrounded by his similarly weary companions, he'd jested a few times, laughed a few times more, and it was a fine thing to listen to.

Stefan drained his goblet and bowed to the Master General, who stood up and embraced him as a brother. A brother of war and blood. In that moment, Aurora understood how deep the divide had been between the two warriors. She also saw it disappear in front of her eyes. In death was redemption, it would appear. Oh, she really enjoyed their ways.

She'd seen Stefan move among her kin of the south, slaying them with carefully trained precision. He had lacked the wildness of the rest. His was a controlled coldness. He had killed and then moved on to the next victim, doing little more than wiping their blood from his eyes, and he was impressive.

He took her hand now, a need in his eyes he'd never shown before. It intrigued her. She lusted for more than blood. Bathing the crimson deliciousness away was an act she'd disliked less than she'd expected, but that was her part to play among these ruthless killers. The lavender essence Lea had gifted her was pleasant enough, and as Stefan led her from the glow of the fire into the warmth of his bed, she was glad her scent was so sweet and alluring. *Different to blood?* It was here she met Stefan as he truly was. Underneath all that self-loathing, he was incredible. As he kissed and groped and swung her wildly around the bedsheets, she moaned in excitement and met his challenge with just as much vigour.

It was desire.

———

The days had finally caught up with the fiery redhead. She drained her goblet and spilled a few drops down her blouse and didn't care at all. This was another life now, different to being the queen bitch of the Spark. This was not ruling a doomed city with endless worry and eternal terror. This was something else entirely. For the first time, she knew where she belonged. She also knew it would not be long before she died.

Roja shook these unhelpful thoughts from her head and excused herself for the night. She was certain she would fall asleep this night, no matter the bed. Stumbling through the darkness, she made her way up through her home and, stripping her dress and undergarments from her bruised body, fell into the warm bedding, only to discover a gift.

A gift worthy of the goddess she was.

A gift worthy enough to incur the wrath of a pack of nasty bandits.

A gift from a man whose heart was greater than any she'd ever known. She almost slid off her mattress, reaching for the lights as her perfect body slid on the silken bedding.

———

"Will we play another hand?" asked Wrek wearily. He couldn't shake the thoughts of Adawan from his mind, but the sine was certainly helping him. He felt like singing, so he did.

A nonsensical few words from a song he'd loved when living in Adawan, about living in the wastes with a one for life, enduring the natural wonder of survival. Even though he sang out of key with the words in the wrong order, Wynn found he knew the notes. For a few moments he felt at home again, and it stung. And reassured him. The world was changing. So should he. Change was natural. Was he?

"And on the first day, I went out."

He took a breath and found the tune's timing.

"And I found myself."

"Fuken far away." He wasn't sure there were curses in the lyrics. It was a small matter.

"And my knees hurt, and it was natural." He didn't care how bad he sounded. In his mind he was weeping for regrets, and melody mattered little to such emotions. He was in the mood to drink and sing until he fell unconscious in front of the warm fire. Any fire would do. This one would last the night. That was enough for him. "And on the next day, I made a new friend... who... oh... wait... shit. Wrong verse."

Wynn adapted and continued. And it was natural.

———

"Walk me home," whispered Lillium, and, finishing the third of Wrek's requests, Wynn nodded and bid a good night to his companions. He ached something awful, yet not as badly as he'd believed he would. His father had warned him of the precarious slope that killing could be. Finding it easier than he'd ever imagined had been a wonderfully dark thing indeed. Better that than crumbling like a waif. He walked her home, drunk as they both were, and it took a time.

She was ravishing in the dim electric light, and he dearly wanted her next to him without the burden of clothes between them, so he kept a healthy distance. She deserved better than what he could give.

She deserved the world.

"Walk me to my bed, my selfish lover," she said, and giggled, falling against the door. His head spun from his own drunkenness, and he stumbled after her.

"You were a warrior goddess," he whispered. It didn't matter if she heard. It was just a thought. She'd been magnificent, and he'd seen her at her most deadly. She was no child, terrorised by the dark, scared and in need of his clumsy protection. She was a deity. She was worthy of her title, and any residual resentment he'd ever held towards her was lost. She was the greater warrior. She always had been. Erroh had been right to promote her ahead of any other.

Her giggling ceased, and he realised his thoughts had actually been spoken aloud. He was also on the ground. He hadn't remembered falling. She reached down and pulled him to his unsteady feet.

"Thank you, Wynn," she said, kissing his cheek. He bowed and assisted her to her bedroom, where he stayed at the doorway awaiting the moment he could politely leave. This was not the first time he'd discovered himself this drunk, this close to her. In this type of mood. She was no longer the delicate creature with a broken heart. This was a fine woman who was confident enough to crave his touch and wake the following morning without regret.

Every time she had offered, he had declined, as graciously as he could. Some of his lies had been rather humbling, and she had taken great delight in his self-mockery. It was more than Magnus's advice; it was the right way to behave. Oh, to spend a moment with that foolish child who'd taken her to bed that first night and every one after. To beat him to a pulp and curse his stupidity. Oh, to offer her such a gift so she might never know the harshness of a needlessly cruel lover. Not to win her over, but merely to remove a scarred memory from the mind of a goddess. His goddess.

I'm sorry, Lillium. I'm so fuken sorry.

He leaned against the edge of the doorway, his mind filled with unsuitable thoughts and honourable deeds. And though the idea of returning to a cold bed held little allurement, he still turned away to leave. "I have returned our first general safely home," he said stoically, then laughed kindly and a little drunkenly.

She undressed behind him, so he took a step towards the stairs before temptation took him.

"Please stay," she said, gliding up behind him and holding him at the waist. It was a firm grip.

"All I want to do is stay, my love, but we both know I can't," he whispered, and tried to disguise the want in his voice. *Don't turn around and gaze at her.*

She spun him around. Of course she did.

She was already naked. Of course she was.

"I'm ordering you to stay, soldier," she whispered. It seemed like a reasonable request. Before he could stop her, she kissed him, and before he could stop himself, he returned the gesture. They sprawled out on the sheets, her eager hands tearing at his clothing. He concentrated on kissing her with all the skill he could remember. She was beautiful and confident, and he treated her as such. Aye, they were drunk like before, but this was different.

This was a gift she would offer only this once, and Wynn, for once, wasn't stupid enough to refuse her. Or ruin her. He kissed her. He touched her. With every body part, he offered. And touch her he did, until she howled with satisfaction and he just continued on. Watching her movements, he swayed with her, watching her eyes for clues of her yearnings, and swiftly he mastered pleasuring her and it was greater than spending himself ten times over.

Hours later, when she fell back in the bedsheets, bathed in victorious sweat, she gasped deeply and giggled delightfully, like a naïve city girl who still believed in hope and romance, deep down. Deep down under the pain. "This means nothing, my love," she gasped as he lay with her. He hadn't attempted to take his own pleasure with her. It was a fine move on his part. He could happily endure a little frustration to hear that levity in her voice.

"Just doing my duty, sir." This moment could last, he decided. He savoured his own exhaustion, the taste of her on his tongue, his stiff jaw and his aching fingers. She was a goddess and he would always love her, but no, he knew it meant nothing. And that was fine, too.

"I liked the kissing parts." She giggled. He said nothing and closed his eyes. He liked the kissing parts, too.

"My turn," she said, and leaned across him and then began kissing him across his chest, and then a little lower. He tried to resist, but his will deserted him as she pinned him down. "And stop hating yourself," she demanded, doing her bit to remind him of his worth.

———

"Was it you?" the stunning redhead cried from the dark. She directed the question at a thoughtful Emir as he stoked the flames and eased himself through his third sine of the night. He had drunk far less than normal, but he was still drunk, because Emir was always drunk. That was fine. He was only half drunk. He was also in a fine mood. It was the little things that made him smile. Like a gift to the woman who needed it most.

Truthfully, Emir had come to the drunken conclusion that he could very well love Roja. He'd suspected such a thing possible the moment she'd dropped from her saddle to die with him a few weeks before. Only now, as she stood in front of him in the fire's light, wrapped in a solitary silk sheet, did he realise he *was* very much in love with Roja. And always had been.

This troubled him less than he expected.

"You looked like you needed a little sleep," he said. He tried to remain calm; his voice was steady. Inside, he was screaming in panic. Was she going to shatter his eggs again? Or follow him around for the next three weeks, eager to make him smile? She walked nearer the fire, gripping the sheets tightly to maintain whatever scraps of her dignity remained.

"What did you do?" asked Erroh, grinning. He tried not to look at her. It didn't matter. She wasn't looking his way. Her eyes were only on Emir.

"He made me a bed of silk," she said.

"Wow—polished manoeuvre, Healer," Lexi said, sniggering as though she knew something that he didn't.

He didn't know at all.

"Come on!" Roja demanded, and Emir leapt to his feet instinctively. Still unsure if he'd pleased her or not, he walked a little closer, just enough that if she struck out, he'd roll with her punch. He really thought he'd done it right, but maybe they weren't her favourite colour. It had been silk he was supposed to get; he had been so certain of that. Maybe she had said she could only truly have a good night's sleep in cashmere. Or maybe she was unhappy that he'd pillaged those they'd saved. Or maybe it was bandit silk she didn't want.

She held out her hand for him to take. It could have been a

trap. He took it tentatively. Turned out, it was a trap. She gripped him firmly, dragging him away from his companions, one of whom was sighing dreamily at the prospect of romance in the air. She led him upstairs, dragging him as if he were a toy. It didn't matter. All their misfortune was lost. There was no Keri, Aireys, or Dia. No fuken trial. There was no apology. Nothing seemed to matter to her now but tearing his clothing from him and gazing upon his beauty, and he allowed her.

"I love you."

"I love you, too."

They kissed. They fell into a silken bed.

Desire.

————

Lea watched Roja and Emir disappear, their excited footsteps fading to silence, and she looked upon her Erroh. Aye, she was still furious about the assault, but had she expected him to do anything else? Had she not been with him when they'd charged? She bit her lip. The alcohol and the primal urge to procreate were overwhelming.

He was jesting lightly with Wrek and Tye, glancing protectively at his little sister now and then. Perhaps her irritation was because he'd embraced Nomi after the fight. Was she being unfair? she wondered.

Nomi, the pretty little whore, had performed admirably with her war hammer, and it had been an anguishing task. That had been no act, Lea knew; no performance for all to see.

She looked at the attractive southern girl, and for the slightest of moments, felt regret for the steps they forced her to take. All Nomi had known had been revealed to be false.

All those she'd loved were lost to her forever. Nearly all, that is. Lea felt the anger rise and stifled it. Mostly.

Lea threw her last chips into a healthy pot and asked for all the cards she could. It was her tactic, her style, and she was fantastic at it. She just wasn't good at cards. Erroh sighed and folded. He'd need a few chips to keep his mate in the next hand, no doubt.

Nomi matched the bet, and Lea narrowed her eyes.

"Lea have no hand," muttered Nomi. She read her cards again and nodded. She looked like she needed a win.

"Lea never does," agreed Lexi, leaning against a barrel and watching the flames. She held a glass in one hand, a folded hand of cards in the other.

"I have a fine hand," lied the deadliest girl in the world.

"Of course you do, my beo," Erroh whispered, halving his chips to keep her in the game. The things one did for love.

"Nomi want more," the southern female said, and pushed in another healthy dose of pieces. Enough to buy Lea out of the game without allowing her the vague chance of revealing her hand.

"I love how Nomi reminds us of her name the whole time," whispered Tye, lying on the other side of the flames. The cards were calling, but he could not answer. He had consumed so much fine alcohol, and slumber was whispering its delicate promises. He wondered, would Jeroen have been proud of him from the darkness? He wondered, would he ever see his mother again? He wondered, would she attain the ultimate step on the ladder of entitlement? Would that make her happy? He wondered, would all the Alpha females want him that little bit more once she did? Mostly, he wondered how much pain his

victims had felt as he cut them down? He'd killed at least a
dozen.

He also wondered, could he handle another drink before
throwing up all over himself? It was irrelevant; he was still
going to drink. He was a man now. Even if his hands couldn't
stop shaking.

"Going to the city, going to get me a family," sang Wrek,
tapping his foot to keep time. "Where is Wynn with the six-
string?" he said, looking around before continuing to sing,
blissfully out of tune. He missed Lara tonight. Missed her like
fire. All around him, he could see the desire that always
followed bloodshed, and he dulled his senses with alcohol
and thought about the woman who consumed his thoughts.
They spoke of bravery in this group, but they had no partner
in the city to worry about, as he did. Aye, it satisfied him to
hide out here with such fine comrades and be brave with
them. But should the Hunt march on Spark City, nothing
would matter beyond getting to her. Holding her. Kissing her.
Becoming her mate. "There's a girl that I want to see," he
sang.

"We're all in," hissed the most beautiful girl in the world, and
stole Erroh's pile. He rolled his eyes and searched for the
nearest spare bottle. He discovered a fine stash where Emir
had seated himself. A quick smile played across his face.
Finally, they realised how much they wanted each other.

Nomi squealed in delight, and Lea cursed loudly at her
predictability. Nomi revealed her cards to everyone else with

glee. Lea nodded evenly. And Nomi swept the chips from the table. Easy come, easy go.

"Nomi best player," Nomi announced. She didn't see the venom in her opponent's eye. She was just happy with the distraction, Lea supposed. "Nomi deal?" she asked happily, and slid a few chips back towards Lea and Erroh. Share and share alike, apparently.

Lea growled a second curse under her breath. She did not want to share. "Nomi win this game," she jested. Her smile did not reach her eyes.

There was something in the air. Maybe it was the exhilaration of their unlikely survival. Lea stood and beckoned her shattered mate to follow suit, and he did. She kissed him on the lips in front of the whore and, joining in the theme of the night, led him away, leaving a perfectly acceptable card game behind.

Instead of retiring to their bedchambers, however, Lea led him out through the main gates into the cool dark of the night. She needed something different tonight. As did he. She saw the grin on his face and kissed him passionately. Tonight, they needed freedom from restraints. No four walls to cage them; no locked door to keep their privacy. None of that mattered now. All that mattered was the taste of the road and the taste of her mate.

Desire.

"I think we're done for the night," announced Lexi. She didn't want to retire to her room, as Emir and Roja needed a little privacy. There were some things nobody wanted to hear. Now, spying on Wynn some night, well, that would be fine.

"The night is on fire," muttered Tye, stretching out in the dust. She watched him for a few breaths longer and thought about how strong his chin was. Stirring herself from childish thoughts, she drained the glass and wondered what exact potent magic was stored within it to inflame all their passions like this. She hated Tye. She hated him even more for trying desperately to stop her from charging into the fray after her heroic brother. Still, his concerned look had been priceless. How could he imagine he'd be able to stop her? She'd only just shed her bindings. Now she was a killer, just like her family. She shook; she recoiled within. Her stomach turned. Her heart hammered. But it was all natural. And it was good.

"What a day," he muttered, and she wanted to strike him. She didn't know why. Instead, she closed her eyes and enjoyed the fire's warmth. Only Wrek continued to talk, though nobody was listening. Not that he cared in the slightest.

"I miss Lara."

"I hope…"

"I hope she misses me."

"I hope she's safe."

"I am…"

"I…"

"… Adawan."

Drunken silence.

Nomi bowed to them all. It was the courteous thing to do. Drunk as she was, she stole a bottle and ambled off into the darkness to hunt. It was something to do. Her feet were clumsy, but she remained upright, drinking from her bottle. Her vision blurred. She was a killer of her own people, and there was nothing to distract her from this cruel truth. So she drank and searched for relief from the pain. No matter how much pain she suffered, she would follow the path taken by Erroh and his perfect mate.

She slipped out of the gate and crept through the darkness, searching for a sign of them. Fortunately, unaware they were being followed, both Alphalines had done little to remain concealed. She followed the sounds of their jesting and giggling, deep into the darkness, until they settled upon a little glade to call their own for the night.

They kissed, and Erroh loved her as much as he had on the day he first fell in love with her. It certainly wasn't the day they'd met, but that was a small matter now. They completed each other. That was enough for him. He held her, and she pushed him violently down to the ground, her beautiful eyes sparkling in the night, her body glowing in the eerie light of the shattered moon above. She leapt upon him and tore his shirt away. He could see the smile. That wonderful smile that eased all his pain, his worries.

"I love you, my beo."

"I love you, too," she whispered, tearing off her blouse, revealing her undergarment. And then she froze for a moment. Only a moment. Every emotion flashed across her face, and then her expression changed to something he'd never seen before: a look of pure, animalistic desire. Lea tore her undergarment free as she straddled her lover.

She wanted to scream out her passion—that they lived, that they'd tasted blood, death and lightning, and come away unscathed. She wanted her Erroh so badly; it was unbearable. And then a flicker caught her eye before she tore her last piece of clothing free.

A girl. She froze and feared for a moment it was the Hunt. It was Nomi.

Leering. Fury overcame her, but she did nothing. She felt his warmth, his craving for her, and she grinned menacingly at the whore watching. What good would a beating do, anyway? Let her watch. Let her see what she could never have.

Not while she lived. Not while she lived.

Not while I fuken live, whore.

Nomi knew she'd been spotted. She froze and tried to turn away from them. She had no right. It was the loneliness. And the alcohol. With her limited words, how could she explain to those she called allies the extraordinary pain she was in?

Friends?

They locked eyes, and Nomi was too ashamed to blink, as if doing so would confirm her wretchedness. She knew Erroh loved only one. That didn't make it any less painful, though. She tried to turn, but her own sadness and loathing forbade it. And then Lea looked away first.

She tore his shirt away and kissed him passionately. Her Erroh, nobody else's. Holding his hair, she pulled his head to her chest and bade him tear the last of her clothing free. This he did with great vigour. She pushed him back on the grass and bowed her head mockingly to the sweet little whore hiding in the dark.

Is this what you came for, Nomi? With his clothing free, she kissed and teased him until he was displayed wonderfully for the world to see. He didn't need to know Nomi watched. As violently as she could, she seduced, gripped, loved, furrowed and howled to the watching audience.

This was no act, either. She was merely herself with him, and soon enough, the vague presence watching faded into the recesses of Lea's mind as he took her with all that he had. And what he had was fine indeed.

Nomi watched, her head resting on a low-hanging bough, tilting to one side. The wonderment of their act left her astounded. Nothing she'd ever experienced within the Hunt compared to the spectacle of their desire. It was more than that; it was love, and she smiled at its simple beauty. She watched with unblinking eyes as their beautiful bodies writhed in perfect unison. Eternal motion, searching for divinity. And when both Alphalines finally spent themselves completely and burrowed themselves beneath his cloak, she slipped away from the glorious lovers like a thief in the night, both richer and indeed poorer for what she had witnessed.

Desire.

59

UNARMED AND OVERWHELMED

What am I doing here?

W Mea stared into the rafters of the Cull above her and smiled sadly. She allowed herself a few moments to remember the event and the questions. It had been fantastic; terrifying too. She remembered his stunningly sharp features. She remembered his wide-eyed pride. Even now, she remembered only the better moments. Not the terror or jealousies. Oh, she had earned her mate.

Breathing out, she watched her breath in the air; it was still cold in the room despite the heat from those present. There were many in this room. But this was the way. She clasped her hands together to conceal her growing nerves. Who knew how easily a sign of nervousness might swing the cause away from her grasp?

As if I have a chance.

Mea wore her finest green silken gown today. She was pleased it still fit. Who knew a life tilling and striving could keep her body in shape? It was small consolation. Today, she felt ugly, old and unimpressive. Hardly Primary material at all.

Beside her, Silvia looked stunning in a dazzling white gown that glowed against the darkness. With arms behind her back in a regal poise, she carried herself as only a Primary could, and she intended to take that prize this very day.

Ignoring the prying eyes of those above her, Mea took a few more calming breaths. It was no small matter to stand before every Alpha female of the city and beg for their approval. Surely, she was allowed a few stomach flutters. Traditionally, the Primary passed on the title; such elections were only a formality. After the recent turn of events, however, democracy would play its part, as corrupt a system as it might be. Particularly where Sigi and Silvia were involved.

She looked at the vile girl and feared the manoeuvrings of a dictator whose motives were questionable. She had heard whisperings of words shared between the city and the south. Whispers of peace. Whispers of welcome guests. All at the cost of only a few dozen fertile miles along the border. Such whisperings might well earn Silvia her place upon the throne. And rightfully so, if she delivered peace.

Mea and Silvia were not alone on the floor of the Cull. Standing beside Mea was Celeste. Her thin frame was draped in a blue and black dress, barely visible in the low light, but Mea appreciated her unwavering loyalty. Any and all with substantial voice were allowed to attend. Celeste had brought a friend. Though Mea believed him unimpressive, Celeste was rather taken with Doran.

To the watching crowd, he was a gambit played in a hazardous wager over thrones. Truthfully, he'd done a fine job these past few weeks, moving a healthy number of wretches from the hovels. He had also grown a fine little army, and that had brought him favour amongst the inhabitants of the city. Who knew removing wretched refugees from sight would prove to be a popular thing? Even if it wasn't peace, it *was* something in her name.

Beside Silvia, and within spitting distance of Mea, stood Dane. He wore his most formal attire. She wondered, was that the outfit he'd worn on the day he'd condemned her mate to death? Her nerves lessened as the anger rose.

Control yourself.

He favoured Silvia taking power. Some might have believed that whatever nastiness he planned for the ruling of the city lay in the diminutive blonde's coronation. In Silvia, there lay alliance. In Mea? Defiance.

There was a third figure, a bastard Mea had almost called a friend. He was not worth the spittle. Sigi stood within striking distance, looking uninterested in events, and she fought the urge to rip his fuken throat out and display it for all to see. That might be an interesting plea for leadership.

He wore a simple smile worthy of a snake, and he directed it to the watching females above. Oh, he presented himself as a kindly simpleton, but controlling the city was no task for a fool. He'd played his part and drawn the attentions of his Alphaline mate. Who had selected whom? she wondered. Regardless, they were an impressive, soulless couple. Throughout Samara, they had spoken loudly of a unified city, and of leading the Four Factions into a shimmering, bright future. They had proposed peaceful times, and it was a convincing argument. No one spoke openly of their vile climb to power. Such a terrible union could bring ruin upon the world, and only Mea stood in the way.

No problem at all.

Above both rival candidates stood the females of the city, those old enough to Cull and therefore old enough to choose their next mother. They leaned over the balcony rail and watched in silence and judgement. The lights darkened; it was time. Each would debate their suitability for such a role. This was the room of the Cull. There would be words.

Silvia was rumoured to be the favourite to take the crown. Her popularity had soared since she'd placed her name forward. Was it not Silvia who had removed Roja the Vile? And was Mea not just a mirror image of the red-headed fiend? Mea had heard other rumours, too, the most important being that fleeing the city after this election would be advisable.

A spiteful Primary was a dangerous thing.

I should be with Tye. Instead of this.

Mea looked up at the shadowed faces above. How youthful and beautiful these wise creatures were. Silvia was one of them. Young, beautiful and feared. Her voice was strong; she echoed their doubts and burned so fuken brightly, how could they not believe?

Truthfully, Silvia was brutal enough to be the Primary. Strong enough to face adversity. Clever enough to manipulate anyone she desired.

She could lead this city to glory, no doubt.

But not yet.

She'd never walked the road, nor lived a life. For that reason alone, Mea would have stood against her. Let alone the thousand sins upon her hands. Perhaps, were things different, had Silvia behaved differently, Mea might have been satisfied with a position as an advisor. She had been ready to stand beside Roja as ruler, but Silvia had put an end to that.

I don't know what to do. I am alone in this world.
Alone.

Without warning, the surrounding lights brightened, and those above faded into darkness. Neither girl left the stage;

neither took even a step. A loud voice from somewhere above addressed the candidates.

"We are at war," she said, and Mea felt the panic most young Alpha males felt when first they stepped into this unforgiving domain. "The enemy is near our gates. This is no time for political answers to curry favour. We demand truth in these hallowed halls."

Mea was ready for this. She had to be. She took a breath. "As you wish," she declared, and her voice was strong.

"Of course," replied Silvia, bowing magnificently. She was born for an audience. "If we cannot make a peace with these invaders, I'm quite certain…"—she looked to Dane, who stood beside her—"… we can hold the gates and walls as long as needed." An impressive manoeuvre, taking the first question for her own and answering it with the appropriate amount of arrogance. "Unlike our grand predecessors, the Wolves *will* answer to me without question." She stepped aside to allow Mea to speak her mind, too.

Well played, little one.

Of course, the city would hold the brutes as they laid siege, but how long could it hold? There were far too many citizens walking the streets as it were, eating the scarce food rations.

However, my dear, your statement is flawed.

Mea imagined the dead would line the streets within six weeks. A difficult thing to admit to a desperate audience. "Fine words, Silvia. However, I believe we should consider withdrawing before the Hunt breaches our gates," she said. It wasn't much of a plan, but it was the Cull: best to be truthful.

"Flee the city?" cried Silvia.

"Aye, flee the city," she said. Already, the hundred voices above in the rafters began to murmur amongst themselves in disagreement.

And the winner is...

Of course they preferred defiance, and it was an admirable thing. They had built these walls for such terrible events. They should stand. They should fight.

We would die eventually.

"And how would you propose such a feat?" the voice from above asked, though Mea couldn't help notice a tone of scepticism in it now. She tried to make out the speaker who hid in the darkness, but she remained concealed. Probably better for the grand inquisitor to remain anonymous should she earn the ire of a bitter, newly-crowned Primary.

"We still have enough boats in the harbour to carry many," she explained. A fine suggestion: sail away down the Great Mother, sail away from the fight.

"They would be hunted down in no time," retorted Silvia. She spoke for those terrified listeners. A fine leader.

"The Wolves would hold the line for as long as was needed," Mea said, shrugging her shoulders and instantly recoiling inside at the gesture. Dane muttered a curse under his breath. Doran folded his arms, and Sigi stifled a laugh. "And those who feel inclined would join the fight, though it is every Alpha's choice." Might as well fall under a thousand arrows while she was at it. "I will stand with them, should it be needed," she said, stepping away. She would offer no more.

"And we would soon stand on the deck of a ship, doing all this over again," jested Silvia.

There were a few sniggers above.

Mea knew there were a few who had been swayed to her thinking. They were no sheep, these wonderful, heroic girls.

"Tell us of your son," the voice demanded, and Mea, expecting this, chose her next words carefully.

"He is my blood, and he was a significant source of pride

to me when he was a child." She looked into the darkness. "And a child is all he is."

"A child with irresponsible zeal and murderous intent?" Silvia suggested, smiling to any who gazed down at her.

"When the Wolves returned, I too felt hatred. Not for their actions, but for my anguish." She held back a sudden sob and silently cursed it to oblivion. She would choose confidence over sorrow. Regrouping, she attempted to play the game. "I hated them and believed them cowardly, but they were following orders that served the city." It was a fine fuken lie, and no one could have known it. She wanted to wail her true feelings, but why sacrifice the world for little more than a personal outburst? "Tye is of my blood, but he is not the first to strike out at injustice," she offered.

"He was wrong," shouted Silvia.

"Aye, of course he was. That is why he fled," she agreed. "Though we can never say for certain what happened. I would favour a trial, regardless of my position," she said, and this earned her a little favour. Not much, but some.

"He is vile. A mark upon your name."

Mea felt the calm, creaking wall she'd built in her mind crack ever so. She turned from the hidden listeners and faced Silvia for the first time since the event had begun. She would face an attack without blinking, even if she were dying inside.

"You see yourself as suitable to lead the Wolves with this blemish upon your person?" Silvia jeered. She was aiming for the throat and hitting the jugular.

More mutterings from above followed, and Mea's head spun. She could only endure so many attacks on Tye. Fuelled by anger, she teetered dangerously close to eruption. "How can I be held responsible for such actions?"

"He is your son," the voice from above argued.

"You challenge my authority as a parent?" Mea shouted

in reply. She'd expected these attacks. She'd practiced for hours as a dutiful Celeste had nodded along with her counterarguments. Standing here was something else entirely.

Oh, please, somebody shut me up before I tear them all apart.
Somebody did.

"I think it a strange thing that he would fall upon eight armed Wolves," Doran said from somewhere behind her. "I find it likelier that they fell upon him, and he merely did what any Alphaline would do, given the proper training and just the right amount of hatred," he said. The crowd listened. He was an injured veteran of war. Had he not earned the right? "Was your former lover not with him, Silvia?" Doran asked almost casually. It was perfect—and a fine question that single-handedly doomed any chance of the outcast Wolves ever receiving an invitation back into the city. For what it was worth, though, he'd earned the respect of Mea for life.

He continued on. "Is that not a greater crime than a grieving mother's?" he asked, and fell silent.

"A fine point, Doran, but to suggest Silvia pay for Stefan's crimes is just ludicrous," Mea said warmly, losing her fury and swiftly playing the new hand she'd been dealt. She stepped closer to the beautiful young blonde in a fine display of sisterhood. Nobody needed to know how she hated the witch. A Primary was disinclined to show that passion.

"I removed myself from him after the events of the Keri assassin," Silvia said. Mea smiled her best dazzling smile. Though she had likely lost ground with that previous question, it was nowhere near as bad as it could have been, or indeed, should have been.

Thank you, Doran.

"We should move on," Mea ordered the voice above. Silvia nodded her agreement. The moment had passed, and she knew she hadn't taken full advantage. These things happened. The day was still young, however.

"I do not believe you can work with the Wolves of the city," Dane said suddenly. "And I do not believe they have any great desire to work with you." A fine manoeuvre, and one she'd expected. He was master of the Black, and he had no interest in her standing as Mydame. It was a hammer blow to her candidacy, but Mea didn't even blink.

"Of course, I resented the protectors of this city for a time. However, how strong a leader would I be if I allowed my own anguish to distract me from ruling?" It was a perfect reply.

Most of her previous words had been Celeste's, but the next point was truly her own. "Sigi is a fine master of the Wolves. He and I were quite the business partners for a time, and I owe him an enormous debt. Were I to lead the city of Samara, I believe we would work together again just as efficiently." She addressed the innkeeper as she spoke, and she spoke as a friend would to another. A shrewd move. "Unlike her former companion, Silvia has chosen a fine man in Sigi," she added warmly.

"I am the leader of the Wolves," roared Dane. It was a fair argument.

"Oh… I apologise, Master of the Black, for implying anything untoward. My mistake." She tipped her head forward, the faintest hint of an apologetic bow. Then she turned to Sigi and bowed deeply. She knew who the actual power in the city was, and she wasn't afraid to acknowledge it.

Sigi smiled. But the crowd muttered unhappily. It was a small matter. Those with their own minds saw potential in her contention.

Before another word could be uttered, three thunderous knocks sounded on the entrance to the Cull.

All heads turned toward the doorway. Disturbing this event was no small matter.

The knocks hammered again as bolts were slid across, and the jingle of keys echoed in the silence. Mea suddenly felt lightheaded, and the blood drained from her face. Whispers erupted from above, for they all felt it too, just as a wild beast understood the thundering charge of a hunter drawing near. Mea shook her head in dismay.

They are attacking.

They must be.

This is too much.

But she faltered for only a moment. Did she capitulate like a grieving widow, unable to take more horror? No: a Primary met terror proudly. Taking one last breath, she stood straight and led by example. Deep down, however, she believed this was the beginning of the end.

She was right.

60

MEANWHILE, BACK AT THE WALL

U we leaned out over the edge of the city gates and
smoked his little tobacco pipe. He watched the wisps
of smoke disappear as the wind caught them and dragged
them off to oblivion. Such was life. He chuckled to himself
for his deep thoughts this early in the morning. Life was a
random gift, and after it ended, there was nothing. No gods,
no everlasting gathering of loved ones, no tables laden with
goblets of wine. He inhaled deeply and studied the little flurry
of movement from behind the sectioned region of the hovels.
Every day, he saw fewer of the smelly little ants emerge from
their dwelling shacks. Perhaps a fine plague had ravaged
them, or maybe the imposing shadow of the Hunt camped just
outside the city had inspired them to flee a little further east.

Good riddance.

Those wretched few who had not fled into the wastes,
sailed a barge up the Great Mother, or joined the outcast
Wolves to die hardly left the cover of their shacks anymore.
After days of riots at the gates they'd lost their fight. They
now merely existed among the dilapidated hovels they called

homes. The city no longer bothered to post a guard for them. It was cruel, but it was the way of things. He should have cared more about their fates, but he couldn't. Their kind had taken Dia and set the city alight in violence and murder. They were no longer welcome here. He was too old to question Dane's orders. Too infirm to stand for those wretched, bastard few. Truthfully, he just didn't care anymore. His fight had left him, too, since the Rangers' betrayal. He should have stayed, should have died with an ounce of nobility, but he hadn't.

Lived to die an old wretch in an old bed without kin.

He was older than most of his brothers of the Black. Tragically, he knew that age would not be the ailment that killed him; nor would starvation. Neither was the proper fate for a warrior. He'd probably find death somewhere in between.

A blade during the first skirmish?

Perhaps today?

Perhaps a year from now?

He sucked on the pipe and discovered his dark thoughts of morality had distracted him from keeping his tobacco burning. *That* was a tragedy of the highest order. He tipped the wooden piece over and patted the dead remnants from the warm little hole. Blowing the remaining flakes and ash away, he heard his friend return from his walk along the top of the wall.

"Have they charged yet?" Wissou asked in jest. His voice was gravelly from long years of enjoying life's finer things. He was taller than Uwe and a little heavier. He had walked as many seasons, and the deep lines on his face matched Uwe's. His black armour rattled loudly as he cast his helm to the ground and lit his own pipe against a small torch they were burning under cover from the winds that plagued this watch.

"Held them off myself, I did. No bother at all."

Word around the city suggested the numbers were ten thousand, but Uwe had seen them for himself as part of an early scouting party. At least thrice that amount had set camp, but there had been no significant movement within it. Idleness and hushed negotiations could only last so long, he knew. When they attacked, they had the numbers to ensure victory.

Every night, they lit their fires, a terrifying blaze of fireflies dotting the land, yet each morning, they had taken no steps closer. If it was psychological warfare, it was a lazy stroke of genius. Terror followed each citizen with every step, and every day the feeling of doom increased. Few dared to stray out into the fields around the Spark anymore, lest a sudden charge occur and they retreat to a locked gate.

Aye, there was always the harbour at Samara's rear. But even if they secured that beast, only the strongest swimmer would have the skill to swim deep below the massive portcullis. And even then, anyone emerging from the waters would likely be dispatched by an eager archer. A hundred brutes emerging would earn the same fate. The rear was no place to attack.

Wissou leant against the wall's edge and looked down at the steel and wooden shacks. "I spoke with Seth," he said, spitting over the edge and watching to see if it hit a wretch. A harder task these days.

"Oh, aye?"

"Aye."

"And what did our precious man of Spark say, then?" Uwe asked. The flames in his pipe took hold now, and both elder guardsmen were briefly enveloped in a little puff of smoke. He inhaled deeply, and the embers glowed.

"The little shit is stirring a brew of trouble out there."

"Erroh?"

"Aye. Word is, he and Roja have formed a fine little army of bandits out in the wastes."

Uwe spat a few flakes from his mouth and then spat again out of disgust. Though he preferred talk of the wanted convicts to tales of impending death, it angered him just how little concern the city had for those responsible for the Primary's murder. Or for those who had fled the city instead of answering for their crimes.

"They need to raise the bounty on his head again," he said. It was all they could do. Erroh of the Sweeping Grasslands and his merry little group of vile outcasts ran through the countryside without a care while they stood alone on the precipice waiting for attack.

Waiting for some fine conquering.

"It's not right," Wissou growled, flicking some flakes from his pipe. He puffed skilfully and inhaled deeply. Uwe knew he'd been meaning to quit, but fuk it. The world was ending, and who didn't want fine flavour upon their lips when the brutes charged in? It hadn't been a rich tobacco harvest, though. Ever since the death of the Primary, trade had taken a turn for the worst, but at least there was plenty of the cheaper shit to go around. Since the southerners showed up, more and more Wolfen brothers had taken to smoking the weed. It was something to do while waiting to be attacked.

Something beyond caught his attention in the distance. He blinked, waved the hazy smoke away from him, and peered far up towards the south. He could see a diminutive figure on the crest of the ridge, walking along the worn path from Hunt camp towards the grand capital city of Samara.

Invasion.

All thoughts of Erroh and his troublemaking were lost,

and both guards fell uneasily silent. The figure was nonchalant in his stride, and he took each step as if some unseen shield protected him. Few wanderers of the road dared to approach the city from this direction, and no new refugees had appeared at the city gates in weeks. The stranger carried a pale white flag lazily over his shoulder, while his other hand held a sheathed blade attached to a leather strap.

"Oh, fuk. What do we do?" cried Wissou. It was a fine question. The imposing barricade in front of Samara's city gates was deserted. No one else seemed to have spotted the stranger, and there was no specifically appointed person to arrange first meetings and indeed first talks. The southerner merely strolled unimpeded down towards the gate with a smile on his face and the wind at his back.

"Meet him at the gate?" asked Uwe.

"Well, someone will have to," Wissou agreed. His face was pale.

They sprang into action, charging down through the gate tower and raising the alarm. But below, they found only raw, terrified youth to call upon; the officers were suspiciously absent. Uwe and Wissou glanced at each other, and then, choosing subtlety over aggression, they decided to greet the newcomer as a solitary pair of Wolves. Less chance of incidents that way.

By the time the pair stepped through the inner gate and out beyond the wall, the city was already stirring as though the market had opened up with fresh supplies and wares.

The southern envoy was already waiting patiently for them in the shade beneath the impressive front wall. "Greetings, friends. My name is Gemmil. I believe today is a historic day for Samara." He bowed. The white flag wavered slightly as he did, and they returned the gesture.

"Speak your business, friend," warned Uwe, stepping

between the entrance to the hovels and the emissary of the Hunt, lest an act of vengeance be taken by some aggrieved refugee. However, the wretches showed little interest in getting involved. He could smell the rot from here. They'd need to torch the area later on to remove the stain from the land.

Welcome to the north. Hold your breath.

Gemmil smiled, showing unusually bright teeth. A smile not unlike a wolf's as it gnawed upon a fresh kill. "I have come for the event," he declared.

His accent was both familiar and terribly foreign. Uwe immediately despised his pale, clean-shaven skin. Too many years hidden under snow. He appeared as though death had gifted him a few days' grace. Uwe wanted him to go away, and to take his army with him.

Maybe he would ask him to do just that.

"Event?" challenged Wissou, though they all knew what event he referred to.

"I speak for the south. There is talk of a divine new Primary, and as an emissary of Uden the…" he said, and hesitated. "… Uden, the leader of the south, I wish to be a witness." He gently placed his sword on the dusty ground and dropped the white flag beside it. He held up his hands in the most disarming gesture he could muster and smiled again.

"I don't think you are welcome," said Wissou apologetically. Behind them, they could hear the rushing movements of a battalion preparing to attack.

"I have a friend in the city who will pledge for me. He is in high standing. His name is Seth," explained the southerner. "High standing for a male, at least," he added thoughtfully.

"We will send word… friend," Wissou said, signalling to the garrison forming behind them.

"It might take some time," Uwe added.

If this unusually friendly character named Gemmil was at all nervous at the sight of the defenders gathering, he showed nothing at all in his features. Instead, he patted Uwe on the shoulder. "Oh, my friends, I have all the time in the Arth."

61

LIES

All talk dwindled away to a surprised silence as Seth announced the southerner Gemmil and led him into the room. Gemmil grinned to the two women who were battling wits over leadership before offering an unnecessarily deep bow. His eyes darted around the room, taking everything in.

"I speak for the fine leader of the south, Uden," he announced to the watching audience. He acknowledged Sigi briefly, then stepped aside to permit him to address the gathering as though it were his right.

It was.

Doran was less than welcoming. "You shouldn't be here!" he barked. It was the type of warning offered at the same time as a fist was thrown and events took a bloody turn. Before he leapt upon the emissary, Celeste stood between them and took his shoulders in her forceful grip. Her calming eyes drilled into his, reminding him of his place. Reminding him of his importance to her.

Gemmil was unperturbed. "The southern faction have every right to attend the grand rise of a pious new Mydame."

He was right, of course. "Are we not a kingdom of Four Factions? Are we not supposed to answer to the pinnacle of Samara?" He placed his gloved hand across his chest and bowed to the hidden females in the rafters who held their voices silent, lest a careless word bring ruin upon the world. This wasn't an entirely needless precaution.

"We have every right to learn with whom we will exchange words, come the end of the southern march," Gemmil went on, still smiling. He spun around, addressing all who would listen and offering what eye contact he could in the harsh light. Unblinking and unflinching, he played the part of a disarming ally and he played it well. "If it helps to soothe your fears, I come in peace," he added.

Not "*We* come in peace." Perhaps a one-eyed god might have enjoyed this performance were he able to see it himself.

Perhaps he could.

"Peace?" spat Doran, turning away to stare at the wall as though it had just insulted him. As though it needed to get a right good kicking.

"Aye, friend. Unlike you warring regions, we of the south are interested in peace," he said softly.

It sounded like he was lying. It sounded like he was a hideous masochist, who enjoyed torturing away the sanity of broken girls, and claiming it was godly work. A murmur of disbelief rippled throughout the room.

"How dare you claim peace, having set up camp here on our outskirts?" roared Mea, leaping to her feet. Her body shook as though she were fighting the urge to tear his throat out. She took a step towards him before better judgement checked her.

"Diplomatic resolution is a favoured outcome," he countered, turning to her. He looked to her feet and then his gaze travelled up until he met her eyes. He gave a small smile, apparently pleased with what he gazed upon. "Though I like your fight," he whispered, and shrugged away her interruption as a small matter. "We have walked thousands of miles, yet your people did not offer us even a taste of northern hospitality once we settled." He shook his head like a disappointed father. "We waited for you, and you cowered behind your city walls." Stepping past Silvia without acknowledging her, he stared at Mea as though she were prey. As though it had been her decision alone to ignore his people. He didn't know her at all. She was a fuken hunter and the worst possible target to test.

Perhaps this is *exactly* why he gazed her way.

Perhaps he knew she was Jeroen's mate.

Perhaps he believed the delicate knitting together of events was no mere coincidence, but actions of his god.

Whatever he thought.

Mea stood her ground and met his stare. "You have torn so many from their homes—cutting, killing, and putting them to the flame," she said evenly. "Yet here you stand, expecting hospitality?"

Above them, in the rafters, a few silent heads nodded. Others feared the ramifications of her outburst. They had come for a traditional election, but this was something else entirely.

"You misunderstand our aggression, Mea," Gemmil said patiently. "You are ignorant of our ways. When we are attacked, we retaliate. If you knew the history of our people, you would know this." He was almost convincing in his words.

"Thousands have died at your hands," shouted Doran. "Those who never desired violence."

"What of the many towns and settlements we left untouched? Unmolested? Or do these truths not taste as sweet to those who seek the nomination?" Gemmil demanded. A flash of anger appeared in his features, but he caught his breath and grinned, and the look was gone as quickly as it had come. "Why not ask the people in the towns who did offer us their kind hospitality? They will assure you that we offered them little threat. You presume we wish to conquer? Nothing could be farther from the truth."

Mea could take little more. "Yet, you march upon us with an army. Yet, you slaughtered the Rangers."

"We sought discussions, many times over. Where is your former Primary to confirm this? Oh, yes: she lies dead—slain by her own people, not by southern hands." He stared at Mea, though his words were for the entire city. "When we journeyed south, the Rangers ambushed us. We did what was needed. We march now in greater numbers to show our strength. To discourage another assault."

"Liar!"

For a moment, Gemmil hesitated, eyeing Mea almost curiously. He smiled again. "So, today I ask a question of both candidates, from the mouth of Uden."

The room waited.

"Will you accept peace between us?"

Mea held Gemmil's gaze. She peered into his soul and decided he was as false as his god. Peace? There would be no fuken peace from these barbarians.

Silvia stepped forward and smiled beautifully, as was her forte. She addressed the watching audience; she addressed the hidden voice, and she addressed the emissary from Uden of the south. "I would gladly welcome peace with the south, come the coronation." A fine declaration. She had the victory in her hand. All who were present knew this as well.

Especially Mea. "Were I chosen, of course." Her smile became smug, and to her followers it was a well-deserved display of arrogance. Everything was falling into place. Even the fact of a southerner daring to march up to the fuken gates was playing out wonderfully in her favour.

"We have one request," he said. "A small matter. Nothing of great importance." The room waited. "Some time ago, an assassin was dispatched to our leader's homestead. And though I imagine he served himself alone, the injuries suffered by our leader were catastrophic." He cleared his throat. "We don't hold your city responsible for this man's vile actions, but he has continued to wage an unholy war against our people, even now."

Mea took a careful breath.

"He leads a large group of cutthroat bandits," Gemmil continued. "They rest their heads in a little town a few days south from here. They ambushed a line of our people and slaughtered every one of them without mercy. Four hundred," he said, and the pain in his voice was clear. His eyes glittered with tears. "Including my brother," he said softly.

"You speak of Erroh?" asked Silvia.

He nodded. *You know him too?*

Silvia knew him, indeed, and was happy to tell him and the watching audience what she thought of him. This was a precarious manoeuvre, condemning a burgeoning legend, but essential if the Alpha females desired peace. "He is little more than a criminal," she said curtly. "On this, both our people can agree. He has a steep price upon his head. When we find him, we *will* present Uden with it," she pledged.

Mea wanted to scream. How could this vile creature slither into this chamber and spin such lies? Far above, she knew the terrified girls salivated at the prospect of peace. No matter how educated her sisters were, there was nothing like a convenient lie, laced with poison, to whet the appetite. She was helpless to do anything.

Gemmil shook his head. "No, no. We are not savages. We wish only to see him in chains. For that, we will swear fealty to the new Primary." It was a fair deal. An entire city for one little cub.

"And you, Mea?" Silvia asked. "Will you sacrifice your little friend for the benefit of the city?" she asked ominously. There was no politically savvy reply.

"It does not seem a fair deal," Mea replied. If what Gemmil had said was the truth, could she sacrifice Erroh? Could she find any advantage to bringing him to the city?

I'm sorry, Erroh.

Perhaps I would.

"Some things are necessary," she said uneasily. She missed the fine old times when all she had cared about was keeping a good standing among the hidden, judging females. Now she was speaking of condemning a close friend to a terrible fate, without having heard his story first. Was this what a Primary did? A bitter taste filled her mouth.

"Well, this pleases me greatly, Mydames. Today is the beginning of a historic day between the factions," Gemmil declared, and she knew him to be a liar. She fuken knew it.

"Whatever is best for the factions will be done," agreed Silvia, and Mea's heart dropped. In that moment, she realised Silvia knew a great deal more than she had let on regarding this matter.

"I have spoken my part. You, too, have spoken your fine words, and I am honoured to be in attendance at this gathering. I am honoured to watch as you choose your next leader."

No doubt pleased with the bartering he had done this morning, Gemmil stood away from the gathering now, moving as near to the door as possible. As he faded into the darkness, Mea, unsure of herself, her ability, her fuken fate, could only look above to the waiting, judging audience.

"Next question?" she asked loudly, and her voice was strong. That was something, she supposed.

———

This is it, thought Silvia as each female cast her vote in a small wooden ballot box far above and the last echo of footsteps disappeared. It was a simple, anonymous way to vote. Each female held two smooth little wooden beads, identical but for their colour. The voter cast the ball of their choosing into the box and kept its twin as a reminder of their decision.

"We would have made a fine team," whispered Mea beside her, playing the fine politician until the last moment. Silvia knew that if she were to win, the shrewd thing would be to appoint Mea as an advisor. Although she knew there was a good chance Mea would flee the city after the vote to escape her wrath. She had greatly enjoyed hearing that rumour. The sisters didn't know her at all. When females were removed from the city, it was for the benefit of the rest of the world.

"I think you could bring experience to the table," Silvia said, offering a bow.

Truthfully, beneath Silvia's veneer of calm and assuredness, there lay a healthy dose of fear. Had she really done enough? she wondered. Had she convinced each sister of her suitability over the past few weeks? Oh, they had pledged themselves to her as she had stared them down. With smiles, jests, and subtle threats, she had earned their favour ten times over.

Walking in here, she had the numbers, but Mea had the advantage of age and experience. Her quiet demeanour, her precise and well-thought-out answers to difficult questions, unnerved Silvia somewhat. Even Gemmil's appearance hadn't solidified Silvia's confidence, as it should have. Mea's strength was not in her canvassing; it was in her very presence. But who knew how the tables might turn now? Just two seasons ago, Silvia had been a reviled female with no glorious prospects, but now she stood on the precipice of immortality. Sigi lit the way. He had ensured her rise, and she almost believed him.

Was it worth Roja's betrayal?

Was it worth stealing Elise from her deathbed?

Perhaps. Roja was safer now. Elise was in a better place. Her actions had been justified, she told herself. She had the rest of her life to explain her actions. She would be forgiven. She had saved the city. She would continue to do so.

As long as I win.

"Of course, Mydame," Mea replied reverentially. Silvia liked that tone. Mea bowed slightly. She liked that as well.

The sound of beads falling into the wooden box echoed around the room, along with the soft footsteps of women returning to their place in the dark. When the last bead had dropped and silence had fallen once more, their fates were sealed.

The lights flared suddenly to life, and Mea hid her eyes from the sudden pain. Silvia stared up, eyes wide open. Primaries did not blink.

———

The adjudicator was an old Alphaline, probably better suited to leading the city than most, but she had not stepped forward. Nor would she ever. She was happier rebuilding the world's finest library, anyway. Her name was Massey. She concealed her white ball in her hand, offered a prayer to the absent gods, and swiftly pocketed it. Silvia was obviously favoured among those youthful girls. She had the most support among her sisters, as well as the viciousness needed and the ability to command. However, Massey hoped her young sisters understood the need for a mother to lead them. A strong and terrible mother, to be loved, obeyed and feared. She stood and presented the sealed box to the gathering, holding it aloft.

"Remove the shields," declared the new Primary, trying desperately to conceal the fear in her voice. The female beside her nodded in anxious agreement. The world waited for Silvia to finish her climb. To take her place among the legends.

Massey removed the key on her neck and fitted it into the lock with as much skill as her ancient hands would allow. She turned it, and all of the box's four wooden walls fell smoothly away. Beneath these four panels were four clear sheets of glass, polished to a shine so that all those in attendance could see the contents for themselves and determine the victor. An official tally would be unseemly, unless it was too difficult to determine the proportion of black balls versus white.

Black for Mea and white for Silvia.

Fortunately, an official tally was not needed. The shiny little beads lay almost lazily against the glass, clearing showing the gathering the results of their decision.

It was almost unanimous, as Mea had feared it would be. Though it didn't hurt her nearly as much as she thought it would. She fell to her knees now, weeping from both exhaustion and relief. She heard the applause, but she wasn't certain she was ready to face any of her daughters like this. Those many who'd pledged their trust in her. With a dizzy head and blurred vision, her emotions awash in a mix of gratitude and terror, she raised her victorious head and smiled back at those looking upon her.

"No," screamed Silvia, facing her tormentors. It was unanimous. The city had thundered out against her. "Liars," the blonde screamed, and pointed accusingly to all those bitches who had pledged fealty and yet lied through their teeth. "You pledged to me, you fuken liars," she howled. Nobody argued. Before the echoes of her last outburst had fallen silent, she dropped to a humble knee and bowed her head, her mind racing. At least she still held some power, and power was all that mattered these dark days. There would be a reckoning. She took a breath and hated her opponent, the city, and the bitches above.

"Mydame," she whispered, though it tore her apart.

62

FUKED

Her name was Aurora, and she was fuked.
I am so fuked.
She held the young cub close to her breast and willed the torment away from him. From her, too. He fought her embrace, his voice hoarse from screaming and his body exhausted from struggle. He could struggle as long as he needed. She wouldn't let go, and everybody was watching. The world shrank to nothing. An insignificant moment of kindness returned to stab her through the heart. Ealis was lost. Without a clue. She was terrified they'd learn of her deceit, though it had been but a minor act of defiance in honour of a dead Ranger. She hugged the cub and desperately tried to think of an escape.

"Let me go," he howled.
Aye, let's go. Run away.
There were tears now. Useless tears, streaming down his face onto her skin, and everybody was watching her.

"Best leave him be," advised Wynn quietly. "He can take it."

Lea must have thought differently, for she joined in the

embrace, wrapping her loving, powerful arms around the infiltrator and the lost little child.

"He's alive," sobbed Tye, and Aurora wanted to take the pain from him.

Aye, little one. Jeroen is alive and in chains.

And I am fuked.

Fuk, fuk, fuked.

All strength left the young warrior, and his feet betrayed him. He dropped from their hold to the dusty ground of the main street and there he sat, crying relentlessly. So much pain, relief, fear, and regret. "They've chained him like a fuken hound." He struggled to his feet, murderous intent in his gaze. "I'll kill them all," he roared, more loudly than his meagre frame should have allowed. And she was proud of her Tye.

Rising to unsteady feet, he swatted the caring hands away from him and marched towards his mount. The congregation followed, a panicked group of Alphalines and lowerlines, working as one unit, pleading to stop the young warrior from making a huge mistake.

"Tye," roared Erroh. "You need to calm yourself." He strode up to the youth but didn't reach out for him like the others had. The child needed a firmer hand.

"We can't wait," Tye warned, drawing his blade on the false god, and for a moment Aurora imagined him striking out.

She watched on, dizzy with terror. It had been going so well, living among the outcasts as she had. In the days since the grand slaughter of the Hunt, she and her companions had traversed the Arth with renewed vigour and silent confidence.

Perhaps there was a delicious taste of arrogance to their movements. Every morning, before the sun climbed above the horizon, they charged out in pairs and hunted the southerners.

Not for killing.

Though most of her brethren rested at the city gates, at least a quarter of her prime lover's soldiers were camped sporadically throughout the region. Though all the southerners had earned the right to march with Uden, he wasn't naïve enough to gather them into one position. So they spread out, dug in and waited for wonderful word of war. And Erroh and his tiny army had found every one of them and marked their position. Such knowledge was worth its weight in gold.

Aurora enjoyed herself among those she was sworn to revile. She was most fascinated by their volatility. They were always just a few harsh words away from tearing each other's throats out, even in jest, let alone in sparring. Yet they didn't. It was an interesting thing. They counted on each other. They spoke, they laughed, they loved.

She'd expected misery after the attack on the bandit convoy. She knew well the adverse effects a fine few murders had on any group. Usually, the tears and regret clouded the beauty of victory. Usually, only the incredibly determined could rise above the horror, while the feeble faded away to shadows.

Usually, there was a river of guilt.

But not so with her companions.

Nay, her friends.

Friends.

She played friendly and enjoyed it oh, so very much. They tore feelings from her like no other group ever had before. Their single-minded dedication to their task was intriguing. And their trust was a beverage to be drained. They were Rangers of a sort. The outcasts she walked with could never be bought. While their call in this life was foolhardy, they had earned her respect. She hoped their deaths would be swifter than most. In a way, she loved them. Every day was a treasure with these wonderfully youthful barbarians. But there was an ominous note in the wind now, because, before she had known them as family, she had condemned them to death.

———

As the battle settled, she'd cut into the dead body several times, swiftly inscribing a message for Uden's godly eye alone. Wonderfully, this dead boy presented a healthy, fat chest to her. All fleshy and expansive. A girl could write a sonnet there had she the time. "Raven Rock," she inscribed. Much of his blood had already drained away, which made her task easier. "Erroh," she'd inscribed beneath it, and her blade work was smooth and swift. "Aurora," was her last message.
Aurora Borealis, not Fyre.

To most southerners, such a name would mean little, but, to Uden, it was a fitting love letter signed and sealed with a kiss. She took a moment and kissed the fleshy, ruined chest and willed her lover to receive her message. Sliding her blade back into its scabbard, she removed her pendant and wrapped it around the dead boy's neck. They *would* recognise the pendant, if nothing else; it was also a glittering beacon to draw their eyes to the corpse. Last of all, she draped the boy's shirt back over her art as the other outcasts began dispatching those on the cusp of death. Beside the dead boy, she heard a low groan from a dying southerner, and she slit his throat swiftly before moving on.

———

733

She felt a stinging pain shoot up through her stomach and did not know why. Perhaps it was something she'd eaten? Everything had been wonderful until Erroh and Lea returned from their scouting trip with interesting news. One captive of the Hunt had been discovered, just half a morning's ride from the town. A recognisable captive at that. Hearing the news of Jeroen's resurrection had caused a stir in both Tye and herself.

Aurora's mind raced. Perhaps she could strike Jeroen down before he recognised her. Perhaps she wouldn't have to kill him after all. Perhaps she could deny all knowledge of their ever having met. Perhaps she could convince them to lay down their arms, given enough persuasion.

"I'm going to kill them all," whispered Aurora to no one.

And now I'm fuked. Her delicate oasis outside herself was cracking to pieces, crashing down all around her. The walls of the town closed in; she was sure of it. It was one thing to ride through the Arth marking positions on a little map; it was another thing entirely to free a broken warrior from the heart of a finger. On another day, she would have taken pleasure at such an arduous task.

Today, she feared the worst.

Tye wailed, and Aurora bit the inside of her cheek. He'd endured far more than was fair. Aurora *was* fair in her dealings. If he asked her to save Jeroen, what could she do?

Erroh followed Tye to the stables as he went about attaching the saddles to his horse. "We will free your father, Tye, but, not today," he said, and Aurora's heart leapt hopefully.

"You think any force in this world will stop me riding out this night to seek my father?" the boy hissed. He tied the buckle securely, then gripped the horse's bridle and pulled it roughly from its stable, and Aurora didn't want him to die.

Erroh stepped in front of the child. He took hold of the beast and laid a reassuring palm upon the younger man's shoulder. *Now is not the time, little one,* his look suggested.

The little one, however, thought it was the perfect time. He knocked the hand away and tugged the beast's head free.

"I ask you once more: calm yourself, Tye. It is a fool's errand to charge into the forest as night falls," Erroh warned.

Tye reached for his sword, and an icy chill ran through Aurora. Please listen to the Master General, she willed, for once a blade was drawn, any manner of horror could follow.

We are friends.

We are family.

Do not do this.

Oh, how she nearly begged aloud. Nearly made awkward pledges to the child.

Lea ran past her, seeing the danger as Aurora did.

Don't do this, Tye.

"Put that sword away, Tye, before Erroh kills you," hissed Wrek in disgust, and Tye looked down curiously as if surprised that he'd drawn a weapon, and suddenly the situation became a little too unpredictable. With a shaking hand, he pointed it at Erroh, his eyes hard. He wasn't himself. Any fool could see that.

"I just want to see him," he cried. The blade wavered. He swished it in the air.

Please, everyone, get out of the fuken way.

Erroh raised his own sword.

Roja gasped, and Emir ran towards the group. Madness had erupted from nothing.

"Tomorrow," Lea cried, leaping in between both blades. Shoving Erroh aside, she reached for Tye, tried to knock the blade back down by his side. It was instinct to protect on her part.

It was instinct on his part, as well.

He twisted away from her, raised the sword again and struck her. Aurora saw the shock on his face, and on Lea's, too, as he drew the blade across her neck.

The world slowed, and Aurora gasped. Lea leapt back with a cry of alarm. She stumbled against her mate and kept falling. She clutched a hand to her throat as blood seeped through her fingers and dripped onto her blouse.

"I'm sorry," screamed Tye. "Oh, no, Lea, Please, no."

Aurora leapt forward and caught her before she stumbled to the ground. But Lea didn't scream; she didn't cry out in pain. Oddly, she merely looked irritated. Nomi dropped down beside her, her eyes wide with terror.

"He didn't mean it," shouted Lea, holding the gash in her neck. "Don't kill him, Erroh." They were fine last words, Aurora thought. Even dying, she looked after Tye.

Erroh didn't kill him. He dropped his blade and fell to the ground beside her, cradling her in shock. Aurora could see how pale he was. As though the blood seeping from Lea was his own.

"Is the blade laced?" he screamed to Tye, as Emir knocked Aurora and Wrek aside and scrambled forward to save her.

"No, no, it wasn't. Oh, god no, it wasn't," cried Tye. "It was an accident."

"Let me see," whispered Emir, gently pulling her fingers away. There was blood. Deep crimson deliciousness, all going to waste in the dust. Aurora imagined Lea bled dry, and found the vision distasteful.

"Save her, healer."

Aye, fuken save her, or Tye is fuked.

"I will, Erroh."

"Is it bad?"

Silence.

"Is it bad?" Erroh screamed.

"I'm fine, Erroh."

"Is she fine, Healer?"

"She's fine, Erroh. I just need a bandage."

"I told you I was fine, Erroh."

"You're sure she's fine?"

"It wasn't deep," Emir said, though the relief in his voice was noticeable. He sniffed once as well. Nothing more; it was just dust. There was a lot of dust in Erroh's eyes, too, as he climbed to his feet with murderous intent. He gripped the sword named Mercy and turned to Tye. And Aurora couldn't do anything to save her boy.

Erroh charged at the younger cub, who defended instinctively. This was no sparring. Tye cried in misery and blocked the strike, knowing death would follow. Erroh attacked furiously, and the young man fell away in terror. Erroh broke the child's guard, and broke it easily, but did not strike him down. Instead, he drove himself at Tye's blade with all the venom he could muster, desiring only to crack and break the sword.

Deep down, Erroh knew Tye hadn't mean to hurt Lea. The child deserved no mortal wounding. Still, that didn't mean it was excusable. He cut on him a little. Just a few grazes on each arm, lightly enough to scar. It was a lesson any master would bestow upon a wild apprentice in need of a battering.

The child took every blow with a whimper until, eventually, Erroh finally knocked the weapon from Tye's hand and leapt forward, his fist connecting smartly with a whiskerless chin. Groaning, Tye collapsed on the ground in a dusty heap and bled into the dirt a little.

You escaped with little punishment.

"I'm so sorry, Lea," he wailed.

"Somebody tie him in chains," growled Erroh in disgust, and Tye began weeping. A pathetic sound for a youth so close to manhood.

Do I cry any more proudly?

Lea's wound was merely a scratch from an unsteady hand, and Erroh learned of this a little later, once the shock had worn off and the stitching was set. He doted on Lea for the rest of the night, and she enjoyed his tenderness.

———

Wrek and Wynn left Tye chained in a little shed at the far end of the town. He didn't resist; wisely, he decided to remain mute until they determined what to do with him. It was a fine punishment, and one he accepted for his crimes. For two days the child remained silent, offering no protest, using no blankets or cloak against the cold. Few visited him apart from Lea, who brought a steaming brew of cofe to him every morning. Every morning, he offered an apology, which she accepted, and then they said little more.

———

On the third day, Erroh appeared before the child and offered a glass of wine. They spoke on matters most awful; they spoke of regrets, and they spoke of imprisonment.

Last, Erroh spoke of apprenticeship and a master, and the child listened.

He began by condemning Tye's tactics, outlining the folly of facing down a raging Alpha bent on vengeance. He displayed the correct form, displayed a few counters, and Tye listened as any apprentice would. There was a stillness in the child Erroh hadn't seen before. He gifted the child a key and an invitation back to the fire and the clan.

———

From her hiding place, Aurora had listened to the quiet conversations of the Alphalines. She had learned of deeper things like love and devotion among a pack. She had learned of violence and control for an Alphaline. She had also learned of forgiveness through necessity. And she wondered, was it possible she could earn their trust outright? Was it possible to atone for unforgivable sins?

63

FIRST OF MANY

S taring into the flames at the centre of the town, surrounded by his comrades and those he loved, Erroh took a few breaths and waited for his heart to settle. It would probably never settle again. Unable to find the words, he nodded calmly and resisted the urge to scratch his arm. Everything in the world was changing. Apparently, he was the first breeze in the gale to come. He watched the flames fight the bite in the cool air. Roja had not yet set the lights running. He knew this because she sat beside her chosen mate, also staring aimlessly into the flames and pondering the latest message from the city.

He wondered how she felt, knowing Mea had taken the ultimate step and now presided over the Four Factions. Erroh suspected Roja felt little jealousy.

Mea's advancement, however, was not the matter that caused such unease at the fire just now.

"I'm the first to bring this news. I doubt I will be the last visitor through these gates," Doran explained quietly. His inference was quite clear. "It would be prudent for you to relocate."

He had brought fine word of the city, news that had lightened everybody's mood. Those who knew her knew Mea would be a fine leader in the dark days ahead. She was wise and strong and, above all else, fair.

Silvia's spectacular failure to take the pedestal was a clear sign that Mea's popularity was unanimous. It was the first sign of unity since the assassination. The Alpha females had chosen, and they had chosen impressively. Silvia had not garnered enough votes to demand either a second count or a place of stature.

Doran's second message, however, was far more sobering. Almost remorsefully, he told them of the requests made by Gemmil, the deals that had already been brokered. Uden, the leader of the south, *would* sit at the table of the new Primary and discuss the future with them—that is, if the Spark agreed to one simple request.

"I will go to Samara in chains, just as they want," declared Erroh at last, finally finding the words. His hands shook, and he held them behind his back.

I can kill him. I can end this.

"No," spat Lea. She scowled at Doran, as if he had announced that Erroh would be dragged to the Spark and slain purely for the pleasure of a madman. Doran looked down at the dust.

"It's one life, for peace," hissed Erroh.

Not just peace. Vengeance too.

"I do not believe Uden would offer peace for one man," Lillium said.

"Erroh not one man. Erroh *great* man," Nomi argued.

"He wants to kill him, and then take the city," warned Wrek, speaking everybody's thoughts aloud.

"No," said Lea a second time.

Wynn dropped his head into his hands. "Can we afford to take that chance?"

"You can't go, Erroh," said Emir quietly. "I'm not ready to see another friend die over a foolish sacrifice. Fuk that. Stay alive and kill more of them. That's a better cause."

It was a fine argument, but Erroh wanted to kill only one more southerner.

"No," hissed Lea a third time, not to the crowd but to Erroh alone, as though no one else in the world mattered. Perhaps they didn't.

"You should rip his fuken head off," Tye suggested. It was a fine suggestion. It would probably solve most of their problems. He was turning out to be a fine apprentice. His eyes suggested doubt, but he followed his master's wishes.

"We can't lose you, Roro," said Lexi. "I'm only just getting to know you." She stood up from the circle of warriors and stormed off, and Erroh saw tears in her eyes as she fled. Her march turned to a sprint as she fled from the town out into the wastes. He did not pursue.

"There must be something to the lack of hostility he's shown Samara," Doran finally said, trying not to meet the sharp, cold eyes of Lea.

"If they bring you to Uden, he *will* kill you," Ealis murmured. "And raze the city, as well. He might simply desire to see you in the city as it falls. Perhaps the safer manoeuvre would be remaining concealed."

She was taking Erroh's decision worse than the others were. He was moved, considering they'd known each other only a short time. Her argument held water, too, but they would not deny him. Could not deny him. He had both eyes. He had no cough. If Uden challenged him, he would finish him.

"I can't believe we're actually discussing this," said Roja.

She gripped Emir's knee nervously, as though she were ready to fall from her seat.

"No, Erroh, just no," shouted Lea, stepping forward. She was not ready to let Erroh throw his life away. Again. He knew that. Still, some things couldn't be helped. If he died killing Uden, so be it.

"I would sacrifice every single one of you if our positions were reversed," Erroh lied. "Why should I treat myself any different?"

"It's a death sentence," someone argued.

"No, it's not," he countered. "This is what we desired. If Uden plans to kill me, he'll do it himself. I may die, but before I do, I'll have at least one chance to strike." He thought it an interesting argument. Few agreed.

As the hours passed, there were many more words spoken. Erroh, Wynn and Doran argued as one collective, while the rest argued vehemently against them. The longer the night dragged on, the louder the disagreements grew. Eventually, amidst a bout of shouting, the Master General declared they would take a vote come the morning when matters had settled and better judgement reigned. No majority was needed; just the numbers. Even though the vote would likely tear the group apart.

———

She lay beside him and fought the draw of sleep and tears. He kissed her, and she smiled despite the sinking feeling in the pit of her stomach. If he did not leave for the city, this settlement would soon be a focus of attack. Some wonderful things just couldn't last. This was a nice insignificant life here, when one wasn't constantly waiting for death to storm through the open gates.

Oh, and for the occasional violent slaughter of brutes.

"Come sleep, my beo," she whispered. She knew he resented her selfish wish to keep him alive, but he said nothing. Why couldn't he understand that the day they had joined was the day he was no longer free to throw his life away thoughtlessly? She forbade him from leaving her behind. Going to the city was abandoning her, no matter how many votes there were.

He was her mate for life, and he had a duty to her and she to him. He embraced her and rose from the warm covers. He groaned unconsciously, and she saw his scars in the candlelight. She loved those scars. Each one was a reminder that he was a man of action. A man of threat. Such things she found more alluring than she'd ever thought possible. They were a reminder of what they'd come through and lived. When she feared for the worst, she remembered his scars and the ones to come. It was a tough life being mated to Erroh, and she wouldn't change a moment of it.

Apart from the river, perhaps.

"I know how the vote will go," he said, and ran his fingers along the blemish on her neck. It was growing into a mighty impressive scar. She would change its origin tale, though. "Why can't all of you just allow me the opportunity to end this conflict?" He pulled a shirt over his naked chest. She couldn't see the scars anymore. It was a small matter. She would see them again.

"They love you, Erroh."

"It's because I'm so pretty," he jested.

"You are pretty," she said, sitting up and wrapping her arms around his neck.

"I know how you'll vote, but I want to speak to each of the others individually once more, before the morning," he said sheepishly. "It might do nothing, but I must try."

She nodded. She had expected as much.

He dressed slowly, the late hour making each move a little laboured.

"It's so late," she said, and threw the sheets aside. "I'll walk with you." She reached for the nearest piece of clothing; the rest were strewn passionately around their room.

He sighed and turned to her, smiling. "If you'd like. But I'm trying to convince them to come to my side. Allow me this, I beg you."

"I'll keep my mouth shut," she promised.

He shut her mouth by kissing her, and then he hugged her and pushed her back into bed. A fine manoeuvre.

"I want to speak to them without your influence," he said, and grinned, and she loved him.

"There is nothing to sway their vote," she warned.

"Part of me doesn't want them to," he muttered, and she wanted to hold him and kiss him and love him forever. Underneath the strength, he was still just a little cub. He didn't want to face Uden alone, but the measure of him was impressive.

He finished dressing and kissed her before mussing her hair lovingly. "Keep the bed warm for me," he whispered as her eyes closed and her breathing changed. Slipping away from the goddess, he left her and walked out into the cool night.

————

Though he remained calm, his head was spinning. His feet felt loud in the night's silence. Each step made an echo sharp enough to wake the dead—or worse, his sleeping companions. He crossed the street and passed the dying embers of the fire. Without looking back, he marched to the main gate and nodded to the one solitary guard on watch.

Tye dropped and embraced him immediately. He did not cry when he heard Erroh's words. That was good. He accepted the responsibility placed upon him, as well as the scroll, wrapped in red ribbon, for Lea alone.

The child understood that Jeroen's fate would need to wait. Though the pain was apparent, Erroh's muted pledge to him a few hours earlier still resonated with him. He was the Master General, and his orders were sacrosanct. There would be a time for actions, but first they needed to deal with the issue of the city.

Erroh pointed into the distance at the dim light shining in the window of their home. "Look after her," he ordered.

"Make it worth it," Tye countered.

Erroh stole out into the darkness of the road and followed the wood and steel tracks. Away from the glow of Raven Rock, Erroh's eyes quickly acclimatised to the dark. His pace increased, and it took him closer towards the lit torch in the distance.

Every moment seemed to fly by. He feared the worst. He fully expected to hear the cries from his panicked mate far behind him, but alas, there was silence. He had exhausted her, one last time.

I broke my pledge to her.

When he reached his riding companion, he nodded a brief greeting and then climbed atop his anxious mount without delay. Doran had the excellent sense to say little as Erroh tightened his saddlebags and braced himself for the frantic midnight ride, all the while thinking about the pain he suffered for leaving his companions behind. For leaving his mate behind.

"Give me a moment," the Master General said, and

brought Highwind around to face the town. He cursed under his breath. He had intended to say a prayer that the absent gods protect those he cared for most, but his words turned bitter.

"Today started so brightly," Erroh muttered to Doran, shaking the desolate feelings away quickly. He had a day or two to dwell on this decision.

"It's the right decision… sir," Doran offered.

"I've shattered something this night," Erroh said, sniffing nonchalantly, as though it were a small matter betraying his mate's trust so cruelly. He couldn't allow his friends to decide such a fate for him. It wasn't fair to place it on their shoulders either, so he had taken matters into his own scarred hands.

He needed to put as much distance as he could between himself and Lea now. Come the morning, when the truth dawned on her, he hoped the message he had trusted Tye to give her would halt her charge. By then, he would be in chains on a long barge, drifting swiftly with the current towards Spark City. She could never catch up, no matter how swift her mount.

"I'm sure she will forgive you," said Doran, bringing his beast alongside Erroh's. Strangely, he reached over and patted Erroh on the back. If nothing else, he had earned the Master General's trust. The day wasn't a complete loss.

"Have you ever broken a female's heart?" Erroh asked, readying himself for the ride. He didn't want to walk another step from her, but Highwind would walk for him. Of course she would.

Fuk you, Highwind.

"I'm working on it," said Doran.

Erroh looked back one last time and then kicked the animal forward. Both warriors sped off into the darkness, following a track that would inevitably lead to their death.

64

JUST THE WIND

S he gripped the note tightly and stared out at the burning haze of the morning. Her eyes stung, and her head spun. She needed some shade. She had survived arrows, swords and a river, but now she was going to die through her mate's actions. She stepped back in from the balcony and took a seat on their bed.

My bed now.

She knew the letter by heart. She read it every morning. Had done for days now. It filled her with hate. Tore away her hope. Held her aloft when her mind tried to sink to nothing. But today felt different. She sensed something in the air. Something primal and terrible. She wondered had he died this morning. Was he dying this very moment? Was she right to listen to her anger? Was she right to follow her instincts? Was she right to obey, and leave him to face the city alone?

I am right.

The scroll was crumpled and torn. She'd thrown it away many times already. As though enjoying the anguish, she recovered it every time. Were she angry enough, she might have burned it, but she had not had the heart. It was her last memory of him. It reminded her of his betrayal.

I can't watch you die, my beo, he had scribbled.

"Fuk you, Erroh."

Oh, they had argued about pursuing him. And she had listened in silence, knowing the futility of the matter. Eventually, they had reached the same conclusion that she had the moment she'd accepted his message from Tye's shaking hand. There was no seeking him out. There was only waiting for word of terrible events. He had denied her so much. Now he denied her her destiny.

She whimpered and cursed him again. Her eyes fell upon the door. Had she locked it? Aye, she had. A good thing, too. They never stopped barging in and attempting to console her. She couldn't take their pity. She was Lea, legend of the wastes, once mated to Erroh, line of Magnus. She had taken the fiercest torments in her life. She could take this. She only needed to count on her anger. She read the next line.

And I can't let you see me die, he continued.

"Fuk you, Erroh," she screamed, falling to her knees.

Lead for me, he ordered, and she didn't want to please him. *Lead as Master General in my stead.*

Honour him? Obey him?

She cursed again. She condemned the absent gods. She pleaded with them to take the pain away. She gasped for air, but nothing came. Was she dying of heartbreak?

"Why?" she howled, and threshed the carpeted ground until her hand was numb. So much pain; no way of releasing it.

It is better this way, he said.

I will love you for all time my beo, he said, signing off forever.

Dropping to the ground, she wrapped herself in a ball and

sobbed. It was something to do; it was all she could do. All too soon, her tears gave way to screaming. Primal, like those she'd suppressed the last time he'd abandoned her at the burned slope outside Keri.

Absolutely fuk you, Erroh.

This was routine. Had been for days now. How many? Time was meaningless when your soul was empty from betrayal.

After a time, when brooding served no further purpose, she struggled to her feet, sat back on the bed and hated him from a seated position. She hated him with all of her shattered heart because she'd loved him so much. He'd left her behind again so he could die alone, surrounded by thirty thousand killers.

Breathing was difficult. She'd never imagined that breathing could be so difficult. As she gasped for air, the world became a blur. Aye, today's anguish was worse than most others before. From her stomach, a burning shudder drew bile to her throat.

Instead, she hit out at the closest thing. Today, it was a fine vase, with delicate designs on the outside. Ages ago now, she'd filled it with water and rested it by his bedside locker. Who knew how many millennia this intricate piece had survived? She slapped it violently across the room and it smashed wonderfully against the wall.

It wasn't enough.

It never was.

Sorrow gave way to anger. Destruction was a good thing, too.

"Fuk you, Erroh."

She picked up a stool that still held a few of his garments. He wouldn't need them anymore because he was dead. She screamed and threw the stool through the window. She no longer cared if her companions noticed her pain.

The stool made a fine clamour as it fell into the herb garden below. It was a small matter. Nomi could have them all for herself.

Like a whirlwind, she spun through the room, destroying everything in her wake. Everything had to go. She could hear the hammering against the door, but she ignored it. This was her private torment; no invitations.

"Lea," a southern voice cried, and Lea smashed one more picture frame.

Fuk off, whore.

Nomi began striking the door.

"Leave me alone," hissed Lea, and threw something else porcelain and breakable out the window.

Silence from the door.

Smashing from the bedroom.

Every object she could find was torn, struck, or kicked, and all were ruined. Eventually, when there was nothing of value left to destroy, Lea, heartbroken and aggrieved, fell to her knees, spent, and wept once more. They had pledged to walk side by side into the dark together. Nothing mattered as long as they were together. He had given his word, and instead had stolen away from her warmth without warning. Without giving her the choice.

How dare he? How dare he believe she would not ride out into harm's way to find him and bring him home to her? Well, he was right.

"Never again, Erroh," she whimpered, cursing her weakness. She cried a little more, each tear a submission to the desolation she felt. Whatever they'd once held was lost.

I warned him.

As the room's stillness struck her, she heard weeping outside her door.

Shut up, whore.

"Erroh left us," Nomi whispered. She was skilled at pointing out the obvious. Perhaps striking out one more time would help some more.

"He sacrificed himself, for all of you," Lea hissed loudly, sliding up beside the doorway, her voice full of venom. "It's only *me* he left behind," she gasped, and fresh tears streamed down silently. She hated him.

Nomi didn't argue the point. A fine move on her part. "We wait for him."

"He's already dead," Lea shouted.

Best leave now, little whore. He was the only thing protecting you.

"Erroh not die."

"Everyone dies," Lea said, hopelessly.

"Erroh not die yet."

Shut up, shut up, shut up.

Lea struck the back of her head against the wall. She didn't know why, but she welcomed the pain. A distraction, perhaps? "Leave me be, Nomi," she growled, and rubbed at the pain. She was losing her mind. "I have no mate."

Worst of all, if he survived? She would kiss him one last time and be done with it.

————

Aurora sat in silence on the edge of the wall linking their fractured sanctuary and the eternal forest beyond. Her mind was awash with unsettling thoughts. She played the events of the vote over in her mind. She'd led a glorious finger for quite a time, but she'd never had an actual voice in greater matters. Erroh had called her a general at one point. It was a far cry from the status she'd held in the shadow of Uden. She would have voted that he not venture to Spark City.

Why?

Because her condemning Erroh would have alerted the others. This settled some of her thoughts, but not all.

Why haven't I left?

She had chosen another path, apparently. The type of path taken quietly and carefully.

But why?

Distantly, she heard Lea wail and thrash, and this upset her. She did not know why.

Roja heard it too, but said nothing. She was beside Aurora, her back to the world, her eyes on the town and the miserable generals of Erroh's army as they came to terms with their comrade's likely death. Too many days had passed without word. Roja looked even more miserable than usual. Usually her eyes followed the healer, but this morning she was listless and lost in her own thoughts.

"He made a terrible mistake," the redhead muttered. Of course he had. A terrible mistake that might have ended with the Hunt's bloody charge on the city.

Aurora, too, felt miserable for his needless sacrifice. Her eyes caught movement beyond the wall. Nothing more than a rabbit, she told herself.

"I don't think I could have done it," Roja said, and instinctively gripped Aurora's shoulder as she climbed to her feet. Ealis didn't flinch. She did not know why. Usually, when people touched her unaware, she would stab them. It was pure habit and had led to several awkward conversations in the south.

"I wish he hadn't left us," Aurora whispered, realising her sorrow was genuine. She was among the enemy, but they cared for each other deeply, and for her as well. A rare and strange notion. Perhaps they might have liked Fyre as much.

Roja nodded sadly and squeezed her shoulder once more before looking out into the wastes. "We're in this together, sister." She watched something in the green. Aurora followed her gaze. The wind was blowing softly, catching leaves in its gentle grasp.

———

"He should have returned by now," growled Lexi, huddled up near the fireside. The embers were dying away in the morning haze.

"Aye, perhaps," Wynn countered. He ran his fingers along the edge of the small piece of metal in his lap. A fine piece of armour, large enough to cover a disappointed face. He wasn't ready to wear it just yet. Or gift away its twin. There were still refinements to make and decorations to add before he strapped it over his face. When he was troubled, his hands immediately sought its reassuring touch. Now was one of those times. He'd created the battle mask himself. Given life to it from a trauma he struggled with relentlessly. No accomplished blacksmith, he'd burned and shaped it over an embarrassingly long time until it resembled something of worth. It was ugly, but he held it now with both love and revulsion. He wanted to put it on. Wear it and feel better about himself.

"You could have argued with him that last night, instead of reaffirming his foolishness," the young girl hissed venomously.

"I'm sorry, little one," Wynn whispered, putting away the faceplate and wrapping it up in his bag.

· · ·

"What's done is done. Erroh knows best," Lillium said. She was as heartbroken as Lea, but she held firm. She would have to. It was what he would have wanted. And what he had wanted was to offer them a chance at peace, or, likelier, to get himself a chance with Uden. He also wanted Lea to become the Master General. And not her.

She chewed on a piece of bread and knelt down to pour another cup of cofe. As disappointed as she was, the world turned; things continued. She could have offered a few comforting words to Lexi, but there was little point. The girl was hard. She could be harder. She threw a piece of bread over to the girl, who caught it and then, after a moment's thought, left it on her plate. A few breaths later, she shrugged and left the fireside completely.

Fine. Be like that, little one.

The camp had become a downright depressing place these last few days. Lillium grabbed the bridge of her nose and squeezed tightly. If no one else would stand up, she would. She swallowed her bread and felt a little better. Today she would lead the charge back out into the wastes to continue their monitoring. They had been careless these last few days, tracking less than needed and mounting no disciplined watch. Retiring to the fire earlier and earlier. Enjoying the terrible wait for word of their fallen hero.

Wynn stirred uneasily, but did not rise. His eyes were thoughtful and nervous. He looked beyond her and beyond the town's walls into the vast nothingness of the road and sighed. She wondered, would he have thrown himself into the path of an impossible threat, in a vain attempt at saving them all?

Lea's Erroh did.

Not my Wynn.

———

"I miss my father," muttered Tye. It just came out. His emotions were in turmoil, and he let it slip. He missed his father dreadfully, and knowing that he had jeopardised any chance of a rescue was tearing him apart. He missed his father, and he missed Erroh.

Wrek sat beside him, and they both watched the river as it flowed past them. "At least if there is peace, Jeroen may return," Wrek suggested, and it sounded hollow. Sacrifice Erroh for Jeroen? It was hardly a victory.

"He ordered me to say nothing of his departure," Tye said. Such guilt could crush a man. Tye was struggling.

"He trusted you enough to know you'd honour the order. We should not ignore that." The behemoth shrugged and watched the sun glinting off the river's surface. Above them, the sky was blue, and the season hinted at some false warmth. It was a nice day, despite the despondency of the inhabitants of Raven Rock. "You recovered his favour after the incident."

"I'm not certain whether Lea will be quick to forgive me."

"No. That is some burden," agreed Wrek. That first miserable morning seeing Lea's face as her heart broke was something awful. She had held herself with composure as she read the note left only for her. The only hint of her agony had been a slight tremor to her hands as they held the scroll. And they had watched, and they had waited, and then they had learned.

"A female scorned," he said.

"Aye, a female scorned," Tye agreed.

There was a slight change in the breeze, and a shudder ran up the back of Tye's neck. Something was wrong. It felt as though the trees sprouted eyes to watch them sitting listlessly by the river. He climbed to his feet. He carried no weapon and immediately felt naked for it. Like a hunter eyeing a fresh meal, he watched the world in front of him. Wrek, sensing his unease, climbed to his feet.

"What is it?"

"Something is out there." He needed a sword, and he needed to redeem himself for following an order given by his Master General. He also needed to save his father, but that was an afterthought.

"It's just the wind," countered Wrek, but it wasn't. Tye watched the sway of boughs and leaves as they danced in one perfect piece, the gentle rustling concealing any menacing footsteps. Tye had spent long enough in forests to sense the turning of things. Wrek reached for the handle of his fine-looking blade and watched the world as terrible things began to happen around them.

———

Aurora felt it before she saw it. Something wonderfully familiar and just as terrifying. Another flicker of movement beyond, but nothing to cause the world to crash around them. A few strands of fiery red hair caressed her cheek, as Roja too caught the movement and slid closer to the edge to get a clearer view of something ominous.

It's just the wind.

Be the wind.

Her hands shook, and *his* grip took hold of her chest. He couldn't be here. Aurora shook her head and stepped away from the edge. *A nasty fall.* She placed the arrows into her new crossbows and feared the worst.

And the best.

Uden was here.

She knew it.

What has happened to Erroh?

It's all over.

No more waiting.

Ride home with barrel in tow.

Oh no, oh no, oh no.

"I think there's something out there," whispered Roja. She craned her neck and squinted her eyes to get a better view of those wishing her dead.

All but one.

Ealis felt herself drown and fly all in the same moments, and each breath took an eternity. A terrible storm of conflicted desires thrashed wildly inside her, as a tempest would toss a lost ship in an endless ocean. There would be blood; there would be home; there would be agony. Inside, she screamed and fought her instinct to kill and love and hate, and all too soon the battle was waged and ultimately won.

Or lost.

Roja hesitated as the realisation overcame her in a terrible instant. The hunters moved silently and skilfully through the forest, but as they drew close in their terrible numbers, there simply weren't enough places to hide. So they charged.

And they did so unnaturally quietly. They carried only swords. No crossbows. On a finer day, with awareness and the proper preparation and led by a dual-bladed maniac and his vengeful mate, the outcasts might have held the town, for they were elite. And they were legends. They were the things of great tales.

But the gate had been left open after Wrek and Tye's return, just one more terrible instance of the Outcasts' languid complacency. They were unprepared. This was the end of it all.

"Oh, please, no," whispered Roja, backing away from the

edge as the Hunt swarmed from the wilderness. She pulled her sword from its scabbard and turned to Aurora, her sister in war.

Aurora knew her intentions. Could see it in her manic eyes. They alone would meet the first wave. They alone would fall in a river of blood while the rest scattered or gathered up among them. She had done this. She had brought the ruin. She was the betrayer.

"Close the gate."

Aurora watched her brethren charge forwards, and she whispered her terror. They were the finest of the Hunt, the protectors of Uden, and they marched only with the god.

Choose a side, she told herself. Choose it good. It was a childish suggestion.

The first warrior appeared in her sights, and she held up one of her crossbows. It was an easy kill, even with such an average piece of handiwork. She missed her divine weapons, lost now, somewhere in the city. But with Wrek's help, she'd carved and smelted these bulky wood and steel weapons, and she'd smiled as they'd taken form. Like a fine wine or indeed a child, with a little careful mixing and a little patience, they could become magnificent weapons.

For now, as she raised the second crossbow and took aim, she threw herself into defending her chosen side. Everything was forgivable, she'd learned.

"I brought them here," she cried sadly. It was an apology. It had been on her mind.

She fired the first bolt. A deadly strike that tore through fine leather, through cotton, through skin and through muscle. The redhead never had the chance to cry. She heard Aurora's lament, and then she heard the chime of a poisonous arrow as it struck her chest.

"I'm sorry," whispered Aurora, looking beyond her dying

friend, gripping the bolt in her chest. Some kills were less enjoyable than others. When Roja closed her eyes, it would bring little joy.

Aurora fired again, and her friend recoiled violently as the second arrow also pierced into flesh.

Don't do it.

Don't watch Roja fall.

She looked.

The girl in red fell backwards from the top of the wall. The second bolt through her chest finished her. Was this what it felt like to die? It felt a lot like falling. Was this how Dia had felt? She landed painfully in the dust below, and the strange thought occurred to her that Raven Rock was a fitting place to die. She wasn't screaming, for the horrific agony was too much, so she cried quietly, for that was all her body would allow. Amid the melancholic wailings of the dying, she watched the sky above and wondered when the light would turn black. When would her unacquainted parents walk her home? When would Dia put the kettle over the hob?

Her name was Fyre of the Night, and she had been her father's little miss golden. She remembered being a child, and she remembered a tall brute mauling her until she died. She remembered the pouring of the blood and she remembered seeing beautiful colours dancing in the sky. Mostly, though, she remembered the taste of the kill and the release from the agony. She was the first. She was the greatest.

Aurora Borealis watched her friend fall in a heap as her brethren swarmed through the gates like a pack of hunting

hounds. She leapt down to watch the light leave her eyes.
Instead, she saw the girl stubbornly hold on to every breath.

She removed the blade from along her side and held it
across her victim's neck. It was mercy.

"I don't want to die alone," whispered the fading girl. The
bolts weren't deep—her leather had held—but her luck ended
there. Ealis could smell the acrid poison, and she stroked the
girl's face gently.

*It's about to hurt a great deal more, my friend. Whisht…
Let Aurora cut you just a little bit more.*

Unlike most southerners, Uden's protectors knew Aurora,
and they feared his wrath lest she come to harm. They flowed
past her into the town and she watched them go.

———

"No!" screamed Wynn, seeing Roja fall. He almost froze for
an instant. The panic and fear he endured was replaced by
instinct, and he leapt to his feet with sword already raised.
The attackers were streaming into the town and he knew his
time walking the road was done.

"On me," he screamed, charging towards the town's wall.
He was doomed, he knew it, and such a realisation was
liberating. He didn't even bother turning to see who followed,
if any did at all. It didn't matter. What mattered was taking
this last fight to the Hunt. Swifter than he'd ever imagined his
feet would allow, the young Alphaline reached the nearest
ladder and climbed atop the town's wall. Dying on higher
ground was better than dying at their level. At least he could
take some with him.

. . .

Uden's chosen warriors separated into groups and charged against little resistance. It was almost too easy. Only one unarmed outcast charged them down. A small, unimpressive young skut of a thing, with scruffy hair and a strong, sharp jawline. He was carrying a healer's bag.

65

GODS OF WAR

Her name was Aurora, and she was a murderer. She accepted that this was her despicable calling. She stroked the dying girl's cheek and watched the wretched healer charging towards her. She thought him brave. Naïve and wasted, but brave. As they formed around him, so silent in their disciplined charge but for their padded leather feet, she screamed and they all obeyed, for they knew her importance and they knew her commands to be sacrosanct.

"Let him through," she cried, and her voice carried far in the morning air. Far enough that those who had unsheathed their blades to meet the enemy knew her disgrace. It shouldn't have bothered her, but it did.

Just as killing Roja bothered her.

She knew the attackers as the Azier. They were Uden's chosen garrison. Only the fiercest could fight for this elite garrison, and they were impressive.

No Outcasts or Rangers, mind, but skilled.

The Azier did not strike Emir down as he ran past. He locked his eyes on Roja's broken form and didn't seem to notice them at all. Aurora tilted her head sideways and touched the bolt, slowly rising and falling in front of her. Roja moaned loudly, and Aurora sighed. Death was beautiful, was it not? Death moulded pain into pleasure. That was what Uden said. She felt his presence, and her heart hammered wildly.

So long.

Please, no.

She wiped some loose strands of red hair from her victim's face and left behind a smear of crimson. Such a pretty face, ruined by red. Then she realised Roja was leaking all over her. She should have relished this wonderful scene of a fading body bleeding dry in her arms, but she craved no taste of warm blood now, felt no urge to smear herself in her latest kill.

You killed Roja, whispered Fyre in her mind.

Of course she'd killed Roja. What else was she supposed to do once her lover returned to her? She was Aurora Borealis, and killing was her gift to this life. And she lived a good life.

Emir slid to the ground in front of her. Dropping his medicine bag carelessly, he pushed Aurora aside and went to work, futile as it was. He took hold of the dying girl and held her face in his hands.

"Were your bolts laced?" he demanded.

"They were."

He froze for a moment, then turned and stared at Aurora. She detested that gaze. Deep down, she screamed and howled. Her grip tightened on her blade.

Stop looking at me like that, Emir.

"I made a mess of her face," Aurora Borealis whispered, trying to wipe the smear of blood from Roja's porcelain skin. She knew it was better to die looking your best.

Emir shook as he tended to her. All but his hands. He

removed a knife from his belt and began cutting around the arrows, and Roja's faint whispers turned to agonising wails. "Keep screaming. Keep fighting," Emir cried, and his tone was miserable and Aurora stung.

The Hunt streamed into the town without the gate to bar their way. The grey of the town turned black beneath their numbers as they washed over it like a tidal wave. And they were too many.

Wynn never knew where Stefan or Wrek appeared from, how they scaled the wall and stood with him, now. It was something for which he would be in debt to them for the rest of his life. No matter how short a time that might be. The three worked together now like veterans and held the climbing attackers at bay, their swords and shields parrying and striking. The air was filled with the clash and scream of metal on metal, the song of the last valiant fight for this long-fallen town. They fought with no regard for their own welfare, throwing their hate into each strike without hope of victory. No better brothers to fall with, Wynn mused.

They were not entirely alone on the wall. Lillium, too, climbed above the surging mass of death and took a stand farther down the wall, towards the town's rear.

"Move down towards her," Wynn cried, spying her, and his comrades followed. He would not fail her. When he died, she would be beside him. Nothing else mattered. And if they all abandoned the fight and leapt clear of the wall, hoping to find salvation in the surrounding forest? Well, that was fine too.

The top of the wall was narrow and no place for swordplay. Yet, here they were. All along the wall's interior rested wooden ladders, taller than a mount's brow and carelessly left behind by the former inhabitants of Raven Rock. Each heavy piece was laden now with a constant flow of enemy reinforcements, eager to mount the wall. With a roar, Wynn rushed the first interloper, slashed at him until he fell back, howling, and then shoved the ladder back at him. Hardly fatal, but enough to delay him and his mates. By the time the brutes set the ladder back up, the three warriors were already further up the wall, driving back another string of climbing brutes.

Wynn had always fancied himself capable of running miles without exhaustion taking him, but the fierceness of war swiftly took his breath. He struggled through fatigue to block, parry and strike, and though he shuffled closer to Lillium with every kill, the distance never seemed to dwindle. He wanted to call out to her. So close, yet far away. To let her know he was coming for her. That she was not alone.

In the end, she came to them. While he had two ample swordsmen covering his rear, she brought the fight to every enemy. Perfectly balanced. She was effortless, her hair whipping gloriously in the early sun, her body pirouetting, ducking and parrying at will, as if the gods themselves painted each stroke in her masterpiece. Her finest moment. She alone was Alpha, and she alone was holding the Hunt with her steel and terrible rage. Effortlessly keeping her assailants at bay while the rest of the town was swallowed up. She was divine. She was of war. She was an impossibility, and she was impassable.

A spark of hope grew deep down inside him as she neared, ever so. He pushed on with all his will and fading strength to match her charge. He would die, but not before he reached her, and fought with her one last time.

A brute leapt forward, his simple attire baggy and

unimpressive. The battle axe he wielded was something special, though. He charged and swung, and Wynn met the attack bravely by leaping back and ducking under the strike. His back touched against Wrek or Stefan, and the world felt that little bit smaller. He met the next follow-through of the axe wielder fiercely. He heard a scream, felt a heavy weight, and then nothing as his attacker stumbled and fell away to the ground below. Wynn didn't hesitate. He didn't wipe the spray of blood from his face. There was simply the next invader to kill.

———

"I'm supposed to kill," Aurora whispered, holding the bag open for the healer as he rummaged deep for something to stem the flow of blood. Finding an impressive tool and wiping it with an alcohol-soaked rag, he worked the second wound. He could hear the pounding of enemy feet all around him, but it didn't matter. He was dead. He knew this, but what was a life if he allowed every girl he'd ever loved to die without him nearby?

Are you there, Aireys?
Watching and waiting?
Are we three about to endure awkward conversations?
You know I'll always love you.
Please, my darling, don't let Roja die.

Her naked breasts were out in the light of day. She was a lady and didn't deserve such an indignity. Instead of hiding her from the warriors who passed them by, he took hold of the arrow and pulled it. Immediately a fresh spurt of crimson erupted, and she screamed louder than ever. The tear in her body held, though. He thought it a miracle that she still took shallow breaths. Further proof that there were gods watching, she had coughed up no blood. At least her lungs were intact. He wrenched the second arrow from her broken chest. This caused fresh agony, and he wanted to hold her, love her, beg her to live.

Instead, he continued battling the darkness. He saw little beyond his beautiful Roja. It was madness he found himself in, and working the horrific injuries was the only thing keeping him from shattering. Who knew he'd been this close to utter destruction? He had once believed himself skilled at recognising those whose lives were wounded by a dagger in the mind. Only now, he realised he was as lost as those he sought to heal. Those like Cass.

"There will be blood," Aurora added, closing the healer's bag and sitting back. Her head swam with unwelcome thoughts. Ideas of another life. Memories? So much pain. She pulled her incredible eyes away from the sight of her dying enemy. Her friend? She gazed upon the ruin she had brought upon the town. She saw them fighting atop the outer wall and doing well. Did she expect any less? How great to stand with them. How delicious to stand with them and put a dagger through a few of their wonderful ribcages. She was no Outcast.

Her name was Aurora, and she liked to kill.

That's what he told me.

Aurora lifted her dagger and slipped it against Emir's throat. "Blood takes away the pain," she whispered in his ear.

———

Wynn waded into two attackers who attempted to barge through their line using combined wooden shields. It was a fine tactic, but fruitless. He hammered at their edges, and as they raised the wooden pieces slightly, he dropped to a knee and slashed out at their unprotected ankles. It didn't kill them, but it was enough to make them stumble. Wrek completed the manoeuvre. Shoulder-barging the brutes with all his strength, he knocked them clear of the wall and screamed a great, triumphant war cry. There remained only one last ladder between the two parties. After that, he'd need an alternative plan. He glanced to the wall's far side. They could never reach his tunnel. There were no stragglers waiting below. Who knew if they could drop and loose themselves from a chasing pack?

"I knew you couldn't manage without me," Wrek roared, turning back to join Stefan. He tried to smile, but the terror in his eyes allowed only a grimace. That was okay. Terror made their acts atop this wall even more heroic.

As they cleared the last flimsy piece of wood and nails, Wynn saw the form of Lillium a little ahead, dispatching another warrior. Covered in blood and wearing fresh injuries along her arms, she stuck to her task. She retreated slowly back towards them, both arms working like deadly machines as befit a goddess of war. Slashing mercilessly, opening deep, poisoned wounds. She brought death, and she brought it just fine. She appeared deliriously happy, tearing the brutes apart. And perhaps she was.

Wynn could hear his own exhausted gasps in every laboured strike he took, and each took a further toll. Regardless, he struck out mightily as Wrek pushed the last ladder from the wall.

"Fuk you," Wrek screamed, and with powerful arms built for leading thieves and criminals, he heaved the ladder held by four faceless killers away from the wooden edge.

Unfortunately, his strength was his downfall, and as the ladder jerked free of any resistance, Wrek stumbled forwards, knowing in that moment that his fight and his life were done. He fell clumsily. His sword clattered down beside him. A minor miracle. He was doomed, but he still would not offer them an easy passage. He would step loudly into darkness. It would be a good death. Striking and kicking, he leapt back against the wall and took hold of his sword. They tried to retrieve the ladder, but Wrek stepped in their way. He had a last mission. It was almost comforting. He would protect the ladder for as many breaths as possible and hope that his companions above would use the distraction he created to leap free from the wall and lose themselves in the forest.

It was almost too simple a plan.

He didn't hesitate, and he didn't believe such an act on his part was possible. He should have died in Keri. Every breath he'd taken since that day had been taken with the spirit of the darkness watching his every move. Men like Stefan were not destined to be remembered. When every step was hobbled by fear and revulsion, it was not possible to live a glorious life. One merely eked out a wretched existence, taking one painful breath after the next. Until now, Stefan had somehow cheated death, but the enemy had dealt the last hand at the table. There were few cards to play and fewer places to conceal an ace of queens. His failures in life were complete.

He could see it clearly enough now. Aurora Borealis was a murderer, a betrayer, and the vanquisher of them all. He'd seen her strike Roja down. He'd seen the same look in her eyes when she'd fought out in the wilds. When she'd dispatched the Wolves that night, she'd stolen his trust. *Their* trust. Through his foolish, wretched need for comfort, Stefan had led her straight to their sanctuary. He had done it because he had fallen for her like a fool. And she? Well, she had simply played him like a discarded six-string.

At least I can do this.

He watched his friend leap headfirst into a wave of evil. It was noble, and it was stupid. For Emir was dead, and soon Wrek would be, too. They'd tried their best and proven to be soldiers of great merit. Nay, more than that: Erroh considered the term "Warrior" to be the highest term of respect, and he and Wrek had earned that title together as brothers today, standing side by side, shields and swords flashing, cutting and killing. Each a brother. Each a god of war. They had fought with tears streaming from their eyes. Killing and mourning in each of their motions. This was the end.

And when Wrek fell, Stefan was alone.

———

It was the metal against his throat that roused the healer from his stupor. It was not anger he felt; it was shock. It was all becoming terribly clear. He was the finest healer walking the world, and he could not save Roja or indeed himself. Not with this mayhem exploding around him. Not with a knife to his throat.

It was horrifically liberating to realise this. He'd always been the finest healer, even when he'd been a mere student in the great city of Samara so many years ago. His master had brutally challenged him, apprenticing him to treat the already lost. To desperately seek healing in a cancerous body, already eaten away to bone and a grin. And he had tried. Fuk, he'd tried so hard, and his master had, well, pushed him further. Every death took a toll, though, and as time passed, all hope and faith had leached away from the young cub. Despite that, he had continued to rage against the inevitable and challenged darkness as if it insulted him.

He looked now at the shattered form of his lover and felt the darkness laughing at him; he hadn't heard it laugh so loud since he was a child. He'd waged a fine war with the bitch, but now, as his own time drew to a close, he conceded that death would take one more soul from his watch, before finally bringing an end to the titanic struggle they'd waged for so many years.

He had always thought it would be the drink that killed him.

Aurora gripped his hair tightly, and the blade broke skin and he closed his eyes and sought out his friends.

66

RUINED FRIENDSHIPS, SOMETHING STRANGE AND A LITTLE DRAMA INVOLVING FYRE

"I t's okay, Emir. This is what's supposed to happen," Aurora reassured the healer as she held his head in place. Even as the life left him, he did not cease his attempts at trying to heal the girl lying near-naked on the dusty ground.

Her name is Roja.

"Uden wills such things," she explained, biting her top lip. She bit hard, and it felt pleasing, intoxicating, and sobering. Her mind reeled. Her heart broke.

Her next victim sighed, and she felt his body relax. He was brave and wonderful, and he deserved a peaceful death. If not peaceful, then swift. It was the least she could do. She gripped his hair tightly and allowed herself a moment of regret. She had always found him quite amusing.

"We were your friends," he whispered. Fine words. Words to think about. She thought on them.

Feeling a trickle of blood stream free, he played his hand and returned to working on the goddess of red. His stained fingers became a blur of movement, cutting, sealing, and cutting a little more. Only a true master could see the difference between the blood, muscle and poison, but he worked through her innards, regardless. He worked as if it were a small matter that his friend had betrayed them all and brought an army to their door. He worked as if such things were a normal part of life.

"I'm sorry, Emir," Ealis said. Her blade relaxed for a moment. A moment to contemplate her actions, he imagined.

He spun around, slitting open his own throat as he did. The wound was not deep enough to kill, but just enough that he wouldn't need to shave for a while. Perhaps he'd have to swallow carefully for a time. He flung his elbow backwards and cracked her loudly in the face. It was a fine technique, learned by every Keri inhabitant during the festival of the Puk. Many arguments could be settled thus from a seated position. Her head jerked as she fell backwards, and he fell on her before she had time to recover. Gripping her blade and holding it up against her neck in one motion, he pressed down and screamed to be heard through her concussion.

"Let me work," he demanded. All around him, the attackers closed in. He couldn't understand why they'd allowed him to live this long, but apparently, striking the infiltrator had spent the last of their benevolence. Their shadows formed around him. The world darkened as they neared, eager to kill but wary of causing harm to his quarry. Nearer they came, and the bitch with the beautiful eyes merely stared up at him without saying a word. And then something strange happened.

———

Wrek met the first brute and batted him away without too much trouble. The rest were the problem. With his back to the wall, he struck with the last of his energy. There were at least ten swords to fear, and he faced them grimly.

For a moment, he imagined himself just as Erroh did: afraid to die, but determined to bring the fight. No wonder Erroh was a legend. Wrek wanted to live. That want would show in his caution. *Fuk it.* He'd played a hand or two in his life, so he feigned bravery. "Come on," he roared, as though he desired war.

When Stefan appeared beside him, having dropped down to join him in death, he almost smiled.

Stefan winded himself as he dropped. After a precious moment to gather his senses, he climbed to shaky feet and raised his blade. He didn't need to nod to his friend to let him know why he did it. Standing beside him was enough. He knew the measure of Wrek as a man, and he was not ready to let him die alone. The odds were hardly fair; they were two magnificent lunatics, screaming and raging in the face of an uncertain and unprepared army. Everything was about to get incredibly bloody and incredibly final. No tales would be told of their last charge. At the end of his life, he was strangely calm. For the first time in an age, he felt worth. He wondered would Aireys be waiting with a goblet of wine in the dark, eager to welcome him to the eternal gathering.

"Come on," he demanded, leaping forward and striking down a southern fiend. And then, before the rest could surge in and send him into the darkness, something strange happened.

———

Wynn watched Stefan slide over the edge as if it were nothing at all. The world slowed. Wynn had never known such bravery. He fancied himself noble and honourable despite his flaws, but Stefan had given up his life without hesitation. If truth be told, reaching Lillium mattered more. They stood together as allies, swords raised, trembling from exhaustion. With her alongside, he felt there was a chance.

She felt differently. She tried to slip down after the others. Her eyes were wild. She had no belief in rescue. All she saw was the opportunity to inflict further death upon the Hunt. There were few attackers standing nearby now, but down below, where her friends were forming a defence, there was just enough fodder to sate her appetite. She turned, preparing to slip down and cover Stefan's flank as he formed up with the behemoth, and felt something take hold of her. Something with a desperate grip.

"We have to escape," shouted Wynn. He held her tightly and pulled her from the ledge. She screamed in reply. A primal cry, the howl of a feline beast denied a kill at the last moment.

"We can't leave them," she screamed, fighting his strength. It felt like the dark. She struck out, but he didn't relinquish his hold. Instead, he dragged her over the edge.

And then, something strange happened.

———

Emir pulled the blade away from Aurora's neck. He did so unconsciously, but she didn't struggle, for she knew full well of his coming. The surrounding attackers fell back and took a knee. Without a word, a flood of serenity washed over the invaders. A surging, slow wave that rose without warning, and each soldier, from the town entrance all the way to the outlining wall, fell to silence and reverence. The world became still, and Emir almost missed the crash and thunder of the battle. His eyes searched for something beyond Roja's broken form. He searched for his companions, but all he saw was the grey of their vanquishers.

And then, as one, they bowed, and the world became quieter still. He could hear Roja's gasps for air. Her eyes were glazed over. He knew that his face was deathly pale; the smell of poison assaulted his senses.

Save her, Emir, he heard a voice say, far away in his mind. Somewhere deep down where Aireys still lived. He returned to the unpleasant task at hand, despite hearing the heavy footsteps of a southern god as he came to gaze upon his victory.

Uden the Woodin Man was impressive. He was dressed in magnificent, dented armour of red and black, yet still it shimmered. He wore no helm, and this added to his grandeur. Erroh had described this mad man in great detail, yet somehow, as he stood over the healer and the fallen females, it appeared that Erroh had done him an injustice. Taller than Wrek and far wider, his body hinted at nothing but muscle beneath the weight of that substantial armour. It was little surprise Erroh had struggled to defeat him.

"My love," Aurora whispered through a swelling mouth. Her words were slurred, but her eyes had regained their lustre. She lay in the dirt and smiled. She licked at the droplets of blood that flowed from her nose. "My divine lover," she added, and Emir finally understood the depth of her betrayal.

Save her, Emir.

He turned from the most powerful warrior in the world and attempted the impossible.

"Is… this… Roja?" a deep voice asked slowly, as if each word was a struggle. As if speaking at all was far beneath him. Emir didn't answer. He was scared. He'd been scared before, but this was something else entirely. This was like standing next to a demon of fire and religious vengeance and hoping hopelessly to avoid its burn. He felt like an ant about to be crushed under an unimaginably massive boot.

When the god knelt down to stare through the healer, Emir was certain he felt his bladder release.

Help me, Erroh, line of Magnus. You're our only fuken hope.

"Is this Roja?" Uden repeated, and it was a godly growl. Emir met his gaze. This was hard when an eye patch was involved. Regardless, he held it as best he could. He even nodded while wondering if it would be wise to send the blade he held in his hand through the god's other eye.

Fuk it.

Emir struck, and the god caught his wrist with impossibly quick reflexes. The giant squeezed, and the weapon fell from his grasp like a toy. Despite himself, Emir yelped. Just enough to delight his opponent. The blade bounced a few times, clattering against the cobblestones, before falling still. Well, he'd taken his shot. At least he could say that. Uden laughed at the effort. Of course he did.

As would Erroh.

And then the god's horrible eye returned to the broken body of Roja. Her chest laboured under the weight of the world and the weight of Aurora's actions. He glanced at it with distaste.

"No one must gaze upon her like this," he roared. A

hundred pairs of eyes immediately found somewhere else to stare. He was their god and what he decreed was to be followed. He had them trained. Exceptionally well trained.

Still holding Emir's wrist, the god slid the remains of Roja's dress back up over her chest, covering her as best he could. If she noticed, she didn't show it. Instead, she just lay in the morning sun, dying all over the place.

He reached down and picked up Emir's blade. He raised an accusing eyebrow, although his look was not without ridicule. *As if a small piece of metal could hurt him.* He returned the blade to the healer and relinquished his grasp on his wrist, though not before offering him a moment to attempt another strike. This Emir knew to be folly.

"Who did this to her?" Uden asked quietly; the words were directed at the nearest warrior. Whispers were heard as the question was repeated throughout the masses of fighters. Someone was in trouble.

"I did it, my love," Aurora stated dreamily.

His massive hands clenched to fists capable of breaking stone. His knuckles whitened, and he ground his teeth. "Do you know this girl?"

"She is a friend," Aurora said. Something was different in him. Or maybe it was different in her. When his hand slowly embraced her throat and squeezed, she almost pulled away. Instead, she gasped.

"You have been busy, my little one," he whispered dangerously. Usually, she adored the torment, but right now she just wanted him to let her breathe.

This he did, but only briefly. She moaned as she grasped her bruised neck and lamented a girl once named Fyre.

Enjoy his love.

Take it.

"Can he save her?" Uden asked, staring through her.

"He is the finest healer in this tainted world." It was the truth. It pleased Uden.

"Well, that is a fine coincidence," the god growled. He turned to look upon the two fighters at the wall, and he looked unhappy with what he saw.

"Do not let little Roja die," he warned the healer.

Emir nodded, as if it was the finest suggestion. Two deep wounds? Erroh had taken more and kept on coming, while Lea had taken one solitary bolt through the back that had nearly killed her. It all depended on the accuracy of the strikes. The body was built to survive and recover until it could no longer. How long before she bled herself dry?

"Who is left?" Uden asked.

"Just those two," Aurora lied.

She lied. She didn't know why. Her mind screamed. She felt the urge to tear out her hair. More whispers. Some attackers had seen others. At least two others, fighting atop the town's walls, no doubt. Still, any delay might help.

She didn't know why she thought like this.

All hail Uden.

Uden pulled a sword from a leather scabbard along his waist. The blade glimmered in the sun. With a lazy, dismissive gesture, he bade the crowd to stand aside.

"Let them come," he said casually. "Let them try strike down a god."

. . .

He waved the two outcasts forward and removed a second blade from the nearest Azier warrior. Testing its weight and sharpness, he strode out into the centre of the town. His temper was volatile. He needed something to ease his dissatisfaction with the events of recent days.

Oh, Aurora, what have you done?

He had lost a daughter a lifetime ago. Now he had lost her stolen cousin.

They moved towards him tentatively. The thick cluster of soldiers parted ways as they neared, and Uden bade them attack. And they attacked.

Wrek was the first to react. With his massive frame overshadowed by the even more massive figure of Uden, he approached his opponent carefully. Stefan looked like a lost little lamb between the two of them, but he never faltered. He stepped alongside his friend, his eyes flickering for a moment to Emir and Aurora as they watched on. He raised his blade and attempted to circle the god.

The crowd formed around them. Enclosing them. Penning them in. The main street became a fine circle of conflict. An arena waiting to taste spilled blood.

"Come take your chance," the god urged. He spun his blades slowly, as though mocking Erroh's technique. Each of his movements was exaggerated and slow. Perhaps he was offering them the illusion of the great metal slowing him down. A cruel jest, if false. Perhaps he just needed the practice of fighting, with his faulty depth perception. As the Outcasts moved to either side of him, he ceased the spinning of blades and awaited the assault.

When it came, he was ready. Wrek leapt forward with his sword and met impenetrable resistance. They struggled for only a moment before the god shoved him back effortlessly. Stefan was already on him, striking without regard for his own wellbeing. The god held his ground and met every strike as casually as Erroh or Lea ever had. This was no practice.

He countered Stefan, who met the move, but the force knocked him to the ground. By then, Wrek had recovered and leapt in front of the killing strike, holding the attack and allowing the smaller man to squirm away. The crowd nodded their appreciation of the move, but they said nothing.

Aurora tilted her head to the side as her lovers attacked each other. Her heart fluttered in anticipation and her stomach churned miserably. How much of her own blood had she swallowed? She fought the urge to throw up as the fight neared its inevitable conclusion.

They stood on either side of him. For the briefest of moments, he struggled to match their aggression, then spun away in an unlikely retreat, bringing an end to the skirmish.

They thought they had him as he stepped away and spun to the side. Both men lunged forward but met nothing. He turned suddenly and, leaping into the air with a display of impossible agility, struck out with his metal arms and caught both warriors across their chests. In a flash, he was on them, striking with all his might. They stopped moving within a few blows.

To Uden, Aurora knew, taking a life with bare fists was an intimate act. She could take no more. She leapt into the arena and then leapt onto her god. Her head was a tempest of fear, anger, and revulsion. She felt a deep, searing pain pulse through her skull, yet still she pulled at her lover. A voice screamed in her mind. Repeatedly. Three words. *He is divine. He is divine.*

"No," she screamed, and attempted to break his deathly grasp on her family.

Her enemy.

Her lover.

Her companions.

Her mind.

"No," she roared, striking him across the face.

"No," she growled. It was primal, and it was terrible, and it was liberating.

She was Fyre. Her nails dug down his face, slicing through leathered, aged skin. He released his hold and climbed to his feet, away from the unconscious fighters. She growled and panted and backed away from him. Not to flee, but to better her pounce. Her beautiful eyes were clear, and she knew her sins. She understood her sin against Roja. She knew it all. She could see it all; she saw more than Uden the Woodin Man.

"No," she hissed, panting wildly. Her movements were those of a cat, cornered and ready to kill. Ready to protect her loved ones.

She had lied, and he hadn't noticed.

"This is my town, now," she murmured through a broken, manic grin. She pointed to everything around them. He'd taken everything from her, built her into something beautiful and beastly. It was the least he could offer. If he said no? Well, she would dance one last time.

The god smirked. He picked up his fallen blade and stood over her unconscious friends.

"Hold her," he whispered, and a dozen hands grabbed her. She struggled, for she knew that gaze. Knew that grin. She knew her crime in bringing Fyre to life.

"Please, my love," she begged, and he stared into her

soul. She felt it burning away. Felt it more as he placed his blade over Stefan's forehead.

"On the night you were born, the sky came alive in colour." She could see his body tense and prepare.

"Please, no. I love him," she wailed, and Stefan opened his battered, beautiful eyes.

"What is your name?"

"Please, Uden. I will do anything."

She looked pathetically at Stefan. He stared right back at her. His last words were for her and her alone. "I love you t—"

Uden drove the blade down, and Stefan's words were caught in his throat, where they perished. His body convulsed and died, and she fell in her assailant's grasp. Her mind shattered and tore. She wailed loudly, and they all heard.

"I give you the gift of blood. What is your name?" he demanded, and she shook, for he spoke the truth.

"My name is Aurora and I like to kill."

"I do this because I love you, little one," he said, and released his grip, allowing her to fall to the ground. "You desire to keep the rest?"

"I do, my love," she wailed, and looked at her Stefan.

Gone in blood.

I never cut your heart out.

"Well, of course. For I am a merciful god. You may have them all. Whatever you desire," he whispered, and knelt over her and loved her, and Fyre died as swiftly as she had been born.

"I want the last Ranger," she whispered.

67

I SAW IT COMING

I t took a moment for the first cries to carry in the morning breeze, Lea looked out through the broken window to see where they had come from, and she knew something terrible had happened.

Erroh is dead?

She hopped over the debris of her rage and stepped out to the balcony to stare out at the horror. Below her, they swarmed like rats, and her heart fell. She'd seen this before. A lifetime ago in a little town called Keri. When the rains had ended that terrible day, she'd seen them stream forward, just like now.

Nomi the betrayer.

And as she had done then, she looked helplessly upon her friends now as they were slaughtered. She almost grabbed her bow and blades. They wouldn't go silently, and she intended to join them. The urge to join her sisters and brothers in delivering vengeance nearly drove her to frenzy.

Instead, she held her charge for Erroh, and she hated him for it.

She had to lead, and a true Master General would lead by leaving them behind.

Defy Erroh's orders.

Do it.

She almost did. Standing frozen for a moment, she watched from her balcony as Wynn led them to the top of the wall. The only tactic, she thought. They formed up and met the charge bravely. There were no crossbows among the Hunt, and they would suffer significant losses. Her friends were brave, and they were doomed, and she wanted to be with them. It would be a fine death. She considered unleashing Baby upon them. A girl could do some fine damage from such an elevated position.

Defy Erroh's orders.

She knew better. She could see the turning of the wind already. The town had fallen and her friends were dead. The killing blow hadn't been dealt, but it was coming.

She saw that not all the southern animals attacked the Raven Rock inhabitants. They spread out throughout the town, hungry little groups, searching for fresh meat. Dozens of different bands charged into the buildings, with swords raised and noses eager to catch a scent. They would easily find her, she realised, and it tore her from her stupor. If she survived, she could spend whatever future she had regretting her decisions, but for now, there were more important matters.

She grabbed what she could and slung her pack and weapons onto her back. Weighed down but familiar with the awkwardness, she unlocked her bedroom door and left it ajar so that no hunter would think someone had ever concealed themselves behind it. She crept to the balcony and climbed up to the roof like a thief escaping with the greatest riches.

Like a crab, she crept along the building's slated roof and

concealed herself behind an old chimney. The dizzying height took her breath, but she knew she was well hidden here. She couldn't see the battle anymore, but the clink of steel reassured her they were still fighting.

Still killing.

She dared a glance out and saw her means of escape. She and Erroh had discussed this once before, in the event they were ever attacked. It had seemed so insignificant then. It had been her idea, and Erroh had agreed it was the smartest move. The building was close to the high wall at the town's rear. She'd been so confident then that a leap to the wall from the roof was a small matter, but now that she was up here, it seemed terribly high. There was only a tiny landing spot as well.

Far below, she heard the distant crash of boots charging into the house. How long before they tore her room—their room—apart? Not that it would really matter. It had ceased to become their room the moment he'd left.

Raven Rock had been no healing place like Cathbar.

She scrambled towards the edge of the roof, preparing to leap. Then she saw something strange happen.

The world fell to silence, and her father walked from the grave into her town and tore her mind apart. She reeled as though struck with a fisted glove by a demon with green eyes.

Green eyes. He had green eyes.

She remembered snow; she remembered fire. She remembered blood. She remembered his green eyes.

No, no. Please, no.

He was older now, broader, but his face was the same. His stride just as intimidating. She'd locked him away. Locked all of it away. She didn't want to remember. She didn't want to believe. She collapsed where she stood, for her horror was too much. She felt her chest clench. She felt her bladder almost release. Bile rose from her stomach and spilled out all over her blouse. Her body betrayed her. She rolled along the roof and allowed herself to die. She could take no more.

How could this be?

More memories flooded into her shattered mind, and she broke further from sanity. This was too much. This was not fair. This was the end.

I want to die.

I hate him.

I can't think.

He never wrote.

What became of my family?

He had green eyes.

Has he killed Erroh?

I am alone.

Lying along the edge of the roof where her body had ceased its deathly roll, she gazed at him as he went to war with Stefan and Wrek, and she gasped and struggled for words, but nothing came. Mesmerised, she looked down to the marching Hunt seeking survivors, and she gave up. Erroh would not come for her. She could just drop over, she realised, and it was so tempting to simply drift away from this life, from its shock. So tempting that it shook her back to life.

Get up, girl.

None of this matters, she told herself. She clung to those words and pulled herself to her feet. She drew away from the horror as, distantly, a girl screamed, and she denied herself further horror. Instead, she defied her bastard father. Her cruel, dreadful sire who had wrenched a world apart for vileness's sake.

"I hated you, always," she gasped, for she remembered hating him, and though her voice was weak, she spoke aloud.

Many feet below, the fall called to her. She tossed Baby

and her swords beyond the wall and offered a quick prayer to the beyond. She felt small and the distance felt vast. Erroh would have leapt without thinking, and she would have followed, ready to pick up the broken pieces of him. That was how it was with them. The perfect relationship, the perfect symbiotic love. He was gone now, and her line was a disgrace.

I am a disgrace.

Who would pick up Lea?

She turned and leapt. It was a strange feeling to take flight into nothing. She made no sound as everything took a further turn for the worst.

Falling.

The hard stone wall reached her too fast, and the impact took the wind from her. She stumbled clumsily and rolled forward, her momentum carrying her over the edge. She tried desperately to stop herself. She felt her fingers rip open as they tried to take hold and failed. To any watching southerner, she was a blur, a slight flicker of silent motion, and then she was gone.

Falling again.

She allowed herself a low groan as the hard, dry ground punched up to meet her. She felt her ankle give with a loud crack. The world turned and turned again. Like a toy doll cast aside, she flailed and rolled and plunged down through the bushes until she came to a painful and sudden stop against a rock.

It was a nice bush, she thought, because she could pull herself beneath its welcoming cover and take a few breaths to gather her senses. Out here, on the wall's other side, she couldn't hear steel clashing anymore.

He's alive, and I want to die.

He's alive.

Oh, please, no. Wiiden is alive, and he is the wrath.

The pain roused her. She spat blood from her mouth and already felt her tongue swelling. A terrible pain shot up her leg. Each pump of her beating heart made it worse, and she could not gather her mind. She wanted to curl up in a ball and give up, and oh, it was a tempting thing. She tried to cry. Tried to squeeze out a few silent, delicate tears. She thought she'd cried her last, but no, there were still more and she hated herself for it.

Cry later, Lea.

In her mind, it was Erroh's voice pleading, and her anger overcame her. How could he not be here now, when they were dying and she needed him most? Summoning her strength, she crawled from the bush and recovered her discarded belongings. Testing her weight on her wounded leg, she almost screamed for the effort and fought the panic. She could walk, but not quickly enough to reach safety before some straggler discovered her tracks.

So, she chose a slow, concealed crawl through the brush over the agony of standing.

It was the longest journey of her life. It felt as long as the walk south, trailing her lover. She pulled herself doggedly along, hand over hand, grabbing fistfuls of dirt and grass and rock and weeds. Her left foot tried desperately to push, while her useless right merely trailed along like a dragging passenger, snagging on every branch and thorn and adding to her agony. Her forehead was a river of perspiration. Every time she hesitated, imagining footsteps behind her, she was certain they'd discovered her. She lost count of the times she closed her eyes and awaited the darkness and no strike came. No foreign shouts of discovery. All she heard was the river and cries from curious crows. They had little interest in her, for there was plenty to eat back within the walls of the town. They only needed to wait for everything to settle.

She reached the river and, after only a moment of hesitation, dropped into the freezing water, only to be dragged down to the bottom with her heavy load.

She did not panic, for she was no longer little Lea of Samara. She was Lea of the road, line of Uden the Woodin Man, mated with Erroh. She held her breath until the drag was manageable. Rising above the surface once more, she took a few breaths and pulled herself back towards the river's edge. Her feet touched the bottom, but she allowed her injured foot to relax in the water's hold. Tucking in as close as she could to the grassy verge, she glided along as smoothly as she could with the current. It was slow, agonizingly slow, but with discipline and hard work, she could slip silently away from the fallen town of Raven Rock, leaving all she loved far behind.

68

BLACK PARADE

A sudden wave brushed up against the bow of the vessel and splashed over the waist high rail, drenching Erroh and jerking him awake. He fell from the stool he rested on, rolled once, and lay flat on the barge's upper deck. A second wave followed and soaked whatever remained of his clothes and he decided this was the worst wake up he'd ever endured.

He lay in desolation for a moment, watching his breath in the flicker of the barge's torches and thought miserably of the wonderful life he'd had before it all turned to shit. The world might have been different had he drunk and gambled less on his merry journey to the city that first time. Had he arrived at the city a few seasons sooner, he might have found his mate and headed east and avoided all this horror. People might have believed he had lived a glorious life, for many of his actions were renowned and revered. He would trade it all for a boring life with Lea.

Lea.

He took a moment for himself. Closing his eyes, he blocked out the dawn's first rays and tried to forget his crushing responsibility. He imagined himself out in the wastes with his beloved as daylight's cold call reared its head.

It was a damp night, is all.

"It's your turn to make cofe, beo," he whispered, and a third wave crashed over him and pulled him from foolishness. So much for self-denial.

Sitting up, he listened to the creak in the barge's body as it fought the change of current, and he knew the hour drew near. This was the end, and it simply wasn't fair. What malevolent entity had doomed him to this constant life of struggle and pain? A right bastard of an absent god, he imagined.

I can't do this.

He knew the city was near, for they had travelled this river without slowing. Catching the breeze, going with the current mostly. His body shook, and he knew he was close to collapsing upon himself. Truthfully, he had lost his nerve.

He regretted not voting.

He regretted these dark thoughts, too.

I can't do this. I can't do this.

Standing up, he kept his face serene. Let them believe he was at peace. Better for all, really.

Holding tightly to the barge's safety rail, he countered the sway. He was no good on the water. He never had been. The bobbing was barely noticeable, but to Erroh, this precarious form of travel was nothing if not terrifying. He belonged on the land, where everything was stable and reassuring. Where a man could get to higher ground and hold firm.

The barge was sturdy enough to hold its cargo, a half-dozen fallen Wolves and two mounts, with space to spare. Though wider than most barges, it was small enough to navigate the river's treacherous bends. The barge captain knew which routes to take, avoiding shallower waters, and until now, their voyage had been without incident.

Erroh roused himself by reaching into the freezing river and splashing more water across his face.

"We're almost there," whispered Doran from behind him, and Erroh flinched.

"Fuk me, where did you come from?"

"Oh, I've been here all night, friend," Doran replied. He sat casually along the boat's edge, watching the world turn from ominous night to ominous dawn. The river had opened up as it neared the city. The last mile before they reached Samara was more a lake than anything else. It had been a fine place to birth a city. A fine place to make a last stand. "Just waiting to see her lights." He pointed to the distant glow, and Erroh's heart dropped. Through the trees, he saw it. A dim glow, growing to a shimmering beacon, rising, giving hope to the world. Unless you were a prisoner returning for sacrifice.

Feels like the end, whispered the absent gods in his ear.

"Did you sleep much?" asked Doran.

"Aye, a little." The barge creaked, one horse whinnied gently, and Erroh fought the rising panic. This was his choice, he told himself. Even as the barge drifted along, he saw them.

He'd been here before. This terror was no different. It felt like a horrid dream. The Hunt were also rising from their slumber now. He caught himself holding his breath at their numbers, for there were many. Any fool could see they had little intention of marching for peace. This was no mere gesture of strength. The breeze picked up, and the vessel glided forward.

So many tents.

Too many tents.

He remembered, a long time ago as a captive in the freezing south, watching a city of animals prepare themselves

794

for war. He'd seen their terrifying numbers then, and he saw them now. He leaned over the edge and threw up. It was little more than bile, but the tearing effect on his stomach and throat was real.

This is no dream.

Lea will not wake me.

He tried to summon courage. When he found nothing, he attempted rage. He thought of his lost friends and the brutal sacking of the town.

Do it for Keri.

"Water?" one Wolf asked, holding out a tankard.

"Aye, friend," Erroh muttered, taking the flagon and drinking heavily, hoping to swallow the bitter taste of fear. He faced the camped army once more, his eyes darting from one large tent to the next. Somewhere within, his quarry lay sleeping. What terrible actions would occur once Uden learned of his shackled return?

"I felt the same when I first saw them," sniffed Doran.

"It's just the sway," Erroh lied, and found the lie agreeable. He remembered the warrior he'd been in Keri. Too furious, too fierce, too foolish to allow fear to take him. He sought that warrior skin now. It was somewhere deep down inside him, frozen, huddled in a cage. Lying made it easier to recover. He wiped his mouth before tossing the canister back to the Wolf. "I'm built for the land."

It wasn't just the numbers that terrified him. At the far end of the town he could see great rolling structures, and his stomach dropped. He'd seen images of these ancient siege engines during his studies with Elise, who knew her histories better than most. Weapons older than the ancients themselves, yet still as brutal today. The south had little intention of making peace. They had come to siege and raze the city. This was the fuken end.

The spectre of inevitable death drew Erroh from his own terror. His mind played the part of general for a moment as the barge moved steadily forward, and he felt that deep, dark cage creak and shudder, if just a little. Were he leading from behind the city walls with a small army to command, he would choose dishonour as a tactic. He would send everything the city had at the bastards in the dark of night. One swift, unexpected attack and just hope for the best.

Bold thoughts for a captive awaiting a death at his enemy's hands, he told himself. He touched his two blades, still down at his sides, and remembered that terrible night in Uden's domain. He had been certain Uden would challenge him, that he was mad enough to believe it was his godly destiny. Had he not offered Erroh the invitation? Had he not charmed him with gifts?

Well, Erroh *would* meet him in the city. This time, he was ready. This time, it was his territory. This time he didn't have a fuken cough. He would not fail. Not with the entire world's salvation resting on his endeavours.

Not again.

Such crushing pressure brought more peace to his mind than he expected. He imagined the cage's gate creaking open and allowing him to go free. Magnus and Elise were known to rise to any occasion. Perhaps he was no different.

"It's time, Erroh," whispered Doran.

With a nod, Erroh removed his swords and passed them to the bald Alpha. He kept his hands out and chewed the inside of his cheek.

Clink.

He hated the familiar feel of metal across his skin, but he didn't fight it. Why bother? They secured the chains and locked him in. A fine move with the city's harbour so close.

"I half-expected to hear a heavy splash during the night,"

Doran said. It was a subtle compliment. Erroh could see he had the bald Alpha's respect.

"I slept in," he muttered, shrugging. The cage opened up wide.

I will kill Uden this day. All will be well.

––––––––

The river seemed vast and serene until the last bend, where it opened up into a bustling harbour, teeming with all manner of floating vessels. They brought the barge to dock at the rear of the great walls, alongside a collection of other boats: longboats, caravels, yachts, and yet more barges, all moored all along the quay. However, it was immediately apparent that they carried no passengers or supplies. Somebody was collecting boats and storing them for safety, it would appear. Perhaps with the Hunt camp facing the front gates, the occupants had sought shelter here. At least it blocked off any maritime forces from sneaking in through the massive wooden and steel portcullis where the city historically set up their trading routes deep into the wastes. Erroh wondered how much trading was happening these days.

As if the city's economy wasn't crushed as it was.

Those who told tall tales argued that the right captain with the right map could sail south until his vessel was spat like a cork into the great endless oceans beyond. Erroh had always sniffed at such suggestions. Still, though, were he asked to test the theory today, he'd gladly attempt the task.

The clink of chain tested him now. He took a few miserable breaths as they dropped anchor and sent word of the infamous one's arrival. It was Doran who noticed the procession first. He ran his hand across his bald crown and shuffled his feet a little. Erroh's heart beat wildly. While

Doran tested the freshness of his breath, Erroh gave in to temptation and scratched his arm. It was something to do while the twenty fully-fledged Black Guard approached the dock.

An attractive young Alpha female led the procession, and Doran met her first. They spoke in hushed tones, while the rest of her companions marched forward and surrounded Erroh the Outcast. He hated that term. Perhaps Emir had been on to something when he'd searched for a new name. They needed something more fitting than "Outcast," which brought to mind a band of nomads. Erroh was no nomad. He knew his home, and he knew his heart. They were the very same thing.

I'm so sorry, my beo.

"My name is Celeste. I speak for the Primary," the woman declared formally, and despite himself, he bowed.

"When will I speak with Mea?"

She laughed, as if his query was both humorous and idiotic. Perhaps it was. Had he thought beyond his need to see a familiar face, he might have seen the humour in his idiocy.

Still, though. Fuk off, Celeste.

"The Primary has little interest in a criminal, let alone a brute responsible for bringing doom to this city," she growled, turning away in disgust. "Bring him," she barked, and a half-dozen brutes in black surrounded him. As one, they took hold and dragged him forward. His chains clinked loudly behind him as they escorted him to his death.

"No need to hurry," he mocked, and met only silence. It was a small matter. He would try to play the lunatic of Keri, with or without their appreciation.

Word spread quickly of the outcast's return, and though the hour was early, citizens appeared at their doorways and windows, eager to see the last march of Magnus's son. They knew him, and they knew of his dead mother. They cast cutting remarks at him as he passed, crude and cruel enough to justify a little violence on his part. He was surprised to realise that they did more damage to him than anything else, and he fought to keep his nerve, his warrior skin. He bowed his head and swallowed his retorts: he was returning in disgrace, after all, not as the altruistic legend he'd presumed himself to be. Not as a brave soul willing to give his life for them all. But still, why did they hate him so? he wondered, although he knew the answer. A good mob needed a scapegoat, and Erroh was not without his sins. They shouted that he had betrayed both the city and the fallen Primary. They accused him of barbaric acts that had dashed all hopes of peace between the factions. They claimed he was just like his father, savage and vile. He stared at the ground and took it. It was not the return he'd expected. He'd hoped for trumpets.

As he walked, the brave Wolves took turns striking him with open palms, just hard enough to shove him forward and cause a little stinging. The crowd jeered and applauded a little more as they watched the procession, buoyed by the wonderful noise and cheer. They knew of the Woodin Man's request. The day of hope had arrived. So they followed the parade.

Those at the front patted the back of each armoured Black brute as he marched past. Then the curses became louder. A child ran out and kicked Erroh across the shin. It barely hurt, and Erroh merely walked on to the chorus of rapturous laughter. Laughter like that could ignite sparks.

"Fuken lowerlines," he whispered bitterly, then scolded himself. Fear simply misled and drove them. It was hard to reason with a mob at the best of times. The child raised his arms victoriously and received a delicate pat on his head from a passing jailor.

Well done, little one.

Suddenly an expensively dressed middle-aged man with arms the size of tree trunks struck out at Erroh. His fist connected squarely with the Alpha's cheek and sent him sprawling into the dirt.

More cheers.

Though not from the Black Guards. A few light taps were acceptable, but this was something else entirely. There was a danger in the air. Celeste spun in fear upon hearing the outburst. She did not interfere as another punch was thrown. Erroh collapsed again and, once more, was dragged to his feet and pulled forward.

Another strike soon followed, and again Erroh took it.

"Enough," roared Doran. He struck out at the nearest bystander with a closed metal fist. It didn't matter who. The unfortunate man fell back against the rest, giving the soldiers a few precious moments to move further through the aggrieved masses. "Brave. The lot of you," he shouted, daring any mob member to challenge him. Only Celeste halted her stride. She waited for the convoy to break through the last street and approach the secured gates of the jail, and Erroh's heart began to hammer with painful, crushing blows that shook his chest. It was a terrible thing to see nightmares brought alive when one had always believed things could get no worse.

Not the dark. Anything but the dark.

I'll take the mob instead.

"Return home, all of you," Celeste ordered in a tone that brooked no argument. Not wishing to anger an already volatile Alpha female, the crowd gave one last raucous cheer and then bravely dispersed. They had made their point, and they had made it clearly. They favoured peace, and they favoured justice.

Celeste turned to Doran. "Keep his swords nearby," she said softly, and Doran bowed. Before he could turn away, she grabbed his hand and held it to her cheek. He kissed her swiftly and placed his hand upon her belly. Incredibly, she giggled at this, and fuk it if Erroh didn't see him giggle with her.

They brought him into the jail, and Erroh's gut clenched in fear. They released him from his shackles, and he stared at the dark chambers beyond.

Without my brothers.

"Don't worry, Erroh. That march was for show and show alone. You are no prisoner here," Doran said, directing him to an open cell that was well lit. In it was a cot, covered in blankets and cushions. There was even a pack of cards sitting on a bedside table. He'd stayed in worse taverns. Beside the cards was a tall jug of cool water, and he almost cried out in relief and delight. When a Wolf produced a block of cheese, a loaf of bread and a bunch of grapes on a platter, he thought the absent gods had played a wonderful trick on him.

"As if Mea would allow you to receive mistreatment," Doran said with a wink, stealing a grape before dropping his swords down on the bed beside him.

"I don't understand."

"If Uden comes for you, Erroh, you will be rested, fed, and fuken relaxed." He grinned.

"Why?"

"She will sacrifice you, Erroh. She will gladly place you in front of him. But only so you might kill him."

It was a plan, a simple plan. It wouldn't work.

Because at noon, the first attack began.

69

CORDELIA THE FOX

How many miles downstream had the river taken her? Not nearly enough. When the cold cut through her, she dragged herself ashore. She knew that familiar, freezing grasp from her march south, and she knew she had to keep moving.

Alone and freezing again. She did not hesitate. Fortunately, the Hunt had chosen a clear day to attack Raven Rock. There was just enough warmth in the air that she wouldn't freeze where she stepped.

A skill Wiiden taught me.

She shook her head and concentrated on the greater task. Moving was easier than standing still, inviting the coldness to engulf her. With enough warmth in the sun's gaze to allow her to delay stripping until she found shelter, she hobbled through the undergrowth. Her hands shook. Her body, too. It helped with the aching leg. Not a lot, but some.

Again and again, her feet tripped and betrayed her as she staggered clumsily through the unforgiving terrain. She reached out and used branches to steady her and pull herself along, one after the other, like rungs on a ladder. After a time, she found a fallen branch sturdy enough to support her—a gift from the absent gods. Though the exertion was awful, and it cut into her armpit, she found she could increase her pace. Pace was all that mattered. She could take the pain.

They're not far behind.

The briars, each more unforgiving than the last, tore into her clothes, her skin, and slowed her even more. Every snag on the ground sent waves of agony up through her leg. Every mile she travelled added to the doubt in her mind. Hours passed in a blur of pain, yet she never relented until at last she felt she could endure no more, and with a cry of anguish, she stumbled and fell. It wasn't the first fall; it wouldn't be the last. Her leg twisted under her, and it caused her terrible torment. She tried to rise, but her arms shook with the effort and she gave up. Panting and weeping, she lay back on the ground and closed her eyes. Her father's face swam before her.

Green eyes.

"No," she hissed. She couldn't think about it. It hurt, it tore at her, it dragged her to miserable depths. Her fingers gripped the little bed of ivy and moss beneath her and strangely, this calmed her. Their scent was bitter and fresh. How many decades had it been since anyone had passed through this forest? she wondered. She took a deep breath, inhaling the magical scent of the plants beneath her, and then, with a colossal effort, she climbed to her feet and continued on. She had no idea where she was going, no clue as to a plan; she knew only that she must keep moving. And so, she marched onwards through the deep, silent forest and towards whatever fate awaited her.

———

On the third day, she could go no farther. Slumped against a fallen log, she wiped the sweat from her brow and gasped heavily. She brushed her damp hair aside; it was a tangle of twigs and leaves.

Her body was a ruin, as was her mind. Having had only a handful of hours' sleep since leaving the town, she could not think clearly anymore. Her head swam with delirious visions of her father's green eyes. His powerful grip. His godly roar. No matter how much she tried to shake the thoughts from her mind, they returned relentlessly. This was the effect of loneliness, she knew. *Desolation. Hopelessness.* She saw no end to this march, no salvation. She simply marched blindly from valley to valley, cresting one rise and descending again, without purpose. They'd lost her scent twice already, but they still sought her out, and she had no more energy to elude their grasp. She had no will to continue living. She remembered being happy once, but such warm thoughts enraged her now. She leaned her head back against the rotten log and felt herself begin to drift away.

I am spent.

Distantly, she heard her pursuers once again, and now, she knew it was the end. She had run her best, but the sniffing brutes with keen eyes had run that little bit better. She was no longer the divine Alphaline of the forest, creeping and gliding, eluding her hunters. Instead, she was mortally-wounded prey, nursing her injured leg, curled in a glade and awaiting the final, killing shot.

Even without her belongings, she had not been able to travel at any pace. That morning she'd dropped one of her blades and her pack to the ground, but leaving Baby behind had been the truest torture. She'd wept silently, kissed it one last time, and then taken a few drinks of water and limped away. She had never felt more alone in the world than she had today.

I had nothing before him. Now I have nothing at the end.

————

As afternoon turned to dusk, they finally caught up with her. They were on foot now. Not far off, she heard the rhythmic breaking of twigs and hushed whispers of excitement.

Aye, she'd run her best, but they had run better.

And then she saw them.

Brutes in leather and steel, bearing the colours of the south. They marched through the forest towards her. One hunter led the rest, his eyes scanning the ground. She cowered against the log, and then… the band of brutes carried on past her and fanned out, searching the undergrowth.

They have not seen me. Yet.

Drawing on her last ounce of strength, she pushed herself to her feet and, dragging her useless foot behind her, made a final break for freedom. One last race to find a miracle. She heard the leader cry out the alarm, then heard his hunters quicken their pace behind her, and her terror spurred her onward. Was this how Magnus had felt? she wondered.

Somehow, she pulled her remaining sword free and held it out in front of her as she went. So this was how she would die, she thought bitterly: alone and broken in a strange forest. Erroh would never know. None she cared for ever would.

She didn't hear the single set of sandals running alongside her, watching, waiting to pounce. In this heavy green, it was easy to remain concealed once a warrior took a little care.

She did however, hear the others closing in, and turned to face her killers, and suddenly the ground gave way beneath her. With a scream of rage and anguish, she tumbled like a rag doll down towards the valley floor, still stubbornly gripping her sword.. The gorse and bracken slowed her descent, but she landed heavily at the bottom and lay sprawled, heaving with rage, and stared up at the top of the incline.

Her attackers stood in a row at the top, regarding her, and then the leader gave a shout and they slid down the slope as one. There were twelve of them in total, and they thundered towards her like an avalanche.

This was the end. Grasping her blade one last time, she took a breath and stood. When they killed her, she would be swinging.

This is a fine way to die.

I will take three with me.

They formed around Lea, savouring the silence before the kill. The leader raised his hand, and then behind him there was a flash of movement. Not from the injured girl carrying the sword. From a different girl entirely. And she wasn't injured. And she didn't carry a sword.

Nomi leapt soundlessly from where she had concealed herself. With all her strength, she spun the heavy club, striking her first victim in one swift motion before following its momentum into a second fatal strike upon his unwary comrade. Only the dull clunk of shattered bone alerted the others as the first man fell, quickly followed by the next. Without breaking stride, Nomi repeated the attack on the next two brutes with equal and deadly efficiency. The club felt right in her hands. It always had. Sparring with swords had honed her skills, but armed with a club, she could best any attacker.

Lea knows that.

Again and again she swung, each blow delivering precise and bloody devastation as Nomi proudly displayed her skills to the fallen Alpha in the only way she could now.

You're not alone out here, Lea. You never were.

Lea stood motionless for a moment, mute with astonishment, and then, like the Alpha warrior she was, she raised her sword and went to task. She fell upon the nearest soldier, driving her blade deep into skin and muscle and then through delicate organs. The man screamed, and the remaining attackers dug in, eyeing the two females uncertainly now.

Nomi was a storm of hate; she charged on them with war club raised. She screamed as she bludgeoned all in front of her, her powerful arms moving impossibly fast despite the extra sword and the bow she carried.

Ignoring her pain and no longer forced to hold her silence, Lea screamed at every move she made, bellowed out her rage and agony with every life she took. And she took whatever Nomi was kind enough to leave for her.

It took only moments to fell their attackers, for they were elite.

When the red haze of battle cleared, Lea gave a last triumphant yell and collapsed. She panted deeply, and she wiped the warm blood from her face. Nomi stepped through the dead bodies and fell to a knee beside her.

"How did you find me?" Lea asked through ragged breaths.

Nomi shrugged, but would not meet her eyes.

"Were you with me the entire time?" Lea asked. It suddenly didn't matter that the bitch had saved her. Nomi shrugged again. Lea took hold of Nomi's collar and pulled her face close. Nomi didn't fight it. "Why?" she screamed, forming a fist. "Why did you leave me, you bitch?"

"Scared." She pulled away from Lea's grip.

"Fuk you."

Lea sat back, speechless. How could this little bitch have tracked her and watched her struggle without coming to her aid? *Fuk you, whore. Absolutely fuk you.*

"With Erroh gone, Lea kill Nomi," the southern girl whispered, wiping her victims' blood from her chest.

"Kill you? Why would I kill you?" Lea asked her, genuinely puzzled. Certainly, it wasn't Nomi who should fear Lea. It was the other way around—wasn't it?

"Erroh gone. Not protect Nomi now," the girl repeated, and wiped a spatter of blood from her stupid southern bitch face.

"He never protected you," Lea said weakly.

Did he?

Nomi shrugged.

"If you feared I would kill you, why save me now? Would it not have been better to see me dead?" she asked, climbing to her feet and moaning despite herself.

Nomi slipped Baby back over Lea's back, where it belonged. She adjusted her own bag on her back before hanging the club down along her waist. Then, without warning, she stepped up close to Lea, closer than she'd ever stood to her before. "Would never leave you to die." That said, she bent and linked her arm behind Lea's stronger leg, and then lifted her up off the ground and slung her effortlessly across her back. Lea squeaked in surprise, but didn't fight it. She was so tired. This was no place to rest and recover.

"Nomi… um…" She paused. "*I…*" she said, correcting herself. "I love Lea, as sister." She shifted slightly, adjusting

Lea's weight. "Family," she said, and Lea could sense the strain on the girl. Nomi swayed for a moment, but held firm. "Heavy sister, too," she mocked, and then began to move forward. Lea marvelled at her strength, and for a moment she saw in this strange girl what Erroh had seen, and she felt ashamed. Ashamed of her mistrust. Ashamed of everything.

"I… um… I'm sorry… Thank you… sister."

"We go find Erroh."

"No. Anything but that."

"As you wish."

Slowly and proudly, Nomi began walking towards finer cover, careful not to leave too many tracks behind. Without a sound, the two sisters disappeared into the dark, eternal green to conceal themselves from those who still hunted them.

70

SIEGE ENGINES

"I'm not sure I like the look of this," muttered Wissou nervously. He inhaled the tobacco and spat a few loose strands free. Something to do while watching the world's end. These next few days would be the end of it all.

Terrifying.

The machines' great wheels rumbled, seeming to reverberate more loudly than normal. No longer weighed down by a great march's supplies, they were now burdened by something far heavier: massive grey boulders, larger than even the largest man. The soldiers rolled the massive machines towards the edges of the Hunt's territory and left them to face the city's front gates, out of reach of even the most skilled archer. The largest machine of them all waited at the rear guard. It had a dozen wheels, and its workings were an intimidating gathering of ropes and levers. With its varnished pine and oakwood structure, its gleaming steel cogs, and fittings of solid iron, it was like a beast from another time. Indeed, its hulking form bore the scars of another battle, a lifetime ago. Seven smaller machines a quarter its size stood out in front of it. These had been built in the surrounding forest, impressive in their own right, yet paling in comparison to their forefather.

"Siege engines," whispered Uwe, his face paler than usual. Even from this height they could see the southerners swarming around the machines, loading huge boulders onto the machines' platforms. The process was slow and terrifying, but neither man could tear his eyes away from the weapons. "I've seen that larger beast before. It's one of the catapults used by Magnus in the last days of the war."

Wissou looked at him in surprise; like the others, he believed they'd all been destroyed. Such weapons had not been seen in decades. And even then, they had not been in southern hands. The great city of Conlon had fallen under such devastating machines, and now Samara, the City of Light, was directly in their terrible path.

"I thought they desired peace," whimpered Uwe, clasping the shoulder of his oldest friend. He knew the stories of the great catapults. There was no place in the world more treacherous than where they stood now, manning the gate.

"They desired the Outcast Erroh to return," he added. "And now he has."

———

They knew their orders, and they knew their tasks, and each one of the brave warriors went to work rolling the legendary machines into place. Many had spent months learning the mechanics of them; the scrolls had paved the way, and the words of their god did the rest. They pulled the levers, threaded ropes through rings until each one was taut enough that it could be plucked to play a merry tune. And what a tune of death they intended to play.

Dozens more warriors rolled the first massive boulder

across the lip of the cart and eased it into place on the ridged platform. Their task complete, they stepped away and brought forward a boulder for the next volley.

The honour of the first strike was awarded to the chosen few. Only those with the sharpest minds and keenest eyesight could fire the magnificent beasts. Now, they lined up the loaded catapult as quickly as its massive bulk would allow— selecting the perfect angle of fire, measuring the wind and praying to their absent god. *All hail, Uden.*

The great central platform shot up with a sharp crack, carrying the heavy boulder with it. The entire machine leapt and shuddered, threatening to snap to a thousand pieces under the strain, but a master had forged this machine. It was built for a lifetime of service, and the rock was no match for its metal heart.

The world slowed to nothing as the boulder took flight. The shot was true and devastating. They did not build the great machine to ruin Samara's sturdy wall nor reinforced gate. They built her to tear the innards of the city and bleed her dry from within.

It cleared Samara's wall comfortably, making no sound but a whistling tearing of the wind as it reached its height and then began its dreadful decline.

It crashed down through the city and thundered through the marketplace, killing an unlucky handful of terrified citizens. The boulder's momentum sent it smashing through stalls and maiming those unfortunate to be in its path. They screamed in fear and misery and anguish and hate. They pulled the dead free of the debris and they called for healers and holy men and they called for mercy, but nobody was listening.

Even the gods were oblivious to their plight.

But this was only the first strike. There were many to come.

It took almost an hour to load each heavy boulder, but the Hunt kept to their task. Every time they aimed the machine toward the city, they chose a slightly different angle, a few degrees this way or that. Each one hit its mark, each deafening crash ending innocent lives and destroying buildings.

It was far quicker to load and deploy the seven smaller catapults. Each of their projectiles was drenched in oil and then set alight. Like a hail of comets, they streamed into the air and rained deadly fire upon the defenceless buildings below, seven at a time in wave after terrible wave. All too soon, the Black Guard battled flames instead of armoured foes. They went about their task with the same efficiency as those who attacked from outside, dousing the flames with damp cloaks and buckets of water, or stamping on them with their feet; it was all they could do. It was just about enough.

A small band of defenders climbed the walls at the city's front gates, bows and arrows in hand, and set their own projectiles alight. They shot flaming bolts at the attackers below, but their efforts fell short by at least fifty feet. Even with a wind, the city was defenceless now. The hail of rocks and fire continued to rain down upon them, and all the defenders could do was run for cover.

It became a constant rain of fire and the city took them all. It was impossible to miss. Fires caught, burned out and scarred the streets and hovels as many desperate hands assisted the Black Guards in their firefighting duties. Day turned to evening and still the relentless assault continued like fireflies on a summer evening.

Evening turned to night, and as night fell, the attackers redoubled their efforts. The larger boulders were invisible now as they sailed over the wall, and the town's inhabitants cowered in terror, not knowing where the next one would fall. The unceasing roar of destruction echoed around the city, accompanied by the cries of agony left in their wake.

And while this ruin fell upon the city, Erroh lay on his back in his cell. They'd left a flame burning, which was nice. He imagined they'd already hacked the turbines to pieces. It was a small matter. A fresh strike landed nearby and despite himself, he held himself against the fear of a large rock coming through their roof.

Doran shifted in his seat by the cell door and sighed. "You brought this upon us, hero," he mocked. It was all he could say. It was true, even if it was unfair. The moment Erroh had stepped back into the city, he had begun her downfall.

Presuming Uden would follow through with the masquerade of peace talks was a cruel mistake. In a perfect world, once Erroh relinquished his freedom, Uden might have dramatised his execution, giving Erroh a chance. All he'd wanted was one opportunity to strike, but the fates had denied him fairness. Some things were not written in the sky. Some stars couldn't be counted.

"At least I returned a champion," Erroh countered. They were alone in the cell. All the others had long since departed, leaving them alone together with their thoughts and fears.

When the first strike had hit, the Black Guards had joined the fight, battling against the fires and reclaiming the bodies of the dead. As the barrage continued, more and more jailors had disappeared from their posts. To the Wolves, there were more important things than an imprisoned outcast. Only the bald Alphaline remained now, as proxy jailor. He didn't offer the front door key, however, and Erroh didn't bother to ask.

Instead, they waited for a large fuken boulder to come crashing through the roof. Erroh had enjoyed better nights.

"You should hate those of this cursed city for what they did," Doran said to him. He reached for a chunk of cold honey bread. He offered some to Erroh, but Erroh shook his head. He'd eaten his fill.

"I want to hate them," Erroh said.

"You're a better man than me."

"I should have allowed the vote."

"This attack would have happened, regardless."

"Thank you, Doran."

"Think nothing of it, Master General," Doran said. He smiled weakly, and Erroh saw how badly his hands shook. Still, he concealed his terror better than most.

They never heard her enter. And why would they? She moved like a goddess, even though she was weighed down with more worry and sorrow than she'd ever imagined possible. She slipped through the concealed door and made her way through the main prison cells towards the dark, forgotten room. She stood there for a few moments before either of them noticed.

"It's good seeing a friendly face on this day," she whispered at last from the doorway. Both Alphas roused themselves from their numb stupor and stared in amazement. Then, as one, they fell to their knees and bowed their heads, for they were once again in her divine presence. It didn't matter the circumstances. It didn't matter their connection.

"Mydame," Erroh whispered.

71

TEARS IN THE CHAOS

S he looked tired. Her eyes were wide and her shoulders were stooped slightly, as though they carried the weight of the world. Dressed in a light blue gown, she was simple in appearance, but elegant. Beneath her steady gaze, something had changed. She carried herself differently now. She was a fine choice as leader of the world, crumbling as it was. He hid the warmth behind dull, predictable, reverence. This was how it was. She was no longer Mea, the kind host and dear friend. She was something else entirely, and he waited now for an indication of how to proceed.

"Never bow in my presence, Erroh," she whispered, stepping up to him. It sounded more like an order. It didn't matter. He remained upon his knee in his cell.

"Mydame, you have come here somewhat underdressed," said Doran. He looked past her, searching for the procession of guards and advisors usually present when a leader walked and finding none. He stood up, but held himself to attention. Outcast or not, he was an Alpha. And a Wolf at heart. This dank, dark cesspit was no place for a Primary, especially one without an entourage.

"They need every hand with the fires," she said. She sounded less like the old, vibrant Mea now and more the quiet queen of a crumbling city. Erroh noticed the long sword hanging loosely by her shapely waist. Why was the Primary armed, anyway? he wondered.

Has it become so bad that she, too, has taken up arms?

"I have not seen Celeste since the first barrage," she said, staring at Doran, who stiffened at the words.

"Mydame…" he began, then stopped. He looked past her to the door like a beast keen to be let loose. "She didn't return to the tower?"

Mea nodded grimly.

Erroh sighed and gripped his comrade's shoulder.

"She is a fighter. Go—find her," the Primary ordered quietly, and the panicked Alphaline tightened his belt and donned his weapons. Hastily bowing, he departed the dark room without looking back. He took off running, and Erroh doubted he'd see the man ever again. Strange that, in the hours they'd sat in the gloom together listening to the onslaught, Erroh had warmed to him, to his wit and his sly intelligence. They'd spoken of many things as the hours passed. Erroh had wanted to ask him if he desired to become a father some day, but the right moment had never come up. Some things weren't discussed in the dark.

"Oh, Erroh, I'm so sorry," cried Mea, once they were alone. Tears streamed down her face. She hugged herself tightly as though she might break apart. "I wasn't there when they took Elise," she said, her voice breaking. "She was alone."

Erroh remained immobile, still upon one knee. He didn't need to hear this; he needed to hear strong words of defiance, defences and revenge. He needed to hear a plan. But these words brought to life the terrible pain he kept hidden away in a little cage. His mother was dead. He knew this well. He'd known it for long enough that he could walk around without falling to pieces.

"Her pain is done," Erroh, line of Elise, whispered, his voice cracking.

"Yes," she said, and bowed her head. After a moment, she spoke again. "On this day of all days, I'm glad to see a friendly face," she whispered.

Erroh looked up at her carefully. Mea had always been larger than life—her tenacity when she'd stalked him in the forest, her casual strength while draining a glass of wine or even screaming of Emir's innocence. She'd always been a presence of strength and reassurance, but now that she was the authority of the world, she whispered like a lost child.

"Is this the day we try to take a stand?" he asked her.

"No, Erroh," she said. There was nothing in her voice. "This is the day they bring us to our knees."

Her words sounded hollow in the darkness surrounding the little cell. The torch flickered, and Erroh felt her hopelessness. She needed something… his queen needed something. He thought a moment, and then found the words. Strong words. Perfect words. Two simple words.

"Jeroen lives."

She fell upon him then, with a sharp cry of anguish and need and sorrow and joy, clasping him in a hold of such desperation that she stole his breath for a moment. A wonderful moment, where he forgot himself and his place and hers.

"What do you mean?" she demanded. "What are you saying? Tell me, little one," she ordered him—begged him. She cupped his face in her hands and stared into his eyes, searching for the truth, searching for a miracle. Her tears flowed freely now.

"He is a captive in the Hunt, but he breathes," Erroh said, and she fell to her knees and wailed. Her relief was contagious, and he sank to the floor beside her and cried with her. For himself, for her, for those he'd been unable to protect. For those he'd left behind.

He heard another screaming crash as a massive boulder landed nearby, and he cried for the doom he'd brought upon this once proud city. He cried, for he knew Lea would never forgive him for leaving her behind. He imagined for the briefest of moments that it was Lea holding him now as he sobbed, but nothing could replace her touch. Not even a Primary's maternal embrace.

"We found him before I came here," he said. "I gave Tye my word we would rescue him."

Her reply was a tight squeeze and a gentle hushing, as her own tears dried up and her loving instinct took over. *It's alright, little cub. Mea is here now.* "When you escape this city, I charge you to honour that pledge," she said, and it was a fine order. It was neither hopeful nor angry; it was simply factual. She hugged him once more and then broke the embrace, but not before kissing his forehead as only kin were inclined to.

"Few will escape the city, but I will fight as it falls," Erroh promised, wiping his own tears away and getting unsteadily to his feet.

She regarded him solemnly, and now she appeared lighter than before. Aye, still carrying the weight of the horrors she'd endured, but now, with the news of Jeroen's survival, there was a glimmer of the old Mea beneath.

"No," she said. "There will be no more fighting. Today we retreat."

———

He followed her through the streets and finally tasted the madness all around him. Like rodents in a cruelly constructed cage, the surviving warriors and townspeople scurried nervously from one side street to the next, keeping low but scrambling aimlessly onward. It didn't matter where they went, alas; there was no escape from this fortress. They glanced nervously at the sky as they fled, in terror of the next whistling projectile. Hours of relentless horror had taught them the art of looking up.

As Erroh and Mea made their way through the ruins of the city, they drew suspicious looks and outright glares. Many recognised him and seemed perplexed that he walked free now. Some looked ready to take out their terrified fury on him, but thought better of it. Better to be crushed by a rock than to start a fight with an unleashed Alpha, they supposed.

"Do you think it is a wise to walk the city with me beside you?" Erroh whispered to Mea after a time. She grinned, and he was almost certain he caught a glimpse of her devilish smile. She no longer seemed like the waif who'd set him free a lifetime ago.

"Uden never wanted peace. Now everyone can see that," she said grimly.

She stopped to tend to a haggard, broken woman clutching a little bundle beneath an old archway. The woman looked ashen, terrified, and shaken to stillness. Mea knelt down and offered a few words before resuming her desperate march. Erroh saw she now carried a small shivering hound within her cloak. Looking back, he saw the woman climb slowly to her feet as though she had been gifted a mission. He turned away again and caught up to Mea as she stormed through the smoke, away from the commotion.

The route they took was not towards the Cull, nor the office of her leadership. They passed the stadium and made their way to the fall walls of the city, where the barrages were fewer. A small crowd had gathered there, preparing a defence.

Mea turned to Erroh, her eyes burning with defiance, assuredness. He had gifted her hope; she now gifted the world a Primary.

"I was not completely unprepared for such an event," she told him, indicating the people gathering.

Erroh nodded, listening. Nearby, he saw a Wolf emerge from the ruins of a home, leading an elderly woman by the hand. He gestured towards the north, and the old woman muttered and dithered and then set off in the way he'd indicated. The Wolf was already moving to the next doorway, pounding on it and calling out. He was not alone; there were dozens of Wolves knocking, shouting, and kicking down doors before escorting the inhabitants towards the rear of the city and the harbour.

"This city was always going to fall," she continued, and he could see the conflict in her eyes. They were no longer brutes she could blame for atrocities and cowardice. They were her army to lead, and petty distrust would do little to help their plight.

"So, you were ready?"

She smiled and nodded. "There will be no separation between us after today. There will be no conflict, no further action aside from pulling ourselves together."

"Aye," he said, unsure of why such a thing mattered.

"I have a plan," she said, and began to walk towards the harbour. He followed, all ears now.

It was a simple plan. As they walked and talked together, she insisted it *would* work.

He agreed.

_____

72

JUST LIKE KERI

T his was how a city fled, and it was spectacular. Every
moment, a new group of people were shepherded
towards the harbour's edge. From the surrounding streets of
grey stone they emerged in a steady stream, as if the city
itself were forcing a poison from its body. They came in their
wretched and wealthy droves, away from the chaos and death
of the first quarter of Samara, and now they herded together,
united in terror and grim hope. They watched the authorities
nervously, glancing now and then at the divine Primary
standing with them. Any time a person neared her, the
Wolves barred the way with a delicate shake of their heads.
The Primary was not taking questions today.

Beside her stood the Alphaline Erroh. They knew him as
a snake who had brought doom to them all. Yet here he stood,
now, free of his chains.

He didn't look that impressive standing beside their
Primary, anyway, they decided.

"This will not even be the great fight that defines our
collective tale," she spat. "Although it should have been," she
added, looking to the sky.

A few hundred Wolves protected the harbour. All along the outer gates where the city was weakest, they were positioned to meet any attack. Bristling with crossbows and all with itching, eager fingers, they watched for signs of movement. Atop the great walls, their comrades lined the wind-swept edges, daring the brutes to move the great siege engines closer.

The city's ragtag fleet of ships strained at their moorings, slowly filling with weary refugees. Some clutched family heirlooms or ancient scrolls; others held their children's hands; some clutched bundles of quivering pups. Under a barrage of orders barked by the Wolves, they scrambled aboard the waiting vessels and settled into their seats.

As the hours of uneasy tension passed, the boats filled one by one. Once a vessel was full, its captain moved it out, away from the gates, but none dared to venture out alone into the open river. There would be safety in numbers. Safety in surprise.

But late in the day, with still thousands yet to board, it became apparent there might not be enough seats for every man, woman or child. Let alone the defenders. Seeing this, the Wolves ordered the ships to forgo safety and take on additional passengers.

"This is taking too long," growled Mea, watching a ragged old man struggle onto a barge. A sea of waiting hands held him, but after a few halting steps, he slipped and tumbled into the freezing water below. By the time they pulled him to safety, more precious time had passed.

Waste of fuken time.

All the time in the world; the city did nothing. She'd tried her best with the time they had afforded her, and it could never have been enough. She had been busy, but the absent gods denied her any true successes.

She'd sent out the scrolls by riders that first day. A great confirming call to arms. A great call for rescue to those she'd made agreements with should the city turn to ruin. She'd ordered the construction of twelve great ballistae to line the top of the wall, hoping to fire great arrows into the heart of the Hunt should they come under siege. Another week and they would have completed the first. Even one beast skilfully manned could have saved hundreds. And those cursed war machines currently tearing the city apart would have never been allowed such freedom.

She'd sent Seth to the southerners in the hope his familiarity might open up genuine negotiations. He'd never returned.

The only official success was in pardoning every member of the outcasts who brought the fight to the Hunt beyond the gates. And here, as Erroh stood nearby, mirroring her every move, shadowing her footstep, she felt better about the day, knowing every warrior or citizen would soon know there was no longer a price on his head. He had the ear of the Primary. And when he spoke, she was inclined to listen.

It wasn't enough she'd accomplished, but she would do better.

"When the front gate falls, we won't be able to hold the harbour for long," Erroh said. He, too, was fretting about the passing of time. The smell of smoke suddenly grew sharper. Turning, he saw thick billows of smoke from the front end of Samara. The fires were growing, mostly untended now with so many Wolves instead tending to the great exodus.

They'd secured the city as best they could, but fallen well short of holding it. Not that it was a futile defence.

Near the city gates they'd used what materials they

could to slow the inevitable first charge. Blocking every route around the gate with debris from the Hunt's own endeavours, every thin side street was covered in shattered fragments of a once thriving marketplace, of every barrel the city offered, every fuken brick they could find, taken from the surrounding ruined buildings. Marching towards the city centre was to walk through carefully placed mayhem. It would stop no Rider upon a horse, but a gathering of soldiers could not move freely in great numbers.

Like Keri before, it was now their best hope simply to delay the final attack, lure the brutes into the fires they themselves had created, and get the people to safety. Theirs was not to win the day. Theirs was giving the southerners hesitation.

Just like Keri.

Erroh shifted uneasily. He could feel it in the air. He could also see it in the sky. The sooner the gates fell, the better. If they waited too long, the brutes would charge around the city walls, discover the fleeing ships, and murder the refugees. No, it was better that the city opened up her gates and invited them right in.

He watched the last of the citizens filter into the last section of the city. He knew full well there were stubborn fools who refused to leave, but there was only so much convincing anyone could offer, before they saw little change in stance. Innocent naïve inhabitants were destined to die this day for no better reason than a refusal to let go of inconsequential treasures and trinkets, or misguided beliefs. Those same treasures and beliefs would be insignificant as a blade went through their body. Erroh shrugged to himself.

"You can't save everybody," he muttered as the street in front of him became clear.

"I tried," Mea said. They stood below the ramparts, watching as the exodus continued. "But what is a leader with no council?" Once, there had been voices of authority, but they had fallen quiet and disappeared. Even Sigi, the richest man in the city, was missing. They had probably smuggled him out within an hour of the first attack, Mea thought bitterly. Dane had also disappeared, though his absence was hardly lamented. He had few supporters, despite his rank, and Mea's rise to power had been greeted with approval by the Black Guard. As the rocks continued to fall from the sky, they had obeyed their new master's orders without hesitation. Sometimes all a Wolf needed was an Alpha to lead the pack.

"A Primary," returned Erroh gently. His hands shook like hers did. He was scared, but she could see the fire in his eyes. She knew his will was iron. Like her, he sought only a way to win.

Truthfully, she had thought long and hard before sending Doran with Uden's message. In a fairer world, she had wondered if a showdown between Erroh and Uden might well have ended the invasion at the cost of Uden's head upon a fuken plate. She'd also hoped Doran would return from Raven Rock empty-handed.

Still, the day had improved, now that she had Erroh at her side.

Stay alive today, little cub, and inherit what remains of our army.

He took her arm now and urged her to board a ship. Gripping her sword, she refused.

He offered convincing arguments. He mentioned Tye out

in the wastes, in need of guidance, wanting to come home. He mentioned her new daughters, safely nestled in the lead galleon. Finally, he suggested Jeroen's life would likely depend on her survival, and oh, he tempted her.

But in the end, she shook her head and watched the last few refugees as they boarded the ships. This was her city to inherit, and her obligation to protect its inhabitants ended only the moment the last person stepped aboard. The Hunt was attacking, and she had little intention of allowing her sword to remain unblemished.

She was Alphaline.

She was the Primary Alphaline.

And she was about to stand and fight.

73

SMOKE ON THE WATER

C louds had formed above the city, but they were not made by nature's touch. These were manmade and cruel. They gathered together and formed a great black mass that billowed skywards. Erroh wondered could the gods see them from their serene, spinning thrones in the invisible heavens.

Fuk you, if you can.

He could feel the heat intensifying as the fires began to spiral out of control. Unable to escape the city walls, the flames grew even hotter than the scorched region of Adawan. He could taste smoke on his lips. It was time: the Hunt needed to charge.

Above the rumble of fire, there came a deep thumping noise. Erroh recognised it at once: buoyed on by the fire, they assaulted the wooden gate with a battering ram.

For hours they struck rhythmically. Never fast and never too slow. Until, at last, there came the splintering crack of reinforced wood and the wail of bending steel. With a cry like a thousand wounded beasts, the city's gates shattered and fell and the Hunt flooded in like water through a ruptured dam.

———

In those last moments before the city fell, Doran found the girl's battered body in their usual place. He hadn't expected she would still make their rendezvous once the first volley had struck the city, but she'd tried.

I have let her down.

There was blood where the boulder had struck her. It had smashed through the roof, careened along the top floor of the building and finally come to rest near the front door. The inn would never again host a fine night of delirious singing or boisterous revelries.

He'd not seen her at first, buried as she was amidst the debris. He'd moved on from their tavern, searching frantically throughout the rest of the burning city for the pretty little thing who occupied his thoughts almost constantly. But some instinct had bade him return to the tavern a second time, and after a closer look, he had found her.

Allowing himself a few precious moments so he might not spend a lifetime regretting his decision, he climbed back into the Pig in the Hole. It was a different world within. The smoke thinner. The heat lessened. The crashing roar of the end of times ever so hushed. Scrambling through the wreckage, he came upon an unnatural gap in the floor with a ladder. He recognised a smuggler's rest when he saw one. Looking down, he spotted a dozen sacks of dark brown cofe beans. Countless crates of refined rock salt and at the bottom of the ladder, the real treasure of Celeste. She was ruined, and he wailed aloud, an animal cry of shock and grief and rage. Her arm was bent unnaturally; twisted and trapped in a rung from when she'd fallen. He knew she was dead, and his heart dropped. He climbed down to her. Pulling her awkwardly with his deformed hand, straightening her arm, giving her at least a scrap of dignity in death. Blood covered her face.

She wasn't even cold yet.

He dared a kiss across her lips. Just one, to accompany her into the darkness. After which he would climb from this terrible storage place, walk through the ruin of Spark City and join the last of the defenders at the fortified harbour. If they'd already left without him, well, it was a small matter. He would survive. Even alone and faced with impossible odds, he was certain he would come out alive.

He kissed the dead girl. And then the dead girl coughed.

———

Erroh watched in disbelief as Doran emerged from the wall of orange smoke, carrying a body on his back. He carried nothing else: no armour, no weapon, only the girl. Even through the thick smoke, Erroh could see the gleam of sweat on his bald crown. Doran heaved like a struggling athlete as he charged through the hastily-erected blockades, then turned his gaze skyward as the first volley of arrows flew out at his pursuers.

His arrival was welcome, and it heralded the death of the city.

Doran, through stubbornness alone, did not slow his pace. He heard terrible screams in the dark smoke behind him, but all he paid attention to was the precious weight across his shoulders. Doran understood love. He understood infatuation as well, for he'd desired another for quite a time. What he had with Celeste was something else entirely. He did not dislike Celeste, but he wasn't certain he loved her, either. He was certain she was no suitable mate, but that had never stopped him from enjoying her delightful body frequently these past few months. Beggars choosing, and all that.

She was tender and loving and beautiful, and he, well, he was generous in his actions, warm in his touch. He had only learned of her affliction a week before. Hardly time enough to become used to the idea. Still, he followed the city's wishes, did he not? Mate and make children; strengthen our numbers for the future. Aymon would laugh fiercely when he learned of his endeavours.

She is worth this effort.

———

As the last barges behind were loaded, the line of defenders stood awaiting the enemy, ready to stave off attacks as the innocents escaped. The motley collection of vessels also carried what supplies the people had been able to scavenge, and what little cavalry remained. A dozen magnificent mounts had been loaded as carefully as possible into one of the holds, though not carefully enough, as it turned out. The strongest of them kicked and reared as she was loaded, broke free of her pen, and galloped back down the gangplank, mane flying. Her name was Highwind, and she'd never taken well to any master below her station.

The thunder grew, and Erroh climbed to the top of the rapidly-created barricade blocking the narrow street in front of him. It was just one of twenty such blockades, sturdily constructed of barrels, wooden furniture and heavy carts. If it was big and heavy, the people had thrown it upon the barricade. This one was high enough that Erroh found it a struggle to climb. They had done well with their limited time and materials, he thought.

A shame they had not enough time to coat the streets with oil or to seed the ground with spikes, though.

He looked around at his companions atop the barricade and counted twenty in all. This was no small group of twenty with a few tricks of war, holding indefinitely against overwhelming odds, however. This was far worse. Together, they would face the attackers atop these barricades, which were twice the size of the wall that had held at Keri. Together, they would hold until the line was broken. And when it broke, they would flee together like rats from a ship, towards another ship. He pledged to stand with Mea until the end. He pledged he would see her safely onto the last barge, or carry her himself, far from the waves of southern animals.

It was a good pledge. He didn't mean to break it.

There was a second volley. Erroh heard the screams this time. Behind the charging Alpha carrying his prize came the rumbling groans of thousands of feet trespassing on their land.

"He'll never get her over the barricade," cried Mea from her vantage point along the top of the rubble.

"Help me," Erroh cried. He dropped to the ground and pulled a barrel free of the mound. Then another, and then another.

"You heard him," roared Mea, and the spell was broken, and suddenly they all came to help, answering his request and accepting his authority. At least for this. They tore and dragged, and within a few smoky breaths, the intimidating barricade began to shudder and sway.

———

Highwind reared as her foreign handler reached for her reins, whinnying in alarm and disdain and no small amount of terror. She could smell the fire in the air and she could hear the rumble of a charge. She'd seen enough in her few seasons to know bad things were afoot. The handler reached for her saddle, for anything to take hold of, and somehow the path opened up in front of her. She had no master, for there were foreign beasts all around her and none carried the familiarity of Master, whom she hated so much. Master, who was still the only rider strong enough to steer her forward. She thought she smelled him for a moment, but then fear took hold. The path was clear, and she charged. Better to feel the land beneath her hooves than to sway uneasily upon water. She cried loudly and broke through the fresh gap in the crowded square of the harbour. She never heard her master's call.

"Ah, no, that's my horse," shouted Erroh, seeing Highwind rear and break away from the handler. He was too far away for anyone to hear.

Oh, Highwind, please, not now.

Beside him, a dozen soldiers rolled a cart free and, with it, half the supports of the wall. Barrels and debris, beds and wardrobes, chests and chairs all crashed down, leaving a fine hole in the middle of the battlements. Doran saw the crumbling defences and with the last of his energy, carried the diminutive female the last few steps to his sanctuary—at which point he was almost crushed by the massive frame of a wild warhorse as it charged frantically back the way he'd just come.

Erroh watched the beast thunder free and his heart felt heavy. He'd hated the animal, and the animal had little time for him, but on one horrific night, she had carried him when he needed it. When Lea had needed it even more. He felt a pang of sorrow shoot through his heart as he watched the beautiful beast charge one last, glorious time into the smoke and fire, towards the approaching horde.

He allowed himself only a moment to lament the horse's passing before pulling himself from his daze and reaching out a hand to Doran and his injured companion. "Take the girl, get her aboard a vessel," Doran wheezed, as hands took his heavy burden from him.

"I lost my horse. I might use you from now on," Erroh said, bravely attempting levity, as Doran slipped through the gap and immediately fell to his knees, catching his breath.

"You and I shall have fine words after this war," Doran countered, gasping, and took Erroh's hand as he pulled him to his feet.

74

THE END OF IT ALL

The Hunt came on without regard for themselves. The city archers above moved as one uneasy unit to counter their charge. They crouched and fired upon the first to emerge from the heavy cloud of smoke. They were easier targets at the beginning: stumbling, coughing, gasping for air, summoning the will for the next charge over the next blockade. It should have been a slaughter; for the southerners were many and the Wolves had plenty of arrows. For the first wave, they were unmerciful. They fired ceaselessly down upon the thundering masses and killed many.

But thousands continued surging through the narrow gates at the mouth of Samara. They pushed those few who'd hesitated a little farther in, and soon the mass of bodies drove forward as though rioting at an ill-fated savage tournament. Through smoke, fire and rubble they rushed, and the archers above began to lose their nerve. It began as a few panicked cries and gathered momentum as the southerners drew nearer.

"There are too many."

"No number of arrows can hold these bastards."

"We are all going to die."

"The ships are leaving."

"They're leaving us behind."

"Fuk this—they aren't leaving *me* behind."

Those furthest from the wave of attackers fled first, and their cowardice was infectious, as was usual in battle.

Far above them, Erroh watched warrior after warrior abandon their post and flee back towards the harbour. Oh, to have Lea standing with them now, holding their fear and driving them to be elite. But he had left her behind.

Like a receding black tide, they fled along the high wall until they reached the harbour, then fanned out and searched for willing vessels to take them aboard. The captains of the vessels were glad to have them; a band of archers was a fine deterrent against maritime muggings.

"Fuken Wolves," growled Doran, standing to the right of Mea and Erroh. He shook his head, and Erroh wondered if he weren't considering renouncing his pledge to them that very moment. "I… they… Ugh."

"I agree," Mea hissed, looking across the barricades.

The clouds formed deathly black over Spark City as she died this vile sunny day. The city was eternal, but in the end, it was nothing more than stone, steel, clay and wood. Many of its inhabitants would live on, and they would need someone to place their hopes and faith in. Losing Mea in battle today would be catastrophic to the war effort. However, if the Primary were to stand in battle and survive to rally the cause? That would be something to build on. Such things were the stuff of legend.

From a brother, Doran received fresh armour and a new sword. Erroh helped him strap them on. As he did, he whispered his concerns for Mea, and Doran agreed with a subtle nod.

Suddenly, there came the thundering of heavy boots through the bitter smoke as the Hunt charged towards the last stronghold of Spark City.

"We're going to regret that," said Erroh, staring at the undefended ramparts far above them. Someone needed to clamber up and bar the way.

"Let us deal with this matter first," Doran said as the first line of attackers reached the barricade. Unlike Keri, this would be no simple testing of the city's defensive strength. The attackers clearly intended to charge, cutting and striking, until they scaled the unsteady wall and came down behind it. When that happened, it was all over. All done. All dead.

This is all my fault.

Seeing the city like this cut deeply into Erroh's soul. Oh, to have another moment to redeem himself. To meet Uden and end his life and pull victory from the fire, so to speak.

Uden is out in the smoke, somewhere.

Coughing in the smoke, searching for the little cub who took his eye a lifetime ago.

And what if he was? Erroh thought suddenly. What if Uden really wanted a second strike at the false god, Erroh? Was he that mad?

A thought occurred to Erroh.

A simple thought.

It was more of a plan.

It wasn't much of a plan.

It couldn't work.

Or could it?

. . .

This was her city, and it was Mea who swung first. Her sword came down swiftly, and she gave a yell of triumph as she took the life of the first climber, an armoured killer who had foolishly gripped the side of the barricade with both hands instead of his shield. Pulling the tip of her sword effortlessly from his carcass, she swung again and sent another of the Hunt to a grisly death. She gave no speech; she led with her actions, and the rest of the Wolves followed her magnificently. And where magnificence was scarce, there was nerve. No promises of riches or suggestions of survival fuelled the city defenders. They stood with the Primary, for above all else, she was their mother now.

The heavy rumble of marching was soon replaced by the screams of the dying and the clash and squeal of metal. The fire roared around them as the Hunt fought through the flames in the last battle their god had prophesied. They were scorched and scarred, but they were relentless. The end of the world was near. It was beautiful. Those who fell today were simply the heralds of his name. Their souls had a special place waiting for them beyond the dark. This life was pain. The fires would burn. But in the end, it would be good.

He said it would be good.

A strange, familiar smell reached Erroh's nose, and it made him smile despite the horror. He never left Mea's side. With his back to her flank, he never stopped moving, either. Never stopped striking. Mostly, he never stopped killing. His blades flashed out in front of him and they sang a new tale of his legend. He was fierce, and he was godly, and for moments, he was the deity they whispered of in the frozen south. He was the Hero of Keri, and he was the champion of the Sweeping Grasslands. He wanted to scream like so many others in battle, but he held his anger in. It would serve him later, when exhaustion took hold and he had nothing else to call upon. He took a deep breath and savoured the aroma of their burning flesh and met the next attacker.

Unlike Erroh, Doran was fuelled by his hate-filled war cries and explosive rage. He appeared larger than life, and each time his sword sliced down through flesh, he roared magnificently. "I need only one strike!" His eyes burned with a fever of bloodlust, as though he were discovering the art of battle for the first time, and Erroh relished the spectacle of his companion at war. He was an intimidating force, and he served the cause. The warring zealots charged his position fiercely and died for their efforts. Within the first hour, Erroh wondered if Doran hadn't matched his own tally, such was his brutality. Things like that shouldn't matter in battle. But they did.

The Hunt climbed the wall more easily than they had scaled those of Keri, but they met far sturdier defences once they reached the top. Each Wolf had positioned himself to meet the attacks as they came. When a Wolf fell, or was weakened by the fatigue of battle, his brother quickly took his place along the top before the attackers could take hold. In the heat of battle, they held their ground. Like weasels, when backed into a corner they bared their teeth, showed some fight. Hundreds stood bravely in the last hours of Samara, and they did almost enough to wash away the shame they carried upon their blood-stained paws. Almost, but not quite.

The struggles continued; the fires raged throughout the city, devouring whatever they could feed upon. Many streets held no more fuel than the cold, grey stone, and the flames only scorched these to a dull black. Other structures, such as the market stalls and the more opulent houses, took light and burned with an intense, blinding heat, weakening the walls of the city like time never could.

Despite the burning, the Hunt never stopped charging forward. Undaunted, the few hundred defenders holding the last free ground in the city met their charge with inspired violence. The streets ran with streams of deep crimson, and bodies lay broken where they fell.

They were fierce, they were brave, and they were too few.

Eventually the line folded in on itself. There were subtle signs as more attackers scaled the different sections and found a way down onto the sturdy ground between the harbour and the barricades. Every time they did, they soon fell to the sword of the nearest warriors, but it was a warning that the tide was turning. No defenders, no matter how skilled, could hold such numbers indefinitely. A day would have been enough. They made do with hours.

———

When Mea saw the signs, she allowed herself an exhausted moan and then, with a heavy heart, she gave the word.

"Fall back to the edge," she cried. She herself was the last to retreat. Blood from the dead saturated her. Her dress clung tightly to her body. It had a sickly warmth. The clouds of smoke stung her eyes and tears streamed down her cheeks, ruining the dark paint she'd applied. It was foolish, but she'd wanted to look her best at the end.

The many lines of Wolves tucked in with shields and swords at the ready. They knew how to retreat just fine. They fell away from the barricade, and immediately the attackers swarmed over the top. Some hesitated, searching for signs of a trap or the appearance of oil, and then on they came.

"We must hold them off," Mea cried, but she knew it was

a desperate roll of the dice now, a terrible game of chance to see who would live. Some of her warriors would die today to give the others a chance at escaping to the waiting boats. She herself intended to stay until the end. "Hold the line, my warriors," she screamed, raising her sword, offering them everything she had in their last moments. Offering them a redemption to comfort them as they stepped into the darkness.

And then Doran grabbed her and hoisted her upon powerful shoulders and carried her away from the melee. He charged through the groups of fighters and they parted, even as she roared and cursed and demanded she be returned. He disobeyed her. All of them did. They allowed Doran and his shrieking cargo through the lines, closing up behind him tightly again should she break free and attempt to return. Doran kept charging and then broke out onto the flat of the docks and thundered straight up the nearest barge gangway.

Without looking back, he roared at the captain to cast off. He flung Mea down at the bow of the boat and placed a heavy shield over her, and then, with both powerful arms, kept her pinned to the deck.

"Now," he shouted at the captain, but the captain, knowing her value, was already cutting loose the holding line. Mea struggled under his heavy frame, but she could not shift him free. "I'm sorry, Mydame," he growled, and held her struggles again.

"Erroh," she screamed suddenly. "Where is Erroh?" Her mind was reeling with rage and regret and sadness. She had left her warriors behind. But nothing hurt more than leaving Erroh behind.

She couldn't have known how far behind he had been left.

Doran knew, however. As the barge steered between the many larger vessels, he saw the last brave act of his Master

General in this terrible battle, and he felt honoured to have stood with him before his death.

He watched Erroh charge forward, and then he was gone from sight, lost in a sea of death. Doran's eyes fell to the last twenty warriors standing at the harbour, slashing out at their vanquishers, blocking with their shields, hoping to steal a few extra breaths of smoky air before cold, swinging steel robbed them of their life.

"Where is he?" Mea screamed, and he held her in place. The barge rocked as it pulled away. The first bolt from a southern fiend, still unable to step into the city, embedded itself in the deck at his feet. He waited for the next volley, and he waited for the captain to steer them clear of danger.

"Where is my cub?" she cried, and then she wept, for she knew now, as he did.

"He has stepped into the darkness, Mydame," Doran whispered.

75

I WILL SHIELD YOU

His name was Erroh, line of Magnus, and he liked to make plans. Lots of plans. Some of them simple, some of them complicated. Most of them never worked. Some were cleverly constructed through deep imaginings, while others began as foolish thoughts and were given flight by youthful naivety. This plan began exactly like that. Like many before, it didn't work.

This did not surprise Erroh. Even as the city burned around him.

He watched the brutes charge along the ledge, and he heard Mea give the last order of Samara. He knew he would never board a barge. He wasn't built that way. He was built for different things, and that really fuken high ledge above was built especially for him. He believed it to be fate. Believed himself to be pushed onwards by the absent gods.

He was right.

The long line of defending Wolves retreated slowly, countering the straggling groups of killers rushing through the harbour. Behind them, their comrades boarded the river vessels, and Erroh thought it a magnificent sight.

The long line shrank now to a few dozen shield-battering Black Guards, holding the brutes at bay along the thin harbour walkway. It was a slow, agonising impasse—until one lone Wolf broke the line and charged forward into the invaders, hoping to catch them unawares. He struck down two southerners before meeting a bloody end, impaled on two long spears. His sacrifice was not in vain. Buoyed on by this reckless bravery, those who'd accepted their last breaths followed behind. The armada of galleons, barges and yachts pulled away from the burning city, while a last charge by a shamed army covered their retreat and beat the southerners back a few steps. The songs were already being scribed for generations to come in the minds of those who had survived to watch their magnificent acts.

Erroh was among this charge for a breath before leaving them to their deaths far below. It wasn't cowardice; it was something else entirely. In his hands was a stolen war horn, gifted to him from the body of a dead Wolf, and swiftly, he strapped it around his back. The dead Wolf wouldn't mind. He was ending the war.

No problem.

As he took the first step, he realised he'd never said goodbye to Mea. It stung him all over again, just like it had these last few days. Perhaps it was a better thing. Had she known his plans, she might have tried to stop him. Or worse, followed him and met the same doom as he would. Following the same route through the last defenders, Erroh found himself beneath the steps leading to the sky.

It was a terrifying and fitting place to end this last chapter of his life. Poetic, really, if one thought about it. He gathered his breath at the first little stone step and held both swords out in front of him. Taking a moment to offer a cautious and untrusting prayer to the absent gods, the Master General began his ascent into the air.

Don't look down.

Taking the steps two at a time, he charged upwards, readying himself for battle atop the great dying wall. He swallowed his fears and shook away the cloying grip of sadness at the events that had led him to this. He would not survive this last battle. He knew this, and that was alright.

Don't fall.

As he charged up through the smoke, away from the thunder of clashing steel, battle cries and the dying, Erroh tried to focus himself. Keeping his head down and his eyes on the steps, he made good time, despite the effort each step took. As the world fell apart, few noticed the solitary figure upon the wall, and that was alright too. He'd always meant to climb this monstrous height at least once. It had just never happened. At least he'd have a pleasant view before he died.

About halfway up, he tripped. It was a fine trip, worthy of some deep purple bruises come the following day—

Idiot.

Climbing to his feet, he felt the exhaustion. Inhaling, he enjoyed the cool crispness after breathing smoke for so long. With his back to the wall, he viewed the city. Through the haze of flame and black, he watched her burn.

And then he realised how far up he was and how a careless step had almost sent him tumbling to gruesome doom below. His vision spun, and he felt himself waver as though the ground were unsteady. As though he were upon a barge.

It was the brutes above who stirred him. In his manic charge, he hadn't seen them march along the wall's edge. He hadn't seen them begin their descent towards him.

I don't want to fight them here.

Summoning all his will, he stepped to one side and blew

the horn loudly. A great, hollow song of war. It reverberated across the battlefield below, deep and penetrating. A warning. A declaration. A beacon. One long and mournful cry to announce himself to the southerners.

He closed his eyes and counted to ten. He still heard them above, rushing towards him, screaming in their language. They were cursing.

He took calming breaths and remembered a little dead town, close to here. He focused on an innocent child, terrified and brave. He thought about his pledge, and then he let his mind wander to those he'd lost. He thought of Quig and Aireys. He felt them near. Perhaps they were. Perhaps they were divine spirits, watching his every move patiently with goblets in their ethereal hands, taking bets, waiting to greet him when this day drew to its end.

Are you there, friends?

He thought about his mother, and pain overcame sadness. He held the pain and allowed it to grow into hate. He opened his eyes as they came to him. A half dozen, one at a time, in single file along the treacherous path. It was almost too easy.

He ignored the great height and the dizzying effect it had on his vision. He focused on the first southerner and met his attack efficiently. The brute struck at him with a heavy axe, and Erroh ducked away from the manoeuvre and slid his blade casually across the man's throat. He fell to his knees and halted the progress of the next. Using the delay to gain a better foothold, Erroh thrust Vengeance through the next man's stomach. The man fell from the steps, holding his gut with both hands as he did, as though stemming the flow of blood was his greatest concern.

Erroh stepped over his first victim and viciously attacked each soldier above him. He was elite. He was calm. Even terrified upon such a dizzying height, he embraced war. His blades cut with every strike; his body was a fluid machine of destruction, and they fell under his attacks.

When the last one lay dead, Erroh steadied himself.

Didn't even need Emir's poison to make sure.

He took a moment to lament his haste leaving Raven Rock without a vial to lace his blades with.

Fuk it, I'll kill him without it.

No problem.

Above him, no more attackers climbed the ledge, and once again he found himself alone on the steps. He took out the horn, and after wiping some smeared blood from the mouthpiece, began blowing once more. The call echoed around the burning city. How could anyone not see this fool atop the wall, calling for attention? He looked back up to the ledge, only fifty steps above, and then behind him. He'd come far. He left his wake of devastation for all to witness. He counted the dead. A fine number. He was slowly gaining on her tally.

"I'm sorry, Lea," he whispered. It was all he had. He hoped the gods carried his words in the wind and found her well. He studied the remaining Wolves as they fought, while the armada slipped away from the city's shadow and surged down river. They were leaving him behind.

Alone.

He blew the horn again. It had come to this. It would always come to this. He walked up the last few steps almost leisurely.

When he reached the top of the city wall, he chanced another glance over the side and again fought the urge to faint. Lea would have loved this view. He looked out through the smoke and saw the surging army thinning out as their numbers spread through the last few streets not yet burning.

Is this a fool's task?

He blew the horn once more, and he blew it with everything he had left in his exhausted, smoke-laden lungs.

"Uden," he roared, holding both blades skywards.

Far below, the city burned and the river vessels sailed away. Strangely, the Hunt didn't seem interested in pursuing them. A few battalions exchanged volleys of arrows and bolts with each other, but no pack of Riders charged along the massive river's edge, waiting for a moment to strike. Their prize was the city, apparently.

He could hear the faint clinking of the Wolves' weapons; they were still gathered together, holding the territory for as long as they could. It was a fine start to rebuilding their honour.

Where are you?

It's not working.

You have failed.

He blew the horn.

"Uden!" He raised the swords in the air again and he waited for the entire southern nation to climb the steps and strike him down. Up here, with the wind in his ears, he found it almost peaceful. He could imagine Lea gracefully skipping from side to side, staring out towards the endless worlds beyond the horizons. He wondered, had she ever scaled these heights while growing up in the city? He knew it was likely, and he missed her terribly.

I'm so sorry, my love. I wish you were here now, at the end.

When I failed.

He dared to stare out into the distance now, as she would have. He gained courage and looked around him. It was no bare place up here. At each corner, built into the wall, was a little guard house. Sturdy and eternal, like the city itself, but empty now, abandoned to the war. He wondered what life had been like for those who had lived and worked up here, and decided it would have been wretched. Especially when they had failed so spectacularly at holding the walls against a siege. He looked around some more and now saw that rope bridges had been strung from the corners, going up and down a few levels. He thought them precarious looking, but understood that they had been built to allow proper distance between marching Wolves upon their watch. They swung gently in the wind and he shuddered again.

Long drop from one of those.

Moving carefully along the walkway, he continued to take in the miniscule world below. He was almost tempted to walk further down towards the mouth of Spark and watch her last moments from this fine vantage point. But he resisted the urge. A few hundred metres beyond, he saw the effects of a stray boulder along the wall's top. The projectile had smashed out a great fragment of stone from the walking path. A fool might attempt to leap across it, but would most likely meet a long drop down the deep crevice and a grisly death on the rocks below. Thanks to this, there was only one set of steps leading to this plateau.

Probably explains why so few come seeking me out.
So far.

Perhaps planting himself at the top of these steps might allow him to single-handedly kill every invader as they surged up to meet him, he thought. He'd knocked bolts out of the air before, so a loose crossbow strike would be no problem. He almost laughed at the absurdity of this plan. There was a limit to his foolishness.

Send him to me.

He blew the horn one last time and wondered what to do should he find himself the last defender in a fallen city.

I will not wear southern chains again.

But it would not come to that. Something had changed in the wind. It began like a wave moving through the burning city below. He squinted, watching. It was almost imperceptible at first, but after a time it became apparent something monumental was happening below. Something unexplainable.

He watched as attackers, mid-step, fell to their knees. He saw their brothers halt, open-mouthed, in the middle of attempting to douse the roaring flames. In a matter of moments, the roar of war dwindled to a gentle murmur.

Erroh stood motionless, unable to look away. What could have caused an entire battalion to fall still upon the field of battle? Their reverence was almost godly.

He couldn't see who they bowed to, but his heart quickened as the wave spread outward and, one after the other, the roving brutes slowed and stopped. The strange wave reached the edges of the battleground and flowed out to the harbour, where the few remaining Wolves, still thrashing madly with the last of their spirit, suddenly met less aggression—and then no aggression at all. Their attackers drew away from the melee and fell to their knees. Theirs was a different act of submission, though. Those on the front line held their swords at the ready. Their faces did not turn towards the ground. They watched their enemy, but did not offer another strike.

Flee, you fools, Erroh thought. It was a very loud thought, and for a moment he imagined that the Wolves must have heard him. No boats remained, but behind them was the gift of cool, open water. Some stripped their armour and leapt from the dock's edge, while others, without the ability to swim, took what small rowboats they could find. It was a fine, unlikely retreat, and Erroh bowed, smiling slightly.

You are welcome.

. . .

He saw the god through simple good fortune, through a break
in the smoke and a great parting of southern bodies. He saw a
monstrous southerner dressed in heavy steel and flowing
cloak march slowly through the streets, flanked by a battalion
of impressive-looking thugs. Even from here, he was
impressive, and Erroh suddenly felt small and timid in
comparison.

Uden moved ever so slowly, as though smoke and fire
were not to be feared. Perhaps they weren't. He moved as
though crushing the city had been nothing impressive.
Perhaps it wasn't. Erroh recognised the slow, lazy movement
of an indomitable force, and he felt the fear return. Fuk him.
He had asked for this tempest to turn his way. He had brought
this fiend down upon him. He had prayed for this opportunity,
and the god had answered.

All hail, Uden, the Woodin Man.

The crowd watched their deity take the first step. Uden
made a casual gesture of his fingers, and the nearest warrior
rose. Then, like a second wave, the rest of the warriors rose
with him. Uden began to move, but they did not follow.
Standing still as death, they left their god to march, and Erroh
stepped along the edge to meet him at the top of the steps.

Uden took his time. If he spoke to any of his zealots,
delivered praise upon them for an invasion well done, Erroh
heard nothing. It didn't matter. All that mattered was
vengeance. And the rising fear he felt in this moment. He
could no longer feel the presence of his fallen friends beside
him, and it was a terrible thing.

Oh fuk, oh fuk, oh fuk.

He felt his heart hammer wildly enough that it
threatened to beat free of his chest. The god began his

climb, and Erroh felt his body quake all over. So alone in a city of enemies. His swords shook. The god's slow march was taking too long. It was a fine, masterful act of intimidation, and Erroh worried his own terror would rob him of his chance.

In his memory, Uden had always appeared a near giant, and many a night Erroh had wondered if exhaustion, fear and sickness had caused him to exaggerate the god's magnificence. He really hadn't.

Unlike Erroh, Uden did not trip halfway up, and Erroh took an involuntary step away from the edge. He knew it was respectful to allow the god a moment to catch his breath atop the great height, but in truth, he stepped back out of fear, and Erroh knew he was to fall to this man. He was right.

When Erroh could no longer hold the fear, he allowed it to take him. Allowed it to slash at every insecurity, reaffirm his own doubts and tear apart his hopes. He allowed himself to tremble and despair, to shatter and surrender. For a few breaths.

Then he let it go, like an arrow released into the clear blue sky.

It's easy. Just die well.

Worry gains you nothing.

Fuk it. Why not?

"Uden!" he roared, so all would hear. The god certainly did, although he hesitated to gaze up. Perhaps hearing Erroh's voice brought forth his own dread. Perhaps it reminded him of the devastating blow he had suffered on that night long ago. It was a small matter. Erroh had something important to say to Uden. To the city, too.

"I… see… you." He pointed to his eyes. His still very intact eyes. "I see you," he cried again, and held the gesture as if it were a weapon. He laughed, for in madness he felt no fear and it was welcome. It wasn't the finest insult he'd ever uttered, but it was a suitable attack in the moment.

Fuk him if he doesn't laugh.

Uden did not laugh. He tore his helm from his head in fury and then, tilting his head to one side, he gazed up. He stared through Erroh's soul with a burning hatred as hot as the blazing streets below.

Erroh stared right back. Laughing. He backed away from the steps towards the harbour end of the city, all the while continuing to laugh maniacally. If nothing else, he would keep his sense of humour. It was ridiculous, and it was glorious, and he felt a sudden peace come upon him. Perhaps it was his mother's ethereal presence that calmed him so. Or maybe being confronted at last with the thing of his many nightmares was bringing closure to his traumas. Who could say? As the god advanced upon him slowly, Erroh knew things could be no worse than they were at this moment. So he became the warrior of Keri. And Uden became his vanquisher.

"I have waited a time for you, Erroh," the god said.

Erroh shrugged as though it was no matter. As though this was no defining moment in the annals of Spark City. He held the tips of his swords out in front, and Uden displayed his own duel swords. Far below, the world watched. They had lost all interest in the departing boats upon seeing the two gods standing atop the great city wall, preparing for the ultimate battle, and this suited Erroh just fine. If nothing else, his allies could use his martyrdom as a means of enticing enlistment.

"I stopped the world so that we might meet," Uden growled. His bald head was covered in perspiration. A few drops rolled down his flawless, lightly-tanned face. His one green eye blazed with excitement. This was the silence before the tempest.

Erroh moved a few paces away from the brute, down towards the city corner and the unappealing rope bridges. He'd have preferred to meet him on flatter, less smoky ground, with a fine view of the Great Mother. It was the small things. They'd waited this long to kill each other; they could wait a few steps more.

"Yet it was I who called upon you to fight, coward," Erroh hissed. His voice broke, and he was dismayed. Would the god believe it was simply the smoke affecting his words?

This time Uden laughed, and it was terrible. Deep, slow reverberations, almost godly, and Erroh recoiled, but he kept his hands firm and his guard set. "And now they watch from below as a god puts a vile brute of blasphemy to the sword."

Erroh was readying a wonderful comeback that involved twisting Uden's words back on themselves, implying that Uden was the brute and he the god. Unfortunately, without warning, Uden leapt towards him and the sudden strike almost bowled Erroh over.

Swiftly, Erroh regained his balance and stepped back into position. He allowed his mind to clear and met Uden's laboured follow-up strike with a careful block before spinning away from a lunge—and, in doing so, almost spun right off the city wall.

"Whoops," he gasped, leaping from the next strike, an ungainly, heavy thrust from both of Uden's blades. A left then a right. So close. Far below, he heard a cry. Someone appreciated the manoeuvre.

Erroh appreciated the manoeuvre, too. It was unrefined, without control. He took another few steps back, and the god slowed his charge.

"Whoa—I nearly fell off there," Erroh said, feigning dismay. He smiled and played the part well. "Did you see that?"

"I have spilled so much blood to get to here," the god roared magnificently, and Erroh could see the weight this meeting carried for Uden. At least as much as it did for him. Still, if he allowed himself to dwell on this, he might lose his fuken mind, as Uden apparently had.

Erroh stepped in to strike, and Uden leapt away. He grimaced with strain as he swung wildly, and a strange thought occurred to Erroh: Surely this great god wasn't foolish enough to allow himself to face an opponent unprepared? Surely, he'd practiced just a little bit with that one eye of his?

As if reading Erroh's mind, Uden roared and leapt in. Erroh avoided him, and he missed wildly.

Easy.

Uden charged again, and this time Erroh, staying clear of the blades, drew a dent across the god's chest plate before leaping away.

Erroh caught his breath and considered his next move. With no depth perception, the one-eyed god was at a disadvantage. Calming his wildly beating heart, Erroh changed his stance and decided to kill Uden and end the fuken war.

Uden was no fool, and neither was Gemmil. For years they had mastered the art of deceit. In life, in politics, in war.

A lesser warrior with an ailment like Uden's might have needed years to master their skill with a weapon. It had taken Uden only a few months to regroup. A few months delaying his grand march. A worthy sacrifice. All the while learning to use his one remaining eye in battle. Watching. Spotting the shadows. Covering the distances. Mastering the timing. Turning a devastating loss into a fine act of deceit.

Knocking fruit out of the air.

As Uden allowed Erroh to misread his technique, he bit back a smile. He could smile openly in a few breaths from now. When the deed was done.

"You really have slowed," Erroh mocked, and he imagined the southerners below, holding onto every flicker of movement.

Did they know their god was already beaten?

Did they know the war was ending?

He could beat this man, and he could beat him well. To stand in close quarters was to invite death, but to keep the fight at a distance while moving was the way to certain victory. Uden dropped his shoulders, seeming to anticipate his defeat.

"I will repay you for your generosity, Uden," Erroh said, sneering, and Uden stumbled forward as he tripped on some unknown snag upon the stone.

I have this.

Uden charged again, but this time his blades swung true. They broke Erroh's defence and almost decapitated him where he stood. Only godly reflexes saved his skin. He retreated, examining the gashes on either shoulder with undisguised alarm.

"What the fuk?"

Misled.

He suddenly saw it now. As Erroh played the jester, Uden played the cripple. Neither was who he claimed to be, and suddenly it became terribly clear to Erroh who would win this day.

Today I die.

I failed again.

Uden charged once more, and Erroh staggered beneath the assault. Blades struck out at him from every angle, and it was fiercer than the first night they'd met; he'd never seen technique like this.

He tried, oh, but he tried to escape the one-eyed god's deadly strikes, but his body tired under the relentless assault. He ducked, received a heavy strike across his back, and spun away, crying out in pain. The blade didn't break his armour, but the force was enough to knock the wind from his already exhausted lungs. He rolled away from the next attack, and his body struck something unusual.

It was a heavy peg, embedded in the rock of the city walls. Wrapped around this peg were supports to the nearest rope bridge.

Run away.

Suddenly, Uden hammered down with both swords and Erroh scrambled away, out onto the first wooden step. He heard the creak, and the world suddenly became unsteady underfoot.

Worse than a barge.

The rope bridge swung in a deep, wide arc, and Erroh watched helplessly as the ground far below swung dizzily from side to side.

Lea probably loved this.

Such a mechanism was against the laws of natural things. Erroh scrambled along the wooden rungs, away from the next strike. Carelessness had almost cost him the victory, and his life. Behind him, he expected to feel Uden strike him down, but nothing came.

There were screams and chants, and Erroh finally pulled his gaze from the ground far below. There weren't many things to prevent his death were he to fall from this height. Nothing but another bridge and a few tarps clinging to the taller buildings. Even then, it would be death to actually leap.

Or would it?

Uden stood at the edge, resting his feet on one of the rope bridge's supports. "You plan to fly away before we finish?" He gave a mirthless laugh, and then casually swayed the bridge from side to side. Relief and serenity now replaced his look of hate, and Erroh realised that as he'd climbed along the bridge, the god had gone to task and cut two of the supports partway through. Not enough to snap them; just enough to begin Erroh's great downfall. The primary ropes were tight, however, and Erroh considered turning and sprinting for the far side. It was a futile notion. His weight would sever the ropes in full before he took a step. Uden had trapped him even in retreat.

"Is this how the great god Uden kills me?" Erroh spat in disgust. It had been a fight he could have won. *Might have won.*

They were all watching him now. With bated breaths, they saw the stories of gods come to life in front of their eyes. Erroh sheathed his blades and held his hands up. He beckoned to the god.

"Come finish me, you half-blind animal," he mocked. "Come spill my godly blood."

We'll fall to our doom together.

But Uden didn't feel like finishing him out on the bridge. So, he did what any near-victorious deity would do when facing a fellow god, blessed with the skills of fire and flight.

He cut the rope.

Oh, fuk.

The bridge rocked violently to the left. It veered out over the harbour. A curious sound of rushing wind filled his ears, and his hair whipped against his face. Even a fall to the water far below was likely to kill him, and Erroh fought the pull of the ground. Momentum dragged the bridge back the other way, and Erroh took hold of another rope just as the southern god cut the last thread.

Falling.

Again.

Erroh dropped from the great height quicker than a quail hunted by his mate. He swung towards the corner of the wall, his arms flailing at the tangled ropes as they fell around him in the desperate hope they might keep him aloft. Bracing himself for a horrible demise, he struck the bridge underneath with a sickening thud.

It felt as though every bone in his body had shattered. Most of all, his left ankle. His descent did not stop, though; it merely slowed, and he kept falling. He plummeted through the second bridge beneath, his hands still waving wildly as he tried to save himself.

Oh fuk, oh fuk, oh fuk, help me, oh fuk.

The third rope bridge hurt the most, but still his velocity was too great. Breaking through the third and final level, he dropped into the smoky air that hung over the city like a blanket.

He fell from the sight of the god above and his acolytes below, into a secluded corner of Samara where few merchants or citizens had ever bothered to step. He fell without screaming, for in his last act he would show them all how an Alphaline met death. He bounced against a tarp above a long-abandoned house, then broke through that to a floor below. The absent gods offered him one last gift, for he fell more slowly now. He broke almost lazily through a last hanging tarp, and with a ripping sound he dropped heavily through to the cobbled street below.

Pain.

Lots of pain.

Fuk you, Uden.

———

Am I alive? There was smoke all around him. He lay upon the ground and wondered if there was any part of him not broken. He dared himself to move his feet and was met with a curious sensation as they followed his instruction. With more pain than he could measure, he sat up from his bed of stone and looked around. He was in a blind alley that led off one of the streets of a once-bustling city. Above, he could see the trail of ruin he'd left as he plummeted. Rope bridges swung wildly where he'd broken through. The tarp owners might rightly wish to have words with him, were it any day other than this.

You are welcome, whispered the absent gods, and he spat in the dirt.

Fuk your miracles.

He looked around, seeking a way out. It was a tight, claustrophobic alleyway, bare and grey. It was no fitting place to die.

He tried to think. How to escape? Through the burning streets? Attack the army at the harbour? Find another set of steps for a rematch?

Best of three, Uden?

All three thoughts were foolish. He was a spent force. He tried to stand and put weight on his ankle, and despite himself, he screamed loudly before falling back against the wall.

He was done. He had the will, but his body had finally

betrayed him. If he met Uden in battle once more, the god would make short work of him. Shorter than before.

I am a failure.

He tried to pop the ankle back into place, and heard a low cracking, grinding sound, and again he heard his cries fill the air. Still, he tried. If he could walk, he had a chance.

Pop back in, you whore. Please pop back in.

His ankle didn't pop back in. It just hurt more. His cries were drawing attention now. He heard footsteps approaching, and he wailed in misery.

It's not fair.

He saw them at the mouth of the alley now, no doubt searching for the false god's body. No doubt they had come to kill him, and here he was, gelded to nothing.

Just die well today.

He had tried and failed, so now he imagined giving in. Sitting against the wall to wait for the fires or blades to find him. It didn't help. When they charged towards him, he relinquished the luxury of defeat. He stood, took the pain, and drew his swords. The first attacker ran at him. The skirmish ended within a few agonized breaths.

A second appeared, and Erroh met him with equal violence. He wondered if Uden, far above, heard his cries, applauded his stubborn resilience. The thought comforted him. He had been beaten again. He would take what comforts he could.

It was the third attacker who knocked him from his feet. It was a fine attack, and though Erroh struck him as he fell upon him, he could not step away. For a few more breaths, they struggled in each other's grip as his opponent attempted to strangle him, only for Erroh to deliver a lucky, disorienting strike with the pommel of his sword before thrusting the blade through the attacker's chest. They both screamed in horror and misery until one fell silent and Erroh lay among the dead, moaning. It was too much.

I give up.

I have lost.

I am lost.

And then, incredibly, he heard still more steps from beyond the smoke, and he cried out in misery again. He climbed to his knees and readied himself. One more kill. He had at least one more kill in him, and if it were Uden, come to see his broken body, he would make the kill count that little bit more.

"Come on," he cried, and the steps neared. Unsure and anxious–sounding, they were heavier than most others. Erroh wiped tears and sweat from his face and awaited his last kill. "Come on," he roared. "I'm right here."

She heard him above the noise. Exhausted and confused, she heard him, and she followed the sound of his cries. She ached and her skin was scorched, but she followed his primal screams of agony and lamentation. She wondered if he would take her home. If he would guide her and let her carry him.

Highwind, almost invisible in her blackness, walked unnoticed through the smoke and destruction and stepped through the thin gap into the alley at the edge of the burning city. Though everything burned, she smelled Master, and she set herself beside him. She quaked with adrenaline and terror.

"Highwind," Master cried, taking her head as she nuzzled him fearfully. She waited for his orders, for his command to flee from this burning place.

"Are you scared?" he whispered.

She was.

"Do you want to leave?"

She did.

"Will you carry me?"

She would.

He took hold of her saddles and climbed onto her back, carefully setting his feet in the stirrups. He moaned with the effort but wrapped his hands around her reins and whispered once more in her ear.

"Trust in me, my lady, and I will get us away from here," he pledged. If she understood his words, she gave no sign. What she showed was her willingness to run, to face the fires ahead. With everything she had, would carry him until she could carry him no farther.

I will shield you.

They charged from the alleyway into the heat of the fires and the hordes of southerners. The harbour was overrun, so he drove her towards the city gates. The smoke burned his eyes and hers, but neither dared show weakness to the other. He kicked her with both aching feet and screamed at her to match her will to his.

Through one secluded side street, past an open area filled with unsuspecting soldiers, they charged. He felt a few hands try and fail to grasp him as they passed through enemies, through vanquishers, through tide after tide of death. He dared not meet the gaze of any lone soldier or platoon he met; he did not worry that arrows might meet their charge, for all he saw was the burning path ahead.

Through countless archways and ruined landmarks of the civilisation of this world, they charged feverishly. He screamed her name; he pleaded that her charge be swifter. He dared her to fear his wrath, and she listened and she trusted and she carried him.

The farther from the harbour they ran, the harder the going became. Fires and smoke marred the routes, broken and shattered blockades slowed their progress, but as one perfect being, they never halted. They chanced another side street, sped past the abandoned Cull and galloped through another break in the wall. As one, they charged down upon the attackers without daring to raise a sword.

"Faster," he cried, kicking once more. Her powerful limbs churned against the painful, hard ground beneath her hooves. Through another archway, through a shattered marketplace and then, finally, under the gaze of at least a thousand burning, watery eyes, they reached the gates.

They did not stop. Nor could they ever.

Through the last roaring furnace, where sparks took hold and singed his hair, where the bulbs exploded and spat shards of glass, and then at last through the great, destroyed gates into the cool blue of a world not burning beyond them.

Many stood, staring in naked astonishment at this godly being atop his mount.

He tested her, and she accepted the challenge. With all her strength, she carried him, her hooves barely touching the dirt, from smoky ruin to cool, clear air. And the only heat upon their bodies now was the warmth of the sun at their backs. She drove herself forwards like never before. Out through the ruined gates they sprinted, away from the last few attackers. Together, they took flight and charged for cover into the sanctuary of the deep green trees. A few who had not yet stepped into the city saw this blur of movement and offered to give chase, but within a few breaths Highwind carried Erroh clear of them before the first arrow could be loaded.

"Aye, my wonderful beauty," he cried deliriously, patting her magnificent mane. She had answered his call and carried him from danger, as she had pledged she would. And at last, under the cover of the trees, Erroh, line of Magnus, brought his heroic beast to a halt and turned her around to gaze upon the city they'd left behind.

He did not cry out. In silence, he watched the clouds of smoke rise, and he watched the last of the mighty gate crumble and burn. It was the darkest day in living memory. There was nothing left to defend. They were now a migrant race, doomed to travel the wastes until it swallowed them up and their kind were lost forever. Everything would change from this moment on. They were all outcasts.

"We are not done," whispered Erroh, the fire god of Samara. He patted his mount and turned her away from the devastation, before disappearing into the endless green.

EPILOGUE

She lay on her back and gasped for air. Her chest was a volatile fist of pain. Each breath was hard. Yet, she took another, and another after that. It was a strange sensation, as if something deep down where all the tightness lay was slowly breaking apart. She wished she could see, but they had not removed the scarf across her eyes. She lay perfectly still, for despite her alertness, she had little strength.

She coughed lightly, the laboured croak of a dying animal, and spat mucus and blood out of her airway. This was no fine way to die, she thought.

However, if she died, she would not cry out. Her arms ached. A fresh pain, unlike the agony in her heaving, shapely chest. The ropes holding her to this bed dug into her skin and cut her powerful wrists and she hated them.

She hated so many things.

Like dying.

She felt a delicate, feminine hand at her brow, while another wiped the sputum from her face.

"Whisht," a feminine voice whispered. There was almost

warmth in that tone. A familiar, motherly tone she herself had once used when caring for her own little cubs.

The person with the kind voice stroked her cheek and offered a drink.

Cold.

So cold, in fact. How could anything be so cold? It was also syrupy and sweet, but undesirable. She had tasted this foul, sweet liquid before. She had hated it then, and she hated it now. The fluid flowed down her throat and she couldn't fight it.

"Where am I?" she whispered, and felt the stirrings of another coughing fit. She felt it grow, and then felt it subside again. Tentatively, she took a few deep breaths. Deep, painful and wonderful breaths.

"You are safe and sound," the voice replied. She felt the soft hand stroking her cheek once more.

"As long as I take breath, I am always safe and sound," she warned, her voice full of a strength she hadn't felt in years She licked her lips and tasted salt upon them.

"I will make sure you keep taking breaths," the female voice replied. It was reassuring, and she knew the syrup was taking effect. "It helps you sleep. Helps to make pleasant dreams, too."

————

"What is your name?" she asked deliriously. Her breathing was still laboured, but the air seemed to move more easily through her lungs now. It was a novel sensation. Her chest ached, but the weight was lessened. It was hard to hold rational thoughts, but in her last moment of clarity before the syrup took hold, she tried to remember.

She remembered the sleeping. Then the pain. Then days

of burning light. Such a heat as she'd never known, and no air to breathe. She'd lain in torment as they carried her from her quiet bed, away from those she cared for.

And now, in this freezing room, she struggled to keep her thoughts lucid and constant.

There was silence for a time.

"They call me Kaya," the voice whispered.

"That's a lovely name. What does it mean?"

"I don't know what it means," Kaya admitted.

"Sometimes it doesn't matter if you know what it means," Elise whispered, licking the salt from her lips. She was thinking about war and vengeance and love. Her mind was leaving her. She closed her eyes under the scarf and slipped into sleep.

———

She awoke without the reassuring embrace of darkness. Her eyes burned, although the room she lay in was barely lit. She shook her head and blinked rapidly. Her arms were still bound, but it was a small matter. She looked around the empty grey cell. She lay on a small bed in one corner; on a table beside her was a single candle. The only decorations were a few jars filled with strangely-coloured ingredients.

Her mind was sharper, but the constant call of sleep still held her. She shook the blur from her vision and let her eyes focus upon the dark-skinned female sitting by the bedside, mixing a concoction of unfamiliar crushed leaves with some honey and water. The medicine her minder constantly fed her was familiar now.

"Are you Kaya? Did you remove my blinding?" she asked into the air, and her voice was cracked and dry. Kaya turned to her and smiled, and Elise thought her beautiful. The woman looked at least a decade younger than she was, but who could tell in this light? A strong jaw, intelligent eyes and long, dark hair like her own. Her clothes were carefully maintained despite their age and crudeness. For just a moment, Elise warmed to her, before she remembered she was imprisoned. She didn't let this show, though. She simply smiled back.

"A lady could go mad denied vision without reason," Kaya explained, stirring the concoction.

"Thank you, Kaya," Elise said. Her mind raced. How could she escape this place? Who would need to die? Was that boar cooking on a spit somewhere?

It was more a cave than a cell, and their voices echoed unnaturally. Elise took a breath with lungs stronger again than before. What had they done to her? Was she actually dead?

Was this the next life beyond the darkness?

Kaya brought over the mixture and bent toward her, holding it to the Alpha's salty, dry lips.

"Does this help my breathing?" Elise demanded, a little more aggressively than she'd intended. Her healer looked at the medicine and shook her head.

"It knocks the fuk out of you," she whispered. "His orders, I'm afraid."

Honesty.

Interesting.

"Then I will have no more."

Kaya went to argue and then thought better of it and shrugged. She placed the medicine down beside Elise, sighing as she did.

"This is no place for Alphalines. Especially legends," she whispered. She radiated gentleness, but Elise recognised deep strength beneath it. *Is she playing a part with me?*

"What do they plan for me?" Elise asked, though she

suspected ongoing imprisonment to be the likely answer. She took some more cleansing breaths and marvelled at their depth. Where was the stubborn grip that had been killing her a little more every day? Where was the heaviness?

Kaya shrugged. "I know little. I am charged to care for you, Elise, mated to Magnus. As I have done these last few weeks."

Weeks? How many weeks?

The syrup had stolen much time from her. "I feel stronger in this place. Stronger than I have in years. You know my name. You know my pedigree. Have you heard my tales yet? Have you heard of my threat?" she asked, licking the salt from her lips. She was restrained, but in her drugged, addled mind was a terrifying certainty that she would prevail.

"Aye, I know your legend," Kaya countered.

"When I rise from this cave and wield my full strength once more, do you want to have earned my favour?" she asked, lying back. As if taking this place for her own would be no challenging task at all. It would not be.

Kaya leaned across her and, with nimble fingers, began to loosen the bindings.

———

HERE ENDS THE THIRD BOOK OF THE SPARK CITY CYCLE.
THE STORY WILL CONCLUDE IN BOOK FOUR: THE ACTIONS OF GODS

Be the very first to hear when *The Actions of Gods* is released. Join Robert J Power Readers Club at www.RobertJPower.com

A NOTE FROM THE AUTHOR

Thank you for reading The Outcasts

Word-of-mouth is crucial for any author to succeed and honest reviews of my books help to bring them to the attention of other readers.

If you enjoyed the book, and have 2 minutes to spare, please leave an honest review on Amazon and Goodreads. Even if it's just a sentence or two it would make all the difference and would be very much appreciated.

Thank you.

EXCLUSIVE MATERIAL FROM ROBERT J POWER

When you join the Robert J Power Readers' Club you'll get the latest news on the Spark City and Dellerin series, free books, exclusive content and new release updates.

You'll also get a short tale exclusive to members- you can't get this anywhere else!

Conor and The Banshee
Fear the Banshee's Cry

Join at www.RobertJPower.com

ALSO BY ROBERT J POWER

The Spark City Cycle:

Spark City, Book 1

The March of Magnus, Book 2

The Outcasts, Book 3

———

The Dellerin Tales:

The Lost Tales of Dellerin

The Seven

The Crimson Collection

The Crimson Hunters, Vol I

ACKNOWLEDGMENTS

For Poll, Jen, and Jill- thank you all for the support and love and kind words. And also for giving me so much abuse about the characters I've punished or killed. I've told you a hundred times, your tears do nothing.

For Jean and Paul. You both have been such wonderful supporters these last few years. And how do I repay you for such unrivalled support? I stole away your daughter. A fair deal methinks. You are welcome.

For Cathbar. You are the fuken best. You've been there since day one. Telling me to keep going when I hadn't a clue what I was doing. I still don't. Thank fuk you keep at me. Your praise fuels me. Your critiques make me a better writer. You've been more patient than anyone else. I hope I don't let you down. I know the penance. Bakudan!!

Eoin. Allowing me vent to you on all important matters involving VAR this last year has been instrumental into getting this book done. I mean, it has just ruined the game. You sir, are a patient calming gentleman. The fans owe you so fuken much. I owe you a beer and a laugh.

Ant. Hey fuker. I just looked out the window and there you were, just painting your fence. I wasn't waving at you. I was giving you the finger. Fairly certain you weren't waving back at me either. When you get this, give us a shout about a cofe. I need to vent!

Army of Ed- my beloved bandmates. I know I've neglected bringing any new songs to the table recently. In fairness, I've been busy. Seeing as most of my ideas are shouted down in practice, I thought I'd suggest something in the written form. How about we finally record that album involving songs from the Spark City world? Just a thought.

Lisa Cassidy. My wonderful nemesis in the writing world. I blew my opportunity to kill you off in this book. Don't think you are getting away so easily next time. Also, your books are fuken baddass. I'll only say that here after everyone has read through my books first. BUY MY BOOKS FIRST. Then check out Lisa's.

John. Any fan who wanted someone whispering in my ear about hurrying up writing the last year should thank this fuker. Seriously, buy this guy a drink at the bar. Every day, a text or a call. For the last twelve months. "Is it done? When is it finished? You really are slow. They're going to be so mad at you. Ooh, I'd write faster if I was you." Well, it is done, John. Don't be going near me now demanding The Actions of Gods.

My wunderful editors - Jen and Steven- thank you both for drudging threw my insanity and somehow putting it together into a semi comprehensible reed. I keept you busy and you guys never complained once about my many many errors. You've Raised the bar. Hopefully though, with the next book I can truly break your will.

A special word for my friend and comrade of the road, Zim Zam. We did it. We finally did it. You got me here and I'm eternally grateful. Though we are a million miles apart, we are only a few clicks away. Thank you so much for everything. Much love, much respect and I'll see you out in the wastes. (Though probably not without the porcupine this time – yeah, you know what I'm talking about… Okay… fine… we'll bring the porcupine. But I'm not bringing his shoes. That's on you.)

Finally, for the fans who've been with me since the beginning up to those who are only getting ready to party now. I love you all. Your kind words and support have motivated me and drove me to make this book as great as I could. I hope it takes you to another place. I hope it makes you smile. This one is for you guys… And… you should talk about it. Loudly. Tell everyone. Tell the world. Because then I'll get all the money and I really want to afford that drawbridge for the moat I dug around my house last year. The wife is going mad about it.

ABOUT THE AUTHOR

Robert J Power is the fantasy author of the Amazon bestselling series, The Spark City Cycle and The Dellerin Tales. When not locked in a dark room with only the daunting laptop screen as a source of light, he fronts Irish rock band, Army of Ed, despite their many attempts to fire him.

Robert lives in Wicklow, Ireland with his wife Jan, two rescue dogs and a cat that detests his very existence. Before he found a career in writing, he enjoyed various occupations such as a terrible pizza chef, a video store manager (ask your grandparents), and an irresponsible camp counsellor. Thankfully, none of them stuck.

If you wish to learn of Robert's latest releases, his feelings on The Elder Scrolls, or just how many coffees he consumes a day before the palpitations kick in, visit his website at www. RobertJPower.com where you can join his reader's club. You might even receive some free goodies, hopefully some writing updates, and probably a few nonsensical ramblings.

www.RobertJPower.com

facebook.com/AuthorRobertJPower
twitter.com/robertjpower
instagram.com/robertjpower